LETALIS ①

By Oskar Holtz

Oskar Holtz, born Oscar Lam, was raised in Hong Kong in
an era of upheaval, during which the exposure to old stories and
histories from China to Japan stirred a fascination with human conflict.
Upon migrating to the United Kingdom, where he resides now,
the stories of Letalis budded and evolved until this very volume
materialized after four years of keen experimentation.

CONTENTS

PREFACE

Did we ever heed the whispers of our histories tearing us from war? Humanity had done all to ensure survival and the creed of destruction. Before in time, there was a peace in our world for seven decades. What of now? The peace had ceased.

Never was 'Letalis' meant to lean for where it lies. Nor its world. Or its inhabitants. But how could a journey, birthed from under the waters of shower to be so simple and thoughtless, grow its soul? Like a being with life and breath, it shuddered from a loneliness. Emptiness. And from that blank white room that houses every idea, the path fate had been woven for us budded into newer faces and human minds. Though never had the thread of the story went pushed by my hands. It was given by the natural dynamics of its residents.

Who beside, some moments have come wishes that I could be joined in arms alongside the blood and soils beneath the heavenly sky and abyss of the sea. Perhaps dreams and mindlessly floating in the void. Hearing the clashes of blades and cries of the horrors yet never divulging to taint the hands of mine. Only to witness. Together with my creations and children. A voice had called to me from within though it may be my own. Guiding and wading through the trenches until the boundaries of a grim tunnel was lightened. But. Reflecting from my pupils. An endless horizon and nothing. It brings me to weep at the nothingness. Knowing that a measly human cannot reach his deity.

There to satisfy only a loss of sanity which I seem to regain on a chair and before the words which constructed this world. Every day and the times that I watch the sprout of the impending sentence. As if living again. Reborn into a distant place not so foreign. There to submit to my desires. To calm my spirit. As the maker. As the god of their existence. That is what I am.

*For the people of Hong Kong and Ukraine,
beacons of modern liberty...*

CHAPTER 1 THE REBIRTH OF PARADISE

"What's the date?" He asked, with a tainted pistol pointed at the face of the petrified guard.

The collected killer cast a glance at a calendar beside a quivering hand and without fault, shot the guard through an eye, spoiling the wall with a viscous crimson red splatter. As the sprinting winds of the underground carried the stream of smoke arising from the barrel, kept stilled before his unwavering eyes, the devil lifted the booklet from the counter. And steadily, he searched. Hoping time had not passed so fast. But the realization of the oddity, that the numbers were unfamiliar, had him paused.

"An old calendar?" assuming from the cyrillic text, his voice felt cold.

Whilst the boots of the hasty guards, clanking in their rush down the drab stairs, grew ever louder, the officer of the detachment yelled for the intruder's halt. Yet, the killer gave no care. His response was rapid. Towards the corpse-ridden corridor, he began to dash across the ponds of blood, and in it, the reflections of the blades and maimed bodies rippled. The soldiers belonging to the realm of the living fought the scent of decay and hurriedly formed two tight ranks. Over their fallen comrades and decapitated heads, bolt action rifles lined the path.

"Fire! Fire! Fire!" The youthful corporal commanded amidst his men.

A volley of an inescapable blanket of brass bulleted at the intruder. But his sharp ears were too quick. He spun and dodged the fleeting rounds with professional maneuvers belonging to an assassin. In the wake of the metallic storm, his hand opened from a fist, and hurled a rain of pellets with the angelic element, *eifer*, gleaming within.

"Hold your ground!" The commander cried as his trembling squad struggled to reload in the face of the predatory foe.

"Do not waver—!"

In the second where their breaths were loosened, the trigger behind the murderer's finger was pulled seven times in a flourish. Embers, in the cone of sparks, ignited and broke the air. A barrage hurtled in arcs shook the flickering lights. On the fated impacts of every round, the lightning concealed within the cartridge thundered, and beaming across the narrow stretch, diverging before the killer's emotionless stare, royal purple rays flowered as if it were summoned from a rising sun.

"G-Gods grant us paradise—" Shakingly, a soldier lowered his rifle and muttered in the path of inviting death.

Heavenly bolts pierced thudding hearts and tore through the walls of flesh. The screams resonated across the corridor until the snapping sounds of bullets had been drowned. Fountains of blood sprayed from ripping wounds as the soldiers clamored for their last gasps whilst few mindlessly fled but never reached so far. Then, for each dropped quiet, gurgling and choking by the spurting liquids, it was before a gradual calm settled above a steaming pile of remains.

He, the angel of death, looked down upon the carnage his hands had raised. The leaking veins of severed bodies. Shattered jaws hanging by a strand of tendon. Hands holding gaping caves exposing the intricacy of beige bones. Everything reflected from the pale light of his eyes.

Unbeknownst to the guilt of a massacre, the man sighed. As the dated firearm was casually withdrawn into a holster strapped beside his chest, the pounding of an enraged pair of heavy footsteps advanced behind. Thickly armored in the extravagant colors of red and gold, armed with silver lances, the party of two elite guardsmen charged along the only path that laid ahead. To the clanking sounds of heels and rubbing metals, the intruder calmly drew to face his enemies upon the glisten of the blades.

Resolute and daring, with the swiftness of an agile desert fox, he darted in a frontal assault. The mighty stood locked in their joints and became an iron curtain. But the killer would not be deterred.

"Aargh!" War cries boomed, for it was enough to return an army from the course of battle.

The soldiers' grips tightened. Their sweat poured. Either seemed confident that the intruder would fall beneath them.

Yet in spite of all hope, the reaper and his shallow breaths were already by the guards' ears.

Their eyes were present on his fluidity, weaving between the shafts. The murderer's glare froze them for his hands to steal away a spear. His inner aura, *kei*, erupted. And however he lacked an eifer, the ferocious slash that smashed upon the duo bisected them with a howling gust of wind, slamming chunks of divided flesh to a concrete crater where the impact rocked the underground bunkers.

In a creaking office chair, gently rocking, an old warrior sat. Of confidence. Almost too confident. Whose opening eyes were the color of flames, a sinister scar ran from the bridge of his nose to his left cheek. His damning grin widened between a moon shaped beard. Impressively, the aged man, appearing to be in his early seventies, had a build of the given legends. That revealed only hints of his war-scarred skin, the rich armor he bore and two silver bears' heads guarded upon his shoulders, with noble gold works of the blacksmith bearing firestorms engraved.

Behind a reaching desk for the council of war, the veteran had been awoken by the eerie tremor. To the dust and peeling paint flinging about the dingy room, the rattling electrical lantern, not so common in the western world, was subdued by the silence. The echoing rumbles had halted. A tightening fist signaled a burst of the entering menace and instinctively, the elder reached for his titanic bardiche. Some joints of small bones taller than he was, the polearm was decorated with the resemblance of a demonic creature's claws grown on the blade's back. Cautiously, he waited. For the looming footsteps to encroach upon the bluish carpets.

"Have you your comfort?" The warrior asked with a slight chuckle.

A shadow was cast over the table, where an asking hand pointed at the blackened hardcover book beneath tapping fingers. As the light shone to reveal the six-foot-tall intruder who wore an ash gray coat, the elite soldier spoke again,

"I find it intriguing how someone would deliver himself here so eagerly."

"For this, your great-grandfather's thesis." said he, raising the book that had summoned the killer's stare.

"The Death Tome." It was called.

The shaded man snatched the relic from the warrior's hands and gently brushed the dust from the stained cover, revealing the imperial eagle of old Zhormann, settled upon the character of a dying tree. Unlike any other book, it did not contain a title nor an author's name.

"Don't bother," told the killer, reservedly, as he kept the tome near.

"It's nothing of a warmonger's interest."

Removing a pair of glasses hidden within his jacket's pocket, the younger cleaned its lenses and pulled his hair back, slickly, before wearing it, adjusting his vision to naturality.

"Then I presume you've held your end?" The veteran questioned him, who had begun trailing towards the emergency exit that was brightly lit with straight white lamps, providing an evacuation tunnel towards the muffled overground.

"They should have done so by now." The intruder replied, prepared to depart when a booming cough sounded across the vast, hollow hall.

"If I find that you've fooled me—" A rather deep voice threatened, tensely glaring at his temporary ally.

The footsteps halted on the border towards freedom, and unable to withstand the warning, he turned to daunt the warrior,

"And, what if?"

As if the leer was a poisonous jab through the soul and mind, a stream of cold sweat ran down the veteran's face. His trembling hands could not be stopped so easily.

"Hmph." But a grunt had drawn the brief tension to a close and ended his failed coercion.

The old man returned to the desk, pretending he had not suffered from the single glance afar and pointed, with an open hand, at the exit and the shadow standing before.

"You're the nightmare of our demons and valkyries," He mumbled, admittedly.

"More so than the Whirlwind, the damned God of War—"

"You speak from the script." The killer interrupted emotionlessly when he attempted to leave once more.

"Won't the Protectorate want you dead?" Another question sprouted from the dried lips of the elder.

An annoyed sigh bit the elite's spine who shortly stopped for a silence. But the devil continued his way on the steps towards the night.

"They've tried..." The intruder raised his reserved voice that eventually grew softer when the paces stamped away.

"And, Grand Marshal Kolchakov," He named the soldier with a collapsing attention, and added,

"Do whatever you will."

When the distant slam of a steel door closed, and that the marshal was undeniably sure the killer could not hear him, Kolchakov slammed the table to break his shudder. From the cursed air wringing his neck.

I

Lycoris

Of the seven continents and seas, divided between forty-six and six states, there were two powers on the stage. Aelon, in the ancient tongue, the Yuruamorikann League of Nations ruled the west and far east. And the Greater Yurasann Confederate Co-Prosperity Sphere. Or simply, the Confederacy. They controlled the second half of the world. Like empires, they never knew it was impossible to reign over four billion people who spoke six universal tongues and thousands more languages, with a spectrum of cultures and ideas. But no matter how far humanity can revolutionize, something would stir in our blood to bring our lives to agony. Subjugated by our sins.

The known world shattered after the Second Calamity that took away a hundred and fifty million souls. Distrust flourished and as a species, growth slacked. Until there was a point where the fuse had been lit, and unable to be blown out, the warring period that would last for under a century ensued. Whilst fruitless wars were raised to deplete our resources and at the cost of numberless lives, the count of conflicts grew without end between neighbors and once allies. And when they thought the past decades would provide a new age of unity...

We never sought for peace in this hell and that senseless dream for paradise was lost.

The world of schisms in this century was devoid of humanity.

But at least...there was once such things as humans...

CHAPTER **CRIMSON**

2 **BLANKET**

On that morning of the fateful day, a gust of freshening air blew through the cracks of the doors. The bright, holy sun pierced the wavering curtains and struck the blankets of the young boy whose body dangled freely over the edge. Marked by uniform scars like window blinds, his arm reached the floor that sent a chill. As shuddering birds chirped in the brisk winter winds, arriving from the narrow, bustling channel into the spacious room.

Decorated rather simply in a darkened gray and wooden tone, the furniture and walls were tidied and easy for the eye. To the left flank of the single bed was a long beech desk, holding a collection of school stationeries, whilst nearer the door on the opposite, stood a blank white wardrobe which was never full. An open shelf reaching for the ceiling was brimming with video game cartridges and books, with one other plank dedicated for the numberless trophies and medals none could count. Where most closest to their master, by the foot of the bed, laid the small black school and racket bags. Though unlike many children his age, he never possessed the luxuries of modern technologies except for his father's ancient mobile phone and a handheld game console, by a lamp, that did not seem too new either. It was no more than an exceedingly average quarters ignoring the peculiar historic objects on the outskirts. Unseen and hidden in the shade.

The alarm rang, asudden, that forced to wake him gradually. Teary eyed, he stretched, knocking his knuckles against the bed frame and carefully shuffled his head onto the pillow before his eyes opened. Picking up the clock to end the irritating alarm, the date, he read, was written across the bleak electronic screen.

31 Sepirus 488. It noted in the Zhormannik calendar, that when his eyes scrolled down, he read the lesser counter,

31.10.12014.

A typical Wenndä. The fifth in a week. For this child, it was another disinteresting school day. But his energy had been drained. Anxious for another short weekend before the cycle would repeat itself again.

Whining and squirming, unwilling to wake, he did eventually rise. Swinging his legs onto the hardwood floor, the boy stretched for the second and yawned. Despite upon his awakening, he began to daydream, thinking of what he had dreamt of the night before dawn, with drool leaking from the corner of his mouth when a motherly voice called for him from the ground floor below,

"Seki! You'll miss school if you don't wake up!"

However, he did not reply. Dragging his half-awake body out of bed, his shadow departed, letting the sun shine on the relics.

And there sat a dusty photograph of many years ago, where a family posed before the scene of Aöure waves and a far eastern hall. It overlooked the below, where one worn wooden practice sword with stains of aged blood leaned against the shelf. Blackened handprints and burn marks curiously littered the weapon with its edges chipped and splintered. They held cruel vestiges within.

Holding onto the pain by his stomach that had hurt for two years, he sleepily shuffled across the room to reach the door that had shut alone from the wind, and entered himself through the corridor to the neighboring bathroom where water began to trickle.

Though it seemed a cold wash of the face had refreshed the ten-year-old who rushed down the staircase in the shell of an alternate persona. Carrying two bags on each shoulder that wrinkled his black uniform, he was improperly dressed for the shifting season, with no such regards for the laws of the school. With a spin around the foot of the stairs, his feet slid across the polished tiled floor into the living room where his breakfast was being prepared.

"Good morning." His mother greeted with a warm smile.

"Morning!" The young boy joyously replied on his halt that swung the school's burgundy bolo tie to rest.

His name was Arminius Reichner. He had somewhat short light brown hair, lightly glittering in the budding sunlight shining through the windows, like the bearing of his true slight smile.

Every air of his aura was soft-seeming, from his hurried walk to the tone of the voice that was never intruding but neither too polite. Gifted by his father's summer green and the mother's winter blue eyes which the latter sat above a small, recent scar, however bright or athletic that he was, the fair boy only appeared as any ordinary child.

"爾之朝飯、阿赤 · *Nei-shi-jōsan, a-Seki.* (Seki, your breakfast.)" Missus Reichner called for him in a foreign tongue of the far eastern, distant, by her blood.

Served the dish of bread and soup with a hint of canned sardines. Its scent of tomatoes was overwhelming and salted even the air. Though the wars had tolled the kingdom, the well-plated meal was enough to satisfy the stomach.

"祢後以！ *Negoi!* (Thanks!)" Arminius replied.

Resting the bags on the seat beside him, he sat and tucked in as his father, however a less expressive man, had dressed in his formal shoes and rose to unlock the back door.

"I'll be off to Luninn for the day so I might not be back for dinner." Reichner told his caring wife.

"Don't be too late," The mother answered heartily.

"You know what they're like. The militia."

Fitting a pair of glasses with his light gray coat and a fine hat, Arminius' father picked up a worn business bag from the low stool and swung open the door, releasing a breeze of wild winds into the lounge.

"I'll see you tonight." He said to his family before departing.

A last disheartened glance at his son did not converse with Arminius. The door closed and clicked, automatically locking itself. And once the engine of the detached garage had driven away, heard by the sharp ears of the mother, she switched on the television to the morning news where the anchor was nearing the end of a weather report.

"Thank you, Jean." She began with a noticeable accent.

"Now moving onto the statement made at the Zhennau Summit this morning,"

"President Kennedy, the lieutenant of Aelon, has declared a policy of non-intervention as Premier Kozlov pledges an additional seventy thousand Confederates to the Baltik with eyes leaning upon the escalation of the succession crises."

"Furthermore," The reporter continued as Arminius dipped

his bread in the soup that soaked into the craters.

"The first President of the Amorikann Union, and the father of revolutions, John Kennedy, sadly passed away in a hotel suite last night here at Luninn..." She started to fade when nothing of remark stole his hearing any longer.

He gobbled down the last of his breakfast and sprung onto his feet with the emptied plate in his hands. For the kitchen counter, Arminius was met with an expected question from his mother's soft voice,

"Are you staying after school today?"

"Mhm!" Arminius returned cheerfully as he placed the dish near the sink.

Sliding to his bags, the child merrily swung the load onto his shoulders and pranced towards the front door, ready to depart. Quickly, he wore his black school shoes, tying the laces with double knots, and once there was satisfaction, he shot upward and playfully flung a key into his pocket. Before departing, as one would do, Arminius glimpsed at his mother and joyously gave his farewell,

"Seeya!"

Missus Reichner flicked her hands dry under the dripping tap and turned to the door with a returning goodbye. But her son had gone.

The leaves were plucked from the naked branches, where the orange of the trees began to disappear, gliding aimlessly onto the rugged pavement that he traversed. His breath iced on that chilly day, along the main path ladened with schoolmates and their bikes. A rowdy bunch yelled for his name from a double decker bus, chucking black smoke, who, he could hear from afar, were his classmates and friends. And whilst they had taken for the easy route, Arminius hiked, tiredly up the steepening hill towards the school crowned atop. Although he enjoyed the backdrop of a coastal Annzhle town, it felt much like an eternity on his journey to school. The freezing breezes stroked his shuddering face that was not made better by the oceanic scent of the morning markets on the scenic waterfront which flourished across the city and the streets, patrolled by the same garrison of soldiers who were greeted by Arminius' wave. Lying on the southern coast of the kingdom named Alben, that was the city of Bristel.

But the settlement, like the thousands of the world, were battling for their drops of life fluid in the night of wars. A gas station, awkwardly fashioned on the side of a hill, caught Arminius' eye, whose walk stopped and pondered the steadily changing numbers,

Two coppers for a liter...? The prices had already risen since yesterday.

That was the equivalent of twenty-six Hannsyatik marks that could buy twenty loaves of bread. As he calculated the values in his mind, uninviting footsteps racing in an uphill climb from the distance, pushed for Arminius to resume his walk.

"Hey!" The fast approaching figure called for him who needed not bother to stop when the other student caught up.

"Armin...wait...!" He panted and reasoned, but only received a frown.

"You gotta stop calling me that, Colt..." Arminius growled before a teasing chuckle came from his friend, if one could call him so.

With southern Sinnik blood, he was a tone of light sand. Taller. Vigorous. Playful. Colt had an odd charm for his attitude. For who bore a punk-like appearance by the azure sweatband around his straight black hair and a bandage over a scar as new as his classmate's, the easterner was never shabbily. Yet being of a similar age holding little difference in maturity, his sizable sky blue eyes uttered a threat of rivalry who seemed incomparable to Arminius' smaller stature.

"Aw...sure..." Colt rolled his eyes and replied with a laugh,

"How about Sekiya?"

Arminius sighed as they strolled, reaching the very summit some minutes later where the school complex stood.

A fluttering flag of a golden lion watched over the entering pupils pass the brick wall into the modernized concrete building. Within the packed halls and regular classrooms, were the students seated. Were they to be late, the duo could not dream of the punishments they would endure, and so raced to class without delay.

The bell soon tolled, and the many who had arrived before too late scurried fast to their homerooms which lined the once bleak corridor then decorated with festive ornaments for the coming winter months. And of course, spending their precious time, Arminius and Colt were the last to enter class. Though it appeared that their teacher had not arrived earlier as usual.

"Arminius! Colt!" A group of five in the corner, by the expanse window that stretched across the room, waved at the leisurely two.

But with eyes fueled, the rivals sprinted over and past the tables and chairs, racing to their seats. Leaping and sliding, Arminius reached outwards and tossed his bags overhead, landing onto the window seat, and claimed his victory for the morning. That was before noon when Colt would often steal his throne.

When the resounding knocks of a teacher's heels approached, Arminius, the head student of the finest class across the year, commanded the pupils to stand at attention with a military-esque salute across his stomach,

"All rise!"

They impatiently waited for the stern, smartly dressed woman to enter. The most hated amongst the school for her arrogance was alien even to colleagues alike. Who hastily stormed into the room, and after her pretense to have taken the register, she waved her hand for the students to be seated. Dragging chairs disturbingly screeched, thus began the longest day of the week.

Arminius took his victor's seat with a serene view of the promenade and unpacked his small notebooks, carrying an olden pen. Their agitated tutor thumped a scholarly textbook, a bulk of text, on the front desk and spun towards the blackboard with a white writing chalk in hand.

"Turn to page one-three-nine!" She told, forcefully drawing the number on the board for all to see.

Everyone, though all but one, scrambled to the page in their shrunken version of the history book. It was he who had forgotten that the lesson had begun as Arminius' book was shutted, taken further from the class by an indiscreet call across the same row of cheap wooden seats.

"Psst," A classmate whispered, but it sounded like a whistle.

"Have you heard?" He asked, assuming his friends knew.

Nodding, then scribbling brief notes as the teacher spoke

over the dispersed mumblings, the group were trying in their best attempt to exceed the top students of the year. Colt, second on the previous exams' rankings, was far too taken by immature sketches on the corner of his book, whilst Arminius, ranked first, mindlessly stared out of the window with a pen clasped between his teeth. Like gods of middle school, the two worried not.

"We've been accepted in the winter tournaments?" Another realized with a careful voice.

Finally! No more countering practice! One mouthed inaudibly to Arminius who had kept his eyes pinned on the squawking seagulls, circling over the distant fishing boats and many piers.

"Don't you all find that to be the easiest part about javelin—?" The leader among the group of friends exclaimed too loudly for the grinning bunch, when, the furious teacher slammed her hand on the blackboard, and named the head student in full,

"Arminius Reichner!"

The class flinched on the eruption of the common temper and from the corner of their eyes, glared at the student who was called. In the room of eternal silence, his friends collectively inched further away, knowing that whenever the teacher pronounced her students' fore and surnames meant inevitable trouble.

"Your book isn't even open, so I assume you know everything about the invasion of Alben?" She asked intimidatingly, in a high-pitched tone.

"Then well," said the tutor confidently so.

"Why don't you lecture us all?"

Pointing her hand at Arminius, the singled student was commanded to rise by the raise of a finger. He gulped, for his pages were closed, but many knew too well that it was no challenge or obstacle to one who could effortlessly vault over.

"I can't...madam—" He, to the teacher's and perhaps the class's unexpectedness, uttered.

"No, no, please *enlighten* us all." Interrupting the apologetic student who attempted a path of reconciliation, their most detested educator interrupted mockingly and unreasonably.

The urge to humiliate was commenced by the support of his classmates, as the tugs on his jacket and taps on the tables agitated his composure as if they were chants of a battlefield. Despite his mischievous friends evidently seeking for a moment of redemption for the years this teacher had disgraced the class with, Arminius was not so willing when a blunted object struck his considerate face.

"Speak now, Reichner!" The woman demanded whilst it was discovered by Colt's touch beneath the desk landed the blackboard's eraser.

Releasing an unsettled sigh, Arminius gazed across the room, knowing very well that the universal yearning for a battle to the final breath rested upon his shoulders against the one who was a so-called teacher. And regardless of certainty that she, herself would defeat the head student and Arminius would find himself bogged in the principal's office, such a strategy could never break the pupil's bulwark's defenses.

"The Battle of Alben began in four-nineteen where the three kings of Zhormann conquered the isles within a week." Arminius informed as if he had become an audiobook with a beginning devoid of any falsehood.

Acknowledging the blunderous bet on the fate she would not win, by the tutor's face had turned pale, the pupils giggled and smirked as the humiliation was set in tracks.

"Heinz of Vrannken landed in Kannten; Erich of Leken invaded through Isö, and Erwin of Zhormann marched on Luninn and killed nine million with his eifer, Blitzfeld—"

"Enough!" The teacher interrupted upon the loss of her fragile dignity.

Returning herself to the blackboard with a shaking hand to the embarrassment, she continued her class. Though, not remembering to sit Arminius down, the head student was dragged to his seat anyways, making an uneasy face as the classroom erupted into the slightest laughter.

"By the way," Colt began aloud towards Arminius, provoking another outburst as if they had not dared fooled around enough.

"Are you coming over for the weekend?" The Sinnik raised his voice.

The sound of shattering chalk snapped in the background, but the inattentive students gave no care despite the feeling of a once more growing wrath stored at the front of the classroom.

"What do you think?" Arminius sharply declined, but his rival was not without a plan when he halted his rocking chair and rested his head nearer.

"Y'know, we've just renovated the sparring hall..." whispered Colt.

"So it's *your* loss."

A pair of eyes brightened aside his best to hide the excitement with Arminius' disinterested face portraying otherwise was unconvincing. Resting his head on a free hand, he flicked his sights from the classroom to the crashing waves, and quietly replied, almost unsure of his certainty,

"Sure..."

Two friendly arms wrapped themselves around both's necks and brought them closer, pointing at one's bandaged nose and the other's scar.

"Just make sure you don't come back with another cut, you two." He mocked, as the group began to ridicule the rivals without end for the coming hours where the sniggers would echo across the five classes of the final day.

The sun revolved whilst the tiresome week drew to a short close, quicker than anticipated. After all, no sane person was too keen to dedicate the remaining hours studying. Rather, most eyed ahead to the practice match after school when nightfall was soon to be marked by the flickering street lamps that turned on upon the setting sunlight.

With a shockwave detonating on an explosive leap, Arminius, as if he floated in the great training hall where a court for javelin had been set, had shed the skin of compassion and unraveled a layer of ruthlessness. His satisfied coaches and bewildered seniors watched him grant flight to his limiting humanity, soaring high above the net dividing the nine players in each half where each held wooden rackets shaped like sickles for the game they played was the true test of precision.

"To your left!" When near the very apex of the launch, an agile teammate called for Arminius.

Glancing upon the floorboards below, where the students had all equally shrunk from the watch above, Arminius' focus followed the hurtling javelin-shaped shuttle towards the far ceiling as he felt the sense of perfection. Fluidly, he launched his racket through the air in an uninterrupted curve and caught the shuttle by its cloth tail. Forcing onwards his entire self in the release of his kei, to the corner of where he was to strike the tie-breaking point, the narrow shuttle was flung with a blast of a lightning pulse whizzing to earth. Within the divide in time, the booming impact thundered and the final point of the match had been collected.

Their coach signaled for the end with a blow of a whistle as everyone awaited Arminius to land with the warmth of congratulations and cheers surrounding him. Though not apparent to the victorious, a number of rested substitutes on the side benches caught a glimpse of Colt's riled face, heated with a challenger's glare.

"Aw man, they didn't stand a chance even with Colt on their team." One grinned as he mentioned, sipping on an energizing drink.

"But no one else could ever compete with those two." Another squadmate beside him praised, though it was not so empty of jealousy which a senior, of the last year in middle school and captain of the squad, had felt it to be frequent among his juniors.

With a towel at hand, the captain wiped his face dry of good near-winter sweat. Supposing his allies were conversing around the topics on the rising rivals, he joined the chatter with inquisitiveness.

"It's a dream for the rest of us." told the captain, sympathetically, gazing at Arminius who had stolen his forgotten glory of the game once more.

The new ace of the team was cheered for, but no matter how often the senior student would hear the voices of Arminius' name being called, he could not water the growing fires of envy. Even if it was so, a chuckle sounded and a smirk had arisen,

"Though, the kinda training they'd gone through must've been..."

From the dense shower mist, the last students emerged from the changing room that had filled the somber evening air with a hint of rowdiness. They had begun their race home before the night would settle for far too long. Trading time with the exits made in scruffy appearances and unconcerned half-open bags, they hurried away.

Being the last of the pack to depart and with another, a neatly dressed Arminius flicked the damp plastic switch nailed near the door for the lights to go as the school grounds closed. It was by the eighth hour since noon at night, that they had gone too, into the cooler calm.

"Sorry, my serves should've been better..." A friend apologized embarrassedly, from the match not so long ago as he wiped his face with a washed white towel.

"Come on, don't be so hard on yourself." Childishly smiling, Arminius reassured with a pat on his friend's shoulder.

"You've only started playing javelin last month." He reminded him as if the classmate had forgotten easily.

On the approach to a bend in the road after a short steep climb to the edges of the school complex, they were greeted by a strengthening breeze from the nearby channel. But as rewarding as it may sound, the wind was cutting. Where they would have to go separate ways, Arminius piped.

"I know!"

"There's a book at home that might help with techniques and other things that you could borrow." The kind gladly informed his fellow pupil, when they came to stop on the beginning of the downhill path.

"Really?!" His friend excitedly cried when the damaged spirit of himself recovered.

"Yeah, I'll make sure to bring it in next week—" Arminius made a promise with the seal of a pinky, soon disturbed by the chime of a phone.

"Ah! Gotta go!" Releasing his lock around his schoolmate's finger, he realized the message must have been from his mother's worry and waved a hasty goodbye,

"Seeya on Lunndä!"

The return of a farewell marked the separation in paths as the two diverged towards opposite routes, jogging for home against the rising wintry gusts.

Under the weakened lamps, cars sprinted along the suburban roads to their local bars for the beginning of another week's end.

Arminius' sweat began to lessen until his face had cooled to his typical paleness. His cheeks grew red from the seaside winds, blowing through every crack and alleyway between the detached houses lining the straight path. Though when the temperature dropped abnormally, for it felt like ghasts were circling, he stopped by a bus shelter and settled his bag on the inclined seat. Shivering, and clattering, Arminius snatched a bottle of tea from the bag's side pouches and gulped unstoppably. However it did not aid him that the drink had been iced.

"I wish I had an eifer that was more useful..." He mumbled to himself, huffing his warm breath into his clasped hands.

Readied for the second leg of his trip, it was then, when the glass of the stop's shelter started to rattle ever so noticeably.

Discreet. Terrifying whirls of engines echoed from the distance which were barely in range and that to the puzzled student, he felt a desire to know what the skies stored that night. Arminius gazed at the clouds and squinted, but had found nothing in his desperate search except for the stars in the infinite ceiling. Lost deep in thought, his expression doubted what he once imagined, however, on the verge to pack and resume his journey, the chilling tones drew closer. The snaps of engines began from afar, sounding almost jet-like. It occurred to him, in the few indistinguishable seconds, when they darted out of the visible distance and zoomed overhead, that a squadron of the recognizable fighters had committed to an invasion.

The Confederacy.

Shockwaves were sent to the heavens, as the blood and fire raged in the horizon, lighting the purple canvas to an orange curtain which provoked Arminius to flee. His breath raced as he turned and sprinted, near the falling bombs, plummeting incomprehensibly, where the screams of the innocent were heard across the hundreds of leagues in every direction. Every wave that crashed against the shores equaled each damning blast which tore through houses, streets, and vivid gardens. Glass shattered around and the ground quaked. Arminius panted as he fought for every gasp. But the black smoke chased him unrelentingly, with the souls of the dead moaning as if they were ghouls, quicker than any living human, much alike hunting thunderbolts.

Sudden shocks bursted through the houses beside him, with no escape from the flanks that had been laced under a shroud of ticking bombs. Arminius halted by a second bus stop to catch his thickening breath. Knowing the real sight of death's door once the shells shattered into thousands of shrapnels, he had not felt the same scent crawling into him since a childhood of terror. A gust of wildfire launched him paces against the frail shelter, shattering the glass, where the tides took with him a flurry of cuts to where he laid against the piercing blanket set by a row of crimson waters.

II

31 SEPIRUS 488
31.10.12014

Friedrich Kennedy

Are we not on good terms, Grand Marshal Kolchakov? Our alliances have stayed our hands from your world ever since my grandfather's reign and to have a little accident provoke your so proud nation? It's laughable. We know nothing of the deeds those Jorzhanns have committed whether you believe me or not. My father. My grandfather. My heart rested upon the declaration of peace and the preservation of humanity. Not total war. Or are we to have a foolish repeat of the Calamities?

Rutenn. You may act as how one would when they are invaded. But do not drag the entire body of Aelon with the blood flow. I presume you haven't even consulted President Kozlov, your puppet, on the terms of peace either—

What are these absurd demands?! Has this all become a joke in your eyes?!

Allow me to tell you this. You've always been nothing but a child in an old man's clothing. Do you know what you've summoned?! The very thing that this world strived for in its survival?! I will never have this! It is unacceptable! To find that you've betrayed my trust by awakening as a fiend! The Protectorate would have your head if it wasn't destroyed itself.

Is war the only option? So be it! Let the Gods curse you to the nine circles of hell and I pray that you be boiled in eternal damnation!

CHAPTER

3   NAIVETY

A darkened pool, from the leaking streams, filled the wasted road. Covered in a blackening shroud, his hands twitched, so slightly, as he woke from what he once thought to be a nightmare. Squinting, Arminius forced his eyes shut again, hoping for the miracle that was to say this was a dream. Whether this reality was true. However, the ringing soon came to him that he had been dazed by a shell. In the real river of blood where his one able hand that could hardly move, was clenched into a fist, as he tried to lift himself. But his energy had been sapped. From the throbbing pain assaulting the mind that ran across his nerves as a blood waterfall cascaded over half his face, littered with dirt and splinters.

He scoured, in search for the alive. Though around, all there was were the heaps of twitching limbs, shattered bones and scattered organs that had been flung to stain the street with a collage of flesh. Peeling and charred bodies without skin became unknown to the world burned in hellfire for they were blessed by luck. Crawling away before the blaze engulfed them were those with bisected selves, barely intact, as some offered a futile struggle before their sufferings' end, with their innards dragged a few feet from the homes in carnage.

The child's heart panicked, hoping the numbness of his lower self was not similarly missing. As he collected his will, to seek for any such mortal wounds, a searing pain flushed.

"Ack..." Arminius cried to the ignorant heavens for not even knowing what mercy they should grant.

There was a fiendish burn he felt to have ignited his entire body, where his every muscle or tendon ached until it had become a purified form of agony. He nervously tilted his head and flipped to lean sideways against the tarmac to where his eyes quivered when the source of the fires laying within was revealed. His teeth gritted with a cold fear surrounding. When he spotted a beam, no smaller than a forearm, impaling his right abdomen. The innocent drew his trembling arm against the wound and pressed deeper for the blood to bubble, leaking between his fingers and onto the tainted beam.

There were no air sirens within the blurred hearing ringing around him. Never calmed breaths. 'The garrison hasn't arrived yet', he must have thought. 'They won't ever come', he probably stressed. Arminius rested himself with his dying eyes facing the above where the shadows of the bombers had left a trail of plummeting fumes. Although nothing mattered anymore. The curiosity of how death would take him drew himself to take a quick glance at his right arm, shaking, and painted with burns. Yet it did not worsen his terror. Where two fingers had been shorn, only a few tendons remained attached to the dangling flesh and the bone which had fractured. Fresh blood spewed onto Arminius' cheeks as he lowered his hand in false acceptance, turning away from the horrors which seemed to be enough to remind him of uncertainty past the end of life. Biting his bottom lips to endure the lessening pain, amidst the anguish, blood tears flowed from his grieving eyes. A tree of severed hands as leaves, and flesh as the soft rotten bark, was birthed into his flooded mind of creation.

A light pair of unfamiliar footsteps, from a boy of similar youth, raced past the inflamed street, escaping the coast to the inner suburbs. He was alone on the hike. Making steep climbs and descents across the unstable rubble, for the desperate child appeared distressed that the uncharted attack not only strangled him. Onwards the sprint went. And although out of breath, his willpower was enlivened, forcing him to summit and slide down ever more hills of corpses.

"Where are you...Wilhelm...?" Rubbing his soiled face, he timidly called for his supposed family.

On the second turn, the other child fortuitously caught sight of a helpless on the heated ground, who spat a mouthful of blood for each he coughed. Though he was completely hopeless as his mind had retreated into slumber, the crippled Arminius and his bold sub-consciousness showed signs of a want to live. But the last standing, well and alive human nearest hesitated. Despite the waning life before his reflective eyes. The question of whether one should rush to aid or not fractured his thoughts, and before he was able to decide, the savior's legs took towards Arminius. Sliding onto the shrapnel-filled ground, cracked and grumbling, the selfless scouted his surroundings for the creeping danger and placed his hands, a feeling indifferent from the frosted air, onto Arminius' neck. The faint pulse beated. The cold sharp touch forced his eyelids to draw open, letting the flickering light seep to produce vision, through a slight slit, where the blurred sights of the injured rested upon the savior's figure. As the last colors faded again, Arminius saw the moving mouth shout, though unheard, to return him to life whilst a helping arm was wrapped around his head. And yet, it could not keep him awake, drowning in the smog of the intimate inferno.

The scent of a fragrant cup of tea whiffed across the compact room where the four walls and roof were surprisingly intact. It seemed the bombings had ceased since many days past, for the sludges of smoke have disappeared, with the remaining clouds of ash settling into the wartorn streets. So, the sun had risen to its morning standard high, above the scorched treetops and the stilt structures retaining some embers, surrounded by the fires on the outskirts of town where the wail of the dead silenced, and renewed a newborn day.

Asleep on a tough, squeaking bed, with a single chair beside him, and a cleaned steel bowl of water, Arminius remained in a dirtied uniform, shredded and punctured with burn holes. Layers of stained bandages were wrapped to comfort his head as he, the child's right arm was veiled from the shoulder to his hands where those deformed limbs, the thumb and index finger, had been stitched and shielded within a metal casing worn over a half glove. His once white shirt, that had been dyed a discomforting color, was fully unbuttoned, revealing more cloth cocooning his fatal wounds.

Then from an imagined sting, hallucinated as the hidden depths dragged his thoughts into the underwater abyss, pinched Arminius to wake. His troubled eyes, shutted by the screams of the dead, widened. With a gasp of air in vain, he had awoken to the same burst of pain remembered by the arisen hell.

Upon the end of his flustered breaths, Arminius gradually entered the calm, and rose upright despite the ongoing strain, irremovable from his stomach. He listened thoughtlessly to the rattling of the windows which steadied as the broken sea breeze flowed through the narrow gaps in the hollow homes and naked trees. As his natural eagerness to recover took form, Arminius shuffled towards the window, desiring the knowledge of the outside world from a better view, although hurting. But on a trip in the path, where his leg had caught the cluster of muddled blankets, he, with a small yelp, tumbled off the bed, hitting his left arm on the creaking floorboard. Though in his eyes, that was oddly considered luck, it was not his right.

Attempting to cover his humiliation in his defeat before the blankets, Arminius kept his torment within. It was then, he could not quite help but moan as the painkillers wore. And for his useless panicking in the fear that one may discover him in such a lowly position, in the corner of Arminius' eye, the wounded boy spotted a shade stalking ever closer, until he who was behind the corner revolved around the doorway, and came rushing to his aid. However, the timidness of his placing down the glass of recently brewed tea on the window sill sent a memory like a jolt, as the same hero of Arminius lent an arm and asked in quite a foreigner's accent,

"Are you...okay?"

"Ngh...yeah..." Arminius groaned, as he lied about the torture he had endured, that not even his legs could sustain to stand alone.

"You should let your wounds heal...before you go anywhere..." The benevolent, by the unsure tone of which he spoke in determined where the other was from was not so near Alben, lifted Arminius and caringly led him to return to his bed.

When the casualty was seated, carefully, Arminius finally found his resolve to recognize his rescuer, who too had rested himself beside. And although the nervous boy, gentle and held little aura that no one could detect, was staring thoughtfully at the ground with his hands clutched on his lap, Arminius could make out the appearance of the kindhearted.

He seemed to be the purest of beings that the shy face was.

With a cutish nose he rubbed from the dust, his short blonde hair was minutely messier than Arminius'. The tentative eyes avoiding contact with the stranger to him were of a sapphire blue, and at its brightest was when the sun shone upon them. Though the dredge of any security sapped him to appear smaller. For the winter season, it seemed most bizzare that he was uncaring of the lack of warmer clothing and was dressed highly peasant-like. However, it was the contrast. A bolo tie, the shade of ice, hung loosely around his neck. It was the very same penchant that a noble would bear if nothing else suggested it.

"Thanks..." Arminius gave a fragile face for the few times that he had done so before.

Lacking a smile that was his signature, he peered dispiritedly at his armored hand. The reflection in the steel was murky. His image was silent. They sat in peaceful coexistence, never shedding another word, whilst the ticks by the minute had passed and no new rays of light had been discovered. The ice on the outer bounds of the thin windows melted, forming beads of freed water, until when all had fallen, both voices, uncommon to be heard together, asked,

"What's your name—"

They flinched in shock, from the unexpectedness of perfect synchronization.

"Ah! S-Sorry..." The savior, still nameless, embarrassedly apologized as Arminius flustered for the blame to be placed upon himself instead.

"Don't worry about it." Arminius humbly excused.

As the break in the stillness had shaped, the hold in the atmosphere loosened. Reaching out, he halted hesitantly at each pace his arm had extended, with a warm hand welcoming the newfound friend. When his expression had strangely, but joyously drawn into a sincere smile, one became the first to introduce himself.

"I'm Arminius."

"Arminius Reichner." said he, taking hold of the other boy's hand then shook it, letting the dubious nature of the unsure personality crumble into openness.

As if there was a memory, alive but buried beneath the years of the past cowered in solitude, the name of Arminius Reichner whispered fervently for the foreigner who could not seem to recall how it was so that a stranger had a familiar scent. The smell of cold steel in blood, from no less than a murder's victim, lingers. Dipping his head, knowing the truth remained unsung, the rescuer replied to the friendliness in a normal tone he had not shown,

"Julien..."

"Julien Carlstadt." The outsider child was named, sending a weaker stun, too similar to the touch of a flashback, to capture Arminius' consciousness.

It was not so strong that the reminiscence would remain.

Raising his legs above the bed frame, Arminius carelessly spun his body, without the tiniest concern to his sore wounds, and faced Julien, timidly watching how the former would inch closer when the rustling of the bed sheet and blankets quieted. The short direct halt caught the shy boy by an alarm but more so when Arminius forced his flattened palms together, sending a bright snap sounding across the room.

"I...I'm truly sorry!" Arminius weirdly apologized, though nothing had pushed him to.

"You shouldn't have been here when it happened."

Julien's face was the equivalent of a frown upon the peculiar individual as he was to say something that would end the nonsense, Arminius only rambled onwards,

"And instead, you were stuck with me ever since that night—"

"How did you know...I wasn't from...this kingdom...?" Julien interrupted in a clearer manner, straying from his typical closure.

"Wha—?" The once endless mound of apologies had ceased, for Arminius voiced discreetly.

"It must've been my accent, right?" A smile lightened Julien's cheeks that the other child had seen, which after all was more human than any else's, with every sentence that he would utter disclosing the cheeriness he was beyond mere strangers.

The bliss of the release in any uncertainty within Julien's mind filled Arminius' face with doubtless glee as he too drove to ask,

"Where are you from?"

There was a pause. Yet, it was not so brief when Julien lifted his chin and saw Arminius' inquisitive glint of his eyes when he mentioned with a trace of paranoia,

"You might think it's weird how I was able to get here in the first place. To Alben..."

"Seeing that I'm a Danne." He hushed, looking over his shoulder to the distant exterior where what seemed to be a clinic, employed nurses and voluntary medics rushed about the wounded hundreds.

It was unusual, how Arminius had received a private room with justification amounting to none before the suffering faces of those far more critically endangered laid on rocks and sheets tagged as beds. Perhaps it was the work of Julien, perceived in his spiraling mind whilst the thousands of questions formed a compacted dune of swift flowing sands, with each grain of an ask tailing another.

"But...what about your family?" A reminder of his own mother and father sprouted that Arminius had retained to himself.

"Aren't they worried?" He provided some care, though ignorant of the delicacy that the question offered.

The Danne's eyes widened from something, no doubt torturous, he had recollected. Then peering down, through the seconds which trickled, the sense of loneliness had been forgotten in having a natural conversation that blanketed his insecurity.

"No." Julien softly replied.

Then the smile eased, though holding no grudge against his family who had not traveled with him, and continued to a tranquil listener that was unlike Arminius' normality,

"They're in Danen..."

The sea's winds pelted against the rocking windows as the ambient bustle livened to their daily routine. Whose ships' horns and marching were lackluster in a collected spirit, different from the calming sounds Arminius had only recently grown into. Their cries were disheartening, for the countless common folk were pained to see their homes destroyed.

In the imagined world where he could have been attached to his personal room, with a game console in both hands, he too was on the verge before the souls crying for rebirth, that was if not for Julien's being there, beside, in the besmirched clinic.

"My grandfather took me here." Julien explained after the short quiet, though not even the mentioned was anywhere to be found.

"Although...he didn't exactly agree to it at first."

Gazing at the rising sun that weaved through the exposed branches and blackened houses, Arminius felt a slit of brighter light shoot into the room drenched in the scent of his blood. And whilst the warmth, like a soothing hand, turned him to return, he leaned closer, curiously so.

"Then, where is he now?" asked Arminius, bringing a highway of troubled thoughts to be unearthed.

Shyly glancing at his new comrade, Julien solemnly shook his head, which nevertheless never showed signs of dejection.

"I don't know..." A polite sigh was huffed.

"And even if he's going to rip the world in half just to find me," His soft chuckle eased the atmosphere, but it was never without doubts that one could feel was being hooked into the softening voice.

"I would be happier if I wasn't dragging him down."

Julien swiftly rose and trailed towards the window where the cup of tea was sitting cooling on the sill, with Arminius' eyes pinned to the Danne's honest back. Where the reflection of his decided face in the rippling tea spun the answer of fate, Julien wrapped his hands around the cup and considered more uncertainty.

Behind the glass and safety, afar on the crater-filled street, there was a confidently-dressed figure, like a proper gentleman, not so far from the hospital in a search of desperation, for his beloved ones among the piles of dead which the maggots and crows circled around and within, plucking flesh and skin from the rot. He paid no focus to the outside world for Julien had been too taken by the heat he could not physically sense, that anything which sparked pictures of the war appeared so distant.

"So, I've been thinking...in the meantime..." Spun around to Arminius, tightly holding the drink that had already become lukewarm, Julien began with the beginnings of certainty.

"Could I stick around?" The Danne proposed.

To a shocked expression, Julien affably smiled at Arminius whose mind could not quite reply, that was, until the breeze of crisp air from the winds of earth rushed into the room and bit upon a fuse in the soul's switch that liberated the blockade of a longing desire the Gods have provided a chance with.

"Sure." Receiving the cup of tea from Julien's loosening grip, Arminius told in time of good faith.

The early winter was at its height, where the days were often dusk. Snow had not begun its fall as many saw it as an omen, a sign for the coming storm before the very beast of the far north broke the desolate sky and rained a blizzard onto earth. And whilst it violently marched through the lands in its reign of terror for the nights until the new year's beginning, bashing the windows and walls of the decrepit room, Julien, as he had promised, remained beside his new found friend. For the time seemed to be a cure of the ailment; as gradual as the stories of Danen were told, the Danne's withdrawn nature imploded. And from whom Arminius could once tell to be no less an introvert, Julien never sounded the same for the better. That even when the nurses would provide their weekly checks and told their patient where some scars ran too deep for normality to be recovered, it bothered the wounded not.

Through the frozen weeks and the month of Jannus, both patiently warmed themselves in the given sanctuary, which since then, housed many more homeless orphans hidden from the storms. Even amidst the mist of breaths and warmth of shivering bodies, the lamenting stench of the young deceased grew greatly, as the era of hibernation passed at a crawl. The rot became unbearable by each setting sun until the pungent smell had encapsulated the room where dawn came, the volunteers and garrison finally sent the truthful numbers of the dead to be away elsewhere but this hell. Their last inviting room that Arminius and Julien had lived within thus far for, became nothing else except a piling morgue. Come Vebrua and its first light of the month, with the dreaded age of winter departed, Arminius and Julien were soon discharged from the precious care of the locals as those of expiring life surged and the need of overground graves grew.

Giving thanks to those who aided him well, the pair departed from the beehive of wreckage and death, as the reapers forced their rampage through the late winter air. They followed the uneven path of rubble, and retreated from the shelter of the skeletal house, where what remained of its walls crumbled and crashed. The infested tents of medics and the garrison filled their visions, where those tending to the wounded in the ruinous background were drained by the massacre. The scents of corpses traveled afar, where hordes of flies flocked to heaps of carts, awaiting cremation in graves of blazes, for the plague was rife, swallowing the definition of any humanity. Those still in the lively realm had to suffer.

Two traversed the narrow, devastated paths with pillaged houses lined in fragmented rows, no closer to restoration. Wild boars and foxes fled from the ominous preying grounds of muddied ice and lumps of snow where limbs or fingers would often display over the meltwater. Arminius' cheeks reddened from the cutting breeze, alike that night of when the bombers struck, quivering in his mangled uniform as if he was a child of the slums. And although he hid the clattering of his teeth to the crows and passerby beggars, his ally was not so fooled by the sight common to his eyes. That was till the distraction came which halted Arminius in his steps, within a puddle of ice.

The hums of a familiar street blindly tugged Arminius across the bridges of steel beams and collapsed roofs, leading Julien, who could only follow onwards to a road of waste chanting the voice of home. It was where one lone, thunderstruck house stood half intact, beneath the brick school's hill, overlooking Bristel and its magnificent havoc, which itself had been bombed and deformed into a volcanic-like crater.

There, on the old forgotten house, dangled an unusually early bloom of a single cherry blossom petal, withered, and hanging from a charcoal beam. In the wind that plucked it from its mother, the petal was delivered to the ground, nearest to Arminius' feet, in the same school shoes he had departed from that home with. As his eyes spotted downwards to the rubble and the single remnant of any flora, he flinched, to a ghastly outline of a mutilated hand, marked by ghoulish lines from the shockwave, that reached for the concrete pavement. They were fixated on the unrecognizable body and led themselves to gawk in fright at the beyond, where it was the shrouded face of a woman, whose head had been twisted, that entered Arminius' suspicion. Appearing to have had her submerged clothes burnt into the skin which although was completely befouled by ash, revealed a few patches of the last paleness. Her eyes had been drained from the heated blast, and were emptied sockets, with a glare from the powder white teeth staring into the souls of the pair, whilst a mere few strands of hair, armored from the impact, remained. The identical light brown shade that Arminius had.

As mournful tears swept down his face, unseen by the Danne behind, Arminius clenched his fists in the winds which adjusted its course and lifted the faded petal into the flow. It snowed again, or it appeared, but that was not so. For ash drifted from a bonfire of flesh, at the height of the suffocating smog and an orange flare ascended heaven, its remains hailed onto hell.

Where one might think would be bountiful meals, decent and ample, were small, inadequate ration boxes distributed on the endless promenade where the populace have fled from the dread of the interior. The enraged and starving cursed the kingdom and some most devout believers shunned the Gods, steady before if the deities would smite them. Others took to riots and protests, sometimes brawls, in need for the sympathetic garrison's intervention. Ignoring those who rambled in the surroundings, bribing one another for rations with as much as one copper, Arminius and Julien kept their path, past the neglected who dared not speak against the fate they've suffered, as the two carried the loads of supplies and equipment which, at least, fulfilled the basics of survival among the seaside wilderness. However, by chance and luck needed in such a world, they happened upon a clear plot of land, far from the clusters of townsfolk. There, the thin strait of meadow sat behind the steep pebble beach, with a marble boulder, shaped like the remnants of an olden statue dug into the earth, for from a first glance, it was the perfect corner to settle on. Their new home had been decided.

The basha, a simple canvas, was rolled out to be nailed into a tidy shape and with much practice long before, Arminius had completed his tasks astonishingly quickly. The Danne would collect branches of fire-stricken trees and beams of demolished houses for firewood, stacked within the ring of varying sizes of rocks and pebbles. Behind the great stone who watched over the children, a meal of stale packaged bread and canned tomato soup was prepared, but nonetheless, was devoured by the ravenous stomachs who have been craving for a hot dinner. It was not so terrible.

Come late nightfall, on the boundaries of exhaustion, the scattered laughter dwindled. Beneath the beaming stars rolling around the untouchable sky, the candle lamps and torches flickered till they were no more, when the last speck of fluttering light came only from the single campfire, enraged and burning. For it was like the pounding heart of those distraught.

As Arminius and Julien waited for sleep to take them into the fantasies of dreams that never came, fatigued and overworked from a simple act of surviving, none could quite figure why it was they kept awake. Perhaps it was the cloaked anxiety of a single thought one could judge.

"Can't sleep?" Julien mumbled, curled up to preserve a faint warmth, staring at the blaze flickering between its growth and decline.

His concerned face brightened slightly, though was weakened, for Arminus had found the troubles knotted around his inner wishes as he leaned against the firm statue before the gale could touch his skin.

"Have you ever wondered about what we're going to do...?" Reaching for the flames, Arminius asked.

With the weightless fuel in hand, he tossed a snapped stick into the pit, flinging a sparkle of embers into the smoke. Whilst another victim of the fires was picked from the bundles of branches and planks, one reminded his ally in a softer tone,

"During this war."

Julien's eyes kept ahead, never diverting elsewhere. Neither to the crashing waves nor the fluttering ash. Only peering into the fire that could not warm him. Who breathed but no steam arose. He did not shudder in the bestial winter.

"Mm..." He voiced.

It seemed that Julien held the same pain of believing his own soul was useless.

"We can't just stay our lives as bystanders...." Shuffling nearer to the waving light, dashing to and fro by the decaying wind, his hug around his legs tightened.

"Or else...it would be impossible for us to survive next winter..." told Julien, determined for alteration in the course of fate, as he too bombarded the campfire with a handful of twigs.

To the snapping and sparks, spluttering from the pit, Arminius widened his mouth, ready to propel a speech into the whistling wind, when his heart closed upon itself and blurred behind his unthinkable reservedness, abandoning Julien to a guessing game. But it was the persistent indecisiveness that forced Arminius to speak again,

"If we're going to wait for peace anyways,"

"Shouldn't we be fighting too?" He endured an honest smile, but the truth of such conviction was eclipsed by the suggestion.

"Wha—" Julien raised his sights from the ground to a gaze towards his comrade.

Springing up, Arminius escaped the coverage of the motherly boulder, under the watchful eyes of the Danne, and casually trekked a few paces onwards to the blasting cold sweeping the currents and its waves unto the limitless beach. His hands were at the mercy of the cold, where the bicolored pupils he possessed gleamed as the moon sat still, and no less appearing willing to take hold of the heavens that began on the horizon.

"Every second that I have spent in these ten years have been preparing me for war." He spoke of the path so lightly weaving over the heights of a far away paradise.

"That is what I've felt, even if my memories are vague..."

Arminius held his fingers, armored in steel platings, and uncovered a harsh sting that bound his hands to twitch.

"This is our opportunity, Julien!" A pause forced the ever expanding curiosity of the Danne to face him, whilst the fire illuminated their backs.

Fiercely clenching his fists, Arminius punched forth, resolutely grasping the distant night above the palms of the sea as if both the divine waves and the hands of man interlocked.

"We'll become legends worthy of Napoleon's order of ancients." The salted breeze blew against his hair, and his face evolved to display an impassioned desire.

But as the sincerity was with no doubt in all seriousness, the air, like a tempest, was soon humored by a childish chuckle from the great backdrop that the one unbelieving of Arminius blurted.

"What? Like the Radilovs?" Julien teased as Arminius returned himself to the burning aroma, with his towering shadow cast over the path he had retreated from.

"No." The slim grin expanded between the latter's cheeks and told,

"Something greater..."

The ardent goal was apparent and ironclad, wanting for the dream to be had that seemed so close in the lush eyes Arminius held that Julien could joke no more about. That was the truest ambition of an immature mind, but for either since that mark in young time, they were genuine.

"Then I'm assuming you have a plan..." After the absence of any answer had been disbanded, the Danne timidly prompted, when Arminius crouched before his friend and answered assuredly,

"Why would I suggest it if I didn't?"

III

1 VEBRUA 489

01.02.12015

Arminius Reichner

Everything about him is barely noticeable. His small soul. His weak aura. I can't help but often feel cold around him. But that coldness does not sting. Maybe because that scent seems familiar.

Julien is one to try. Blending in with the everyday crowd. But he cannot after all. Unable to be defeated, he would continue the fight when I would easily give up. I know that he's not the strongest I've ever met. I know he's not another commoner. These questions keep me awake and wondering...

What is the truth?

Not once has Julien complained waiting for me to heal. Despite sensing his hiding troubles when his grandpa hadn't come for him, even days and weeks after the raid, he stayed beside me. How could anyone be this patient?

It's unnatural...

But every doubt has been emptied.

The stories of his home. The local legends that I'd never hear of. The pain of being left alone.

To think that after three months, I finally feel the same warmth another would have when they've known each other for their entire lives...

Then...

I wonder why his name still stings me everytime I say it...

CHAPTER

4   RECRUITMENT

Seagulls cawed over the sea of fog that was cleared by the rising sun. Above the solemn waves crashing in the graveyard wreckage of sunken planes. On the dreamy Jupdä morning, the fourth of a week, that was the second day of Julyus in four eighty nine.

Curled up, with his bad hand being rested upon, and his other tucking his legs against his chest, Arminius peacefully slept. While under the basha that was mild and tight, he was cornered at the edges of the imaginary chamber. All in avoidance of Julien. As if he was laying on a king-sized bed, the Danne selfishly conquered the neutral grounds, resting with his rising and sinking stomach exposed to the sunlight. And with whatever odd spell that the warmth had casted, the boy shuffled into another position by the moment the skies had cleared. The wrathful seas of the night and early morning soothed. However, that was much unlike the sleeping fury of Julien, gently wiggling across the thin, tattered mats, who flipped over and rudely smacked Arminius to be awake. With a shock in a flash, the latter coughed. His miserable eyes explained all as he rose and squinted, in search of who had attacked him.

Stretching and yawning, exercising with twists and turns, Arminius kept alert for perhaps, he thought, revenge should be best executed then.

"Julien..." Sleepily, Arminius nudged him who only squirmed.

Faced away, Julien soundly ignored the irked expression of Arminius' gloom, near surrender and defeat. But with a sigh, the awoken boy spun around, not without stirring a scheme when his plan had been revealed from the glint of a light surging through his fingers and an open hand.

"Wake up already!" Arminius yelled, brushing lightning coils along his friend's neck.

A cruel alarm rang across the jolted nerves as the awakening was far from kind when the favor behind karma had been repaid. Julien, shuddering from the biting pain, leapt across the boundaries of a dreamy heaven and returned himself into reality with a shaken cry.

"What the hell—?" Albeit softly, he complained, scratching his neck that had become a reddening sore.

Whilst the dying populace across the meadow had dwindled since the end of winter, that morning appeared and strangely sounded too serene. As intended for Arminius' noting finger pointed out that the fated day had come.

"Ah! I almost forgot!" Julien realized his faults, though to Arminius, he could never assume that the Danne had remembered at all.

And whilst Julien mumbled to himself, blaming his flustered thoughts and his mind in combat, hectic over clothing himself in a frayed jacket, Arminius, who seemed most prepared, fitted a stolen colorless flat cap and escaped for the outer world.

Into the summer, where a broken hunting spear resided beside his feet, he inhaled a generous gasp of the pristine air, for so long had the skies been violated by the smoke plumes, the clouds had recently reversed its state into the untouched white. He watched packs of grieving homeless ready their shovels and market trolleys, beginning the tedious tasks of clearing the rubble that remained common across the city streets. They banded together, for the less enjoyable recovery of aged corpses had turned into somewhat of a duty that each wholeheartedly felt, rather than voluntary. But it was no job for children that Julien knew and recalled, with a tap on Arminius that brought him to the tight scope of the campsite.

Beneath the heavens protecting the heads of the innocent humanity, an honest smile drew across Arminius' face, who, with understanding eyes, retreated from the memorable boulder which beside, he had called home for a great many moons.

"We should get going." Arminius lifted the spear from the pit of befoul ash that left a trail of the dust-like gray and cloaked the weapon in a torn sheet of cloth.

But as his body dragged further away, treading across the bland drying grass, Arminius' sights were only set upon the other who had not budged. Whose mind was entirely drawn towards the supplies, tools, and foods, it was clear for one so close to perceive what Julien thought as worryingly wasteful.

"Shouldn't we pack everything before we go—?" Julien asked, yet upon being enlightened alone by the very same idea that Arminius had conserved, he paused and resolved,

"Nevermind, you're right."

To the opposite of his contemplative friend, Arminius restarted his journey and approached the deceased fire pit, distancing himself from the circling gulls riding the sluggish waves.

"It's best we leave it here in case someone else might need it." Arminius reassured, spinning the splintered spear between his fingers until it was surely caught in a taut grip.

"I'm sure of it." said he, adjusting his cap so that the shadows would not bear weight unto his eyes.

Whilst Arminius walked excitedly by to the pavement and the fractured road, Julien dipped his head and sounded of slight agreement with a muffled voice, when unaware of a hand hooking onto his jacket, felt a firm tug pull him out of oblivion.

"Come on, what are you standing around here for?!" Punching ahead with the spear in one hand and Julien grappled with another, Arminius shouted with the highest vigor of the wartime months.

"They're gonna leave without us!" He warned, eager for the coming happening.

Away from an unforgettable life, within they had spent well lighting fires; hunting untamed boars; and easing the ailing of those wounded around. For them to abandon and search onwards was troubling. However knowing the desire to progress their dreams, the two advanced. To a saga awaiting beyond the dying meadow and the urban roads.

Upon the setting of the desolate townscape in a heated urban environment they passed. As it was for any second day of Julyus, the town was swarming with limitless waves of crowds. Those who sought to join the great patriotic war or had been tamed into this endeavor fought their first battle to the desks of registration and the path to fame. It was better than waiting for peace. For most, the question of recognition as some glorified hero in the eyes of the king and the kingdom outweighed the answer of likely death itself. Yet the battle against the weather was the true initiation test.

Sinking into the sweltering summer, worsened by charging gusts of hot, arid winds, Arminius desperately dragged his legs along the rugged paved path. When he would usually babble and complain, the heat kept his mouth dry and unable to speak. The sweat silently dropped in beads from his wetted hair. His jacket had seemed to have stuck to his skin. And if ever he had the chance, he would childishly hop into shadows where the cool air was his definition of paradise. His comrade, Julien, though strolling from behind on the scorching earth, could not find it to be as deathly so. Instead, enjoying the warm breezes which he could barely feel, skipped his sights across the high street of craters and ash. The populace who rebuilt were less monotonal. Through his beaming eyes, some smiles and coarse chuckles began to reveal. Laboring in the long effort to recover, it bore a gentle warmth.

Soon the summit was too in reach, where the crumbling walls and a ruined spire of a scenic church poked above the sloped road. The memorable clinic they were once granted the hospitality of had become dimmed. No longer was it the core heart of the settlement when there was little need to treat the dead, except for mass burials near.

On the grassy mounds, icons of saints and flowers watched over the graves they commanded. In the new homes of the hidden souls, they could rest for however long eternity would endure. The town in its portrayal bore a striking scene that only reminded him of the voices from home calling for his return.

"If only this war would end all wars..." Julien muttered behind with an unsure face.

Through the narrowing street, soon into an alley, the two allies slipped past the pipes and beams of houses leaning against their fellow roofs and walls. As one paid caution treading over the sharp corners and cracks in the treacherous route towards the square, another had his mind set in division. Holding onto Arminus' shoulder in lead, Julien could not help the sense that their paths were leading them towards different destinations. Tentative over the decision made to fight in the coming battle, his expression grew troubled then blank. Until the sun came to shine upon the duo again, the shock of light broke his wordless ramble.

"Hah...hah..." The huffs of his ally gave no will to the aura emitting worry on the stop before the heavier air.

"What's wrong—?" Julien showed himself and found Arminius' eyes flickering about the town in a search.

Needless of a spoken answer, the rumbles of his stomach replied.

"There! A ration station!" Arminius, who had monstrously recovered on the distant thud of a single grand war drum, spotted with a predator's instinct.

On the outlines of the drear town square, stood a single stall. Away from the crowd piling beneath a shelter, at quite a length. There was hardly any steam or signs of cooking food. Neither was there a queue. Believing their luck was due to be had, Arminius grabbed Julien by the hand and raced towards a meal.

But of course, the fortune was little less than a mirage.

"Oh? Our little jaeger?" The kind lady named Arminius.

Aware of another's recognizable Danne accent, she portrayed nothing but a mask of discontent despite all the aid Julien had provided the town with.

"Sorry," The quartermaster returned to Arminius with a hearty smile.

"We're nearly out so you'll have to share." She apologized upon handing out a tray of a meal.

The portions were tiny and were never full in bowls. Perhaps enough for an average child but the contents were old and the least filling. Somehow, the leftovers they had were more discouraging to see than the canned foods each faced daily. However these fumes were better for their bodies than to run on the stinking air.

"That's alright!" Arminius brightened and cheerily turned themselves away.

They never saw the shaking head of the lady whose soul knew to give more, yet, could not.

To an isolated corner, with Julien close, Arminius slumped down against the remains of a blackened brick wall. Fallen pipes and disintegrated stones surrounded their small bodies as the monument was spotted with shrapnel wounds and blood shadows, reviving the memories of that night. The remains of a shop or whether it was a home for one or few. No one quite knew.

They watched ahead, at the people who flocked towards the town's center. Lines of conscripts and volunteers dismally marched onwards, to the engines unseen but heard behind the splintered corners of streets. At the gong of the collapsed bell, the boys looked at each other. One, with an optimistic grin, at the other bearing an unclear tone.

Laying the tray on his lap and the spear on the rubble, Arminius took hold of the hardened loaf of bread. And with all might, he tore it unevenly. Naturally, his hand lifted the larger piece for Julien as the wasted crumbs fell onto the grayish ground.

"Thanks..." said the Danne, slightly.

Whilst he watched Arminius dip his bread in the soup of potato peelings and onions, his mind was elsewhere. As Julien's friend had felt his strange lack of appetite, he stopped chewing before concernedly asking,

"What's wrong?"

Who was plainly staring at his lifeless meal, Julien tensed under the fleet of clouds. Mumbling to himself, the expression on the Danne's face darkened as he hesitantly disclosed his inner stresses.

"Have you ever wondered..." He held his penchant in a loosened fist as invading crows swooped across the sky.

"What might happen to us on the battlefield?"

With a puzzled face, Arminius turned to Julien, who pondered limitlessly. About the strings of the future that had already been weaved into fate.

"What do you mean?" Gulping, Arminius burdened himself beside the terrors of doubt.

"My grandfather..." told Julien, briefly beginning.

"His only desire is to fight a rewarding battle."

Knowing the same will, Arminius' glance was thrown away. The light in his eyes lessened and the ambition was no more. He wondered whether the solemn tone of his friend was a simple clue that this plan to dive with the currents into the war front was but a forced choice upon Julien.

"I can't understand why not one soldier," The latter mumbled.

"Not even him...fears death..." He shied away.

Of all the entangling indicators sprouting from Julien, that it may be war was not his chosen path, the shades had been defeated under the naivety summoned in Arminius' fixated eyes.

"You'd be stupid not to fear death." A soft grin surfaced from one's face as a slight snigger was freed.

"Either of us will know," Peering into his reflection on the clouded armor, he recalled.

"From that night."

Julien, whose cheeks turned bright red, flinched as Arminius patted his head and promised with a candid smile,

"If you're *that* afraid of it,"

"Then I'll be the one to protect you." He knew no bounds to embarrassing his companion.

But for the very least, it seemed that Julien's worries had been driven away. An innocent glint returned. He stuffed his bread between his lips and dipped his flustered face, hidden behind the fatty crust as the apparent answer had been given.

A chuckle came from Arminius, yet it drowned the shy thanks that his friend gave soon,

"Okay..."

When he eventually took a bite, Julien's appetite rose. Though realizing for how long his stomach had been starved of, the Danne raced between the soup and bread, pulverizing the last crumbs with his quick, immature manners. Watching over, who resumed his own meal, Arminius gathered a brief smile. It was then that the crisp chimes of an announcing bell rang twice.

Suddenly, the boom from a croaky voice of a stumpy man, redressing his height on a podium, exploded through his newspaper cone.

"De convoy'll be leavin' now!" He announced in a thick, southern Yurupe accent.

"If y'all enlistin', please make away to yer station and await fer de next 'un!"

As the masses scrambled to the counters, where the recruiters were posted, they could only watch in bewilderment by the fanatic race to the lines. It was their turn too, they knew.

"C'mon!" Arminius dropped the tray on the ground, which then had been emptied already, and took Julien by the hand again.

Excitedly, one, with a spear, pulled the other to rise, and sprinted to the shortest queue they could find of the dozen which there were. No matter where, it was as impressive.

There must be at least a thousand signing up. Arminius thought, slipping between the gaps of towering adults and the taller, through the unseen lengths of bodies crowding around the ruinous square.

Skipping the chain of soured faces who glared at the unmannerly youth, their turn was due at the front of the counter.

Records, in innumerable stacks, layered like clothing over the desk. The leaning towers of folders and snapped books shielded their heads, that merely a single strand of hair stood upright over the menacing pages.

"Here." Arminius pointed, directing Julien's eyes to another ledger below.

The names were messily scribbled and were hardly eligible. Some words were not, at the minimum, recognizable. And they realized, the recruiters nor their overlords, the officers and country, must not have paid any concern for the list to become an abstract art piece. Statistics, was all these words meant.

Who was first, the Danne spun the bandaged pencil into his grip and knowing that the course to war was resolute, speedily wrote, without much hesitation,

Julien Carlstadt. 8 Vebrua 477.

From behind the desk, the squealing chair rolled nearer. Intimidatingly, the bored recruiter, picking at her fingernails, loomed over the duo.

"Age?" Despite having the birthday, cleanly presented before her, the volunteer asked abruptly.

"Twelve…" Julien replied with a tensed gulp.

From the rear storage compartments in the hundreds of boxes, cluttered in rows, the recruiter snatched a white armband and carelessly tossed it over the records. Landed in Julien's hands was the poorly sewn cotton piece. With hints of beige, it was a soiled white color, unlike the standard reds, blues, and yellows of old Alben which the generations above wore.

Strict on their code of enlistment, the isles' law had divided the cadets into colored bands. By age, it was the White Band, who were of the youth's section that Arminius knew well. He did not quite meet the lower bounds.

With the pencil in his hand, anxiously pinching upon the sharpened edges, he worriedly stared at the sheet of paper whilst the recruiter had looked away. Arminius caught a glimpse of

Julien, beside him, although his friend was never too troubled as he had been long distracted by adjusting his armband. Then, slyly concluding, he forced his hand to forge a new birth year,

Arminius Reichner. 11 Apelyotes 476.

Casually resting the pencil on the record book, Arminius breathed again. As if time had resumed its path, Julien returned his sights on his calmed ally, and the recruiter spun around, with a white band ready.

"Age?" She robotically repeated, though the same answer was expected.

"Twelve." Arminius faked with a glance at Julien.

Another band glided across the table and was settled in his hands. Unbelieving of the dream that he had always once had, of a life in war, or perhaps it was his role in nature's giving, Arminius stared longingly. A bottom most step to fulfilling the honor for his house had been conquered. But not so soon, his imagining of the noble future was broken by the next in line.

Rudely shoving him to be away, a conscript shot a blunt, brutal glare at the youth as Julien brought his friend to departure.

Uncaring for the disdain cast amongst the seniors, Arminius' mind had been encapsulated by the want to know what route his soul would run. Burrowed distant from the present. And whilst the fantasies circled in an infinite vortex, a poke on his back startled him most.

"I didn't know you were older than me." Julien cheerfully mentioned, as they neared the rumbling convoy.

Pulling up his armband, Arminius took a short look at the Danne.

"I was never to begin with." He smugly responded, silencing his perplexed comrade.

On the turn of a corner, the pair were greeted by the sight of archaic engines. The smell of rare black gold struck Arminius to awaken from a dream. Scouting the vehicles in wait, Julien childishly counted each truck, brimming with fresh recruits, seated like sardines in cans when the last transport wagon, that was not yet filled, was found.

An open topped supply truck showed beyond a haze of steam and smoke. Its paint had begun to peel from the elements. Exposed rust spotted the chassis. And even more dangerously, neither the wheels appeared to be anyhow healthy. Despite the dread of embarking on some treacherous machine, unseen ever before, Arminius eagerly leapt onto the vehicle. In a swift spin, he leaned outward with a hand, for Julien who latched on tightly, the Danne was pulled aboard. But before a given chance to be sat, the brakes creaked and unclamped. Huffs from the exhausts spurted, and the convoy stumbled onward.

The backdoors were shut by the garrisons overlooking the transports. Thumps of fists on the plated wagons sent a signal for the vanguard. Whilst passing by the other bands, as the ages progressed towards the conscripts and recalled veterans, the youngsters of the new modern army saw the faces of their elders. Emotionless and found less thrill. They were the stark opposite of the laughter sounding ignorant of the unknown war afar.

The scenic route peaked on the rolling hills and lush flora with valleys surfing over the lands. Streams flowed from the peaks of shield-like mountains aside the raw summer winds, distinct from the ruined town's smog. Flowers of the meadows sprouted and revolved their bodies towards the eye of the sun. Shining rays of warmth landed upon Arminius, but not Julien in his shadow where both savored the view of forests. The lungs of the world. The vast emptiness of farmland and fields. Plains stretching yonder to the lines of the horizon. Their gleaming pupils told only of the expression that could explain a feeling of awe. That awe was to expand to not knowing bounds.

At the turn on the highway, the convoy swung into the treeline. Tiring to endure, Arminius and Julien held onto the truck as it rocked up and down. The path that led deeper into the woods only narrowed, and few paces from the bustling carriageway, the road was impossibly already no wider than the height of a person. Branches stuck at their faces, depressed by the seesawing of the vehicle from side to side. Wheels slipped and dipped into the mud as if it was an unending torture. Then at the wide stream, the convoy plunged into the currents. Like a ram, the recruits were thrown ahead where some were drenched in the tides.

"Gods dammit!" They screamed as others moaned before the few, dried and warm, smirking.

The final stretch was in sight after the bothersome barrier

when until then, they had suffered only the unlivable. Upon arrival, the painting had been redrawn with a strange blessed light.

A standing blossom within the burning hell of the blighted kingdom. Most surely, the unique flair gave the site a certain tint of brilliance from the counterparts who were imaginably drab. There, a bridge linked the banks together, cast over a shallow stream flanked by pebbled levees. As after much of the reservoirs had been diseased, hordes of laboring folk heaved water from an olden mill to some places else, yet to be discovered through the gawking eyes. The urbanization of the vast cavity within the woodland left a single lone tree, standing beside the bridge and the headquarters that overlooked the shimmering flow. In steps like stairs, the far cliff had been chiseled. Barracks and storages coated the far background whilst cubical wooden towers bore on watch on the elevated borders reinforced by palisades. And dressed like a Rus fortress, hidden in the holiest valley was the White Band's camp.

Where the convoy braked and halted beyond the broken gates, the many instructors watched the flood of fresh recruits leap onto the gravel ground. Lifting the lock of its hold on the backdoor, Arminius followed the crowd onto the sand, lifting a small dust cloud upon his disembarkment. As he watched for Julien, stumbling on his unsteady jump, the awaited first command came.

"Get yer arses over 'ere!" The sternest instructors repeatedly yelled.

"Hup hup!" Others playfully added.

In little bundles, it seemed most cadets had formed the bows of beginning bonds. Given gestures, pointing fingers and waving arms directed the herd to a small barn-shaped depot. Behind, where once made sure by the garrisoning soldiers, the chortling engines restarted to a retreat deeper into the forest. Though the noise never gave so much as a stroke on Julien's ears.

Mesmerized by the camp, he received the splendor of the postcard-like landscape.

"Ju-lien!" Arminius, with a prolonged shout, called for his friend.

Raising a thumb at the warehouse where all else had gathered before them, he hooked the Danne from thought.

_____

In the queue that could compete with those of Bristel, the two watched the rush of recruits hurry with uniforms in delighted hands. Blithely chasing each other across the narrow stream to the dorms which castled the layered ridge, the cadets headed. Perhaps the excitement flushed Arminius and Julien with the flow of impatience as the nervousness arose from their thumping hearts before their wait had been paid.

Entering the shades beneath the high curving roof above, the breeze submerged the great heat. The echoes that would once sound from the beating heels were curbed under the chatters. Around, the encircling crates were chaotically littered, with junk sat atop, and wherever they tread, it turned to be a winding course around the heaps of wasted linen or metals.

Whilst avoiding to wound themselves in the maze, there carefully, over the path, a cheerful young man waited for the next battle-ready pair. As his fellow instructors dispassionately followed the common practice of measurements and distribution, that certain officer seemed rather joyous. Who was overly enthusiastic about this dull job tending to the cadets, he seemed lighthearted even if his greetings and goodbyes were not always remembered.

"Oh? Who's 'ese young'uns?" The youthful instructor twisted his voice, searching the crowds beyond and the line ahead.

His accent sounded forced. As if it was an act played to pretend.

"Ya guys might be de youngest 'round 'ere!" With the last quarter of a cigarette, clamped between his teeth, he presumed.

Lightly tanned with an absolute and unserious face, he had sun gold hair drawn back with a blank black headband. He was not particularly handsome by high standards, but averagely well-looking. His charm of some typical high-schooler divided this man from any encounter thus far. Dirtied with grease and grit, his appearance was unlike that of a model soldier. Although, matching his keen brown eyes, he certainly possessed a confident stature that was ordinarily tall and tough. Though it was not seen because of his incredibly strange uniform. Unprofessional but fashionable, it was profaning the code of conduct that stole the spotlight for such delinquency.

Stunned by this unexpected introduction, Arminius and Julien stood speechless.

"O'course," The instructor remembered, crushing the dying cigarette in his bare palms where the marks of old ash were dotted.

"Haven't introduced m'self have I?"

Upon removing yet another smoke, buried in a pocket of mess, he held the small roll of herbs, unlike tobacco, and a matchbox close as in another time of the day, made himself better acquainted with future comrades,

"I'm Adam."

"I normally oversee de kitchen, but…" Adam removed a match and lit his cigarette in a flash.

Breathing in, to the embers which paled and regrew, the instructor unsheathed two tape measures and gladly assessed them before his aiming eyes.

"Sometimes, bein' an instructor ain't too bad eith'r." He had no gaps for the recruits to interfere.

Memorizing the numbers his quick mind had taken, Adam scrolled his eyes along the toppest shelves and spotted the perfect sets. Without a ladder, however, who never shocked Arminius nor Julien, their instructor nimbly climbed to the apex and swiped his hand along the boxes. As the earth returned him to the hard floor with a thump, he laid the uniforms on the table, more agile than Arminius in a javelin match. Patting the two neat batches of clothes, his calculating sights bore upon their feet.

"What's both ya names?" Adam leaned over the table, scratching the sideburns of his hair.

"Reichner! Arminius Reichner!" One proudly replied over the rising smoke.

"Julien…Carlstadt…" Another softly said for himself.

The instructor froze. His inquisitive eyes turned upward and were latched by the sparkle of an ice-like jewel. But to him who cleared his mind with a shake of the head, he found it impossible to be.

"Carlstadt…?" Adam repeated.

Returning to his work, the stumped soldier rummaged the cupboards behind and below, though was not more so than who he named.

Scaredly, Julien paced back, but it was enough to arouse such suspicion.

From the corner of his eye, Arminius had felt the sense of hazed secret, wrapped like foil around his friend. And certainly, within the subtle mumbling, Adam bore a flick of a thought. But annoyingly, it could not be made out what was spoken.

"Hah! I guess dat name's common 'round dose parts, huh?" The instructor sprung into view again.

"I'll remember ya both!" Adam chuckled, pushing onwards the full uniforms across the counter.

"Just make doubly shore ya take care o' yer selves." He tipped and let the duo free of his voice.

Recovered by the force away from the obscured truth, Arminius and Julien cheerfully nodded and thanked him with a synced smile. Taking their uniforms off the counter, and like the many others before them, they were pushed to be gone by a memorable laughter in the background who greeted the following few.

To the splashes of the current against the boulders and the bridge's stilts, Arminius led his comrade. The shadows of the broad dark leaves fluttered, as it screened their heads from the afternoon sun. Unto the flat wooden crossing, raised slightly over the stream where the running water made its course, Arminius stopped at the climax. Daringly, he trailed onto the edge, watching the free, soothing flow. But for how long he submerged himself in the homely camp and the forest around, something had impaled him.

"Carlstadt." It was out of his character to speak of this name so formally.

Paused behind, the Danne could not reply to such a shock, and between a step, he lined his feet together.

"Why does your name silence everyone...?" With merely a heart of unknowing, Arminius faintly asked.

Those of the earlier call raced to the banks where most would be idly by, lazing and conversing about the newfound bands of recruits. Gazing at the endless bounds of the camp, flanked by the lodges overlooking the parade square, Arminius was taken by the breadth of contrast between the shrine-like peacefulness of the wilderness and the near-forgotten war. Things which concerned him reminded that a baseless belief such as by his comrade's name was the lesser and saw a snapping change of his young curiosity.

"Whatever..." told he.

On the softening of the ripple from the weakening wind, Arminius turned away and advanced on, leaving Julien alone, in a developing abyss of answers he could tell and not. Quiet and enclosed, he wondered,

Arminius...should I...say anything...?

But... Julien countered with a slap on his face, as Arminius casually passed by.

What if he hates me for it—? In thought, then when there was a jolt that disturbed the curse of aimless doubting, he yelped,

"W-Wait!"

By the shirt, Arminius dragged him along the resumed path. But the ride was not so terrible. As if both were with memories short, had erased the tension, Julien and Arminius rattled themselves anew under the nature of forgetting.

At the bridge head's tip, the road ended and diverged into branches stretching to the reaching corners of the encampment. Where one instructor defended, towards the point that his finger pinned, was directing the pair onto the farthest barrack, that along they went. Hiking the blocks of weathered stairs to the trail that faced the sizable dormitories, they breathlessly, who could not take mere rests, sprinted beside the blocks. As they had eyed, it was before the last barrack that they dug their feet into the gravel that the ground would break their run till a stop.

Gazing across, the cadets surveyed the flattened face of the lodge. It was a longish construct of timber and arches, as simple as any encampment may appear. Dual windows guarded its entrance, with curtains drawn to retain the surprise of unfamiliar allies awaiting within. Then there was the rumbling door and steel handle that tempted Arminius' excitement.

As the Danne steeled himself with a sharp breath, Arminius approached and reached for the entrance in a relaxed demeanor. The gateway opened into the hive of trainees.

It was nothing more than a simple, casual dorm, plagued by the often creaks when they stepped on the wrong floorboard. However, may it be luck or not, that poor noise was suffocated by the rowdiness of the interior atmosphere that stretched along the twenty four bunk beds lining the candle and lantern lit room. Where the sun beamed through the dusty windows into the wide hall with its high ceiling, made narrower for the number of recruits, the youthful vigor was illuminated. And as the two strolled through the corridor-like path, they found a charmful corner that had not been occupied since most had found their retreats nearer the door.

"Looks like home." Arminius searched the hard mattresses amongst the disinteresting stronghold.

"It isn't too bad." Julien shyly spoke in the presence of a lack of recruits.

"You think so too?" Arminius chuckled.

Swiping a thick smudge of dirt from the poles that he grinded on his armor, and upon finding a broken chest at the foot of the bed, they had decided. Opening the trunk, he was first to stash his spear, and both readied to lay their new equipment on the beds. Though there was one thing left to be called.

"Bottom or top?" Arminius humbly asked when Julien hurried up the unstable ladder towards his bunk, that it was expectedly his choice.

Smiling gleefully, Julien swung his dangling legs and enjoyed the panoramic sights for he was usually shorter than most, the Danne was able to guard the half-filled dorm with his fascinated eyes with a feeling of his figure surpassing others for once.

"We should get changed—" Arminius suggested when they were interrupted by the distant click of the door.

Swung open and through came an unwelcome comrade's face who was shaded by the sun's sideway glare. For his surprise reflected in Arminius' eyes, was a provoking dismay, the newcomer's leer was settled on his rival discovered in the building's remote corner.

"Oh?!" The cadet who had walked in, was gifted by a challenger's grin.

To Arminius' disillusionment, he bitterly revealed the recruit's name,

"Colt?"

IV

7 APELYOTES 488

07.11.12014

Julien Carlstadt

Danen has finally declared war. The last nation of Aelon to do so...

Something calls for my return. To fight with my people even if I don't know how to. But I can't bear to leave Arminius alone. Yet, a hand clenching my heart tells me many other things. That I should sail home. That I should play my part in bringing our world to peace. Wilhelm should've found me by now...unless he followed grandfather into war...

I don't ever want my disappearance to drag down their effort, so in the meantime, we'll find a way to help however we can. Even if it means to dig graves waist deep in the dead, or bandage rotting wounds. I'll do it.

But for now, I'll remain here, in this quiet room. Beside the first I could call a friend in this life...and once he wakes up, we'll decide whatever we will do.

For now, I still wonder...

Where have I heard of your name, Arminius...?

CHAPTER 5   THE EVENING OF FATE

For the same pride within the rivals, unwilling to scatter, a clash in the band was to come. And although neither felt that way when the gap between was further, it was when Colt began his way towards the rear of the dorm that a spark ignited their instincts, blasting Julien beyond the clusters of rage. Who could not fathom the startling aura tenfold of any regular recruits, he gulped as his eyes followed Colt near their beds. Julien's fists tensed, on the railings of the upper bunk, as the antagonist halted beside Arminius. The natural enemies stared ahead.

"Did you think you'd rule over these extras alone?" asked Colt, drawing his leer upon Arminius.

"Aren't you one of them?" The latter taunted with a lightning-like glare.

"Arminius..." Julien tried breaking the stench of lust for domination, lest the instructors would catch them inciting a riot.

But he could not do so alone when the heated troublemakers were unwilling to cease the duel.

As the cadets, distant from the commotion, carried their way, the rivals' eyes locked settled on the growing embers into a colossus of fire. The door opened and slammed shut. However, the shaking bangs could not tear them apart. Until unpredictably, the blue blaze of one's soul dwindled.

"Tch! Whatever." Colt snapped, passing by to the bunk of the opposite.

Slumping down onto the bed of screeching springs, he collected his breath and eased. With a quick glance to the allied enemy, whom Arminius could not so simply ignore, his thoughts remained fixed on the terrible competition he had not expected him to appear.

Stammering, by the malice absorbed into the air, Julien leaned over the bed and asked with a desire to unearth the

grudges,

"W-What was that about?"

Bearing the face of irritation and specks of envy, Arminius removed his coat and slipped his arms through a clean buttoned jacket. Though, as if his emotions had been false, upon a sharp exhale, he gathered a relieved expression.

"It's nothing." Arminius peered upward and told Julien with a forced smile.

The rage stilled in the atmosphere was weak and disintegrating. But in the dorms, for Julien who could not be convinced by the uncertainty of Arminius' answer, he seemed to be stranded in no man's land waiting to erupt once more. The bystanding sensed his uselessness. Unable to divide the roaring winds.

Knotting the last laces onto the rear of his boots, Arminius swung his body from the bed and slipped into the vacant corridor with a Alba red and white kepi hooked around his fingers. Treading across the barrack, his footsteps weighed heavy. The shadows of the bunks and himself lengthened beside the lowering sun. And without a word to his closest companion, he reached for the door and swung it awide. With a hint that Arminius was longing to escape the darkness from the need to share the same sullied air as his antagonist, Julien watched the outlines of his friend bind with the blinding orange light till it closed and trapped the scent of lamps within.

The crisp forest breeze blew past the trunks of trees and lunged their weightless bodies against him, overlooking the parade square below the steps into the valley from the gravel pathway. Towards Apollo's star, his dim, shaded gray cloak flicked along the waves of winds, partially veiling the carmine red field blouse, the pride of the kingdom. As he calmly breathed, ridding of the clouds obscuring his thudding heart, he brought his hands to tighten his leather belt, though for how irremovable the trousers were, there was little need. And somehow, it was in spite of his juvenile face, Arminius bore some maturity in the imperial uniform of august Alben.

Whilst he fitted his cap, tightly onto his head, the light shut of the door behind turned Arminius towards a recruit. Hurrying to his side, the Danne figure swung the cloak around his shoulders and made sure not to entangle the invaluable jewel around his neck. As Julien appeared from the dormitory, shabbily dressed, he embarrassedly asked in a flustered tone,

"Is this…is anything wrong…?"

Arminius shook his head, near to laughter that Julien never understood. There was indeed one thing that he had his eyes upon since his comrade approached. And that, any would do, was the raised collar that Arminius adjusted.

"Thanks…" mumbled Julien when a shadow pushed past.

It was the same cadet who had given such a hated scowl at Arminius earlier.

Not flinching, and thinking that he had needed to voice something as the disrespect before him remained unparalleled, Julien prepared to lift the barrier on his voice. It was most irregular for his normality. Storming ahead, beyond Arminius' care, he reached for the recruit. But in a turn, Colt turned to the threat of aura that he could detect, and with a stare, an equivalent of a seasoned general's, flicked himself free from the paralyzed grasp.

No longer were there words. Only a touch of fear sprinkled like a preview to the gross fires attacked Julien. Watching Colt chase the freed currents of a gust to the river, the Danne stayed caged in an ever shrinking cell of terror.

"Don't mind him." Arminius held Julien's stiffened shoulders, which when the protective hands eased him, relaxed.

"He does that sometimes."

"What do you mean…?" Julien held speechless.

Drumming the thin windows and door, the winds battled on for the rattles against the dorm's frames fell into sustained thuds.

"It's a stupid dream." Returning to the Danne's flank, Arminius grinned as he had remembered what burden Colt desired to tug.

"By defeating everyone he would meet, that Colt believes this way, he could become the greatest warrior." He faced Julien with an embarrassed look, filled under a library of memories of that night of a thought alike.

"Even greater than…?" Julien paused for his friend to answer.

"Yeah," Arminius softly endured.

"Even greater than the Whirlwind."

"The living God of War." Bearing his sights down and ahead, onto Colt, whose figure subjugated the courtyard in a cover of an azure kei, they uttered.

The crowd enlarged in the flattened rays of sunlight sliding onto the square before the instructors who began their march to attention on the stream bank's edges. Amidst the stamps of an officers' column, some three hundred recruits were present. It perhaps meant nothing in a war spanning continents, the number which was there, but who had gathered as one entity, despite scattered and disorderly, formed an impressive lake of grays and reds. There lacked visual disparity.

At the rear, into the masses, Arminius and Julien joined their comrades lastly. Nimbly slipping into the force, until all units positioned in some shattered structure or otherwise, the two stood beside unknowing of the welcome they would hear. However, in the wait that passed slowly, the doubt that anyone would appear wore at the impatient.

"How long are we gonna stand here for—?!" Colt voiced, within the center ranks.

Though his ask had been answered from a ground-trembling voice that shook the valley of the flocks of birds.

"All cadets!" He spoke, ceasing the courtyard with an echo-like shockwave, which to think, a mere human produced from the depths of his lungs.

With their ears deafened and a call that summoned them awake, the White Band hesitantly shuffled and listened for further orders. Still as boulders, they had anyhow irritated the man from the formation that baffled him.

"A hound could do better!" The head instructor raised his shout and commanded heatedly,

"Into six damned ranks!"

Julien and the many aside him scurried to new columns and ranks, in a neverending orchestra of stomps. But whilst his eyes were not on his own in line, amongst the dust clouds rising from the dragging feet, there were three alert and unmoving. Who were unwavering too. Arminius, Colt, and a girl seemed bizarrely familiar with the protocol. The Danne, composed by those he copied and practiced in standing at ease, could not rid of the curious scent of odd veterancy.

"Anyone would know to stand at ease, fools!" An angry yell stormed as the court desperately shifted once more, with their marches sounding like machine gun fire.

"I swear on my honor I'll execute you all for the next time you blunder!" The instructor rampaged.

Short and somewhat fat, he was a middle-aged man. His face was old, and had eyes deprived of sleep. With a white mustache and stressed graying hair, presented himself wearing a slacked green beret, neatly placed on his head. The squarish armor, fitting of his arrogance, was undoubtedly unliftable, but he seemed able and adaptable to his slowed body. However ineptly appearing he was, by his feet, a weapon belonging to a deity napped standing straight on the loose gravel. Arminius, peering over the heads as his own held straight, spotted the glimmer of the stream-like blue maul hammer of ivory and steel that stood twice the height as its wielder himself, whose one hand gripped the enchanting weapon and another cast from view.

And as if he had lost all breath to battle the petrified trainees, the instructor withdrew his terror-striking growl.

"Hear me, cadets, and know my name." He was hinted as calmed, then released an outburst again,

"In the later two years of your sad age here, I am your commanding officer and head instructor Major Thomas Ascot!"

Giving way, by the tip of the hammer, Ascot pointed at his fellow subordinates and introduced a familiar officer at the head of the instructors' detachment.

"My second-in-command is he!"

"Vice instructor Mister Adam Skowroński!" His foreign name was revealed but without a rank.

"Do not better expect him to be a winged hussar." The commander added in a casual manner.

Immaturely waving his cigarette, it was by accident that Adam launched the smoke at a cadet's face who flinched from the meager burn. As whilst the major babbled and named the every officer in line, none too interesting, for at least, the boredom was overshadowed by the vice instructor's ignorant self, unapologetic and noisily scraping his shoes on the parched ground.

"All must know that as a subject of our kingdom and its army," Ascot cleared his voice after the mundane opening act.

"There is but one trait that we shall need!" He explained.

Spotting the perfect victim for a question at the vanguard of the White Band ranks, Ascot marched towards an unfortunate recruit.

"Mister Gin Calenzo!" The instructor called for the smirking cadet.

"You ass of a delinquent!"

With a face and structure quite clearly defined and sharp, the proud soldier, older than the average cadet of the band, had the brawns and tan of a farmer's child. Carelessly dressed, his prayers rested in wait for battle, as he was not so different from someone named Colt. Although one could take, this Gin Calenzo was most definitely slower in the mind. Told from his whiskey-colored eyes, the recruit emitted a brute's aura, intimidate ahead, past his spiked hair in the shape of a surfing wave. It was the shade of sunset gold that matched his warrior's spirit for when he stood to answer, the grounds felt to have quaked.

"Let us see if your thick skull can recall what I've told you repeatedly before," Ascot reminded him and asked,

"What is that one trait, as soldiers, we all require on the battlefield?!"

"A trait, huh?" Gin repeated, in a thinner accent than Adam's.

Then gathering his lacking intelligence, answered ever so surely,

"'Course that'd be da wish to kill!"

As he found the head instructor to be nodding, appearing satisfied by the answer, the recruit smugly smirked. Then Ascot paused. When the shoe of his hammer drove itself into the stomach of stubborness.

Felling Gin, gagging and vomiting on his knees, the major smashed the titanic shaft onto the yard and muttered with fissuring annoyance,

"You truly are a waste of air to have spoken at all—"

"Devotion!" Then, another cried in interruption, and spun the commander's head to the source of the answer.

"Exactly..." Ascot, impressed by the most definite reply, trailed for the tensing cadet.

"Devotion and duty."

However, from that, his mind sharply fractured again and erupted.

"But silence!" The major swung his hammer near the trainee's face, exploding a gale from the halt before the ivory met bloodshed.

"Speak when you are told to!"

"For you will die by my hands before the Confederates'!" He observed the frightened face and quieted his rage before allowing himself to continue.

Raising the hammer above the cadet, who slumped from the horrors drilled into his chaotic and feeble mind, Ascot retreated to the sides of his instructor comrades. And paying no pity for the one petrified recruit, he only returned to the two hundred ninety nine alerted by the roar of his aura.

"I was taught too late, two decades ago, in the Fourth Danne War." began the commander to a short lecture.

"A good soldier does not think of its adversary as a human,"

Although, it was within Arminius' memories, this quote that had been forced upon his throat to swallow, he could not yet remove the coldness which the words blanketed, dispersing an outbreak of goosebumps.

"Once one realizes the humane soul of his enemies, he is no longer so." The major ended, then keeping his hammer high, he fiercely warned,

"These dual years are not for the frail!"

"Devotion to *our* kingdom, and, *our* people will determine how this war shall change!" Ascot shot a short glance at the quivering boy and with the blunt fervor for war, sent the final message to the White Band.

"I am merely here to guide you on your duties," said he.

His mammoth hammer was lodged into the dirt, unwilling to falter even in the shoving gusts which could topple a pyramid of shields, as the lead instructor brought his hand into a strained fist before the cadets.

"If you cannot see yourself of use to our defenses and assaults, there is no dishonor in disbanding." He added threateningly to the class, absolute on their role in silence, so as not to anger the unstable man anymore.

"But know this!" Ascot grasped the gradual dipping of

heads and slack in their stance, and like puppets, launched the individual consciousnesses to the induction speech.

"Without devotion nor duty, we are nothing but a rotting pile of litter waiting to be trampled on."

The unforeseen introduction, straight and true, began to stir murmurs and doubts among the indefinite cadets. Arminius cast a glimpse at Julien and who returned the same, they were filled with enough certainty to remain, kept on the journey as if they were on railways.

"Now, all units!" The major tore open the heavens' doors with the claws of his voice.

As the second-in-command, Adam braced, who prompted the instructors and showed the band to perform so too. The cloud of sands levitated from the attending square and floated as mist over their knees.

"The training will commence tomorrow!" Ascot commanded in his return across the bridge before the ceremony had concluded.

"May you suffer a missing finger if you are late!" His speech had completed with the evening order of the decaying sunlight.

"Dismissed!"

The thundering of the march, the recruits and instructors saluted. Open-palmed with the thumb pressed onto the chest. They bore the sign of an honorable blade upon the heart. With a farce of waving the recruits, hurriedly sent to be away, Adam overwatched his aides and allies falling out of formation. And thus, the dispersal began the two year journey through the White Band.

From the bank near the commander's office, the vice instructor guarded the retreat of Thomas Ascot into the immense sanctuary of paperwork and faint candles. As the square was all there he was alone, he scrolled his eyes along the path taken by his superior. Till unseen by any recruits, the door slammed fastly closed, but it was by the shaking hand the major had kept reserved.

Hiking through the grass, beside the stairs then lined with lounging recruits, Arminius dashed to the top with Julien latched onto his cloak. At the last arm of the climb, they grappled and leapt above the valley's slope, and furthered with an easy jog towards their far dorm.

The Apollo had plummeted, abandoning a slight orange border, clamped and thinning beneath the delft blue sky and above the darkening forest canopy. As whilst the intimate torches and braziers were alight across the camp, gave no naturality that full Luna, risen from her slumber, had provided nightly illumination over the lands of mother Terra. It was the beauty of a world, so contrasting, that they had ignored, despite the scenery of it steadily changing alongside their run.

Exhausted of breath, the pair slowed and declined into a stroll. And before the same entrance was presented, Arminius and Julien stopped and summited the three planks of steps, resonantly from their heels. The chatter that their sharp, hunter ears could detect, was livelier. But nonetheless, where nearest the door, so whilst believing peace and serenity in their corner had been promised, they reentered the dorm. To that, they were introduced to a barrage of bickering voices roaring from their retreat.

Accompanied by his suspicions that one sounded terribly familiar, Arminius cautiously returned for his bed, leading Julien past the recruits who had been shaken by the unfolding of anarchy.

"Ya gotta problem, huh?!" Gin latched his hands onto another trainee's collar who Arminius expected for him to be.

"How did someone like you get in the white band?!" Colt wildly returned as ferociously so.

"Did ya mean anythin' more dan dat, Colt?!" The golden haired recruit fought in return.

And whilst they battled with words and little action, on the verge of a brawl, a reserved cadet sat uncaringly, peering emptily into the storm. That he sighed, never attentive before the fight, the unsociable, but sane, was met by the pair who casually joined the audience.

"What are they up to now?" asked Arminius, leaning against the wall, though he would have known who had given birth to the fire.

The unhelpful recruit did not answer.

Something, in a way that the recruit cuttingly stared ahead, spoke of a mildly cavalier attitude. He had slim, midnight blue pupils, sharp to bear resemblance to a preying feline. With a fringe that hung from the left, his longish hair, covering an eye, was a dusk gray color. His frame was ordinary, and whose blood was of the south, was a figure between Arminius and Julien's height. Neither appearing apparently potent nor powerless, he showed no interest in anything beyond his inner circle. Whilst it was that which gave him a first impression of slyness too.

Then, an ominous shadow, with gleaming red eyes took hold of Gin and Colt by their collars, and lifted the two, whom to him were hardly weights.

"Are...you...done...?" Bellowing, he startled his comrades.

Seeming unknowing how to communicate, the demon appeared from the void. With especially short blackish purple hair, his nose was tall, befitting of the cadet's squarish face. The irregularity of his aura had drowned the dorm into a time of silence. There was but a sole reason for the lack of need to negotiate. The giant was taller than the six foot high bunks and the bulk he carried doubled those of his comrades. That is, he was only at the age of fourteen. The seriousness in the glare could bring an early winter to the heat of summer.

Heartlessly tossing the numbed rivals who choked as they rolled along the floor, that rocked the barrack, and with a ghastly warning, the demon watched over the fallen when a pat tapped his shoulder to cool.

"Come on, Miklo," A light hearted cadet approached the group that had formed.

"You're scaring them." He joked, confessing his brightening nature.

Colt hushed and began to rise, rubbing his sore ribs and arms bruised by the giant. But Gin could not stay so still.

"This titan..." The sweat on the brute's face began to steam as his rage churned.

The recruit, whose companion was the demon and was not so much taller than Colt, advanced past the living wall and welcomed himself into the lantern glow.

"Sorry about him," An apology stemmed for the one who could not quite speak, pointing at the huffing colossus.

"This is Miklós Dragosavac." Then, the aiding trainee introduced him.

He leaned nearer the squad and whispered, yet Arminius

could hear him from afar,

"Some might call him the Sorbe Impaler, so I wouldn't get on his bad side."

A pair of damning eyes gawked at him. The air sent a cold wave along his back and flinched, not daring to look back at his comrade, the good friend released a cautious smile.

"By the way, I'm Lev Hayek," The carefree recruit remembered, rubbing the back of his head, before he was lost in a ramble.

"Nice to meet y'all." His wide smile had stolen the light of the crowd around him.

Lev was of modesty. Never explosive nor too insignificant. He was of Eurasian blood, like Arminius, but was far more obscured by his Yurupe half. The beautiful, if one could name, twelve-year-old had a proper and lean body, who towered over his comrades except the giant, but it was without a sense of rulership, despite his lion yellow eyes whispering otherwise. Beneath unkempt black hair, his pupils were like torches which stood in the fore of a crawling flood of fog.

"I'd say likewise but ya better chain dis beast." Gin stomped onwards and took a razor glimpse at Miklós.

Then boastfully pointing to himself as if he was a revered war deity, the farmer's child boomed,

"Gin's my name."

Though it was sure that for how reaching Ascot's shout was, the entire cadre knew of this delinquent.

Marching proudly, across the wheezing floorboards, by how indifferent he was towards anything but himself, Gin slapped his hand upon the reserved boy's shoulder, beside Arminius, and gave his comrade to show as well,

"Dis mute's Arber Konstantin."

From within the shadow beneath the bunk, with an aura more piercing than Miklós', Arber glared at Gin with a vicious stare, who, without thought, pelted from the dark.

"I guess...I'll introduce myself too..." gently, Julien stammered, in honesty to break his timidity.

The squad, who had not taken notice of him, lifted a brow, utterly puzzled by his presence.

"Y-You can call me Julien." Dipping his head slightly, so he would not find eye to eye with any of the recruits, the Danne had taken long to say.

A bulky shade neared and overshadowed the measly figure with a domineering scent reeking of trouble. And at an inch-long gap, their faces were held close, as Julien leaned away.

"Stop stutterin', will ya?" The punk growled.

"It'd be too much fun breakin' yer teeth—"

The slap on a face stunned even the squad, trailing away as the tough Gin froze in submission under Arber's kei and open palm. Their bodies were in a standoff, with neither side determining the following. But the victim had not been thrown into a frenzy.

Exhaling a surrendering sigh, he slacked his shoulders.

"Hold on…" Gin mumbled, realizing the last who had not been acknowledged.

Peering at another beside Julien whose name he could not quite remember, but have most definitely seen before, he shuffled closer until his slow memory widened and stopped when the bulb of recollection shone.

"Right!" Gin punched his fists together and cried aloud after a revelation.

The warrior-like soldier aimed his finger between Arminius' eyes.

"You're the ace of your javelin team aren't ya?!"

"Aurelius…no…Argent…?" Gin quietly muttered to himself whilst wronging his new comrade's name for every guess.

"It's Arminius." Arminius interrupted with an awkward grin.

"The one who scored twenty five to one." Colt blurted out, swinging his kepi around a finger as he spoke for his old classmate.

Veins popped in Gin's head and clenching fists as his enemy keenly remnicized.

"The one who buried your team last summer and *that* Rus in the finals." Aiming at Lev, it was added as salt on scars which ran deep in the unforgetting heart.

"Fuck off, aight?!" Gin's rage erupted.

"How was I supposed to defeat any god of junior school like 'im—?!"

He was paused by a particularity lurking within Colt's humiliating words.

"Hold it," The brute, whose eyes sharpened and stilled

bitterly, spun to Lev.

"W-Wha—?" Lev stammered, pretending to be unbeknownst to the source of the wrath.

Inching closer to the tallest pair before Gin was beneath Lev's chin, the aggravated leer glared upwards at the black-haired soldier. The two uneasily stared at one another before Gin advanced and yelled,

"Did I hear a *Rus*?!"

Whilst his allies were distressed at the flustered, with soured and unbelieving expressions, Lev hastily waved his hands in declination.

"W-Wait a minute! You got it all wrong!" The singled soldier tried to explain.

Some, whose faces burned with the sin of wrath, were not so in the mood to hear out the comrade.

"Well…maybe you got it half wrong…" Lev muttered.

"Make up your damn mind!" Gin and Colt screamed, with fists to be thrown.

But Julien, who too felt most foreign, kept understanding of the dragged pain concealed behind Lev's cheerful smile. Of what life unwanted visitors endured beyond the borders of home and amidst a country like a foe.

Yet as his hands were brought closer to Arminius' jacket, he knew his friend need not be urged to say.

"We can't just blame someone who was born half-Rus." Arminius spoke up with a slight laugh, and that soon calmed the squad.

Withdrawing themselves to their bunks, they sat in serenity whilst one stayed at the core, trailing from the windows to the center in an irritating cycle. After the barrack had taken too quiet a turn, he stopped in Arber's shadow.

"Pah! Dat doesn't change anythin'!" Gin wildly slapped his own face until his cheeks had reddened.

"But as long as you're not with the Confederacy," The brute aimed at Lev and affirmed, though with a disgruntled face.

"Dat's fine by me."

Curled on the edge of Arminius' bunk, Julien, with a pleased smile, lifted his head. Peering outwards to the seven around the rear of the barrack, the facade of discomfort broke.

"Sounds like we've summoned an international coalition…"

His silence became a distant shape of a soul.

"It is what it is." Gin sniggered, confidently punching upward to the dull arched ceiling.

"With our strength, the Confederacy won't last a month!" He declared when a hand shoved him away from hiding the light.

"Only if you can survive longer than that." Arber mocked monotonically.

"If it's a matter of survival," Arminius chuckled, peering out of the window beside his crossed arms.

As the arisen squad took their sights to bear upon him, he answered with certainty,

"I'm sure we would."

V
- - 493
- - 12019

Julien Carlstadt

I didn't think much about our squad at all. On the day we met in this corner of the world. We were average students trying how best to survive and only by coincidence, were we there. In the same ray of light.

You question yourself. 'If we were to lose everything anyways, then why did we choose to fight?'

But, if all life leads to death, would there be no meaning?

To have gotten this far already, it's enough to satisfy me for ten short lives. We might not see victory. But that doesn't matter as long as they'll win this war for us. You could say I'm glad, in a way, that I hadn't immediately returned to Danen for my people, or maybe that thought is just to relieve me for this coming battle. No matter what anyone else thinks otherwise, I'd say we were lucky in this life…

Then if so! If everything was to truly end here! Why won't you battle to your last breath?! You chose this path didn't you?! Fate didn't decide anything!

See! I'm not even shaking anymore. Every last drop of that feeling has been burned out.

Is this what you felt ever since we escaped? The pain of remembering the ones you fight for?

We should go…they can't carry the currents alone…

CHAPTER

6 RIVALRY

A shot pinged from a metal plate, under the clouded sun over a few dots of orange clouds cast onto a sunset red sky. In a range where the recruits in the fore laid prone on the ground, were discharges and sparkles of gun barrels alongside the rising hazes of heat. The lazing waited for their comrades to have their round and joined the boredom of lasting fire. For the many days that had passed, everything seemed routine. But the furthest of all, under the watch of the ever encroaching skin of the hammer that the head instructor breathed, the squad was there. The least fatigued by the harmless competition between the seven imagined within the tasteless training.

"Nice hit." Julien praised, in his wait behind.

Arminius relaxed his hold on the rifle and steadily released his held breath as a shade creeped over.

"Just watch!" Gin laughed when smoke began to shroud their sights on the targets.

"Shut up for a minute if you want to keep your throat." Arber coldy replied, resting his head against the barrel of the rifle with a peculiarly immense book that he read alone.

But it seemed his ally was so spirited that day nothing could rile him. However, not that he could return the fight even if he had decided to.

Whilst Arminius had given his position to the restless brute, he widened his grin, knowing his mark could not have been surpassed. Yet Gin seemed as equally sure he would. Besides, the idiot knew that he himself could not do worse than the ending row.

There, Lev, sagging into the dirt, was thrown into crisis from the careless barrage barely striking the target. The Rus mumbled with a self-conscious dip of the head, whilst Julien reassured him as he patted him on the back for all a good try.

Aimed, without a crack in his sights that held the slate in the distance, Gin watched for the perfect line to appear. His vision had tunneled. His senses felt the wind falling faint, as he pressed against the trigger. But when the sound of a magazine clipped into the chamber of the other neighbor's rifle popped, it startled his aim. The round was struck and smoke rose freely. Though as the breeze of gravel and sand cleared, Gin saw the peaceless crater that the shot had dug.

"Colt!" The recruit's fury boiled, pointing at the target that his bullet had steered away from by a full laughable meter.

A smirk turned upwards, waiting for another brawl to be unleashed. But as Gin poised once more for another round, the impossibility that a riot would not be stirred became unusually possible. He never gave up.

Bullets clinked and pinged, inching further by the mark. The unyielding brute helplessly retaliated with ever more burning want for a single strike. It became otherworldly. As he had exhausted his ammunition pouch, once full then empty, blown away by the arid dust of the high summer, Gin panted in defeat.

"Gah! Why won't it—" The punk screamed in frustration, rubbing his head furiously on the ground.

He punched the dirt and bruised his knuckles as blood was prepared to be drawn from his self-harm. That was, whilst the sniggers and laughter had been summoned across the squad, the glimpse of an angelic being watered his fire.

"Who's—?" Gin, whose perverted thoughts silenced his voice, blushed as bright as the chains of gunpowder sparks igniting along the rows of rifles.

It was to his eyes, the heavenly figure had descended into his sights.

In the safety of her squadmates, the cadet emerged from the brief blanket of gray swirling outwards of the innards of the gun's chamber. But she seemed like an average recruit, who was no better than an ordinary shooter. As the bolt of the rifle was pulled, the emptied shell grazed her hand. But she did not flinch.

Who Gin had spotted was a girl. Her nose was scarred along the bridge as another comrade did. Of hardly shorter than the common height of her age, she was slender, but was roughened by the training with cuts and smudges littered over her skin that was not cared for. Sand gold hair that battled the code of uniform was tied into a Vrannch braid. The killer-like eyes of a desert shade, were as if she housed a predator's soul. As elegant and straightforward as one hunting valkyrie, the girl bore no concern for anything else except the target ahead of her.

Surprised that none had even realized, Gin whistled to his allies before he was too engrossed. Tapping Arminius and his comrades on their shoulders, he had done good for once and discreetly pointed at Colt's very nearby neighbor.

The seven halted in awe. Stunned by the holiest soldier. The being was enough to open a highway to heaven when a face steamed like a freshly baked bun, and scrambled to the forefront.

"Uhm..." Colt foolishly began.

But he could not catch the admired as the squad sat embarrassed, in bewilderment. For even Arminius, sipping a flask of water, he had not predicted what his rival would say.

"Mind if I joined you?" Then, the bold cadet asked.

His comrades snapped away, toughened to keep their chuckles shut. But as Arminius giggled, he spurted a fountain of water over Julien, and broke the quiet with a choir of laughter. When the apologetic friend wiped the Danne's face with a clean white handkerchief, the ask, the gathering saw, had been heard.

Boredly, the girl faced her admirer and rose from the earth, swapping for a queuing ally.

"If you could shoot." She frostily exposed how poorly Colt had been trained.

Not a humiliation could surpass such. And before he could return a little yelp, the valkyrie had unified with the sand, and retreated beyond where the squad could stare. Colt's face thumped onto the dirt and suffocated himself of shame. As the blasted mocking filled his ears from beside, that was, the irritating Gin inept in keeping his jokes in check, the Rus boy uncovered a chance to include himself.

"What kinda pick up line was that?" Lev cried aloud across the row towards the failure.

"This isn't a ball, you know—" Leaning over the border of sandbags, he quieted to a whisper.

"Hayek!" Ascot named him solely from atop the ridge, administering the range with an aide by his side.

The feared voice froze Lev. His nerves were paralyzed. If so for a moment, he felt the cold streams like glaciers pierce him. Then once the heat of the sun warmed, the young recruit hastily crawled away to Miklós' protecting shadow. But the giant was much too taken by cleaning the grime from his rifle to offer any aid.

As the squad humiliated Colt with terrible imitations that had only degraded his mind, there were the both, who were not so keen to trouble themselves.

"Haven't seen her before…" Julien curiously mumbled.

Hugging loosely onto his rifle, the Danne was latched and locked by the encounter. The questions, as he would often find, erupted and brought his mind to dream when the rustles of pages disturbed.

"Her name should be in here." Arber spoke, for it was a first, that he was not answering another's.

Stunned by the twist in openness of the reserved cadet, Julien spun towards him, enlivened. And it was not from nothing, that he would search for the girl's name.

In Arber's hands was the same scholarly book. A bulk of paper clamped between a timeworn leather cover was all it was, with the history of the yellowing pages darkening as Julien's eyes saw lower. However, there was a sigil that disturbed him more so than the task before.

"Wait," said the Danne.

And that paused Arber's quickening flicks through the book as Julien asked,

"Where did you find this…?"

"Ascot's office." told Arber, in his typically collected tone.

"A-Ascot's off—!" Julien stammered.

For one who had thought his squad were crowded around Colt in the unending torture, it was a surprise that Arminius had shown himself, but with a slap over his friend's lips to cease his uncontrolled exclamation. Yet before Arber could speak another word, the roar of Ascot commanded the White Bands to halt their fire,

"Pack up, maggots!"

"I've had enough of your play today!" The head instructor thundered, turning back alone.

As the rocking mechanisms of bolts rubbing against gun chambers rang, the recruits raced away to the central encampment, drawn by the savory scent of dinner that Adam had mastered. Though knowing they would never win the sprint, the squad rose late after.

Slinging his rifle over his shoulder, Arminius reached for Julien who peered up, gratefully. Their hands were held together and the latter was pulled to rise. The grit stained their uniforms and faces, but it was in a day's worthwhile training. And whilst they trailed far from the flock, dashing along the river where their mirages were blurred by the muddied current that would soon clear, Gin and Colt resumed their neverending brawl that no one would bother to disturb.

"So...?" Arminius prompted amidst the storm of hurling insults.

The book shutted. His comrade's eyes closed as he recalled.

"Her name's Alexandria Zygos." Arber restarted, hoping that he would not be interrupted.

"Alexandria von Libra?" Gin and Colt emerged from their baseless squabble and dissolved the hundredth battle.

The dynastical name felt familiar in Julien's archive-like memory. But there was, to him, in the maze of records harbored within his vast mind, a spot of knowledge that he could not remember.

"That's what you would call her here, in Aelon." Lev added for the unknowing two who nodded.

"Aged twelve, she was originally from Hëllat—" Arber read the profile written in faded ink.

"A prestigious member of the thirteen Inntorklus dynasties..." Julien muttered for he was eventually able to recall.

"The Libra were the first to be defeated in the civil war."

Though the Danne could not have known, then, there was an extra note scribbled on the margins that told of a valuable fact.

"There is a great possibility that Alexandria has already inherited an eifer." Arber recollected.

"An eifer?!" Some screamed.

"She's one step ahead of all o' us?!" Gin madly yelled into his comrades' ears.

"I wonder which attribute it is..." Placing a hand on his chin, Lev pondered depthfully.

And whilst the squad flustered over the note, there were two cadets, silent and conserved. Their eyes were unsettled. Focused on the dirt below. When alarming them, Julien breached the quieted atmosphere.

"Arminius, Colt." The intrigued boy started, holding both in nervous sweat.

"Do you think we'll be able to inherit one?" He questioned with a sudden desire to know.

The two stalled on a step. But before Julien could notice, they smoothly resumed.

"An eifer?" Arminius sped to Colt's pace and weirdly nudged him to answer as well.

"W-Well...yeah...I guess if we train hard enough—" Colt replied.

"Dat ain't no matter to me!" Gin exclaimed, excitedly.

"We'll see tomorrow." Colt slapped his rivals' backs and demanded,

"Nothing will stop me from dueling you, Gin, Arminius!"

With a relieved gasp, yet he did not hear what Colt had promised, Arminius found the disturbance to be his savior regardless. His soul had neared the verge into the dark abyss, as he was unwilling to tell of the growing kei to his comrades that his lie remained true to.

On the path to the barracks, to the rear of the wait for a hearty meal that was unlikely to be had beside the armies and training bands, the squad enjoyed the flying night through fast time. Fantasizing what the following day would be. And although, on their return to the dorm, no one could rest easy. For knowing that by the morrow, there they would engage in the core of war. That was if their drunken and frantic screams and shouts would not lead to their demise by execution under Ascot's hammer. There was anarchy by midnight that the howls traveled afar in the dark to the commander's agitated ears.

Gently pushing past the creaking door, Adam demanded of them with a sharp, ear-splitting whistle,

"Quiet down."

He knew to save his soldiers from the havoc if Ascot had come. And with an odd reason, his two words had been respected. Before the major could discover for himself that the mead had been bribed for by the lawless recruits, and assured by their bitter looks collapsing onto their pillows, the vice instructor shutted the door to contain the thoughtless creatures from ever ravaging the outer world.

A sharp sigh huffed when the lantern lights were dimmed. His hand naturally reached for his cigarette box and slipped a smoke onto his dry, crusting lips. Unsheathing the method of fire, a matchstick sprouted alight and lit the uneven roll of local medicines. As he hopped down the flight of stairs, there came a chill. Shaking his head, the carefree officer broke free a warmth by the scent of incense and disbanding the thought of the unnatural instance, he carried his tiring body across the stream, where soon to meet the headquarters.

The commander was scribbling on the book that had been smartly returned. Not that he had realized it disappeared in the early hours. As Adam entered after a brief knock on the door, he hurried to the jar of grounded coffee. Without a word or an ask to whether Ascot would have preferred a refillment, he poured lukewarm water and a dash of powder into a cup. Mixing the drink until it formed a whirlpool, the lesser instructor leaned against the single table and watched the flickering pen intensify.

"Dat's unlike ya." Adam mentioned, with folded arms and a cautious sip that would not spill his drink.

"Ya would've been chasin' 'em 'round da pen till sunrise."

Ascot's writing paused. As he reclined, his hands were placed on his stomach.

"And what, to break my frail self?" He asked very plainly to Adam's chuckle.

The head instructor rose from the antique chair, with a squeal of the arm rests. He strolled to the window, with his eyes wandering, watching the calm narrowed stream trickle past the tree. The grayed bark, aside the moonlight, had a bullet wound that still held the round.

"Humans are weapons of war. To be used." In his blankness, Ascot taught Adam, who listened, but knew before.

"Why would I discard such vital resources that precedes even technology?"

"Oh? What sorta turn did ya take to become dis soft?" Adam returned with the major's sigh.

Nearing the commander's desk under the wave of pressing wonderment, the junior questioned as if he had discovered the source of Ascot's abnormal benign behavior,

"Der are a promisin' few, aren't der? 'Course you'd know."

"Da second man to have survived de Whirlwind—" He haunted the aging officer's memory.

"Can't you answer that yourself, Adam Skowroński?" Ascot grunted sourly.

"For how long are you going to hide yourself here?" His shackles upon his anger freed and stormed over the disintegrated fence of a bipolar mind.

"In this shithole." The major interrogated.

Adam gazed down upon his coffee with a smirk when he took another loud sip. But he knew too, that no answer could follow as he mumbled,

"Who knows…?"

"Someone of your caliber belongs on the battlefield," Ascot perhaps praised, yet the tone of his proud attitude told the opposite.

"Or else you'd just waste away."

Returning to his chair with a tensed expression, his wrathful eyes were unlike the usual senseless face. They were judging but knowledgeable, when he faced the delinquent and demanded of him,

"Do something worthwhile with your talent before you grow old, lieutenant."

The chirp of the morning orchestra by the forest life was the band's waking call. Gushing through the crosses of windows, the light bore an unwelcoming heat that was the dread of the middle season. Where it could not shine unto the corner of the dormitory, none, for most were too drunk, could remember whatever day it was that had arrived. As the cadets dragged themselves to dress, there a sober boy dangled, halfway from the bed, as his drool cascaded from the pillow's side. His mumbles were unheard. And it was the serenity of the waking air that kept his eyes closed. Until, a shadow was casted upon his face.

"Arminius!" Julien called awake.

With a frightful scream, however not too deafening, Arminius sprung into Julien's face, felling him by a fatal headbutt. The Danne crashed onto the ground. His cold hands were placed on his head as the bruise that his friend had given reddened more slightly.

"What the hell..." Moaning quietly, Julien held his pain.

Arminius rubbed his head as he searched around for what he had struck. Vast emptiness and no one that he could see. The boy slumped off, with a coat in his hands when he began to change that a tiny grunt caught him to spot Julien, curled on the ground in misery.

"What are you doing...down there...?" Sleepily, Arminius asked.

"Ngh...it's nothing..." Julien twitched and peered up, nearly with tears in his eyes.

But when at the gong of the morning call, the pair were turned to the bellowing bell. A dull clank. With searing headaches and paled faces, those who had yet to be awoken sprung to rise.

"Damn...what the hell did Adam put in that...?" Lev groaned as he rocked and stumbled.

Though it was most unfortunate that he had crashed himself into Arber, whose face of dawn darkened. A punch and a slap boomed across the corridor. And to where Gin had finally risen, the Rus fell unconscious by the side of his bunk. His face bore a frightening hand print.

Within the racket that had pushed the unfamiliar cadets of the same dorm away, with faces of dismay, the Danne stared ahead. Then, he felt an arm wrap around his own that selflessly assisted him to stand.

"I was sure you hadn't drunk half a mug last night." Arminius joked smilingly as the squad scrambled.

"Really, it's nothing..." Julien had to assure, hiding his eyes beneath the kepi.

Led to be gone through the doorway into the wild, without his comrades but the Danne alone, Arminius held his trust in his companion's words for all that it sounded false.

The crowds of the White Bands flooded the warehouse on the opposing bank over the stream. That they watched, sat on the edge of the valley, Arminius and Julien twirled the blades of dying grass around their fingers. Savoring the winds from the horizon, it blew softly upon them. Lifting their hair and too, calmed their minds in their wait for the slower five till they came to show scruffily so on the passing of a closing door. At which, the two stood to greet all. And, with a flick of his head towards the glimmer of silver, Arminius had set their sights on the sea of cadets. So be it that they were the last, downhill they chased, to the bridge and the path for the queue that had formed before the head instructor whose shouts of commands and threats ferociously brought the early birds' songs to lull.

Squad by squad, the line shortened. Recruits entered and exited from yawns to joy with their long awaited reward in trembling hands of soldiers who could not believe that the simplest of cold steel would excite them. And whilst the squad was binded by sight to the glee and honor of bearing strangely outdated arms, there were two perverts whose beaming gazes laid elsewhere.

With her cloth-wrapped polearm, shaped to be a spear, the Hëllennik girl marched by without a glimpse at her admirers. The braid swung in a pendulum across her back as her cloak fluttered ever more so beyond the shade of the barn. Though Alexandria knew that it was often the both, Gin and Colt, who gaped longingly.

"Oi, ye two, stop starin." Adam netted them with the snap of his fingers.

Tossing a spear and a sword over the counter, the instructor gave no care that the pommel and shaft struck their faces and made a bleed from one's nose. But it was possibly the arousal of a recruit that unclogged the waterfall of blood. When it was the last cadet, next in turn, that impressed him most, Adam shoved the perverts to begone.

"Arminius Reichner!" He warmly welcomed him.

Casting his cigarette onto the table, the instructor killed its embers with a thumb, before grinding the ash away that smudged a dust print on his hand.

"I 'eard yer de top play'r in de induction exams." Adam congratulated with his own mannerisms.

"That wasn't anything compared to what we're going to face..." With a humble grin, Arminius embarrassedly acknowledged.

"Shore thin', soon'r er lat'r." agreeably, Adam told, as he lifted a weapon for his cadet to see.

His childish eyes gleamed, that Arminius found the sword to be so dangerously captivating he could stare at the blade for hours in a day.

"It's de last *an'* de sharp'st."

"But don't overuse it. *Yet*." The lieutenant pleaded as he placed the blade on the counter.

"Ya might have ta last fer years, even decades with dat."

Seeing the sparkle of the pommel, Arminius held his hands back no longer. Then, unsheathing the sword by no more than the length of a finger's joint, it revealed a silver shine of a normal blade. It was cheap, without a guard, and nothing unique. Except for it was only sharpened on one side, and was wider than a standard saber, resting in an abomination of a scabbard. When holstered on his belt, the glint of steel shone that his eyes could not be removed from.

"Thanks, Adam!" Cheerfully, Arminius linked his palms together like a clap in a display of gratitude.

The voices of the youth's comrades called for him. And with no short notice, he had dashed away, rejoining the squad. It was pleasant to witness. For one lieutenant who had never felt the same.

He grinned and hopped over the counter, hooking two faithful tape measures onto a chain dangling from his jacket. As it was ordinary for him to do, Adam uncovered the last stick of smoke entombed in his pocket of junk. But it was bothersome that his matches had all been consumed. Sighing, as his head began to itch, it was unseen how a fire burned so brightly after a simple flick of the cigarette.

Along the stream upriver to the furthest of the complex, the allies strolled. Where the valley deepened and the ridges heightened, the body of water was no wider than an urban drain. As Arminius held carefully onto the gripless hilt, the first droplets of sweat squeezed out of his skin. Yet the heat did not bother some. Gin who despite that Ascot would have his head if he saw, playfully swung his sword about. But it was soon, when the light penetrated the thinning canopy, that he knew to stop unless he desired a wish for death.

There was a lone barn in the infinite space, on the edge of the encampment, a flattened plain awaited. Beneath the hellish sun and a cloudless sky, the dirt cracked where no grass survived. But it was fantastical to behold. Where the three hundred wooden swords and spears laid standing asleep, their glazes shone. The scorch could not reach far, and in the bare lands without rain, they miraculously had not set alight under the blistering weather that doused even Ascot's fury.

"Into ten ranks!" The head instructor ordered in the drought with his closest aides drawing heavy and stale breaths beside.

Panting, the cadets marched into formation. Of those lines, they were displaced and jagged within the desert-like heatwave. Yet it was no matter to the major, wiping away a lake of sweat with a rugged old handkerchief. If ever he spoke any more unnecessary words, a stroke, he thought would take him of life.

"Hear me!" Ascot rolled up his sleeves in preparation for another of his stodgy lectures.

"As you have been honored no other of Alben has," He dramatically commended, which certainly had the traits of a competent general's speech.

But his White Bands heard him not.

"The blade you bear will serve as the backbone of our armies..."

His voice faded. Goosebumps grew from the warmth of the air. It was sure that the atmosphere had augmented the scale of time. Where seconds became minutes which seemed to be hours. The cadets murmured and grumbled. Sweat dripped, along the individual strands of their eyelashes as they stared into the distorted backdrop by the warm waves ascending above the ground.

"How long is he gonna take?" A cadet complained, with one hand resting on the flat pommel of his sword.

The desire for a shade became a dream for luxury. For the

next hour they sat, the force wearied. No wind came to relieve them. Water flasks emptied. No clouds flew to shield them. And the river dried quickly. Arminius' eyelids felt to be pulled down by the flatness of the instructor's speech, who he himself began to sag. It was then, that when the recruit was near to fall asleep, he heard one phrase that his comrades yearned for.

"If you scraps of flesh dare fall behind," said the commander, scanning his soldiers.

"Do not hope to find yourself back in my barracks!"

"That is all!" Ascot concluded with a boom that had revived the breaths of the recruits.

Shuffling and rising, they stretched for the three hundred pairs of eyes teared from yawns and hopeful sighs. Though not so later, the wild creatures of the band's souls regenerated. Like raging clouds, a storm scrambled, and the crashing thumps between the false backswords and spears ensued. And it was much like Arminius, who only watched onwards at Gin and Colt flustering over whichever was the best, he kept reserved and waited for all to have chosen before the time to advance presented itself.

"Looks like we drew the shortest stick." Arminius offered a last fan of his face with the scrunched kepi and pointed at the distant swords on the rim of the sector for Julien to see.

As they rose, he found it unusual how it was that his friend was the least bothered by the heat. The Danne's uniform was stainless, and his face was dry. Neither had he uttered a single complaint.

"Hngh…I don't think we had a choice…" Lightly laughing, the Danne drew onwards.

The marathon the both had embarked on, weaving through the cadets' reckless swings and jabs, was a challenge nonetheless. Whom Ascot had been eyeing, the king of the White Band slid by his destination and swooped a wooden sword into his hand whilst the least active comrade who was less so familiar with such simple devices of war had only found his grip.

"To hell with this, Adam." The major groaned.

His watch shifted to the trail that led to the headquarters in the calling milder camp, guarded under a loose smog from his lieutenant's smoke.

"I'm not staying for this farce." Ascot decided.

As he himself, the commander, departed from the sector of close quarters, the chain of control flowed into the delinquent's hands. But Adam knew that the head instructor had gone for the cooler air under the forest trees and then at his fingertips, was the pressing training to be taught and polished.

"Well, I ain't dat carin' like ya." Adam flicked his cigarette onto the ground.

And from the dead air, under his shadow tracing to the barn, the embers fainted and sunk into dust.

Eager and willing to aid his clueless companion, Arminius drew himself poised for defense, and aimed the sword at Julien's two-handed grip in brace. For not knowing how so to defend, the Danne anxiously asked,

"How should I…?"

When he had remembered that Julien had never held a sword before, let alone one for practice, Arminius eased his hold and realized a suggestion.

"You know, I got an idea." told Arminius, inching ever slightly away.

Swooping his hair back that soon fell into its regular shape again, he wondered whether there was another route to help. But redrawing to a new posture, his aura told that there was a single method. His body was open and guardless, that if one saw on a battlefield, would curse him to be an idiot blinded by arrogance.

"Try striking whenever I say so." He raised an instruction.

His friend's eyes widened, in doubt.

"Are you sure…?" asked Julien, hesitantly bringing himself nearer.

"It'll be fine." Arminius smiled.

The practice sword rose into a slanted hold. Then, out of the short silence between the two cadets, he cried,

"Above!"

The voice that he had never heard uttered by Arminius exploded, and in shock, Julien stumbled. But on a sharp return, as his joints locked and bursted into a fervor for a duel, he charged into practice with a mild war cry.

"Hagh!" Slashing downward in the first strike of his life, Julien's cut was effortlessly countered.

"Left!" Arminius commanded again, giving no ground for

his comrade to recover upon.

Swinging his sword from the below to the side, Julien drew a line of dust which followed the strike and smashed the wooden sword into his friend's. Followed by another swing as Arminius called, Julien's aim was inaccurate and gravely random that the experienced found easy to parry.

In the duel of stamina that seemed to take a toll on the novice, the spirit of Danne blood had taken more minutes than Arminius once predicted. His mind was stunned. Though he hid his true thoughts. When it was finally that Julien collapsed from exhaustion, Arminius' heart had sped too.

With his palms on the sand and hilt, Julien panted deeply. His arms and legs were his only pillars lifting him from fall.

"You okay?" Arminius, whose frame blocked the distant sun, reached for his comrade.

"I didn't...expect it...to be this tiring..." Julien took the helping hand and was brought to stand.

"You'll get used to it." His ally sincerely encouraged, patting Julien's back which was still strangely dry and lacking sweat.

"It took me years to learn, so..."

"Just don't rush it." Arminius advised when the sounds of dense wooden swords clashing echoed across the flat sector.

Heads turned and the paired clashes ceased. Recruits began gathering around an arena in a circular crowd yonder. To see that everyone had all nerves on yells and thunks of swords in the background, Arminius' eyes were drawn to the masses as well.

"What're they doing?" Julien wondered.

Irregular clouds of dust blew to the skies behind the cloaks and kepis. And that their curiosity was chained no more, both hastily raced to the cluster of students which Adam had not broken apart yet. Diving into the sea of pushing and shoving bodies, the same question surrounded them.

"What're they doing?" One, too short, found his seat over his close comrade's shoulders.

"Those two again?" Another shook her head with a sigh.

Those two...? Arminius and Julien repeated in a cycle when they came to sense that it must have been the two cadets that they knew too well.

As both closed, the brawl sharpened and its sounds grew more pronounced until it was before them that the faces of the combatants unveiled.

"Not this again…" Arminius slapped his head and gazed at the turbulent bulls.

"Hyargh!" Gin screamed as he launched an overhead strike into a waiting spear.

Sliding back, Colt spun his polearm and landed in a taunting pose, tensely gripping the shaft as he aimed the blade, in the partial shade for Gin. The brute, of all cadets, lepat away in the defeat, who seemed to be exhausted of breath and ideas. It was whilst his enemy toyed for longer.

"Gods dammit, Colt!" Gin shouted as his foe prepared for a dash.

"Yer good, I'll give ya dat!"

The squad, though once dispersed, inched closer to the circular border and had found themselves joined together. But it was rather and perhaps of Alexandria's being there who lured the cadets.

"I wonder what it was this time." Lev pondered, stabbing the ground by the shoe of his spear.

"He started it," Alexandria pointed her spear in a reserved tone, at Colt.

"Something about a duel." She added.

Then, the squad had evoked the time when the challenge was agreed.

"You're kidding…" Arminius delivered all he could say.

Almost as if he took flight, bounded from the ground, Colt charged at his newfound rival. Like a true arrow. The spear tip lunged at Gin, who was so proud, was perturbed from the appearance of a dragon-like enemy.

How could I be defeated by someone like him?! Gin gathered his thoughts.

As he collected all the shards of his kei, the brute charged his near splintering sword until it sparked and locked. Before Colt came piercing. His spear flicked about, lightly tickling Gin's block in a whirlpool, where it was unclear where he would next pinch. But where the instinctive brawns saw an opportunity, his defense was unhinged for a second. The tilted sword was ready to strike. Yet that had been the bait. Colt flanked around and spun his spear into the sword's hilt, flicking it away as an opening was made. The battle had been decided. As he sped his polearm to the perfect center as reflected in his eyes, the strike drove Gin down onto the ground that kicked alive a small sandstorm.

The winds blew outwards and sent a cold front of shocks through the speechless cadets' nerves. Then the smoke began to clear. Although it was a wooden spear, at the tenacity of how the strike was dealt, the weapon was dense and carried much weight, sufficient to inflict a severe wound on a measly recruit. Most especially when Colt had aimed for Gin's neck. But an arm was there, instead, to take the blow.

Huffing rather heavily, dirtied by a dust cloud blown from an easterly wind, a layer of steam rose from where Colt had struck his arm.

Looked down upon by the victor whose glare was that of a mystical beast, Gin spat a spot of blood onto the dirt. Whilst his squad thought him to be in somber trauma, a roar of thrill by the brute changed their beliefs,

"C'mon, Colt! One more round!"

Colt collected his breath and mockingly stared below at the defeated by his feet.

"That wasn't half as interesting as I thought it'd be." He spited.

"What?!" Gin thundered.

But despite his wants to battle, his standard toughness had been spent. Unable to rise alone. He had not apparently realized that his bruises had stolen his last strength.

"There's no point," Turning away, Colt mumbled.

Gin's eyes heatedly widened upon noticing his rival's air where his words held weight. That their individual strengths were farther than a whole valley or ridge. When the doubt was cleared that from then, they were poised oceans apart, he finally gave in to defeat.

"Damn…" The brute slammed his fists on the sand.

As the vice instructor overlooked the crowds from the warehouse, Colt gave no time for the cadets to remnicize. A second battle was to come. His eyes had decided but no one knew who would face him.

"Come on!" Trampling over his uninspiring triumph, he brazenly exclaimed.

"Gimme someone to fight! With an eifer!" Colt demanded with great conviction.

The challenge was met with a similar silence as how

Alexandria had watched his terror through the clash. The squad had thought her to be the following act. But neither was the girl willing to step forward.

"Who the hell are you asking for?!" The audience of recruits clamored.

"This isn't a battlefield y'know!" Another hollered.

"What'd you expect from us?!"

As Colt spun around the arena, it was sure that he was in search of one counterpart. Someone he would find an equal who would not bore him so well. At the third quarter of his revolving body, the cadet spotted him in the midst of the average soldiers. Quiet beside his squadmates.

"Arminius!" Colt called aloud.

With his name cast throughout the valley, Arminius kept shut when the presence of the angered crowd hushed. The camp shuffled away to leave him be, and out of mere strain, the squad soon retreated as well.

"Are you sure about this—?" Julien asked as Lev tugged him from the site of a gathering duel.

"No." Arminius faintly replied.

"I haven't even answered."

His rival chuckled, awaiting eagerly for an answer that never came. The crowd murmured, taking another step back from the springs of the heated duo.

"Ain't this better than the hall we were imprisoned by!" Colt cried across the emptied distance.

"Why wouldn't I take it?" He questioned.

"You're not seriously thinking about using it, are you?" Arminius brought his wooden sword to his hips and aimed its pommel at his rival.

"Why are we stuck here studying with the lowly lot?!" Colt sneered, thrusting the spear into the ground.

"Us both!" He punched his chest and tread onwards.

"We're ahead of everyone!" The soldier revealed his mind to the three centuries of recruits on the bounds of outburst.

"The only reason I'm here is to prove my dynasty's legitimacy—!"

"Training has always been the one thing we were born to do." Arminius argued and turned his stinging eyes to Colt.

"Don't talk like you know how unnecessary it is…"

"When you can't even get a good shot with a rifle." He insulted, inching his feet closer into a formidable stance.

"Hah!" Colt interrupted.

"As heirs to our ancestors' eifers, we only have one goal in mind!" The zealous boy stuck true to his beliefs and lifted an open hand.

"That is to become the next God of War!"

Onwards the rivals marched that Julien's mind could not be taken from. There was a light in his search through the inventory of memories and hailed the discovery of the voice from before.

Is that what he meant by wanting to become even greater than the Radilovs...? The shy recruit clenched his fists.

To surpass the Whirlwind...

The squad restlessly tapped their fingers on the wooden swords and spears for he was not the only one who found the straining air difficult to breathe within.

"If this chance was here to prove that I'm enough to fight under our banner," Colt boasted.

"Why would I throw this away?!"

Arminius' eyes burned again. As it did on that night he told Julien of the distant dream. His smile expanded, ambitiously like a devil king.

"You're right." said he, loosening his grip on the sword.

The rivals dropped their wooden weapons and unsheathed the cold steel, both grasping the hilt and shaft tightly as they drew into a stance for a clash.

"I wouldn't throw away this battle either." Arminius continued.

"Heh," Colt cracked a light laugh, twirling the spear above his head before switching his hands into an obscure grip that Arminius was certain to have not seen.

"Lemme see your eifer, Arminius."

The crowd shuffled further to safety by their instincts which told the truth.

"Adam!" An instructor yelled at the vice commander from the balcony of the double-decker warehouse, watching the creeping prelude of the battle.

Adam raised his arm, barricading her from interfering, who was nonetheless bewildered by the calmness that surrounded her fellow officer. And despite the morals provided as tutors in the army, no more were the subordinates going to battle him for they knew the duel was doomed to happen under his watchful eyes of curiosity.

"I've kept an eye on dese two since 'eir arrival," The lieutenant juggled his tape measures whenever in need of intrusion.

"If da legendary house of Chō could be defeated by sum flea in de system…" He revealed to another instructor, watching the two fatal enemies pace nearer.

"It'll make fer a show." Adam balanced on the ledge to live a daredevil's view.

VI

- - 461
- - 11987

E.R.

Beyond political boundaries and beliefs, ideas and innovation, even deities and their heavens and hells, there are two supreme elements who ruled above all since the birth of mankind hundreds of thousands of years ago. We see them in everyday practice but are also the cherished weapons of war.

I had done well to realize this. But terrible deeds with it.

The aura of a certain person is derived from how strong that being's kei is. They intertwine, but are not necessarily the same for the aura is something others can feel, but the kei within cannot be sensed by another. Yet the capacity of us as a species remains the same and thus cannot be increased through laborious works or decreased through crippling the mind.

Whilst all are born with kei, not all possess an eifer for this element is inherited through rigorous training and exhaustion. The stark opposite of kei. Its power depends on the particular master, as one could range from a gentle breeze harming no leaves to an eruption of flames devastating a city of ten million souls in its wake.

That perhaps was my mistake.

Where kei was, there eifer shall be. The energy of the body paired with the zeal of the soul where the former is to be stored and the latter discharged. It is what warriors, us, or some average soldiers use in the heat of battle. Though to control one's kei and eifer to perfection is like…searching for a paradise in hell.

Young Joshua. It was impossible.

CHAPTER

7   DEVOTION

In the form of a greatsword bearer, Arminius carefully drew his blade. Airily and low. It was defensive. As the opposition was a spearman, it was odd he would not take the initiative. Not against the youth of a prestigious house, whose glare intimidated even the spectators behind. Colt was welcoming to an attack, with his weapon aimed from battle.

Dey're well-trained... Adam scanned the both.

Patience in waitin' fer dat instant.

The two recruits remained at a stalemate. Neither side wanted to be the aggressor. Until the sands shifted, Arminius realized then he was caught in a trap and shuffled back. As his rival kicked and lifted his wooden spear, the leer of Colt's eyes sharpened, and with all his might, hurled it straight with a whip-like throw. The spear, disintegrating as if were a crashing meteor, broke even sound. With a boom that washed the dirt away, it rushed at Arminius, who although in a poorly, flustered stance, lightened his grip and flicked his sword upwards, sending the hurtling javelin into the skies. The crowds' eyes turned up till the splinters plummeted, paces from the feet of the stumbling cadets. A violent wind of the first impact blasted.

"Of course!" Julien punched his fist into a palm upon noticing the plan that Arminius must have strategized.

"What's up?" Gin asked, scratching his bruised arm.

"He chose an unstable stance from the beginning that would give him time to react," The perceptive Danne thought.

"In case he had to counter quickly."

Though that thesis was certainly true, the glare of Arminius' failing fire told a hidden story.

He got me...? Despite the upperhand, he found his defense to have been breached.

His kepi had disappeared. That was before it parachuted to

the earth. Where half the cap was there, a burn marked around where it had ripped in two. Surely too, Arminius threw a glance at his right hand where his touch did not betray him. From where the spear had skimmed past his armor, the graze left a blackened burn from the deflection. If he had not had such wear to protect him, both his fingers could have been torn off one might think.

"You're slacking." Colt provoked on the midway.

Arminius wiped his hands on his uniform, shrouded in sand from the shock of the unexpected volley, and readied his posture for another unforeseen strike. Knowing he had the momentum, Colt finally charged in, with the malicious intent of a killing blow.

He rammed his shoulder into Arminius' chest, pushing him away and abandoning his needed range, Colt stretched his arms along the shaft. The spear was then a dagger. With a new advantage served, he swooped from left to right, that grew into something that could not be caught by human sight. His rage had taken him into the depths of senseless battle whilst his intuition was all there was to drive his four-pointed jabs, forming an eye-catching gust of cutting winds.

Pushed to the retreat, Arminius lacked any air of aggression. His bruises within of his grinding and hammering bones multiplied and was forced unto the boundaries of a loss as his rival slashed and thrusted onwards.

"How's Arminius losing this...?" Lev commented, nervously biting his hand.

Flicking his spear as he had done so to Gin's defense, Colt slowly gnawed at his enemy's breath. But it did not mean that he was neither worn from the prior duel.

Calmed and recovered from the opening act, Arminius' breathing steadied. As he had times where his spirit would be shattered under undeniably more brutal events, that was never one of them.

"No..." Miklós groaned.

"His...eifer...is...conserved..."

The sparks from the clashing steel began to quicken, ever so much for every strike. Colt's flicker was devastating, which transformed into a tight ring of pummeling stakes. The crowd failed to catch them in their views as the sand clouds began to swirl. But what seemed unseeable, for the combatants it was as if time itself had been slowed four times. Where every deflection and attack was precise. On a self-made battlefield, they fought over the inches of land.

Caught you! Colt yelled in his mind.

He leapt back, as if the body and the tool was one, and propelled into an offensive in the familiar form of a spear. There was a spark of azure fire yet the eifer had not shown its entirety. In shock, Arminius' eyes widened, but in favored time, he was thought to have dodged the fleeting blade. Then, before Colt was near the defending boy, his shadow snapped across the field like a firebolt and rocked the skies with a jet-like bang.

Landing at the halfway of the square, Colt wildly slashed through the ground ending his savage assault. His feet dug into the dirt and gravel some paces away before his body came to a halt, leaving a trail of smoke and blue embers behind which was a sight to behold from Adam's overlook.

Pivoted with one anchoring leg and lowering himself into a second stance, Colt ominously grinned. The both had reappeared from the storm on opposite halves of the court.

"How'd you like my eifer?!" He cried proudly, and to know that of twelve years in life, the cadet was capable of such immensity.

A shallow cut on Arminius' cheek gently opened, letting free a rosy droplet of blood that flowed down his face. Two flowing gusts cleared the stage of the sandstorm, revealing their faces to the crowd who was astonished, for a surge that ran through their veins.

Sekiya... The voice named him from a broken vestige that he remembered well.

Always have the intention to fell your enemy with one strike, The old man reminded that was of an accent from home.

So that they may not have to suffer. Even in death.

"One...strike...?" Arminius muttered to himself.

The scent of iron in his blood reminded him of the only ideology that he needed in battle and thus, gave birth to a new revived lust for the death of another.

The winds heated but the summer sun had fogged. Adam peered at the heavens that rang of a warning whilst the sword of Arminius rumbled with purple coils. His eyes were the devil's glare.

"Aren't I lucky to see it again?" Colt chuckled, sinking himself ever more.

With his spear displayed beyond his body, his eifer began to roar. A blaze which protected him burned the roots of weeds stuck within the gravel, blackening the soil with a whirl of unrefined embers. On Arminius' blade, lightning gathered in an arc that only the hilt remained to be seen. The sword thundered and cackled, that the master of the eifer could not control.

"Time ta go." Adam commanded, leading a party of stunned instructors to the fight which soon marked the end of the beginning.

"Don't hold back!" Colt yelled.

Flicking his foot into a push, the onslaught of his twirling spear charged before Arminius. Two trails of fire formed as Colt dashed, closing the great gap between their humming blades. Where it was only a scant fist's distance, Arminius gathered his blade at his rival. He lunged with his lightning bolt and a cry from his ancestor, slashing through the spear's shaft, until the blade met fabric near flesh. But Colt had not been defeated as sung by the tensing grip on the broken spear that was driven for his fated enemy's neck. The threat that they would kill the other, from the shouts and roar, shook the audience with a callous truth.

"Had 'nuf fun yet?" Adam suddenly appeared between the duelists.

"How—?!" Arminius and Colt lost their bloodlust and turned their eyes from the battle.

Two tape measures were released and hooked onto their collars, pulling them from the fight before any realized under the severance of adrenaline that the battle had been interrupted. With the strength of a dozen bulls, the lieutenant launched the cadets into the crowd and although unknown where they had landed, the dust clouds of hurrying allies flocked to their comrades.

"De rest of ya get back ta trainin'!" The vice instructor called for the recruits.

The skies were still bright in the tint of the middle season when the spectators eroded. Those who heeded his command scrambled away beneath the watchful eyes of the instructors dispersed into the crowds. But those too close to the reckless fighters could not obey.

Below the high ceiling of the warehouse shading the squad, they circled around the fainted recruit whose hand rested atop his forehead. Arminius' eyes gently widened with the amplifying mumbles quieting asudden to his awakening.

"Did ya black out?" Gin waved a hand over his comrade's face.

Held by Julien and Lev, guarding his flanks, Arminius came to wake. Squinting, he scouted his squad whose faces were written with an array of expressions.

"You really went all out, didn't you—" Lev laughed when the damned pain of a kick stung his shin.

"Ack..." The tall giant squirmed.

"Don't encourage him." Arber mumbled with his scalding aura.

Watching the fallen Rus by Miklós' feet, drowned in agony, there came a surprise at the corner of Arminius' eye that Alexandria too was there. But knowing she did not belong to such a squad, the girl looked away and had reserved herself in a corner beside a ladder.

"You okay?" Julien concerned himself whilst he helped his friend to rise.

"Yeah..." Arminius replied as he struggled upwards.

But his legs were so frail he could do little to stand alone. In a coat of dust, the recruit was bruised on the joints that his nerves had not realized nor felt.

"Everything..." Gritting his teeth, he uttered.

"Feels numb...again..."

He looked at his hand, twitching as he tried clenching it into a fist.

"Is that your counterbalance?" Julien held Arminius' hands and pressed upon the weakest points of the palm.

"Ngh...sure..." Arminius gave a muffled answer.

"A counterbalance?" Lev repeated.

Heavy footsteps approached them, who had the gall to show himself after the brash challenge. The stalwart figure, unattached to any wounds to his strength, tossed the charred, wooden splinters of the old practice weapon onto a table. The tool breathed out streams of steam that in its rest, resembled an object birthed from hell.

"In simpler terms," Colt began, driving the snapped spear into the planked ground.

"If you overuse an eifer,"

"Your body injures itself to prevent you from discharging your abilities." He told them, crouching down before Arminius like a crooked delinquent.

Showing his blistering hands, smoke arose from the skin that Arminius lacked sympathy for with his childish ignorance.

"Y'know I used to get worse burns than this." Arminius' rival sniggered at his past and stood, tearing the spear out of the floor.

Walking to the field to work his training, Colt faced away and waved a hand.

"Thanks for entertaining me this time, Arminius." He reluctantly said, casually.

Following him to the plains, Alexandria gave a blessed last glimpse at Arminius and departed for her sparring partner. Though finding herself once more in the companionship with Colt who had returned to his immaturity, joking and chortling till a word was spoken wrongly so, there of the Libra's power was a rapid fwoomp of a divine kick into the his leg that left him, squealing like a siren, to melt away in the near-setting sun.

But a brief laugh from the shadows behind, ended their smiles, who, tossing his tape measures high, snatched his hook-like weapons before it would fall.

"A-Adam..." Everyone met him with fright whilst the instructor halted his steps with a stormy stare into Arminius' eyes.

Cared for by Julien, the culprit held a troubled face that felt forced to turn away, ashamed by the duel. That was startling, when a light hearted chuckle flattened the fear.

"Heh! Don't worry, I know what y'all thinkin'." Adam forecasted.

He, who sought to end the training, nodded at a lower ranked instructor. Knowing the order, a shrill sound of a whistle bursted between the sergeant's fingers that delivered a report to the headquarters where the gong and drums rolled from the distance.

"I'll deal with Ascot." The lieutenant promised, rubbing the back of his head.

Gazing at the squad who kept tensed from the eventful day, he lit a cigarette, hoping for the whiff of incense to loosen the cadets.

"Calenzo," He called, pointing his smoke at Gin.

The brute responded with an irate grunt, but he was cooled by an odd ask.

"Stay 'ere fer a while long'r, will ya?" Adam directed him as he waved the squad goodbye.

"An' de rest o' ya, don't tell Ascot a word."

With a volley of quick salutes, the squad rushed on their return to the main camp along the dried stream yet to have recovered. Where Arminius, hinged around Julien and Arber's shoulders, enjoyed the path to the barracks without shedding a tip of kei, his comrades escorted him with laughs and praise. And it was whilst Gin watched the field rumble as the three hundred sprinted towards the serenity of the forest valley where the conditioned air of nature awaited, he spotted Adam's shallow grin, taking in a fresh breath of smoke.

"Dat was fun ta know."

"Ya might just take my spot on de podium, yet." The vice instructor mumbled, softly exhaling.

"Or maybe even teach's…"

No one heard. Neither did Gin. Not even Arminius so taken solely on the ambience, which Adam's voice was mixed with the settling calm.

By the sun's down, the doors were tightly closed. They did not speak of the happenings of that day. And though with an early end after the last parade, by the mid evening the camp fell silent.

Unwilling to return, Arminius laid resting with his hands pillowing his head on the waving grass. With a worn bandage slapped onto his only wound, it was a pointless attempt to dampen his bleeding which had not stopped. As he gazed at the stars with a faint lantern beside, allowing for the ceiling's shine to appear, the sting of aridness in the air ripped a new fracture from his cut. From atop, the rustling of fabric turned his head, spotting lower into the valley a figure climbed. Behind the shadow, the headquarters was still bright and alight, lit with a row of candles by the window where the blinds could not hope to hide Ascot's shade seen scribing. The figure was Julien, who neither had a second to change from his soiled uniform. Rushing uphill, clawing at the grass which wavered like a great ancient beast's back in the serene breeze, the Danne was holding a satchel of sorts in his hands.

"Arminius!" He called out.

Arriving at the ridge's summit soon, Julien placed the bag of clattering goods in the gap between himself and sat next to Arminius, whose eyes returned to the stars.

"Here, don't move." Julien kindly asked him, picking a jar of alcohol from the cluster of monotonal liquids and items.

Splashing a drop of the bitter substance onto a rugged piece of cotton, he sat Arminius upright. Then, without one false move, Julien ripped away the poorly bandage.

"Can't you be more gentle?" Arminius squirmed as his comrade rubbed his slashed cheek with the cloth.

The cotton bloodied, but no more was the wound at least plagued. Through enduring the hardship, a fresh bandage was neatly taped by its four sides. Then the dressing was complete.

"Thanks..." Touching the soft slab that felt like a cold blanket on his cheeks over the cut, Arminius murmured.

The two were still, before Arminius laid onto the grass once more, with his eyes fixed on the constellation of abandoned satellites curving around the earth, which resembled a protective scarf. Julien peered down at the empty square, and the stream beside where the shadows of the yellowish leaves cast a net over the pebbles beneath the bright full moon when the thought that he had wanted to speak of burgeoned.

"You never told me you had an eifer..." Julien drew his friend's eyes to him.

His look was dispirited, by the drowsiness hidden behind his legs, curled against himself. The lamp started to dampen and flicker, dimming itself for the shadows to be merged with the night. But Arminius never mentioned anything. For his mouth opened and closed, indecisively.

"I've always wanted to have something that I can fight with." told Julien.

"Wouldn't your mind be the thing you're searching for—?" But his friend answered briefly.

"Even then, it's not enough on a battlefield..." The Danne sped in return that declined into an inaudible mumble.

"Let me handle the frontlines," Arminius urged again.

"You can strategize behind—"

Yet Julien had become so agitated that he grabbed the other's shoulders and shouted in his face. Unlike his timidity, he had gone mad.

"Arminius! I envy you!" Julien confessed.

Suddenly, the voice of honesty balanced within the core of those words that his ally could not face straightly took Arminius' dulled pupils from the stars to the earth below.

"There's nothing to be envious about..." He pleaded under the same loyalty to the truth.

Twisting a strand of grass around a finger, he sighed and gazed at the swelled stream.

"Others like me," The recruit watched the reflection of the moon glisten on the water's surface.

"Being born into a warrior's house..."

"We weren't ever intended to have a life without two deaths." With the final word, he distressedly plucked a handful of the earth's green blades.

The litter in his hand that Julien had his sparkling eyes upon floated to be carried into its burial miles away in the river of winds.

"Would you ever want to live in a world that freely torments you?" Arminius asked.

Julien sprung up heatedly, in the midst of the rage. Clenching a fist over his penchant, he faced Arminius, with a persistent gaze as the lantern returned to strength.

"But isn't that the same as not being able to fight a war with your own hands?" The standing boy questioned.

"I know I'm not the best at combat..."

"Even so..." He paused for the breeze to settle, before insistently following,

"That's why I want you to teach me your eifer!"

Picking up the lantern by its small hoop, Arminius rose with the unsteady light. The good friend knew that this was the Danne's resolution all along. Turning to the sky, he worriedly huffed when no answer could be said. His mind was in scrambles and divided between the schisms of will and morals. He could not reject the request yet could neither accept. When a squad of footsteps brushing along the grass neared the two.

"Is this what you called us out here for, Julien?" A friendly voice spoke from behind.

And when Arminius revolved towards the approaching shadows, he found a squad of four with an awkward brute hiding behind a giant whilst it was Arber and the Rus who headed the party.

"All of you too…?" Arminius unsurely asked.

But he had not seen Colt nor Alexandria, where he could guess was his rival sleeping and another uncaring for additional labor.

After all, they have eifers anyways… The cadet thought to himself.

"No hiding things now, Arminius." Lev smirked as Gin stepped ahead, out of the shade.

"I didn't wanna say dis, but…" The latter muttered unclearly, wildly shaking his head.

"Show me how ya do thin's too!" Slapping his hands on Arminius' shoulders, he begged.

Staring at the lantern that he held beside, swaying as the trees did too, Arminius' eyes quivered in uncertainty. Waves of the night breeze stroked the tips of the grass and his fingers. He finally came to be, to decide.

"I can't…" He released a dejected answer.

"What do ya mean ya can't?!" Gin exclaimed, shaking his comrade about when Lev restrained the troubled brute.

"It might be different for another wielder," Arminius held onto his forearm as he felt his lively pulse.

"But you'd need my blood."

"Hah! That's easy!" Gin broke free of Lev's locking arms and stormed towards his eifer-holding ally's face when both were narrowly apart.

Then holding a loosened fist over his arm, he pressed his thumb on the vein. and though Gin never sounded to have, he joked,

"You just have to inject your blood into us—"

"That's not how our bodies work." Appalled by the brute's undeniably bewitched intellect, Arber tugged on Gin's hair and pulled him to be trapped behind Miklós' arms' unbreakable cage.

The eyes of distraught were too in a search for a key to attain the dream of bearing a desired eifer. However long they stood awaiting for an enlightenment, there was an oblivion of obvious solutions.

"But…" Arminius began again.

In hope, his restart snapped the squad's absorbed minds and turned their focus unto him.

"There's another way." He had discovered.

And which drew them, trailing closer, all eagerly asked with brightened faces,

"What is it?"

Arminius, who discreetly told them, held his breath and whispered before they would be caught by the patrols lurking about the lower encampment,

"Only if all of you are able to last until the hour past midnight."

"Everyday. For the next two years." The recruit warned them who could not be dispelled for their hearts were too ironclad to change.

Hesitant for everyone's answers before one would reply, the squad glanced at each other's eyes and collectively told Arminius with a determined nod. Eventually the last, Julien, also sounded agreeing for the test of endurance.

"Alright," Arminius replied to their conclusion.

"I know a place in the first sector."

From beneath the graying tree, an instructor watched. The recruits who chased their chosen leader rushed towards the desolate grounds that was the barren desert of the crater. Along the creek, the six were bright and clear, neighboring the crescent moon that tracked their reflections.

"Even what I've promised Gin…." Adam sniggered with a grin at ease.

Leaning against the old, crusting bark, he flicked a cigarette into his mouth. But never showing the smoke the glint of fire, the vice instructor chewed on the end of the stick.

"Are y'all willin' ta go dis far, simply fer an eifer?" He pondered.

Crossing his arms, Adam peeked through the leaves to the path, where the young soldiers had disappeared beyond sight into the tranquil valley.

VII

2 JULYUS 490
02.07.12016

Julien Carlstadt

To think that it's been a year since our recruitment and another to follow when our squads will be determined. Major Ascot and Instructor Skowroński will decide those worthy to become lancers of our future elites. They are the ones to lead us into battle from the vanguard. It is an honor for all. Most likely, the cadets chosen would be those with eifers...

Although we've done so for many months now, I still find it tiring to have to wake everyday before the sun's arisen. Train until the hour past midnight. And before we could sleep, the day would revolve again. Unsurprisingly, I've yet to see myself bloom, unlike my comrades. Their actions seem fluid and natural. But all I've ever felt was little lightness and nothing more. Not to say I won't change, but maybe I'm doing something wrong...

Why am I complaining? I was the one to ask Arminius in the first place. I trust him after all. But I know that he can't shoulder everyone.

Importantly, I need to ensure my place as a soldier who can fight his own battles...

CHAPTER

8   IN TWO YEARS

The scent of an undying battle was fresh, and the blood splatters' reek flowered out of the silent trees amongst the red bog of a seared forest. Haunting their commanders who led them to tragedy, the dead slept beneath the howling winds. A row of flares lit up the foggy skies and blinded the heavens above. Whilst the sound of gunfire halted on the rims of the woods, the rustling of blades and scabbards began their growth. Out of the gray, a wave of soldiers in the sparkles of armor charged into the pit of death. Another scream came from the second front. Tips of swords and spears, bayonets and maces raged through the no man's land. And in the current of bodies, the vanguard were trampled into a mash. Their comrades' boots were polished in their splinters of bones and skins of guts. Where they clashed after the stretched lines of infantry met, hacking at their hated enemies, one could only tell apart ally and foe by the colorful standards furring the battlefield of sorrow.

Far, safely behind the frontlines there was the rearguard. It was impossible for even such a grand army to be sighted over the flat terrain, that near his tent, a commander of Aelon stared on in dismay. With a pool of sweat swarming his collar, he felt the air shift against his luck. Afraid, and so the field general could only watch on with his aides beside, anxiously waiting for the unheard reports to arrive. Since the hour has passed, not one messenger showed their face. Until, in the distance, a blast of fire delivered hundreds of men flying to their deaths as they plummeted from the skies like an infestation of felled flies. A wave of flames ate away at the frontlines, by a turbulent ripple of slashes that struck down the last stragglers within the hell ditch.

Amongst the charred trunks of trees, afar from the headquarters, a Confederate grand marshal beamed and glared death-like upon the petty officer. Crawling away beneath the near two-meter-tall man's feet, he could not escape. When the veteran swooped his mammoth bardiche along the ground, the blade quaked the earth, bisecting the armorless man, tossing innards and mud into the canopy above. The sharp strike, by its haste, had not caught his spine and halted by the corpse's hip. A trail of gore drew along its journey of carnage. The elder's eyes glowed in the face of a crumbling force, as truly being the great who could vye for the title as God of War.

"Kolchakov..." huffed the Aelon commander as he observed the field of an inferno, gritting his teeth with his fists clenched tightly.

"Why did he have to appear at such a time...?"

"The firestorm." He named the Confederate beast.

The allied frontlines disintegrated into nothingness as the foreign flags and coats poured through the forming fissures. Whilst the heat of their morale soared, Aelon's cooled. And amidst the disaster that had lasted for a matter of a few short minutes, the gallops of riders drummed nearer.

"Sir!" A messenger of the right flank, dipping his head, cried for the commander.

"They've pierced the third line and are en route to the middle guard!"

On the left, another stumbled off his mount, holding his entrails from spilling. Falling to the ground, the soldier, whose life was fading, bore an even tenser look than the last.

"G-General..." He spewed viscous blood, almost as if the remains of his organs had been coughed up.

The soldier withstood the pain no longer and emptied his last breath to deliver the final report,

"Vice General Marko...fought with honor..."

"He fell valiantly...in battle..." His voice was lost in a tearless lament.

The subordinates' faces divulged into a heightened panic where they knew not what to do.

"You don't mean the Right Wing of Sawunn, d-do you?" One colonel stammered, but there was only one of the same name he knew of.

"Jan Marko...?" His lieutenants murmured.

Before the commander who sat quietly, the camp of higher officers tripped into disarray. Yet no doubt, the general of the army was most devastated by the losses that had reached his ears. That he had hoped those words did not.

"That's the seventeenth." Another aide commented when his comrade gathered his courage to hail the commander's name,

"Nikola—"

A raised hand halted him. The general had eyed the suffering for long ages, who had seemed like he was doomed to fall alone. Then of his heart as a leader of the thousands fallen under his command, Nikola kneeled down before the messenger. Apologizing with a whisper he had repeated too often, the commander soothed his death. By a relieved sigh, the messenger's face appeared to thank him. Closing his eyes, he finally released his hand of work and allowed himself to be opened by a slash of a saber. Blood sprayed as the dead fell onto the hard dry dirt, staining the armchair. The poor man's life dripped down Nikola's face, as he retreated onto the humble wooden seat.

"Nikola!" Whilst the closest medics rushed to the body that was carried away, the subordinate repeated.

"We should reform our lines!" He suggested.

"And what?! Let the Confederates plague our elites in the rear?!" The colonel captured the party's ears.

"We should withdraw for the day and end this clash!"

"It is unfavorable!" Hence, the next opposed.

As the staff babbled without any agreement or parallel judgement, throwing their ideas and predictions at random, the general stood.

"Retreat." Though reluctantly, Nikola told the idle messenger and the aides plainly so.

"What?!" His second-in-command lunged himself at the general, over a table with a single map simply marked in vast batches of red crosses and snapped pins.

"What will we gain from retreating?!" He advised his superior.

But the commander ignored him, with a bronze flare gun at hand and a finger on the trigger. Lifting the barrel towards the sky, a black flare popped into the clouds. The soldiers around and in the distant fronts turned away from battle, as the dark light shadowed the ranks, and saw that their day was closing. That the clash had indeed concluded despite the impossibility.

"Let us give up Baltik." The general impatiently tapped on the map.

The wise colonel slammed his hands against the table and startled the staff officers, but the general did not flinch despite the booming shout,

"This is outrageous!"

"We are the last army covering the retreat of Marshal Piast—" Reminding his commander, the soldier was brave to battle the order.

Till of collected rage in good time, Nikola grabbed hold of the colonel's coat and held him near with a petrifying aura stilling his aide.

"I have seen half the concerning battles since the rebirth of Beuoe." He spoke in a deep, demeaning tone.

"There is nothing outrageous."

The colonel gulped as he had been silenced completely but words had not changed the fires a few leagues north. When Nikola finally calmed, dropping his aide on the ground, he told briefly,

"We've no choice."

"It is either Buruʃʒ or downfall." His predictions were clear.

For they had lost the decision of battle, no one could believe the reality displayed and waved ahead of them.

What could they gain from stepping back except for condemnation?

His staff, guards and soldiers shed tears as the order was guaranteed with a second black flare. Thus, the Aelon army began its cold withdrawal, beginning a march to be chased by the Confederate cavalry who came to stop at the edges of a razed city. The headquarters; the tents were burned, leaving no evidence of stratagems behind. And with the rearguard soon following, no matter how pained it was to be defeated within a day, they could see that the great field general was seeming lesser too, beneath the shadow of the mighty colossus called the Confederacy. To the rims of extinction, the sluggish troops dragged their wounded legs in full retreat.

The morning of the first day in Julyus began under the serene skies four hundred and ninety one years after the Tyutunniks'

rise. A ring of smoke revolved around the window beside a bed that came from the burning of a herbal cigarette held by a soldier, sat on the three-legged chair, whose hitched scabbard dragged along the smoothed wood floor as he crossed his legs. The scent of a hunter's garden filled the room, covering the qualities of a good cup of hot tea, lying motionless on the table. As the squad began to wake, he took a reserved taste. His drowsy eyes peered outside where the engines had begun assembling. Where bags and satchels formed rows across the field as Ascot directed, in his typical tone, new supplies into the complex before the next shipment of innocent souls would have to endure his satanic training.

Taking another quiet sip of his tea, the cadet admired the unchanged view. The blankets and shuffling of a pillow rustled above him, who another recruit had awoken, dangled off the top bunk. He sniffed the crude air that stung his senses, ridding the thoughts of returning to sleep.

"You should stop..." Julien mumbled, but he was so muffled by his deprived power that his ally had not heard him.

He pushed his body upwards and rose with one eye shut, rubbing the other by his fingertips. Under the shades of his blanket, a mantle over his head and body, the Danne gazed down and was shot by an alert of the sun's rising light. It was enough of a burst in energy that moved his hand to a uniform stack, tidily piled at the foot of the bunk. Agilely, Julien slipped into his attire. Buttoning the cloak loosely wrapped around his shoulders; fitting a belt which tightness would not choke his interiors; and adjusting the kepi so it would not fall. He was dressed impeccably without a ridge of wrinkles. And once his bed had been neatly made, the cadet leapt off and landed softly on the creaky floor.

"Morning." Julien shook Arminius by the arm whose eyes brightened.

Arminius' hair was slightly longer than it once was when he first attached himself to the White Bands, and certainly, by a morning glance, he had grown somewhat taller.

His head lifted off his right hand that was wearing an unfamiliar layer of polished armor that he would have never done to clean. And dragged out of aimless daydreams, Arminius turned around with the cup and greeted his companion as they would do daily,

"Here..."

To the Danne tying the final knots on his boots, the squad's leader reached ahead, uncomfortably sitting facing the chair's spine. Returning with a bothered smile, no doubt by the smoke still with embers, Julien was passed the drink who took a gentle sip too. Then standing as he returned the tea, not any warmer than an affectionate palm, he tossed a coat onto Arminius' face with a request prepared and repeated for the numberless times.

"When are you ever going to quit?" asked Julien.

"It's for my eifer." As his friend pulled his jacket away, he excused himself.

Where it was an outright lie that he heard to be spoken, Julien shook his head whilst rummaging about the chest for the pieces of junk or tools that had been kept buried in the spare mountains of cloth bandages and reeds. But amongst the rubbish, heaps of unwanted items and the undeniable stench of some forgotten blood, there was one blade that he knew his comrade would hold close. Unearthing the collector of dust, nothing more than a child's broken toy, Julien kindly placed it beside Arminius for him to see that it was his old hunting spear. Casting a glance to the weapon of memories where himself appeared, Arminius lowered his stick of smoke and grabbed it by its snapped shaft.

"We should go." Julien voiced, suspending his sword higher so it would not bury itself in the ground.

As he wore a jacket, Arminius grinded the cigarette into ash, giving his thumb's silver plating a black smudge whilst the squad had all awoken. He did not reply.

"I wonder where we'll be deployed." Though sounding unexcited, Julien dreamed.

"About that..." Gin yawned loudly, filling the deserted hall with a short echo and yelled, eager for blood,

"I heard from teach that they needed extra manpower on the frontlines—!"

"Not this early in the morning, Gin." For only the brute's booming fervor led a hand to heartlessly slap him from Arber who growled.

"But that could be anywhere." Arminius noted for his comrades.

The giant, Miklós, had not shed a glimpse whilst the last specks of litter in the isolated emptiness was emptied outside. And whose question had been answered saw no dissatisfaction. From a continent away or be to the far north or extreme south, where they were to be deployed did not seem to be a bother. Not that the one unwilling to wake noticed that the day was not any usual.

"Colt!" Lev punched the lazing comrade on the shoulder.

Springing up to a tall shadow looming over him, Colt's body froze. But upon the revealing light, shone unto the Rus leaning into the rays, his muddled mind quieted.

"You're gonna be late." Lev reminded him.

The morning attitude remembered little, that Colt gave a sickened face.

"What do you…" He slurred when the wildest imagination of Ascot's demonic grumble shadowed the blue skies of his eyes.

"Crap!" Colt shouted.

For knowing if he was delayed to his graduation ceremony, it was too horrific that would bear. With the thoughts of his skin serving an eternity as the new platings for his commander's hammer, the last recruit scrambled about to make his entrance in time.

"Let's head." Arminius rose from his bed with a hand on the pommel of his sword and said to the squad with the revival of a bright smile.

There at the bottom of the simple valley on a field not so large, from hand to hand a lieutenant juggled. The tape measures were caught in the canyons between his fingers and lifted away into his firm hold as Adam heard the heels of his recruits on the race down the weathered stairs. Ahead of the last squad to appear from their stronghold, he stopped to form the White Bands into the prologue for the coming ceremony that Ascot was so eager to conclude.

"Why'd ya take so long?" As Gin came sprinting by, Adam saw his chance to smack his student's head.

"Y'all are up front." To the first rank where the troops had dispersed from, the instructor pointed.

Winding through their comrades, the seven hastened into the century where the head of the cadets amongst the free positions to be taken was Alexandria too. Stamping into post, it was an eight-strong squad of varying designs by prowess and intuition by the Gods creations but uniform before their kingdom who governed the vanguard. As the most content and arrogant of members, Gin and Colt smirked, those smiles sat unseen by the three hundred near-soldiers behind their lead. Keeping a professional presence, Arminius watched ahead for the head instructor marching onwards to the parade square where the recruits were ready for his final address in the dual years in hard labor. Needing not his heavy hammer, Ascot's military soul had returned to him, of a young fire that had once been blown wetted. A calm pale color, with no nights of sleep, and yet he certainly seemed joyous inside, despite not showing on his exterior.

Clearing his throat with his hands behind, he waited for the drums of distant encampments.

"White bands!" Ascot yelled, raising his hand high into the air for all to see.

The courtyard braced and saluted for the last day.

"I'm glad to have had this honor," The commander lowered his voice and thanked in his slight, sincere tone.

"To have trained you; to have revived you; to be able to deliver you to the battlefields anew!"

Ascot gulped, forcing his second nature, the uncontrollable outburst, away from his speech.

"A fruitful century of three hundred very weapons have ripened,"

"To you are new gendarmes!" He erupted.

But it was by good fortune that the ranks fell into a roaring storm of celebration for the completion of such a mark of achievement. The decided squads praised their neighbors and rivals, equally allies alike. Their words of thanks and luck reached every's ears. Till the clamor was slashed by the pounding shout.

"However!"

"As with a unit who are to see their first battle," Ascot hinted, pointing upwards to the dots of clouds.

"Comes an elite squad." The instructor finally lowered his arm from tiring.

He took a quick glance at the rank before him of the eight he had confirmed long ago.

"Hmph." There was a forceful chuckle, unheard of ever before.

"Yet I am sure for the first time in my twelve years as a head instructor," Ascot told with much certainty.

"We have never seen such a complete landslide in our mutual agreement to their names."

The instructors saluting beside him, gave no signs of rebellion. And when he glimpsed at Adam, the vice instructor only nodded, for the givings to be granted.

"The following are the lancers of the present!" The major declared, resounding through the placid trees and heightened air.

"Miklós Dragosavac!" Adam narrated the list of where there were the myriad annotations on every of the three hundred names.

This demon colossus will hold a frontline alone. Why would he not be an elite? Though he was a mediocre student, Dragosavac could bisect ten sandbags in one strike of a spear. Perhaps more if his brutality could be polished. But he is no more than a battering ram on the field. He lacks a mind of his own. However, there is no such need.

"Lev Hayek!"

Incredibly yet terribly inattentive, Hayek was nothing we had expected. And that was his ability to control. His psyche brought a squad of ten parallel to Reichner's in our ten league march. He was the second recruit to inherit an eifer this soldier had created for himself, that is, after Gin. The thoughts he possesses are capable of intricacies but Hayek locks his intelligence tight and plays the foolish role. Of course I'd know of his name mere weeks after induction. The lieutenant's eyes were first captured by this fine art of manipulation.

"Alexandria Zygos!" The vice instructor continued.

Adaptable and a top student, she would make for the perfect assassin if not for her house's law on warfare which denies her role beyond the forefront. Those wishes are keen, but she does not stand out as they would hope. And whilst everything else was to be expected of her prestige with an undeniable warrior's heart, the choice to why stay here in this shithole is the same as one counterpart. There was not a second option.

"Colt Chō!"

Ranked second to third in practice and theory. He is never first which hadn't I thought so since his blood could be traced to The Azure. Despite this, it was clear why. The conservative nature of traditionalism does not lead him to strive amongst the generation of this day. It weighs upon him like a boulder to be dragged alone to the cap of a hill. But for this so-called unsolvable problem, Chō should not be too far behind the two ahead of him for his presence, if not overshadowed on a battlefield, could single handedly redirect the course of a clash.

"Arber Konstantin!" Flicking Ascot's notepad to the opposing page, the four remaining names were called.

The perfect marksman and a hunter. The small goliath. Konstantin certainly has his talents in combat, no doubt by the individual strength unreliant of squads. This Makedunn is no more than an opportunist, where his natural accuracy of intuition is but a burden on enemies. His capabilities are bewildering in addition to any slyness that this cadet, future lancer, possesses. We, ourselves, do not know of any boundaries that hold him tight.

"Gin Calenzo!"

Adam's student, and first to inherit an eifer within these walls. Calenzo is sluggish in the mind and brutish in battle. His brawn is ahead of his questionable intelligence. However, by a thousand leagues. In the endurance hike over The Folds, in spite of having taken the wrong route that had cost him some five thousand ranks, he reached the lodges firstly and proudly. Some good has come out of this joker after all.

"Julien Carlstadt!" He neared the end.

Unparalleled in the sight of tactical and strategic warfare, his expertise is natural. I could dare say if the Whirlwind were to appoint him as a right hand aide this very day, there would be none disagreement that Carlstadt would lock the Confederates into a stalemate with one army alone. His excellence in waging war on chess boards is commendable. Yet, he cannot be paired to battle that young genius, a boy of the Confederacy, in the real world. Carlstadt lacks the strength to. And his ideals are to never attack. To fight till the last in a defense.

"Then there's this one..." The lieutenant mumbled to himself, with a somewhat fascinated look, as he studied the said soldier's notes.

Reckless and resolute. Indecisive and an imperfect perfection. Reichner ranks first in combat and second in studies. Certainly an impressive recruit from the years I've lived as an instructor, surpassing the incompetence of many I have seen. What talent. To perform conflict in his form and dauntless manner. This lancer was *a veteran before we trained him. But he suffers from a fatal flaw. That be his severity whenever he is to assault, never to defend. His unbreakable sense of duty to end a battle before it had begun may become Reichner's downfall.*

"Arminius Reichner!" So, Adam called the final recruit.

The cadets marched onward, stamping down onto their new grounds before the gendarmes, and saluted together to the man who had watched over them. Though he had done close to nothing in training the distinguished eight.

"These eight lancers of the White Bands have proven themselves!" Ascot exclaimed upon the finished list.

Spinning them around with a simple gesture of a wagging finger, the head instructor peered ahead, past the forward-looking squad and aimed his eyes at the remainders.

"This is your new elite squad." He hushed, drawing his hand along the vanguard row.

"In the many years, they will lead a path of victories."

The squad could do little to hold back their grins, proudly so.

"I will bestow my honor upon this unit." As he adjusted his beret, Ascot revealed his shaking hand, which he had kept hidden from eyes.

"If you understand that much, then never curse my name with defeat."

"Thus the thirty-sixth White Band disbands!" The commander announced to an uproar of the crowd.

Into the region of the same sky where similar strokes of smoke signaled the heavens for the earned years of training had concluded, Adam fired the last green flare amongst the flung waves of kepi and arm bands. The cries of relief and delight were heard with embraces. The elites banded themselves together by the pebble banks of the slow-flowing stream, to be cheered and praised by the recent gendarmes, Ascot made haste, that he alone, followed a lower gravel path of solitude into the thicket.

A small meadow, not too far, where the one willow tree, no taller than five men, slumbered beside the widened stream, but still shallow enough for the bed to show. The graveyard of heavy chalk slates, like a henge, surrounded the central monument that had the statue of Nike announcing her victory soothing the silent names. There were a thousand. Carved into the sides of the marble pillar, most were abbreviated where some whose were embedded into a silver plaque were written in entirety. For every two years, this list would unstoppably grow.

"I thought you'd be 'ere." With the ruffling of leaves yet unheard steps, Adam called for the commander.

Peering higher until the sun was in his eyes, the major took a gasp of Terra's lungs' reserves.

"Want to place a bet?" Ascot asked before the murky reflection of his face in the decayed stone.

"How many of the three hundred are to return alive this time?" His head dipped down and silently read the names across the plaque.

Adam drew a smoke from his last packet and lit it with a prayer for the honorable members of the fallen, failed to enter the chambers of the valkyries. A puff of ash glided onto the path that the lieutenant advanced upon.

"Eight if I'm bein' optimistic," He replied and sighed.

"But seven'll be my bet."

Scrolling his eyes along the names of the five previous elite squads, Ascot pointed at an empty spot of the forty second member,

"Last I heard, he defected to Danen."

The head instructor glanced at Adam who huffed the cloud of smoke and released a faint chuckle.

"Oh? Tell me 'bout it." Adam turned towards the training complex, waving his hands, uncaring of the story.

His final glance at the void of alphabets, around his comrades the traitor had deserted, was not so full of bitterness. For a smile has been drawn since the last, decades in the past,

"A shame,"

"I heard he had much potential." told Ascot, detaching from the garden of memories.

The major pivoted and returned his way to the headquarters from a short visit to the lifeless yard. His vice instructor laughed, unsure to be feeling of a spoken reply. But it was the truth that he knew, the words were the furthest from a joke. Scratching the side of his head as he tossed his cigarette onto the stone brick path, Adam eyed the sun that subdued the light into his own.

VIII

1 JULYUS 491
01.07.12017

Lev Hayek

After our marathon in the dark, I can finally see the edges of the tunnel. It felt like an unending chase where the last stretch of the run in the breeze is most refreshing. It didn't smell of blood or gunpowder awaiting us, but the nearing of our chase for the one dream of becoming the greatest.

After I've followed him for all this time, I'm beginning to sound like Arminius. But maybe it's not a bad thing. Perhaps that's just drunkenness.

Then tomorrow, we will be off, in a foreign contingent to relieve our allies in Buruſʒ. I wonder. Are we enough to turn the tides of war? Or am I too naive to think so? That we are too minor to be regarded as change. Those two could answer. Not that I want them to. There are so many questions which have awoken, that keeps me from losing consciousness over some ciders.

Ah! I shouldn't think about it now!

CHAPTER

9

ARRIVAL ON THE CONTINENT

It was the fifth hour in the morning when the sun was barely in the sky, being lifted by the clouds which formed pillars on the base of the horizon. On the cooler summer day, within the wreckage of the night's celebration, every soldier had long been awoken by the spurts of engines. With a sword attached and a rifle slung, Arminius fitted his hands into a pair of gloves as he made ready his comrades equipped for early departure. The skies remained a bloody orange whilst the ranks and files stood attentive before Adam whose sleepy voice helped none who only yawned. His thanks and harbored thoughts cleared over the hook he found attached to the three hundred in a short tempered speech. And after a brief salute that brought a sigh to the instructor, he pointed at each of the thirty squads to the twenty seven antique automobiles. But the elites were the last to embark for the passing of luck from Adam's voice to his most outstanding successors. With gratitude, and a look of surety that victory would find herself over their heads, Gin punched his half-drowsy mentor on the arm. It was the sign of good hope that left the last impression before hopping on, they filled the box to the brim with their instruments of war and selves under the absence of the solar gaze. There, after the pat and knocks on the trucks' frames, the dirty diesel rumbles disappeared, as the open ceiling began to clear away for the sun's due course. One by one, beyond the gate. Adam waved the last squad away with a burning match in his hands beneath a roll of tropical tobacco whilst the imprinted tracks from the encampment filled the lieutenant's eyes under reflection.

The complex was shrouded by the dust behind from the exhausts and sand on wheels and tracks that the soldiers' eyes watched fade into the forest. The dips and bumps eased and on the sharp turn onto a highway, the lands which filled their eyes two years ago were too unfamiliar to believe it true and same. Departing the countryside, the cycle of engines circled around the path that connected the capital and the southern coast. It was only that day, which was after the midsummer, the Rumann roads of the southern county were packed by a discoloration of black and steam gray smog. The smell of war. When eventually, the opening of the path into four wider lanes, the formation evenly opened and finally, the tarp over their heads released.

Revealing the heavenly sun into the shadows, Arminius shielded his eyes. He looked onwards at the rolling hills of Alben by the soft sea. At the summit, where the trucks had slowed, and the sounds of a humming fleet growing ever louder, they admired the silver glints from the innumerable ranks of centuries. Like ants from afar, they marched aboard repurposed ferries docked on the grand royal port of Dubren, pumping a series of smoke, like harmless chains.

"Kah! How many are there?!" Gin laughed aloud, as he climbed onto the edge of the wagon for a greater view.

"One thousand?! Ten thousand?!" He reached out for the wind, battering the lancers.

Arminius and his comrades showed their heads beyond safety. There to witness the grandiose short-lasting sight.

Undivided, the uniform clacks of hooves and tingling armor with chains to blades trekked along the waterfront from piers' edge to edge. They, the mounted officers with voices and their calls roaring, indicating the presence of each column, it seemed there was a new league apart that Ascot could not have compared. The standards of every graduated century bobbed across the ranks in response to their bestowed names. Backed by another force to their rear, thus when one unit had been documented, they were directed onto the ships as the slow march drove on.

Upon the passing of a tunnel, that view was lost. But by the moment of darkness faded away, the convoy had exposed itself amongst the crowds where it appeared thicker bands of soldiers. The brakes' screeched at the journey's end. Hooks around the wagon's door swung away and awide the exit was made. Alighting at the rear, of the fifth century in wait, whilst the trucks departed soonly, the elites kept their heads fixed ahead at the vanguard of the three hundred. Though not properly, they led their comrades into the queue.

To their own dealings, they did not quite know what shall be done. And with the harsher directors, mere common officers who thought themselves were atop everyone else, presented them a terrible impression as prideful soldiering fools and an unhelpful lot.

"Gendarmes!" They yelled, waving their greased black fingers at the ranks in line.

"Get yer arses movin'!" One added uselessly.

Reluctantly, the century listened to whoever those orders may be from and posted themselves in a column before the ships. Their entrance unto the concrete port was made, and after a short rest, the fated turn was there.

At the vanguard, of the eight lancers, they were welcomed by a battle-scarred face. Riding a brown warhorse, the officer had his eyes and long, combed mustache peeled onto the booklet in his palm.

"Now..." His deep voice coughed out.

Flicking through the pages until he had found the numbered order of battle, a pencil in his hands tapped on the honored titles.

"Arran Century!"

At the very head of the fifth row, the first century, at the end of the port, waved its flag of a golden sun high.

"Steiner Century!" The colonel continued for the one with an abstract mountain banner.

The standards fluttered in their raise each band was named to be recognized. Till it was the last unit. The tenth in line, to be called by the officer,

"Ascot Century!"

The bearer between the elites lifted the colors high. For Arminius who watched the cloth rise, he was filled with a transient ardor upon seeing the sun illuminate the golden lion laying over a crown and dual crossing swords.

"Order number zero two zero seven four nine one!"

announced the colonel, shutting his book.

"Godspeed and Gods save the King!"

With an outbreak of cries and cheers of fanatics and staunch nationalists to be the background tunes, he rode off for his fellow officers, and opened way for the units to march aboard.

In lead, the lancer marched into the ferry before them and alongside their allies, through the agonizing twelve blocks of stairs to the topmost floor. But it was rewarding. That above past the haunting exercise was the open roof of the vessel. And Julien, in all manners of a child, ran onto the upper deck and spotted a good round table. Expanse enough to house eight members. He pointed at its welcoming seats that Arminius, naturally, stole a chair closest to the sea.

When the clock's hand struck noon, the horn blared and the bell chimed twice. The steam and smoke blended, pumped from the single funnels, into an ash-like bunch of thin volcanic clouds floating away in the wind. Propellers churned. Then there was motion. One could not feel the waves crushed beneath the mighty weight of the ships as the fleet sailed off, leaving the plot of safe, motherly land. Bound for the terrors of the near continent.

By the cruise across the northern sea like valkyries on clouds, there was yet the sign of war on the shores to the flanks. No fires nor smoke. The villages and ports of the coasts seemed at ease at night. Any traces of battle nearing from the future was dwarfed by the laughter around, and the noiseless sea breezes of the calm summer. When morning came again, the canal of the grand fortress of Kilunn was in sight. But on the same hour of when they departed Alben, something more magnificent was showcased.

The coastal gray walls of Rustuk, some extraordinary twenty meters high, rose over the waves of the curving Earth. Where nearer, the clarity of the welcoming mood stretched beyond the town's cobbled streets and monuments of the royal regime. Acres of wheatfields covered the closest lands with a golden paint no less like a fantastical artwork. Whilst, the scenic tour a hawk's eye could give caught the flourishing port where within and beside were lush green woods thriving in such civilization. The lancers and soldiers could forget history, how these territories were once ruins only half a century ago.

Turning into the city's harbor, eight ships came to dock, for its troops to disembark. But though their engines had ceased and the skies cleared of the black clouds, two smaller ferries were set upon a course to a narrower path. Not far upriver the ships dragged. Until, in the forest opening past the gates and battlements, the elites spotted a cadre of a few idle officers beside their mounts, gossiping, as one may not call it concerning chatter. As the ships piloted closer to the wooden docks, which timber were senile, the naval horns blared a low-pitched grumble, as if it were used to summon the devil. The commanders halted their nonsense babbling, and mounted, fixing their uniform, armor and arms, before the ropes were thrown to bring the ships to dock. The drawbridges lowered. A landfall chime rang from the hidden bell chambers. Leaning out, Arminius watched his allies flood on land whom a few made a horrid scene, who had not been naturalized at sea, bothered themselves by retching into the river.

"How long are you gonna sit there for?!" Lev yelled at Arminius whose sights finally turned from the currents of stomach juices.

Drawing his cloak around his shoulders, the last of the lancers rose and trailed towards his waving comrades, awaiting him by the stairwell where the echoes of rushing steps resonated.

Two battalions on guard, and centuries beside another and another. The Ascot Century was excessive at the least. With the standard alongside the elites, the numbers of young gendarmes eclipsed their comrades. And they were sure that whoever of the ten majors ahead would take the mantle and lead the three hundred, their luck had run out. But eager to meet their new leader, the youngsters' eyes swirled around, searching for who was to command them soon. Though not any later, the officers had discussed the matter to a conclusion. With one of the many, rode up front, he was the voice of the shy colonel aides reserved under an old oak tree.

"It is good to have y'all here on Zhormannik soil, Albas!"

"Welcome to your new home!" He began with an intimidating voice that could defeat any other.

A straight mustache swept along his face that reached the edges of his ears, and his curling facial hair appeared as if strands grew from his nostrils of a tall sharp nose. The black mace he bore was ready to strike and the aura he kept from awakening was imprisoned in the silver of his armors. There was no doubt he was the leader among the pack, serving as the deputy for his seniors, by the pridefulness of his beginning tone.

"Silber Cohort!" The major announced.

"To know that you shall face your battles under the heavens,"

"Your names will be carved into the annals of history!" Waving his mace about, it came to be by Arminius' face who never flinched when the blunted edges, chipped and diseased by rolls, was halted before a gap.

Galloping away to the second century that his honor could be instilled in another's heart, the commander pledged with his shouts which could uproot the trees wholly,

"The alliance remains loyal to us, and we shall remain loyal to the heavenly Aelon!"

"There is no slightest doubt that we may win this war!" Briefly declaring, the man raised a fist, but to no roaring response of hollering.

"Pledge your souls to victory!" He furthered louder.

"I *promise* you all that *we will* be at Muskau's gates by year's end!"

With an ignition of cheers and cries by everyone he knew, it was except Arminius and Julien who remained utterly quiet. Knowing that such phrases had only been repeated over history for morale, it was no easy fight the major had described.

"Now, it is only natural to have assigned you to us Zhormannik warriors!" An expected wallet of patriotism uttered from his lungs.

"Lest you forget we are fighting for the König in *his* lands." Turning away, he wasted no extra breath in ordering his juniors to commands by the flicks of his mace to the standards.

But of course, the senior's choice mattered more to himself and could not shed a glance for the three hundred youngest.

Please Gods, give us a strong commander. Gin prayed in his head.

His allies searched for who would lead them into battle. Impatiently snapping and fidgeting their fingers softly. Arminius too took a run of calming breaths. Then when the century's turn came to be, with the commander pointing his shaded comrade at the high banner of the lion, the Ascot's gulped. Anxiously, the troops waited for the shadow to show. The sun slowly crawled over his head, releasing the stressful turn of awaiting. Then before them, stood the new, promising major.

"Good to know you all." He said, but his lacking voice had been drowned in the mighty shouts of his senior officers.

The enthusiastic gave greater speeches and divided, there was this man who introduced himself, boringly,

"I am your century commander, Major George Codrington."

With a carbine in his hand, and who looked to be nothing short of a traditionalist warrior, his face was dispirited and had eyes half to shut. An unremarkably thin mustache made the middle-aged major no worse nor better in the wear of a standard red Alba uniform. Though his iron paddings called armor had seen younger days, there was not one scratch. Most probably since neither had the sheathed saber seemed to have moved in the past decades. The most noticeable gimmick was his old, bronze baroque helmet. Otherwise, there was nothing. Pure emptiness and who had no soul to wage war.

Him? A major? Everyone thought, catching the speechlessness of their own comrades.

The colonel aides beneath the maze of leaves and the nets of branches turned their reins and loosened their grips as each took notice of the working majors. Snaps of twigs and the creaking of the empty ships soothed the minds of all but it was disturbing that the slowness of one particular Codrington stole the two pairs of criticizing eyes.

"Is he even supposed to be here?" One asked with a yawn.

Infected by his comrade's fatigued howl, the other responded,

"I heard he's a veteran of some obscure war."

"But that was over twenty years ago." He recalled.

Removing their helmets which were clamped beneath their arms, they watched the troubled unit, who were bewildered too, by the new unsettled commander. As the elder centuries were nearing their ends of a string of contrasting speeches, the recently promoted provided the entertainment of overlooking failure. But the colonel aides still bore respect for the major's aging life and past.

"Damn that Ascot..." Eyeing his seniors, Codrington muttered, but it was unheard.

"I should've become an instructor."

The elites pondered and looked beside cluelessly. It was only to see that their allies were also struck by confusion. Their thoughts soon turned into louder mumbles, and when Codrington had once departed the world of unsurety, the blast of a commander's lungs shot through the ranks,

"Codrington!"

The lancers and gendarmes froze by the halt and change of air. The pace of their breaths quickened as they peered along the columns to the foremost century.

"Are ya done, ya sack o' shit?!" The deputy energetically exclaimed, as if he had no control over his own mind.

"Yes, yes!" Codrington returned yet he knew to have not done so.

But I still haven't explained anything... Alone, his troubles grew.

Unsure of what such a large century entrusted to his command entitled, the major worried quietly, mumbling away from the glares of a doubtful force staring upon his back as the many stood stilled by the one factor Ascot would have shunned. That this man was surely the definition of any incompetency.

"Do ya think we're gonna live past a week?" Gin whispered beside Arminius and Julien.

"Look at 'im."

Their commander bit at his fingers and knuckles. And without knowing what so many things were flowing through his head, the brute continued,

"At this rate—"

A calamitous kick, but the swoop was heard of before, swung into Gin's ankle. With a low cry, the barbarian lost his stance and plummeted, thumping heavily on the patches of grass. Yet, it had somehow miraculously snapped Codrington awake. And it was when he took his first glance at the squad before him.

"Hm?" The major made his concern.

"He slipped." Arber covered his faults, staring at his comrade by the edges of his view.

There, held a tensing quiet between the unbelieving look of the commander and the resolute leer. Until a cackle, in spite of the strain as he had felt soon after the Ascot Unit's appearance, bursted from Codrington's mouth.

"Just watch your feet next time, elite." He noticed as the colonel aides called for himself and the officers.

Elites...? No other force held their elites in the foreground but in the rear guards that the squad thought from the shock, for their commander knew despite not having been told.

The majors gathered around the colonel aides, and pleasantly whilst leisurely, the bouts of agreement were thrown beyond the hearings of the best in the cohort. And anxiously, the squad who were still too flabbergasted by the sharpness of a blunted officer, kept with eyes gaping and blanked. His hands tensed as his knuckles dug into a palm. Arminius felt it most odd that the rank of major would have existed to cover the flesh of veterancy.

No soldier with that experience should be leading a three hundred man unit. He judged, yet the past of Codrington was unknown.

Someone who could tell from a glimpse that we were elites... should be no less than a legate...

On the sound of clanks from the salutes on iron, the meeting concluded. Whilst Arminius withdrew into reality, the rowdy speeches restarted beside when their commander returned with his usual vacancy. But weirdly, he projected firstly without the often delay,

"Ascot Century,"

"We're up as the vanguard in this march." Codrington began, then held a pause.

The incitement of excitement bounded around Gin and Colt, that their comrades could notice the inspired hearts that were reflected on their faces.

"Twelve days long." informed the major, raising his rifle to rest upon his shielded shoulders.

"The march will be to save our allies in Burufʒ."

Heads turned and lips flapped. The century whispered and murmured amongst themselves. There was perhaps more discontentment on the distance they had to engage that was incomparable to the scale in training. They were alien to the real war in patience and endurance.

"But fret not!" Codrington assured before his command fell into disarray.

"Our commitment will surely aid this war effort!"

Then, which he had never done, the major placed a hand on his chest and saluted with hope and the pride of the military.

"When we drive the Confederates back,"

"It will be a straight road to Muskau from there!" He exclaimed with false certainty but at least the century had been fooled.

A hearty cheer forced neighboring units to sound a war cry too, raising their fists high in the air like pumping engine pistons. The machine of war that relied on the blood of humans ignited and the fuel gave birth to rallying shouts of glory. The ten flags waved as the cohort began their march onwards to forgotten victory.

Every sight opened in the vanguard to the vigilant elites, whose stretching views were never disturbed by the emptiness of the country roads. Like the front seats of a car, the ride by foot was once breathtaking across the flatlands of the wheat fields, until the many hours that had passed at the same marching pace made the naive children realize the core of war. The wait.

The first day departed, with the end in night in a camp not too far from a humble Zhormannik village. Arminius held his march onwards nearest the major and colonel aides, bringing Julien to hurry by shoves and tugs. On the second sun of the journey in the trail of fields and farms, a repeat, the warm winds died for the best. Bright but cool and dry under the half sunlight, the breeze satisfied the trail with a bearable day. Though to due, a lancer could not restrain his thoughts much too long.

"Gah! Can't we hitch a ride?!" Swinging his sword out of its scabbard, Gin steamed.

From the colossal shade of Miklós, precise hands, if he were not to be cut, clasped the flinging blade between two palms. But who could not turn back without being disarmed, the unknowing brute endured an enragening mumble that seemed to be belittling him.

"I wonder what goes on in your thick head sometimes." The joking voice chuckled, yet it was not Colt.

Behind Gin's back, in the dark, the black hair rose high till the lancer whose face was unseen before then, was shown to his comrade. Releasing his hold like chains on the sword, Lev strolled alongside and told his idiot friend,

"Fuel's run dry because of the constant warring, and at this pace,"

Leaning into his hands, locked by their fingers, the Rus stared into the dreamy sky of two tones of white and blue.

"We'll run out in less than a decade."

"Tch! That ain't my problem!" Gin grunted, unwilling to hear the truth.

As the first squad's chatter drew an eavesdropper's attention, Codrington slowed to match their pace, but never too close to provoke them.

"Look on the bright side, Gin." Arminius encouraged, and asleep on his back was a Danne, carried ever since the early morning.

"Us new soldiers are usually dumped on the frontlines—"

"The frontlines? The frontlines?!" Without a breath of air needed by his ally, Gin clamored again and again whilst he would make certain the squad had been deafened by his kei.

But on the ramble in desperation for battle, a man of boredom, bored by the scenic path, spoke as equals to his soldiers,

"Exactly that."

For a few counted seconds, there was silence that the brute followed too. Beneath the short shadows of the clouds, the slightest glint of the unpolished helmet flickered. Perhaps, to a regular soldier, that knowing it was true when their fates were due for the frontlines, that they could not accept the command lightheartedly any more.

"So I was right after all." The cheery smile of Arminius twisted into demise but he was not saddened nor troubled.

A forest gradually came to be, sluggishly surrounding the cohort when all around were the thin trunks of the temperate lands. The road sunk into a dirt path. The snapping branches, and chatter of the forces echoed louder. The trees humbly waved. Removing his saber from its sheath and readied it beside, Codrington armed himself for the chance of bandits' ambushes. Known to be rife through Yurupe.

Yet knowing that much, the brief silence was not of the sickness of unpreparedness. The elites wanted more insight from the major that as the eight pairs of eyes were upon him, Codrington sighed with a grin.

"The elder soldiers before you at Rustuk are part of the second cohort." The major explained.

"They are the contingent tasked with reinforcing the defense of Warsau."

As the path they took began to darken by the light could not pierce the impenetrable canopy, the flick of a match drove the splint alight. And impossibly with one hand holding Julien and another with a cigarette, Arminius puffed a breath of smoke that was the scent of herbs.

"And us?" Colt asked in place of the reserved elites.

With a quick glance at the columns of followers, the despair of commanding some youngsters to the tongue of death filled the void under a surge of fire. As projected by the flash of eifer in his eyes, Codrington strained his grip on the sheathing saber.

"We are to be integrated into the Sudetes Gale Army at Akülunnarchs," Pausing before the short tour of the dark forest that had ended, the major and his century reemerged into the spacious country.

"The next site of a decisive clash." He predicted.

Some proud grins, too confident to be measured, dotted across the many faces of the elites. That even Arminius could not hold even a pinch of a laugh, when the atmosphere had woken Julien, unable to enjoy a quiet nap.

"First thing we're thrown into is a battle?" Neither could the thought be pressed under his typical act of maturity.

The eastward journey was shortened by the days and passing, to the mark in the linkage of Aelon forces at every crossroads met. Elites kept awake, the flames that had bursted in their souls were remembered for the impending war. From where the heavens watched, the grand coalition had formed. And it was nigh, the field of steel.

IX

6 JULYUS 491
06.07.12017

Julien Carlstadt

It will be a week before Akülunnarchs come into sight....

Before the possibility that anything could happen...

My hands tremble. Because of a stupid fear like death. How useless am I? Should I have stayed home aiding from afar? Deciding to join this war believing that there really is a chance of me becoming someone like my grandfather. How stupid was I to have listened to Arminius? He's different. He's been trained for his entire life anyways. How could I compare?

Yet I can't ever hide my curiosity for things such as war.

In my fourteen years, conflict has been a fascination of mine. Why do people fight? What would it be like fighting? And how would taking the life of another feel? The strain of the upcoming battle has invaded my body.

This atmosphere of waiting bloodshed...

It often reminds me of a hidden torrent of five years ago...

CHAPTER

10

THE MARCH INTO THE OPENING VOLLEY

The thousand of the Silber Cohort marched with haste, knowing there to be an ally to be saved. But it came at time that their bodies were submerged, to become a spot of a detachment within a crippled division commanded by an unknown savage whose plain-headed and unruly self swore an oath of ill omen. Before the border was marked between two formidable kingdoms, there on the coastal way of the sea, they crossed the legendary bridge of colorless bricks over the river's mouth. Where the passing across the site of battle for King Lech was a blessing, at long last, the cohort traversed into the central Yurupe state of the continental hegemon. Leken. It was not so dissimilar to her neighbor. Nothing had altered. The core remained mere militiamen and drafted peasants from neighboring Zhormann. But they were in a last attempt to save their nation. All had the morale of elites. As they told themselves in belief that they were the saviors of their homes.

The sun broke the clouds and emptied the battlefield of the sorrows. In the early day, the unit marched, quickening their pace after the past leisurely stroll. Where the air grew heavier and the high drums' pounding captured the senses of the century, first to arrive. Eager, Gin and Colt raced ahead as the faithful comrades chased in their dust. But beyond any hold over his thudding heart, by he was gripping his sling so tightly it could snap, Julien shuddered at the nearing of the ridge that Codrington led towards. Then, when they finally climbed and reached the summit of the plateau, Arminius took the leash and his eyes were first to rise above the grass. As one grand line of reinforcements, casting a shadow over the battlefield, a burst of war cries and clashing iron were blared into the division's faces.

As Gin sniggered, with his arms stretched before, the scent of blood and the bashes of blades refilled his veins deprived of kei. And before the mesmerized, the brute sucked a lungful of the red curtain cast across the lands.

On the battlegrounds, heads and limbs flew, with an occasional gunshot's snap drowned in the waves of cries. They could spot that within the chaotic frontlines, there was some order. But it was a reckless Confederate general who led the charge of traditional cavalry into Aelon's weakened core. There was no resistance and not one shield could defend. The lines bursted like a dissected heart. It shattered. For Arminius knew he could do little but to await new orders, his eyes were simply peeled upon the carnage crushing the souls. Trampled by the hooves of war horses. The youth felt the adrenaline rush in his nerves. The eifer he carried could burst.

"I've never seen a battle of this scale with my own eyes." Intensely clutching the pommel of his sword, Arminius could only say.

Though shakingly, Julien sensed death as something unlike honor or glory. He nodded yet was troubled by the snaps of bones. Both flustered and fascinated, the Danne had not distinguished whether his mind was fearing the inevitable or jittering over the thoughts of a dream.

Codrington's arm drew along the lines which had been shaped; he calmly passed orders for the shift in formation. But as well, the century commander knew to keep weary of the coming command that was soon to arrive as his allies marched to a still. The shafts of spears dug into the mud and the squelch of unbalanced stamps on sinking ground ceased.

Then, at the height of a heart beat, thuds of the lightly rumbling ground came.

"Order!" A yell flew to the division commander who administered the field.

A backline messenger, told by the tall banner borne on his back, galloped on his mount across the field from the distant safety of the headquarters. From where a white flare shot into the sky, the pale stone cottage stood. The blinding light lit up the gunpowder gray clouds whilst the heads of the soldiers were captured by the temporary shine. Like an automaton, the army began to withdraw without a single word that was the genius of signals. Even strangely to one unfamiliar to the code of war, their enemies halted too.

"For Third General Isak Bodén!" The messenger delivered, harshly tugging on the reins.

"The Eleventh Division is to descend for the vanguard and await!"

The armies retreated from the clash and a stalemate was drawn again. But amidst the loosening clouds, the bountiful layers of corpses emerged. Swallowed by the ground and forced to the earth by the prints of a stampede, the many, some alive but most certainly senseless, were disfigured or mutilated that from afar, the elites were lucky to have not witnessed beforehand.

"Aight!" A coarse call thundered that was from the general in mention.

A stout man of his late forties, in the noble dress of scarred armor that covered not every inch of the body. He was taller and greater than any warriors noted till then in the lancers' campaign and had quite the vicious diagonal scar running along his uncombed, bearded face from a nameless war and a nameless axe that had branded him so. Curled dark gray hair, short and unwashed, was the barbarity of his nature, bucketed beneath an exotic pickelhaube that was of a royal blue with a yellow plume. The priceless center coin on the helmet above his forehead held the order of a golden vase. From a family of prestige.

"You heard 'im! By the wills of the gods!"

"For I only ask for the heads of those Rus rapists before your wives and children are made toys of the Confederacy!" Bodén roared for his forces to hear.

The incision of his words were crisp and short, but it was sweet enough to have given his division the fuel they needed. Cheers and clashing swords; the punches of spears into the air. Neither Arminius could hold his feet and maintain a steady look as the zeal of patriotism swept to ignite the same excitement as his comrades.

"My Eleventh Division! Advance!" The blade of the general and his personal guards charged and as reinforcements, the fresh current of the division rushed downhill.

The Ascot Century traced the narrow gaps of the army in the tides of the advance. Their banner weaved through the shielded rearguard of fanciful armor where stares of disdain were but a trait from the veterans and highest elites. Then there, though not so far, the middle guard they had arrived upon was a melting pot of standard troops and conscripts. Their eyes were calmer yet still many had the frowns of fury. But, at the frontlines, the disintegration of any orderly system arose. It was no less a segregated sector that within were the peasants and militiamen scattered apart. As the unit joined the third party of the army, the disciplined were found more so foreign to the faces of shell shock and hopelessness. There was not the ordinary glimmer of appreciation for life that the commanders thought could have beaten the Confederates to their homeland. The speeches that Arminius and Julien once predicted were lies.

"There's no way..." Lev spoke of what seemed obvious amidst the oblivion of souls.

"They won't survive a single charge."

Codrington readied his carbine as the divisions awaited for the last survivors of the previous clash to fall into line. Returning to the vanguard. Arriving alone with flesh and splinters of bones in their hair and atop stained clothes. But though for the soullessness of the depressed, they gathered the courage and joined the next onslaught before the waving sabers of commanders.

"It's only natural..." Julien explained as the unit beside him inspected their rifles from butt to muzzle.

The squad turned to him, curious, as each loaded their first rounds of the twenty shells. Pings of bolts snapping into place reverberated down the allied lines like a shock wave from the center files.

"The weakest in the vanguard are only thrown away as a cushion for the clash." The Danne continued, but quieted, most definitely.

"So...that their bodies could pile into a slope for high ground—" His voice was perhaps more timid than usual when Arminius halted him with an assuring hand.

"Sure, but it won't turn out that way for us." The latter boy concluded, disabling Julien from his rambles.

Surprised that there were often new insights about this peculiar elite squad, Codrington asked with his shadow protecting overhead,

"They would never tell you ordinary soldiers. But the academy?"

A light chuckle, sounded as little as a sigh, when the Danne placed his flat palm upon the bolt and locked the bullet with a gentle push.

"Not exactly..." Julien embarrassedly replied behind a smile.

"It was probably my grandfather who taught me."

Probably? Arminius wondered how it was odd for him to have phrased a memory.

"Is he a soldier as well?" The major questioned the lancer.

But there was not an open answer where the joy of a vestige had broken. However his nerves had been calmed by talks of distant matters. Though the stage was claimed by another who intervened.

"Ah! Major!" Lev drew the commander as the remnants gathering within their unit held horror.

"We know our third general but what about the commander of the army?" He curiously peered upwards towards the tallest banners of the cliff edge's headquarters.

Pointing at the cottage and the ridge, the lancers' heads were spun around by the discreet finger of Codrington.

There was an elder, but not too old, a few years senior to Bodén's. His nose was fractured and had a distinct squarish jawline that was paired with a short, narrow goatee. With arms crossed and a glare watching the distant Confederates, there was no doubt, the flurry of simulations for the battle ran like a rusting turbine in his head. In a golden brown uniform that only one nation of Beuoe took pride in, he appeared of average height and brawny. Yet, despite his somewhat warrior build, the man's complexion was telling that he had not seen any duels nor close battles for years and decades. Perhaps it was fear or laziness. One could not name.

"That's General Adrien Nikola." Codrington introduced the army's commander to the squad.

"He's a good man, but he oversimplifies every concept of war." The major gradually hushed, hoping no one else, too foreign to like, would hear him.

"Which has proven problematic over his aging years."

A bang of a revolver filled the air with the echoes crackling across the sacked, and razed field. That, the ringing signaled the completion of the army's formation. Wherein like a weighty bowl, three divisions were stretched into the shape, hoping to hold their enemies within the curve. The vanguard, the middle guard and the rearguard. All accumulated to form barely eighty thousand soldiers remaining. Some rested reinforcements whilst most were worn.

There was no one ahead. There was not a sign of comrade life before Arminius and the lancers. Only the distant specks of shining armor and barrels could be seen, lined along the horizon by the field's outskirts and the treeline.

"Draw and aim!" Bodén commanded for the ranks.

Kneeling, the first line in wait soaked their knees in the mud and dug ever deeper into the earth. Their heels were submerged when the iron stance was made by sharpened pupils resting in their rifles' silver sights. It was soon the minute that would bring the battle to war again. The heating breath of Arminius exhaled as a brief stroke of steam.

The plated coats of lightweight plates; black iron and silver helmets filled the opposing front with an imposing aura. Their distinguished commanders pointed the series of blades at Nikola's forces, and was more prepared to unleash an unforeseen terror upon the Aelon. With the two grand batteries primed to incinerate the lacking eighty thousand, they waited for the last fog to clear before a Confederate aide rushed to the heights of a crumbling temple tower.

Her feet were agile. And soon, she had reached the outlook overlooking the Rus machine below and vast, glossed on the invaded land. The war engine of mankind themselves without any needs of complex steelworks of machinery stood superior to the westerners of the world.

"Vice General?" The young lady called for the commander.

Whose grin told of immediate victory, it was within the ruined village of Akülunnarchs the vice general's arm was raised with an ensuing order.

The barrel and the abyss of the flare gun rose into the air, pointed at the heavens, as Nikola scoured the flanks to the left and right. His commanders were in position. Every soldier was eager for the taste of blood. Without the loss of the malice and rushing stress of plunging into uncertainty, the fanned flames of loyal hearts, for he was willing to deal first, the trigger was pulled. Shooting a swift green flare to the above, it was tailed by a wall of similar smoke from the lower colonels under his command.

Reflections of the light illuminated the rifles and the tiniest metalworks on uniforms. Then when the sparks were due to fall from the clouds, a blossom of the same word dashed across the front.

"Fire! Fire!" Codrington and fellow commanders cried after Bodén.

A volley of yellow and amber sparks from the muzzle of the rifles erupted like thunder with a cover of smoke that blurred the darker row of pinkish explosions firing upon the allied army. Bullets hurled across the field of the dead and in the last thought, the waves of brass skimmed over the elite squad. As if a hook swooped around his head, Arminius felt the stream of boiling air navigate by his ear. The screams of horror and crunches of guts was before the blood squirting at their backs. Rounds ricocheted from Codrington's armor and were sent to the heavens who frowned upon such unholy massacre.

His head lowered whilst the second rank discharged another torrential volley. The air splitting noise assaulted his ears, that Julien flinched but his comrades battled on. Under the rapids of firing guns, the leading lancer searched about.

"Still here?!" As loud as he could over the blasts, Arminius asked.

The nods and lively shouts in reply were barely heard, but luckily, the elites had survived the greater peril of the first volley. But behind, where the chunks of flesh were flung above the rear ranks, he turned towards, holding steady his kepi. His eyes grew in shock as a shadow of despair filled his face.

A leaking lung and a geyser-like puncture. Two younger soldiers laid drawing laborious breaths. Their faces paled and the trembling had ended. They were only waiting for the lanterns of the valkyries. He wondered why it was that no one aided them, for the past two years they were the closest comrades. Not a human soul could care for the suffering.

"We should get them off the field—!" Arminius reached for them but his arm had been latched by a tight grip.

"It's no use." In a tone seeming nothing but cruelty, Arber intervened.

"They'll be trampled anyways."

Arminius watched his comrades drown in their blood, gurgling and spewing over their faces whilst their lives were snatched away by death's fleeting grasps. The same breathlessness of the inability to protect circled Julien. Closing his eyes, the Danne spun around and took aim once more, but was trembling. By the uncovered slaughter ensuing, Arminius hesitated for long. Where only he thought he may be capable of saving them.

I should! The lancer battled his mind.

No! I might be able to protect them…but what about everyone else?!

Will I cause too much trouble—? His body stilled.

Then, a punch in the back broke his eerie silence that was unlike him, a typically reckless and strong willed soldier.

"Arminius!" Arber yelled to the captain of the elites.

Shutting his eyes with the force of a seal, the shade of nothingness reminded Arminius of his duty. And when the choice came to be said, his voice was forced to submit into the nature lacking humanity.

"Damn this…" He muttered, returning into formation.

The fuse of the fifth rank's rifles seared. Sparks exploded from the gaps of the chambers. But the result had been the same, closing to the tenth line before the cycle would repeat. Any chance of striking an enemy was a simple game in a lottery. The Confederates knew too and so the machine that was to break the equilibrium was brought forward beyond the low and distant clouds.

A monstrosity of grand Rus guns were wheeled to the front, ahead of the corporals and lieutenants holding the battle lines, mesmerizing the many gendarmes that the foot soldier's volleys of rounds halted. Yet, the ember had already grown before their ignition. And a firework-like garden of flowering blasts bursted in the dense smoke from the Confederate army which the Aelon third general had realized soon.

"Don't lose your heads!" Bodén warned, though he was nowhere to be seen.

The shells zoomed with trails of fire and were launched across the army shaped like a bowl. Peering up to the sky, there was no sun to blind their eyes. As the rounds withdrew from the momentum, the shells quickly dipped.

A deep laugh blared. It was the division commander. He foresaw the flaw of the field howitzers. As luckily for his troops, the quaking of the ground had not come from the blow dealt on the army. Tossing boulders and the pieces of flaming skin from the earth that showered onto the rearguard like a mud storm, unwavering, the ridge had swallowed the lion's claws and for then, the Aelon had been spared from the plate of catastrophe.

"Nil casualties, Vice General Vasilevsky!" The Confederate aide reported with the binoculars pressed over her eyes.

Furious by the petty assault, she slammed her hands against the quaking rails and leaned into the shallow rising fog with a yell,

"Fix your sights and reload—!"

But her commander held the uncontrollable subordinate and patted her shoulder in good will, easing the flustering reddened face that had besmirched the lady's fairness.

"Do not be so hasty," Vasilevsky pleaded, drawing himself to the edge when his hold clenched into fists on the fences.

"That was to test you." said he, but it was not to the aide.

As the two armies went into another bout, volleys unending and warriors chanting, the general devilishly chuckled. His proud demeanor was unaccepting of the fatal loss of the artilleries, but was sure that it was only an ant amongst a colony of methods victory could be guaranteed by. Vasilevsky slammed his hands onto the railings and aimed his eyes upon the Aelon forces.

"You've avoided enough." He grumbled to the regiments beneath him.

A grin drew wide as Vasilevsky moked, swapping his sights towards the far ridge's headquarters,

"But how long can you sustain your mediocrity for, Adrien Nikola?"

Nikola's brows lowered into a frown as the thickening stain of dying luck was felt to be a puncture in his heart. His groan in pain was quiet from the aching poison of bad weather looming over his shoulders. He knew that the defense of the headquarters would do no good. The fires of Vasilevsky's pressing claws were peeling ever more into his lines. Witnessing the frontline rifles and soon the center disappearing into the whitish gray thicket, the general could only spot the rims of his rearest guards, sprayed by showers of dirt.

"How many thousands have we lost?" The commander asked of his aides, by a warring map, circling their fingers around the northern forces.

"Two thousand in the first volley." A colonel responded before a second staff added,

"Hundred and a half, about the second, and no more than thirty succeeding."

The troubles grew. Amongst the grumbling of disloyalty and conspiracy, many spun their sights to the Confederates shielded behind the curtains of gunpowder clouds. Their desperation became unmatched.

"Where does the Seventh Army sit?" Nikola requested that it was for the formidable Vasilevsky.

"One hundred fifteen thousand." The highest ranking subordinate reported.

Awaiting for a mild silence between the thunderous cackles of firing ranks and ruffling of kneeling soldiers for the next volley to be charged, the general retreated to the table beneath the broken sky. He held a red colored pin, clinched by two fingers. The needle of the wooden marker slowly pierced the crisp paper at where the circular checkers surrounded. And in good form, the same formation of a bowl was seen to be the three pillars. It was the vanguard that Nikola's fingers pointed towards.

"Corporal!" A loyal messenger was called to the commander.

Summoned like a war hound, the sprinter swung about the tent, half mounted. He rose himself to the saddle and paused by Nikola, dipping his head gently to the general. Though the order came unheard by the gust of wind, the sharp ears heard the command and were rapidly adapted into words within a small notebook his pockets kept ready. The pages fluttered but the scribbles of the pen were quick. Till soon, he nodded again telling that the order had been printed. Lashing the reins with a fierce shout, the messenger began his descent for the battlefront. His banner, once dulled by the staleness of the air, waved again on the ride.

The heat of colliding hammers and brass drew lakes of sweat in the fierce cheers of the troops. Immune to the fear, the crashing waves of spirit struck. Reduced to fifteen rounds, the elites took aim and pulled the stiffening trigger. Except the ground or grass, they hoped to wound their enemies. Yet no one was sure to have murdered any.

"We can't let up!" Arminius inspired as nothing was borne beyond mere meters.

"The smoke will keep us concealed for now!"

As the chambers were opened to the elements by the draw of a bolt, the hollow thuds of emptied shells sunk into the mud. Spots of bronze clustered by their heels and the smoke blinded comrades near.

"But the same goes for those Confederates!" Lev reminded the squad who no doubt knew by then.

Their stocks of ammunition had not dwindled much in the slow march of bullets and the troops on the field failed to fall. Impatiently, the razor-like-bladed glaive of the back and forward trailing third general bounced on his hand. His soul was able to erupt a flow of eifer if not checked by the words longed for.

"Make way! Make way!" There was a distant bellowing voice.

"Order! From General Nikola!" The corporal hailed from the fog, darting through the gaps in the ranks.

When the messenger neared the third general, he never bothered to greet the commander with the slightest salute and came to be by his ear with a whisper,

"Plan Lannes. Full autonomy."

Whose face exploded into instant joy, harnessing his inner wantingness to finally act, his lungs contained only one command needed to sound. Bodén's fidgeting fingers halted. The glaive landed in a grip that even his joints and bones clicked. A mumble beside the unrelenting barrages sent the messenger to his return to the hill where whatever the request was, however absurd or reckless, to be granted.

But unseen by those captured by the rage of battle, surging through their veins, none had noticed the change in strategies. The common soldier had no wearies if the battle would remain stale as long as their lives were preserved under the blessed veil of the smog.

"Hold, men!" Codrington raised an arm to the sky.

His hand was clutched on the stock of the carbine. Eyes fell upon him as his command was given. When catching wind of the exhaustion blighting the hard fighting troops, the major turned to the banner with his head raised.

"Elites! Rotate to the rear rank and freshen yourselves—!" He granted, to the relieved stares of the lancers.

The gasps to replenish their squeezed lungs were thought to have been a breath of peace whilst each, readily easing their strained shoulders and lowering the rifles, rose from the knee. However, then on the shuffles of the reinforcements, a light tweet of a war flute rang in the dense descended heavens. Elites searched around. But it was not near that the tune was sung.

"Halt!" Abruptly, Codrington held a fist high for his unit to see.

Of what the signal was to be, the memories of the veteran rushed into his mind like a scorned stampede.

"This…" The commander realized.

His face grew pale. Whilst he looked about, everyone had paused, startled by the forced bulk that shattered the momentum of battle. It was an eerie calm. Before the hooves of a sprinting horse came more pronounced. The third general's image from afar enlarged till a roar, as his flight by, was beside Arminius.

"My glorious division! Their breaths are due!" The slaps of the reins and the galloping bashes of the beast rocked mother Terra.

Who caught the general's plan, it sounded like that the Confederates' volleys ceased too. On the great deep thumps of a high drum, all rifles retreated. The forces of centuries began to merge as the many cohorts. Commanded to, the files narrowed and were bundled. As the drums' pace steadily rose, the rumbles were louder.

"The hell?" A face of frustration was what struck Gin.

But the elites were dumbstruck by the signal that they could not answer, hence his rudeness called for the commander,

"Hey, ya've frozen solid—!"

"A charge..." Codrington broke the stillness with a mumble so quiet.

"What?" Leaning ahead to hear, Gin blurted.

"Ascot Century! Ready for a charge!" The major erupted as he reared his stallion.

His carbine was holstered and the untouched saber was drawn, and that could answer Gin with one obvious clue.

To the drawing of blades sliding by the swift screeches beyond their scabbards, the Danne boy was pounded by the flooding fear. Allies armed for a melee but his rifle remained rattling from shudders. His pupils shrunk yet Julien's eyes stayed widened. Not a gulp could break the sweatless cold breaking into his swelling pulse. From the dread he was removed by a friendly flick on the head and an assuring smile beside.

"Just stay close." told Arminius, dragging his sword and spear to be faced against the enemies' equalling unsheathing of steel.

There, the fright stayed but was sunken for the time by the relieving faces familiar to Julien. The elties bore a contrast of willingness. And he knew not to fail as once before he promised to fight with his own strength. There was a brief blankness that loosened the defeatist stare. What had arisen was the parallel zeal.

Blades of the spears and swords. Mauls and maces. The vanguard pointed their noses and silver tips at the Confederates. All awaiting the next cry. For when the harsh drumming halted, Arminius watched the tail of a red flare whistle into the air. The prelude divided into a hellish arc of crimson smoke, like the chains of chariots that the invisible devils casted overhead.

X

14 JULYUS 491
14.07.12017

Adrien Nikola

One hundred thousand. This number plummets. Ever since this war beg: two years ago, not once has our allies won an engagement. I pray this does not turn into another blunder then catastrophe. We would have to retreat yet again. More lives lost to the jaws of the Confederacy.

This should be the perfect field for a pitched battle. Akülunnarchs. Impossible for I to be outflanked around the bog of the east. However, my staff disagrees repeatedly. Pretending that the greater chances of a cavalry detachment sweeping around is beyond my eyes. I know what is what. What do they know about commanding such a grand force? Easy to presume this battle will last for long. If we simply grind at the Confederates, they will eventually withdraw and this victory will be ours. Vasilevsky needn't chase me more and our people will suffer no longer. Hear my prayers, god of the Sudetes winds for tomorrow's bringing.

Night is here, and the red waves have come.

CHAPTER

11   INSUBORDINATION

Like flames in the sea of fog, the enveloping cloak of flares burned. Drowning the voices of the afar, their tensed eyes were on what laid ahead beyond the clearing smoke. As the stomps of the cavalry rode in a charge, within the guards of elites, Bodén roared,

"Eleventh Division! All advance!"

His words echoed against the invaders' shields in waves that pierced the fog. The tip of his glaive pointed ahead, leading a triangular formation. A dust cloud, like his very own cape of forty thousand men, followed the thunderous war cry. Screams to inflict terror filled the turbulent air. The lines broke rank by rank. By the rear pushing ahead, they forced the vanguards to charge ever faster than their own known capabilities.

"Ascot Century!" Codrington yelled, with his saber raised above his head.

"Onwards! Follow the commander!"

The elite squad cheered alongside the major in an unstoppable storm broke free of its shackles. A light jog evolved into a run and the ground quaked too. Beside the lancers who kept their heads towards what was awaiting behind the cover of gray, the banners of Aelon rose. State by state. The colors of the flags fluttered, waving away the mist that revealed their bodies to the sights of the grand rival. Ahead, there was one, whose expression kept in a birthing rage. Fixed by a single target that no one else knew of, Arminius was latched into the flow.

Without need for an extended sight, an aide peered at the emerging frontline. Columns and files pressed onwards. Across the field of trampled corpses; the flowers of death, the plains were

nothing but bodies of desperate souls. At the spearhead that soon entered the light from the darkness of the fog, it seemed that Bodén was to offer the Confederates the day's second clash. A madman, his fury craving for blood sent a shock of goosebumps for those who heard.

"They're charging?" The aide reported to Vasilevsky, watching over his troops with arms arrogantly crossed.

The vice general bore a smirk. Sure that the iron curtain his army was, he believed, would not be moved. Not an inch of the tower shields would be pushed in the grappling mud. They glared at the rising dust clouds together, from the echoing stamping and cries, incoming for his head. There were few troops who sought glory quicker than the charge. But they were foolish and wasted to have been cut down by the disciplined Rus.

"Is this what you're playing at Nikola?" Vasilevsky grunted, expecting better of his opponent.

"You gave up *your* command?" When the frustration expanded his veins, the winds broke around the steam of his eifer.

Marching to the stairs, he descended the crippling tower but without his subordinate holding her ground. The encroaching hunks on the bent white stairs landed at the ground till the shadow showed out of his nest. At the mouth of the doorway at the forest behind the slanted church, the cavalry guard of the great warmonger was found resting, however hardened for battle if it would come to face them. They had been awoken. The screeching and rustling of their heavy scaled lamellar was a response to the commander they cherished and protected. Every rider was a giant. Titans who were hardly shorter than Vasilevsky himself.

With self-righteousness that dethroned any claimants. As the vice general mounted his war horse, he was equipped with a great curved sword and a sun-shaped shield. Ornamented with solar flare-like spikes reaching outwards that weighed as much as pure gold. His face was scarred with a shallow slash along his jaw that a small mustache did not reach. The golden and metallic hues of armor that he wore was the heirloom of his family, and like a lord, it was backed by a plain reddish cape. Pinching his pointed beard for good fortune, the commander fitted his helmet that was the head and jaw of a lion. Only natural for a man as terrible named Leonid Vasilevsky, the *Summer Lion.*

"Third General Rzhev!" He called for another.

"Sir!" The man reported, with a flat-handed salute along his chest.

More extravagantly dressed than the commander he answered to, the series of sparkling red and gold cloth and metals was his form. But his face was unknown, unable to be seen under the shade of the polluted branches and brownish leaves.

"I place you in command." Vasilevsky temporarily promoted him to a ranking of his own.

"Of course, sir!" Spoken in a weird dialect, Rzhev flamboyantly bowed.

"I will look after this place as I would do to my home."

The vice general warmed his joints and tendons, swinging his sword from side to side and clicking the buckles of his spine. As Vasilevsky pointed the blade at the frontlines, laid outside the forest, Rzhev retreated into the church tower and watched over his loyal commander before an order was made.

"Now, Igor!" The vice general yelled to the sailing clouds.

"Trap them in my snare of machines!"

From above, his officer dipped his head that Vasilevsky had not seen. Lifting the flare gun of the higher general's, Rzhev reached out, pointed to the scalp of the canopy and raised his arm.

"Elite guard, let us bury those fools!" Leading his personal squad, the Confederate commander galloped past the church's door and was past the village.

Diving into the forest where his army awaited his leadership, he was under the thin plume of two falling green flares. Weaving faster than a leaf could touch the earth, the charge journeyed. Unbeknownst to the brewing ploy, Aelon became a vulnerable prey to the steppe beast's claws.

Over the vast meadow in the no man's land, there was a path few of rot, the elites were without signs of slowing. The sprint of the eight caught Codrington at the pace of the gendarmes but though the formation seemed to be intact, the vanguard's spearhead had broken from the shaft.

"Elite squad! Slow your feet!" The commander pleaded but to no avail.

He was ignored. The lancers had shot away from the century.
As on the high of adrenaline, they sensed the end of the static air.
A fresh wave of wind blew over their heads, and in no time later,
the clear skies unraveled from the thinning smoke like an untying
ribbon on a present.

This battlefield... Arminius dreamed before the opening.
Just like home.

A deep wall of iron reflected the sun, dragging the surreality
of what they had imagined before the clash of the frontlines. Skins
of spears, as if the army was the jaw of a shark, never wavered
in the developing breezes of the forest dark leagues behind their
backs. It was a straight dirt plain, of lifeless weeds and brown,
decaying greenery lying unmoving in the sights of an army before
his eyes. But before their blades met flesh too, Arminius peered to
his right on a bash of a blade against shields. Waterfalls of blood
washed through the Confederate ranks. Bodén, whose beastly
shine, crashed into the fragile lines and penetrated the ranks.
Slashing right and left with his razor glaive, heads flung above,
sheared from bodies.

"Look at ya third gen'ral go!" The heartbeat of the brute was
most impatient.

"Let's getta puncture in da Confederates an' make a way for
our unit!" Gin suggested to the lancers' leader.

Yet he was not one to listen to any other strategy, Arminius
nodded at his squad who were with confident grins.

"Miklós!" He called for the giant.

The colossal of the rear sped past his comrades. A hunk of
flesh, bones and blood with a dash of lust for a slaughter. Alone,
Miklós raced by Arminius with a spear that was as tall as he, and
charged onwards for the squad slowed for the Sorbe's show. With
a demonic leer, the cursed eyes shocked the Confederates of the
first present rank.

"Who's that supposed to be?" A soldier squinted, trying to
make out the figure in a haze past the mass trail of clouds.

"No matter!" The corporal of a squad swung his arm and
commanded,

"Just kill him before he even sets his breath on our shields!"

Spears dropped and aimed at Miklós, whose stomp at full
sprint began to weaken. But it was that his dash was unimaginable,
his footsteps had become lighter than nature's stalking predators.

When a secondary row of spears dipped ahead, the elite was yet to end his rush at the lines, like a train which had no brakes. A blackish coil burned in his spear. Then all of a sudden, he came to a halt with a stomp of a foot. His neck was barely before his foes' spear tips as the demon stretched his grip and twirled the spear into a whirlpool of glowing blood red and black.

"Hah! What is this mockery—?" The corporal laughed before his eyes drew blank and his lopped head was in flight.

The hunk of flesh landed by the great devil's feet, with a plop not dissimilar to a butcher's toss of meat. Its face was conscious and twitching, but by the mud seeping into his carved neck, his eyes were in agony. The spear swung across the bodies of the first soldiers, bisecting its enemies before the blade. A gush of their lives' fluids detonated in a tidal wave to the air. The shafts of spears snapped into splinters. And what remains of the corpses thumped onto the ground. A shockwave of the monstrous strike launched those unhurt hurling through the lines. And it was some lowly lancer, a fiend incarnate, who had unleashed an infection of fear. As guts and brains splattered across the dirt, liquified into mud, the trauma forced the Confederates into a shaking retreat.

"H-He's a d-devil!" Shattered, one's soul could only stammer aloud.

A few steps back in withdrawal they took. But as keen were their legs in advance, the Confederates were pushed onwards by their commanders' rifles and swords.

"Do not waver!" A lieutenant was sure to hold his ground.

"He's only one man!"

The inspiration was a drug for the troops. Gathering their courage in a maelstrom for vengeance, the holes in the dubious hearts had been repaired inhumanely. Their weapons locked upon Miklós. The devil's eyes expanded. In a stance for another bull's charge, the instant was met by a figure leaping over his head with the shine of steel obscuring his face.

To the Confederates in dismay, a boyish yell was paired by his crashing, and slashing into the ranks. However blood did not flow so easily from the lightness of the agile strikes. That had pushed his foes away on his landing of both feet, they were stunned, but suffered gentle wounds. The elites rushed through in an unstoppable flood and smashed their blades along the cave of the army. For the coming century, a canal of guts and limbs had been dug.

"Everyone here?!" Arminius cried over his shoulder to the uniform charge of comrades that had arrived.

"Yeah!" Julien replied from the center of the formation.

"How long are ya gonna sit 'ere for?!" Gin stirred, flicking dry his blade of a coat of fabric and sinews.

With a fury of fluid cuts, the momentum of the major dived into the second ranks through the opening the elites had made. Ringing of steel on steel. The prompt cease of cries. The regular flight of inner organs. The division rampaged upon the Confederates and the close battle ensued when the names on the God of Death's expanse ledger would be troublesome to keep count of.

"Elite squad!" With his saber lowered, Codrington rushed to their side.

"That was too reckless!" The lancers were scolded.

"The division can't keep up and if we continue with our way—" He said, deflecting the whirl of a spear pitched towards him.

The Confederates tightened their encirclement. Like water around a stationed stone, the emptiness was quick to be filled by reinforcements.

"Commander!" Arminius acknowledged.

"What is it?" Codrington asked, sliding his saber into the throat of a spearman whose dissected tube bubbled.

"We should keep to our pace—!" Suggested the desperate lancer.

"Did Ascot not teach you anything?!" The major finally boiled in the heat, that none would have thought to see.

"Arminius is right!" Julien interrupted as well.

It seemed every soldier had gone mad from the chaos. But it was the Danne's call that the enraged bickering halted.

"We could draw some of the attention away from the Third General." Pointing at Bodén who had sawed into the thickening lines afar, Julien judged.

"There's a constant flow of troops behind us so we can withdraw from the spearhead." He analyzed to the surprise of the major.

"Even if we don't break through, the commander would have an easier time."

Leaning against the saddle's spine, Codrington pondered. Appearing as if his aim was for the headquarters, Bodén drove further than the bulk of his division. He saw the commander was soon alone, plunging to the depths with the noble guards. If one mistake in a step was made, his self could fall into the abyss of blades. With his awed eyes closed, the major listened to the blows between blades as the elites shielded him from the impending Confederates.

"I wasn't in the right." Wondering quietly, Codrington shook his head.

"Alright. I'll take your word, Reichner." The century commander showed some appreciation to the soldier whose eyes held faith in success.

To the nods of both lancers and leader, the major raised his saber to the clouds and issued a rallying cry,

"Ascot Unit! Hear!"

"Reform yourselves at the vanguard!"

The century composed a formation of an arrowhead, with the elites of the outer edges placed like a coat of poison.

"Charge! For the Aelon!" The offensive began at the signal of Codrington.

A cheer of the lessened century freshened their kei. Felling a soldier threatening to seal the channel to the second column, Arminius was the spear's unbreakable tip. The drive was unending. Yet the blade was still as sharp with drooling blood. The absolute might was gaining and there was a renewed hope for the conflict to be won. As the cracks widened along the front, many units trailed into Codrington's path or had formulated their own. The strength felt doubled could not be any higher they thought.

The Confederates are close to breaking. Arminius felt the air lighten and an allied victory in sight.

All we need now is for Bodén to reach the headquarters, then—

Rumbles of veteran engines approached. His mind was reminded of the familiar sounds of that night over two years ago. The distraction came by the break in the wind.

Those aren't bombers... He thought whilst the strikes on enemies slowed.

The elites heard too and the sprint became a crawl. To the blanket of the risen fog and the spreading sky, the lancers peered upwards and the major was aghast.

"You gotta be kidding!" Colt raged with a gust of wind from his gentle swipe of the spear, flicking a squad of Confederates into their advancing allies.

The ground began to rattle as well, as if an army of titan was nearly upon them. Mixed in the hurricane of aircraft, there was another recognizable metal foe. Noticing the fleet of steel birds emerge from the clouds, there was one answer that Arminius doubtlessly announced to the horrors of the division found in the trap,

"Fighters and armored cavalry!"

A squadron of aircraft stalked the air, with their humming shroud and rattling of machine guns. At the edge of the ridge, General Nikola watched the flies near like winds cruising along the sky. There was not a fighter able in his possession. Nor were there any guns that could offer battle. That was the downfall of Aelon that the common people of the world knew that they were most lacking in revolutionary technology. Yet he was in no panic despite the slight agitation of the sight.

"Sir, a squadron of light fighters!" His aide reported.

Squinting, it was spotted by the old pair of eyes that the planes had begun to dive shallower towards the front. Their route was confirmed. They aimed for Bodén's head no matter how many Confederates they would waste for a taste of victory.

"This isn't going to be enough." Nikola patted the hilt of his saber.

He took a step back and sighed, counting the spinning propellers drawing closer.

"Twenty three, twenty four." Exhaling his troubles again, Nikola concluded.

The general tugged on his sword and the buckle unclicked. His single blade dropped to the grass to the bewilderment of his subordinates as he retreated to his tent. Their mouths were gaping. They had not known whether the general had surrendered by his gesture. It was all the while Confederate fighters locked Bodén in their sights as their throttle was pulled back with the winding cogs of old guns.

"Sir!" They ever more worriedly cried.

The winds lowered. The dust clouds settled. As the division's charge had dissipated in the twilight of an endless enemy, a perfect line of Aelon troops was formed for the fighters to peel upon.

"General Nikola—!" The colonel sounded for the last time.

Rising out of the tent into the light, a new man was clutching onto a greatsword whose blade was the width of a plane's full wing. Armored from head to toe in dense layers of bronze studded platings, he may have been named a mediocre general when the warrior meant for leadership. But he was never mentioned in songs of duels and brawls, may it be of the obscurity of his strength that the aides knew not wholly.

How long has it been? Nikola remnicized.

"General..." The aides gazed ahead as he approached the ridge again, with the broadsword under his faithful command.

Before the fighters' guns opened, Nikola widened his stance. Launching his sword behind him with both hands, an eifer gathered in his weapon, glowing with a dirty mountainous color of Aurelian. He held a breath as his foot dug deeper into the ground that his comrades had felt to tremble. Then, the eifer snapped within him, as it was to explode.

"Hargh!" Nikola thundered, swinging the hunk of metal in an entire curve.

A berserk blade of the gale launched like a wind god's huff, traveling at such greatness time itself slowed. The clouds around its path deterred and the skies rifted. For the Confederate pilots saw the brightness headed upon them, they were in an impossible attempt to steer from its path. But it was at an astonishing rush that the gust slashed across the squadron. A firework show blasted awake, into chunks of flaming aluminium. Dark shadows above the Confederates' heads expanded until those fiery meteors crashed into the ranks, tossing evaporated blood, skin and bones into the air like shrapnel from a grenade blast.

Vasilevsky halted his units for the fire to pass and the bodies of his pilots to disintegrate. One corpse dropped before his eyes. Whose guts had been sucked out of what remained of their ribs. The general could not tell whom it belonged to.

"Adrien Nikola..." He began to rage, gritting his teeth furiously as his body steamed.

"Where did you find your reason to fight?!" His voice echoed across the battlefield.

"What could machines achieve when man can perform twice as well?" Nikola scratched his head on his mount for war.

The storm of flames burned their backs. A curse to the Confederates' pride. He watched as the wrinkles between his brows eased when the light steps of a messenger dropped to the ground on one knee.

"Urgent report!" Holding a palm over his heart, he delivered.

"A flanking brigade of infantry and an armored contingent to the west!"

To the field, the general scouted the near ranks of the hill's base and the charging detachment towards his allies' exposed flank. Bodén turned wary. But he was too long wedged in the frontal army. Of a dozen tanks and three thousand soldiers wearing the lifting flags of Rutenn, the fatal seal was approaching.

Had the madman not dug so deep... The hand on the greatsword tensed with a grumble of Nikola's mind.

"*That* old man's grandson will see to it." He allowed a sharp exhale.

Turning to the tent, encased by shields doused in water and secured by a council of guards, the commander called for a soldier,

"Lieutenant Lienz!"

Upon hearing his name called, his swinging legs stilled from the bed by a dim, dying candle. A knife, he spun between his fingers, slipped into the sheath of his thigh's belt. The glow of a bow and the rustling of arrows rose with their master and leapt for the entrance. And from the unseen interiors of the lavish quarters worthy of a duke, a youngster was present.

He was small, who met Nikola's command by the second. This soldier, appearing firstly unbelonging on the battlefield, bore a welcoming boyish cheeriness that was with viridian green eyes and brownish-orange hair like matured fire. His smile had to be so wide and innocent. Yet he was carrying an exotic bow on the left hand gloved by a gauntlet, in the manner ready to seize a life. Otherwise, he was not assumed by many to be a warrior. To be clothed like a lowly hussar, of the Lekann red and white, it was half-spectacular and enough. What more was the playful prance he made in such a disciplined place for no child his age.

"What is it, uncle Adrien?" Lienz referred to the general whose voice was that it did not seem to matter.

"I'm to join the middle guard." Nikola bluntly told him and checked his flanks with quick glances.

"Do not heed any other order, understa—?"

"The middle guard? Can I come too?!" The lieutenant, although unbelievably he was of this rank, cheerfully asked.

"No," answered Nikola, facing Lienz.

"I do not need to know what your grandfather would do if you were seen on the battlefield." The commander unhesitantly mentioned.

Lienz's cheeks puffed with a sour look in disdain. By the strangling hold on the bow, he only responded to his name when the thought that battle for his young self had finally come. But it did not. He did not understand any reason.

"However, Lienz…" Nikola reassured the youth.

"The fields need to be cleansed." Pointing at the forces of armor and looming Confederates to the west, they were one league from the clash.

"Mind if we borrowed your flames?"

Reinvigorated by the ask from the general, the lieutenant's face surely brightened once again.

"Not at all!" He happily accepted.

Swiftly, he dashed for the cliff and balanced his feet on the loosened rocks. As he drew the bow's silver wings of a Lekann hussar, his commander made ready his men. The lieutenant brought an arrow from his thin quiver and laid the nock on the string. He aimed for the mechanized cavalry, slowly dragging the arrow till the fletching was by his cheek. Lifting his bow, the arrowtip sat steady like a mortar. Lienz leaned backwards as he gently bit down on his lips. Then as if there was not a charge of an eifer, the archer released his grip. Into the skies the arrow was shot. A flourishing shockwave of fire lifted the soil from the earth. The missile was lit in a flaming vortex, swirling in the air. There was a splitting boom at the height of its path, when it began to drop no slower. Then by the eight longest seconds past, the tip of the arrow pierced the thin shields of the tank. Detonating, the small firestorm spun across the tight ranks, throwing a party of black smoke plunging into the brigade.

The terror of the scent of overcooked barbeque was the results of a joyous massacre. Bodies of crawling crews had the slightest chance of escaping the inferno. Their skin had boils if not peeled away by the unthinkable heat and to reveal the cracking bones under the paper-thin stroke of remaining flesh. But the oils and gasses ignited and sent a second wave of horrors. There was no choice. The advance had to halt before the fires would clear.

"How was it?!" Lienz cried his victory, swiping a slither of the bowstring's dust from his cheeks.

The storming of the downhill ride with his personal unit was brisk to arrive at the middle guard. Whilst the soldiers gave way to the century-large cavalry, Nikola had broken the code of his morals. The defensive, marked by the shot of a flare, soon turned to be the aggressor. Of thirty thousand men advancing beside him, the pitch of rested cries was pictured nearing to reinforce the vanguard. And the least glorious of generals, Adrien Nikola, was its head.

Hiding in the mist, the dust cloud enveloping the hill, Vasilevsky spotted. His arms, in natural swings, caved his blade and shield into the fallen spearhead of fatigued troops of Aelon. The once sharpened tip of Bodén's charge was no more. They stood still for the Confederates' stubborn defense to gnaw at their shins. Whilst the lion marched nearer the skirts of the feeble division, he hacked and bashed, till the gold was painted under the red of his enemies.

"Hah! Have you finally committed yourself to this war?" His nerves were struck by laughter.

The charge of a cavalryman, who thought his measly cry would stun the general, was faced by a growl that reared his mount. Spikes of the sun met the thrust of a spear. An impact splitted the shaft and through the bursting fragments of steel and wood, a crashing plate of the shield slammed the foe's skull into a cavern.

"You are far too predictable." The Confederate's eyes sharpened.

Raising an arm, his demand was caught by the sight of an aide who raced by the dropping corpse. The thump of the deceased fell beneath the shadow of the banner of the Confederacy. Towards the odd, lone rider of pearl silver and shining carmine red garb, Vasilevsky ordered,

"Send in the cavalry."

The unknown aura. Nikola's charge was unstopping. His senses could detect a single hint of a trap. But he was too far in the fray to save his men that not a bead of sweat could be shed for the feeling wrenching his guts.

As the elites pushed onwards with their tiring comrades, an opening they had delivered themselves into was a sinkhole of divided allies. Of different fronts and ranks, Arminius glimpsed at the pockets only in orbit around the commander's god-like powers. The monster clashed alone. And though Codrington had reached the third general's guards, there was a swift current slashing between. But the cuts into his enemies were still deepening. In squads of ten they were flung from Bodén. However, every pair of ears had noticed. The shouts and chants were another's tone. It had changed and surely, the clamoring did not come from the nearby army.

"Their voices..." The third general searched the lines until his eyes were met upon the distant picture.

The dust cloud of menace had grown on the east and west. The scenery of battle cleared. Like pincers, there were two contingents advancing for his death.

"All halt!" Bodén commanded for his hearing on the epicenter of the annoyance.

The thundering hooves of a heavy cavalry force grumbled across the field. And by that, Nikola had come to realize he had been reeled by the bait on the hook.

"General! Two forces to our flanks!" A subordinate pointed his head to the old force Lienz had halted.

But they did not seem to be delayed. Perhaps the short victory had eased the timings between the two magnifying forces. Where beside the general, the magnet-like Confederates were compelled by the magnitude of Bodén's bold maneuver.

Knowing he had been played, the general pulled on his reins. The shock brought the middle guard to a sluggish march as he waited for his aide to confirm the besieging presence of the *Summer Lion*. More colors of the vanguard fell. On the darkest of minutes, two banners of the alliance from opposing fronts were at a sprint, whisking through the shifting columns. But they had old, undesirable news.

"The three thousand has restarted their advance on the left!" A scout reported before he could drop on his knee.

"Another ten thousand on the right!" Another messenger added.

The paleness of the general returned. His face was as if he had seen the future of the dangers. The predicament, he felt, was another nightmarish déjà vu. Of a yet one more complete disaster.

Was this a trap all along, Vasilevsky? Nikola pondered.

Eyes shaking, the adjutants had not put their alarmed stares elsewhere. As the commander raised his hand, disheartened and in a usual fashion, the man could not resist the temptation to grind his teeth.

"Damn this war…" The screechings of tooth on tooth was a vulgar sound.

"I will never allow more unnecessary losses." He mumbled before lowering heads.

Clashing against squad upon squad, the queue thinned before their eyes as if the elites had not given their toll. But the Danne, once overly cautious, was drawn ahead by the restlessness of his comrades. He wondered to do the same. But Julien stumbled ahead and by his face, was an encounter with the appearance of a Confederate soldier. Twice his height, and who had thrice the brawns, the shade crept over and grinned ominously.

The lancer silently yelped as the soldier flung his blade pummeling like a lumberjack's axe. It was only by a miracle that the training with Arminius had saved his shortening life by an overhead defense. Yet slowly, his unequal strength was draining away. Soon with no room to escape. By another charm of a devil, a hand grabbed his collar and was tugged away. With a strike of a blitzing cut, the jugular was slashed awide. The decapitated soldier threw a splash of blood over the savior's face and soaked his coat in the crimson rain.

"Arminius..." Julien named.

With a caring glance, Arminius sheathed his spear and reached for his comrade. Holding onto the helping hand, they locked and the fallen stood. A print of a smudge of blood was wiped on Julien. His nose picked the scent of the cold iron in the warmness of life. But one whose entirety was drenched found the jacket, stuck to his skin, only a damnation and nothing else.

"Gods dammit..." Spun in range, he undid the buttons of his blouse.

And at a notice of the dual assault, he slipped free of the fabric hindrance and tossed the wetted veil into the wind that blew against the soldiers' face. Charging at the hidden corners of the agitated Confederates, the boy arose from the rims of sight and slashed their chests with a fatal blow to their hearts. As he had hoped, the gendarmes' lives seemed to have faded.

"They just keep coming!" Lev yelled discontentedly, backing towards Miklós whose spear had begun to bend from the uncountable hours.

"What are we even aimin' for?!" Cutting through seven bodies of unfortunate riflemen, Gin cried.

It was the ravaging battle that stole their minds of sanity. As both fronts wondered when this hell was to end.

"Even Bodén stopped advancing!" Colt pointed to the largest warrior, mounted and higher than the human waves.

But even he, a third general, was clueless to his men simmered down by every cry and short clash.

"We need more troops!" A lancer suggested as he pressed his back on Julien's.

"The eight of us aren't enough!" Their feet held steady, though shaking, it was Arminius who offered.

"For what?!" Lev only encouraged.

There was silence amongst the lancers, battling on the outskirts of their unit. Until the impatience of the leader in the pack called for the major,

"Commander!"

Codrington turned to his elites and the shift of the unit followed. In a protective schiltron circle, the lancers had returned to their role as the core and heart of the century. Yet if they were not quick to say, the unit of one hundred would become a void on the field.

"What is it now?" The unnatural fever of the major burned.

But it was not Arminius who answered, whose plan in his mind was often or not relied upon. He nudged Julien on the ribs, when the passing of the torch was enough to catch the elites off guard.

"W-What?" The Danne stammered when a second poke on the back brought himself ahead.

"Lancer Carlstadt!" Codrington and his roughening voice barked fiercely.

"Do you have a say or not?!"

With rising mass crushing his hesitation from the certainty of a set of eyes gleaming behind, Julien was in the prelude to enter beyond the scarf of the squad.

"Yes..." With a simple answer, he told.

Before another word could be uttered, the curse of an unwanted flare lit their backs in the regular tint of whiteness. Rocketing high into the sky, there was one signal meant for the color. The stares of disconcert followed the smoke until it disappeared into the singular graying cloud cast before the sun.

"A white flare..." Arminius spoke as if he was regarding the Apollo dragging himself to the horizon.

"Withdraw! Withdraw!" Nikola's new, and unwelcoming order passed across the ranks.

The Confederates hurried their advance, storming the inches gained over the piles of the dead of Bodén's division. With their main army on the offensive, even the mad dog such as he had to obey if the ascension in glory could be reached.

"Rally and break!" Bodén waved his polearm in the air for his standards and units to see.

As the rally and retreat flustered and was disunited, the smirks of the Rus were ever wider by the softness of easy prey. Chasing the most hopelessly damaged rear once the forefront, the deranged flight of human bloodlust took every to hunt through the eyes of berserkers.

"Ascot Century!" Raising his saber for an assembly to his call, Codrington shouted with the unhelped break in his voice.

Those too wounded and taken of breath to fight were all but half. They could fire a few luckless shots with their rifles but then, the junk of guns had to be forsaken.

"F-Follow the division and withdraw!" The major's soul shattered.

The height of panic swept the ranks in the flow of retreat. The hundred soldiers became fifty weakened. Confederates swallowed the remnants of anything gained before. But Arminius, surrounded by his squad, did not surrender an inch. For he stared into the distant forest, the soldier spotted the church tower whose spire poked like a hideous branch from the high canopy.

"Arminius!" Julien tugged on his shirt.

"Come on, we need to withdraw—!"

"The headquarters is right there." Arminius replied as he was slowly pushed by the tides of rarely uniform allies.

"If we can take it…" He revolved and looked at Julien with the same ambition of his eyes reflecting the backdrop of the lush flora.

"That's too reckless!" Julien tried reasoning but his comrade had not heard his plea.

Before Miklós and Alexandria at the onslaught's meet, Arminius drew himself. A Confederate thrusted his sword but with the slide of a blade, the lancer pierced his eye by the brunt of his snapped hunter's spear. Falling to the ground, the scream was short as another came to challenge. Arminius dodged the careless swing and took the next life with an angled slash.

"The quickest way to end a battle…" said Arminius, charging his eifer as he prepared to dash into the human maze.

"Is to take the head over the army."

He lifted his heels and slanted his sword. Distraught clouded the Confederates upon the sparking lightning coils of royalty. Around his body and blade, the trails of bolts thickened.

"Wait—" Julien tried to grab him.

Within a snap, Arminius shot into the army. A tail of lightning in his path had split the ground and air from a burn so intense. Every particle of ash airily floating beneath his shadow was shocked into nothingness. The vortex booms in rings of vaporized blood turned into thunder clouds on his landing and from there finally, the elite squad's ears caught. As Arminius flicked his sword outwards, purified of not a touch of bones, the heads, and limbs were brutally tossed to be above. Dissected bodies collapsed whilst there was not one cry in agony. Geysers of blood ushered.

Although their hearts told them not to, the Confederates endured the fight. But Arminius had distanced too far that he was to drown in steel whenever the limit of his eifer was seen.

"Wait up, Arminius!" Energetically, a brute pranced over his enemies' heads and made a way to the leader.

Without a dash of thought, Julien was escorted away near Miklós, by the path that their comrade had so willingly forged.

"You aren't gonna steal my prize, are you?!" Colt twirled his spear with the slither of a grin.

A Rus had held his wantingness to join, but the temptation of a devil's campaign was distressing to ignore. And so the grunt of Lev sent him on the journey yet there were two too tentative to depart.

Alexandria, who never agreed to such recklessness, held her spear close but never spoke a word. To Arber, the expression written on her face was the look of the fruitless outcome. But in the former's stead, the last soldier was willing to enter the closing gap.

"No matter if you're not going." Arber plainly told her, marching ahead.

Nodding, Alexandria spun her feet and made for the century once more. In safely joining herself with the rear, the last of the lancers was no more in her sight. Not another glance could satisfy the troubles hanging like a boulder on an old net over the heads of the passersby. The perils of glory was only a ghast tapping their shoulders. There was no shelter between the charge and the high-standing tower.

XI

15 JULYUS 491
15.07.12017

Julien Carlstadt

Who am I to say? We promised each other, didn't we? When one was weak in either offense or defense, he and I would fill that gap for the other. It was clear for anyone during our studies. If this is true, then why can't my doubts seem to disappear?

We both know that we could've waited for a better opportunity. This plan's too reckless. The headquarters is too far and there are hundreds of ranks between us and them. Without the support of the Third General's main forces, breaking through their lines will be near impossible. But now, there's no way we'd make it with just the seven of us. It's the truth. What will happen if we're trapped? Unable to escape?

I once thought that I could trust every judgement Arminius makes. But it's all to chase this one dream that was wrong from the beginning...

Yet...I can't bring myself to tell him...

CHAPTER

12   RECKLESSNESS

There is one thing I do not understand. There were such thoughts revolving around Arber.

If you're capable of forming strategies that no one can see past, He peered ahead at the one he chased.

Then why are we here?

By the swash of blades along the narrow path, it was not their haste that caught the leader. His spending of his eifer was like an addicted gambler. Unstopping and drawn for more blood to shed. Although the strikes were still cutting, his senses had numbed.

"Arminius!" Arber called from behind.

The propelling blade like the bolts of a ballista whooshed. Ducking beneath the missle, Arminius watched the spear pierce the ranks like a sporting javelin, skewering half a dozen soldiers before it was harshly met by the scarred ground. A survivor, slowly awakening to the blur of the seven lancers, felt a flash of a strike on his neck. Then there was no pain. Beheaded by Gin, the Confederate sagged to the mud. Whose face was carved by the stomps of the brute. Wasting no seconds, he rushed across the ever deepening ranks, scalping the fools fated to face him. Launching himself with his eifer crashing, Colt burned through the lines. With Miklós hammering the Confederates into the ground by the bluntness of the snapping spear, the fight was puppeted by their hands it seemed.

"Arminius! Wait!" Julien repeated for his comrade.

Who removed the spear from the stack of corpses, Arminius flung it to its wielder.

"Thanks." The lancer slowed his strikes when he caught sight of the spire of the tower.

It had grown. The target was much closer. And ahead only remained a thinning column of fresher troops, stampeding over their comrade's leaking bodies to encounter the rampaging elites.

How many have we killed? Arminius wondered with his eyes set on two rampant dragons.

"Colt! Lev!" The boy yelled, pulling Julien by the jacket.

"Your move!" He prompted his squad to leap away, for space to the duo.

As if they were closing gates of a fortress hill, Lev and Colt lined beside each other. Their spears pointed to the earth in a sloped form where hoops of fire, like a legend's renaissance, circled. One of azure jade and another oil black. Burning like the gods' wrath.

"Now?" They sniggered, to each other's nods.

The five lancers reached ever further, protecting their backs as both eifers roared. Staggering the Confederates, Lev took to a run, stylishly swooping his blade from his flank to flank. Ramming his spear into enemies' bowels, he let free their guts to flow. The shuddering bones snapped and impaled their innards whilst the trembling of the defeated grew before they were struck, by the boosting swishes of his form of a mythical beast. He vaulted over one and the other until at the sprint's distant point, Lev slashed clear an arena of orbiting foes. But none bore the courage to battle.

"Hold your head, Lev!" Awaited long enough, Colt began treading in light steps.

Jabbing his spear, a pulse of flames shot through the lines, opening a way to the Rus by the hellishly burned. Coal-like, the seared bodies crumbled. Alight, some fled. Though most who saw the true sadistic art of war had only the mind to fall away. Before the whirl of mud and pebbles, the soldiers marched for Lev. Yet when he peered upwards, the curious eyes of the Confederates did the same. Their hearts were dazed when they saw. With an inelegant leap, the burgeoning embers were in flight.

Like a wave in empty air, the cavalry charged. The helpless in their armor were flattened under the offense. Rivers and streams, like veins of a lung, trickled into the craters of the field. Over the last old charge, the renewed second assault had broken. And in layers, the sheets of flesh, rotting and dying were pressed against the earth. Soon there was emptiness before his eyes, the

Summer Lion and his soaked blade. As the two forces converged at the general's assault, the slaughter was diminished and the dishonorable Aelon was granted the wish of withdrawal.

"Vice General!" A captain rode to Vasilevsky's side, whose eyes were on the sorry figure of Nikola retreating to the hilltop sanctuary.

"We should regroup our forces and prepare for the next day." Watching his forces swing about the vanguard, the Confederate suggested.

"That way, our men would have rested and we will have the upper hand—" He told, when a gust, faster than sound, ended near his throat.

With a blade, dripping and of a stench of death, inches from the cavalryman's neck, Vasilevsky returned to him under a bitter aura.

"Do not forget your place, Serov." The vice general interrupted but the captain held a composed look.

"I never took in a cripple because I ever pitied you for not bearing an eifer."

The two soldiers glared ahead in the unending standoff. Winds breezed over the heads stilled. Until, Vasilevsky flicked his sword away and calmed.

"You should be more reserved." The tone reminding him was softer than what Serov was accustomed with.

Through the length of the backdrop, a spark of flames filled the skies. As a missile meteored, the impact dealt a flash fire of blue and green. Fierce, that the boom came later but it had not shaken any war horses. Then the slow slash of the shock was only hollow, lifting some caps or not. But the height of the daunting smoke was circled by a storm of ash and limbs. It was not a bluff or by accident. Sure they were that themselves were familiar to the thunders of eifer, the Confederates advanced. However, as he and Serov had realized, the lake of an emerald inferno had sprouted all too unexpectedly.

"How...?" Crushing the hilt of the sword, Vasilevsky growled.

His pupils sharpened in the overcast beneath his helmet. The provocation by the Aelon general had once already irritated the irritable man. And at the climax of the climb in the swell of heat, an outburst traveled to his arm and grabbed a guardsman by his collar.

"How did a force of that magnitude seep past our lines?!" He demanded, rattled at no other perfect time, a rhythmic gallop neared.

"Who is the commander of that contingent?!" The vice general stormed.

When the flat notes of the rider showed himself in the commander's company, the messenger coughed from a burning heart ache.

"Urgent from Major Petrov." The soldier had not shouted.

Pulling the guard to the ground in a fit, Vasilevsky held his rage to hear.

"Seven are due for the headquarters!" reported the courier, unafraid of the reviving tempest.

"Where did they find seven thousand?!" Serov interrupted but the same thoughts had misted in the general's mind too.

As they waited for the gale to settle, and for the banners to be carried in another current, the runner of the Confederacy adjusted his helmet and tightened the belt. The plume swapped its flow and the straps of his pauldron fluttered. The tensing atmosphere was unlike any other message from a lowly officer.

"Just seven." The messenger corrected him.

The shock was divided amongst the guards who could question but would not. There were no heard sounds but the doubt of Serov.

Seven? What a terrible number, Rzhev. Vasilevsky sighed in the deepest huff, clearing his breath of bad mouth.

Like a psychic's snap, the pinch in his third general's distant mind was but a coincidence that reminded him of the looming souls approaching the gates of the headquarters. Where they would not expect, the seven lancers knew not the prowess of a higher warrior awaiting them.

"Serov!" The vice general turned to the colonel.

The blankness that outlined his face flashed into color when the cavalry legion he commanded blossomed before him.

"Of course!" Serov's saber unsheathed when the rallying cry of the units repeated across the ranks.

Steady for the final charge, he whipped the reins and opened a path like the crossing of the Rubre and plunged himself into the lines of the vanguard. Yet, whilst the victory of the day was fast coming, Vasilevsky had his hopes laid elsewhere. The reflection of the waving trees and the crossed spire appeared in his drying blade, when the seven remained wild.

Enviously, a dreamy face stared into the glimmers of the great red army. The back lines melted away from the charge and the squad, though masked by the many thousands, had broken the rear from the flames of the elites. Blows and sparks flung between clashing blades upon armor. The break in the battle replaced the stinging hunks of steel with disordered calls of commands to give chase for the seven. Twisting a white dandelion, the lieutenant sat on the hill's steep brow.

"I wonder who that is..." Lienz muttered when the step of a foot from the dismounting general awoke him.

"Which unit are they from?" asked Nikola upon his return to the encampment.

Like the good archer, his focus was only on the unknown force. Who were little but scattering the uniform standards of the Confederacy.

"Dunno..." The lieutenant gathered a hefty breath and blew free the seeds of the flower.

"They must be no larger than a platoon at most." Nikola sighed, knowing the force was lacking.

He dug his greatsword in the dry soil, loosening a few strands of grass which glided towards the bog. Crossing his arms, the general was not so sure of the act before him. Insubordination and autonomy Nikola was troubled by only if the elites could return.

"But they look strong!" Joy filled Lienz and brought his commander beyond scouting the unpredictable future.

"I'd like to meet them sometime."

The shine of the archer's eyes. Nikola saw. It served its purpose as a reminder that the chance had not been lost.

I admire such fervent soldiers. The general had a change of tone, lifting the greatsword from its rest to be above his head.

A cascade of dirt and rocks slid from the blade under the amber afternoon sun.

Even by means of insubordination, I will not let their sacrifice go in vain. He caught a second wind.

"Warriors of Aelon!" Nikola boomed, launching the point of his sword at the village of Akülunnarchs.

"Our courageous has won us time in piercing the once impenetrable Confederacy!"

"We must devote ourselves now! To the defiers of the butchers!" He waved his sword at the innumerable files whose heads spun to the voice of their general.

"This is not yet lost if we can drive a stake in their rotted hearts!"

Fixing his blade by his side and the rising archer, the blood of the commander boiled till the heartbeat could be felt in his neck and ears. The veins in the soldiers' eyes darkened. The strains of their grips steeled. When the last tear in defeat dried, the tailing shadow of the goddess victory arrived.

"Eleventh Division! Eighteenth Division! Thirtieth Division!" The forces were named by Nikola.

"Bring the storm to the prey!" Then, the order came.

"Hagh!" Cries of the rocketing morale bore upon the flustering enemy.

The Confederates restrained no longer the beast arising. Bodén's vigor doubled from the grand speech. Slices of throats and felling his foes rushed at twice the force and agility. There was a resurgence of level bloodshed. As the spearhead was adopted again, Nikola snapped his reins and charged downhill whilst all Lienz could do was bravely cover the plains with his fire-tipped arrows. Launching his gale into the opposing army, and flinging the common soldiers from their feet, the general bravely followed the madman into the open clash. When the day was due to end, there approached the rebirth of a spirit.

Snaps of branches and the crunches of leaves. Panting in the escape from the fronts. The howls of the woodlands' winds channeled through the vast forest ceaselessly. For the spire had dived under the canopy, the winding lights and scattered shadows were the only compass for the elites. But never minding their path, the seven soldiers crossed the exposed roots and leapt from opening to opening. Until the borders of the village were in sight.

"We should be able to find a hideout before dark." Arminius

charted a simple plan.

"A night attack?" As Julien stayed close, he paranoically looked over his shoulders for any Confederates who gave chase.

But knowing by the entrance into the barrier of Akülunnarchs, they had since retired from the pursuit. Yet it was something uncanny, the feeling of the limitless emptiness. There not a single patrol was marching about the wilderness.

"You'd think this reckless kid could wait for that long?" Lev chuckled.

If not...then when...? The Danne muttered to himself though what the Rus realized was true.

After the battle...

Another lead after the other led him like a chain on a hound. The answer emerged from the cavern of the intricate mind then was noticed in the shine of his eyes.

Does he plan on taking the headquarters before the army's returned?

After the battle but before nightfall... Julien unveiled the revelation of his comrade's brilliance.

Taken by the possibility that such aggression would work, he clenched his fists and faced the earth, hiding the smile blooming from the gloom of his face. His reason to trust the first comrade had not splintered so far as he had minded. Amongst the squad, Julien quickened. But around him, the rustle of uniforms hushed. Unseeing on the path ahead, he felt a thump on his head when he bumped into the unwavering pillar that the giant stood still like.

"What's up...?" Loosening his kepi, Julien lifted his head and peeked between Miklós and Lev.

Afore centuries of rifles, there was a warrior who was no ordinary officer. Over his shoulders and in a ring around, the ranks were laced by numberless hundreds. He had yet to speak. Only his arm held steady to draw their trigger fingers on the command.

"Has the general come out to face us?" Streams of sweat glided to Colt's chin as his hands, shaken by the eifer of his own, retreated to hide his infirmity.

"No matter, I'll kill 'im like I did de others—" Gin readied, advancing carelessly by the steps.

"Hold on," A hand held his shoulder when one, as more reckless, revealed himself before the brute.

"They had to have expected us if they had this many at the headquarters" Arminius detected.

His caution advised his allies, withdrawing in slow shuffles. But their rears, they heard, approached another force of the depths. The aura on the Confederate officer was mesmerizing. It was not the animalistic strength Arminius sensed on Bodén. His kei was a stark holy light never referring to the real soul beneath.

"You there!" Rzhev called out, pinching his small, pointed beard.

"Are all here the scoundrels who leech on our marvelous army?"

He had an odd accent when he spoke, though, with a serpent's glare, he was almost desiring battle. Not aged was his face, whose cheekbones were definitive, matched by a long sharp nose and slanted eyes, he had the appearance of an overseer. When the blade he wielded lifted, the squad had spotted its swirls like a drill, finished by a coned hilt, similar to a jousting lance. Anything otherwise was also most noble-esque. The absolute suit of gold and dark bronze armor was sparkling as if it had been polished by the days, and the undersized shako hat he wore was too small to fit. Though the third general pointed his rapier at Arminius in a weird arrogant stance, he was not yet so assertive as some.

"What if we aren't?!" Arminius answered in a riddle beside the gritting of comrades' teeth.

"Haha! Nevermind your games!" Proudly, Rzhev laughed as he pointed at himself.

"You have earned your prestige to know my name!"

Lowering the rapier, he bowed with his grayish hair touching the forest ground but his hat did not move or fall.

"I am Third General Igor Rzhev!" He introduced in the most flamboyant manner.

A snigger by Lev broke the strained air whilst the Confederate rose upright and opened a palm by his ear.

"So surrender now, I demand it!" His men marched five paces nearer on the order.

"Or as a pupil of the Summer Lion, I shall strike you down under heaven's watch!"

But not at all, had the elites retreated. Not one step or a half was taken away. The foothold was stubbornly firm before the imminence of battle.

"Like hell we're surrenderin'!" Gin poised for his allies when the bolts of rifles were struck in place.

"Arminius..." Tugging on his comrade's drenched cloak, Julien whispered.

"Your call." Arber was backed by the fires of the squad.

For the next void of time, neither parties spoke. The watches on a few Confederates' wrists sounded over the zephyr. The ticks of the seconds passed amidst the distant calls of the village's officers. The church's fallen bell did not ring when the aide atop watched the stand. A seed of a pure dandelion floated onto Arminius' hand as he tread with the church's in his eyes' lightning spark.

"Just try it!" Drawing his sword, he taunted.

"We'll take your head and your headquarters along with our victory in this battle!"

They gathered their breaths and on each raising their eyelids from a blink, the spears and swords pointed outwards. The brief wonderment of the Confederates' perished, and ascending, the contempt of being ridiculed had grown. Before the pack of wolves, the barrels' cavernous bores locked upon the seven. Both were to loosen an undying horror.

XII

11 MARS 492

11.03.12018

Arminius Reichner

I was so sure of victory. That any strategy of mine would work. Despite the odds stacked against my will, I've always broken through. To defeat the Confederates was no easy task but I've done so already. With the elites. Wanting to be at the forefront has been a long lasting dream and so even when we were trapped by the third general, my naivety remained unchanged. But because I was that blind to the happenings behind me, it didn't matter when the decision…that burden was placed upon my back.

The ice is thawing beyond this window that cages me from my comrades every day. I may never battle with them however much I long for the opportunity.

I was too immature to know the truths of war. When one strike has provoked an entire army to act the same, the morale which soared that day has brought a devastation. If I had known that it was to happen because of me, then I would not have chosen this route…

CHAPTER 13 A QUESTION OF DEFECTION

The seven cautiously reeled the Confederates ever nearer, until each soldier was shoulder to shoulder. In a tight guard, the elites rotated carefully, pushing for their foes to make the first move. When Arminius spotted one of the few who bravely advanced, locking their finger on the trigger, he held half a breath. As Rzhev raised his rapier, the rotating besieged troops came to a halt. The dual fronts watched ahead until the third general mouthed so slightly.

"Lancers!" Arminius signaled, raising his sword, for the blade to be stabbed into the earth.

"Fire!" Thrusting his rapier, Rzhev yelled.

A volley of lead and smoke piled rank upon rank, skimming past the narrow air in the arid forest as a light streak raced across Arminius' eyes. His cry, and all his eifer was forced into one blade breaking the ground. A crack in the earth shot a wave of bolts blasting into the thin canopy. Thundering beyond the sheltering trees that formed an impenetrable shield, the sphere of lightning cast the bullets for the heavens.

In the dense veil of remnant eifer, the only sense of direction was blinded. Unknown to the murmurs around. Unknown of any happenings. A Confederate's gun rattled of fear till a noise spun him to a swinging shadow. By the chance that it was an ally, he could not gamble his life and fired. The crackles of gunpowder snapped through the fog and the figure fell. But as he made his way for the dead, a blast pierced his chest and a burst of blood gushed. There, the chains of bullets swerved into allies and the battlefield had become anarchy in gore.

"My brave soldiers, halt this play!" They could hear their commander calling, though his pleas were drowned by the deafening screams of his own men.

Then, out of the fog, Gin leapt, and slashed one's face before
the next victim whose death was delayed by a feeble parry.
A spear rammed through his lung and through the leakage
unstoppingly flowing, the fleeing Confederate sunk into Arber's
blade. With deathly strikes, Arminius beheaded a row of riflemen,
lying in wait for the enemy to appear before them. Bodies flung
into the air from the gusts of slashes by titans behind him. On a
fiery rampage across the freer openings of the field, Colt forged
a ring of fire around the heavy clouds. Yet alone, Julien, found
himself cornered by two nearing him. Their eyes were set on the
only apparent inept, made for an easy prey.

There's…no one…around… Julien thought, pleading in his
mind.

That's not…! He shifted his demeanor, raising his sword for
the throat of the soldiers.

What was it that I said?

In a new mode, Julien inched his feet forward, brushing the
carpet of leaves which were caught by his heels. And whilst the
enemies' blades were launched overhead, a corridor opened for
his charge.

"Hyah!" The lancer cried, driving his sword through a
soldier's stomach.

As the Confederate stumbled, deepening the wound, he
reached ahead with paling skin. His eyes flickered when his
bloodied hands had nearly touched Julien's face. When by a snap
in his soul, the man crumbled before the lancer leaned away and
tugged the blade from locking flesh. Striking his skull on the
sword before it met the ground, the body slumped.

"N-Nikolai!" The comrade of the fallen raged.

Dropping beneath the careless swing, Julien swept around his
legs. A sword slit the soldier's ribs and a wall of blood dashed onto
his cheeks when death had come. The thud of the corpse ended
his instinct of survival in his stand.

"What…did…I…" Julien panted, rubbing his face of the
paint of life.

His fingernails and palm, he stared at, were reddened as
if he had submerged his hands in a bucket of innards. When
the disgust and awe lingered, from the smog, a friend hurriedly
approached.

"Julien! You okay?" asked Arminius, as he defended

themselves from the strikes of stray bullets and steel.

But beside his boots, there were two bodies, buried in a shroud of mud and leaves. Twitching, they were far from the realm. And he assumed that it was his Danne that had taken them to the afterlife.

As they dreamt over the bodies, whose limbs had finally found their rest, a distressed shout of afar was heard like a punch to their ears. Clashing, unlike the lightness of the lancers, took hold of the battle. It was nearby that the cry attacked. However, it sounded terribly familiar.

"Was that..." Julien muttered.

"Gin!" Whose aura shortened from the unmasking of a beast, Arminius called for.

There was a third entity. A colossus greater than Miklós. Though the sounds of the hooves resounded, he could not say where from amidst the mist that the invader would strike.

"I'm going for that idiot." Arminius told his comrade.

"Wait, we should regroup instead before—" Julien held his shirt tightly that pulled him nearer.

The songs of iron and clanking armor exploded before Arminius and Julien, as a shadowed titan steamed on a spotted horse. His golden eyes shone like a ghast's beacon. The sword was of gold and had a strait of blood. Swinging down upon the Aelon lancers, the blade crashed like a storm surge into Arminius'. Who was interrupted so, he could not have readied entirely.

"Wha—" Trying the fight, Arminius groaned.

When the duel kept Julien agape, the ground around his comrade began to sink. The fissures of the earth heated and the sparks of flames bursted. The impact was impossible. The roar of the gale knocked on his ears. His teeth's gums bled from gritting. Deeper into the crater he was pressed that the Confederates' blackening blood filled to his ankles.

I can't...my eifer... Yet to be broken, but baffled, Arminius fought.

He could not escape a hand to draw his spear. Their blades shook as the vibrations were dispatched across the body, tilting till his back was nearing the forest floor.

"Gyargh!" The field general screamed for his strength to blast awake tenfold.

An inferno of cutting wind, hammered its prey over and

over. Rocks split like feeble shells. The crater dried and it was no
more a desert than the plains of the south. Arminius' sword was
at a great bend, barely held by a slipping grip. Then when his
mind suffered an instinctive jolt, a strategy came to him. But the
air between his hand and hilt broke. In disbelief, he sounded to
have gasped beneath the shape of defeat. The flash of the lion's
blade drove onwards victoriously. The shockwave sent the clouds
away, and boomed into Arminius' shoulder. Blood poured before
his comrades. A red mist enshrined the elite. Kneeling, his eyes
had blanked like the quivering mind of the six and the cascade
flowered when he plunged asleep in the cold.

"I'll bury you!" Julien screamed, conflicting his timidity.

Without the notice of anything else, there was only one
enemy ahead. With what his comrade had taught, his blade
slashed. He felt the fluidness from training. His form was well.
But so, the strength was effortlessly parried by the vice general's
shield who finally showed his glare. Launching his fist in a hook,
Vasilevsky struck Julien who could only curl with a cough of
blood. Something had fractured within. The strike was as if he
had been tortured under the wheels of a carriage. He battled his
locking knees as the Confederate held his head and lifted him to
his height. With arms and legs disabled from the unclear pain
whether his neck was tearing, the boy could not squirm. The
squad were reckoning with a fiend. No human they had seen
could compare with the leader. And that Arminius had been
crippled, none had the ability to match this man.

"The five standing!" Vasilevsky referred to them, pointing his
sword at Julien's throat.

From the cleared air, Arber lent a shoulder to Gin whose self
had first witnessed and felt the cleaving blade halt before bone.
Hearing the babble of the general, that was all could be done.

"Surrender." He demanded, tightening his grip on the yelping
Danne.

The naivety of the elites were not so vulnerable to concede.
Pointing their blades at the center of the troubles, three were able.

"Still putting up a fight?" asked Vasilevsky.

The lancers' leers followed the golden sword, unsure of its
path, until the threat had become unable to forget that their
armaments were lowered.

"Or should I take an arm or leg?" The Confederate growled.

Digging the toppest limb of the blade into flesh at the arm, blood oozed from the severed skin. A sting he had not felt before infected his nerves. Cold sweat and its itch showered his body. The hot terror filled his heart.

"Gah...ngh...!" Tears trickled from Julien.

Clenching his fist, Arber watched the blade slice deeper. His comrades could not face the sadist demon who would have found torture to be enlivening. Unwilling for a potential victory to be buried away, the lancer's nails punctured his palms and a row of his own life was dug free. But when the blade neared the bone, the clanks of his spear ended his choice. The elites knelt and placed their blades beside. For how little it was, the church was almost there that they could not reach. With that single needle at the heart of the fallen and the hostage, they had done nothing.

The courageous charge and their most holy beacon had disappeared before Nikola. Not a spot of their remains were sensed. Even ahead of the lands they had regained behind the lance of the Aelon could not equate the loss of those aura. Whilst he tugged his reins to a leisurely march, beside and farther into the Confederate tide the third general leapt over the walls of infantry and crashed his blade against their backs. The madman swung his razor glaive and freed the gendarmes of their heads. Like the forging of veins, the division swept and clawed at the rib cage towards the heart. As a major had come for the vanguard once more, his flank was joined by Alexandria. But she had not spoken.

Where...where are these elites...? Codrington searched.

His eyes could not spin from watching the girl. At the clouds over the forest, Alexandria frowned. The unease of her face had been so ever since her return.

They can't be, can they...? The century commander spotted the general at a breezy pace.

There had to be an answer, he felt, and rode for the elder.

"General Nikola!" called the major.

As he passed the guards, cladded in bronze, the greatsword filled the sight. Without any such towers or wings, it was impressive that the general could track every step around him. By the change of touch in the wind. Perhaps the rallying cries he could tell by. Even when Nikola had been taken by the sails of war, the break in the ranks turned his head.

"Oh? I do not think I have met you before." said Nikola, gazing at the blandness of Codrington's character.

"Please excuse my rudeness." The major lowered his weapon and steadied his mount not too close nor far.

"I am Major George Codrington of the Ascot Century and the Eleventh Division." He introduced himself with a dip of his head.

"Bodén's?" The general named from the hint of a smile.

Loosening his hold on the hilt, the blade tipped to the ground. From a mount, the sword reached the mud of the spilled blood. Then swerved from duty temporarily by the disturbance hidden beneath the salute, Nikola asked,

"What is it, Major?"

"May I request the scale of the flanking force?" Codrington bluntly questioned with a pounding desire to know.

But the general's mouth kept shut. By half a minute, the answer was delayed. The observance of the glare unwilling to depart drove his eyes elsewhere. To his rear. To whoever was glancing over their comrades to the headquarters of the army. However, the tint of light that shone from the major was not the essence of a traitor or loud-mouthed fool. So, he finally spoke,

"Do not speak of a word you hear here."

Leaning over his stomach and the flicks of his horse's ears, Nikola pointed at the treeline of where the battle cries had vanished and told quietly,

"I was last informed seven."

"Seven…?" Codrington repeated.

But the elite squad has eight members as far as I'm aware. Peering to the clash and soldiers taking flight from the charge of his allies, the major recalled.

And, without Zygos who's here with the century…

A darkening storm casted over his face upon a glint of realization.

There are seven in the elite squad…!

"General!" He called Nikola once more whose aging heart chose to stutter from the cry.

"I believe those seven are of my century." Codrington informed.

The savage purged the battlefield in the pursuit for horrors. Their comrades, mashed under the hooves of the cavalry, sparked a disease of frenzy that blossomed over the rolling hills of corpses. To see skulls leak what held within. The yellowing bones and strands of flesh exposed to nature's glory of war. Holding their legs shattered by the rush, the wounded sat dreaming of haven. But the cries and screams were the same. There was little sense of individual suffering.

"W-Where's the vice general—?!" Amongst the staggering ranks, a soldier exclaimed before his throat was slit.

The terror was the lacking command. None gave calls of orders any longer. The sergeants and lieutenants had silenced in disunity. Spreading, a few spoke of fleeing. The once great Confederacy was nearing its height. Its downfall, to their own men, was to ensue. Without a banner of leadership, the commoners' will to sacrifice their lives was but diminished. When the sight of the glorious flurries of Bodén's glaive plunged into the sea of the red army, some laid their weapons to rest and turned their souls to the forest.

"Traitors! We'll have you, and your families doused in tar—!" A sergeant cried as a blade met his spine.

His ruthless charge held the blood of his berserk ancestors. The state and people the third general fought for had lived to hear the legends and rumors divided through the Yurupe front.

"I'm amazed." Nikola simply watched as he himself drove onwards along the columns of infantry.

"I truly am—" A rogue glimmer of a foe's kei held his tongue.

Of the breaking battlelines, an old man stood in wait. Quite surprisingly tall, his stance was wide and direct. A bardiche rested in his hands like a suspended bridge as soldiers escaped the hell. It was unmistakable that he was a marshal. Higher than that of a general. But this particular Confederate was not spotted on horseback. Neither was there a helmet. His armor was gold like Vasilevsky's, however much more sporadic were the decorations of flames and gales it appeared as if the fires were stolen from the underworld's wrathful fifth circle.

What is this fossil doing here on the battlefield? The third general smirked, nearing the prey.

No matter! It was your fault to have appeared before me this day!

Whilst the Confederate's cape waved in the wind, he did not shift a foot or hand.

"Gagh!" Bodén drew a train of dirt and grass from the trailing blade, and a whirlpool of hail and winds forged.

Standing his ground who did not think to move an inch, the elder was patient. His eyes were only on a mark when the first hoof of the horse passed a row of crawling troops, he lifted his polearm. When knowing that the shadow of the blade would not end, the goliath bardiche's presence choked Bodén's mind. Sweeping through the frozen air, the straight charge of steel chopped cleanly upon the stallion's neck. With a final neigh, its legs tripped and crashed into the plains, tossing its rider towards the skies. There was not a thought that passed him in the catapulted flight. Watching the steady leakage of his companion's severed neck whilst everything was overturned. He landed and was lucky to have done so. But as he stood guard, ready for another strike, his legs buckled.

What is this... Bodén had never encountered the sense he bore then.

Fear?

Without a signal, the bardiche hummed behind and the two generals' blades clashed. In a storm, the third general was tossed across the field. Gusts bursted from the impact that carried ripples of waves along the grass.

"This is beyond ridiculous..." Digging his spear into the softening mud, Bodén halted himself from being thrown any further.

"I should not have been defeated..."

The battle around had paused. For all to see the duel before their eyes. A circular arena formed around the duo, as the war cries of the Confederacy were forced into their heads like gladiators of the ancient worlds.

"You're but one worm waiting to be trampled." The grand marshal joked as he approached the warrior of Aelon.

"Frail. Foolish." He scoffed, loosening his fingers around the shaft.

The footsteps echoed in the ringing ears of Bodén. The

squelches sounded as if there were replicas of his body circling the predator turned prey.

"Even my students would have felled you with one strike." taunted the Confederate ever more.

"In a century's time and still, you would not compare."

The chants of the factions and screams of their names rocked the battlefield. That so far, even Nikola had heard to have driven a spike through Bodén's knocking heart. His terrible fit of fury canceled his allies' shouts to the repeat of the words,

"Hold your tongue, gramps..."

Lifting himself before the Rus' eyes, the third general spat a blot of blood as the humiliation saw no halt.

"The last general I had taken from this world was but the scent of junk in my path." said the marshal.

"You need a plug in yer mouth..." A tundra gale sprouted from Bodén.

Beneath his feet and blade, the ground and life froze as a winter storm gathered beside him. His eifer charged and the temptation to end the babbling had come for the peak.

"And you, a mere blade of grass on a dying meadow," The elder man chuckled.

"Are nothing worthwhile."

"Have you ended yer speech?!" A growth of phantom arms snapped out of the third general's back.

The card he was once so forgiving to play shot loose in a vortex hurling across the summer field. Like whitening scales, the last green furs of the scalp of Terra shattered under the frost. Volleys of iciscles blasted in a tantrum and struck with a cold mist, screening the marshal. With the pre-emptive strike dealt, Bodén charged his razor spear. His blade was on the course of a decisive sweep when the bardiche dispersed the heaven granted powers in a swipe. The hums of the vibrating slate of steel dulled on flesh. Before an expression could be made, a head was ripped from its spine and the flat tone was like a hack into a tree.

The voices in his head were hazy, who called out his name as he gently rocked back and forth. Buzzing lamps shunned the dark. His vision was stained by drying blood. As he woke to the

sounds of the gates rattling behind the thick stone wall, he tried
to wiggle his hands. But with tough ropes and reeds, his wrists
were tied. Within a half-broken church whose pillars showed its
story of past burns before, he aimed for the tower looming over
the roof's skeleton. There, it was a pace away. The lancer dipped
his head and felt a familiar knot of a bandage rub his cheeks. He
had come to wake. To the beside, his comrades, unimpressed by
the sanctuary they had been granted, stared at the cracks of the
church's floor. Poor masonry. The slabs of stones were uneven
and unkept, sometimes unpleasant to lay on. But they were lucky
to have not witnessed the wholly wrath that the Confederates
reserved.

"Hey, Arminius…" A weak groan called for him.

Grinning with a busted face, Gin leaned on Arber's arm.
However, those were not wounds from the clash. They seemed too
new.

"War's a bitch, ain't it…" The brute mumbled.

Yet that was all that any could say. No one had thought
otherwise. The hope melted in the weighted heart.

"A-Arminius," Softly, with a spot of a tear at the lower rims of
his eyes, Julien muttered.

"Sorry." He apologized.

His comrade's face did not lighten and the frown in failure
deepened. To the endless bounds of dread that he believed the
attack would make him an upstart to be revelled became a distant
entity of childish thoughts.

"Y'know…" Colt grumbled.

The elites knew of the fires burning in his nerves. Who was
not so grateful that he was breathing. His annoyance welled inside
detonated before Lev could calm his rage.

"Was this part of your plan as well?" asked the lancer, with a
hot scowl at his rival.

"What are…" Arminius staged his defense but the rant would
not break.

"Because it seems like ever since we followed you," The
torment of Colt added atop, shuffling nearer the leader of the
elites.

"Shit has been going downhill for us."

"This isn't the time—" Lev gently patted Colt on the back but
he too was shoved from a clear sight of the elite in question.

Staring with a furious glare, the rage had infected Arminius. His ears could not bear to listen to the rambling. His voice could not be shut from retaliation. What more were clenching fists though his itching knuckles were imprisoned.

"You're the one who wanted to follow us, bed stain—" He barked.

"Ach..." A second pain nailed his body to rest.

The wound in his shoulder tore and the soaked bandage began to leak. Sliding beneath the tightened cloth, a red tide flowed no matter how better Julien had eased his cuts. Dazed by his own accord, Arminius' senses grew airy. But when the rivaling lancer had not heard in burning agony, Colt fought again,

"Aren't you forgetting something?!"

"You forced our hand because of your recklessness!" He reminded him.

Never has the squad been as still. The hoots of owls traveled through the many leagues. When Colt settled in the corner of his own, the lancers could contemplate whatever they were held prisoners for.

Was it our wrong to have encouraged this attack? Some questioned as some argued,

What could've been done otherwise?

Drawing breaths which were sharp and quick, the steam was warmed by a fever. Sweat beads shone and dripped. Arminius could do little. The faces of his comrades turned side to side. One glance was taken at the wounded. Another glimpse of the church's door. When the slither of light beneath the gate darkened into the night with mumbles and the clinks of keys, the elites turned to the entrance's creaking.

With steps of the troop, the way opened and introduced to their presence two extraordinary giants. Bears in the skins of man. That would shrink the being of Miklós. They marched to the flanks with double-headed cleaves and through the salutes, a trail of officers bumbled. Their mouths puffed smoke that was an odor of booze and tobacco. Pairs holding onto their comrades shoulders as each drunken soldier poured into the house of the gods. But at the rear, a greater man of a fathomless character held the lancers shriveling auras under chains and rocks. His nose pointed ahead and took a short note of Rzhev's whispers when he spun to the Aelon squad.

"You seven have made quite some noise today." Vasilevsky praised.

"Somehow, this little squad has achieved more than Nikola will ever in his lifetime."

The breaths the elites took matched each other. But with scorn, they gawked upwards. Was it perhaps the humiliation of being told kind words by no ally yet it had not seemed so. There was a striking balance in the general's choice to feed compliments that Julien found devious.

"Do not give us those eyes of disdain—" The Confederate's shaping tone deepened on his approach to the lancers.

"What...do you want," Arminius rudely interrupted.

"Vice General...Vasilevsky?"

The drag of a chair halted at the crevice of the floor's slabs. Rzhev, whose nostrils and eyes widened for a slit of a second, was astounded by the bravery of a return so impolite. Not Julien could hold his tongue to save his comrade but Arminius' vision was only concerned by the end of his tunneled sights peering into the pupils of the vice general.

"Oh?" Kneeling before the lancers, of one drawing profuse sweat and heavy breaths, Vasilevsky rested his hand on his grand golden sword.

"What is your name, soldier?" Unexpectedly, he asked, inspecting his bloodied face.

"The hell do you need that for?!" Colt swung from the corner and interfered.

A keen glare faced the general. Like the thrust of a burning spear into the neck, his aura was supposed to stay the Confederate's feet. When a common gendarme may shudder by the deathly intent behind Colt's eyes, Vasilevsky was too iron-skinned to have felt the slightest pinch on his nerves.

"We should better know each other," told the vice general as he rose with his hands against his knees.

"As comrades." He added casually.

"Comrades...?" A cough took the man's head downwards and saw Arminius folding over his stomach.

Flicking alight the excessive beauty of a silver lighter, a cigar burned over the flame. With a filling soak of the smoke into his lungs, he patted the tip of the roll and ash flicked onto Gin.

"Would it not be a sound achievement, if you can prove

yourselves," Vasilevsky kept a short pause.

"To be colonels by the month's end?"

The spark in Julien's eyes realized that his thoughts had been in the right. Plans to have imprisoned enemies of the state alive and under the good care of fresh air diving through the church's ceiling openings, Vasilevsky had forged a dangling bar of gold waving beyond the pale of Aelon eyes and ears. For the hunters of only glory.

"What...?" Arminius drowsily peered up, where the moonlight shine embraced the blank stone walls.

"So that...we could fight...for the...Confederacy...?" The lancer's fever burned over his inaudible mumbles.

"The Confederacy can only grant you victory." Vasilevsky could only emphasize, drawing nearer until his feet were by the lancer's rocking head.

"What could a mediocre party hope to do but whine in defeat?" asking furthermore, his voice sounded ever more desperate.

"Under someone..." Gathering what little power he had, Arminius raised his head with a laugh.

"As average as you?"

Steam arose from the skin wrapped above the thickening veins of his hands and neck. Like a ripening fruit, Vasilevsky's face was stricken with hatred by the gall that the elite was able to utter words the general had not believed he would hear said before him.

"Laken..." Arminius named a place that was not too far, but the single word was enough to move Julien.

Shaking his head; tapping his hands, the Danne tried to drag his comrade from a grave too deep that he would be buried within.

"Nikola..." Another name was spoken.

"Half your army...one hundred thousand..." He provoked beneath an irritating smile.

"Just how much mold have you grown in your mind to have a wish for death?" Vasilevsky muttered quickly.

As he paced away, the staff and guards peeked over their shoulders and dipped their feet in the storm of rage that was swirling. The pencil in the third general's hands snapped. Flying, the tip of the lead tapped the floor.

"Sure...it was your victory..." The lancer taunted, unsure of any punishment that he had spoken his mind.

"But...Kolchakov...babysitted you in command..."

The tingling of the blade against the scabbard's stomach slid into a rustle of the vice general's sling and belt. Twitching from the boiling blood waiting to erupt, his hand skated onto the hilt. Shines of gold casted a flash of moonlight.

"The only...mediocre general...here...is you..." said Arminius.

Without hesitation, he released a lighthearted chuckle. There was no regret. But his comrades saw him as foolish. Gazing up, his eyes were fervent, fueled to ignite the Confederate's fuse which eventually happened upon such insanity when he had thought his words had gained a victory. Only as the shadow retreated, the jet-like burst of power of a boot smashed Arminius by the stomach. With a cough, choking on the bitter taste of his organs, he was hurled to the wall. A horrible crack of the wall and bones sent Julien, aghast, scrambling for his fallen friend.

Heaving a narrow creek of blood that spewed in bubbles surfacing over the corner of his mouth, Arminius' eyes were half-blank. Anyone whose human soul was curling was tied by their hands and feet. They watched and listened to the calls for their faded comrade. But alas that sound was hushed and the rising ringing oppressed the outlines of the Danne before him. Blackness with a spot of light crawled into the blur.

"You will pour your heart as a slave for the Confederacy," In his immature tantrum, befitting of his eifer of the summer fire, Vasilevsky snarled at the squad.

"Even by means of chaining your eyes to the purge of your old allies—!"

At a coincidence, the unlocking door of the church interrupted the quarrel. The staff officers dropped their mugs and shattered bottles on the blessed site. Spilling mead and the sweetness of wine seeped into the cracks of the gods' own floor. Over the purplish red blend reminding one of a children's story of how the fields of hell would seem, they saluted and scurried from view, disbanding to the corners as if work had taken them. The giant who had grown a shade over the vice general whom most had thought was titanic anyhow, encroached.

"Teach..." Vasilevsky noticed the sigh of the old man.

His breath was pumping with fire. Through the whirling lungs of a warrior and the throat like a tale's scaled demon, the orange tint lit his neck.

"You should not be so wrathful, Leonid." The blaze of the elden soldier cooled into a cloud of smoke that drained from his mouth as he spoke.

"Or else it would be no different from my enemies."

Resting his bloodied bardiche on the wall; the blade dripping of flesh, the marshal of the Confederacy tossed a malformed head onto the ground, more inhuman than the dirt on his shoe. As it rolled towards the elites, even a fool could make out the dead's name.

The third general...? The squad stared at his face, as if he was still wide awake, unclear of whether his role in the world had been realized.

It was no doubt as they peered up that before them was the only man comparable to the God of War. The *Firestorm* and a thousand other names to be called, he was Grand Marshal Ivan Kolchakov. As the stories he had read of were often fables, the legend of a tale had been unbelievably summoned before Julien who could not discern a nightmarish dream of inhaling the same air as such heroes would. Or the fantastic reality of enemies.

"Who are these children?" A dark frown swiped across his wrinkled face when Kolchakov asked.

Gulping, the vice general loosened his collar as his master strolled towards Rzhev whose hand on a new pencil had stopped. However, when the marshal's back was turned, all could still feel the itching warmth of his eyes overseeing from the heavens.

"They found themselves snared near the headquarters." Vasilevsky adjusted the truth that the tutor's sharp ears caught a fine part-lie.

"Had Igor not been there to stop them—" He pointed at his own student, lowering his head behind a mirror.

"Execute them." The grand marshal coldly ordered, swiping a bottle of clear rum from the desk.

"How...?" Even Vasilevsky stumbled.

The formidable cork withstood the pinch of the grand marshal, but like foes before him, there was a pop on the loosening of the mouth that burst a fragrance of fruit and a burn in his nose.

"Hang them, burn them, however you will do it." Kolchakov offered as he washed his tongue and flushed a glassful of the booze.

"But they could become assets to our state—" Sheathing his sword, the student pleaded.

"And what of them in ten years' time?" The old man questioned once more but it was checking the loyalty of the vice general.

Kolchakov slipped the bottle beneath his arm and lifted the bardiche from the wall. Dust and debris crumbled. Where the stone showed the blade its hospitality to lean upon, there was a lasting dent.

"When will they rebel? When will *he* make you his vassal?" asked the marshal, pointing at Arminius who could not wake despite the stop of bleeds by a comrade's tied but easy hands tightening the wound's dressing.

"Leonid, I've seen their eyes before." Kolchakov showed his last, damning glare.

A wind broke through the cracks and swung the door open for the exiting man. Vasilevsky was speechless. Silent before his tutor who stepped into the light of lanterns. When the marshal was to mount the stallion brought awaiting him, he added quite straightly,

"I will be taking fifty thousand,"

"Sure as I am, they are not needed in your army." Holding the saddle, he leapt and mounted smoothly.

"What are you planning?" The church became unguarded by his presence as Vasilevsky stormed beyond the sanctuary.

"Warsau." Kolchakov plainly answered.

"But that's over two hundred leagues to the south, beyond the frontlines not to mention—" His student delayed him again.

"Sink your acting of like how I'd picked you up three decades ago." His patience ran dry when the menace of Akülunnarchs solidified, gawked at by the Firestorm.

"You know that your mentor can burn his way through hell and return with the devils' heads on a pike." Reassuringly, Kolchakov told.

Waving his hand, the personal guards were told to be away. Into a diamond, the cavalry formed. But whilst they marched, the force was without their commander.

"Next time you request my assistance, make sure you are to be defeated." The marshal mocked jokingly.

"I do not want to travel across a country to simply watch your victory ensue." There was a proud laugh that did not ignore his age.

He flicked his reins and spun his horse for the guards. When a second lash reared the stallion, the marshal rode at a sprint for the forest of nothingness and ash. His companions sped and escorted the departing Confederate. Yet he had some words to say that did not face his student.

"Mikhail may not be as strong, but you ought to learn from him sometime!" told Kolchakov.

Then, the riders dissipated to the blackness of night and the coal-like trees. Vasilevsky saluted and held a pause of his arm for some seconds before he was sure his tutor had gone. For the church, he headed, after the gallops gradually quieted. The door shut behind by the hands of his colossal guards. So paranoid the man was that it was an awkward time of wordlessness before the vice general approached a bottle of beer and unwrapped the paper seal. The crumples echoed, bouncing through the collapsed nave.

"I have no choice." The general sighed, finally removing his helmet, and placed the delicate art on the table.

Taking a sip of the beer, Vasilevsky dropped onto a chair and rubbed his sweat from his head of short, curled hair.

"Never can one be against his will."

He unsheathed his sword again. To take a lasting look at his own reflection as ash began to fall upon his golden blade. The ground grumbled then rocked. There was no nature's quake. That would be extraordinary. The staff around him halted their hands and steps to listen. Towards one direction, they all turned. A faint cry from afar was cut short by a gunfire-like snap. As Rzhev looked up, disturbed by the dust gliding onto his writings and cup, an explosion, too near, cracked the glass panes.

"What is it?" Who could not bear to remain idle, Vasilevsky marched for his officers, huddled around a single window that stood overlooking the street that fed into the town.

Shoving past them, the general peered to the outside world. And utterly baffled, his eyes opened two-fold. The burning soil. The torched roofs. As his soldiers in the reserve quarters fled, there was something that pillaged the path for the headquarters.

A young man, of his early twenties, came beyond the flames. A cigarette hung from his lips. His tape measures swished, knocking those surrounding him to be dealt an ordeal by fire. Who dared challenged him, the temper of the heaven eifer was both the spear and shield.

"Who is it?!" Vasilevsky raged at his officers who had yet to provide an answer.

No one could. For the lone soldier was someone seeming so unknown. Untidy with no sense of maturity. Aimlessly flicking his whip-like blades, launching razor gales in disorder that a fighter would not be able to predict his next.

"Hey 'Onfederates!" The soldier's first yell was recognized by the once hopeless lancers.

"Who 'ere's got my cadets?!"

XIII

5 JULYUS 491

05.07.12017

Thomas Ascot

I had lost my moment seventeen years ago when a Whirlwind battled our stand in the north. It crippled me. But more so now whenever I see soldiers such as he who may spend their life in isolation from the very nature of themselves. Skowroński is no different as a foreigner in an unknown state. Why would this man bother for Alben when he can be with his people in Leken?

His soul does not belong in peace. The talent he possesses belongs on a boundless battlefield that would be a boon to our allies. Why remain in such a hell hole when one can enjoy their youth in war?

A man of your stature. A warrior of a prowess only children could have dreamt of. Yet you are here!

Rot in a hell, Adam!

CHAPTER

14   APOLLO

The storm of ten years past crashed on the shores of the far western beaches of the three-crowned kingdom. Laying wasted, a fisherman's boat. Spared of sinking, the wooden hull had splits. Within, the defector was worn by scratches and bruises. But what this boy's drenched Alba uniform spelled ill luck was that he had found land on the last enemy the isles would see to face. The scourge of the sea flushed into the boat when the chiliness of the coastal breeze woke him to a taste of salt on his crusting lips. Seagulls cawed, gliding in a halo. Clouds broke on the entry by the sun. It lit only him. Stilled there with his eyes barely open, holding a rope-burned fist. Waves thrashed and splashed him. He found his second wind to rise and move from his traitorous adventure into a new home across the tides. Only when the sea quieted and retreated, abandoning marshes, the young soldier climbed over the pools and rocks; firm dunes and fine land to concrete asphalt that led towards the magnificent islands of Danen.

It was by chance that there was one man in his mind to seek. The road signs. Bridges stretching and winding over the island clusters in its complexity. Most roads he marched took for the grand fortress city. Three days and two nights. His socks had been soaked yet never did he bother to heal the whitening skin of his feet and swelled toes he felt peeling away. No one was selfless enough to present a bite of biscuits to someone so distant and foreign. Until the walls were there, he found way to smuggle himself in a carriage of slaves no older. Their eyes met, but the purpose of their lives differed when the traitor of Alben leapt from the coach and roamed the cobbled streets. In search of the lonely house that stood singled amidst an aristocratic park. That was hard to miss. Though there were a century of guards, its gates did not endure the stubbornness that stole the common sense of even scaling the spiked fences of the villa. Tight securities had holes that were unavoidable to have given this trespasser the first unwelcomed access to the porch.

When the knock on the door was met by an opening, the defector flinched. A chamberlain in his early thirties answered. His frown, like a proud man of the upper class, stared. Through the door, the unity of a party of gentlemen beside the *Great Danne Wind* glanced at the uninvited reeking of fish and an odd sour stench twice as pungent as a pig's pen. But the three children chasing about the lounge did not bat an eye. Knowing what message he had brought before the God of War, the door shutted, and the begging traitor was thrown into the alleyway slums.

Of the whole world, thirteen million subjects of humanity had requested this man to become their tutor. But any sane person had realized. It was impossible. Regardless of rank, strength, blood. None could harness the wisdom of the Whirlwind. Then it was the naivety of the gendarme that was one exception. Thirteen days, he climbed. And each hour, he was tossed to another unwanted dump of the city. But by nature, someone willing to sail the northern sea in a broken vessel through the winter season of storms had the very same patient mind of a good soldier. And before he landed on the porch on the last day, the king personally faced the nuisance.

"You again?" The words the Whirlwind spoke were to the first student.

Six years passed like a child's forgetting mind. Ascending the two league fjords of Nurwezh bearing the Whirlwind's axe. Diving the cold lakes of Sueken until he was latched onto shore from drowning. Escaping the sea swallowing a sinking island before the waters would bite at his bleeding legs. Every day, he was felled of exhaustion. Then the next Lunndä would come for his times, quelling rebellious armies of the subjugated peoples. To be taught the art of war. But it was not eternal.

"What'd ya mean, teach?" With a wrapped gift in his hands, the student asked from his tearing impatience.

In the small lounge, the teacher sat with his vision rested before the warming sun of the coming spring. The seventeen-year-old took a short glimpse at the longish box that was cheaply decorated in a small bow. White and golden, like the sols on a kind day of his eyes.

"What's dis fer—?" He marched to the old man's side when a raising hand halted him.

"To have trained you; given a new eifer not my only grandson could see..." said the new king, breaking the rapid of questions.

"It is enough for one life."

Unletting to depart, the soldier, filled with too much youth for a household of elders, latched onto his own hair and muttered,

"No, teach, ya haven't..."

"Adam!" The Whirlwind yelled but the passion behind his voice was unlike the thunder in training.

The curtains of the lounge wavered and hid the star. A cold wave strolled into the room when the front door gently widened for the chamberlain to enter. He paused at the carpets and dared not venture further.

"Do whatever you want with your life," The king stood from the couch and swung his gargantuan body towards the student whose head hardly reached the warrior's shoulders.

"Just as I have done."

Unraveling the box, the shimmers were reminiscent of the paradise granted. Platinum hooks, with the mechanisms of tape measures, the blades laid on burgundy silk.

"I only ask for one thing." He added, lacking the joy in a desolate heart.

The student stammered within. No words could be collected that would stop the presence of inevitability.

"Harvest your life on the battlefields,"

"As the God of War's fated heir." Since the dawn of his journey in the world of wars, it was then that again the king called himself and the youth only once.

The church crumbled in the ray of the deity. Hidden behind the panes and walls, the phantom of the sole soldier flickered in the shadows of flames. From witnessing what terrific agility, the officers paced away as the glass cracked and the debris collapsed. When two hooks swooped into the chamber, the heads of Confederates were ripped towards the vast heaven sea with an orange hue. Unseen and unheard before, the vortexes that rolled around the platinum tongues drilled the bodies into eight parts where crosses tortured the fleeing. With their blades unmoved from scabbards, they had let the man have his frenzy. The generals' legs were forced from the ground and by the wind, they were lunged like toys to the desk beneath the tower. Tearing flesh, the hooks were filled in a burst of light, sending whips that bore monstrous marks in the stones of the ancient.

"Teach…" Gin mumbled, avoiding the checked blasts from the lashing that protected the seven.

When the generals had capsized and the clumps of flesh could do nothing to tie his feet in a stalemate battle, Adam eased his blows of eifer, imprisoned for too many years. The dust of the church dropped like heavy ash and the air was cleared of the murk that cloaked the intrusion. But the brawl entered the two cleaves of the guards by another name. They were the true elites of the present.

"Yer gangin' up me?" Adam grinned at the faceless creatures stomping to his way.

Spikes embedded into their skulls, the pain reminded the duo whether a life in suffering or one to cause was to be followed. Olden bandages which had yellowed from the unchanged years were bleeding like the grayed faces behind the masks. In a rock tight formation, the armor, no less chunks of steel, were as if they had cladded together. Marching closer, the aura drove a menace that the instructor failed to compete.

"What is that fool planning?" Lifting from the ground, Vasilevsky squinted but he could not see through the unpredictability behind the confident smile.

As his subordinate third general stroked the scratches on his pauldrons, he peered to his side and saw the humiliated face angered to heights that was unusual. Veins reddened in the whites of the Summer Lion's eyes.

The guards saw the gaps in Adam's defense and dashed for the opportunity. Charging, the walking pillars swung left and down. At what momentum, Julien watched the afterimages trail behind the blades that gave their instructor no ground to gain. But leaping side to side; bouncing about like a boxer, he dodged every strike. As if he was taunting them. Yet the squad could mostly comprehend that the slashes were hefty that could cut air and sound and nothing more. For Adam, the attack was sluggish.

A jaw dropped and it was Rzhev who had realized as time appeared to have stopped.

"I-I recognize this form…"

"This elegance!" His excitement bursted.

Spitting his cigarette at a giant's face, Adam leapt over a thrust of the blade and landed insultingly on the steel body. He dared to chuckle when the delinquent hurled a pocket knife that slowly spun into the precise hands of Arber. An efier glowed and the cutting of the ropes and reeds were distracted by the clanks of the instructor's shoes hopping on the cleave.

"Ain't dat 'nuf?" Adam began a dance that had weakened the soldiers he toyed with.

Hooking around, the tongues shoveled into the giants' necks. Their bodies paralyzed and a crack blackened the veins that had staled from the stop of hearts. From a flick of his arms, Adam collided the two dazed heads and a fatal whip slashed along the openings of the helmet. A gaping ravine widened and the tendons were pumped out with thick blood falls. Like an oil spill, the soulless lives leaked. The legs who still marched for the instructor alarmed the generals. But soon, for they were mortals, snapped their bones from the fight against death and thumped before Vasilevsky. The breaks of the church floor were then rivers, seeping into the patterned soles of the Aelon and Confederates.

"Was this another reckless attempt to take my fortress?" The vice general tread, printing a sticking stamp of gore.

Drawing his sword, without a shield, he pointed at the young man whose mouth was already busied by another smoke. But he had not noticed the squad who had been freed and were flocking in a chain to the lieutenant's flank. A whistling blade hurled for the Summer Lion's head. His instinct was instant. Batting the pocket knife, the slight blade swirled into a crack in the wall from where the trail of azure steam vanished.

"Let us handle it." Colt sniggered, patting Miklós to his side who raised both bloodied cleaves.

Whilst Arber borrowed his back for Arminius' ride, it was lastly Julien rushing to the aid.

"How did you find us?" The latter boy asked as they stood their ground, unarmed, around the savior.

"Well, it's only a coincidence I'd arrived as yer comrades fell back inta line." Adam recalled, sighing and clicking his tongue in disappointment.

Turning to the only lancer who could not hear, he chuckled, "Y'know ya shouldn't 'ave left a girl alone."

Alexandria? The elites came to sense.

Almost pleading, his arms were widened and his knees were bent before Vasilevsky. As if he was a blockade to halt the hunter, Rzhev lowered his head and muttered before speaking his thoughts.

"I remember now!" Worriedly, the third general exclaimed, as his face slowly rose.

The expression was irked but was charmed by the uncalled arrival of Adam. Yet it merely gave more reason for Vasilevsky to act rashly.

"What is it?" He snapped.

"You should remember those years ago when Danen retired from the joys of war." The lesser general spun to the lieutenant on his knees, and pointed at the man with his nose.

"We had thought how odd it was for the God of War to have retired so early..." Rzhev added that seemed to have struck his tutor like an incendiary.

Every memory of all talks and dinners he had that was for months, to have sought a lasting conversation of the Whirlwind, had been speculation until his hands eased when his eyes confirmed.

"That man couldn't be..." said Vasilevsky, knowing it was the truth.

"The *Apollo*!" Rzhev glorified.

He questioned his mind. His palms sweated. Glaring at the one named the student of the Great Danne Wind, to the veteran Vasilevsky, Adam was barely a circus master, juggling and spinning his tape measures.

"Sheesh, ya guys aren't lettin' us go, are ya?" The lieutenant rubbed his head as he shuffled back from the generals taking no steps forward.

It was unlike the proud men the Confederates were. Upon hearing the name of the warrior before them, their shadows had not been overtaken but had shrunk alone.

"But! This ain't an assassination." Adam joked, as he hid his blade from plain sight, that if the generals were to move their hands to the hilts of their swords, the tongues could gouge out their eyes.

A whisper to Lev prompted to push the squad to be away after a brief nod. Colt grunted but too followed Miklós, never questioning the command. And fleeing, the lancers passed the wreckage that sealed half the doorway. There was not a reply nor an exchange of words between the parties. Only for that the two factions were leering at foes before Adam was the last in the church. A wave from his temple left the generals in wonderment. As a drop of sweat sprinted from his sideburns to his jaw, the soldier of Aelon had escaped the hands that had done good to hold their prisoners in the cages of the Confederacy. But alas, the scraping terror of facing a warrior trusted by the Whirlwind's strength was too much a horrendous screech.

"My holiest tutor, we have the numbers to give chase—" Rzhev, unwilling to accept the defeat in having been fooled, pressed his chest ahead but a sword was held against him.

"Igor. Let them be." Vasilevsky halted the third general.

He drove his blade into the stones and severed the church and the earth. As the pillars holding the tower collapsed from the nearing fires, the ruble crumbled outward. Sliding like an avalanche, the stones and beams crashed. Though the trembling ground did not shake him. There was one bottle on the floor that had not broken into shards and Vasilevsky was lucky to have found it to have not been emptied.

"We'll have another chance on the battlefield." Hesitant to remind himself of the tragic coincidence, his voice echoed softly in the bottle.

"They've bested us." A broken spear in a pond of blood took his sights for the shaft and blade in red.

At the fourth hour by the morning, the night birds sang for the squad, ascending the mound of a fleet of flags on each stake and spire. The dead in piles awaited the fires of the high judge, where they slept eternally longing for life. Mourning for their fallen friends, the living knelt over the bluish flesh. They prayed, yet knowing that the past would not return. In time as the tip of the sun, still dark, rose into the sky in the pinkish clouds, the field had settled. All was calm. The fog crawled over the surface. There on the ridge's summit, a general bathed in the skyline when a shock to his soul woke him from meditation. Seeing that the squad had returned from their failure alive, Nikola's heavy heart was relieved. With a blood trail, Arber hurried for the camp but there were not so many cheery faces. Those who watched the recovery of the seven-manned squad were in a divide of feelings.

"Major, yer elites are back!" Adam showed his way to the front.

The small drum and bell tolled, awakening the army whose eyes had dark bags beneath. No common soldier was to greet them except for one particular lancer who rushed to the elites.

"Elite squad!" A voice the squad was familiar with was unfamiliar by his tone.

Summoned from his tent on the outskirts of the fortified hill, there came a major with a stormy look. Racing past the lieutenant, Codrington unleashed his rage,

"Do not act so selfishly!"

"All seven of you could be executed for insubordination this noon!" told the major whilst he and Vasilevsky started to sound alike.

Ah, I'd prefer not ta... Adam awkwardly smiled and calmly bathed into the smudge of soldiers.

"It doesn't matter as long as we get Arminius to—!" Julien interrupted from the rear of the squad, nearing Arber and his comrade.

The major reached for the Danne and drew him nearer by the collar. Gripping his commander's wrist, he tried to free himself. But it was as if his other hand was warming to strangle or clobber that had sealed his mouth. His lungs were dry. The scent of a stinking dry breath. He had not taken a droplet of water since the elites had disappeared. And that, Julien could assume well enough why it was so.

"It doesn't matter?!" Codrington raised his fist and barked.

"Your endeavors got over fifty thousand killed in a single clash!" He revealed.

The struggle halted. As the sighs and mumbles of the crowd that they had lured quieted, their eyes were on whatever the major was to charge the elites with. Whether it be a public beating or a dimwitted execution. Yet from the tone of the air, he loosened his grip and tossed the soldier onto the mud.

"Major. That is enough." The general moved aside his men when the chain of blames stopped.

"The fault is mine." Nikola judged.

Contemptuous of his own doings that was no fault of his, Julien dragged his arm across the flattened patches of grass and rested his hand on a knee. From his sleeve, tributaries of blood snaked to fingertips of dried soil. Wetting the slabs of crusted dirt, the mergence of mud dripped from his nails.

"Infighting will twist our duty." told the commander, kneeling down for the Danne.

"But we mustn't forget what it is that defines our roles."

Refusal to look upwards was the shame Julien carried without reason. As the drops of life fell together at the same dull beat, he could only face a lightening Arminius.

"Get the boy inside." Directing Arber for a tent adorned by a ring of red swastikas, Nikola told.

A path opened by the poleaxes and arms of the guards in bronze. Through the crowd, Arber raced for the medics with his comrade huffing in undisturbed pain. But alas the squash of a heartbeat lifted.

"When a plan failed to yield results, I would do my best to save my men." His truest intentions were unveiled when Nikola returned to Codrington with an anxious look.

"But I was too distracted."

"War isn't so two dimensional." said he, forcing division amongst the witnesses.

Murmur began. Though their anger for the general's decision did not seem to have been quelled, it had somewhat eased. But of those who found more justification to blame those unloyal to the absolute command of the hierarchy, a few aides approached.

"Do not let the armies hear of this." A whisper was from behind.

"Your authority. Ninety and nine whippings and reprisals." Glares of the higher officers struck upon the squad.

However, the camp of the personal staff had split. Whilst some grumbled in discontent, the younger found their own kind praiseworthy.

"They are the heroes of this battle." One lieutenant pleaded with a dash of envy.

"Is it not our first victory to have retreated the Confederates?" Another argued as a third soldier narrowed his eyes and agreed,

"Of course, we would have little idea what would happen to our integrity."

The crowd were detached by beliefs and laws. Punishment or reverence. One could not easily tell how the factions had formed. Officers and gendarmes encouraged the squad with distant mutters that what the elites had done was in the right. With words that broke Nikola's reputation of harm. But another party would stare at the youngsters in disdain, gathering talks that a radical route would best serve Aelon. They were both senseless. Who remained on the fence were only sensible not to interfere.

"Before your mind comes to a decision, Adrien," Then, an ederly man spoke up.

From amidst the waves of pushing and shoving bodies, a gap in the crowds was widened for a way to the general. With his hands behind his back, he entered the presence of the many aides who withdrew away. The guards did not stop the lone intrusion but disbanded the onlookers who fled the axes and maces of the protecting ring.

"Tell me what it is that these lancers did wrong?" Casually, a question sprouted.

Rising from the ground, Nikola slowly turned towards the voice when the figure entered his view. Awide, the eyes of the general shot awake, startled by the chance of his happening on the same battlefield.

"G-General Warneńczyk?!" Nikola stammered, watching his comrade near.

"Another general?" Colt frowned but the two commanders did not speak of one another on the same podium.

A simple glance of Warneńczyk moved Nikola from the stage where Julien stayed himself close to the earth. Their kei were bizarrely distinct. There was a pressing force around the foreign general that none could find in the Boëm who had become a cheap, middle-aged man.

"I cannot see how such brave youths should be chastised." Warneńczyk offered as he halted before Julien.

"Right?" asked the general for the Danne as he was tightening the tails of his burgundy red beret.

The wrinkles around his eyes, fueled by an unnatural shade

like ash on the blue seas, showed that he was in his late-sixties, if not for his narrow, combed white mustache and short platinum gray hair. His face was long and defined with a nose similarly so. Bearing the same odd stature that the elderlies of the battlefield were, Warneńczyk stood rather straight and was only a nail beneath six foot tall. He was a simple man. In what baggy, and unfashionable uniform of his younger prime. But something of the royal colors of the Lekann hussars held more mystery than the appearance before the elites.

"I did not come here without reason, however." He said, stuffing his hand for an inner pocket.

Returning to Nikola, there withdrew a letter for his ally. Before they had read the contents within, their eyes were on a seal denoting the enraged wind that any could have recognized the emblem. His mouth was agape and could not delay longer. Nikola broke the wax and stretched the folds to its fullest. The order was bolded and too large to ignore. It was a short, handwritten note of three lines that told plenty.

"The Wanal?" Nikola read aloud.

"Yes. That fossil means to reform our defenses." told Warneńczyk, pinching the letter from stopped hands.

"Even if half of Leken is to be—" Tearing the paper, corner by corner, the wasted fragments of ink were freed to be with the seeds of dandelions.

"This is your motherland. How could you surrender so easily?" Nikola whispered but it seemed he did not understand one thing that was the essence.

"For victory," General Warneńczyk interrupted his mindless comrade.

"You must first sacrifice another of equal importance."

Pulling a fist, he raised an arm and the guards of Nikola's headquarters hastily marched away. What authority the old man had and was used in another's field. It was as if he was the host to the one who had invited him.

Whilst Julien stood by a hand hooked around his elbow, the elites saw the commanding gesture who waved for the squad to follow. Behind the duo of veterans, a sudden burn impaled his arm. He grabbed where he thought had stung most and between his fingers, blood began to ooze. But Julien did not squirm or whine. There was not a complaint he could utter. Like his younger self, he bore his agony.

"Another thing, Adrien." Warneńczyk advised once more to the stunned Nikola and sharply informed the latter,

"You've been redeployed."

They stopped before anything could be seen over the southern ridge. The Boëm general had paused, reconfirming what the Lekann said. But in bouts of the words running around his head, Nikola could not fathom whether it was the truth.

"Where to?" He had questioned.

"Line Two-Five-Nine." Straightforwardly, Warneńczyk answered.

Restarting their journey for the summit at the rear of the hill with the generals leashing the elites nearer heavier air. Like scaling the pinnacles of Terra, their lungs sensed the great strain they had not felt since arriving in the midst of the flows of battle.

"Then who's to—?" Nikola blurted before a storm had swept him into the new current.

The war chants. The stamps of shields and spears. Marching to the beating drums and bells like gongs. His answer was carried by the wind. Unbelievingly, Nikola rushed to the edge's peak with the squad chasing behind. There they had not found the prior emptiness that faced the Aelon's backs. Rather, a romantic sight to behold.

Lush silvers and gold of the winged hussars with feathers drawing awide. Leken was the continent's predator and in her grandness, was present. The armed peasantry and commoner core of the army were shabbily dressed and wielding unconventional blades. They cheered fanatically with a voice not a professional army could find for their dear general who arose over the hill. Warneńczyk gave a slight salute but it was sure to have sent a jolt of warring passion through their hearts. There were at least two hundred thousand stationed beneath the plateau. And all whose faces were bloodied and dipped in sweat were as loyal as the nobility to its king.

"How? You brought the Winged Lance?" Quivering at the picture pulled from a propagandist film, Nikola mumbled.

"I had stressed we would not have enough." The old man chuckled as the seriousness of his tone had become ash.

"But these Rus were too easy to fool." He had even dared to brag.

Easy?! The squad, in collection, yelled to their minds.

That's another story here! Lev remnicized their troubles with the Confederates of the front.

However, as the youngsters had believed that he would go no further, Warneńczyk proposed to steer fate towards another course.

"If you do not mind, before you leave." The general began, pivoting to the squad.

"Hm?" Who had accepted his future soon as his soul had lightened, Nikola hummed.

Before his senior would speak again, the Boëm realized the desire behind the eyes glaring upon Julien whose body stiffened. But not only for the Danne. The squad had the same weights pressing upon them.

"Hmph. Of course." Nikola sighed, stuffing his pocket with a shard of the order as he agreed willingly.

"That will take some stress from my hands before I make my retreat." He added, to a nod.

But when his mind was out of luck busied by the realms of military matters, Warneńczyk sharply swiveled in a return to the long clinch in his heart and asked quietly,

"By the by, where is Károly?"

"Oh, Lienz?" Nikola mentioned a lieutenant's name.

A shadow peeking from the tent was caught by the glimpse of Julien. As the archer had been spotted, he leapt from the dimmed quarters that was hardly brightened by the ascending sun, and sprinted for the general with open arms.

"Grandpa!" Latching his small self around Warneńczyk's waist, Lienz hugged him tightly before the squad awed by the swift curve in pace.

"Good morning" Warneńczyk softly greeted in return, patting the lieutenant's morning hair.

"Did you behave yourself?" Yet knowing the answer, he asked.

With a pleased look, Nikola saluted the both and retreated from the ridge. But smiling at the elites, it carried another meaning as the departure started. Swirling his arm in the air for his officers, the whistles and hollers of his subordinates were carried along the awakening ranks scrambling to the crackling fires heating pots. The destined retreat was coming.

"Y'know, y'know, I was finally given an order!" Lienz cheerily exclaimed that was too energetic for the early day.

"My eifer *fwoomed* through the tanks and everything went *fwpaa!*" He explained, throwing his arms about like a dramatist.

"Károly, your gramps is proud of you enough." Warneńczyk pinched his cheeks.

When the scene of family could warm another, there was still a coldness and emptiness that Julien wished for it to be away. But watching the corners of their mouths widen ever more, the Danne did not retract a slight giggle that caught Lienz's hunter-like ears. For a moment, the archer spotted the elites awaiting the command of dismissal from Warneńczyk. Together and alone, and embarrassedly in the presence of the general and lieutenant, the squad did best to ignore when they heard the joyous rush their way.

"Wait up! Are you the squad who charged into the Confederate's headquarters?!" Prancing around the lancers, he took good close looks at everyone except those too tall to reach.

"Are you the leader?!" Before the squad had anything to reply with, Lienz exploded in glee again as he assumed for Julien who was only coincidentally at the elite's vanguard.

"No, no, no!" Waving his hands, Julien flustered for his modest soul could not take the role.

"That would be Arminius." He added.

Scouring around, Lienz peered past the gaps of the squad as if he knew who the lancer was. But of course, Arminius was nowhere to be found.

"Arminius…?" His search continued.

"Ah, he's in the clinic—" Julien spoke, but it was in a manner he had never felt before.

He was not so shy when Lienz had approached him. As if they were playing a game of catch up.

"Károly." Warneńczyk called for his grandson.

"I need to speak with these valorous soldiers for a while."

Pointing at the trains of wagons lining in files beside the overseer Nikola, he asked of him surely as a mild distraction,

"Could you please help uncle Adrien load his rations?"

"Alright!" Without a fight that he would have most certainly engaged in with anybody who was not his own grandfather, Lienz jogged towards the mounted general.

His grin passed by the elites who had to shed an uncomfortable smile that was not so rude as a little response. And as Nikola was poked on the leg by the archer, the lancers followed the mouthings of the Boëm. Whilst the child was driven from the work of his grandfather, the swishing of grass shifted further from the squad.

"Come, lancers, we have much to discuss." The general led the six.

Lastly, a glance by Julien took to the archer. His hands were already occupied by the crates and cloth whilst his face reddened by as many folds humanly possible. Settling the stack some pounds heavier than he was, Lienz swiped his wetted head that had heated too far. But afar from the honest work and the shell of the compatriot who was displayed before him, he wondered the same as years ago,

His name...Károly...

Where have I heard it before? It arose.

XIV

- - 492

- - 12018

Adrien Nikola

Shall I seal the noose that dangles from this ceiling? It is burdensome that I must be confined here to my sorrows because of one simple blunder. Or has it always been? Had I not chased the glorified hero named Arminius Reichner where his name has only become the cursed daily words, would then the battle have been ours? Do I still retain that stubborn belief that this outcome was inevitable to begin with?

I pray to you again, winds of Sudet, guide me onwards to this victory that may suit me more.

The Confederates are here. Still like rocks in a pool. I had expected Akülunnarchs to have been the same. How naive. When simply we've never won a battle as an alliance, it had given me hope I was doing no wrong. Then as those defeats piled atop over the days and months I've spent sitting before the frontlines, the wounds have blighted my entire body.

Warneńczyk, I was a fool to ever diminish your blame on me upon my departure—

Now who is it at the door...?

CHAPTER

15   ONSLAUGHT

Flayed by the encounter at Akülunnarchs, the measly twenty thousand rallied to the headquarters in a farewell to the sight of battles for the known days of the morrows. And in no sense was there a celebration despite the relieving sight of the Winged Lance folk. For his face had the long impression of a sour failure, as when he had decided to give up Baltik, General Nikola dipped his head as he mounted. Leading the officers from the hill's toppest haven, they descended in crippled columns. Their faces were portraying the same. Who thought they had escaped from the horrors and yet there were other woes to replace. Under the flags drawn down by the still air, it was the last of the frontlines for Adrien Nikola.

As the last sparkles of helmets and the groans of infantry had dissipated over the camp's back pass, the old general lifted his beret in an adieu and flicked aside the linen doorway. The squad pursued into the chamber of rustling paper and flickering candles louder than the whispers. Before, none had dreamt of the chance to be beside the cabinet for war. Not within a decade they had thought but achieved in the first days. But as an impression, not all headquarters were so easygoing. What little staff they had planned along two wide boards set behind a long table. The chairs were even. There was not a seeable grain of dust fluttering beneath the banners hung across the ceiling. Noble coat of arms, Julien peered upwards at, were of an eagle and its lancer. But as he was tapped on the shoulder by Lev, the Danne spotted another leaning over a chair. The officer was laying a map with two apparent subordinates of the general. Yet he was not Lekann. He had a shaking hand.

"Major?" Julien seemed wholly unsure but it was the man there in his eyes.

Beside Adam who too responded with a quick glance, their instructor coldly asked before his face was shown,

"Is this the lot who's left?"

Gah, it's really him... A sickness whiffed over the lancers' heads when their stomachs turned.

It was truly a dismal presence for the major himself to have come to the field. And through the faces of many twisted grins, Adam read their minds. But under no command was he required to remain if ever Ascot would begin another lecture. So with a cigarette and a match in his hands, the lieutenant lifted from the table and retraced his steps for the entrance abruptly where an opening was presented to the bumbling delinquent.

"Den, I'll leave ya to it." Lighting the smoke as he abandoned the elites, he said but with a huff that Julien held his breath from.

However, when his hand reached for the curtains, ready to scurry away, a boy rushed through rudely and paused when he found himself to be in the presence of a commander.

"Excuse me, general." Arber dipped his head but it only halted the elder's trailing with a pin in his hand.

"That is quite alright." replied Warneńczyk, plotting a winding road of markers as Ascot moved the fronts of chess pieces to the direction of a subordinate's pointer rod.

The splash of blood on his jacket and the pond that soaked through his back. Arber stunk of rusting iron that Julien was the only who had been disturbed and turned away by the splatters and scent. Even if it was to release the quietness he hoped not to, Julien concernedly asked,

"How's Arminius?"

Giving an honest look, that once was never his casual slyness, there was nothing to hide but to give the assuring truth.

"He's fine." Arber replied.

His eyes were still sullen. Albeit it was less so. The clouds had cleared but the sun had not risen. Julien felt it odd that not even his comrade's words could satisfy him as a smack on his back pushed the storm from the soul.

"Don't worry 'bout it!" Gin blurted, singularly collapsing the politeness before then.

"Arber said he'll be alright, so he'll be." He patted, shameless of the bruises and stains ignored.

Warneńczyk had been hearing. His palms were flatly placed on the map's torn edges where the fiber had loosened into strings. He saw the thanks be uttered from Julien's mouth but it was softer than a whisper of a waning ghost. Though the elites had not known whether the general knew of their captain's name, a brief grin caught his closest aide's sight.

"I haven't properly introduced myself, have I?" Sliding his hand along the table with his beret slipped into a belt loop, the general reminded himself as his speech began at last.

To the unbottling of a flask, the lancers held their tongue. But not before continuing, Warneńczyk took a slight sip of sweet rum that the aroma of alcohol could put a bull to sleep. It had hardly punched the old man. As Julien held his breath for the scent to fade, the general set the bottle on the table and spun it by a light push.

"I am General Władysław Warneńczyk von Krakau," He was ordained by the holy name.

"Second in command of the Lekann forces, and first of the Winged Lance Army." Warneńczyk did not dip his head like any aristocrat would.

Perhaps he was not. From his randomness that was unlike the single route of courtesy from a nobleman. Everything that stretched between his aura and devotion on the skin was misleading.

"It seems you and the major are all the more acquainted." He pointed to both his personal advisors and introduced the other,

"But, for him…"

Bearing the insignia of the Lekann crowned eagle, the kepi of the red and white lifted from his black and pulled back hair. With honor and pride, he gave a quarter bow and fitted his cap once more. The young, serious aide of his late twenties stood loyal. Clean shaven and far less tanned that the officer did not seem to be born of the field with untrained hands which were not roughened by the hilts of swords. But though he was shorter than the commander, there was nothing particularly small about the air he forged. Like his general, no one could doubt that this man was only equally capable.

"Colonel Aide Jacek Florek, second to the Winged Lance." The man saluted with his hand beside his shoulder, dissimilar to the Aelon's sign.

"I pray that our alliance will grant us fortune." He had to add.

"That is enough…" Shaking his head, Warneńczyk dismissed his subordinate.

Although acting so vigorous, the limit of the general reached its peak. For how long he had marched with his army of the peasantry, the pull of a chair gave the elites their response. With a slight huff, he sat, scratching his brows and scalp when the officers of the quarters held their work and faced the conference. Patient stares were not welcoming but perhaps, the lancer had sensed that they were newfound allies disparate to the outside fiends searching for their deaths.

"So, you are the squad the general's been tearing his hair about." said Warneńczyk to the silence of the room.

"They call you the heroes and butchers of Akülunnarchs."

To the names bestowed upon them, the seven lancers flinched.

"I understand the latter." He softly ridiculed his stolen soldiers, then the sharpness of his lungs pumped a spear of words,

"For all I have heard were the cries of failure. Recklessness. Traitorous."

A glare of a phantom diverged into the wings of lances. Through Julien's eyes, it was as if he was being suffocated by a thousand blades held to his throat. Not piercing. He was uninjured. However, the warning of the single leer was cursing the lancers, stricken by the cold wave.

Who…is this gramps? Colt took a half a step in retreat as sweat ran down a brute's face.

"I had sustained my reputation by adopting you from the Sudet Gale's hands." Warneńczyk reminded the party.

"Whilst, you could have lived a long life on an inactive journey to a fortress for another…six years?"

"What worth is there taking you in?" asked the general.

Like night blowing across a desert circled by the curving horizon of the four winds, the heat had submerged into the dark. For then, Warneńczyk contained his kei. Nevertheless, any mumbles or littlest motion never recovered in the truce. When the watch of an aide snapped by the next second, a soldier reeking so much of evaporating blood forced his comrades to lean away. It was even Warneńczyk who had to subdue the stench with a refillment from his flask.

"Gramps, ya haven't been listenin' to anythin' have ya?" Gin stood before Julien as he presented his figure for the tent bewildered by his unhumorous manner.

Gramps?! They shouted in their minds but the general gave the freedom of no concern.

"Have I not?" Warneńczyk played along, pushing a fist and a palm together as he leaned ever nearer to hear what this delinquent would have to say.

"Were we not de only ones who managed ta break through an army?!" He threw his arms wide like a dictator declaring his speech.

"Was that not your recklessness?" questioned Warneńczyk yet the rant did not stop.

"Whilst dat Nikola was sittin' on his ass, de headquarters were thrown inta hell!" With good reason, Gin twisted the truth.

The wise elden man knew too well from his lasting life and dealt a hand in an attack again,

"That was Lieutenant Skowroński if I recall."

"Even if we failed dis round, the chances of scorin' big—!" Lastly, Gin tried as the general's hand raised from its rest on a fist and ended the spent arguing that would be infinite if not stopped.

With his eyes and finger running along the map of the trail from Akülunnarchs to the western reaches where the shades of borders devolved, there was already certainty in his language of the body. As if he had been plotting a strategy for long, Julien did not discard his awareness that Warneńczyk had been prepared for the rant of a lancer.

If so...why is he spinning us in circles...? thought the Danne.

"General," Julien voiced, snapping Warneńczyk beyond his simulation of the next days.

"What are we really tasked with?"

The tapping on the table, like the repeating knocks on a door, eased then ceased. Warneńczyk peered upwards and once more, Julien was the lancer before him as the brute was detained by his comrades in the shadow of the backdrop. The general's wrinkles folded and released around his squinting eyes. They appeared to be analyzing every essence of Julien. From his childish face to his innocent aura that fed a bowl of worry to the lancer. As Warneńczyk relaxed the odd look of a snap of despair, he began twirling his mustache when a blatantly false grin widened.

"Of course you would see through me." In the form of a riddle Julien understood not what the old man muttered.

A glance at Florek and Ascot were shot, who granted him the reassuring and inviting nods that kept him from plunging too far into the mist of memories that had been forcibly forgotten by the persons of the present.

"All right," Warneńczyk wore his beret and addressed in a revival of confidence.

"If all are as willing."

Snapping for a delivery of a blank note, he readied a pen from his pocket. And on the drop of the paper onto the desk ahead, the series of sentences by quick scribbles painted a letter of sickly runes that was no different from a doctor's writing. With a flick of a lackluster signature, and a spot of ink at the tail, folds of the page transformed into a thin slip. Without a second opinion from his own doubts, Warneńczyk rose himself and reached the document for Julien.

"Show this to your captain when he wakes." Warneńczyk ordered.

"Reichner, was it?" He confirmed by Ascot and a reply of a grunt.

From the fix of his collar and his tucking of the chair, the seven elites found themselves amidst a ceremony. As the atmosphere tensed by the salutes of aides directed for the squad, the lancers realized the course was near and fixed their ranks. Proper and clearing his throat; with hands behind his back, Warneńczyk finally called,

"The eight saviors of Akülunnarchs!"

The squad braced and saluted, heeding the commander. Orderly, they looked on, at their general, proudly bearing their heads higher.

"From here today, all shall be honorably disbanded!" Warneńczyk declared, sending a short scare across the lancers.

"No longer under a standard, they will serve this war autonomously!"

"In accordance, except for I, no order may be heard." Unholstering his pistol of baroque antiquity, the general gently laid the barrel, surely threateningly, pointing for the center of the squad.

Still. Silent. A gulp failed to hide itself. As Julien could only watch the finger further from the trigger, then his angst came to rest.

"When the first betrayal sees the light," Warneńczyk told them, resting his fists against the table.

"The second comes twice the darkness."

Waddling his finger, the old man shook his head and quieted.

"I assume you know that your fate now hangs over the blade of the executioner." Dishearteningly, the general cleared any misjudgement that the squad had been freed of the military court.

The long table that was the river between the factions of the officers and lower soldiers rocked. Whilst ease flooded through the gates the lancers were still felt to be choked by the throat. Eventually, the commander waved down. And however stressed each lung suffered, the easy exhales concluded the induction.

"I haven't felt dat tense since we're cadets!" Gin expelled the last of the strains.

"But isn't this your third time?" From behind, a sneaking Colt whispered in his ears, chuckling as he told so.

A vein popped in Gin's temple as one sniggered away. But before an elbow crashed into Colt's stomach, the giants, Miklós and Lev dragged them from a brawl that would be so humiliating seen by a general's eyes.

Whether it was talent or father death's luck, Warneńczyk sped a glimpse at the convening lancers.

It would be senseless not to have. He confessed.

"Shoo, you children," The general dismissed them with the flap of his hand.

"We old men have no need for the youth in this matter."

Abiding by their first commander's new command, the reborn lancers hailed for the last in the day. And one by one, the elites, latched around each other's shoulders of grime and brownish blood, sought the light that had finally arisen in the outside world. But once the last had his hand on the doorway's curtains with a foot stepped beyond, Warneńczyk called his name,

"You are Julien Carlstadt, are you not?"

Halted, the boy had remembered he had never told his name. And yet the general knew.

"Yes...but..." Turning to the table that Warneńczyk had departed and was in his stroll about the boards, Julien returned.

"Arminius Reichner and Lienz Károly." Out of the blankness, the commander listed that one was Julien's comrade, and another the old man's grandson.

There was no prompt for the general to have asked. He simply did so of his curiosity that layered his mind.

"Do these names remind you of anything?" asked Warneńczyk as if it was an informal interrogation.

Approaching the table, though cautiously when he answered, Julien's mumble sounded split of his answer,

"No, not exactly..."

Upon a failed intrigue, Warneńczyk's eyes landed on the plan of a board where there was no crowd like the other. Though none had attention to the conversing duo, the general was rather secretive. And it was when Julien noticed the odd reaction that the elder portrayed, he knew only to answer whenever the officers were caught in the thunder of redrawing strategies and predictions.

"But, their names...they sound familiar..." Julien unsurely muttered.

"Yet even so that you say this is, it leads me to wonder," said the general, brushing his mustache.

"Why is it that you are fighting for Alben, *lejepëa ëape uent keaoenpeajens tëa Teajkeaenjceajke?*"

The bell tent. A dirty beige linen shelter. Its coned ceiling was high where the tip was raised by a single pillar. Near the ground of leaves beneath the lush forest forgetting the plains of Leken. Within, there was space for at least ten with mats laying on the flooring cleared of grass. It remained a field of dirt drained by the fires found from charred marks. But the smell of burns stayed. From the incense of a smoke, it burned upright, in a small cup beside his rest. A thin blanket covered his body to the shoulders as his new uniform was placed by his feet. Under the shade of a chair that was occupied by a bowl of steady water, he wore an unbuttoned jacket that had no trace of his. Over the decency of bandaging in the same knot, at last his wounds had closed.

To the eleven days Arminius passed in a slumber, the world shifted far. The company of the Confederates were in pursuit.

Across the marshes they had been chased, the Aelon broke and reformed only to be fractured again. And in fragments, the armies fled alone, detached by any sense of a frontline. It was like the wars of the middle ages. Not one soldier could know where they could step aside at ease. Even in dreams, the pain slashed across his back as the fiends chased in an unending void of whiteness.

His eyes twitched as the revival in the world slowly drew awake. He felt a towel, seeped in iced water, on his forehead for the fever to wear away. Yet, however real his touch on the mat or his breathing was, the looming figure over him was dreamlike.

"Julien...?" He mumbled but the shadow did not depart.

Until the swings of the lanterns found light on his face, the being was blurred. For it morphed into a face as the stars crackling in his sights cleared, Arminius was caught in a stare between. His face paled, and scaredly, leapt out of his cocoon and scattered backwards.

"W-Who're you?" A usual calm did not seem to find itself in Arminius.

The intrusive officer, in the coat of a hussar, leapt onto his feet and smacked his pants of the dust as he kept far. He was not much younger but a cheerful smile was otherwise. When the racing heart of the rudely awoken paced easier, another rushed into the tent. This lancer, he had known.

"Arminius! You're awake!" Julien lunged for and hugged him, throwing his friend against the ground that nearly thrashed a hole in the wall.

"Ach..." Holding his shoulder, Arminius squirmed as the Danne quickly scrambled away.

"Ah! Sorry! I forgot about that..." The latter sat upright when he apologized.

Pivoting his arm around if anything ever felt unsafe, Arminius checked. But after a click that did not hurt so well, he relievedly sighed,

"I'm glad...you're safe..."

Who brought himself cross-legged, Julien excitedly nodded as the towel on the comrade's face plopped on the ground.

"By the way, Julien..." Arminius remembered, although it had happened mere seconds ago.

"Who is he?" He pointed at the soldier who dashed at the two, hopping from the gaps between the mattresses and blankets.

"Oh, him—?" To the archer, the Danne turned around but he was already before them.

"I'm Lienz Károly." Introducing with a huge smile, the lieutenant reached for Arminius, and harmlessly, he followed,

"Can I call you Armin?"

As if he had grown out of childhood, a stretch of embarrassment could not be hidden behind the blush that reddened his cheeks and the bridge of his nose. Impossible to deny this freely child to call him a name that he had despised since the tongue had been learnt, Arminius took hold of Lienz's hand and replied,

"Sure...Lienz..."

Although he was brought up, his reply was met by a pair of waving hands of Lienz's who gestured to stop.

"You can call me Károly." told the archer as Arminius bent over for his boots.

"You're Mazhiar?" The latter made a guess, almost as if he knew before, whilst casually spinning his knots around and buttoning up his jacket.

"How'd you figure that out?!" Károly surprisedly exclaimed.

"They have their surnames first, don't they?" Sharply sighing for the last top button to be tightened, Arminius explained.

"Just like my Sinnik name..." The squad leader softened.

He tugged his jacket's skirt and straightened the creases when a cloak was flung over his face. Whoever the perpetrator was looking for a chance to distract his hand from making for his pocket. But it was foiled. When the packets of importance, of smokes and matches were brought before Julien's eyes, he frustratedly pushed his hand against his comrades' backs.

"Come on." Shoving them from the tent, Julien took them towards the wilderness Arminius had not yet seen.

"Wha—" The two voiced together.

"Not in here. Do that outside." His friend commanded the one unbeknownst that he had lit the incense.

Unwillingly, Károly and Arminius were brought beyond the curtains by the typically gentle boy and were shunned from the fire to the nature of light and dark.

The bells, strung like a chain between each sentry of the redoubt across the city, unnoticeably chimed. Where the moon was smiling teasingly upon the elites, there was an array of stars and floating satellites. For another thousand years or more, they would circle the earth without a know of any happenings over the world they mothered. With a campfire in between the sentry post and the sleeping quarters, burning bright, the breaking wood were attended by some lancers. Crouched down with parts of a hunted boar at the tips of their spears, Lev and Alexandria tended by a felled log and stump. It was hacked open by a swift slice. And there despite being regenerated, Arminius was not alone to be found livelier than ever. One could forget that the Confederates could prance on them and they would not bat an eye.

The leaves and branches crunched beneath Arminius' feet, whose trek was met by the Rus' sights of disbelief.

"Arminius?!" Lev yelled.

"He's awake?" Gin turned from his post but his head was forced to the sights of the rifle again by Arber's harsh discipline.

"You took your sweet time." Colt hissed at the awoken.

"Not dat you've been doin' anythin' either 'cept for starin' at Alexandria all day." Gin returned with a dumb grin.

"Shut...it..." Miklós growled at the dueling duo, pressing his grip into their heads and lifting them until each was blessed by a headache.

Exhaling a ring of smoke that dispatched Julien to Lev's side, Arminius neared the fire and warmed his hands over the slab of meat.

"What's this?" He asked, sniffing the aroma of the boiling pool of fat and herbs.

He and the two slumped onto the log and watched as Lev's soul slowly spurted out of his breaths from the two hours wasted fanning the flames. Slowly, the juices cooked its host, wrapped in leaves, and stuck to a stolen Confederate spear that reminded Arminius of an emptiness that his own was not by his hand.

When did I lose it... In a blink, he wondered but it was best not to think about such tiny matters.

It was in the current that Arminius lived. The past would not disturb him as he followed Lev's hand unfold a pocket knife that ran along the boar and tested its tenderness. The melting meat touched his tongue like spreading butter and lifted a thumb.

"It's done!" Alexandria expelled a shout for the squad in the sentry.

"Stay with yer crap, Colt! I'm gettin' mine first!" Gin tossed his rifle onto Colt's lap as he sprinted for his awaiting dinner with a growling stomach.

"Wait up, you glutton—!" Colt tried to release himself from duty.

A giant took his arm and flung him into the post, cutting his consciousness cleanly until a smack of his face switched his mind alight. In the cold of night, whilst Miklós tightened his clench on a rifle, Colt laid under the spray of stars. A flick of a paintbrush by a deity seemed to have covered the blackish blue canvas.

"Gods. Why does it have to be at this time?" He contemplated with the soul of a philosopher when it was answered by a girl irradiating his life.

Resting a piece of leaf, there were three hefty pieces on his chest. The heat stroked him with the blow of steam gliding for his nose. As he looked up, the face of Alexandria had pelted away after she had been caught in her long stare at an admirer. Colt quieted.

"Oh, right!" Julien remembered, taking shy bites whilst Károly had begun begging for his second.

"Our new commander has orders for us." From a pocket, he removed a letter that saw it treated well for it had not scrambled or ripped and passed the note to the squad captain.

Like blinds over a window, hiding the words on the street, Arminius stretched the sheet and revealed the scribbles of the general. He scrolled down, line by line. Some meaning could be made out of the illegible writing but it was enough to have weakened the corners of his smile.

"Where are we now?" Noticing that many days have passed since the transfer and Akülunnarchs, Arminius asked.

"Bizhust." Arber answered before Lev, whose pleading for the last slice of meat was met by contempt.

His comrade stuffed the cut in his mouth and the Rus, in defeat, dropped to his knees and befallen by depression, he lowered his head.

"We...lost...?"

"And retreated this far...?" Arminius tensed and gripped onto the leaf with an expression between a blend of regret and fury.

"Don't worry, we couldn't do anything about it either." Lev assured, as if he was not a belligerent.

That's reassuring to know... His comrades thought with flames in their eyes towards him who spun from the fire and whistled to a random tune.

"The Confederates outnumbered us; they outplayed General Nikola too..." Julien remnicized as it was whilst Károly keenly listened to the lancers' story.

"What can you expect from Aelon?" Punching a hole into his plate from nature, Arber critiqued.

"They should've reformed the Reich before the war—"

"Whatever," Gin broke the sullen atmosphere that was supposed to be a heartfelt gift for the lancer risen anew.

Waving his knife in the air with the last piece of the boar, the brute chattered,

"Ya guys are complainin' too much."

With the meat torn from the blade by his wildling teeth, he sipped the broth and tossed the leaf into the fire. Cooling by the sap feeding the sticks, the camp began to darken. Yet soon, the breezes of the river enraged the flames and sent the blazes higher than it once was.

"If ya can't move on from de past, den how're ya supposed ta fight a war?" Mouthful, Gin still spoke.

But it was with great wisdom that the squad had not expected from a foolish warrior of brawn not of the mind.

"Gin's right." Julien agreed.

"We shouldn't be dragging our failures."

The last stretch of the cigarette burned out and what of the end Arminius flicked into the campfire. A trail of ash chased the burning hint of tea and dived towards its own kind. Releasing the last huff of smoke, he muttered,

"Speaking of the past..."

Holding his hands over his stomach that was filled and satisfied, he slid onto the ground and cushioned his head over the log. Towards the heavens he looked as it gazed in return for him. He felt two pairs of eyes on him from Julien and Lev, anxious for what Arminius was to say.

"Who did the hunting?" asked the lancer.

There had been relief; the sighs rested their tensed kei. Their worries that he would fall into the steep pit of saddened rambles, they could not have hoisted him to bliss. But to his question, none answered of the original squadmates when all turned to Károly.

"Heh heh. I thought you would ask." The archer chuckled proudly.

"With this. I did." He basked himself in the glory of the slight achievement.

Leaning back, Károly swept a jewel of the dark and returned was a bow and a quiver. Arminius' eyes shone as he was given the honor to hold what could be an heirloom in his hands. The silver and crimson adornments of carvings was like a spit of fire that served an intricate grip but was smooth to hold. Its lightness was only a casing of the strength that could withstand his eifer. Which was so spectacular, the bow could be the eighth wonder of the world.

"Have you heard of Pelsut?" Bringing an arrow from its pouch, as Károly inspected the tips, he asked.

"The Military College of Balaton?" asked Julien, curling his hair around his finger.

"I heard they only accept a hundred students a year out of a million." Arminius backed.

Though he knew it had been odd how Károly was dressed or armed, that was no more uniform amongst the elites than the shapes of leaves on varying trees. His suspicion grew more when Károly had asked of Balaton.

"Yeah! I was selected for the ninetieth place!" Károly informed his comrades who was fastened by his meriness.

"You got selected?!" All cried.

As Arminius returned the bow, the lieutenant sheathed his arrow. For he shook the quiver with the rattles and clacks of shafts, the last addition slipped into the slackened pouch that laid on his lap, pressed together.

"I've been training since I turned four." Fixing his quiver to his slanted belt, Károly told them.

"It's only natural for where I come from."

He posed for a sign of victory and held the moon between his fingers. The radiance of Luna, slowly swallowed by the rushing clouds, disappeared that did not hold his hand any longer. Yet on the ground below the skies, there was an infectious beam that was restored.

"To become the first to shoot down the sun of course!"
Károly declared for the lancers.

His objective seemed far fetched. Arminius saw his own
embers in him. It was not impossible to gain if it were not for the
illusionary goal he chased of felling a star from the universe. Like
the aiming eye for the title as a great general in Napoleon's order
of ancients, the pledge was ultimate.

"How old are you now?" Julien questioned the comrade by
his side.

"Thirteen." Replying with a grin, Károly lifted his hands and
formed the number.

"Twelfth of Apelyotes, four seventy seven." His smile looked
to have shifted to his eyes too.

"No way!" A thump onto the forest floor was accompanied
by a cry at the loss.

"What do you mean?" Lev patted his comrade's back as
Arminius raised his head before the fire and answered,

"He's beaten me by a day!"

"What—?!" The entirety of the squad rose, stunned by his
unveiling.

"Quiet down," Colt was summoned from behind, shielded by
the rustling of the nightly leaves.

"Movement in the treelines." He whispered towards the blaze.

Until their breaths were silenced so far that they could be
mistaken for the dead, the chatter extinguished. But so luckily,
Julien's clever realization replied,

"Keep talking."

"Staying too quiet will only alert whoever's out there." His
judgement was sound.

Turning to Gin with a mischievous smirk, Lev responded,

"Uh, I guess…"

What the brute had not expected, only as the Rus brought his
hands into a cone over his mouth, he sat and let the devil take his
comrade's thoughts to idiocy,

"Gin's fly's undone—!"

As a bash by the fist like hail smashed into Lev's skull, the
lancer crashed to the ground with his arms slacked and the back
raised. Whilst the turn of the mild talks spun into a show of
comical resuscitation of the background, Arminius tapped Colt
on the shoulder as they made for the sentry.

"Arber, Károly. With me." Cautiously crouching, he told them.

The three by the camp behind, though with only two pairs of working eyes, they curiously peered past the post into the abyss which howled with a bleak breeze creeping from the night. Their feet were fleeting. In a file, the lancers and the lieutenant slid onto the raised step of the small fort and took cover beneath a fern green tarp.

"Here." Colt lifted the rifle leaning against the post for Arminius.

Who looked through, searching for the creature lurking that the sentry had spotted, Arminius aimed about in an arc. It was a while that as Arber aided his captain steadily, the foes were not yet found. Agitation bred impatience. For nearly thrice, Arminius locked his finger on the trigger when the branches bounced or the sight of the changing shadows alerted him.

"Where is he..." He mumbled, gliding his hands along the stock oiled by his sweat.

Then a shine in the bushes took their watch. Arminius lowered the barrel and pointed for the obscured shade over the texture of leaves that seemed most unnatural and often shifting.

"Should we ring the bell?" Károly suggested but was shutted by another's finger on his lips.

"That'll alert everyone and everything in this forest." Arminius calmly denied.

"Who knows how many have infiltrated already..."

To Alexandria, who knelt down with her wrist on her knee, he returned a glance.

"You and Gin should warn the other sentries." Pointing at the louder brute, Arminius advised, never an order.

Which with a nod, the girl launched from the sentry and dashed for the campfire as a quick circle of a finger drew Gin to quieten his bothering voice. And in opposing directions on the river bank, with and against the fleeting flow, the lancers set for their distant allies hinged together by the ropes and bells. But there remained the lone soldier whose Confederate standard was shown. Whatever he pleased, the troop spied and noted from trunks of trees. Perhaps they had thought that the noise of the camps would drown his own before his return to the headquarters wherever it may be. Was he gravely wrong.

"What are we gonna do with him?" Colt asked, taking charge of the rifle whilst Miklós had the Confederate's head behind his sights.

"Capture him. We could interrogate the scout." Arber placed a hand on Colt's shoulder and proposed.

"Are you sure?" Arminius remained fixated on the lone predator stalking the woods.

"Do you want to give up any chances of gaining information?" To the captain, Arber settled the plan.

At his hands clenching, Arminius peered down. He wondered if it would break the bonds that tied him to his code of honor. Controlling his breath, the soul in the heart stabilized. His doubts were glued to him. Yet with Arber's conscience dragging step by step, it could not be avoided that his own was altered on that second of decision.

"Károly," Hesitantly, the archer was called.

"Try not to kill him if you can make the shot." Arminius gave him the passage.

"Mm!" Károly, the lieutenant, noted from one of a lower rank.

He had his bow dipped. And at an arc, it was passed sideways to fit through the space between the tarp and wall. Károly's breath began to beat in a rhythm. As a barbed arrow was nocked on the bowstring, his fingers relaxed on the draw.

Thirty...thirty-five...forty... The lieutenant counted until his stance was in place, and his vision was upon the imaginary tube that reached for the soldier's shoulder.

Half his contained breath he exhaled. Then before the strength would snap, Károly released his hand and a short burst of air blasted open the tarp, alerting the scout whose pupils narrowed on the edge of death. The feathered arrow whistled through the leaves and branches, sending a small gust of wind close to its tail. In a vortex, it struck before the Confederate could dodge. And in unbearable agony, he fell, as gushes of blood ushered from his wound. Unable to unbind the arrow that was enslaved by his flesh, the soldier began to crawl from the lancers of Aelon hurrying to his aid. Groaning and wheezing as his hands clawed at the forest floor, a strike by the butt of a rifle threw him into a limbo.

Midnight was nearing. The moon behind the thin slates of gray had reached the apex brightened by the splatters of declining blue and red lights. Rallied to the fire under the untouchable gods merely watching from their paradise, the squad rotated their sentry. Though they desired rest, it was hopeless. Even so far that they could flee, the screams chased them. As a sharp horror pierced the air, Julien flinched whilst the torturers were unstopping in the drive for thriving pain.

"I already told you, I don't know anything—argh!" The scout endured when Arber tore another finger out of its joint.

The index dangled from the chair's arm as the Confederate prayed with his trembling words.

"Isn't that enough? He doesn't know a thing." Arminius raised his voice as he held his comrade by the arm.

From eyeing the next finger along the hand, Arber stopped and faced the other with a cool expression that had no remorse or wrath. It was simply blanked that no one of his age should have portrayed.

"Would you think that I'm doing this for fun?" He replied, holding the third finger.

"This is all for the sake of victory." Arber told to the crackling of bones and a scream.

Kneeling before the Confederate, the lancer watched his face twist as his lips were split from his bite in torment.

"Besides," On passing a glimpse to Arminius, he woke him from the false fantasies of wars,

"I wouldn't believe a word until we break his wrists."

For the soldier pushing his weight on the fourth limb of the first hand, Arber shuffled closer to who appeared more likely his own victim.

"What was your purpose? Where is your main army?" The soldier of Aelon continued the interrogation.

The terror shorn for Arminius to witness. His eyes could not water knowing that such were these peoples of the Confederacy that drove a stake in his heart two years ago. Unable to stir fate in elsewhere, he looked on, to the man's slides of tears and blood.

"Edz loudzoy…dïvïmy myanaj jaežlaebj…(Please…gods save me…)" He begged in Rus.

"Myanae Katja…edz edzmyoy vjnjeadz pejdeÿajs…(My Katya…I'm all she has…)" The soldier wept.

But Arber was without naivety as his hands tore sideways. The fracture of the joints pulled for the butcher forced a damning tug and ripped the bone of its socket. A cry for mercy again, so mind-broken that his voice broke, resounding through the forest when the screams could travel far at night.

"Arber! He's broken!" Arminius repeated his plea.

A wave of light took his hand and ushered him to reality once more. There was clearness and cluelessness in his inhuman self that shook awake whilst his soul had been stolen by his torturing. What of the past in his memories flushed into his library of the mind. The bayonets of the earth littered without bounds. He saw an eruption of fluids. Then a shock cleared the scattered flesh to the misted image of a girl. Of his same midnight blue eyes.

"Arber!" There was a call for him again.

As he met the glare of Arminius, panting from the shouts, Arber spread his hand. Drawing a canal in the leakage of blood, like a dish of soup with jittering tendons and veins, he flicked his fingers dry.

"Arminius…"

"Is it true that your only goal is to realize a dream?" Arber's curiosity impaled the change of air, from the shades that seeped into the tent.

"Or is it to win this war?" The lancer asked.

"What are you trying to get at?" Arminius stilled on the spot, deepening his tone.

Closing his eyes a good sigh released, of the rewarding sensation that he had predicted well on Arminius' traditionalist dream.

"I spoke with Julien on our journey here." told Arber, glaring into his comrade's eyes.

Leaning back, Arminius sensed it an honest attack.

"Shouldn't we all make the necessary sacrifices even if it means to cause suffering?" Arber advanced onwards.

A knife was taken from its sheath and aimed at the sobs of the soldier for his fingers in a croaking voice, sludged in his throat, the blade circled over his neck.

"I noticed something in Akülunnarchs." told Arber to the tensing grit of Arminius' teeth.

"The way you fought wasn't how we saw you train." He mentioned.

The lancer weakened his grip on the hilt and spun it towards his captain's eyes. But Arminius never retreated. As he stared below to the shorter comrade, his spirit enflamed. To the rocking of the chair and body, to and fro, whilst the Confederate's eyes were indefinite fountains, the allies stood in a standoff.

"It was recklessness. But you were limiting yourself." Arber warned him, lowering the knife.

"The Confederates couldn't have stood a chance—"

The torment of the past rushed to the hive of the consciousness as the tides of fury bent a wire that held his temper. Whilst the glitters of lightning caught an ember in an eye, Arminius clenched a fist and blasted,

"Then did you think I should've waited and watched as our allies were slaughtered?!"

"W-We were fighting a battle of attrition that Nikola would've never won!" In breaking words, he was shaking in short bursts.

"Don't fuck around. This isn't a game of chess." Arber denounced, monotonically, the other to a limit before ignition.

"If I had known you weren't suited for war—"

"You don't want me to hold back right?!" Aloud, Arminius checked his comrade, that where the sentry and squad were wearily waiting, bouncing their knees and tapping their heels, they readied to interrupt.

"Then I'll prove it here!" He snatched the blade from Arber's hand and raised the knife above his head.

With a short grunt, the plummet like a vortex from the tip that swirled the slashed air rocketed into the tortured hand. Cleanly, two fingers bounded off its bones and plopped onto Arber's boots. Wailing, as if a grand battery of howitzers were fired, the Confederate's body seemed to have jumped from the pain. The chair with the soldier tipped and crashed, kicking and screaming, leaning for his hand that was firmly roped to the arm. More blood squirted from there than the breaks of fingers before. Arber peered down, lacking tones of emotions, and kicked away the sagging limbs as he spotted his comrade storming for the wilderness. But madly, Arminius' hands were quivering.

A calm breeze sailed to the camp of disturbed expressions. Perplexed by the happenings in the chamber of the torturers, the bawls and few whimpers filled them with what their ears could have only heard. Yet none could bear any guilt to simply ask. The yells seemed to have ceased. Perhaps the elites' victim had lost his voice. As the fires brightened when the shadow of an approaching soldier held the winds by his back, the moon shifted sluggishly into its decline. Clutching his shaking hands, he shuffled into the ring around the flames, kicking and sliding over the leaves on the march.

"Anything?" Lev asked lightly and peculiarly politely.

Fearing that he would not stand if he sat, Arminius held his hands by the fire and warmed the blood in the creases of his palms to dry.

"Not yet—"

But so fatedly, the curtained doorway of the tent flapped aside and the last lancer rushed to inform his squad with the usual unsurprised tint of his eyes,

"We need to get to the general."

Bells' dark ringing. The alert passed by one ear to the other through the old man's head whose scroll was upon his face. His first aide moved aside the cup of half-drunk coffee as a major ran his eyes along a ledger. Locked by a crisis, the staff sprung to their feet and gathered what might to widen their eyes. The forest and its city had awoken. Troops marching and the shouts of officers hurried to the roll calls. To the alarm so immediate many found themselves barely dressed in the warming woods. Soon sentry by sentry, the barrels raised and rested on the logs. Rifles loaded by the snaps of their bolts and bullets and the trigger on a soft hold of the finger. Nudging the general, Florek awoke him to the rude soundings of afar.

"What is it…?" Who had slept lightly, Warneńczyk lifted the paper from his face and shivered from the gust that found its path into the dully headquarters.

The curtains flicked and the sucking air turned the flames of the open lanterns, like puppets, to three lancers on the entrance. Their feet stamped and positioned in the form of a chevron. The leader saluted for the elites.

"Report, sir!" Arminius released his aching shoulder and eased his stance apart.

"And I presume you are Arminius Reichner." Warneńczyk fitted his beret and greeted.

"Want a drink to wake you up?" He thoughtfully offered.

Holding his hand flatly, Arminius kindly declined with a puzzled grin and continued,

"We've successfully captured and interrogated a scout around two hours ago."

Warneńczyk disbanded his drunken behavior and in an uncanny change to a serious demeanor, he leaned nearer the desk with fists holding up his chin.

"Vasilevsky's army's stationed five leagues east of here, across the river." The lancer informed the cadre that held every officer on the spot.

Their hands drew to their sides with whatever pencils or pins that they were to plan with. The blunt falls of tools filled the core of the army. If it was true, to the inner circle around the general, the predicament had invaded too far.

"That's within the range of their batteries..." Warneńczyk considered.

"If I were them, my main force would've already begun advancing through the forest." Julien added to the response of the general again,

"Under the cover of night and the woods..."

"In other words, they are planning for an all-out assault on the town." Arber suggested.

Yet for the silence to have gone, a brief chuckle came as Warneńczyk stood. He gave the table and the map two taps. And it seemed the machines of the force's brains were revived in reverse. They pulled the pins and scratched the markings of any plans. There began the clearance of evidence that the many prayed to the gods would not find its way into Confederate hands.

"Hoh, Leonid. I did account for this." Boastfully, Warneńczyk told.

"However, this does mean for Kolchakov's theater will soon follow—"

"Not soon, sir." Arminius interrupted that gently closed the elder's mouth.

The lancer took his hands to his side and breached his formalities by allowing himself onwards. He boldly reached the desk without command until the boy had to look up for the taller general.

"The scout had mentioned Vasilevsky was the last to position." quietening, Arminius closed his report.

Inching towards his general, a subordinate's tone whitened that then not the light of lamps could console. The pages in his hands glided free from his fingers and slipped to the table's underside.

"T-That can't be..." The lower colonel stammered, waiting for Warneńczyk's genius to save them.

However the old man's look was not so frightened as the aides of the camp were. He sat. Clasped together, his hands were in every calm gesture. Fingers rolling around knuckles and feet tapping the grass who were not tense but carrying the impatience of excitement. As if he had expected so far that unexpected happening too, Warneńczyk glared ahead.

"Just like the days of the Reich on the porch of Leken..." He recalled a history never experienced.

"Their blitz intends to catch us unarmed."

The lancers kept their will steady whilst Ascot's face worn down. Warneńczyk rested his arms and leaned against the chair, meditating with a few sighs nonetheless. The headquarters were thrown into shambles. They were restricted by the atmosphere, picking their pencils from the ground but it was nothing to be contributed to the war effort.

"We must hold the Wanal!" Stunning his comrades, Florek raised a speech in what patriotic enthusiasm the young man had.

"They cannot be by the Udor at the week's end—"

As the aide was to gather any more morale, he discerned the climate of the quarters. Sagging, the hope had diminished. All before the Confederacy, the titan, continuing its stampede across the world. The defeats had come to strike the closest subordinates. They may have witnessed a thousand failures in the two years of battles. And no human could comprehend such losses.

"You know it is impossible, Jacek." The general noted, shutting his eyes as he spoke for his men.

"We have thirty five armies of three and a half million on this front."

With the loudening rumbles and whirls from the sky and land of machines, the elder held the desk and peered up.

"What can *they* achieve against forty contingents and eight million—?"

An explosion rattled the tent, sending the officers and lancers to one knee and arms over their heads. But Warneńczyk had not. The pillar quaked with the ground. Scents of a cursed kei layered the canopy of the forest that was unavoidable. Volleys of fire banged from the near distant hills.

"W-Were those howitzers...?" Julien faltered, standing with Arber's hold around his arm.

On the second wave of shocks swaying the curtains, Arminius raced out of the shelter to the command's park on a square that watched over the city below. As the officers rose, the slit of the doorway contained the sights of the lancer grinding his boots to halt his body. The road was not struck. But the rubble of old attacks barricaded any convoys from ascending. Through the rows of dereliction, above, the shells, like winged stallions with fine white tails, flew. From afar, the smoke revealed the Confederate's measured advance. The dust storm from the charge and the war cries. And of course, the stench of the Summer Lion was there too.

Between the sizzling barrels and smoke of giants that polluted the air in a smog of grayness, the vice general raised his arm with a flare gun for the setting moon.

"Rzhev! Break their will!" Over the pounding, yelled Vasilevsky whose echo was found in Arminius' ear.

A red flare in the night sky popped and sparked into clouds of lighting. Across the valley, the voices of the Confederates aimed for the descent into a new battle. The union of the soldiers terrorized the forward redoubts and in seconds, the line trapped and stalled by the river to their backs were pending to fall.

A flurry of meteors from hell rained above his head. Blasting before and behind, two waves of fire roared beside as spheres of flames engulfed the town. Smoke, as thick as tar, and a scent of burning flesh twisted around Arminius. What few feeble shots in the dark did little when the Aelon resorted to a counter charge. But against the pyroclastic flow of troops, they were simply devoured by the blades and lead.

"We have to return!" Julien jogged for him as Arber followed.

"They won't be able to hold out!"

Overlooking the river of stumbling allies, the bank was overrun by the onslaught of the human wave. Mercy, as the soldiers had seen, was not granted. And in a fate worse than the disgrace of being amongst the corpses crushed into the soil, the drownings were in masses.

"Before that, Carlstadt, open your eyes." Warneńczyk pointed at the through arched bridge, held by a single squad.

In a crushing defense at a blockade, the only checkpoint choked the Confederates' spearhead. Releasing the flow of those in total retreat, they fought bitterly until the threat was no more a shadow and was the fiend that stormed the roads.

"I did not think that bridgehead was to last." The general thought.

"But the armies should have decided to issue a retreat as well—"

Florek placed a black flare in Warneńczyk's hands who snapped open the chamber of a worn flare gun. The bronze ornamentations were majestically illuminated by the razed roofs and weeds of fire. Loading the colored shell, he clicked the barrel into its lock and raised the gun to the air. But as his finger shifted from the guard to the trigger, there was a shout for him,

"Emergency, general!"

A tragedy-bringing messenger, carrying the banner of the king rushed over the dip in the hill. As Warneńczyk lowered his gun, the soldier slid to the pavement and dropped his head.

"Another report…"

"What is it this time?" asked the general, ready for another disaster to be heard.

With tears and cold sweat watering on the corners of his eyes, hardly holding a salute, the messenger delivered, shivering,

"T-The capital, Warsau has fallen!"

XV

28 JULYUS 491
28.07.12017

Julien Carlstadt

Since the outbreak of war, the Confederates' advance was slow. It was as if they had been checked by something holding their necks. Now, Leken had to be abandoned. If Aelon cannot stand against the horde, then how many more years will it take for the Confederacy to fall like the Reich? This Blitzkrieg. It should have never worked against a united...front...

Then...unless...our defenses were shattered to begin with...

Has it been for the past two and a half years? Had no one recovered our armies? Were the Confederates too immune to our resistance... too weak?

Anything would mean nothing for Grand Marshal Kolchakov. Everything we've done up to this point was just to delay the inevitable. I'm sure Arminius should've realized it by now too, but our forces are too divided. Communications are barely functionable. We're sitting in the dark surrounded by hunters we cannot see. It'd take a miracle to halt their advance...even for a day...

CHAPTER
16

A BREAK IN THE PACES

Not one hour was there to levitate their spirits. Like the differences between a good dream and a bad. The restless pushes, day and night, hurried the Winged Lance in a retreat by a pace of twenty hard hours a day. The march became a crawl. Starved. Unsleeping. No matter, its soldiers sailed and shuffled for the Udor. But Warneńczyk's desperate face told them that his own men had to halt the Confederates' growing drive.

It was the day after the fall of Warsau, and the defeat of the Wanal. Convoys of barges glided down a river where its banks were guarded by the angelic winged hussars, glimmering in shining armor even in the deadly rays beneath the nightmarish sun. Soaring, the heat had dried the lands. The river could not be passed as the hulls of the boats rammed against the bed. And so, they took to the ground but there were yet two hundred leagues before them.

The soils had started to boil and crack. Struck by a drought. Its people of the country in the valley of death watched the withdrawal drag. Saving chants of pushing their resolve, snacks were offered but the old farmers needed them more to survive the high summer. The able locals pledged their arms. Of fathers and daughters, mothers and sons, they banded to aid. And those still hesitant had found to be with the escape too, from the invaders of the east. But their minds were plagued daily such as though at that time, so far, Arminius could turn back. There would be fighters like flies circling over the churches and homes. The smoke rising in the fierce weather. What of the innards of the city were drained and a shell of the corpse remained.

As the days pressed, the Confederates who gave chase had halted in a wait for their frontlines to reach. Set upon by the underworld's awakening, the once great river that spanned twenty five paces devolved into no more than a gentle stream that even the littlest, like Károly, could traverse without his legs being swept from balance. It was the thirtieth day of Julyus. Heatwaves seeped out of the fissures in the earth as the squad journeyed in the stroke of water. Their boots splashed about. But there was no worry that their feet would wet for the depths were shallow. Whose ears were ringing, hallucinating of water, iced from the rivers of Sibir, Arminius and Julien led in the elites' vanguard as something kept their minds sane.

"Your turn..." Arminius huffed, dazed by the scorch.

He leaned on the hilt of his sword, but it sizzled so horrifyingly that Arminius' hands instinctively flicked off.

"Then, cannon to green five three." Julien replied, but he appeared undisturbed by the baking air.

Chess, however tedious the idea whom one had given was, they had done so for the past three days. In the windless valley that saw rare flourishes of warm breezes, it was not that they needed any more heat on their skin.

"Dat's dull..." Gin groaned, dragging his legs across the sand.

"It might be for some useless eater." Colt weakly mocked, but his chuckle could not sound.

I can't... Mumbling in his mind, Gin tripped and planted his face on the riverbed.

"Gin! Hold on!" Lev knelt down to douse his comrade with the trickling creek.

Dripping, his eyelashes flicked a streak of sweat on a blink. As he rubbed his eyes, the thought of the game reminded him of Julien's voice. But Arminius could not seem to remember.

"Wanna continue tomorrow?" The latter dishonorably excused himself.

"Sure, that's if you survive another day—" Julien laughed.

As Arminius gave a sigh, in the aridness that pained his throat, there was another chasing downstream with the toppest of his lungs. Together, the two turned their heads slightly for the cry and wondered whom it may have been that held so much breath. When a shadow cooled their backs, and with a breeze brushing the sweat beneath Arminius' blouse, he saw a pair of flinging arms hoop around their necks.

"Arminius! Julien!" The soldier screamed, tugging themselves into the narrow stream that sprayed the basin on the toss of the heavenly water.

Pinned to the current washing his face, Arminius and Julien's eyes opened to the altering waves that slowed and winded around the bodies like boulders. Shielding the sun, there happened under what they thought to be a cloud. But the figure had brownish and orange hair and a bright face grinning upon them.

"Károly? What were you doing?" Calmly, Arminius asked as his senses were cooled by the stream he refused to rise from.

"Don't you wanna feel the wind striking your face as you run?" The lieutenant responded.

A drop of sweat from his chin struck Arminius' cheek whilst he rose, in clothing so drenched that a slight gust could send him into a cold. Holding his head, tarnished by what terror, wet sand, Julien pointed at the path of devastation that Károly had unfolded and asked,

"Is that why those soldiers seem weirdly mad?"

He directed his friend to those behind with foul faces and wetted uniforms. An awkward laugh was uttered. As Károly lifted Julien from the stream, the advance of their allies eager for vengeance rushed their pace before the three could escape into the columns once more. And in the chase, the ambiance shifted to the beats of the drums and quickening steps.

The valley shrunk. Encased, the ridges narrowed the plains till shadows surrounding the army stretched, by the hills and swinging trees. When the cool summer winds blew across the ranks, it felt more pleasing than seeing gold in pockets.

"We're saved..." Lev opened his arms and basked in the chilly breeze.

As if the forces of two hundred thousand mouths breathed again and sighed in relief, the chatter only grew. Then, as the lives of the Winged Lance Army recalibrated with the return of their lost souls, Arminius and Julien surveyed the lands of fields and forests. Warneńczyk looked ahead, shut from the voices of his men. He analyzed the tightening path that not only he had spotted. Wondering if he was destined to battle there.

They must know. The old general gathered, knowing the fine young warriors.

Our purpose here was never to retreat as such.

"Jacek." Turning to Florek, he signaled.

After the spiraling amber flare, the people of a small humble village widened their doors and windows, to witness the march. Two larger banners, in the first of the vanguard were raised for all to see. The Lekann winged hussars, whose valkyrie-like wings spread as if for take off; and the standard flag of the common white and red. As the army halted beyond the gates, their chief approached Warneńczyk and knelt. But Arminius could not make out the words except for a pledge to their king named August.

How does he have this much authority? Arminius thought, watching the elderly men exchange conversations.

It wasn't just here. Nikola's army too...

When the bells rang and the folk were told, the village scattered on the command. Taking whatever belongings they found to have use, and bringing away the refugees who had the brief hospitality of the Winged Lance Army, the retreat of innocent hamlets in the valley was dispatched by a hundred-man escort.

By the hand of Warneńczyk, his troops assimilated themselves with the rugged streets and toughened homes. The afternoon came and the wagons were unloaded. The settlements of Da Vinci guns, whose bodies were like organs, as the nine barrels of each were assembled. Woodlands steered away as the eifers cleared the land for stakes and barricades of a short wall in a perimeter. And it was natural for the general's headquarters to have rested on its throne on a hill. He overlooked the encampment with ease and to the furthest bank across the valley grounds. With the ditch of a drained river, a hundred thousand men marched for five leagues north. They held the same banners. But none had been told what their purpose was. For as Arminius hammered the last nail of a tent, he stared into the storm of dust that had risen for the clouds.

Nightfall went. The braziers, scattered across the camp, diminished. Ash chased the crisp leaves falling. For another day, the rising air was born again. There were no marches. No calls of names or the addresses of ranks. Yawning, the sentries on the short battlements held the guns with peeling paint. Though there was no telling what the enemy could perform aside their sights. Beside the intruding creatures of humanity, the forests wavered hoping that yet another axe's swing would not disturb their kingdom. As the grass of the plains and crops of the field had not revived from the yellowing curse, the trickles of the stream could finally be heard. Their river had swelled under the white blots drifting in the eternal sky. And soon, when the army arose, they were greeted by the hand of serenity.

In the morning hours, it was usual for the general to wake early and gather his studies. His senile face was the only in the headquarters. Alone. With a single book, of a cover of an iron cross, keeping him company. Then for hours until the common soldiers would rise, he would sit and sip his sour coffee. The sun, glaring sharply past the breathing slits of the doorway, reminded him of his duty. As he shut the text and lowered his glasses, Florek and Ascot passed the exiting general on a stroll to the ridge's watch. Beneath, the path along the bank, was there a wandering pair.

The two offered themselves to the peace of a small pier. Narrow and shallow, it dipped into the slow flowing river. Sparkling, the bumping ripples diverted from the shore like curious fish. As the winding path was concealed by the length of reeds, Arminius and Julien rolled up their pants, and together, slid onto the edge. Their legs dangled above the current where it was at times enough to brush their bare feet. But soon for Arminius' mouth itched to hold something, he removed his cigarette box and tapped a smoke free of the pack. With one flick, a match was thrown alight and lit the roll of herbs. Burning leisurely, its scent of tea leaves streamed towards Julien's nose.

"You should stop..." Quietly, his inevitable remark turned Arminius' head as he swung his legs.

"Quit nagging." Puffing a thin layer of smoke, Arminius flicked the fading match into the water.

"You're not my mom..." It became a mumble.

As the writhing awkwardness spiraled to their bodies, the certain calm found time. Gazing at the myriad of flowers and the waving lone tree behind the bridge, it was rare to have enjoyed such sight in a war of no rest. There needed not to be words. Poems by the scene formed. The illustrations of the sweeping vines over the other bank. What a welcoming atmosphere that they could spend till old.

"I'd do anything to escape the north." Julien spoke softly, clamping the pier's planks but beware of splinters.

"To here. Or any place warmer."

As the wind took a sudden change, the river fought in a war of its own. One wave downstream and the ripples splashing against the beast. Dabbing his toes on the ever shifting surface, Arminius felt his feet shudder.

"You might like it in Bäuwar." He piqued the Danne's interest.

"I'm sure—"

"Come to Hünnzhar too!" None had detected him before the cheery archer attacked his comrades with his strangling hold.

"Finally awake?" Arminius clutched the lieutenant's head to free himself of the struggle.

As he was pulled nearer the edge to the water mirroring his smile, Károly released the two and straightened his back of the soreness. Stretching, his lungs loosened into a chuckle.

"Grandpa said I'll only grow taller if I sleep for longer." said he, naively, still in belief of old folk tales.

"Don't worry, you still have time." Arminius reassured.

"You're not much shorter than *him*." He pointed for Julien whose face declined into a slight frown.

With the pat on the pier, invitingly, Arminius offered a seat beside. To the affable gesture, the third of the band tossed his boots to the foot of the slope and rocked the infirm dock on his leap to the seat. He kept a sign of looser tenderness. For the same ridge they admired together, and the hill tops of the distance, their backs seemed fitting. Whilst one sighed, another would. The bond of some and few days could not have been so sure and strong. Like young neighboring friends, there were no stutters in the chatter.

"Sure is nice being able to laze in war." Károly muttered, widening his arms with no care for his comrades.

"Soak it up while we can." Peered away with eyes of disdain flicked onwards at the battlements, Arminius groaned.

"Just wait till it's our turn on guard." The troop snapped the harmony.

"It can't be *that* bad." Julien convinced them but they did not seem to have been.

The three shadows had a similar tone of kei. They seemed oddly untensed and appreciative of the world. Towards the wind, their faces held uncaring for anything beyond what they could sense. As Károly puffed his cheeks to hold a gasp of country air, he leaned back, dropping onto the pier, with his eyes closing. Sighing, taking in the sunlight whilst the sky was still emptied of clouds. For long, his daydreaming was uninterrupted. Until a tap on his stomach shivered him.

"Huh?" Károly asked with no notice.

"Look!" Arminius excitedly called out, pointing at the waters.

Searching around, Julien leaned ahead. But he found nothing but the regular churning pebbles, roughed back and forth. Yet the stubbornness was short lived. And Károly, who could not hold his curiosity any longer, sprung upright and reached ever more outwards from the pier.

"What is it? What is it?" The archer repeated.

Then, as Arminius distanced himself from the tide, his hands were placed on their backs. Too soon they had realized. After a shove pushed them into the river, two yelps cried before the crash. By the rise of Julien and Károly over the flow, a faint, sweet laugh in their clogged ears was like a mumble.

"That was for yesterday, Károly—" Arminius smirked, lifting the cigarette from his lips when four hands latched onto Arminius' shirt.

His mouth gaped and a short cry spat the smoke into the stream. Tugged for the drenching vengeance, Arminius was dunked into his own mischief. The spout of the fall sprayed the bridge and banks. Planks of the dock, once too light and dusted, were splattered by washing waves. The splashes of the joy revealed its colors that divine day, caught in the eyes of the overseer.

From the tent, Florek trailed a path of pressed grass with a map rolled beneath his arm. The specks of bugs, not often hordes, glided wherever the gusts pleased as the march terrorized the front meadow. Warneńczyk, the colonel aide spotted, rested on the slanted fence line where the ridge provided good sights over the three. Though with a duty, his desiring inquisitiveness brought him under another purpose. For the general he approached. He followed the old man's pointing nose and found the lancers and lieutenant skipping and chasing in the sparkling turquoise. His questions for what it may be that kept Warneńczyk so engrossed were answered by as brief a happening.

"They act as if they have known each other since the day they were born." Wearing his kepi, Florek thought.

His eyes were somber. Drowned in the past which he could not flush away. For Warneńczyk seemed despairing upon being reminded of what dread worse than war.

"They did." He worded that pressed Florek's brows.

Waving a glance at the general, the colonel aide cleared his throat and steadied his expression.

"I do not doubt your grandson's ability." Florek mentioned that turned the general towards him.

"But Reichner and Carlstadt..." The man named Károly's comrades but as he presented his face, his eyes were fixed elsewhere.

"You seem to have put your faith with them so soon."

From the fence, Warneńczyk lifted himself and rose higher than his aide. Gazing at the elites whose fires of the camp drew a slim line of smoke to be joined with the sea overhead. Ahead, the three children of tragedy climbed ashore. For a minute, the elder could not see them. Yet the worry that they had disappeared was foolish. When the soldiers arose from the hidden dip of the river bank, his soul entered a clam in the blankness.

"Hmph, it is only natural for the blood they carry." Warneńczyk exhaled, scratching his chin.

"To have faith in them. For my soldiers to have faith in I." Wisely and softly, he lectured the younger.

"Or it would be no more another *Protectorate*."

In circles though the old general spoke that Florek brightly understood, the officers watched for the trio's safe return before they spun away. Taking his trusted flask that poured warm wine into his mouth, Warneńczyk blended the bitter mixture between his teeth. Shuddering, his mind had revisited the present.

"Ah, Jacek, what was it?" He asked as they headed.

"The radio's collapsed, just a few minutes ago." Florek delivered, sliding the roll of a map from his arm for his commander.

"Seventeenth; eighteenth. Lost all contact as well."

"So, Pusnnann and Krakau have fallen…" Warneńczyk analyzed as his voice faded into the chaotic cheers and deafening laughter of the squad.

Until the four days from then, everyday, the sears of red meat from hares and hapless deers flooded the plates that Károly gained. In his hunt for game, so much so was donated to near comrades and the headquarters on its nature's throne. As Julien learnt the bow, the law of the sword was taught for the archer. From wrestling their prey, they would be smeared by dry mud. The elites would shake their heads and recover what spoils of victory the three gained in the day whilst the nights would fly like chariots of the glorious daughter of Luna.

In the dark of the third sun of Auzhustus, the campfire was at a mild blast. Restrained by a ring of wet leaves and rocks around the flames, the pyramidic blazes ushered against one point of the meat which scorching fats rolled like wildfire. To Julien's helpless dislike, Arminius gushed a thicker mist from his mouth. But it was an odd combination that smelled of coffee and tea. As Lev burnt every cut of the hard-earned venison, Alexandria stayed to her corner, steaming potatoes delicately wrapped in herbs.

"Lev, how are you gonna become a cook at this rate?" Colt asked, waving a mug of fruits, risking poison, and rum.

"It's just a little black." Lev poked the reptile-like block of meat and offered a taste for Arminius.

"Here!" He showed it to a comrade who leapt closer to Károly.

"N-No thanks." Arminius awkwardly rejected, holding up his palm against him who insisted he tried it.

Pushing the hand with the knife for the lieutenant, the lancer had prayed that his friend could be tricked. But in a swift maneuver, Károly swiped the chunk of meat, no less a piece of charcoal, and frighteningly dared chew it.

"Your cooking's getting better, Lev—" That was hardly a lie, Károly encouraged as by the devil's luck, he choked.

"You really can eat anything." Julien patted his back.

Around, his fond comrades were too drunk for any meaningful chatter. Perhaps the joy was the purpose itself. Such nights had always been too quick for Arminius, whose memories were not so easy to forget these minutes in time of hells' doors waiting beyond the walls. Remnicizing of home, the embrace of safety placed on his shoulders. Taking another sip and watching Károly cough up the wasted venison that had not been punctured once by teeth marks, Arminius could not help but spurt a laugh at his friend's clumsiness. Yet there was one touch alien to the atmosphere within the fort.

Ever since the lights over the walls had enlarged, Arminius would glimpse on occasion at the canvas swashed by a gradual rise of colors. The cycle of the soldiers on the battlements pressed against their guns as they stared at the heightening chants and deepening thumps of a march. Nudging those around him, the squad captain could not dismiss the crackles of thousands of torches paired by cries lasting a thousand years. The bellow of war drums beated. The chiming of bells. A flare of an unwanted amber reversed all smiles.

XVI

2 AUZHUSTUS 491
02.08.12017

Arminius Reichner

An archer from Balaton. His talent shows. He once struck a boar across the forest, something I could never match even with a rifle. It humiliates me to say that someone who had been born a day after had already fought in two wars. There's no doubt that he's more experienced than we are. Maybe Károly's the arrow we desperately needed in this squad for the elites to be complete.

Being around him has always reminded me of something that would distract me from the world. Because of his immaturity and comfort that doesn't fit his actions. But aren't we all? Aren't we all as childish? He wants to become the greatest archer, which is only my own dream no matter whatever way we pursue it.

I guess that would explain the familiar scents that I know I should've detected before...

Ever since he joined us, both their names have rung even louder. As if two puzzle pieces have collided and formed an image before me. It's vague but familiar. I feel like a child who's forgotten everything where not even the slightest hint can get rid of this annoyance of not knowing.

I can't seem to...remember...regardless of the joy in knowing that I could've met them earlier...

CHAPTER

17   GATHERING STORM

"All units! To the battlements!" Florek commanded in the general's stead.

Slumping like a rocking ship, Colt drunkenly looked on. Before him, the distorted twists of the luminous flares were casted in his drooping sights. His eyes were unevenly open when Arminius dragged him for the tent.

"Haargh! Dey're 'ere!" Gin stomped into their quarters with filling glee.

The lancers and lieutenant scrambled for their uniforms. Fitting their caps and flicking their cloaks over shoulders and arms. As Károly tossed the arsenal of swords and spears to the elites tightened by the clock, Arminius grabbed the last rifle of the squad upon the buckling of his belt. Together, their hands were armed. Amidst the flustering fort, the force of nine were first to emerge to the hiking strain. Through the doorway of curtains flicking for their passage to battle, the squad entered the open. Where there was never a bang of rusting chains from metallic creatures, their minds minded not what eerie emptiness there was above. But the might over the walls could still taunt the warriors with the clanging of steel.

"Lancers! Lieutenant!" In the settled wind that was absorbed by the clamors, Warneńczyk roared for, that sent a gale by the prowess of his voice in the descent along the hill.

Curling his finger, with one hand hidden on his back, the general ordered for their ascent. By his word, the squad abided. With a kick in the dirt, the surge slain the fire. As the steep ridge of a winding slope led the elites, the headquarters gradually rose from the earth and over the brow, the beret then the kepi were seen.

"General!" Stamped onto a hold in formation, only Arminius had saluted.

Whilst Warneńczyk returned a Lekann greeting, he strayed from the safety of the homely hill. Patting the lancer's shoulder the old man led onwards for the edge.

"Come." told the general, waving Florek begone.

His staff hasted. As if all were in competition to outperform another. The rustles of paper and the calls for messengers. It was that every half a minute, a new runner would depart and be replaced by their comrades. The thundering of distant hooves traveled the front in complete unity, from wall to wall and the revealing gates. Arminius stared at the tempest of the command. To the dictators of battle.

"Jacek!" Warneńczyk ordered.

A wagon of a bell tower in the distant opening was rolled by one man alone. To the underside of the pyramid like the Kuschites of the southern continent, it was scaled. Holding the string of a hammer, Florek held his stand on the ladder. And with the nod of the general, the bell tolled and the five blaring bellows had the attention of the brave hundred thousand. For the winds had dived in politeness, and the soldiers were still, their eyes and the minds of Terra gazed at Warneńczyk. His feet reached beyond the steps. The ground fractured beneath him. But he could not give so much care for his own life as the guardian of the kingdom.

"First, fourth, fifth, and ninth legions!"

Reaching forward for the wash to the north that joined the nearest stream, his eyes darkened with the glare of a haunting beast.

"To the Sorrmul! We, the shield, shall serve the august king!" A boom of his voice jolted glass and shattered the heap of windows.

The men cheered in the eruption of glamorous shards. With their blades waving and tall banners swinging in arcs, the forces of the protector charged in the swoop of the releasing ropes on gates. Forward, they forged the preludes of a frontline before the Confederates who had come nearer. As the elites pondered how the brawl would ensue, a lancer crashed their thoughts.

"Gramps! What're we doin' up 'ere?" Gin asked.

"Shouldn't us elites be down on de frontlines?" Eagerly for a chance to storm the grounds of war, the brute punched his chest as his comrades' voices were with him.

Warneńczyk gave a mergence of a sigh and a chuckle.

Hooking his fingers around his belt, the general pushed his thumb till it could go no deeper as it released the weight on his lungs.

"I had thought you would ask that, Calenzo." The general simply filled the interlude to his answer.

Pinching the wearing leather, a slab was pulled from the interior. He held it before him and rubbed the decayed piece free to glide.

"Certainly, you would have been stationed at the tip of the vanguard if this was a battle of attrition." Warneńczyk explained whilst the single chant of the concluded formation layered the left plains.

"But we are not Adrien Nikola." Held up a finger, it paused the lancers and lieutenant.

The Confederates seeped through the gaps. There the silence of rifles remained in the crowds of unsheathing blades. The unsettling tension of the two armies like plates were about to quake on the clash. Yet they almost seemed baited within the realms of a ploy the Aelon had drafted. Arminius had not rid of the scent in trickery. From somewhere, and sometime, there must be the climax that would determine a strike in return against the vice commandant heading the Rus vanguard, in his glistening armor that reflected the flames of his commander's charring eifer.

"This was never your everyday field battle." said Warneńczyk, before the news revealed,

"For a man as lion-hearted, you must snare him in hunt of fools of Aelon."

Vasilevsky...? The squad's common burning blood bubbled.

The wings of the armies collided. Eastern and western. By the center of a flushing river, the torrent of bullets splintered on the plates of steel. Their pace to the river steadily crept. Three hundred thousand Confederates inched for the thinner ranks of the foes. On the next rising sun, the scorch returned in an unbroken torment. But beneath, the clashing maintained a will of iron. Yet the malice could not keep the defenses high. They were overwhelmed by the bullheaded superiority that forced the Rus over the bank. Knee deep in the currents, the disorderly battle became one of survival. Drawing away, the Aelon commander decided best to issue his retreat in a short defeat as in the while, the elites rested their war horses overlooking from the hill. The nine anxiously awaited for the old man to say that it was their time. The hallucinated voice was nothing in the silence of winds.

"Is gramps just gonna sit us here?!" Gin itched his head heatedly.

"Soon, Gin. Or else it wouldn't work." Julien reminded him, however quietly afflicted Arminius was.

Hoping for their blades to be wet with blood, the squad waited. Though once the yolk of the sky had set to its home under the horizon, it was sure that Warneńczyk had decided not to plunge them into the fight once more. For the fifth, the sixth, and the seventh days of Auzhustus skipped by. Allies retreated beyond the river, then retaking what they had lost. Over and over. As if there was no definite end to the slaughter. They had bore enough in the boredom. The minds of the lancers and lieutenant split between plotting to ride into battle without the general's call or to remain true to honor. That wedge, in luck, sealed by the ninth.

The sun had barely risen and the moon was retiring beneath the earth's curvature. Confederate battle drums knocked rhythmically opposed to the lightening chime of the Aelon concealing the marching troops. Most were still in high spirits on the seventh day of the clash. But the elites could not predict what was to take them into the next morning. Whether it was battle. Perhaps another damning delay. Nonetheless, none were awake to think otherwise.

Within the shroud of incense, an old Zhormannik cross hung on a rack by the arms of the tent. It was probably a spoil stolen from some poor veteran's home. But for Gin, the last Kaiser's eagle was the first symbol of the squad. Obeying the ideals of a dutiful force, the charm pendulated nearest Károly sleeping soundly. His body was flung widely in every direction, who had rested his head on Julien and his legs spread across Arminius' stomach. He treated his comrades like trees holding a hammock. Whilst at the late time when the clatters and splatters of iron and blood resumed, the elites were in whatever world they fantasized. A horn blared and a profound smash on the command's drum wobbled the ground. The shock flung a bolo tie around his chest that Julien caught strangling him and to the rudeness of his own penchant, the Danne woke. But like falling dominos, he had struck Károly on the head whose legs kicked Arminius then his cry captured the squad to waking.

"What the hell…!" Arminius flipped on the mats, rubbing his bottom rib in the awakening.

Without a need by a call, the elites rose to the drumming that halted on the last dual pound. Yawning and squirming. They flicked their blankets free of their bodies and leapt to the attention of the command repeated over at dawn.

"Get hitched and running, cavalry!" The general thundered with liveliness.

"The Confederates will not wait!"

Darting from the haven, the elites formed at the foot of the hill over the olden fires of the dark. Their hurriness flung a case of ash and dust but for the fall of the cloud, their faces and salutes were revealed amid the untouched ray of paradise.

"Understood!" To Warneńczyk, their responses matched the commander's yell as each broke for their mounts.

Reins around their hands tugged the companions over the path splashed by the slant of light. The hooves hollowly knocked. An impending charge awaiting to chariot the clash. Scaling the ridge in a cautious march, the squad readied their cramped legs for the ride into terror. Their cloaks were like those of veterans. Stained by the patches of blood. When the snorts of the horses and the growl of a brute summited its path, there the lonely elder was.

"Good morning, children." Warneńczyk greeted, pulling his hands from pockets to behind.

"Have you all rested your heads before the great turn?" He suggested with a grin that curved his mustache.

Before the general, the elites halted. The wonderment of what opportunity had come of the crumbling patience inspired their eyes. As of those thirsting for palms to be soaked in death. Unimaginable how the dystopia for a commoner unknowing of the warring youngs' desire was ever more terrible.

"Our eifers must've rusted resting for so long." Leaning his arm on Lev's shoulder, Colt smirked.

"Can we finally be let loose?!" Yet it seemed that Gin was the last to have understood the old man's meaning.

"Indeed, lancers. *And* Károly." Warneńczyk furthered to the elation of the lieutenant that the trust of his strength had arrived.

He pointed at the road, which clustered columns of infantry binded. Blinded by the walls, the contingent knew nothing of their allies and the warriors of Leken amassed in another retreat that only the headquarters could have seen. But too far they had gone beyond the river that the banks became unguarded. Trampled, the first lines of wagons and guns had submerged. Unletting for a simple victory, the Confederates pursued their arousal for a massacre. There was an aura that breathed the same air Arminius felt since the beginnings of the fort. The similar play of reeling a bait.

"You are to take up positions in the vanguard of Florek's detachment." said Warneńczyk, lowering his arm before needing to emphasize,

"But you must wait for my flare."

"When the gates open, you will fall under your autonomy on how to proceed." The scheming general blankly informed them.

"Alright!" The lieutenant mounted and exclaimed.

"I won't let you down, grandpa."

For those who could not bear not to submit a smile, the lancers followed the enthusiasm. But as the leading captured his foot on the stirrup, a chuckle of the grandfather put their wild pulses to ease,

"Hold for a minute, Károly, elites."

Arminius and Julien, from the saddle, turned their heads in a wordless reply.

"Do you not want to witness the overture of our orchestra?" Warneńczyk asked, readying his flask for the show.

There was no option in his right mind for the frail to revive another counter attack. This, past the river far, was to be the closing strike of the hammer. The Summer Lion had poise. His men could tell, by the one plunging charge across the slowing flow of shallow whiteness, that his wrists had not flicked the last card to play. Vasilevsky, who had not engaged his sword in the rotting resistance, was staunch enough not to worry himself so much. But his monstrous impatience became predictable.

"Pairing your peasants with my veterans?" The vice general

scoffed, widening his fearsome glare.

"This cannot be the last stand you hold."

Raising his arm for the turning heads of his soldiers, Vasilevsky sucked a deep hunk of air. The veins in his neck and the cage of his chest expanded whilst the mist seeping through his teeth spat into a slight work of blazes.

"Machine gun corps! Advance four hundred paces and hold!" A burst of his voice tried to equate his tutor.

"Panzer division! Support for a second rank!" The commander directed.

The mechanized beasts rolled beside the clustered duets of gunners. Tracks and the studs of soles assailed the waters. Razed barricades and war wagons crashed and crumbled. In the scorched earth, the pressing steel hurricane crossed the time of breakthrough to the failing borders of Aelon Leken. The trails in the mud thickened by blood slithered. With that fine slow down by the obstacles catching the infantry's hurried feet, the Winged Lance had reformed their ranks.

"Shields!" The frontline's officer commanded in a shout.

By the rows, the conscripted and wavering stepped two paces back. For those cladded to take the Rus ahead. From the mass, the desert-like breezes shifted over the foundations of a true iron curtain. Their tower shields stacked and burrowed. A dam of noble gendarmes stayed unmoving before the permanent terror.

"Shields?" Lev had set his heart to panic before the general.

"They won't hold against the panzers." Arber flatly thought.

"No." Warneńczyk replied to the elites' petrification.

However that he said so, the lines began to alter. The longish and irregular shape shifted. Like closing doors, the flanks pivoted by the corner and castled in a squarish hold. From the rear, there a standard block of footmen scattered their stance. They did not appear so important they needed to be protected by the headquarters pledging their souls to the caving vanguard.

"But would it not make for an absolute distraction?" Fitting a flare in his gun, Warneńczyk aimed for the battlefield.

The pop of the trigger shooting a yellow flare loosely echoed. Exploding in the air, the magnificent arc rained as if it had hit the sky's short ceiling. Squinting need be, the squad gazed closer. It did not aid their worries that the compartment of soldiers was the worst equipped force they had seen in the weeks of war. Blades were not drawn. Never was there a dab of armored garbs. But it came at the instance once Arminius sighted Károly's gleaming eyes nailed to a colonel in the force's forefront. That irregularity of the army was a conspirator of Warneńczyk's plot.

He was not so much older than Gin. And to have surpassed his eighteenth birthday days ago. The energy of how his commands skied the ranks, even in the midst of a losing battle, was peculiarly the same as a certain archer's. Of high youth was short but elevated by unembarrassed pride with short, pin black hair and a confident, handsome smile on a fair face had across him a spell of appearing younger. And bearing a necklace, it was with the insignia of an ancient retainer family.

"Let's show these cunts our silvers!" Foul-mouthed and the teacher of the Mazhiar lieutenant, that colonel cried without a need for his name.

Fanatic cultists of his sect of archers cheered in a wild bringing of the next hunting wind. As he took pose at the head of the core, he widened his footing whilst attending his ears to the barks of the Confederate hero.

"Men! Let this day be etched into the histories learned by the thousand generations!" Lunging his arm free of the reins, the vice general punched forward.

"Down with the Aelon!" A choir of roars intertwined.

Shells in volleys, discharged in surrounding sparks. The stampede, such rounds holding death's scythes, snapped across the flower meadow of corpses. Spinning lead, piercing cones forced their drilling heads into the shield wall until the cracks blasted for holes to tear apart. But though the fleet knew nothing of morals, before the race through the ranks would end upon the archers, the gaps were restored by another series of iron slabs. So thick in bulks, the tower shields had halted the lawn mowers of all wars.

"Onwards!" Thunks and chimes; the sizzles of muzzles were smeared over Vasilevsky.

"Delay your eifers!" The Aelon colonel grasped his vermillion longbow, which carried a small charm of a fox tail's fur.

"Nock!" He ordered, drawing an arrow, a length of his arms, from the quiver strung on his back.

For the shine on the blue, the archers aimed. Above the heads of their brother gendarmes. His right arm bended till the elbow had nearly touched the ground. With all breath drawn from his lungs to the strings of his body, the colonel released the quick grip. A burst of air shook the earth, and like a rocketing missile, the fanned gust of flames purged the unlasting flora. The eifer on the arrowhead glazed with the launching of a feathered crescent dashing towards the apex. As Vasilevsky gazed up for the blackening shroud, whose shadows pierced the Confederates' hearts, he muttered,

"What is—?"

Before his sentence could be ended, the dark lines swallowed the machine gun corps who were felled by the traditionalists' tips of arrows. The darkened tsunami of bolts chased them. The swarming rain speared hearts and ribs; bursting eyes; whilst the unlucky many were impaled by the dozens to their backs. Soaking the grass in blood, the artillery of titans struck the panzers in the advances.

"What is the meaning of this…?" Vasilevsky growled.

His pupils quivered who could not bear to look. The delay ignited before him and pounded the shards of tanks easily conquered by the simplicity of eifers. Its final mother of the collapsing sky, the colonel's who had shot so high, came in a rush like the stroke of rivers. Engulfing itself in a golden flame that roared like a warrior king, the blade crashed for the middle grounds and detonated on the snap of impact. Limbs flew in the disintegrating heat. A ball of a volcanic hell torn and casted into a mushroom cloud tall enough for anyone confined within the walls to see. Where the headquarter's ridge felt the booming clap of the shock, the flames soared above the greatest hill that Warneńczyk witnessed from.

In the black smog, Rzhev was in a search for his commander. But the hindrance of a cough of dust and dirt which had invaded his lungs was all there was to answer. Vasilevsky flustered, beholding the fallen. All his treasured machineries. The mechas of the Rus. It had been annihilated and yet the arrows kept their paths flooding into his army that was in shambles. Like dry air on water, some had bounced from his armor. His rage in the sword and shield were curbed when the rumblings of the ground impaired the glorious Confederacy by a restored wave of light.

"Your fall is nigh, hounds!" A winged hussar leapt before his eyes and rammed the lance into a foot soldier, skewering him away as his comrades were in the stampede.

Towards the tinted river that the trap had been sprung, Adam and Ascot forwarded the moving hill. Into the densest smoke with a charge, they fought in the rallying cries of the grand cavalry.

"How'd ya like that?!" Adam exclaimed as he leaned off his saddle, with one foot in the air, smashing his blades on skulls by the major's reservedly appearance.

"Where did they come from?!" A bellow of Vasilevsky reflected amongst his adjutant.

The avalanche of the flanks had pledged for the attack. Their backs pushed by the hundred thousand others deceived to have not existed. In the entanglement of division, the head could not wage battle without its legs. There when the river had bisected the Summer Lion's army, the prey was abound. He who did not portray the slightest smugness, Warneńczyk fitted his flask in his hold and lifted the wine for the gods.

For the second evening, the invitation to the headquarters dragged the elites from midnight. The caws of reapers' crows fissured the sky of clouds. Beneath the spire and the stretch of a banner, the busying command quieted when the squad had shown themselves through the curtains. A table sat shabbily dressed with stains detailing the cheap works of the carvings inferior for a general. As Warneńczyk scribbled across the assortment of stacking ledgers, he mumbled for Florek's name. Then a nod and the click of his heels brought for him a jug of a comforting fragrance and shallow mugs that he laid on the table and offered by an open hand for the squad to take seats. Awkwardly, they heeded. Dragging the chairs on the flattened dirt, like hoes on a field, the ploughing and scraping took Warneńczyk's eyes from the beige pages.

"I remember the night when the hussars marched through Krakau." The general rose, clearing his jacket of biscuit crumbs and the tips of snapped pencil lead.

"Was it that it made me realize when I needed to fight the Three Reichs?" asked he.

Grabbing the jug of tea, Warneńczyk bent his old, creaking back and leaned for the nine mugs. Whilst the lancers and Károly's eyes and ears were on the commander and his story, the waterfalls of the drinks poured.

"The resistance of the sewers provided me warmth," told Warneńczyk, swinging the last drop from the jug as he pushed the closest mug for Arminius.

"All there was to sacrifice was the breath of mine." Gently laying the emptied vessel, the general pulled his hands across the desk and slumped against the chair.

"How could I have ignored their first task—?"

"Spit it out, gramps." Gin cut the stillness with his arms crossed when his comrades dared not to speak without order.

"What'd ya call us for?"

The backdrop of candles flickered. As the flask reentered the children's sights, they prepared themselves for the pungent scent. But once the cap unsealed, the bottle never gave the horrendous whiff. It was quite pleasant. A perfume of ginger and lemons which tensed Julien's hands clasped together.

"As impatient as ever, huh?" Warneńczyk chuckled.

He leaned ahead and grounded his elbows on the table. His fingers locked as the elder breathed into the gap between his palms. It was that the glare and air he gave was often littered by solemnity but with a gravity of ambition whenever a priceless idea rummaged in the mind.

"When the time has come," The lungs of his' bloated.

"You must take the head of a general." He revealed collectedly.

For those eavesdropping on the conversation, that was most amongst the aides, they muted. The squad hushed, whose memories reminded of the encounter of Rzhev. Yet the appeal of confidence in defeating that third general was there in spite of the unnoticed other.

"Of course that would be of no difficulty in collaboration." Coughing to clear this throat, Warneńczyk unbuttoned his collar for the trapped zenith of the meeting.

"But if not Vasilevsky's head."

By an enlarging stare at the general who had uttered something as ridiculous, Julien rose from the seat and repeated in a stammering voice,

"L-Leonid...V-Vasilevsky?"

Gin gulped for the flash in the past when a single strike of the lion had nearly wiped his life from the heavens' chart. The equality of unease was the very same sense. As for the times with mumbles between his allies, Arminius rolled the tea in the mug where the curls of steam molded into an upward cone. He rested silent.

"There's no way outta this, is there?" Lev spoke which seemed worthy of a joke.

"Perhaps." The general's one-worded answer was enough to have gathered the squad again.

"But..."

From an interior pocket, a wallet of brown leather and reddish-orange stitchings were pincered by Warneńczyk's fingers. The wrinkles of the skin were the likes of its master's, where the spine had degraded by the grease of aged grips. He opened the capsule of histories and had a thoughtful gaze at the relics within. Sliding a photo from the holder, a picture of black and white spun as it skated across the table.

"Are you willing to chase a dream or fight a war?" With the question arisen in his eyes too, Warneńczyk proposed for the elites to judge alone.

The preserved edge of the photograph struck the belly of a mug. Arminius pressed his plated fingers on the vestige for it not to fall, which grasped both Florek and the younger comrades. Their heads poked between the gaps and leaned over the squad captain when the visage of a lively character was held dormant.

Before the steps to nowhere, plains of rubble, his smile was twinned with Károly's. Whose face was darkened by mud. The foot of a Lekann flag and the studs of his boot staked their claim over a corpse in a well-known uniform. An iron cross was half ridden by what was blood whilst the plates of the shoulder could only affirm the superiority of the fallen soldier. With a pistol in the killer's hands, the innocent face was in joy over death.

"Whether you fail or succeed," Warneńczyk returned the lancers and lieutenant to him.

"It will not change the outcome of this battle."

Standing tall, the general saluted for the first appearance before anyone as the concoction of ginger and lemons cooled under his shade.

"For I intend to cast my net around the valkyries no matter how many I will sacrifice." Under the conviction of youth, the old man declared.

"Libra. Chō. Dragosavac. Hayek. Konstantin. Calenzo. Károly. Carlstadt. Reichner." He named them.

"Take the blessings of war, and earn us a victory."

The honorable elites awaited glory at the gates when the red flare was given. A brigade of five thousand chanted behind them. Were them, they led the pending charge. Hence, the nine greats of Sorrmul. Restlessly watching the slow opening. By the twists of the squealing hinges; the heaves of the soldiers working the wheel; the grumbles of the Sorbe giant. Arminius rested his eyes and looked towards the clouds, peering past the walls as the rays of light and wind passed by the gaps of the gate. When the air had stilled and the gatekeepers did their work, he lowered his head with a spirited gaze into the reflective blade. There was Julien and Károly, and comrades past behind in the metalwork, and where a trail of ash and corpses with fires raging and dead hearts beating telling as the oracle of the future.

"Let our names be carved into the annals!" He raised his sword high in the air.

"For Aelon! For Leken!"

The drums banged slowly with a roll filling their souls. The garrison, proudly before the contingent, dug their spears in the streets. His allies heard the gratifying short speech by a boy who was so little a leader.

"We were the gathering storm!" Arminius reared his horse.

Taking the words in remembrance of Warneńczyk, their five thousand pairs of lungs released a cry of victory. In the uproar and under selfishness that would not change, they rode, hoping for glory in the vanguard, for the burgundy death's valley.

XVII

3 AUZHUSTUS 491

03.08.12017

Władysław Warneńczyk

*The reason for harboring the rebellious elites. It was never to free
them from Nikola's strangle. That was to acquire my podium in this
war. If I am that hand which feeds them, what says by the end of
this calamity? Would they be legends or heroes that would collapse
the Confederacy with their nine pillars of blades? I care little for
morals. Any warrior should never. It will only bring upon their
downfall and the destruction of who they fight for. I need to protect
my family, king and kingdom. Whatever the cost. Take my honor,
reputation or prestige. I care not.*

*This is the difference between you and I, Leonid Vasilevsky. Are
either of us willing to sacrifice some things to present a victorious
future? I know I am for this, it is my drive. Hence, see, even as I am
forging your death's note before this chance we must steal. Tell me,
how so will you fight back?*

When I take your head…

CHAPTER

18   DUEL

Two clouds converged, descending the flat ridges of the expanse valley. Without the command of the severed head, the foul surprise took the Confederates into a shattered withdrawal. The gap, the passage to peace they had forced open, began to seal ever tighter and again. But it was the horrendous nature, assuming that the repeated maneuvers of a breakthrough then retreat would ensue. That thought had broken. A surge of a new unknown suffocated the vanguards as the blood in their veins were frozen. As the armor of the heart melted, the molten streams of troops fled. Who only had the will to bully in a one-sided battle was never to recover from such fierceness of a counter-attack.

"Sir! A hundred thousand from the northern right!" Serov reported, composed, unlike his comrades in nervous breaks.

"Five thousand to the south it appears." Rzhev gazed at the encroaching front.

By the buckle of the scabbard, Vasilevsky held. Sweating, profusely, the heat of the great turn crushed his ego. The fractures of the mind seemed irrecoverable. What blunder he had played would be made a laughingstock if ever the general returned home. Unable to think, the shock had come. His face flushed as the torridness of failure climbed his nerves.

"My mentor," Rzhev, speaking elegantly, twisted his pointed beard.

"Is it not so possible to defeat our enemies?"

The vice general kept ahead with an arm shielded by the sun. Emanating the budding temper by slow depthful breaths, there was a groan and a sigh.

"Speak!" Vasilevsky demanded.

A snicker spun Serov for the general's student who was so lighthearted in the nightmare as their army was poisoned. Raising an arm for the sky, Rzhev peered upwards to the tips of his fingers, touching the heaven above the accursed mist of low-lying ash.

"Would it not be unfavorable to battle against the flow?" asked Rzhev, lifting a brow.

Returning to the earth, the third general turned his mount and body for the hill beyond the fort. Where the spark of silver shone on the tip of the blade, at the ends of the rapier, the Aelon's old man, yawning, stood staring and lounging. The adjutant's sights need not be on the lion to have sensed his wrath.

"We shall either retreat that may take so many precious lives." Rzhev firstly suggested, staying with a glare at the Lekann flag.

He theatrically lowered his arm and dived it ahead, towards the village.

"Or that may be we borrow their currents and thrust us to their general's head." The third general offered lastly.

His hand came flat on his breastplate. And acknowledging his teacher's highest authority with the dip of his head, Rzhev presented the two strategies for the commander who had stalled,

"It is by your order, should we advance with either."

Vasilevsky released a huff of luckless bad breath. The wrongs of hesitation he was humiliatingly corrected by a student. But for him, as there was an opportunity nonetheless of the careless blunder, the man of arrogance would take it. Forcing his helmet tighter, until it felt like a part of his head, the squeeze cleared his mind. As he lifted his sword and rested the curved blade on his shoulder plate, Vasilevsky took little notice of the smaller force that appeared neither elite nor numerous.

"Hmph. You never fail to amuse me, Igor." The commander grinned as if that smile was of a reborn predator.

"O' I would never dare." Rzhev chimed.

Aiming the sword at the southern contingent where the flanks troubled at wrapping the spearhead, Vasilevsky's roar revived,

"Captain, with me!"

"Third general Rzhev!" He called, pointing to the routing wings of the Confederacy once the arrows of the enemies had yielded for another succession of volleys.

"Take a third of mine." The general cooled his lungs.

"I wish to see your banner over the fire by the day's end."

"Of course, sir!" Rzhev twirled his voice.

As he rode, the third general gestured for a close aide. In his camp, it seemed that every underling was equally lavish in the cloth of nobility. However similar he may be, the young officer was softer. Never telling a doubt of his mind. Even within the shade of his greater superiors, when his face sought the wrongs.

Soldiers collapsed under the plunging missiles. The sides of innocently drafted shields in war amidst the fluttering feathers of shafts. The air had darkened again. Whipping their backs beginning to crawl, the arrows flicked wounds awide. Screams in the chase. It was no different than whenever the Aelon had retreated. Only that the will of constant victory had diminished into a void. Tower shields lifted and marched whilst the spears struck the exhausted. Taking so many lives, the generals had their dance of armageddon.

In the eternal stream of the five thousand, Arminius searched the thickening clouds. By the gray sourness he could feel dabbing his lips as the sailing wind pressed, it had the taste of the deceased. The compass of the Apollo was no more. Relying on the whispers of kei, his sword hacked through the spines and hearts of those in doom. The grace of the fluidity of the squad captain gave the fallen the last warmth of life that his comrades would not grant.

"That's forty-two!" Gin yelled lively, digging his blade into a conscript's arm that cleaved the fellow open to leak.

"Focus." Arber reminded the loosened creatures.

"We're not halfway to Vasilevsky." Taking lives only in necessity, the lancer judged with his quick eyes.

Blood, like veins, supplied the soil in a reddish-orange coat. Where nearer the river, the earth weakened and had been churned by the charge into sludge. Its viscous current was of a blanket of floating eyes and limbs like a boiling stream, bobbing over the surface that could not be seen. Unstoppingly, the rear guard waded through the lukewarm waters but that formed a trap for carbines of hussars to peel away, thus to toss more ingredients into the hellesque blend.

But the distancing cavalry and infantry was what had crept on Julien's mind for the while. Never minding what lay trampled by the hooves of his companion, he sped to Arminius' pace, tracked by Károly. The archer had the bow in one hand and a snapped, bloodied arrow in the other. As a spearman stepped outward his lines to confront the vanguard, he cold-heartedly rammed the head into his eye, peeling the organ from its socket.

"Arminius!" Julien called from close, till the three were parallel.

Taking a glance at the tip that had pierced the eye which juices leaked down the shaft into the gaps of his palms, Károly took a short swing and flung the arrow into the bodily sea.

"Florek's falling behind!" Holding a pause to avoid the winding slopes of flesh and stake-like bones, the Danne reported to Arminius.

"The spearhead will detach—!"

"But we'd lose the momentum!" Arminius looked over his shoulder and watched the sagging assault to the breadth of resistance.

Staunchly, the Confederates' columns replenished through claws hooking their own flesh giving a package of refreshing blood for the mass to halt the advance. Florek who had never appeared a warrior finally bore his saber unsheathed and courageously swung in great arcs. But that was hardly an effort to the push of the footmen, fatigued.

"Damn, we're almost there..." Aiming for the tallest banner of the *Summer Lion's* sigil, Arminius could not let away the moment of victory.

The wind around their ears to the clinks and clanks of iron doused their bodies in inspiration. The elites held ever straighter for the headquarters, crashing by the fire in the junkfield of splintered wagons. He thought not to be reckless with the backdoor reminiscent of Akülunnarchs to not perform the same.

Taking a glimpse at Julien beside in the ascension of Dante's hell who swallowed the hides of the Rus, the lancers' leader bit his lip and carried his verdict,

"Let's slow our pace!"

"Regroup at the core—" Arminius faced Károly when the manifestation of an alien glow vibrantly shone from his comrade's pupils.

A wave of ferocious gold swung from beneath, drawing an ominously bright hum. For Arminius' chest, the swish of the eifer skimmed the air at an unavoidable span. Yet in time, the lancer drew his sword close and deflected the strike, forcing the rapier in a curve to miss barely. Immediately, Arminius pulled on the reins and forced the squad to halt with him in the dispersed crater of battle.

"What was that...?" Arminius exhaled after the scent of death who had crept too near.

Whilst the few divided strands of hair, separated from the head that could have been taken, drifted before him, his working pulse tried to settle. Upon realizing the familiarity of the warrior in confrontation, the thumps of his heart never rested.

"Oh? You again, youngster?" asked the third general.

Brushing his beard, Rzhev's eyes expanded by the sight of Arminius Reichner who had shunned his recklessness but his nature endured.

"Tch." Slapping the reins, the lancer charged for the officer without much hesitation.

Holding his target at one point of the body, exposed, the insanity on the swing caught the Confederate in a startling pinch.

"Hoh?" The man rang.

He lost his hold on the mount and leapt from the saddle. Twisting and somersaulting in the air with his rapier in perfect form, Rzhev elegantly landed with a spin. A small dust cloud kicked up from the ground under a drought and with a stupendous bow, it ended his dodge of Arminius' slash.

"Are you not the reckless child of Akülunnarchs?" Rzhev mocked, pointing the rapier at the lancer's neck as the elites would bear witness to the prologue of a battle within another.

Nearly dropping his shako, the general refitted it, holding the cap sideways for a show off of his glamorous armor.

"Him?" Gin's instincts returned with his stare on Miklós' rifle.

His hand had nearly stolen for a path into treachery had Arber not pressed his panther's eyes on the brute and emotionlessly growled,

"Gin."

On the outskirts of the developing ring, the infantry had broken into but happened by chance around a new surprise. Florek tugged the helm on the horse and reared the mount into a standstill whilst the lancers in his shadow troubled themselves with the blockhead needing Ascot's lectures.

"Lemme take his head!" Gin fought but his allies would not let their hands free.

"No wonder you got kicked out once before." Cautiously, Lev pulled the brute away from the clearing stage.

"It'd be dishonorable—"

"All o' ya!" A yell with a swing of his arms tore Gin from the grips over the sweat-soaked jacket.

"Like my ass gives a shit 'bout honor." He grunted as the encircling battle suspended.

Only if it had meant locally, the soldiers had ceased the conflict and lowered their weapons. Knowing that they would not need to fight for a duel that decided the fate of that one clash, the troops merged on the opposite banks of the swelling arena. Like the pits of gladiators, the spectators were as one. There were no factions. But prayers and hopes filled even those irreligious. That even Julien's gritting teeth and the shudders in fear with Károly by his side, they could do nothing. Letting the strings of fate steer in the fogged pass.

The center of the crisis. Still on horseback, Arminius weakened his stance and brought around to face Rzhev who fortified on his own two feet. With the rapier held to his face, he seemed at a blatant disadvantage.

"My! I could not have predicted this." Rzhev perked, driving the blade into the cracks of the field.

Arminius frowned upon him from afar, as if he was higher than the third general. He had prepared to make a second charge but, even mounted, there was a stink in the sewers of doubt that something in Rzhev's pockets of tricks placed him above.

"Is this what a duel is...?" The lancer mumbled with no distinct expression.

Releasing the reins from his grip, he wondered more,

"They won't have to fight if we do."

"And if I don't, then would it be impossible for victory?" A thought curbed the sliver of annoyance surrounding the veil hiding the truth of his real humanity.

Two droplets of sweat fell from his cheeks. The devils in his ears chanted to fight, whilst the armies of death calling for surrender were massacred by the larger voices. His will was ironclad when the decision had come.

Arminius' feet left the stirrups and slid from the saddle. With the single blade he needed be wielded for victory. The trustworthy sword. The lancer held it in a standardly and quaintly open form, taunting the third general with a challenge he could not depart from. To the center of the dueling grounds, he walked.

"Oh? You're approaching me?" Rzhev accepted the invitation, menacingly drawing his rapier from the earth.

The third general had once expected Arminius to cave easily. But twice, he had been wronged and fooled. When the battle was to be decided then in Sorrmul, that from atop the hill, Warneńczyk had his eyes peeled onto the ring. Knowing there were stalemates of the center and northern flanks by Serov and Vasilevsky's hardy hold, it was the south he searched for a victory. No matter how small Arminius may have been before the prowess of Rzhev, standing as straight and sharp as a needle, the aura matched a fierce field general. Although the veteran found his greater standings over the duel, Rzhev could not shake the piercing teslas he saw sparking around his foe's hand and sword.

Like a lightning storm, there was no warning. Arminius dashed. Before the sounds of his shockwave were caught, he swung his sword widely, taking the third general off his balanced guard. In a mere second, Arminius was beneath him, clamping his teeth as the sword winded to face its tip at the soil.

"This little cretin—" Rzhev's thoughts whistled when a sandstorm was forged from Arminius' blade.

Impairing his sights, the commander coughed as he scoured around. Aiming his rapier wherever there was noise. But from the distant clashes, he could not predict for until the last instant. When Arminius leapt from the clouds, striking down, the bringing of the blade hammered the silver with the anvil-like defense of the rapier. The loud snap in the deflection blasted the sand away and cleared the onlookers' views again. Grains of embers rubbed as Arminius tensed ever more, driving the metallic curve for Rzhev's face when the brief shocking shout and strength repelled Arminius to the ground.

In a single roll onto his feet, Arminius dragged one hand along the soil to slow the slide. A controlled fall, the lancer took that proved to the enemy Confederate his capabilities. Both sides panted. Yet none of the eifers had been seen. It captured the spectacularity of the artistic definition of war. Why humans were so dying to join for what they believed for their individuality in units and armies. The burden they shouldered on the lives of many.

"Third General! For the Confederacy!" From what was a battle of attrition, the overly sure juniors cried.

An uproar steamed. With the chants in a united stand against the Aelon, they called,

"Rzhev! Rzhev! Rzhev!"

Their booming voices were heard. Encapsulating the battlefield and Vasilevsky's ears. Who had heard his student's name be finally glorified, a smile arisen of his proudness.

As if it were holding him down, violating his body by rude grasps, a tree of hands began to rip his human face from the death shriveled under. His heart pounded, jumping around the body in his ear, hands, and mind. Before the lunacy of becoming trapped in the prison of foreign cries, a trying cheer pushed his back.

"Armin!"

"You still have another after!" Károly held a hand in a cone around his mouth.

"Reichner! Reichner! Reicher!" Lev began a second surge for the Aelon troops who gazed on.

Unheard of. Low ranking. Hardly a novice in war. Although there was that, his allies poured and pledged their faith as the loops of his name were sent to the gods. When they themselves could not hope to stand against a third general, the shouts gave a silent meaning for the lancer.

If one sacrifice is enough to save this entire army... Arminius sighed, resting his eyes.

"Fine." He took a gasp of air and held it for slight light-headedness to appear and disappear.

Releasing all his breath, the fogged thoughts in his mind were blown away, and a certain normality returned.

"Enough of this theatrical nonsense!" Burning afterimages, Rzhev's rapier circled.

Like a deva, his blade held its place. Waiting. For the younger to make his attempt.

"See the dying life, taken by the wind from I, the restless

forest—" He spouted before the interruption by a swift wind, razor sharp, cutting across the drowning fields.

"Hahah!" Rzhev laughed, dodging, and launched a flourish of dagger-like jabs.

Golden needles in the rapids, his fiery drill stabbed and flickered. Tiny thumps and crashes into his sword broke the wind beside, marking its make of the own current that flowed through the trampled grass. Arminius held his stance, quickening his steps to parry every strike. But to the ten jabs there were, only one could be averted. His habitual swiftness was hardly enough to prevent a few shallow cuts to his face and arms when the rage brought his sword and gathered a clustered eifer charge.

"Hyah!" Arminius cried as the boulder of the strike crashed, spinning a whirlwind of lightning coils.

But who all had narrowly escaped again, the third general stepped on the hilt of Arminius' sword and drove a kick against his face. Felling the younger whilst the warrior landed gracefully. The act was met by an applaud from his comrades. Those cries and chants submerged the Aelon in a sea of a pure Confederate fleet.

"Ah..." Arminius rubbed his nose as it bled onto his hand.

Rising, enduring by his sword, he stood. The vision of the duel collapsed. Whilst the blood was smudged across a cheek, Arminius flashed a glance at the elites. Julien shuffled nearer in dismay but Károly had held him tight from the square. The disbelief and the irritation of their inability to fight. With the eight, there was only Arber whose voiceless warning gawked to signal an awakening.

Beneath the ribs... The summer of Arminius' green eye thrusted for the target.

He leaned, addressing the third general's unbreakable defense with the offense of his speciality. Ramming his boots deeper in the ground, there attained a good hook for a launch. In the one more gasp of the tough air, the crackle of a failing eifer accompanied the shooting rush.

With a heavenly strike! cried the Aelon fighter to himself.

"Hoh, this again?" Rzhev voiced, smugly unmoving in the course of the reckless lancer.

An accelerating dash by powering pushes. The soil beneath his feet cracked and bursted from the charge. Too unnatural to follow even by the trained sights of the squad, Arminius lunged his sword at the foe. The twin figure, the god of lightning warfare broke the lines of the many dimensions until only one could be left. Driving black and white illusions that blinded the world, Arminius thought as his blade entered the cells of the Confederate aura,

Got you—

The armor glimmered. It had come from an eifer. As the blitz submitted, Rzhev sprung for the heavens but not too far from earth. He grinned. Watching the mouth of Arminius widen in the loss of the battle. Who released himself of the spent stress in the offensive, it was to have found that his blade had missed.

"W-What—?" Arminius stammered, upwards to see the third general who had stilled.

Thanking the gods, Rzhev held his head high. The unforeseen had presented its entrance for everyone shuddered beneath the holiness of the devils' sins. On heaven and earth, earth and the hells, the crime of the living is shown in a facade of human goodness. By the golden wave with circular blisters behind his back, the presence of the eifer was no longer so simple. Anything that was humane in punishment had departed.

"T-The Diogenes Circle..." Arminius realized.

There was a certain ring in the development in life for all eifer wielders. When one had learnt an eifer, they had never mastered its potential. But upon their true martial capacity, the scholar's work would prove that the form of the capital beyond the heart, mind, and soul would be achieved that the gods would not be able to bind anymore. Letalis. As the story told for hardly three millenniums goes.

"See the true nature and blessing by death from my hand!" Rzhev proclaimed.

Shining and capturing the purity of the battle's field, there held a sense that an object of this value should have remained banished from the face of Terra. Yet his rapier glowed. Like wealth and jewels of a king's chambers. Placing a hand spread over his face, he aimed the tip of the blade, held close against his chest, for Arminius. The chanting had stopped. For the Confederates and the Aelon. When both fronts had seen what the brightening star ominously foretold.

"I must say, I have not encountered such delight." praised the third general.

"However, sadly, we are done tea-partying." Then, the smile hollowed.

A rumble shook the colorless sky. And there, his blade filling with all his eifer burned as hotly, greater than the sun. Noting the perplexed Arminius below, whose feet carefully retreated, Rzhev thanked, casting the rapier in the propelment of the capital eifer,

"High gratitude for entertaining me, youngster!"

The shower of gold, meteoring needles of eifer plunged. Crashing waves of arrows in lengths and explosivity of artillery. Its train of thrusting pikes flared into a cloud and flames blasting the topsoil to be away. Every strike was torment unleashed. Choking the earth by her throat with the motor-like tunes pumping and resounding across the plains.

XVIII

1862 YEARS BEFORE THE ZHORMANNIKS
9664 YEARS AFTER THE BIRTH OF OUR HUMANITY

Diogénis o Ikesías

This young fool that they call the Exile. What have you ever time to be summoned here to mine sanctuary?

Son of a slave, be mine hound and deliver such records to the rapists of Romulus or make mine own geniuses thine if thy wish to be Diogénis is here.

You may well see mine practices and enlightenment. Use it however thy corpse might be, there is no sanctuary to live under the Léthē. The oblivion of humanity. The lethal. The chance for a zeal must always be there to enhance one's self. Depending on what human the cruel man is, it may fall on blessing to collapsing a city, or be as worthy as mine of bodily fluids. But indeed perhaps it may draw any's inner heart to become more than once they were.

Now begone, thou has prolonged thy stay, halt sucking mine precious air.

CHAPTER

19 THE UNKNOWN

"Arminius!" Julien cried his name, nearly falling from the saddle in the gusts.

Their faces shielded from the storm, driven by a selfish rage. The ground near the Danne's feet began to crack, and of the turbulent whirl of drills diving for where Arminius once stood. The golden grass that soon inflamed, burning through the soil as the craters merged to form a deepening pit. Devouring the earth until the underbelly, the stone and the waters flooded. Were the strikes so insufferable that from Arminius' eyes, there were nothing but the terrors of sparks that broke his defense and shattered. Slowly tearing his soul from its body, his hands started to burn, such as was of touching burning steel.

"I can't...hold..." Arminius gritted his teeth until the gums bled, harshly keeping his mind stable in an asylum.

"There are no exits..." He scanned around him.

Only a wall of eifer, so thick it could keep an army out, laid before. As Rzhev's machine of thrusts, unknown of the fate his enemy had endured, to him Arminius could have been long dead or not. But his teacher would not have doubts. His pillars of pummeling stakes boosted. The rapier was no longer merely an object to be wielded, but to be controlled in the crazed waltz.

Although that he was forced, bearing into the ground, his will was unflinching. Holding the same resistance hoping for leverage in a gap where none appeared, the dilemma he faced, like others in the past, gave him the necessary intuition of a cornered prey. The brain circled. For a counter charge, the possibilities seemed endless yet far.

Above? Ahead? Aside? He thought though alas stayed caged within Rzhev's bars.

"It's...impossible..."

Steam arose, not from his eifer but a foreign power whose

heat ruptured the averaged mind, disintegrating his shortening life.

The filthy fog and the looks of an unruly sun growing in the womb made of clouds. Beneath, the general's army was halted in their advance but the drop of Warneńczyk's had been spent. Fortune placed his wager on the three fronts that had their attempt to assemble on the base of Confederate corpses. It could not be then that a bombarding chase would wipe the Rus home. Another day of grinding teeth would wear at the armies and that knowing the encounter cannot be won under the thought, the general exhaled the poor contemplation on defeat.

"Report!" An aide ran to the commander's ridge and shouted with an underlying breath of anxiousness.

"Our hussars have stalled; Ascot has withdrawn," The soldier paused for the distant cries of a general's name to pass.

"And Rzhev's engaged in a—"

"I am only so old, you know." Warneńczyk alerted him.

Whose knee locked of the scare, the subordinate bowed until his sorrowful, twitching brows were not in sight if the general ever turned.

"Forgive my rudeness." asked of the lieutenant.

"No. It is no fault." His senior gently itched his head, sighing apologetically.

As the young man raised, another plain theory braked his voice. However alone Warneńczyk seemed depriving his years of hardship, he could not think of another maneuver to break the stalemate that would engulf his duty as the days of the First Calamity would.

"Should we send in our garrison?" Hence, the aide recommended.

"Hmph." Warneńczyk grunted, reluctant to throw a show of a gambler's power.

"And you intend me to lead the five thousand we have?" He asked on the spin to the officer that stuttered his heart.

"Little chance." told the general.

Where the prized archers were exhausted of arrows, their hands held nothing but short blades of daggers and knives. When the north were caught in Vasilevsky's wedge, tearing the corners that was blind to the commander over a hundred thousand. Warneńczyk surveyed the sites of the dislodging attack. There, his eyes skimmed the path of the legions and rolled to the southern sphere.

Reichner. May your child rest with victory. The prayer sounded.

Cuts slashed his face. The shudders of the cold, in becoming a forgotten spot in the world, drove the lancer's grips tighter. His sword cracked in the attrition. Drowning in the inescapable landed storm, surges of shooting stars opened the ground. The sturdy stone dried and detonated, but yet, did not let up in staying firm with the earth as Arminius had done by the ticking clock on his limbs.

"I can't…retreat here…" The suffering muttered.

Though Arminius' mind stilled like a calm lake. After the flash flooding rain had passed.

What…am I doing…?! Shaking his head, he searched the emptiness in the crowded city of lances with a keen eye.

"This feels wrong…"

The blouse began its tear, exposing bruised skin from the punches sustained by his fastness that hammered at the bones. To the second where Arminius had been numbed by the painless sensation, lost in thought, Arber's words returned to him.

I've been looking for exits the entire time… Arminius raised his voice in the descending revelation.

It's no wonder there aren't any… His hawk-like instincts gazed at his predator above where the lines of the figure were merged.

What I need right now… He thought.

"Is an entrance!"

A gap in the dashing barrage rend unto a new opening. Rzhev's self was past the clouds. And finally, where the desperate need of a purpose was there, the boy buried the crack of a grin. Deflecting the incoming streaks of golden javelins, Arminius knelt. When the poor sword gave its remaining kei to charge the master's eifer, a wave coiled, circling the blade as the sparks gave it the final life it heads.

In space that seemed desolate, yet brimming with energy that flowed in his veins, Arminius took one last glance at the next spire and drew his sword. Reimagining the petals gently gliding towards him as if the world had stopped, the unknown soldier took a step to the side and dodged the strike. Then, releasing the constricted nerves of his legs, the eifer stored within blasted him for the skies like a fervent missile. The rocks below exploded into crystallized blocks, like the perfection of marble chunks, and sunk in the thunder torn by the lift off. Tryingly, the only pyres were rendered. Flesh wounds were given but they sealed with the stitches of lightning.

Spotting the clouds below that gave way to an electrified bullet, Rzhev halted his fires and recollected his eifer in preparement. Yet was shocked by the darting spear whose lungs could not waste for a cry. A burst of a slice upwards through the armor and flesh before the third general realized.

"Gah...?!" Rzhev gasped in the stun.

It had nearly pierced his heart in one strike. Spinning in the air where the colossal shadow of his own had then succeeded Rzhev, Arminius twisted his grip overhead and swung before the Confederate's recovery. In a demonic wave of unholy sounds, the colliding metals clanked. The hellish fwoomp crashed, jetting the commander to the ground. Another cutting rush of wind, blowing the dirt and grit from the dueling circle, surfed the lands.

The ground, burning from the leap, was in havoc on that he lightly landed, with no more than a small thump. His sword, almost breaking, was alive, strangled by his paralyzed fingers, trembling by the impact. Rzhev's eyes pinned ahead whose body was captured by the rubble of around. He flusteredly grabbed his rapier, removing the loosened rocks from his armor and tightly aimed its chipped tip at Arminius. Whose appearance was out of the smoke, he was almost untouched. Loosening his wrist, the lancer twirled his blade. Flicked sideways as its origin was. The tattered jacket flapped in the calming wind that blew a sheet of embers and dust their way.

Julien opened his eyes when the gale had been beaten. For the results of their comrade that they had missed in a blink, the squad stared who were oblivious to the reality.

"What was...what happened...?" Julien murmured with the

air of a silent victim.

Resonantly, a shocking slap across his cheeks left a faint red mark. But who had done so, he had the reasons in the right.

"You looked like you saw a devil." Károly recalled the Danne's shrinking pupils, shaking from the cold aura surrounding the two duelists.

Though he had felt, regardless of the call to light, that Arminius' illusion was more the blizzard engulfing the sun in eternal darkness. That for Julien, it was never felt before. The coolness of a killer's heart.

"Youngster…" Rzhev called him, coughing cups of blood that splattered onto his arm.

Arminius trailed the path that had been dragged by the tracks of battle. Showing taller than once at the openings of the duel, the lancer stopped beyond his foe's reach whose weapon was intact. That was unlike its wielder whose eifer had perished.

"Oh my…how shall this dance draw…" The third general spewed.

"Isn't this enough…?" Arminius interrupted in an attentive voice, slackening.

"How far will you go before you'll surrender?" He asked in return.

Swaying, the third general had risen from rest. Rzhev's ears bled from the counterbalance. Drawing yet another slice of his kei, the man gathered another gasp.

"No one…I…or my mentor have fought…survived another day." He had his talk of nonsense, but it was of pure grief in witnessing the drama of defeat.

Unable to witness the truth of a loss, nor gather a sense of accomplishment, Rzhev spoke on.

"To fight…that is the will that we must bear…"

"Our noble duties to protect…" Clearing his face of the blood, wiped away by a dirtied handkerchief, Rzhev freed, allowing the cloth to smoothly parachute.

"That is why…"

"I will not surrender!" Rzhev stubbornly yelled, charging his final eifer, the field general raced across the path at Arminius who watched him sluggishly run.

The lancer readied his feet. Slowly, the build of the climax ensued before unleashing a quiet gale. Snapping along the field, there left a lightning highway. Scorching and sparkling with Rzhev halted a half away. A heavy blanket of blood rested on Arminius' sword that had blackened. Seeping through the cracks that eventually carved away, the blade shattered and was sunken onto the earth.

"Sorry to have worked you this hard..." told the soldier to the blade.

A geyser of Rzhev's life ushered from his side as he collapsed onto one knee with the spectators, whose jaws' dropped, holding nothing but their silence. Warneńczyk felt the breath of a godly eifer blow from the valley. The aide and he gazed at victory herself.

The third general could not bother to hide his tranquil agony. A spillage of black blood dribbled. Grasping his vicious wound, his vision at last had clouded. The defined sounds he heard were of Arminius' boots, timidly treading the thunder field. Unarmed, and doused in the brew of blood, he neared Rzhev's rapier that had escaped his hand.

"Ah...splendid..." The third general moaned, relieving the pain.

"From how you have survived...my last spring, queenly card...I may have given up..."

Halting on the step of the blade, Arminius muttered to Rzhev who received a muffled audio. But unknowing of the sounds from the mouth that moved, the Confederate groaned without hearing the lancer's speech,

"Know this, youngster..."

He removed the shako of his childhood, placing the keepsake before and facing him so that he may find peace on the sigh.

"Hesitation will only see more death...and believe me..." The man looked to Arminius.

"There is nothing less spectacular..."

From the wounds, Rzhev removed his hand, letting be dark liquids naturally take its flow, draining him of any will to survive.

"Now prove that you are worthy of this magnificent world!" He pointed at the rapier, with an aching sight of crimson handprints.

Reminding him of the numberless innocents he had taken to the gates of red, Arminius discovered his persona in the underworld. Where the piles of hands, holding heads, stacked into clumps of souring flesh that the death tree parted to join its leaves.

"The God of Death will grant you mercy in the afterlife..." Arminius recited the passage of the old, lifting the rapier above Rzhev's neck.

"Wherever that may be..."

"Then take my life!" The general exclaimed his closing words in the theatrical impression.

"I will happily give it to become one with mother Terra!"

Through the spine and from the chest, the blade drove. The layers of ribs and a lung bursted until the tip met the shako. Like a banner, the rapier ended its journey of a skewer. A last ring of blood flowered in swirls over the blade as if it was crying from its master's death.

The high laws of war had been mutilated. Such happenings of an unknown soldier taking the life of a general had not occurred for over five decades. Together, they were speechless. Unable to make sense of how it had come to be that the lancer, who had lived a life for half the years of the Confederate, was subject to a miracle.

"Arminius..." Julien clenched his quivering hands, but his eyes were forging tears on the rims.

"T-That's not possible..." Troops, no matter which banner they cried under, their disbelief were together as one.

Lev raised his spear in the air near the shaken Florek who had uncovered the impossibility despite the general's pledge. The gamble the old man won. Once clashing armies mumbled and their blades tipped on the releasing holds of the soldiers' swollen hands. As Károly lifted his heels from the stirrup, he dashed for the captain beside Julien's taken gaze when a cheer of the comrade Rus grabbed the allies' ears,

"Arminius Reichner's slain Rzhev!"

The repeats as they shared the names along the ranks bustled into an uproar. Echoing the frontlines, the asks of whether it be true or not was dispersed in conspiracies. For the blood masses, the acceptance of death was there in the beads of tears.

"Rzhev? Dead?" Serov heard on the halt of his battle but never told Vasilevsky to turn his back.

Under the command, the faithful wept and mourned when one fallen warrior had brought together a dissatisfied peace. Sighs of relief were many amongst the conscripts who saw no attachments to war. It was as Arminius had hoped. The victory there he desired. But captivated by the robbery of another life, the lancer stood with waning aura, over the hilt that shivered in the gales. Blood that had not dried navigated to the westward of his skin. A break of yet more memories of a cruel past flashed through him like fire as his eyes plunged into fear and sickness. Arminius felt his stomach turning. What he had never found before becoming so disturbed by a single death was haunting that perhaps it was not who he had killed. But for how many in the thirteen years of life.

"Armin!" Károly's laughter snapped the lancer from the hypnosis.

To the approaching clatter of hooves on the deserted plains, barren of mother's hair, Arminius turned to the squad, but not fully. The remnants of eifer drained. Whilst the younger comrades hiked the treacherous path, shattered, Florek stayed his own, with an apology he did not give.

"Károly..." Arminius called with the name of his house, Reichner, flooding the small, known world.

There was no smile, grin or chuckle, suchlike. The contagiousness of the crescent the lieutenant was branded by could not find itself seeping into the lancer's veins. Except for when Julien's palm was easing his stiffened shoulder, Arminius flinched from any touch that was anyhow familiar.

"You did well." A praise from Arber was unheard until then.

Yet even when it was rare for such words to be said, the squad commander blinded his sights to his comrades whose snowing compliments melted for one brute to unchain the kindness.

"What're ya spacin' out for?" Aside the heart of the good, Gin punched Arminius on the arm when victory was due.

"Are ya gonna take 'is head or what?"

A new blade, however battered and splattered in the dips of innards, was shoved against Arminius' chest as Gin strolled to be before him. The sticking blood clung to the flayed jacket. Chilling the drooling wounds, the steel had the reflections of the elites.

Scattered and eyeing elsewhere, in a rounded defense, the seven others spied on the shifts of the Aelon and Confederates before the pending clash.

"His death saved this front..." Arminius took the sword from Gin's hand and shared a glimpse at the mirror in the silver.

"Of a massacre."

His face was ridden with the blood of old foes who told him otherwise, forgiving the needed honor of felling a general.

"No." Holding the blade for the brute, Arminius replied when the soul of joy casually restored.

"It's nothing like home..."

Julien perked his ears. Afraid to question what it was that he suffered, the Danne could not build his courage to, when the dread of ripping his sanity weighed greater than knowledge. The troubles of Arminius rooted at the rear of his mind.

"Then don't mind me." Colt crept towards Rzhev whose lifeless head began to gray.

Before he dared steal a trophy, Miklós stepped in the path and the plotter knew another entity of death. Dragging Colt by the head with a crane-like hand, the giant dragged his comrade to the mounts.

"In this case," Arber spoke again in a record for his voice.

"We should report this to the general."

"But..." Julien held his fingers in his mouth for a whistle but no tweet came from his blow.

Károly wrapped his arms around Julien's shoulders, leaning close to his face, and showed the artistry that evolved from an exhale to a sharp whistle. The pierce of all noises bolted in a recall for the horses and as the beasts neared, Lev tagged the question for his own,

"Are we still going for Vasilevsky?"

Onto the saddle, Julien mounted, and reached for Arminius whose own seemed to have fled for the wilderness in the tempest. And in a tough struggle, he was pulled on that luckily, the two were almost weightless to the creature.

"'Course we gotta!" Swinging his sword to free the strictness of his arms, Gin exclaimed.

"We have the momentum." Arminius brought a suggestion that herded his squad to the mission that was set astray.

"Vasilevsky might fall before anything else—"

"Hold!" A cadre of great officers, incoming, was raised by a new voice.

The supposed leader lifted his arm and waved it in the air, calling for the squad to halt in their place. But as he rode closer, his bannerman and armor revealed the lethal allegiances that smothered the task in a chase for a second victory.

"Confederates…" Gin readied his sword and comrades followed.

"What the hell do they want?!"

Though knowing the cautiousness of facing a foe, the Confederate pulled on the reins and stopped before driving his neck for their blades. As Gin and Miklós held the vanguard, Julien stumbled away, cloaking the half of Arminius' face behind the nimble shifts in the ranks. The intimidation, the lancers wish would take the Rus far. But he was completely unshaken by the odd greeting sign and indeed brokered a truce,

"Forgive my rudeness."

Frowning, the squad failed to believe the snake and the lie and trusted their spears and swords onwards. Yet the officer never leaned from the threat.

"After the passing of the commander, it's only natural to join arms and talk…"

"For now." He revealed, removing his scarlet helmet, winged and with a silver plume, which the soldier clamped under his arm.

The man was twenty years of age. Around the prime for battle. Of purity undeserving of the frontlines, he did not seem to have cared for any to smother his attractive face or pearl white hair that shone even amongst Rzhev's closest staff. And even so, there was not a scar. With skin that was pale-tanned, and a build of a noble warrior, as he opened his rose red eyes, the whole glory of the shaping aura bloomed. Who was enshrined within his blood and silver armor, where no skin was exposed from the neck to toes, the bombastic core of this soldier was not simply for meeting Rzhev's grand demands. The eagerness for a skilled fight was in the light grip on a boringly thin and straight glaive by his gloved hands hiding a history, never the peculiarly relaxed demeanor.

"Rzhev was a fair warrior." told the officer in the ordinary remembrance of the commander.

"But he lacked honor."

Placing a hand on his chest, the Confederate offered a bow and apologized in the stead of the headquarters,

"Please find the heart to forgive his actions."

Once on the rise of his head to the nine who had eased, his eyes flicked around the crowd. And there in the background, he had discovered a cowering Arminius for then, lurking to see who that may be, his tone soothed.

"Lancer Reichner?" He asked.

Singled of the nine, there was no escape from an exchange of words. His dual colors of the pupils were too easy to match by rumors and stories that undoubtedly, the Confederate officer had realized.

"I have seen and heard much about your achievements." The strangely realistic admiration took Gin to give way for Arminius who dismounted and invited himself to the presence of the enemy.

"Although I was not present at Akülunnarchs, the stories of Rzhev traveled far." The young man continued.

"Recklessness. Defeated. Fled." Arminius listed the attributes of his name since.

"Were they what you had in mind?" In a game of trickery, the lancer asked.

Unafraid to be in the range of a glaive or a sword, both glared at each. Not approaching further. There was a looming feeling of fiends shielding either that none could fight. But the scents of their souls were the same. The iron of blood.

"No, that's not the case—" The Confederate calmly breached the quiet.

"What are you here for?" Colt pushed through the brainless guards and yelled that would pause the storytelling.

Smiling, the young officer had to alleviate the party, but there his warning had come unexpectedly in the exchange,

"Do not attack Vasilevsky."

"What—?!" In bewilderment, the elites synchronized their shouts.

Though a quickly raised hand broke the tail of judgements and assumptions that soon could be said and thrown into an epitome of an abyss. The suspension of the talks had the elites calmed.

"I will make an attempt to slow his march." The Confederate

guaranteed, that prompted the winds of confusion to battle into the conference.

The vital traitorous act did not concern himself over the possible consequences. He had a neutrality that held not the atmosphere of an enemy. Neither a potential ally. The unknown officer had an encrypted style that blanketed the colors beneath which Arminius considered, numbed as the elites were too.

"Why?" Having found no reason, Arminius mumbled.

His foe, a bystander of the fronts, fitted his helmet and rested his polearm.

"Why?" He repeated.

"We may be drawn by fate to clash in the future."

In a path to the return to the Confederacy, the officer spun his horse and flicked his head for the army. Enduring the next authority of the headquarters, the banner and the aides smacked their reins and galloped towards friendly lands.

"Perhaps you carry the same prestige as I do."

"That I realized." Unveiling something as simple, a grin grew.

The metals of his armor shined when a sun ray broke the clouds, releasing a dark warmth for the gap between the two. To his belt of the back, there was a plain broken spear. Too familiar. It was dented and wrapped by a brownish bandage that was pierced by the shaft's snap. But for Arminius, he never voiced.

"Your name?" Before the Confederate could be let free, Arminius halted the elite soldier.

"Ah. Of course. Please excuse me." The former turned to answer, placing a salute along his stomach as a nobleman.

"I am Colonel Regulus von Eos."

The sense of rivalry drew closer. Though the tensing air was somehow lifted by three black flares, like rockets, shooting to the day's star. That unwelcoming strain of the spirit was of an order for the Aelon.

"It seems your general has recalled you." Regulus watched the blackness fall then emphasized,

"However, it is *your* victory nonetheless."

As a promise he held, his blade looked for Vasilevsky, the Summer Lion. Calmly riding with his glaive directing the curve of the route from the battlefield and dust, his last words before withdrawing out of reach came,

"It was well to have our paths cross, Arminius von Regen!"

The headquarter's tent rested from the falling pillar and loosening nails. Carefully rolling a flag, Adam smoked on a cigar that had the prints of a corpse. His face and uniform was drenched in rotten blood and flesh dangling from his fasteners. Who had yet to clean himself despite many calls of his superior, the delinquent was berated by the major's volleys of poor temper.

"You should never have charged up this hill without orders." Ascot complained.

"Relax. I just want'd ta see what dey're up ta." Adam excused himself, drawing a pin from the ground, he pressed it into the hoop to bolt the flag down.

"As mindless as Reichner that you are." The major added to the humiliation.

A squadron of cavalrymen ascended the uphill way. To their left, the camp was torn despite the works that prepared the fort till the times of the festive winter. Campfires and braziers were watered, where the river flowed like lava, thickened by the wash of blood. The battlefield had been emptied and the dead were abandoned to be burned. It was as the promise Regulus von Eos had endured, the Confederates retreated hesitantly.

"Speak o' de devils, ya kids look like ya've seen hell an' back." Adam welcomed, tossing the flag onto the wagon.

"I'm glad you made it safely too, instructors." Julien greeted.

"Gah, c'mon. We couldn't sit 'round when all da fun happened ta be in da south." A lie took a liking to Adam's voice again.

The elites dismounted and upon the immediate landfall, they were welcomed by the seniors whose eyes could not be taken from the youths reminiscent of their memories in the decades ago.

"Are they the general's guards?" One colonel asked.

"You've done well." Another admirably thanked them.

"Do they not remind you of our days, Władysław?" An older staff laughed beside Warneńczyk, sharing a memory of a near-forgotten past.

But for his adrenaline and drive to survive had gone, Arminius suffered the gush of numbness in his legs and tapped

Julien for aid. His two closest comrades, without a delay rushed to his side and carried the squad captain by his arms as they neared the slight crowd whom the general led.

"General...sorry...Vasilevsky...he..." Arminius despaired, but Warneńczyk somehow saw otherwise.

"No, do not be." The commander raised his hand and pushed his every staff to work.

"Rzhev's death caused the southern flank to break." He pointed at the plains where death was rife and soaking the earth.

The terrible flask of wine unbottled and the odor had returned. Never needing to know what the elder had blended in the ghastly mixture, Julien and Károly inched from the scent with Arminius closing his lungs before safety was reached.

"The reformation will take the lion until morning." Sipping the wine, the general told.

"He has provided us the perfect opportunity to retreat before an encirclement."

As Warneńczyk wiped his mustache, stained by a dash of beetroot red, the square of the ridge became devoid of officers unfamiliar to the closest ring of the general. There remained the trusted folk. Arminius wondered whether he should grant the report of the ceasefire when another decided to tell,

"About the Confederates..."

Stuffing his handkerchief in the chest pocket, Warneńczyk grunted and asked,

"What of it?"

"A colonel promised to slow Vasilevsky's advance after Rzhev's death" Julien documented.

The general did not interrupt. In the delay of his mind, he knew not what to say of the oddity. Even if a thought or a theory arose, the old man could not be so sure.

"I don't know...or understand..." The Danne quieted, knowing nothing of the enemy's senses.

"Have you a name?" Warneńczyk scratched his chin, unaware of the name to be called.

"Regulus von Eos." Arminius recollected.

A rivaling set of eyes hid on him. As if dragging his body into battle once more he had tried to ignore. But still, he could not shake the coldness that had seized the flow of blood. Amongst the well-learned, the colonel emerged a thousand fold greater than the person they had met. Yet the few who had never heard his address minded the stolen colors of their comrades' pupils.

"Eos?!" Florek erupted, unlike his professional guise.

"The family who had fought the Rus for over eight centuries," Julien began an account, shortened of a vast history.

"Only Tsarevich Alexei conquered them in a year."

Observant of the Confederates, the squad faced the vice general whose search for his comrade Rzhev was nowhere in the ranks. The roars of infuriation were negligent of what his adjutant had told him. Unwilling for the belief, he rose an arm for the summon of Regulus as an elite voiced her tale,

"Like the Libra,"

"Their family is dying." Alexandria had said her first words of the day.

"Then would that not make Regulus von Eos…" Lev voiced among those who would not for Julien and Arminius were not the only who had surfaced a forbidding fact.

"The so-called genius of war?" asked the lancer.

The pounding understanding of what they had faced and dared threaten, Arminius clutched onto Julien's shoulder ever tighter. His wounds had settled by the heat, fusing with the runs of sweat. However, on the picture of the Confederate's departure, the elites remembered the last word.

"Do you know each other?" An interrogating act rebounded all's ears to Arminius.

"No…how would I?" The latter lowered the frown of pain and held higher to his ally's blank curiousness.

"Why did he call you by another name, Regen?" Arber recalled.

"Was that not one of the three imperial families of the Fourth Reich?"

By the morrow, the Winged Lance had gone. A heavy fog had descended into the valley. Carried by the scent of burning homes, raped of loot, and of massacred militiamen from the last stand against the Confederacy. The reputed greatest of all, the Summer Lion Army, mobilized upon the forgetting of the disaster the previous evening.

From the lush grassy meadow beyond the river, crossing it, brought Vice General Vasilevsky to the wasteland. Muddied by unrecognizable faces, mutilated by arrows and eifers that had dissected and blasted the bodies into quarters. Both Aelon and Confederate troops of a few found the humanity to spare their enemies before a calm death swept. They came across a young soldier, whose limbs and face were shredded, but horrifically breathing with a wasting throat, reservedly. He had laid himself against a sturdy spear, before a new friend found of the site. An Aelon soldier who was so fortunate to have already begun to rot. The stench flew by Vasilevsky's nose.

"We're close." Regulus led the general closer to the grounds of the last duel, where there was a stark contrast in the stages of destruction that had torn the world apart.

On the approach, the fog thinned, lifting a shroud over a single soldier collapsed in the center. With his rapier stuck through his chest that held him, like a skewer, kneeling, hands dropped and a dissatisfied death face.

Vasilevsky's heart thumped, dismounting, and walking towards his late student. The staff caught the general and saw their comrade, shriveled from the leaking blood that had ceased. Their eyes watered, ever so slightly. Regulus never found anguish. His commander, reluctant to grasp the truth, whose eyes and hands were madly shaking, knelt before Rzhev. A narrow stream of tears ran when he clenched his palms on the cold corpse's arms.

XIX

11 AUZHUSTUS 491
11.08.12017

Leonid Vasilevsky

The disaster that I had suffered in Laken paled to the one I've witnessed. That old geezer has beaten me numb. And now once more, I've failed to uphold my teach's wishes of encircling the millions by fall. Sorrmul was a shitshow. To blame it on the innocent women and children we massacred was the last thing we could've done as sacrifices for Rzhev's entry into his reincarnation. I haven't been able to see my own for two days by my will, except for those occasions where Eos would catch me with another reconnaissance report.

Hah…!

General Igor Rzhev. You have finally exceeded me. Naturalized as of Kolchakov's courts. His style and exemplary talent, he was a few years younger than I was. But as the ages passed, that narrow mind of a street urchin became overconfident and loyal, as if he was born to the upper nobility. The acts he performed, were, and always had been a theatrical nuisance. But now a part of that light in the headquarter's flair had been swallowed by the God of Death. If there was one thing I should've known before throwing him into battle with a fiend's aide-de-camp was how victory ensured his painful death.

Then otherwise, I would not have done so…

CHAPTER

20

A DEMON IN
THE WOODS

"Sorrmul. Our promised victory sees the anarchy of the devils."
Warneńczyk flicked through the pages of the papers titled
L'État, marked the fourth of Apelyotes.

"Only sixteen thousand losses we have achieved and over
sixty thousand Confederates." With his reading glasses slightly
dipped, the general addressed aloud.

A refreshing aroma from his warm cup of coffee circulated
the corner. The staff were working tirelessly. The rubbing of
nightmarish stacks of files and clacking of heels about the smooth
stone floor. That was except for the three. Ascot, Florek, Adam.
His only audience stayed lazing.

"Is this the beginning of an end for the mechanized in
warfare?" He told onwards with a grunt.

"With the complete devastation of the Summer Lion's armor
with the blades of our glorious alliance."

Tossing the paper, Warneńczyk removed his glasses, stuffing
them in the single chest pocket, and leaned against the mayor's
chair with his hands gently resting on his stomach. Contemplating
whether the earn of praise was worth the battle, the old man
huffed.

"Dey need ta catch up." Crossing his arms, Adam chuckled.

"I do not blame them." Ascot complimented as he
remembered for the inner circle,

"We have not won a battle since then."

Rising from the creaking chair, Warneńczyk strolled towards
a map board nailed to the marble wall. He tapped the crinkled
paper twice whose markings had three great crosses slashed
across nations.

"Leken capitulated a day after we arrived." Warneńczyk read.

"Nurtözh and Sueken a week later."

A classical town hall they resided within. The building had

been repurposed into nothing short of a military headquarters. Its toppest floor had been transformed into a glorious revolutionary cabinet reflecting the days of the partisans, overlooking the river flowing with tugs and boats, surrounded by the calm snow on the banks whitened like toothpaste. His army patrolled the city, marching the same streets until it was another's round; whilst some played with the children of the boulevards, tossing snowballs and sliding on the pavement's ice. In the distance, the medieval walls of Sedinn stood some twenty meters tall, protecting the jagged perimeter reinforced by the city militia manning the cannons of their homes. Lined with natural barricades, the many rivers and an impressive lake, it was no wonder the Confederates had yet tried to assault. It was equal to a meaningless suicide charge. Before the Plan Green line.

"I'm still quite taken." Florek admired the untouched skyline of red roofs and white walls that blended into the snow, with splashes of greenish bronze smeared across the city.

"How is it that this place remained undisturbed?"

Warneńczyk slowly moved his index finger along the map, from Rutenn to the main continent, and asked,

"Remember the bombings?"

"How could we forget?" Adam poured a new cup of hot tea into his flask and shook it around to dispel the heat.

"Four million..."

"And not a single one here in Sedinn." Circling with a light-colored pencil four points on the map, Warneńczyk informed his subordinates.

"It's one of the fortresses the Confederates desire."

The officers neared, to hold them for the general who turned back to explain.

"Basil."

A valley fort that had held necessity for only two walls to the east and west. Wedged between two mountains. Dictated by the Hëlwet canton in Zhormann. Who held Basil had the ordained authority over the Alpen.

"Kulunn." The mention of a second.

The city of three walls. Each some thirty meters high, rested on the River Rennen. It laid the sole reason why the three Zhormannik kings were able to launch a counter-offensive against the Allies that recaptitulated the world of four-twenty-three.

"Tschrewen."

Certainly, the impression of her sisters were greater. But the two thousand and four hundred canals and the port, the maze of the fortress was never subtracted from any mind who wished to conquer Yurupe.

"And Sedinn." The general ended.

An eastern redoubt across the river could match the fire power of any of her counterparts. It was the first step for the beast in the east nevermind the fields of the continent. If they could not scale or break, wade or sail the walls and rivers, the Confederacy was no giant.

"To maintain a foothold on the mainland before shifting their invasion to the isles and the far west." suggested Florek whilst the burn of tobacco leaves in an odd solution drifted over their heads.

"But are dey willin' ta throw everythin' at us?" Adam added, soaking his lungs in the smoke.

The expanse hall was soon shrouded by the scent of the herb. A pale grayness lifted the yellowish tint of the lanterns and the eclipsed light of the sun. For its windows, Warneńczyk trekked towards and smiled before the blur of the dust-covered glass. His hand was on the desk and a pile of reports that bore a known name of his ranks whilst the aides found homes, leaning on the wall, and chair. Only Ascot ever stood upright.

"I would not worry myself over the vanguard." The old man confessed.

Held a finger for the walls fogged by the season, his nail was directed at the forest beyond the eastern redoubt.

"Our nine sergeants...no...lieutenants are enough to deter." Warneńczyk smirked, raising his mustache by the corners.

"If only three hundred and sixty could pin them in their place," Scanning the new reports under the general's palm, Florek commended.

"Imagine what they could do with barely ten times that."

The lieutenant closed his eyes and snickered, lifting his cigarette above an ear, scratched by his thumb. Long he had been blessed by a talent that whispered the hiding essence in a voice and so which the commander had, Adam pushed for an answer,

"And dat's not it?"

A breath of the general paused. Revolving to the desk by

his heels, he pulled closer a chair and took his back to rest. With the restored heat of the brew in his hands, the elderly senses gathered the rising steam under his nose. Not fearing a little burn as he drank, the coffee brightened the needed vigor of a winter heartbeat.

"Hmph." Clicking his tongue when the mug left his lips, Warneńczyk answered,

"I must admit there was always a second."

The dirt tracks slushed under the banner of a white, crowned eagle. Like a cold shake of snow and mud. Its gravel roads, plunged into the dry cold sea, were non-existent. The occasional howls that felled tree branches shook his squad from the ever growing cold that began to sink from the falling sun. With Julien and Károly, Arminius marched in the deep snow that swallowed their knees. Shivering, the common occurrence of snow seeping into their boots, they marched on. As a band of ninety men, they feared not even if an army descended upon them. The trust held in their hearts could deter the devils' force if their band fought together. But it was still troubling that they, the infamous elite squad, were forced to patrol the woods so far from a warm brazier.

"I can't...believe...my grandpa would...make us do this... achoo..." Károly sneezed.

Wrapped in a thin blanket by his comrades to trap any heat, the onset of winter in the Lekann lands found its way through his layers of clothing that were never sewn for the freezing climate.

"When we were training...in the mountains...it wasn't this cold..."

He sneezed again and sniffled, clutching Julien's arm as the Danne dragged him along.

"You need to walk to warm yourself, at least." The latter hinted but Károly would not budge from the ride.

Sighing at a loss, Julien untangled his frayed scarf and tossed it over the archer's head, drooping onto his shoulder. Quickly wrapping the gift around him, yet he still shuddered.

"We're almost there." Pointing at the open forest grounds in their sights that was luckily, shallower, Julien said.

"How is it...that you're immune...to the cold?" Arminius' teeth clattered, puffing steam as he spoke with a paled face.

"Not you too..." Julien sighed, unbuttoning a satchel that held a bottle within.

The cap he spun opened for a fragrant scent that smelled like tea. But it was mildly sweetened and had a speck of spice that was exotic to their noses.

"Here!" Cheerily, the lieutenant offered.

"Some ginger tea."

A common drink in the northern nations of the old world. Though it had originated from the far east, somehow, even as he had never mentioned, Julien, unbeknownst to the typical human warmth, knew how a brew could fill a heart at ease.

"Thanks..." Arminius nodded, unbinding his splitting lips for a sip when Károly dove his head.

Gulping the last drop that not a drip for Arminius could be saved, the lieutenant captain exhaled loudly, ushering a thick cloud of steam from his mouth.

"Hey, Károly, save some for Arminius." Julien flustered but the plea was late.

"Did you really make this yourself?!" The concoction of a fantastical attitude invigorated Károly.

"I knew that would happen..." Arminius and Julien murmured, resting their arms over the archer's shoulder.

Near the opening, by tall pine trees stripped of their leaves and left to the breeze, the sag of energy drained from the hike of the morning and noon. It was only so by coincidence, that they had stumbled upon the perfect station for a gathering before their return to the city for the monthly rotation. Logs and tree stumps carved into what appeared to be a camp. Frozen over by a thin layer of ice and snow that dripped onto the mud, filled the grounds with new snow. It did not look as if anyone had come recently. But for the understandable harshness of nature, no one would.

"A hunting post." Károly detected, swiping the snow away beneath his feet to reveal an old fireplace.

There with a flint stick, but empty. Ash and small rocks formed the outline.

"Seems abandoned for the winter as well." Arminius halted the march and scouted the site.

He searched for the barriers which protected them. The hollowness between trunks of trees and branches that kept their vision clear of the rounded hold. Signaling for all to the arm stretching for the canopy, Arminius waved with a call to their troops,

"Let's hold here!"

Clatters and shudders. The platoons gathered their bodies around the growing bundles of firewood. From barks and branches into piles across the camp, Károly fastened the clearance of the woods. Once the ash and snow had been brushed aside, he unsheathed his knife and held it firmly against the flint. Throwing a handful of sparks into the dried sticks in one flick, the camp lit with a single brazier that soon expanded to the seven there were.

The ground began to thin of snow, although the blessing of the clouds still fell elegantly from the sky, and the camp warmed. Huddling around the stones and flickers of flames, the loyal soldiers awaited with chatters on one name. The retreat into Sedinn and the hearty meals of civilization.

Close by the blaze, Károly and Arminius warmed their hands. The heat was fanned towards their faces from the single current of the forest.

"Ah…" They expelled the last inch of frost in their lungs with a breath sucking the flying embers.

"I'd forgotten what warmth was like…" Resting his eyes, Arminius mumbled with a disturbing moan.

"I'll make sure to mark this camp for our replacements." Julien drew a notebook and sketched a map.

But as Arminius' hand reached for his pocket, the Danne stopped. A parental stare eyed the other, tapping a cigarette from the box and sticking the smoke beneath a dying match. Arminius pretended not to notice a disturbing glare with a renewing of another conversational topic.

"So, uh…" He stammered, avoiding Julien's eyes.

"What are we gonna have for dinner when we get back—?" Arminius forced a question out of his guts.

"I can't believe you sometimes." Julien huffed and lifted his kepi as he sat opposite him, further from the fire.

"Before anything, we should report back to the general—" He flicked the pages to the end, where there was a list detailing the skirmishes and scouts they had encountered for the past month.

"Arminius!" A call for the lieutenant turned him to the guarded perimeters, where several guards have been autonomously posted.

Two soldiers of the same youth sprinted for the trio.

"Arnau? Siegfried?" Arminius leaned from the fallen tree and inhaled his smoke.

Siegfried. His age was never told but it was clear he had not struck the teens. With a gentle face, cheerful in his dark green eyes, he was considerably shorter than his identical comrade in height and blonde hair. Who wielded a short sword, so for its scabbard would not drag, his black and green jäger's coat was the noblest wear one could find in an armory. But of poverty and unfortunate belonging, that must have soaked his family's lacking fortune.

"Lieutenant." By the name of Arnau Rieding, the compatriot greeted.

Like Julien, he was of fourteen harsh years. An aged Siegried. Though sincere and steady knowing his role, it was often the shell of a heart beneath that held a childhood never experienced. Bearing a raised sallet helmet that covered his longish hair, the shadows of the steel darkened his emerald pupils. The lightness of shades and inexpensive market clothes that he could surely afford ten pieces over. How he carried six blades, of swords and knives, and the hunks for defense for Arnau was able to move in his boyish build was absurd.

"A message from Lieutenant Calenzo." said he, placing his helmet on a tree stump by a hand that was scarred by burns.

"He'll be late home 'cause of a skirmish!" Siegfried pushed Arnau aside and delivered the report in happiness and simplicity.

"Another battle...?" Károly repeated, spinning to Arminius for new orders.

Yet the commander shutted his mouth on the feeling of a disturbance. He turned his focus to the north when the earth quaked beneath. A trail, a smudge of smoke rose by a howling boom seconds after. The burst of a gale racing through the winding gaps of the woods blasted Siegfried into fright as he sheltered behind Arnau. From the settling storm, when the forest snapped to their return to naturality, Siegfried felt his head be grabbed and locked in a fierce rub by his friend.

"I still don't know why you're afraid of little things like this."
Arnau laughed at the youngest.

"That must be Gin…" Julien thought.

"No matter how many times we tell him not to use his eifer."
Arminius shook his head and scolded without the brute being in
the present.

"So, are we just gonna wait here?" Arnau checked as he
released his strangle.

Without an ask for a favor from Károly, in joy, Siegfried leapt
onto his back and was taken with a dash of a whirlwind.

"Yeah. We might revise our plan." Announcing to Arnau's
surprise, Arminius steered a finger around the snow.

Károly toured the camp by hops and sprints, following the
breeze wherever it blew, with Siegfried latched tightly onto him,
laughing and giggling from the freedom that provided a kind
show for the older comrades of the force. They searched the fires
for rumors and half a joke that occupied themselves with the
recruits who feasted on the last rations of biscuits and candies.

"You mean to retake Stellpurt?" asked Arnau of the
Confederate town beyond the forest.

"It's too vital to lose," Julien analyzed, drawing a map with a
stick on the ground.

"That will be our wedge into Leken, large enough to flood
two armies…" He drove his comrades' eyes for the depot of the
town.

"Or so Arminius says." Arnau finished his sentence.

Landing where he had begun, Károly dropped Siegfried onto
his feet whose knowledge of the day had achieved fulfillment.

"The general's entrusted it all to the three hundred sixty of
us!" Siegfried keenly peeped.

"Then we'll be able to become guards for the König, right?"

"But won't you just cower behind me once it really comes
to it?" Arnau wrapped his arm around Siegfried and drove his
knuckles against his skull.

"Who said that?" The younger fought away, wriggling and
slipping from the choking clinch.

"You'll surely become more renowned by fighting with us."
Chuckling with smugness, Arminius secured their stay

Who with no reply, the two knights embarrassedly smiled as
the commander stood and inhaled a pour of smoke for the final

stretch of the cigarette. With the strange interlude of war merrily silent of spilling blood, the soldiers of the Aelon had been sedated by the tranquility. Tossing the roll that was saved from the burn by the melting ice around, although there was no such need, he lightly crunched the ash with a boot.

"No matter what, once we get this war over with," Arminius placed his hands on their shoulders.

Nodding, Siegfried and Arnau grinned at each other who had once agreed before the moment.

"You can decide then—" The lieutenant told them.

"Arminius…" Julien knelt beside where the smoke had sunken into the meltwater, wiping away the cotton-like ice that stuck to his glove to reveal an unearthly dent.

"What is it?" Strolling with the three by his flanks, Arminius examined the revealing hole that had collapsed.

Bending down to see what wild thing caught Julien so interested, they staggered by their bewilderment. Their pupils shrunk and shone. Except it was for Károly, all the more curious, to tread onwards to the mammoth print from a beast who's paws, made of five claws, eclipsed their heads. It had been frozen, under the ice, as fossils were. Unmoving and untainted by any outsiders, the snow had preserved the fantastical sight.

"H-How could something this big live here?" Holding Arnau, shivering from the cold and ascending fog, Siegfried cried.

"I don't know," Arminius watched the lines of the deathly shrubs and said.

"And I doubt anyone's willing to find out—" Waving his arm for his men across the camp, the lieutenant readied to drag the ninety into battle when a comrade's hand brought his shoulders to rest.

"Armin, wait." Károly whispered whilst the mumbles of Arnau and Siegfried screened the officers' voices.

"It'll cause panic with the exhausted." Julien assessed, from the decision of Arminius that would have thrown the thirtieth day into a hell.

"We can't know for sure but," adding to the untold chill, Károly snatched his bow and told.

"It doesn't look like the beast's been here recently—"

Arminius felt a shadow stalking in the treelines. Its kei was not human but other-worldly. He heard Julien and Károly's voices calling for him as he reached for his sword. But before he was quick enough to unsheath it, a blizzard leapt from the fog, casting a grim shade over the officers. A beast, four times the size of a grown man growled, with a mounted warrior whose gleaming eyes shone like a terrible omen.

XX

4 APELYOTES 491
04.11.12017

Władysław Warneńczyk

Whenever you were frightened, beaten, robbed, we sought help when none gave any. Seek the nearest forest where a shrine always awaits. But do this quick, during the winter, when the snow has set. Before the melting season burns down whatever's left. It is only then, the Stunnebyar, a bear of stone and ice, will appear for all our Lekann children in distress.

That is the story, at least, that has been told for the last seven decades. Everyone knows of this modern legend. It was never some folklore of the old.

In urgency, I would often go pray for him. Even as the occupation spanned my life. Before the liberation. Before a battle. After the resistance. After the calamity. He and his keepers were not simply characters to be told as bedtime stories. The state, especially the King, believes this bear as their very protector. The problem is, we do not know whether this creature is alive. No one had ever deliberately gone searching for him...

A fictional legend? Hah! Major, I would never lie of that...

CHAPTER

21   THE STONE BEAR

A flesh wall pranced at Arminius, like a preying creature, growling as if it had been rung alive. Roaring for a feast of blood, its claws were the size of their knives, perhaps even sharper, that has seen its veteran days in this forest, scarred by impressive cuts to the bone, but not a single wound on its body which carried a monstrous man. The warrior with eyes that taunted their minds shone bright like two red stars, wielding an alarming double-headed axe with a blunderbuss built into the weapon that carelessly swung at the lieutenants.

The unit caught sight of the vengeful spirit and were thrown into an unplanned panic. They clamored, unable to move, and were stilled in their shaking legs who seemed too afraid to aid their officers. The sky-scraping mounted beast shadowed everything beneath him. But Arminius found his resolve to fight.

"Out of the way!" He pushed Julien and Károly aside who took the two knights with them.

Tensely, with gritting teeth, Arminius brought his sword in a charge of the eifer before the blade was unsheathed, illuminating the scabbard. As he drew it, the axe, for it had skipped time, quickened towards Arminius' head when two spears, together, clanked before the duelists.

From the sparks of the grinding blades, Arminius flinched. Noticing two tall soldiers had caught the blade, holding the monster with a crossing shield of spears as the axe pressed.

"Sup." The black haired soldier turned to see if Arminius had been saved.

"Lev? Miklós?!" Arminius cried, abandoning his powers.

"Two children have stopped my time-devouring axe." The monster lowly groaned, bringing free an inner demonic rumble.

"That's impressive, I'll let you have that." He said conservatively.

Steam puffed from the skin as the heat generated with simple breaths. It was unclear how far his limits could be stretched, but that strike still seemed lenient towards his prey.

"Name's Lev Hayek!" Lev introduced himself, transferring the pair of eifer to one hand.

"Miklós...Dragosavac...demon...of...my...people..." Miklós grunted.

The miracle of the two began its push against the warrior, breaking open his strike that tossed a whirl of snow and small black embers into the forest. Pulling on the reins, his bear clawed into the ground, ripping open the earth as it was thrown along the white, bottomless carpet.

Retreating towards Arminius, protecting the lieutenant by the spears, Lev and Miklós panted. As Károly slid, locking his bow and grabbing the quiver, he nocked three arrows in the valleys of his fingers whilst Siegfried and Arnau drew themselves behind the commanders whose swords plainly aimed for the demon's head.

"Are the others not with you?" Arminius asked, helping Julien from the snow whilst the haze over the unseen face thickened.

"No. They're too caught up chasing Confederate ass." Lev replied.

"Scouts?" From the report received, Arminius could only have guessed.

A drop of sweat fell from Lev's cheeks that burned from his eifer. The bitterness of the dual authority in winter and death he could taste by the ash and snow fluttering onto his lips.

"An entire battalion." The Rus disclosed.

A battalion?! Nerves of Arminius' mind echoed in loops of voices.

Are they planning for an attack soon?

"We can talk about it later." Lev's hands stayed firm, steadfast, clicking the spear when he targeted the tip at the monster.

"For now, this titan needs to be excused."

But the giant's ghastly gaze spoke of death, stealing their souls from an immeasurable aura. He and his beast took a step onwards and revealed their colors in the sunlight, barely penetrating the clustered clouds.

Their eyes widened and pupils shrunk, shuddering from an unforeseen surprise that uncovered the man's unthinkable size.

"He...He's a colossus!" Lev took a step back.

In the bright ray, not one portion of his body was short of brawns and widened veins. He, the man of horrors, had a maze-like bushy beard connected to his dark brown hair shaped into a thick slabbed crew cut. His skin was slightly darker than Gin's, and although the climate he lived in was the lowest extreme the unit had visited, all the man wore was a white undershirt with a military jacket branded by some flag. Neither his pants, too small, or morning routine slippers were for the winter. A thought, like the bluntness of his eyes, could give all chills.

Yet what was more stunning was the bear he rode. A Kaukasann brown. Some two meters standing on all limbs, patches of his shining fur had been whitened by ice for the past however long years he had witnessed. Together, they stood over four paces tall, as if they were a distant star, incomparably enormous. And despite all the features of a tyrant he carried, his eyes were not that of a heartless killer no matter how terrifying they seemed. There was a mediocre hint of compassion.

"What's an invading army's purpose here in my forest?" The man bellowed.

His forest? Arminius thought, turning to Lev, bracing his stance as the ice around his feet began to melt at the swirling void of embers.

Though he was not alone. Károly's arrow was engulfed in a flaming blanket and Aranu had exposed his two longswords with an intent of an agile victory.

"Are you Zhormannik? Boëm?" The warrior asked, conserving his strength.

"Perhaps the Suedes of across the sea."

His foes remained silent, unknown of what to say. Another word could be wrongly taken and their heads would take flight.

"Fine. My task here is only to protect this land."

"It matters not if none answer." He growled.

Raising his axe above, a reflection of the future was shown when the blade was to be embraced by the sludge of flesh. Mirages and shockwaves forged, splitting the air from time and space.

"Gah! This is a pain." Lev faced his spear downwards.

The black dragon danced, revolving around its master like a deity. Embers from the tip of his blade spun into flame from a bright orange into a cold black fire. Whilst Miklós' footing cracked the earth, a devil erupted from his back, like a phantom colossus whose razor teeth made its jaws that frightened even his own men. There the matter held in balance for whoever would give the first blow.

"Wait!" Arminius cried for either factions to halt, spotting the flag sewn into the warrior's jacket and the colors he bore.

"Arminius?" Julien uttered.

Lev and Miklós retrieved their eifers on the order but Károly was not so willing. From the simple word of Arminius, the messengers Arnau and Siegfried had little choice except to obey. That it seemed to have doused the festival. The warrior's axe had stopped rumbling when he was paused too whilst Arminius pointed at his sleeve that caught Julien's eyes.

"Shouldn't we be fighting together?!" Arminius yelled, slipping past the protectors who were spoken to calm.

The lieutenant halted beyond the warrior's reach, far enough from his axe that did not provoke the man who addressed,

"What would make you think that, brat?"

"Aren't you the protector of Leken?" Arminius had noticed and for the warrior looked upon his own sleeve that had exposed his unsure allegiance.

"The Stonnebyar..." Károly heard of the childhood fiction, only to know that the being of such a monster could appear.

Stone bear of the northern star? The unit muttered amongst themselves as the uncertainty shrouded the foreigners,

Have you heard of him?

As the unit had arisen from panic and the air had quieted, a sense of curiosity lingered. Irremovable from their hearts.

"If so, then how has the nation fallen?!" Arminius clutched his collar with the rupture of his temper that was a little act to ridicule the great protector.

Not without a vision on his mind, Julien jogged for the center where the baggage had been bunched and attached to the lieutenant by an invisible string, Siegfried followed.

"You've got nerves to say so, kid." The warrior's eifer blared a horrendous bellow, as if it was sounded by a battleship announcing the dawn of battle.

"Do you wish for death?"

He stormed, clouding his judgement, who rashly held his axe above for the tracks to be set on a strike. An iron heart bulged and the crushing weight of his world pummeled.

"The answer's here—" The devil boomed.

When the warrior was held, it was by a flapping flag. Raised above the campfires to the middle of the troops, behind Arminius, it stole the beast's senses. Waving a cloth standard of the royal Lekann flag, Julien and Siegfried bore.

Dismounted at the sight of a familiar banner, the being towered over Miklós nearing the two meter mark. The protector patted the bear and approached Arminius, casting a heavy shadow over the gloom whose inner soul had seen disintegration.

"I presume you are here to recruit me." The tone of the monster changed.

Recruit him? I haven't even thought this far ahead. Arminius questioned himself though in the exchange of thoughts, Julien calculated,

But we shouldn't let this opportunity go...the general might need someone like him on the frontlines...

"Were you sent by King August?" asked the warrior, but the deepness and the blare of his voice did not alter.

Cold sweat ran. Allies were fated and tied to the lieutenant. It was no childish matter. Afterall, there was the impossibility to deflect the stone bear's charge. Yet Arminius still surely replied, shocking the unit of life,

"No."

Lev drew away, realizing an antagonizing aura forming around the warrior. The archer appeared before Arminius and held his shoulder, trying to drag him from the bounds of death.

"Armin...maybe say...yes?" With a shaking core, Károly explained for a better choice in words.

"Then what are you here for?" The protector asked, chopping his great axe into the ground that firmly mounted upright.

There, tearing his mind between one doubt and another with nothing but a strand of hair attempting to hold the enveloping crack in place. Arminius' cluelessness in stranded times was infamous amongst his closest. But neither dared or judged that they could answer, else it might do away whatever plot the lieutenant had planned.

I could lie...but would he see through it? Arminius drowned himself in an infinite layer of hesitation.

No...I shouldn't gamble with our lives. Then this... He clenched his fists, and finally answered bluntly,

"We were ordered to bring back the protector by a general."

A gale separated their breaths, as if protecting Arminius with a division in space. Branches snapped when the weight, stacked upon, was too heavy to endure and collapsed into the snow.

"Is that so?" The stone bear growled.

Julien gulped. There was an eerie silence before Siegfried broke by whispering to Arnau,

"Did it work?"

"I hope so." With his hand on the pommel of a sword, Arnau prayed.

Grunting for the last, the warrior lifted his axe from the soil and brought a heavy blanket of roots and mud with it, flicking dark brown specks of dirt onto Arminius' uniform.

"Very well." said he in agreement, mounting the bear and bringing the creature towards the path that they came from.

"Follow." The protector demanded.

Their faces brightened in a silent cheer with Arminius' hands regaining some color. The thumps of hearts had stopped and restarted by a catch of breaths. Sighing from the unbelievable outcome that could be dreamt but untrue, Arminius commanded a subordinate of the unit,

"Arnau. You're up till the rest arrive."

"'Course, Lieutenant." Arnau and Siegfried saluted, smiling at the victorious.

"Lev, Miklós, Károly, Julien." Arminius called for.

"I'm glad that's over." Hugging the spear on his chest, Lev relieved the knots of his guts.

From a distance, the five lieutenants tailed the beast. Each with the respect of themselves and the elites' captain. By either the demon or Confederates, they were readied for an ambush if need be, blending into the surroundings. The vision of their backs were removed, in the further march from the units. However the disappearance of the high smoke and the awakening of chatters pinched the vow of silence from the protector.

"That was a poor lie, child." He spoke to the demise of the truce.

"Any idiot could have seen through that." The titan added as Lev and Károly solidified and braced for an assault.

But the stone bear never stopped.

"I am only curious for what you have to say." Admitted to the truth of the soul, for that the warrior hoped to ally.

Where the snow thickened, far from the camp, in the turbulent ocean of the woods and ice at a leg of the journey was a depthful trench Károly fell through. That covered half his body, he was tugged to the surface by Lev's arms who carried the archer across the ditch that swamped the elites. When asked anything, they would answer without fault. About such ideas as the Third Calamity that had drowned the world. So during the lengthy hike uphill, Arminius told the happenings of the outside world for the warrior had seemed to have lived his life in seclusion. No news of the turns in the decade had reached his ears except for the knowledge of the late King of Leken's tragic death. And though there was much more to be said, the stone bear and the master were familiarized with the present by the return to his lodge.

Placing his axe on top of a slanted shelf, the warrior picked six tin cups from a cupboard, nailed to the roof that his head nearly touched, and sat them on the kitchen counter where there was a sizable bottle of tea leaves.

"Chai?" He asked under a roof of hospitality from someone appearing unlikely.

"Yes, please." Most answered, though half had not known what it was.

In the regular cabin, brightly lit with numberless lamps and torches hung from pillars, there was not much that piqued the squad's interest. As expected of any lodge dotted in an uncharted sector of the map, there was a humble rack of rifles. Dusty, and antique, waiting to be used, beside an old cobbled fireplace, blackened into odd patterns on the rim. Whilst in the corner, most impressively laid a set of armor that did not appear to have been worn once in its lifetime despite the priceless craftsmanship it showcased. And sat, some standing, around a squarish table beside a window with curtains drawn, were the officers and the huge warrior, each holding a cup of tea.

"This Confederacy has pushed their way into *our* world."

"Is His Majesty, the King, safe?" He asked with a clear concern for the royals though it was not expected from someone who acted like a hermit.

"Yes. It was on the papers." Arminius answered.

"King August was flown to Borulinn."

Seeing that all were weary from the cold, the man tossed a match into the fireplace, igniting what was left of the firewood until it burned like hellfire. Almost too instantaneously. As if he had fanned the flames with omitted incantations, the lounge was warmed.

Knowing his king was safe satisfied his questions, and left a blank reply. A gentle nod.

"They were half right about the Stonnebyar." The man revealed, looking to the snow where his bear was resting beneath a five hundred year old evergreen tree, a sky blue color that blended into its habitat, yawning at the winter birds flocking to him.

"Wojtek the Protector."

"A beast who would live a thousand years, right?!" Károly piped.

"He's only seen seventy five years." The warrior told them.

Then it would have meant the calm creature was barely a yearling in the eyes of a millenia.

"And I am merely his third generation,"

"Wojsław Ashur." He was introduced as though his eyes did not seem to have care for the guests' names.

The glare had the same aura as what they had felt from Warneńczyk months ago, but there was something unusual about the demon that appeared less threatening than the general's. Lacking heart to scheme or ambush potentially. As the leader of the front removed his gloves for his own hands to be heated by the mug, the elites tensed in the wait for one to end the grave stillness. Gin was not there. Rocking his cup in a circle that spun a whirlpool in the strange foreign tea, Lev wondered aloud in fascination,

"That's a weird name..."

"Are you not Lekann?" The lieutenant asked.

"My grandfather was Porsann." Was all that Wojsław answered with, a nation of the ancients.

"Not that any *Menschen der Alten Welt* would know of." A blend of an elden language stayed the boys baffled even the sharpest ears of Arminius understood not.

Settling the tea that he did not sip once, Wojsław grunted,

like in disdain of sharing the same air as the people granted invitation to his home. Was it the intolerance of seeing the colored eyes and pale tones of the soldiers that soured the taste of the chai's incense on the outskirts of his tongue, but there was one who he spoke more leniently towards whom had stared at for the longest time.

"I presume you are the fellow demon I had sensed, Miklós." Wojsław knew not of random.

The giant dwarfed by the other titan blinked slowly and dipped his head.

"A fellow d-demon?!" Károly clattered, feeling a chill along his spine as he thought of the impossible twists that paralyzed him.

Arminius knocked on his skull and pinched his comrades cheeks as he cleared the lieutenant captain's imaginative mind,

"Moron, he's talking about the eifer."

"Us demons have the ability to sense another," With crossed arms which were as thick as tyres, the protector shutted his eyes and said.

"Hear them talk from afar. Follow their lives."

As his back pressed with his flanks wider than the seat, the groaning legs of the chair and floorboards sounded near to snap. The tea had lost its radiance. The steam had dissipated. Half full were the cups, the ripples were no more like the locks on their voices. Motionless.

"We could know every detail." Wojsław alarmed the elites with the truth of the demons.

"That's why many of our people remain quiet or silent."

Lev's face lightened, as if discovering a new person within his friend, he found Miklós' blink and a nod again.

"However, I did not encounter your unit out of coincidence." The warrior accounted.

Drawing a heavy gasp of breath, briskly exhaling steam that almost turned fire, the air within grew weightier.

"There was a *fiend*."

Both sides halted a mutual trust. Hard earnt and fought for. Lost in a single sentence. To denounce anyone by that word more so within their squad closest was a bane.

"Who are you calling a fiend—?" Lev fought as Gin would do.

"Lev." Arminius called, stopping his near rampage.

A growl of the beast's lord tapped on the bear's ears. But he was simply put to sleep by the closing day. The tension of the living room eased for Wojsław withdrew,

"It seems I have deceived myself."

"Then, who was it that sent you?" And he finally questioned.

Arminius' hesitant fellowship glanced at one another, then eventually, their sights were placed upon the helm. The commander shone a slight dip of his head for Julien whose reply was nonetheless the equal of his comrades.

"Władysław Warneńczyk." He answered.

Nearly ripping his flesh from the bone he had dug his fingers into, the shine of Wojsław's eyes matched his strengthened grip.

"That's a dangerous name you speak of, child." The warrior took a sip of tea to weaken the beats in his chest.

Yet not for once, in the past three months, Arminius considered, had the general ever shown a sign of threat. Perhaps it was the induction that he never realized but for even the protector to speak of an old man in such a way, it was unfathomable.

"I was told by my father..." began Wojsław in a low tone.

"The Phantom Hussar. That was the name he bore on the battlefield."

Returning to his usual self, the great beast sat upright and committed a story with the squad quietly listening. Károly had never been so still in his life for by then, he would have stomped and shouted about in awe.

"He was said to be the ninth wonder behind the Whirlwind." Wojsław explained.

"Capable of chaos. His phantoms could sweep away a hundred thousand lives before noon." told the brutish man.

Unwrapping a block of rations stored in his coat, he tossed five biscuits into his mouth and rudely, he chomped on a snack, flapping crumbs over the table like a sandstorm that blew.

"But...he hasn't taken to the battlefield..." Julien pondered, breaking the warrior's story.

"Even if he truly possessed something of that caliber..." The Danne held his chin, never coming to realize the phantom of the general.

Drained of tea, crushed leaves and spots of sugar laid the bed of the steel vessels. Snatching the five mugs and his own, towards the kitchen, Wojsław stomped. Under a simple copper tap of trickling water, he began to wash the cups, not wasting a drop to the sink. As the elites admired the forest's dusk to the tapping of ice beads falling to the snow, the watch of his thumbs rolling about had Arminius quietest.

"It smelled of sin, five years ago." Wojsław carelessly blurted.

Three soldiers felt a stab in their spine as if the plates and joints of the body were split in a common shudder. Their faces had paled, corpse-like. But it was not by memory. There was nothing that could be explained to the minds of what stimulated a jab of pain. The unpleasantry of befriending death loomed beside their shoulders.

"The Protectorate." The beast emptied the water of his cup and sat it in a rack hung before his eyes.

The squad was silent. With the howling winds alone bashing against the thin rattling windows. Wojtek had fallen asleep and the birds had stopped singing at the turning daylight into a soothing sunset, darkening the early evening sky.

"W-What is th—?" But set aghast, Arminius stammered, forgetting all known languages of humanity.

At the gap of seconds in the unknown, the door flung open and a gush from the wild blizzard thrusted its way past a youth who opened it. Everyone spun around, taking a gasp as their eyes represented a grievous snap in their minds. When the young soldier, petrified of whom he had disturbed, once believing the lodge was empty, was seen bearing the enemy's flag on his great snow coat.

"A Confederate...?" Julien noticed.

"A-Ah...!" Frightened, the scout stuttered, slowly retreating to the outside.

A slam on the counter froze the Confederate as an animal growl of Wojsław neared. The warrior stamped for his axe, fluidly sliding from the shelf into his hands. He aimed the barrel at the soldier, who so unfortunately encountered the demon of Yurupe.

Weeping streams before true death's face, the Confederate stumbled and tripped over the doorway, falling into the snow as he crawled back.

"Death holds you..." Wojsław was a fly from his finger on the trigger then a sprinting comrade rushed for the barrel.

Holding the axe from its aim with his might, keeping Wojsław steady from firing, Arminius freed the soldier who stumbled as he fled.

"Did you not say they were our enemies?" The warrior boomed, rotating his eyes for the lieutenant.

"Or was I mistaken, again?" asked he, callously.

Their enemies' scout burrowed his hand in the snow and flung a white cloud at the two, before escaping with pants, running and tripping. Wojtek woke from his slumber, hearing the desperate crunch of snow, and spotted the scout speeding for the forest. Prepared to chase who he thought was prey, he roared loud that birds of the woods flapped away.

"Wojtek!" Arminius yelled determinedly with a sorrowful look.

The bear turned to him. Then sniffing, the creature stared at the scout disappearing downhill. Hesitantly, the protector of the kingdom heeded his words and sat against the tree, yawning.

"Are you going to stop my hand every time I bury an enemy?" Sending a rising shadow overhead, Wojsław gnarled.

He tightened his grasp on the axe and swung the shaft into Arminius' chest.

"Ack!" The lieutenant coughed as his meager self was flung across the floor, landing beneath his comrades' feet.

"Arminius!" They cried, clamoring to his aid.

Without a helping hand, he stood, banging his fists on the table to hold himself. Cooled was his mind, Arminius wiped a creek of blood flowing from his mouth and answered as he would in a normal tone,

"He's just another conscript...a kid..."

Lowering his axe, Wojsław's figure sinisterly towered over Arminius. However intimidating, the latter's will was strong enough to believe he was fighting for the right cause and comparably, their auras battled in the equilibrium.

"Age has no place on a battlefield." The demon drove his axe through the planks of his home.

"There are only enemies and allies."

The blade that was the weight of a boulder rested itself on the lieutenant's shoulder. As Arminius turned his neck for a cut to burst on the skirts of the axe, a hum like a bellow drummed in all ears.

"Know this,"

"I will never fight with someone of your kind." said Wojsław.

XXI

Lycoris

The time-devouring demon was the third protector of Wojtek the Stunnebyar, carrying a family's legacy that had been passed down from his grandfather. A man from Porsen. Once a kingdom in the Schatten. During the Second Calamity, it became a national legend, fabricated by the Entente but not false. Aiding the partisans across the continent and the eventual downfall of the Reichs. However, once the world had settled in the period of the warring states, not much was known after the treaty.

Wojsław had inherited the fate he was bound to. Alone. With an heirloom axe and eifer of the Dahayuku. In his blood to stay loyal to King Jan's dynasty. No matter what they did, he obeyed. Even if it had the slightest moral wrongs. Not any nobles sought him out until a squad of young officers lifted him from retirement and into a general's care.

When I had first met Wojsław, I felt that his martial had remained unchanged in the many years he spent fighting under banners. I was too young to understand anything. Upon him being killed by my father, it was only then when I had begun studying the greatest of the ancients.

And so I am here. Documenting, in brief. The lives of those I would never meet...

CHAPTER

22   GUILLOTINE

"There's a storm coming." Arnau peered to the sky where the snow had begun to fall again as the evening shaped.

The flakes glided onto his eyelashes that flicked the icing sheet with a blink. His face was lightened but except the reddened ears and nose in the frost. Near the fire, only the coat and scabbards dried as he turned for the path his commanders had taken, sighing with a burst of white steam into the current of the gray smoke. The three hundred and sixty soldiers forgetting the five had banded at the camp. In what started as light rains and hail to heavy storms from the eastern winds, not one life was lost during the month of toil.

"Dey're takin' their time aren't dey?!" Gin squeezed his head and yelled for his comrades' return.

The prelude of a blizzard picked its winds to flood the unit. In the swap of gusts, a kepi had nearly flown away if not for a hand anchoring the cap to his head.

"We could've joined them if it weren't for you—" Colt berated.

"You're one to talk!" Gin exclaimed, drilling his finger against the rival's forehead.

"All o' us disengaged but you were too caught up with shit 'bout glory!"

Grabbing Gin by the collar of the scrunched jacket, Colt shoved his comrade from his face and reintroduced the brute to their avenue of conflict,

"If it weren't for me, then we'd still be stuck chasing the Confederates around!"

"Dey didn't need killin' if you'd just listened—" Gin returned when a knee was rammed into his stomach then Colt's.

Into the snow, they were thrown by a second kick that leapt at their chests, hacking the two to the earth. With the rushing torrent of Alexandria's leg, she had swept her comrades' neutrality if ever were Gin and Colt conscious.

"Do they always fight like that?" Arnau pointed at the both who held their stomachs as Alexandria dragged them by the ears.

"Since our first night." Arber answered.

The shades of soldiers, their outlines unclear, came before Siegfried. From the shadows of the evening and the refrigerated forest, the smog lifted off the figures until their faces were cleared of the snow. Waving for them, the lancer shouted for their names and cried for Arnau who answered with a smile.

"They're back!" Siegfried hopped over the fire and crawled through the flurries.

By a titan, the pack were led to home. In sky blue armor, like a bright star of the night sky. His helmet pictured the jaw of his bear, Wojtek, whose gleaming eyes were as frightening as it was kind. Heavily plated, and his back plate studded, he carried his double-edged axe that was heavier than Siegfried. And more scaringly, the sabatons over his shoes were with short spikes appearing sharp enough to impale two ranks.

"This is Wojsław." Arminius introduced, as the warrior rode towards the center and as if he was the medusa, hardened the unit like stone with a simple glare.

"Woah! He's huge!" Mesmerized by the excessive colossus, Gin and Colt shouted, shielding his eyes that exaggerated the beast's height.

"Are you sure he's worth taking along?" Arber coldly asked to test the demon's temper.

Wojsław's eyes, with creature-like constricted pupils, revolved and ominously stared piercingly into the lieutenant's soul.

"Hmph." Unafraid of a slight taunt, Arber's smugness restored the warrior to his tracks and told Arminius,

"You've hit the jackpot."

"Sure..." The commander grinned when a slap on his back jumped his heart.

It was the lieutenant captain, awaiting for what order to bring to his troops that reminded Arminius of the last call in the wild.

"We should get going." Károly suggested, throwing a sack of goods over his shoulder.

"Yeah." Arminius began his journey to Julien who was laughing at the fell fools aiming for each other's throats beneath

Miklós and Alexandria's watch.

Taking his friend by the collar, he dragged him away. For his comrades dispersed, one by one they carried their voices and the final marching commands before hibernating in the city for the winter.

"I wonder what we're having for dinner." Arminius starved his stomach with thoughts ever more.

"Hopefully food that won't get cold so easily." Julien gazed at the towing comrade, pulling him along the soft snow.

"You're not wrong…" The leader chuckled.

Then lifting Julien onto his own two feet, they made for the vanguard, passing his unit who were tightened in a formation to deter the cold of seeping in. Stamping his feet before the raised colors of the bearer, Arminius overtook Wojsław tailing Julien's platoon and rose his order,

"All units! In three files!"

With an arm risen, and a smooth command for the eight bands, he cried under the streak of the failing moonlight,

"We march for Sedinn!"

In the columns of the centuries, the force departed the refuge, yet letting the camp still bright in the blizzard that engulfed the flames. The lights of nature switched off after a white fog behind the backs of the uniform rumble swallowed the vision whole.

The night life excelled, overflowing with the populace in a merry cycle of drinks. A creeping moon found its way, peering through a clouded window pouring unrelenting snow that settled in the exhilarating settlement. Its city gates opened to the Apelyotes scouts, passing the redoubt across the river, bunched with romantic floats that shipped more drunks. Where some vessels were awkwardly tied together as the tugs housed black market stalls overlooked by the wall's garrison. Soon, Arminius and his squadmates could join the welcoming celebration, lassoing them into a civilized flow. Within the confines of the fortress was so surreal. The atmosphere had changed in a step within the borders from the outside forested world to the inside of a renaissance artwork. It was certainly strong. The wind battering the high walls, fluttering trees and uplifting depressions of white powder across the plains. However within its battlements, the gale had died, leaving only a pure festive rain of calming snowflakes littering the streets. But the results of war were still clear on any front. Half the street lamps, illuminating outside seats and tables, shone, and yet some still flickered. Whilst lights of main roads which connected the four flanks had been replaced with braziers and torches, refueled by the region to the west, until it was too far out of reach. Then most fireplaces and stoves resorted to torn houses, demolished by axes and eifers, slowly shrinking the town. It was the toll they had to take, simply to satisfy their needs to survive.

"Do you smell that, Arnau?" Siegfried tugged on Arnau's sleeve, catching a whiff of a mix of ingredients, drinks and satisfactory meals.

"It isn't the scent of ration packs, at least." Arnau sniffed.

"Heh heh, we'll make sure to have our fill fer tonight." Gin chuckled, stomping towards a restaurant he had eyed for the past minutes as they have stood idly in the middle of a cobbled square, waiting for the units to catch their breaths.

"And guess who's paying?" Colt winked at Arminius as he chased Gin along the avenue.

Once the last comrade had joined the rear in no real formation, Julien nudged Arminius in the side, prompting him to give the final order of dismissal.

"Alright! I know…" Arminius whispered.

Standing before his troops, taken away by the baroque and classical backdrop, he raised his arm for everyone to see.

"You've all done well to endure the month!" Their commander shouted.

"Without a single loss," Punching his arm forward, Arminius praised the prayers which were answered.

"We've kept the Confederates from our trenches!"

The units roared and cheered, stamping their spears and boots on the hard ground in a battlecry applause, rumbling throughout the inner town, catching those on board the tugs by a warm surprise.

"Who knows?" He furthered, and implied the planned offensive on the Confederates' lines,

"The war may be over by the following winter!"

Another applause stormed the streets, backed by

commemorative whistles of the citizens and fighters of Aelon.

"He hasn't changed." Arber commented beside a mumble of Julien's,

"Arminius...he's run so far ahead I can't trace his old self..."

For his journey, the Danne had long been with Arminius and though their objectives were so far a variance, he had found himself to be across a narrow creek, dividing into a deep schism whilst his comrades attempted to construct a bridge for where Arminius was. But alas, that wooden plank had collapsed by too many chasing to catch.

"Take this night to recover!" His friend's voice heightened again.

"Afterall..." Arber exhaled peacefully.

"Celebrate!" The leading figure yelled.

"Our little brother needs no changing." said the typically wordless boy.

"For our turning tides!" Arminius cried.

A last cry for the commanders' names chanted in a swirl that merged into one smudge of noise, louder than the last. As four officers strolled down the riverside boulevard, the final dissipation brought units away, departing in squads to nearby bars and searching for apartments to entrench within. That remained Arnau and Siegfried. They who preferred to stay by Arminius and the officers, that was including the great warrior, yet to have said a word since his arrival into the community of sporadic commotion.

"Good evening, lieutenants." The voice of an old man broke the youthful crowd.

"Grandpa!" Károly, as always, was the first to meet the grandfather of the nine.

But it was not only the general who had shown his face.

"Instructors. Colonel Aide." Julien greeted, and in return, his squad was welcomed by the seniors of the headquarters.

"I hope no one was lost at the last minute." Ascot mentioned but to the shaking heads that cracked a slim smirk from the major.

"We've also looked over your plan to retake Stellpurt." Florek added.

"So, am I gonna 'ear anythin' from Gin?" However, expecting the lack of wisdom of his student, Adam nonetheless pressed.

"He misused his eifer, again." Arber snitched on his comrade.

"Huh...I'll cripple 'im next time..." Shrugging with his hands raised, Adam sighed with a composed threat.

Ran for the distance to a fanciful restaurant, marked by a carved frame swinging in the wind, above where they had sat, Gin and Colt, with smug faces, waved for the squad. It seemed that they had smartly reserved a feasting table of exactly eleven seats, with forks and ceramic plates arranged.

The brown bear, unseen, growled softly, holding all to turn to face Wojtek joyously nodding up and down with his protector leading him onwards. As he saw their march nearer, releasing a devastating kei, the thunderstruck Florek and Ascot were muted.

"Y-You...?" Adam stammered, taking a step away from the path to open for the general.

"You weren't joking, gramps." He remembered the old folk tale, watching as his commander took to the fronts.

"I see you've found new allies." Warneńczyk approached the creature calmly with a senile smile.

Placing his hand on the creature's head, he reached to rub his fur, and told it in a soothing tone,

"You've grown, Wojtek."

There was a lieutenant among the crowd, separated in their inner thoughts, that drove distress rather than the high perplexity.

We never mentioned his name... Arminius could not fathom this bizarre reality.

Even after the story told by Wojsław, more mysteries surrounding the general crept into the open, as if an ancient animal, buried beneath the earth had sprouted from hibernation and uttered a mystical instance. But those around him were as easily dazed.

"Hah! Wojsław. Last time I saw you must have been thirty years ago." The general let free a crashing laugh.

"You were so small." He recalled, bringing his hand flat, level with his thigh denoting the young lost height.

For if the stone had scratched his armor, the warrior bent his knees and bowed aristocratically for the general. Feeling an emptiness at the reunion, he kept his rigid demeanor.

"I await your orders—" Wojsław had pledged.

"Now, now before all that, you should tell me what happened." Warneńczyk held up a hand.

And by that gesture, Wojsław rose.

"We have a lot to catch up on." told the general.

The quiet giant remained silent. Hesitant. But did not walk away from his kind invitation that was impossible to be declined from his new master's offer.

Partaking in a ritual of the same prayer that had fallen on all Lekann children, mumbling a series of incantations that straightened his mind, Wojsław joined the staff party as Warneńczyk desired, taking Wojtek, sniffing the old man's coat.

"General." Arminius halted Warneńczyk whose hand gestured for his comrades to carry themselves for the town hall.

"Hm?" asked the general, to the lieutenant demanding answers with an uneasy face.

"The Protectorate." Arminius recalled what the word had come with pain that the protector of the forest had named.

"What is it?"

Half the squad was baffled. Each with a shadow wanting for questions that the general should have answered. Of his eifer. Of the past. With every piece of the puzzle unresolved and doubling, the general had become too distant to know. And there the familiarity of the peculiar note of such a thing as a *Protectorate*, not Károly nor Julien could hide their troubles.

"To know The Truth, you must know its price." Warneńczyk cleared his throat as the suspicion was ignored.

"But to you, it is already invaluable." He spoke to Arminius and only to him.

His feet returned on its tracks, tracing the footprints of his comrades who were shrinking images on the promenade.

"Enough of this."

"Youths need their talks on dreams or you'd gain my wrinkles." Waving his hand for the squad watching the officers' backs depart, Warneńczyk had abandoned their questions with ever unknown.

Knowing the general had always been a man of paranoid intelligence, sly in every manner possible to attain victory by whatever means, he had his reasons. Though to Arminius, that was hardly the truth.

Our general's been hiding everything from us. He clenched his mouth in agony of a sense of uselessness.

His eyes widened at an uncertain revelation.

As if that was by nature…

Perhaps he's running from something. Arminius changed his thoughts.

"All o' ya!" Gin called from afar.

"Are you gonna stand around or what?!" Colt jumped from his chair and the impatient soldiers slammed their fists on the table like a pair of toddlers.

"We're coming." Arminius replied, accompanied by his comrades who seemed revived from the shade of the blank truth.

Sliding his kepi onto the table, Arminius messed his hair and sat by the interior that shone an intimate tone of light. Beside him, by nature, Julien and Károly seated themselves whilst the places around the long table were filled. The waitress who took their orders was with a truthful smile, and tensely, the commander listened for how many dishes the babbling mouth of his comrades would ask for. Before the wait could starve and dull the chatters, a feast worthy of nobles was presented.

Siegfried lunged from his seat and gawked, near-drooling over his plate at the exalted dishes. A fruitful platter, though without fruits, was before them, unlike anything they had seen for the past years. Extravagantly such showed the prosperity of the city much alive. The cuts of rarities were the center of the stage, dominating the dinner table of all hunted meats and delectable vegetables in the unforgettable stews that each had a bowl of. When the war might have been forgotten of the bland grains and stale breads. Helping to pour a cup of ale into the eleven vessels, Julien was first to raise his own.

"Let's just hope the war will be over by next year—" He began when a brute dove for the platters.

"To hell with yer speech!" Gin interrupted, ripping a chunk of the boar from its flanks by his greased, bare hands.

"Sieg, not you too." Arnau saw the child lunge for another plate.

The feast had been set for the elites and the messengers. A vividness of peace in the darkest hours. An easy feeling leapt around him, captivated with a sense of home. Although amidst the overture of a blizzard setting, there was a warmth hugging him. He looked around. To his allies battling against Gin's gluttonous hands as if there was a familial quarrel over the last slab of meat. As the reserved laughed on the rims of the foreground. With a sincere headache, he took a glance at his plated hand.

Maybe this wasn't so terrible... Arminius thought for the nearing future.

But I wonder, will it ever be the same...

"Still..." Gushing a sigh, he counted the coins in his pouch.

"Only they can be so easy when I'm the one paying."

A cup then was held by his hand whose wielder took the lieutenant from the cavity of a broken mood.

"Arminius." Julien's comforting voice was by the right.

"Don't be so tight on money." To the left, Károly mumbled upon stuffing an unhealthy mass of food in his mouth, lifting his drink too.

Tightening his drained wallet with a rope circling the opening, Arminius shoved his funds into a pocket and grabbed a drink. He raised it ahead of Julien and Károly's then replied with an amused manner,

"You're lucky we aren't using bonds yet."

Clinking their cups together, rejoined the squad in the meal. Admitting a semi-ravenous behavior to the friends that knew him not so well, the chuckles and half-grins evolved into what the street was proud to hold. The expanding smiles and drunken laughters were uncaring for the neighbors in the flats above.

Their stomachs were satisfied. Only bones remained on the plates. Drunk over the table, Gin snored loudly in a sleep that found unconscious reasons to deliver kicks to Colt's shin. As Lev mumbled, pointing at the vibrant street that had bulged with townsfolk strolling around the alleyways and shops, Miklós filled his tenth cup of ale, yet awake and still thirsty. When the Rus slid onto Arber's shoulders, not a slap could bring him to his senses. Then so another stinging blow to the cheek put Lev to sleep from his hallucinatory adventures.

"After this war...if this plan succeeds..." Julien swirled his cup of ale that he could not finish, reflecting a persona of himself.

The comrades still sane listened closely, relaxingly sipping their drinks until the Danne asked, glancing at Arminius whose lips were sealed over a cigarette,

"What do you all plan to do?"

With his gauntlet wedged by the cloth tied around his jacket, Károly sprung and yelled with a return of optimism,

"Nothing's changing, just letting you know!"

"The first to shoot down the stars." Arminius mumbled but another was not so enthusiastic.

"Károly, you're being too loud..." Julien embarrassedly hushed, apologizing for his friend upon taking a few looks at the passersby who had come across a gang of oddities.

Huffing over the stretch of the table that was slowly cleared and wiped by the waiters and waitresses, the smoke from Arminius' mouth was brushed to the skies by the rising air. The snow fell as the ash of the incense would, for a thin coat of ice to carpet their soles.

"Is it going to be the same for you, Arnau? Sieg?"

"Sure!" Siegfried righted his back and nodded excitedly.

"Maybe I'll get a chance to become a noble if I impress the Kaiser." The youngster dreamed of a distant life.

But though it may have been said by the youngest that their dreams were in collaboration, the exhale of the elder messenger was less noble. Quite humbly appearing.

"Well..." Leaning back and swinging the chair imbalanced, Arnau gently rocked the seat on its hind legs.

"I would be lying if I said I wanted to keep fighting." He revealed, taking a glimpse at Siegfried, unbeknownst to a seperate path the closest comrade was willing to take.

Awkwardly settling the chair on its four legs, the soldier continued,

"At home, I was a well-known inventor."

"Ever since six, my hands were tied around blueprints and machinery, but..." The messenger held a long pause.

A short sword drew and Arnau held it between his eyes. Staring into the shining metal of the blade with the discolored mirage of the far clouds.

"Its thin walls could not cage me forever." Taking a short breath, he told the keen listeners the story of an unheard world.

"Though, I still hope, one day, I can return."

Peering to the winter, reminiscent of the day he had never forgotten. The night of the thirty-first under the tenth moon.

Dreaming of the embers and smog that cast a screen of death over the town of where he once stood, Arminius puffed a light gray cloud of thin smoke that was brought, like a chimney, to the lamp hung from the restaurant's exterior.

"Your turn, Julien." Arminius voiced, knowing that Arber and Alexandria would not answer no matter the pleas he would humiliate himself with.

Although there was a goal that only diverged from Arminius' pride, Julien thought for his answers but in a depth of ideas. There was something else stirring. But when his mumbles had ceased, they knew that he had come with an answer.

"Wha—?!" His face went red and his grip tightened, scrunching his pants.

"What is it?" Arminius raised his voice on purposely, with a stupid smile, knowing widely what his friend had thought of.

"Why has your face suddenly gone red?" Károly joined the closing circle, bullying the Danne.

"N-No, no. It's not what you're thinking!" Covering his blushing face, Julien stammered.

"I've only met her once…!"

The expressions of the squad dispelled any doubts and it was clear what Arminius had wondered was certain. That even Arber released a snigger upon Julien's realization that he made a mistake in a choice of words.

"Oh? So it *is* a girl…" Arnau concerned himself too.

"Afterall," With a joking and twisted voice, Arminius shrugged and shook his head on the trail to shame.

And with his cheeks pressed against his comrade's, he gave the grin deserving the accounts for the next centuries,

"Who wouldn't wanna chase after someone as cute as you are?"

"W-What are you saying?!" Julien's blush ripened ever more by the praise that paralyzed his unexpecting mind.

"Enough of me! W-What about you, Arminius?" He pushed the lighthearted commander away from a tight embrace.

As the calm after the storm gradually seeped, they regained some sanity after the whirlwind picked gaping holes in Julien's enclosed heart. Taking his kepi, Arminius swung the cap on a finger and slouched, sinking. Kicked further from the table that let his legs crossed, the lieutenant accepted the oblivion of his dubious dream.

"I don't know...anymore." He halted his hand and bore a glimpse at his comrades, of those asleep and awake.

"Maybe...a plot of land in Bäuwar would be nice..." Arminius noticed a second ideal that was unlike the childishness of the first.

With the small streams of Alpinne breezes blowing across the temperate meadows, it was the perfect sight to behold despite it imaginatively. That, it was enough to remind one's self, the lieutenant, of an old home he had never reached in memories.

"Settle in a small village..." Twirling his hair, Arminius invented an illusion that the squad could grasp.

"Our houses near..."

Their chatter quietened, and their bodies stilled. Blushing, a tender smile took their faces around him to flush as well.

"Y-You can't say random things like that!" Still heated from his flustering reveal, Julien held Arminius' shoulder and rocked him back and forth.

"That ain't a bad idea..." Arnau chuckled.

A pair of heavy running footsteps on the stone street, desperately merged behind him. Arminius, facing outwards foretold an unfortunate happening arousing. Two soldiers, as if they had sprinted from one town to another, slowed from the flow of urban crowds, panting unstoppably. They were soaked with sweat, needing to ease their hearts. But impossibly in the damnatory blades of cold and heat battling a war in the lungs.

"Fu, fu, fu...what'd you call me here for?" One demanded an apology of his fellow, huffing heavily.

"Did you hear?" The other questioned, leaning over the uneven pavement.

"Borulinn..." The capital of the Zhormanniks was named.

Deciding it was time for the slumbering to wake, Alexandria brought a thunder strike kick to their shins, tearing Gin and Colt from sleep.

"Ah—!" Waking Lev, Gin cried, rubbing his shin before his awakening was met by a stare from Arminius glaring past his shoulders.

The disruption was found short lived as the unknowing elites perked their ears to the conversation, too far a coincidence that seemed almost cliched of where they stood behind them.

"She's fallen." A corporal told his closest ally.

"Then we're surrounded—!" shouted the second.

"Not so loud. You'll incite panic." His comrade hushed, slapping a hand on the blabbering mouth before their heads could be had for treason.

"It won't be long until everyone finds out too."

They scouted the undisturbed crowds where no one could grasp the turbulence that had unfolded behind their backs as the joy of the frontier was strange since the prelude. For when the Confederates had never tasted for an attack, only Lev shadowed his knowledge on the mischievous foe.

"I tuned into the radio by accident..." A man spoke, almost to a whisper that the unparalleled senses of the elites could not hear their gossip.

"Grand...Aelon...Meyer...defected..."

"Kaiser...presumed...ablaze..." In parts like a tunnel with spots of light in the mountainous valley, seven words they heard behind the chorus.

"Summer Lion...Eos...Radilov...Sedinn..." Coldly announcing, a dash of goosebumps ran along his body.

Vasilevsky?! The squad knew.

But the shudders never ended there. As the two greatest houses of the western Confederation hovered beside the vice general's, a luckless omen eclipsed the realm. Two men that they have heard of, the third, a Radilov, was a new weight to battle. And without hints of who he or she may be, it was useless to war against a legend that was the tome in the arts of bloodshed.

"Not only that..." continued the Aelon corporal.

"You wouldn't wanna know...King August's family..." He gritted his teeth for then his news was none wanted to hear.

The soldier's voice broke and his eyes teared as the words he spoke became more muffled, caught in his throat,

"T-They were strung up...alive...on the Branenn Gate..."

"Nine million...our own people...King August himself..." Listing, shakingly, for the dead, the corporal shared guilt with the elites who heard.

A rage surged. A real anguish. Through their veins, creeping from their heads. Holding the storm melting in his pot of temper, the squad neared a revolution as those heartless enemies of the alliance counted the seconds to the festival of guts.

On the impressive battlements, colossal in size and length that ran around Sedinn's redoubt, stood a young man, wielding a shadowed spear. He held a severed head by its hair with a cruel, twisted face, painlessly screaming without a lung. Its body, twitching in a bath of blood, was kicked off the walls, into the bottom pen of mud. Then releasing a light sadistic chuckle, he raised a fist in the air, and ordered with glee,

"Fire…"

His grand battery of howitzers, aimed for the city, above the walls where it would devastate the populace on that fateful day. The inevitability. For forty-eight gunners pulled the lever and covered their ears, dropping down onto one knee when each gun saluted in an enlightening volley.

Tossing a heavy smoke screen visible from the distance, there were infinite crackles, like fireworks, popping across the river. There was a short delay, before a chiming boom ruptured the city drawing all towards the origin. But that was before the shells had landed.

Enemy artillery?! Arminius adapted.

Low velocity…could be air burst…no…shrapnel? With the innocents staring at the clouds that sat hollow thus far, he wondered in the limited time, concluding alongside dread,

Incendiary—!

A shadow of whistling projectiles captured the unmoving crowds. Striking across the town like napalm, suffering blood shadows graffitied on the pavement. The flames chewed at houses, tearing roofs from its walls, and ripping families apart with a breath of disaster. The impacts sent the bodies to the heavens, and flesh burning, with a dozen sharp shells penetrating the main street, seeable from Arminius' bright eyes of hellfire. As those on the open slid across for cover, the lieutenant impulsively flipped the table over, catapulting their cups into the air, and whilst the party had hidden themselves, he grabbed Julien and Károly by their jackets and held them closeby, lunging, together at the ground before a shell impacted where the two soldiers stood. Sending a tide, a fierce inferno.

XXII

4 APELYOTES 491

04.11.12017

Regulus von Eos

Obeying my orders. To keep silent. Should I ever forget my place, then I'd be no less dishonorable than Vasilevsky. When news found its way to Kolchakov's ears, the marshal was more than delighted. Though it was by my words that drew this to happen, to watch the tormentors enjoy the tortures.

We observed. The square of massacre. Quartered, torn limb from limb, his wounds spurted from the thumps of the heart I could feel poorly too. Screaming. The young prince was strung, hanging alive, soiled by his own blood. His sisters found the same fate. Their bodies were split from below upon losing their voices. For the sickening fun of my men. The eight royals' life rained and were by then nothing but the butchers' pride.

Even I, as a warrior, in all life, could find my stomach turned aside. I was cruel. But no one should suffer fate such as they did. The innocence of humanity has become a one-sided victim.

But I had realized the general was only human after all. If not for Rzhev's passing, we would not think for him to become more ruthless, and to steel himself before throwing millions at the backlines of Udor like shields of war. And yet the loving fiend who had created such a wreckage in this middle world, I still admire so.

Arminius von Regen, who shall you ascend to be…?

CHAPTER

23   DIVIDE

Fires submerged the river bastion, the final hope of any chance
of redemption in a quick war disappeared into the underwater
trench of flames. Like it was fed fuel, explosions ruptured one by
one, pouring incendiary from devilish howitzers that bit into the
human flesh and transformed a perfect town into a pit of blazing
snakes.

"Isn't it beautiful…?" The young third general fiendishly
smiled.

Second in the arts, he was the epitome of a rebellious
persona. Sly and twisted. An eighteen-year-old Aurel Radilov.
Slim and fairly smaller than the average. In the reflections of
flames, his short unbrushed hair was a chocolate red, the blood
flooding the walls alike. Despite his innocently youthful face,
whose ocean blue eyes were sharp but gentle, his sadistic grin was
there. Blowing with the course of the high winds near the clouds,
the general's wardrobe was stylish but casual in a sweatshirt. All
was bloodied. Soaking by the dribbling spine of the severed head.
Held in the other hand, was a three-pointed spear, with engraved
letters along the jewel blue staff. Its standard silver blade seemed
newborn from the blacksmith though for whatever horrendous
behaviors were in play, the crimes had been forgotten by the
pristine beauty.

"Kakakah…" He chuckled.

The face of the headless man sagged, almost rotting-like,
by the draining of the last blood holed in the brain. Aurel tossed
it over his shoulder. Splashing a few drops that stained his arm,
the lump of flesh fell aimlessly towards the ground. The hunk
thumped on its old host body and was greeted by a swarm of fire,
with a click of fingers from the general's aide.

"Is the young lord done playing around?" The subordinate
asked, igniting the hundredth body that night.

Ripples in the blood pond traversed from his boots knocking against the heavy walls, wetted by a frozen crimson waterfall. As he approached the edge, the general leapt onto the merlons and pleasurably watched his victims burn in his purge of disintegration. Panic was rife. As he had hoped, the ideal insanity he saw in witnessing a buffet of death.

"I will never lose a wager. Regulus..." Aurel spoke across the skies.

"Will you take Tschrewen before I devour Lubek?"

Reaching for the impenetrable fortress, a lie on the banks, he clenched his fists with the resolve of a hunter.

Protector... A demonic howl called for him.

O' ye the protector... The devils chanted in a maddening loop.

Toying with his mind that was half in the real world and half in the eden of hell. There were no fires. Nothing of resemblance as seen in the stories. No torture. Only infinite emptiness bordering the lone tree, made of hands that reached for him as creatures lurked about. Their eyes gleamed at the endless feast of skinless bodies lying in one clump, as the mattress beneath the boy, chained with iron bones, unbreakable and sealed to the ground. There was no sky. But the ceiling of red veined eyes, bleeding cascades of blood, who oversaw him.

Held close to a heartless life in our ancient world... The ever-bleeding tree growled, beaming with joy.

Have you been forgotten...o' greatest...?

Your humanity for an eternal world... It grumbled.

Ghosts climbed from the creaks in the piles of bodies, and dragged him beneath, into a boundless sea of calamity. From a spike impaling his heart, Arminius was recovered before the tree.

Are you unknown to death...? The souls surrounding echoed, across the vast crimson cavern.

Or bound to it...?

Slowly, Arminius resurfaced into reality. First feeling a light, shining outside his eyelids. Then a dozen warming hands, holding his shoulder, shaking him awake as blood dropped, like tears onto his scarlet-red tainted face. His sickly pale skin regained normality, and found the will to at least find his senses. Noises of horror flowed like flash floods, of those stricken with terror. Weeping and the pain in cries, until their voices were lost into the void of hopelessness. A phantom's scent scoured the ground. The reeking smell finally brought Arminius to wake.

Realizing there was a fading memory, or a nightmare of those calming hands, Arminius opened his eyes, face down to the ice cold pavement. Holding Julien and Károly in one arm each who surely rose. Both, luckily, were uninjured. As his comrades around him started to rise, they sat upright, rubbing their heads to ease the short surges of soreness.

It...still stings...

"Has the barrage stopped?" Károly searched the shadowy street, running with rapids seeping into the overloaded cracks in the stones.

Ash and debris of material and flesh were on the avenue. Some bodies were intact. Yet barely any had survived the impacts unscathed. There was nothing but a sense of emptiness, clenching his heart. As one held a bitterly silent child in his arms, sat against a lamp with a leg shattered beneath the knee.

"Arminius!" Julien noticed his comrade, whose jacket was covered with splinters from the table, though none, fortunately enough, struck.

"Are you okay?!" He placed one hand on his back and felt a light eifer shock to his fingers.

Sighing, Julien helped Arminius and scanned for any wounds.

"That's a relief." The Danne lightened his heart again when his friend had fully awoken.

Standing, drunk from the attack, his ears were still ringing. Shaking his head to clear the mist his sights as Julien had gone to aid the squad. Oddly, Arminius felt something weakly clutching his leg, above his ankle. And of curiosity, he peered down and saw a hand wringing his boot.

"H-Help...it...end...I..." The ghastly soldier pleaded.

Flesh under his torso was not of existence, blackened by a vulgar burn mark. He had crawled as far as he could, leaving a trail of guts laid on the pavement. Half his face was missing that revealed a sector of his intact skull, holding his pinkish leaking brain and a disfigured tongue, dangling from his mouth.

"Ah!" Terrified by the horrors, Arminius let out a small scream, falling onto his back that loosened the grip, leaving a bloody handprint on his shoe.

Remembering the words he heard from the dream, the lieutenant stood and pretended no one had heard his cry.

"Is everyone else alright?!" Arnau stuck to Siegfried, protecting the officers.

"Why...the hell did they attack at this time?!" An anger powered Colt, scratching his sealing wound with the heat of an eifer.

"It's still winter!"

Gunfire rang from across the river. The Aelon were unguarded. As one bridge fell, the next crumbled. Engines and the stampede of trucks and troops charged into the city, opening an unchallenged massacre of the defenders, broken from the pre-emptive strikes.

"Don't tell me they've breached the city walls..." Lev drew his snapped spear.

"Speak of the devil!" A pocket of infantrymen found themselves running along the very same street once vibrant then a grave.

"We thought everyone had perished." Their supposed leader, a lancer, sprinted ahead and met the lieutenants, recovering from the shock of the shells.

They were of the Apelyotes scouts too, marked by the golden autumn leaves on their collars. And upon recognizing the loyal squad who were the surprise to the eleven that they had fled the battle, Arminius asked,

"Are you all that's left from the west?"

"We couldn't confirm. Everything happened so quickly." The lancer saluted his seniors.

Rallied and with weapons drawn for whatever foes awaited them if ever the Confederate broke the last line, the elites turned to the chaotic howls of the city.

"The Confederates are attacking from the east." A report was delivered with a terrified light in his eyes.

"It won't be long before the next bridge falls."

Gazing at the burning waters where explosions were set, countless, Julien trembled. Uncontrollably. Told by his shaking sword that rattled in spite of his hands trying to still the blade.

They endured the choir breaking the soul. By a rope, the voices that called for mercy amongst the merciless demons, the squad was dragged to a self-destructive clash in honor of the vanquished. But knowing the senseless suicidal mania, many bore the disgrace of halting with a sharp screech of their rubbing teeth.

"Shouldn't we consult the general first?" Lev suggested.

"Fuckface! He's given us the ability to act on our own!" Swinging his sword like a maniac, Gin drove the blade towards the falling bridges.

"We just gotta charge and hope!"

"That's impossible..." The trembling voice from the infantry spoke.

"E-Even if we wanted to consult the general..." He held his head that suffered a dire bleed with both hands shaking.

"T-The...the headquarters was hit..."

Károly's eyes shrunk from an underlying fear. As his limbs helplessly quivered after calming Julien's, the lieutenant captain dropped to the ground. His bow fell from his hand that grabbed the snow, melting, merging the rainwater with phantom tears.

"Don't go spewin' shit like that!" Gin yelled at the wounded soldier, pulling the poor man by the collar.

"But...but...I-I saw the top floor go up in flames..." The soldier stuttered.

No matter what excuses their conscious mind told them otherwise, their subconscious imagined what had occurred and was gone.

Julien knelt beside him and held Károly's head by his chest. In the scenario no less a nightmare, he nearly cried in the shared sorrow found. For Arminius portrayed a disheartened face, watching his friend weep aloud into Julien's jacket. That sound. It was fine to make him stand unnaturally still.

"What should we do, lieutenant?" The lancer restlessly asked.

Traumatized by the figures of death, fidgeting and biting their thumbs; rubbing their hands ferociously to rid their torn skin, the people of Aelon were already crippled. Inept for a fight and yet remained.

"We have to assume, at least, you're the new commander of this section." Another pressured him.

"Lieutenant, please give us your orders." The able ushered a fountain of pleas.

Their voices swirled into one pot of words, and unable to pick apart what they were asking, Arminius was overwhelmed. He had been clamoring for the top of the chain. But how he inherited such a large command was never what he desired. And that his mind was frail before. His best to competently lead whatever troops were there shattered.

"We can't afford to lose Sedinn."

"The fortress is too valuable." Arminius reminded them with an innermost feeling raging.

The people in this city... He doubted who had broken the promise of peace with that heart.

If we leave them here, then the same thing will happen as it did in Borulinn.

"Regroup at the headquarters and cage ourselves." A command spouted from his desperation.

"Our units will be freed of the stretched defenses who we could use to flank."

However thoughtful the plan to retake the city was, there was something that had bugged Julien for long. Staring at Arminius by his feet, listening to the orders of the returning recklessness which were sporadic. Unrelenting. It would destroy rather than construct a selfless counter-offensive. And there nothing would remain.

But that'll kill more than we could hope to achieve. His eyes of sorrow, wanting to search for a cleaner route to end the conflict, sought for another solution with Károly in his arms for he knew his oldest ally too well.

There's another way. The Danne convinced himself.

Not to attack. But a method that keeps us alive on the defensive.

To climb out of Arminius' shadow had been a distant dream, but not unattainable. They were equals afterall in thought.

I should say something... The lieutenant decided, yet as he opened his mouth, no words escaped the tip of his tongue.

No...I can't betray him. A doubt crawled.

He's always been in the lead.

Julien clenched his fists, so drawn between a schism that either banks pushed him forward or pulled him back. But both outcomes seemed feasible. It was a matter of willpower. To break free of the shackles holding him down within the colossal shade.

"Arminius…." Then he called him.

"There's another option…"

Everyone swung to Julien who now felt the same immenseness Arminius had shouldered on his own. The aching muscles that imprisoned him like the earth on Atlas.

"We should retreat to the west and regroup beyond the walls instead." suggested Julien, surely however of a submerged courage or a belief in his judgement.

Arber nodded at him, approving a new beacon. Though the lower infantry never had the thought similarly. The loyalists had trusted every maneuver Arminius made and thus, were not so willing to change strategies in the notice of the decaying allies.

"That would bait them into the city and—" The Danne continued.

"No." Firmly, Arminius declined before his comrade could finish.

"Armin—!" Julien argued through the spirit of the commander whilst the gates of his ears and mind had shutted to any reason.

"Do you not want to get this war over with?" Arminius interrupted again and glanced at his companion.

"This strategy to outflank the Confederates within the walls is desperate, but it's the best we've got."

"Arminius." Sheathing his spear, Arber spoke in the stead of Julien whose timidness was softer than the tyrannical child.

"Are you really trying to win this war, or is it about the discomfort of suffering?"

The clock's second hand in Arminius' mind ticked, and an aura engulfed the squad who were shoved aside for the winding gasses of a dormant gateway to the dark fantasy to creak open.

"You're being reckless, again, lately." Arber reminded him, tearing the honor of his captain plate by plate.

"What do you mean?" Facing the revolt, Arminius scowled whose demeanor he was painted with was hostile to the youthful cheerfulness that was himself three years past.

"Didn't I tell you about your limits?" His comrade scolded.

By the remembrance of the torture chamber to the ambience of the river flow, the picture of their present was the same. Except the blades were different. And the enemies were the punishers.

"If we don't advance here, it won't take long for all of us to be encircled!" Arminius told them, losing his short patience in a growing pace to a shout.

"Do you want to die in a crater and lose this city altogether?!"

"For war and victory, we need to sacrifice some things." Arber lectured him further to the borders of boil.

"And am I not fighting a war here?!" Arminius yelled for it seemed his capacity of sane sense had loosened.

"Then start acting like it!" Arber returned that pressed his comrades to cower, believing he had gone mad to have roared.

Winds picked its tides. The hopelessness in the soldiers' hearts watching their officers fight in the harshest of times and still, were buried in a no man's land. Wretched and wringed, they listened and witnessed the unfolding infernal turmoil.

"In the back of your mind, you can foresee thousands of methods." Arber pushed on.

"Or is your aim so narrow that becoming the greatest like some genius fills the corridor?"

Arminius refrained himself from punching a friend, but a tightening bomb inside him raged into a tropical storm. Suddenly forming a fist, he swung a left hook into Arber's face. With a shockwave charged by his eifer, he flung him into the broken table behind. Crashing against the floor, the splintered wood cushioned his fall as the elites rushed to him, dismayed by the grand escalation.

"Arber!" They cried, pulling him up to show a bloodied mouth from a bruise in his cheek.

"The fuck was that for?!" Tending to Arber, Gin wildly cried.

Left in a cold sweat, realizing what he had done, Arminius was backed by his troops who looked on at the torrent. Unknown for who they should have supported. The lieutenant dropped onto his knees, and stared at his reddened knuckles. His tearful eyes watered, completely aghast by something that did not seem like what he, himself had done but by the personification of the fiends whispering in his veins. And despite the lightning bolt to the face, Arber rose, keeping to his reservedness as he wiped the blood away holding no grudges, with a smudged stain on his hand.

"I admire you, Arminius." said the emotionless boy, lightheartedly.

"How easy it seems to lead; how powerful you are; your strategies." He added that would forge a list of the traits of worth.

Stumbling towards his kneeling comrade as a spot of blood dripped from his lips with a split, Arber told Arminius,

"But you shouldn't always look into what comes next."

"Save some space for the present." The lieutenant with the feline pupils advised.

Mounted, taken from the stables, the squad hurried a major sprint across the plains outside the intact western city walls that opened to a force numbering some four thousand soldiers from all corners of the army. A dust storm from their charge caught the eye of the enveloping Confederates, encircling the city at the pace of rivers.

"The right flanking force is picking up the pace, Lieutenant!" A messenger galloped to his side.

Julien remembered what Arminius had noticed during the brief war council an hour before.

"Your prediction was right!" He shouted.

"The guillotine..."

The guillotine advance requires three main forces from the center, left and right flanks. With the left unmoving, the opposing flank would sweep from their side and pincer the escapees who would be forced to meet the spears of the infantry on the left. Thus, completing the snare whilst wiping clear the besieged defenders. But the flaw was daylight rising.

"We won't fall into their trap." Julien resolutely declared, signaling for Károly a few paces to the rear who was the unit's core.

The lieutenant captain, having wiped away the last tear left on his cheek, removed an explosive arrow from his quiver and drew his bow upwards at the starry night sky. Towards the brightest stars, the archer released his hand and shot the arrow, releasing a short burst of wind that traveled with its flare. A high pitched whistle ensued, burning the last of its eifer borrowed from its master, and exploded like fireworks into a unique fire of orange, tinting the ground below.

"Advance! Don't drift to the left or we'll be caught in their blades!" Julien directed his men who followed him to the book.

To predict the strategy employed to annihilate the defending forces entirely was no such feat performed only by soldiers. Arminius could look into the thousands of paths possible for defeat or victory, whilst the execution sat fairly with Julien. They had realized, in the midst of the years into their journey, that a combination of themselves could tower splendid heights. An unbeatable titan.

"Sorry...Julien..." Arminius apologized, concerned of the unscrewed tantrum that quaked his comrades.

"I should've listened to you...earlier..."

Over a shoulder, Julien watched, for that he was in the lead of the dashing chevron.

"We've been fighting beside each other for three years now..." The Danne lieutenant softly said.

"And it's only recently that we discovered *how* we should've been all along." Slowing to Arminius' rank, Julien kindly smiled at his friend who could not bear to look him in the eye.

"You have my back." Arminius was warmly assured before returning to the road ahead.

"It's a promise."

Surveying the ground of the battle, Arminius regained his will to face another. Then there was to his behind Károly, wearing a falsely cheerful face and an exaggerated smile.

That's not...it...Julien... He felt his voice breaking, thinking to himself, sniffling.

Pleasantly, the cutting wind brushed against Arminius' face, holding him in a soothing way as an eye bled like tears that no one saw.

XXIII

10 APELYOTES 481

10.11.12007

J.R.

Dyattumetesis plezhët unne Kalamitj schall stërazhännster hais Pat avure Hümannitjisrebirt berigtet. Vur Sinnen an uös, uë suworet. Vrum Hëll tu Paradise. Annkin mudeklinnër. Ryasunnbetat Unneprutekturate, uö Korborus, sitschinn schambën. Kasen tär Tälen vurwik Kause? Lazhrake vallsupunn uë? Sülen kann neworrepenisch echsket Zhrazhzhentau unntuer Neueazhe beseworet vrum Haisturj. Kumemuster Trëpözhën be.

Vurzhiwen Neuelive, Dyatzhut schall reburnner. Bekumër Annkienntsiweßel. Hais Ultueurlt. Hais Neueueurlt. Hais Medyum. Pösuen unne Zhryam newor unne Ann houpetukunntänn inn Hanen, Tetschrut migt besilennt.

Vurzhiwemj. Itisbe juö Time vur Bet.

Prumisevur teteller annutor Sturj nechst Murrau. Minnekilt.

CHAPTER

24 THE LAST STAND

The titan. Marching to the war drums banging, closed their suffocating grip. Feeling a tightening noose around their necks, the cohort quickened their pace to escape the wrath of the onslaught. Comrades of the Winged Lances were abandoned in the sluggishness by their wounds. But they had no choice. Either few survived to pluck a victory ripe from battle, or all to perish in the gray of defeat. Even for as insignificant as four thousand, they could pray to change the tides of the hundreds of thousands. Yet even as their will could carry like an ironclad, it had distracted the failings of their bodies in the blizzard. Gales and hail were unforgiving, freezing their fingers and toes until they could not move. Some, who had said for themselves; able to endure, dropped and were stolen of air. Despite the blinding front that battered their eyes, neither the Aelon and Confederates' visions were so impaired that their mutual enemies had sunken into the vast whiteness.

Atop a spire of a burning tower, dangling his legs over the arch that slipped into the darkening smoke, uplifting a scent of bodies in cinders caught within the building, sat Aurel. Feasting his eyes over the inflamed roofs, he caught the winds of a march that had escaped his grasp. Pointing his spear at the core of the slowing unit with an eye closed, the third general watched on.

"Ah...? Is that the cohort of the soldier you couldn't stop talking about, Regulus...?" Aurel passionately wondered, holding a hand over his face.

"Was his name...Arminius Reichner...?

Resting a hand under his chin, and the blade against his shoulder upon finding an interest he grinned at, the playful face grew engrossed towards the rout,

"That's odd..."

"I could've sworn you said he would throw his head into the

dung." The general thought, whether the commander was truly the soldier he named.

From his pocket, Aurel picked a deformed candy and unwrapped the sticking paper that had decayed into the melted sweet. The crackling flames spurted like solar flares inching to the ceiling. He gave no mind to the slithering arms of the blaze.

"Maybe it's not him..." Tossing the snack onto his tongue, Aurel considered, though not that he could believe his own words.

"Or..."

He chuckled, gradually swelling into a childish, but inhuman laughter. Standing with an ovation in his spirit and seen in the eyes, the envisioned claps and clamors for his name and body erupted before the purge. Aurel balanced himself on the wooden skeleton, heating as the burning veins began to shave the grand temple. And with the words of praise, the young man reached for the clouds and asked the gods for an embrace,

"Kekekeh...you have me interested..."

In the dissatisfaction, ascending the hill to a plateau, painted by a once dense forest, for then tainted the scenery with the remains of rotting stumps that provided no shelter for their declining soldiers. The daring unit was at the point of the rally. All that was there was an incapable fighting cohort and certainly never enough to take how many were there storming the river. Sucked dry by his heftiness of breaths, Arminius tried to ignore the gray snow falling from the sky, reminding him of the lives he had nonetheless forsaken.

"Sedinn has fallen." Arber calmly told them, riding through the ranks with Gin who had joined the vanguard and dismounted.

Arnau hiked for the officers, sheathing his short swords, and said with an unusual timidness,

"There's no point in saving a limb without blood."

"Sure, but we'll still—!" The inspiring Siegfried was sure to convince his comrades but the shake of a messenger's head held his tongue.

Across the plains below, and over the city, the pour of Confederates was every last wager cast into the assault. The vibrant lights had spun into an urban sprawl of slaughter.

Although the gunfire had halted from surrendering, the cackles and clicks of guns were replaced by slashes of iron and bludgeoning sounds. And when the rear guard arrived soon, the guillotine was complete. Its last meters sealed between the north and south courts, rotating and stamping into formation facing the city to choke the unfortunate in their escape.

"'Sup, Arminius." greeted Colt, before his head showed itself above the curve of the hill as Alexandria safely marched from behind, beside Lev and Miklós having the flanks.

"Did anyone fall back?" Julien questioned, feeling his heart compressed by an uneasiness.

Sticking his spear into the ice, cracking the bottom most soil, Colt gushed a breath of hesitation and meditated before a grievous reply,

"Two hundred..."

A punch on a log that was stoned from the season was no more the collapsing entity of the spirit amongst the squad. That only Arminius etched before ten loyal allies near his side. The fury of a backward temper shot his fists into the stump until his kei had depleted. Until his knuckles and the palm under his nails bled. His mouth was clenched. For a stream of blood oozed from the lips of becoming so harshly trapped by his teeth, he could not utter a word without the thought of a tear.

"Hah, what is this?" Gin fell, back first, into the snow.

Each soul took their seats on the snapped trees, surrounding the broken fire, dying, that was half-alight within Arminius.

"It all happened within three hours..." Julien took a glance at the moon, at the midnight height.

"And now the Confederates have found a capable leader..." joked Lev, trying to lift their spirits.

Silence, together with a despairing sigh, had forced him into misery. Twisting a small strand of hair that stuck out of his helmet, the awkwardness had found Arnau too. The morale, whatever it may be, had seen so far beyond redemption, the fogged mood was not so easily uplifted. And somehow, with a desperate set of footsteps crunching the snow, an omen of good will shone upon them.

"Urgent...order!" A man, of the unit's many wounded messengers, cried.

Sickly green and sweating in abundance, he sprinted uphill,

slipping sometimes but managed his path towards Arminius. Whose immaturity dropped, the commander wondered what changed the murky atmosphere.

"What...an order? From who?" He asked quietly.

The elites bounced up at the hearing. Knowingly, as it was pledged before, only one man could command them in direct.

"I've been asked...to deliver it to Lieutenant Reichner." The messenger passed.

"Are ya deaf? He asked who it's from!" Gin irritatedly boomed, demanding an answer from the soldier who fell at the thought of his voice that snapped like a landing shell.

"A-Ach! G-General...Warneńczyk..." Stammering, the good soldier crawled away from Gin's frightening attitude.

When Julien placed a hand on Károly's flame-toned hair, the archer's sniffles returned that inclined steadily to hiccups that had his eyes water for each noise. Seemingly, Arminius had calmed. And to the extent of the broad welcoming of the general marooned in life, the same clamps in his comrades' hearts weakened.

That's pathetic... Arminius scolded himself, releasing the flow from the creases of his palms.

Did I really need new orders to hold my hand...? He said in the mind, peering at the crimson linings on his nails.

What have I been doing...?

The tragedy was lenient. The recklessness of his eyes faded. Of impulse, he had forced his trembling fist to lean against the bark. In the freeze, the wounds submitted to the snow dabbing the bruises and cuts. Before the lieutenant received the letter, he turned to the messenger and lent a hand, mentioning with a short sigh,

"Rest yourself in the core." Taking the wetted envelope, Arminius offered.

"That'll at least ensure your recovery."

Yet as the soldier was ready to depart, he was promised by a pair of eyes holding a brute by a glare,

"Don't mind him, he can get hot-headed."

"Who are you callin' hot-headed?!" Gin yelled to prove the commander's words.

The messenger nodded and propelled himself upwards. Saluting to thank him, he descended the slope with joyful tears that he wiped away lest the lieutenant could see.

Exhaling his black luck he had been bound, Arminius peeled the seal, tossing the string that binded it, fluttering with the wind. And reading with an average tone, he brought the squad closer, anxious to hear.

"I write with haste, Reichner." The general had scribbled.

Wojsław was here. I live well. The encirclement is at hand. We must forget this fortress and retreat west to Plan Yellow on the Albunnt as due the new grand commander's wishes. Advance onwards. Do not wait for us. To southern Lubek. There will be one bridge standing. But you mustn't cross it! No matter the cost! It was hastily written in cursive and with hard carvings onto the page like a doctor's note.

"Take the blessings of war and earn us a victory. Warneńczyk." That order concluded.

Brief and sure. The aimless hours like circling crows marching around the fortress were no more. Observant of the fated tides crashing onto the ridge, the squad whistled for their mounts in the security of a higher command. But the general had not shown his face. The doubts of his capture or death drifted in the foul air.

"The Whirlwind must've foreseen everything." Arnau climbed onto the saddle and wrapped a hand around the reins.

"We should get moving whilst we have the chance..." The resolution of Arminius' revitalized in the bringing of a forbidden hope.

Recognizing his comrade's old self, piecing like a forgotten puzzle, Gin sneaked his breath behind and slapped the elites' captain in the head, scoffing as he mocked,

"You're finally back, huh?"

"I guess..." Arminius mumbled, resting a hand on Julien's shoulder.

Though his plan had been foiled by the transparency of a thought. The Danne calmly lifted his friend's cold hand knowing what he was to say.

"Then, mind staying our captain?" Julien suggested, spiting Arber's disheartening stare that disappeared with the enthusiasm of the elites.

However the trust of leadership may be hazed, the individuality believed what sat well for the war. And in spite,

Arminius doubted his senses worthy of award again,

"Why…"

"I'd planned to return your role since the beginning." told Julien, holding Arminius' shoulders.

"Isn't this what you wanted?" Clutching ever stronger, and unwilling to let him be gone before an answer would reach his ears, the lieutenant asked.

Who was speechless. With his mind muddled for what he had pronounced, the latter was stilled.

"It's like…death's chasing me…wherever I go…" Arminius' voice softened, avoiding the eyes of sapphire blue in the terrible wonderment.

"When could I have hoped for a dream when I've stepped into hell—?"

Julien aimed his fingers on Arminius' forehead and flicked, printing a small mark beneath his hair that waved in the elegance of palace curtains.

"Even the brightest can be fools at times, you know." The Danne chuckled, taking the chance of revenge for the years of companionable harassment by calls of idiocy and calls to be awake.

"This was never a dream." The kind friend advised.

An expression of disinterest in the title blanked and revived an affection for the battle he grasped. For the grace of people and the Aelon, the hints of embers and semi-gladdened flakes in the grin shaped. He studied. The path for the war to end all wars. Perhaps nothing like the delicacy of joyousness must show. Only that be the duty anchored.

Arminius placed a hand on Julien's head and rubbed it, making free both spontaneous blushes.

"Cut it…" Julien called out but he could not dismiss the smile on his comrade who blessed the help,

"Thanks, Julien."

Bearing the sword brushed by the snow, the Danne lieutenant looked over a shoulder and scouted the thousands. Rested and sealed of wounds, but the trauma never did, there was no banner that took the folks to march. Stateless, no drums played, the cause

of the Aelon disappeared. Only for selfish survival that the blades were like hounds on the battlements of vengeance.

"Units! In centuries!" Julien directed for a comrade to lead.

Whoever of those with rides, the officers beside, gendarmes took to the saddle. Unsheathing steel, the scrapes of the cutting edge grinded like an anarchic orchestra. Straightening the sleeves of their uniforms, the preparement of the long advance was due in the night of the elites.

A dream...? What is it...? Of a great embarrassment, Arminius blushed at the slight vision of his tantrum

He tried to blunt the sharpness of his sighs, but never could the boy take his eyes off another who had yet to mount as the cohort shuffled in the outdoor icebox. Károly's position did not lie. With a considerate fire aiming for his grandfather, been thought dead the hours of the moments. But if he could not watch his escape with his own eyes, then there the archer would not sleep well.

"Armin..." called Károly, quietly bringing himself to his side.

"How can you be sure?"

The city was dormant. Neither the armies on the outer nor the interior showed the tiniest breath.

"I'm not." Arminius' sympathetic smile, not too apparent, showed.

"What do you...?" Gazing at him, Károly sensed an alleviating belief of one thing.

A rumble, cast upon all lands, began a miniature quake. Arminius caught a glimpse of a shine in the lines preventing the escapes, yet like a cage, was weakened by its vast gaps between its snapping columns.

"But does that answer your question?" He pointed at the sparking shockwave.

An explosion from the walls caught the Confederates, flinging hundreds into the air above their ranks. Like ants from afar, dotted the sky like close by planets with the thousands of shadows converging to form a growling shade. When time froze, seven white stars attached to the floating corpses beamed. Launched from the ground, a gust of wind from his leap lifted the snow and changed the course of the flowing winds. The maddened warrior zoomed about the seven, razor sharply, and delivered a demonic strike at his enemies, flinging the bodies towards the earth as if hailing meteors crashed, savagely into the tightly packed. With rays of light, their impacts collided. Coming together to form a beam, it turned into a stone bear wreaking havoc on the formation that tore between its dark claws. Its waves of gales rippled across the field for each hurried strike until all the blizzard could not bear and was blown aside for the escape of Warneńczyk, leading a colossal force with his great war scythe.

Four straight days, in the dense snow; marching eighteen hours from colorless mornings to black evenings, only lit by dim torches and lamps that often diminished. The legendary cohort lost its momentum as the wounded dropped beyond the rear guard until their figures could not be seen. Every day, the camp would shrink, pushed onwards by the cavalry who lent their horses to the unfit. The inevitability of freezing and poisoned bleeds captured the souls and snatched them before they could be recovered.

Villages passed were abandoned. And whenever they marched across a major town settled along the main road west, only hundreds remained. For on their second day, the cohort was upon a frozen swamp, whose lengthy icicles gradually grew until the tip met the snow on the streets in the densest town of the region. A sixth, only the militiamen stayed to defend their homes. And yet they knew little. That wives and children, sent to flee the war, clutched in their gray arms, had been preserved by a thick blanket of ice and snow a few leagues outwards. But never going to give up their stand so easily.

Half the path through the forest, the march bogged in the mud, suffocating many, and catching most with sinking traps. Where in time, the unseen thin ice would crack and swallow a squad whole. However, on the third day, blinded without radio, the cohort encountered a century of scouts. Although the golden horde outnumbered their foes, they could not keep a fight and suffered swathes of dead at the hands of an ill-fated ambush. Barely escaping with their lives, what remained marched on, bleeding until they had found camp at an old ruined castle beside a serene lake. Had it not been for the streams of blood that fed into the emerald waters and deafening screams of Siegfried, thrusted by barbed bolts. Despite knowing they were those who crossed this hellish line, Arminius was reminded by the need to push onwards until the bridge was within sight.

On the bright and settling morning, the sun just rising over the treeline, what remained of the cohort, numbering a numbing one thousand, were the first to enter the final hold before the only bridge over the river within ten leagues. The path was unpaved, with construction banners warning them of the unfurnished road that was once replaced with new tarmac. Two rows of trees lined the road from its flanks that was eventually cut off by the crossroads before the crossing. Its sparkling river had not stilled, leaving way for the clear, cool water to majestically carry downstream. The bridge was ancient, built in the middle ages. Its arched cobbled path remained intact and its two small watchtowers that guarded the choke point were perfect for a river defense. Upon spotting obstacles and cover around him and having his mount borrowed by a pair of casualties, was on the ground, Arminius straightened his arm above and cried,

"Halt!"

The cohort paused and their footsteps slowed like an overheating machine.

"Castle the bridgehead!" Arminius commanded.

Dissipating into a semi-ring around the bridge, the riflemen were directed to lay out a jagged perimeter whilst the regulars formed the core of the cohort, in a tight square behind.

Shivering from the loving sun warming his back, Arminius sighed. Removing a cigarette from his pocket of goods, he held a stick between his teeth that could not not clatter. The lieutenant's shuddering hands lit the smoke that suppressed his mind as the squad flocked to him like magnets.

"It's gotten colder..." Károly sneezed before rubbing his nose.

"Sure sounds like someone..." Lev teased who was felled with two spinning strikes to the leg and an impressive axe kick to the head.

"Ack!" The Rus' face planted on the ground and was left as he was beneath Arber's glare.

"And we still gotta wait fer gramps!" Gin screamed

maniacally, scaring a neighboring flock of birds to take off for a calmer home.

"Quiet, Gin." complained Julien, covering his ears.

"We're still in enemy territory."

"Neither do we have enough supplies to last through the weekend." Arminius counted the days they had spent on one hand and the remainders on the other.

"But it should be enough till Tschrewen."

"Is that where we're headed?" Siegfried's head slipped through the gap between Arnau and Károly.

The lancer's arm was slung, tightly against his chest whose spirited heart would have agitated his wound.

"That's my prediction." Arminius said unsurely, flicking his cigarette.

Gazing down the southwestern path that followed the river on its drive, it was dissimilar to the opposite bank, forested and appeared to be untouched by the filth of humanity. There was no mistake when he spoke,

"This road directly leads to the fortress on the Albunnt."

"From what I know..." The lieutenant continued.

"It should keep them at bay for a while."

With a click of his tongue, and comparisons drawn, a corporal rested his arm on the commander's shoulder and forewarned the degraded luck,

"But wasn't Sedinn supposed to be impenetrable?"

"And still, it fell in one night..." Colt dragged the sorrows of Arnau's voice with a carefree accent.

A stallion neighed in the backdrop of the typical low Zhormannik village and the same messenger, with his face brightened from a well recovery, ran to the officers and dropped to one knee. Saluting Arminius before delivering the message.

"Lieutenant." He first greeted, with his head honorably dipped.

"The general is four hours till." Informing them, still knelt, the man told in a tone as if he had seen the savior.

"Gramps' caught up already?!" Gin sniggered, stomping his feet in the mannerisms of a rowdy child.

"He's quick fer some wrinkled bastard! I'll give 'im dat!"

Four hours may not have seemed so much, but whenever the threat of becoming skewered by blades from the shrubs was plausible, anything could become a great turn. So time passed slowly.

"Alright…" With the intelligence heeded, Arminius tossed the ash of herbs to the ground and returned.

"Ride to the general but lead him with the shortest path."

"Right away." The messenger saluted the officers and departed hastily, leading his horse away before he had mounted properly.

Galloping down the powdery path the cohort had taken, the squad ignored his disappearing outline into the forest which rattled like rifles.

"I wished we had radios…" Arminius sighed.

"It would be simpler—"

Then before an occurrence, the lieutenant felt an ominous breath looming over them. A gunshot rang and a splatter of blood splashed onto the stone gray road that was unevenly paved, leaving for the thick blood puddle to flow into the side drains.

Appearing from the forest, a sadistic smile greeted the petrified, watching the blood leak from beneath the Rus commander, stepping over the puddle into the light. His fiend-like grin revealed two sharp canines barely showing itself, as the spear he wielded gnawed at the flesh of the messenger, hooked by one of its three tips and was flung onto the grass.

A ball of water, formed of his eifer steadied beneath his blade, growing into a head-sized globe until it stopped expanding. The liquid darkened and began to echo as it shifted into a sharp blade, rotating so fiercely, the road cracked from its swirl. Aurel's eyes were fixed on Arminius alone, ignoring the riflemen unluckily between. His pupils were constricted. Clenching the spear tightly, a tidal wave of an oceanic deity lunged with the swing of the polearm. The accelerating train curved and split the heads who nearly ducked to safety and before the lieutenant could draw his sword, the blade of water skimmed past Arminius' neck, striking the tower in the background. Its bricks began to fall from that single strike, until it all collapsed, crashing from the bridge to below as half was taken to the depths of the river.

"What…was that eifer?" The dumbfounded squad had their feet stuck to the ground, unable to move.

A paper thin cut on his neck bled, horrifying Arminius whose adrenaline could not keep awake.

"I missed…?" Aurel shrugged, ordering his troops to take

their firing positions.

There were at least fifty thousand in the sights' distance through the span of the plains and desolate houses. If not more, who had the thousand-strong cohort surrounded on the three flanks. Aiming their rifles at the thin barricades that kept the formation intact, except for the backs that remained open for escape. But the lieutenant remembered, no matter what he did,

Do not cross the bridge no matter the cost.

"The Confederacy…" Arminius gritted his teeth, drawing his sword.

The general's shadow merged into the frontline, laughing at the frightened faces of the squad.

"They must've followed our messenger all the way here…" thought Arminius.

Angered, of becoming so utterly puppeted on a battlefield cleansed his share of fear, and determinedly announced to the elites,

"Take eight hundred men each, and defend this bridge till the end." Arminius briskly responded.

"Siegfried." He patted the young's head who peeped a startled gasp.

"Command the core, but if I ever give the command…" The lieutenant guided his eyes to the crossing, the taboo in the last order.

"Cross the bridge."

"Leave it to us!" Gin punched his chest, scraping the scratched blade on the dirt.

"We'll make sure to kill a thousand each!" A roar seized the cohort's ears.

"You better." Colt poked him with the foot of his shaft.

The squad dispersed, sprinting evenly, like a sprouting flower towards their commanding century as Julien and Károly took charge of the groups beside the center. Of the lieutenant whose broken hands carried the fates of the battling warriors, he shone himself in the midst of the border. Between the warring packs, stuck in emptiness. Flowers of the flakes of snow, finally pure of human ash, clung to the strands of his hair.

"*Blitshünntorkoeurt!*" The lieutenant bestowed a name on the wounded unit, pressing their rifles on their low passable walls.

The hunters of lightning. The Blitzjäger Cohort. Perhaps

slower than a storm. Perhaps in the guise of the prey. That noble title was instilled into their minds. Some missing an eye or an arm. Many dressed in blood-dried bandages. All fought equally. Aiming their barrels at whoever they found the easiest victim, laid their fingers close to the triggers.

"Once the battle is over!" Arminius shouted.

"No matter how many of us may perish including I!"

"Our names will forever be engraved into the hearts of the generations to come!" He inspired, stepping onto the barricades like the descendant of kings.

"Fire at will!" The ten commanders raised their voices.

"Front rank...fire..." Aurel issued the reply.

Two veteran lines opened their hearts and pulled the triggers, launching crackling sparks and sprays of bullets bursting flesh as the volleys ripped through their lines that shrouded the bridgehead with a dense blood smoke.

XXIV

8 APELYOTES 491

08.11.12017

Władysław Warneńczyk

We should be cautious of Aurel Radilov's hunt with his fifty thousand veterans. Afterall, he is Admiral Radilov's boy. The child of the Scourge of the Hannsen. Who could believe such fate, if by awful luck they find us in this vast forest, then we'll fall before reinforcements can be pleaded to save us. And all that we've done to preserve the integrity of the army will be most lost. Our ten thousand who barely escaped with us are no match for Radilov's elites. But it worries me more that there is a slight possibility of having Reichner's force being discovered earlier than ours.

Even if it may take us four hours to reach them, we must make haste!

In case that clutch in my stomach is true, I will make the necessary precautions.

My wisdom never fails to amaze me, even in the darkest alleys...

CHAPTER

25

BATTLE OF THE THOUSAND

The smoke weighed heavy, guarding their visions from enemies who surrounded them with no escape. A reckless charge into the defense, in hopes to overwhelm, crashed into the barricades. Blades, of bayonets and swords, casted waves of steaming blood onto the snow as the fronts tried for ground. Inch by inch, the cohort fought them, until a second wave poured like boiling water, melting the rooted frontlines, and stampeding across their comrades' corpses to satisfy their lust to protect.

Arminius slashed until his blade had been repainted by the color of his devil. Holding his eifer, the lieutenant firmly held his ground, cutting down the Confederates flanking his century through the gaps that began to form.

"Our reinforcements will be here soon!" He rallied, kicking a soldier out of stance then rushed to slash his throat and spine, spilling a waterfall.

A heavenly light shone upon his vision, at the corner of his eye. Distracted by a boom, Arminius retreated and saw a blinding glow, like an amber sun that looked too familiar.

"Shit...it's too early for him to use that..." Lev drove his spear into a dozen men, exploding their guts with his gush of black fire.

Dashing through the field, Alexandria neared Colt, spinning her spear that ignited a trail, sparked by her ruthless golden sweeps. Cunningly, she deceived her enemies with a fault in her defense, luring them closer before sending a ring of blood splashing at the pace of her blade.

"Has the left fallen already?" Colt floated from a great jump into the air, aiming his spear at his enemies so cruelly pierced by rounds of azure spires.

Behind the cracking lines, led by the countless suicidal breakthroughs that kept the Confederates pinned on the theater, the brute's men started to fall back from their enemies' swarm. But in the distance they fled, a berserk Gin was there. Having his jacket and shirt torn to thin strings, the blood and sweat ran down his pulsating body. His veins glowed as the eruptions of his heated eifer came to life. Heatwaves seeped from the earth and opened a jaw that swallowed the flames burning into his sword until a terrifying, grand prince-like creature crawled out from the clouds.

"Hyargh!" With thunder, he widened his stance as the ground exploded into slabs.

Riding on the solar flames of a quadruple-drawn chariot, the son of Apollo bellowed with his double swords, spinning, for it created a rushing trail of fire. Tailing Gin's gliding sword that ruptured the road as he flung a rampaging chain of solar flares, the wheels disintegrated as it traveled further, and like a fireball, his eifer rammed into the fleeing Confederates who saw an expanding dead end. A sea of flames engulfed the street that burned through the ice, riding for the rear that tossed charcoal bodies, empty and evaporated, into the air which rained, clump by clump, into the river and battlefield around.

"Heh..." Gin panted, catching a liver on his shoulder.

He brushed the innard to the stones and crushed it beneath his boots. The black smog circled his burning body. Its embers slowly died from the cold. His sword did not seem like it would ever cool as legs of its iron melted, having nicks to widen on the blade.

"I got more where dat came from."

"Would ya like to see?" A beastly grin showed.

As his men charged across the flaming grounds and attacked the flustered, hacking their chests apart in a frantic assault, it was that the brutish century maddened and had revoked their humanity.

Two hours were by. The right flank was holding with a stalemate. Neither was willing to commit. So concerned with Gin's anvil defenses, the soldiers were left with a delirium in a skirmish that befitted machines of rifles and bows. Arrows and bullets flew. Drawing spots upon spots of blood as they fired, returning the favor. However, knowing the need to stay the bastion of the cohort, the lieutenant's bottom-most hunch could not feel the same way.

There's no point sticking around...

Arminius wouldn't sit by, would he? Lev asked himself.

A whistling stray arrow had his head on the path, but who dodged the mortal scythe of the reaper in time, he was struck on the arm. Dropping his spear from the snapping pain, Lev crouched and held his wound, gushing creaks of blood soiling his uniform.

"Ngh...now of all times..." He held the thin shaft.

"I don't want your love...whoever..." Pulling out the arrow in a clean tug, Lev joked; releasing a sigh.

The iron tip seared with his black flame as he leaned against a tree. Biting onto his arm, the Rus pressed the burning arrow along the length of the wound. It sizzled, that made his blood bubble until the opening sealed as he had hoped. Gasping desperately for air to rest a headache, Lev tossed the arrow away that burned into the snow cover.

"Now that you've just changed my mind..." The lieutenant huffed, picking up his spear with his nose pointed for the giant of the fray.

South, a few hundred paces to Lev's flank was Miklós grabbing a soldier by the head. He lifted him to his eye, where the demon stared at the choking swordsman, gagging before his comrades who dropped back first, in fear. As the aura of the Sorbe inflated, a runner sprinted down the lines, drawing his cap as bullets and blood flung over him.

"Lieutenant Dragosavac!" The messenger called.

The demon reacted simply with a thrust of the spear into the Confederate's jaw, letting him slide to his hand until Miklós dragged the soldier from the slimed shaft. He thumped onto a mound of snow that had his comrades scream in horror at his white eyes of the dead.

"Lieutenant Hayek has asked for reinforcements to the flanks" told the man of Aelon.

Approaching the crawling Confederates, Miklós swung his

spear close along the blades of grass sticking beyond the draining snow, and hurled a bucket of blood splashed to the side, tainting the whitest floor with a sharp painting of a scarlet liquid. Three heads plopped, who kept their same expression at the face of death.

"W-Will you answer his request?" The gendarme's voice trembled.

Miklós blinked, nodding to assure the messenger. Not a single humane thought ran through his mind as he took to the field beyond his own lines and flattened his enemies with flicks and swoops of the spear he wielded. No bullet reached the commander. Nor an arrow that could be stopped by his perfect arc in catching the fleets mid-flight, astonishing the archers and rifles. Then finding a small soldier charging from a textbook path, the giant drove the arrow into the Confederate's eye, tormenting his allies with the squelches.

"Agh!" The Confederate screamed before it was driven from the socket then thrusted through the soldier's neck.

In wasting none seconds in simply sealing another's will, the robotic devil howled an endangering mist. Miklós' forces looked, retching in disgust at his demonic self, traversing the Confederate lines like a mechanical saw to wood. Unstoppable through bodies that piled into a row of the high trail.

"F-For Lieutenant Dragosavac!" An awe-stricken corporal from the century cried, waving his sword afore the troops.

His warcry mimicked the blitz into the veins. Detonating like a falling dam, the kei surged aloud into a devastating mode. Charging out of cover, the raging forced themselves onwards at a vehicle's pace, and so suddenly did they advance, it caught the Confederates slacking.

"What—" An enemy soldier was bisected before another word was said.

To the right of the clash against the traitor countryman, they spotted their comrades crushed by Miklós' blunted spear. Flung in a single sweep upwards, his fury did not halt. Then perhaps they had forgotten, the giant soared ahead.

"Ee—!" A Confederate was taken by the head, praying for eternal help but alas none aided him when he was savagely disemboweled, pouring guts onto the soiled blanket.

"Miklo!" Lev waved from afar, diverting his foes whose

retreat had begun.

The thrilled soldier darted to the Sorbe and held himself in a guarded hold beside his comrade, tossing the corpse onto the stack of curled intestines.

"Ready?" He tapped his spear.

Miklós grunted in reply to a mystic black mist, rising from beneath Lev's feet. A flying dragon of flames caged his arms and spear, attaching a roar from his bursting eifer. In a click, the shade of a devil spouted from Miklós' back, laughing with a gate-like jaw that huffed the armies of hell, in the form of a dense blackish cloud. The settled layer of snow on a branch wavered in the wind, until the seat it held splintered, with a sharp snap.

Turning his spear outwards, Lev thrusted the weapon forward, ripping open a blooming cone of fleeting flashfire, plummeting into an ominous flow engulfing everything that was in its lane. Devastatingly, Miklós whipped his spear in unstable crosses. The afterimages of his slashes threw numberless blades of winds, groaning for blood at flesh and cuts to any organisms reduced to mere chunks to be swallowed by his clamping jaw, chasing those who fled. Caught in a black pool and a hunting devil, the Confederates were trapped in a neverending nightmare. Until it came for them, clawing out of trouble, many leapt into the river, not knowing it was filled with shallow pools of rocks and boulders. Then in the last second of their delicate lives, were crushed by their own demise.

His eifer tapped into his resting mind, napping on the great Wojtek. Waking him with an excruciating sense, tingling along the nerves of his fingers, he braced his grip on the giant axe, as if wringing its soul, and sniffed the air that smelled of his own.

"What's up, Wojsław? Smell somethin'?" Adam rode beside, under the empty trees grown by the many lakes in the richly colored and bright marshlands.

"Perhaps…" Wojsław growled.

"A demon…"

The warrior deterred his senses to the trail of frosted leaves, sitting like a winding carpet that bent from each subtlety, and named,

"Dragosavac."

"Dragosavac?!" The lieutenant repeated, unhinging the buckle that held his tape measures.

"How far?" asked Ascot.

Wojsław relaxed his focus, holding the strength of the scent he judged. The bitterness whispered before his answer with a creaturesque nature.

"Just under four eastern leagues." The warrior replied, for Ascot to signal Adam to the general's diamond of staff.

It was an hour's march away, nearing the high noon of the battle, the cohort was far from the number of a thousand it pledged with. Gin's hammer and anviling charges on the far left and the devil's flames on the right gained ground, but near the center, the curve of the formation had flattened by the brunt of Aurel's human wave. Arminius, Julien, and Károly's units were soon to break under Radilov's iron fist.

If the center falls now... Arminius parried ten spears with one strike.

They'll be cut off from our only escape!

Vaulting over the back of a Confederate, the lieutenant drove his sword into the swordsman, tearing his body into two whose severed spine was torn, having no suffering.

"It's my fault, Gin and Lev..." The commander apologized, leaping to safety behind the wavering lines.

"Centuries!" He shouted and grasped the cohort's rigidness to halt.

"Fall a hundred paces!"

In a united front, the hundreds retreated. Supported by Siegfried's two hundred who rushed to carry the wounded, exhausted of ammunition and kei. Whilst the semi-ring regained a sane shape tighter, the lines were still too thin to fill every crease. But to retreat another hundred paces would mean enemy fire would only become no more than a graveyard trap.

Juggling a knife from hand to hand upon dropping his spear

into the snow below, he leaned against a valley in the tall tree, able for the general to watch over the battlefield. Aurel's eyes were pinned onto the Aelon foe and the two who retreated beside him. Though an enemy, his heart did not feel so.

"You're one interesting character, Arminius..." The third general casually named.

"First, Regulus tells me you're the offensive..." He holstered his knife and leapt softly, feline-like, onto the snow, undisturbed by his phantomic walk.

"And next you do otherwise..."

Kicking his spear from the ground into his hands, Aurel moaned,

"Ah...but I find it weird..."

"Why haven't you fled across the bridge?" The high youth shrugged.

Spotting an unfortunate foe, crawling with a crippled leg that did not look too serious a wound, Arminius' strategy came to light.

"Oh...?" The general realized, stamping on the wrist of the whining soldier whose lungs breathed a yelp.

"Are you waiting for a savior...?"

"Kakakah..." Aurel chuckled with a smile, driving an even harsher force onto the poor soldier's wrist until a crack was heard.

His scream drowned the laughter who lifted his spear above the man's back and sliced away, skinning him with shallow slashes like a torturous fiend that made him cry for saving path of mercy.

"That's amusing,..."

"I'll make sure to give you a little push..." He sniggered.

Aurel ended the torment with a last draw, dividing the soldier's head from its body with one swift swoop of the sharp spear that not even one drop of blood was caught on the blade. The neck's pumping vessels sprayed like hot springs onto the general's heels who stopped over the rolling head. Twirling his spear above into a whirlwind, he drove it to his front. Overlapped, the weapon sat on his left arm and aimed it at the graying sky, throwing thunder sparks in the clouds at an arc as his sapphire circle, rotated around the tip of the spear, showed in its simplest form.

"Let's see your tears..." said Aurel with a smirk.

A turquoise beam, stored within his shaft glowed.

Discharging from the circle in liquid form, it dispersed into rails of water, looping around the prevalent shot that broke the first sound barrier before it slowed. Clinging tightly until it reached its apex above the frontline's heads, the formation began to break as it rained like the undirected rockets into the retreating men. As it appeared an unconcerning and a futile attempt, many of the unbeknownst soldiers stood to watch the spray sharpen, but soon found it to be a rumbling before their expiration.

"Run—!" Arminius tried to unfreeze them.

The attack diverged into millions of raindrop bullets. And only then, they noticed. A splash, like grape shot, punctured the troops, blowing holes into their bodies. In synchronization, fountains took to the air, felling all who could not flee before Arminius' eyes. Growing in despair, he turned to Aurel with a snake bite glare.

"I'm not one who enjoys fighting..." Aurel coldly giggled upon the massacre that was his pleasurable toy in war.

"So if you're looking for one, little Armin..."

The general put his arm ahead, clenching a fist, and challenged,

"Come get it..."

Thousands seemed to have prance on the lieutenant, with immense lusts for blood, charging the straight road that only Arminius defended.

"Tch." The lightning in his eyes coiled, in short waves of sparks that flowed across his body, and tightened his grip on the dulled sword.

"Is this some test?" He wondered only for the pledge he made to decide his mind.

"I won't bury myself before I've wasted everything."

The lieutenant straightened his posture, and began walking backwards, for his forces in withdrawal.

"Eh...?" Aurel grinned at their meeting sights, stretched afar by the glass cord that pulled Arminius further from his natural trait.

Into a run for the new defense line, sandbagged by Julien and Károly's centuries, half his unsensible spirit told him,

What were those deaths for...if I'm never going to kill him here...

His drying tears dripped in small drops as he eased his eifer.

"I'm holding out until the general arrives..." His choice was sealed.

"For the sake of victory."

The fleeing soldier slid for cover beneath the volleys of fire at his back behind a young creaking tree that shuddered for every shot that struck its bark.

"Julien! Károly!" Arminius cried for his comrades who were pinned by the pings of lead.

On the reloading after the great minute of fire, the two dashed to Arminius who hung his blood drenched kepi on a branch. Forever alone.

"We should retreat an extra fifty paces!" Julien suggested, trying to conceal the screams of his soldiers who could not return much fight, depleted of ammunition.

"I've already lost my entire century to that one attack!" Arminius shook his head.

"It's impossible!" The unbelievably self-righteous had admitted.

"Then what other strategy is there?" The Danne stole the chatter to the destined conflict.

Bullets whizzed past their heads, with derailed shots flinging into Siegfried's lines. Their messenger captain ducked from too close a call by the hells.

"Shouldn't we cross the bridge?" Károly budged in.

"No!" The heated duo shouted together.

"Your grandfather told us to never cross this bridge until everything's lost!" Julien spoke for the reckless archer.

"We still have our arms and legs!" Arminius exclaimed and punched the earth.

"And even if we don't have our blades, I'll fight them with my fists!"

Before the arrival, there was barely thirty minutes. But the three argued on methods of survival whilst their men were mowed into mince. The unyielding shots gradually ceased as the Confederates were too drained of missiles. For they drew their swords and spears, the march into the defenses with one single wave chipped the skins of their enemies. Fatigued, the Aelon slowed, yet the ferocity of their individual battles did not stop. Whenever they found themselves pushed back, in squads, they forced the Confederates away again, like an unrelenting tide that would wash against the shores of a blood moon night. With corpses at their feet, the warriors climbed, using bodies as shields to ambush the stampede of the Confederacy. However, they were taken away by the current that no matter drowned them.

"Kekekeh, I thought you would've attacked by now, Arminius..." Aurel chuckled at the sight of their infighting.

His growing laughter, tampered with his temptation to join the fight as two minute yet broadening dusty white clouds developed towards the bridgehead.

"But it's a shame I won't be able to fight you again..." said he.

The ground beneath Arminius shook from a rolling force in the nearby trees. Shaking and waving as if a war machine had flown to. They must have been thinking what it could have been that created such a thunderous march when an encroaching shade of noble cavalrymen descended upon the streets that directed the forces of menace towards Gin and Lev's checkpoints. His glaive glimmered above the scarlet-armored commander's silver plume, flapping like a flag as his men braced their blades and lances.

"Cavalry on the left!" Gin shouted for anyone to plainly hear.

"On the right!" Lev yelled for his troops.

"It's over!" A soldier in the tremor and purge cowered behind his comrades who slowly retreated from the vanguard.

"It's over! We're done for!" Another panicked that drove the cohort into disarray.

With the thrust of the illustrious units, the flanks shattered grandly, for everyone who had seen his face realized, crossing death's door was imminent.

"Make sure to savor the blood on your glaive..." Aurel muttered.

"Regulus..."

Slashing the soldiers trampled, Regulus von Eos' blade collapsed the barricade in one devastating blow revealing the light he carried on his back, as if the sun rose from the shimmering armor. Throwing his enemies high into the air, they fell, unable to stop, to their eventual deaths as skulls and legs snapped like thin biscuits and those who unfortunately survived were crushed by the clampering cavalry, splitting their heads for brains to leak.

Like two knives at the spine that would sever the head, rode over the fleeing forces. The left and right were incapacitated as the center was at threat from an encirclement. Gin drove his sword into a horseman's thigh and tugged him off, executing him with a silent cut and exchanging for a saddle of his own.

Storming towards Lev, a largish group of riders aimed their lances at the lieutenant. He flicked his spear in a dozen strikes into the ground, throwing a handful of snow and smoke that disrupted the charge until their visions became no more than a slit. Then before they saw, twelve jabs into their throats made them gag blood that bubbled when they fell, behind Lev riding to the haven.

Arminius bolted from soldier to soldier, cutting open their chests and thrusting his sword into their heads, leading a painless death. Not even he could keep with the drive the Confederates felt in needing to soon decimate the cohort.

"Julien!" He spotted, trying to dodge the three who cornered him.

Then, from the rear, Károly and Arnau took flight over his head. The bow was drawn with twinned arrows ready and Arnau's two short swords at hand. They crossed each other and the marksman fired in a fluid form, as the lancer carried his blades in reverse. Near landing, Károly's arrows struck the Confederates in the chest, punching them backwards for Arnau to thrust his swords through the collars of the last. Without hesitation, Julien cut the closest across the torso as Arnau swung to deal hasty slits to necks, toppling the patriots.

In his blurry sights, Arminius watched the two who saved Julien reassuringly punch each other in the back and there he heard the muffled,

"We should do that again, Arnau!"

Károly bounced up and down but Arnau never knew how to answer the unbelonging excitement.

If we don't fall back across the bridge, then everything will be lost... Arminius thought alone in a gloomy six-sided room.

But why is the general so concerned about crossing it?

Near to indulge in the void of assumption, Arminius slapped his cheeks to wake himself.

Think! Think! There's no time! He cried silently.

His mind clogged like a set of cogs broken by the one blank problem he could not see nor solve. Coming to realize the threat of becoming trapped by the converging cavalry, Arminius decided,

We don't have much of a choice...

He turned to the last unit that had seen the least, and at the lancer who stood in the center of the formidable square, miserably onlooking his fallen comrades.

"Siegfried!" called Arminius in his loudest blasting voice.

That was the order if all hope was lost. To cross the strange bridge forbidden to retreat over.

"Quicken your pace! Our allies need us!" General Warneńczyk heard the distant cries of the battling troops.

The air thickened and it became unbearably pungent in the metallic scent of blood particles, carried by the flows. Through the thickets of poisonous berries, wrinkled by the snow, his army compacted into marching columns. Regrouping with the vanguard, Warneńczyk's nervous cramps in his guts worsened, paining him so far his age started to show with grunts.

"C'mon now, gramps. Ya aren't finally agin' are ya?" Adam joked as if he never shared the same feeling.

"Hold your immature act, Skowroński." Florek loosened his joints that had been raising his silver war fork for the days.

"Of course, Colonel Aide." The lieutenant sarcastically apologized, turning to the warrior.

Wojsław was resting his eyes, concentrating every layer of his kei into an audio focus that preyed on the nearing enemies. He tracked near the treeline. From their chatter to the scents they wore. However, an ugly sensation of sensing a fiend among the soldiers made his nose bleed.

"Wojsław?" The general asked for his reassurance.

The protector did not answer until his eyes unexpectedly widened. Patting Wojtek on its fatty neck to halt, he announced to the officers,

"We're here."

Few paces from the column in stealth were the backlines of the army, holding the patrolled forest. Yawning, a soldier stretched, between two small trees that blinded the sunlight, unable to reach him past the thin shadows. It struck a rustling bush catching his hearing though he could not quite make out the figure hiding within.

"Huh?" He groaned.

Casually strolling closer, the Confederate stopped at a distance out of an arm's reach. Peeped through the branches and dying leaves but again, failed to identify the disguised being.

"Must be a hare—" The soldier thought when a shadow loomed over him, darkening the skies above.

"Wha—!"

An axe drove into the soldier's mouth, thrusting the barrel against the poor man's throat. Wojsław pulled the trigger. Gunpowder sparks bursted from his head and blew a gaping cave into his skull. The thunder of the shot brought the Confederates around to an emerging ambushing legion of ten thousand storming past the trees and into the death snare opening

"Guards of the Winged Lance Army! Charge!" Florek appeared before the general could say a word.

Driving their bayonets into the rear guard's backs, the ambush sent a pulse of fear across the ranks, barbarically cleansed from behind. But the vanguard units were still determined to break Arminius' cohort and had not anchored themselves in turning sails.

"General! The bridge!" The colonel aide pinpointed his allies being driven from.

The cavalry closed the gap and forced Arminius onto the bridge, leaving a mere dozen stranded in an island encircled by hunting Confederates, until it too was no more but a cemetery hill.

"Károly..." Warneńczyk mumbled, intensifying his hold on the scythe that began to break his oath of a humane phantom but there was not a hint of eifer.

"I'll never let you cross this river..."

His blackish stains on the blade dissipated and the fanned aura of an ancient mirage was only imagined.

"Wojsław! Thomas! Adam!" The three vanguard leaders rallied with the general's cry that none had ever heard.

"Drive your blades into the enemies' hearts and take the core of our army!"

"I will never accept defeat!" Warneńczyk commanded.

"Let's get 'is done, vanguard!" Adam ecstatically rounded his men and snapped the reins, with the rescue cheering as they charged towards the bridge down the paved straight.

Thus, crashed into the Confederates like a wedge in the formation, in high hopes of bringing back the heroes of Akülunnarchs with a link to their nerves.

Deflecting an arrow that raged at him, Arminius pulled his sword to trap five spearmen in his parry. Locking their spears together, the lieutenant thrusted, throwing their stances from balance and divided their throats with an electric slice, burning the sense of living warmth.

"The general's here to save us!"

"Long live the Winged Lances!" His men clamored at the ambush.

Aurel had adapted soon with forces of two. The bulwark crashed its head against the old man whose cavalrymen had hardened to battle the flow whilst the Eos pierced deeper in the continuum of the unfavorable front. A pot of the hunters had crossed with Siegfried castled on the opposite bank. And so the ten great warriors were to defend the bridge from the congesting Confederates, stampeding in a fruitless attempt to overrun their enemies that held nothing but a blockage from the blades of the formidable Regulus. Where the more who tried to battle, the cycle of eifers tossed into the thickening ranks. The murdered piled.

"Kakakah…" Aurel directed his eyes at the Lekann wedge from the rear that was taken as a glorious surprise

"That's a bold move, general…" He looked over his shoulder.

"Just to save what once was a cohort reduced to nothing but a century…"

"Too bad, old man…" The general mocked Warneńczyk tirelessly, sending lives to the brawl with no care to his backside.

"Your grave will be marked here, forgotten by our next generation."

Gleaming eyes from the bushes and concealing pine trees, hidden far. Their scents blended with the huddling Confederates that toyed with Wojsław's scent when he was last present. A red front of several thousands of men camouflaged within the snow lunged at the prey they had stalked in a frenzy, thrusting and cutting through those caught beyond formation and terrorized Warneńczyk's flanks.

"Impossible!" The general noticed his depleting troops.

A great foot soldier, with the helmet of a golden lion, and his gilded armor, tore the sword into bodies numbering in the twenties as if they were no more than training dummies. Ripping innards from fractured ribs, the Summer Lion rose to tower over his enemies with an eifer shadow.

"Aurel Radilov." Vasilevsky growled, grabbing hold of a soldier by the collar and whose stomach was met by a sword, gushing a geyser of blood onto the crimson snow.

"What did you call me here for?"

"Fly swatting?" He acted in the voice of his teacher, Kolchakov.

The two generals glared in a standoff as the factions clashed. In struggles to force their foes to submit, under the glaze of the thawing ice.

A reverberating hum of Wojsław's axe pummeled, blunting the barbs that tried to catch the eclipse of soldiers. Taken by Wojtek, who drove his protector in bursts of sprints, the double headed blade beheaded in a rhythmic beat. Splashing curling iron and blood that soared across the resolute lines, they sped ahead, overtaking Adam and Ascot who were covered behind his stonewall back. The warrior gestured, lowering his empty hand and the two commanders pulled back and away for the strike of time.

Wojsław slowly brought his great axe, pressing the shaft against his ribs when the midnight tint of his eifer fired into a highlighted sparkle at the tips of the blades. Everything paused. Or for at least the world had slowed so that no human eye could determine. As he punched his blade forward, the punctured air, time and space between the head fractured, bringing onwards his demon that bellowed a spell of doom. Fastening his grip onto the axe, Wojsław briskly swung across the panel of Confederates, bearing a grumbling horizontal rift, like a void was empty of anything. Then as time resumed, the attack dashed at his enemies' backs, tearing through with an indomitable hidden blade that smashed unforgivingly. Chunks of flesh, bisected bodies, and disfigured heads erupted like a tube of lava-like colors, channeled into a spring.

Catching a glimpse of Aurel, hidden within his own men who watched the burgundy rain shower into the burned sludges of mud and snow, as limbs and parts fell thumping onto the earth, the trio of officers advanced despite their thinning ranks. The Confederates began to close the breach with thick double-lined bayonets and spears where cracks in the once tight formation began to open through the attempts to bombard their foes with catastrophic defeats in the local battlefield. The thousands of ambushers dropped as their enemies' spawn of blades doubled for each replaceable death.

"The bridgehead is open!" Ascot hollered to his troops' three cheers.

Arminius spotted the centerline of the allied wedge revealing an opportune moment, and cried,

"I'm going ahead!"

But the lieutenant's arm was grabbed by Julien who held him to stay again.

"Arminius, with us!" said the Danne, as the squad paced back for a breathing court to chamber the final assault.

Drenched in sweat and its steam piping from the spaces in his clothing, panting whilst he tried to control his breath, Arminius nodded and took his steps behind the nine. Flicking the blood from their chipped blades, the squad withdrew defensively, unveiling an open drive to a leading charge. The bricks below cracked, from the escalating determination. Digging their boots deeper into the snow, a mark in the march broke from the unnerving figure of the formation the squad took.

Now! They all spotted the break, and leapt at a spectrum of paces.

Like a diving swallow, a thunder clap darted across the narrow emptiness. With a lightning streak of strikes as if they were a volley of artillery shells, bursted through the clustered front. A surge of shocks against the bridge weakened its legs, hammered from its flanks by the astounding attacks in figures of eight. The chainsaw glided from side to side, offering precise bursts of eifers in the creaks, until the hammer struck the nail that split the world of Confederates into carved caves.

Their flashfire fury moved Adam to the brink of tears. At the sighting of his student's explosive chariot that burnt, forging a blast of shining smoke combined in arms with roaring flames of Sol that was a rich gold color, the lieutenant raised both blades and yelled for even the general could hear,

"Let's bury 'eir heads, vanguard!"

The allies in halves approached the bridgehead of the wavering, struck by Ascot and Wojsław's ruthless blades.

"I'm not leavin' till every last Confederate's bled fer dis battle!" cried Adam.

A quarter of the wedge crossed the border of the unpaved track, onto the destined bridge, as some sped ahead in anarchy without the unity.

"Look, Arminius!" Károly pointed, battling with Arnau's knives.

Holding onto each other to stand, both grinned at the sight of the retreating Confederates before Julien ran towards them with a blissful glint in his eyes and blessed,

"We're saved—"

But two deafening screeches from the rear turned their alleviation into pronounced horror. Armored cavalry rolled through the corridor on the crossing, chopping the Aelon blurred by the rushing growth of the Confederate countering maneuver. Cruising and commanding, Regulus took a brief glance, with eyes of a hunter at the thunder, forced to halt before an encirclement again. His rival's eyes quaked, thinking with their rescue, everything would have ended in their victory. But perhaps he was being stubborn in the thought of becoming saviors of the legendary battle of a thousand jäger was the only path fate could swerve towards. And yet when an iceberg appeared before him, his mind did not steer away.

The ambusher's vanguard who had yet to pass by the crossroads disappeared in the cloud of rose red petals whose screams were heard afar. Then nothing came to be within a minute. Their voices were swallowed by the clashing blades. The genius had annihilated the bulk in the seconds of staggered behavior.

Stranded, the officers halted. Turning to the Confederates, who first routed, stopped on the spots. Pivoting on the soft flesh peeled from the bodies the army had massacred, bursting lives' juices onto the dirt-turned mud from the voluminous blood spilled that day, the soldiers regained their morale before the grandeur Regulus whose glory shone like a reborn god.

"I never expected you to put up for so long." The colonel thrusted his spear to a closing victory.

Regulus lowered his blade and removed the helmet with another hand, opening way for his nobly tied hair, into a short tail, to waver along the brief breezes.

"And yet even with your allies on the brink of fall, you fight with such certainty." He wondered and praised his enemy.

"Lieutenant von Regen. Your honor exceeds even mine."

His troops cheered twice at their wavering enemies, powerfully changing the barren mood of the battle to the Rus' favor,

"Long live the Confederate motherland!"

"Long live the sacred tsardom!" A flood of footmen hailed the alliance and their ancient nation, like a blaring horn.

Their voices echoed throughout the forest and distant plains and were heard from the towns nearby. Into three columns, Regulus readied his units and shouted with the high tide,

"Advance!"

Gathered along the bridgehead, they charged onwards, crying for battle at the lesser hundreds held still on the bridge. It was the climax and one, in particular, thought he had been played from the beginning.

"Everything...our defense...the bridge..." Having a loss of the fake omen of hope, Arminius mumbled to himself.

"Even the reinforcements who were supposed to ambush them..."

"When I'd thought we were one step ahead of our enemies..." The somber boy stared at his hand where a handful of wisteria purple discharges sparked near a muted cry for his name, over and over.

"Has my doctrine really harmed more than it had saved...?"

A meadow that he could not have forgotten appeared before him. Though Arminius could not tell reality from a hallucination by seeing such horrors transform into a beauty. Blood waterfalls, and a floating island, chained to the eternal hell that held a glistening shard of his mind, eclipsed the rotten orange moon. The extraordinary sights beheld looked distant from the boundless cavern of faces he once saw. Arminius stood in a shallow lake, whose crimson waters flooded his boots, holding flayed floating bodies and eyes that all gawked at the boy where some flesh and skin clinged to his legs, unwilling to let go. Whispering evil spirits into him, the eyes seemed to have spoken, until he was led away to a river, feeding to the growing fiend that he had seen numberless times.

Your life... The tree of a million fingers and thousands of severed mouths pointed at him.

Eyes grew from its skinless bark, bleeding and weeping dreading tears.

For an eternal world of an utopia where death is your prominence...

Its hands branched out, forming a chain of dripping lifeless flesh and bone that reached down for Arminius' head.

This world is our paradise called heaven...

A revelation for the coming day where choice would quarter the soulless being you will possess... The voice faded as the cries from the outside drilled into the cloudy ceiling.

"Arminius!" Someone shouted into his ear.

Waking from the subconscious world of far stress, Arminius turned to him whose quietened voice begged for his friend,

"We need to retreat."

"Our cohort will be overrun." Julien informed the commander.

Arminius held a short pause. But the time he closed his eyes in prayers and meditation, the figure of the terrible death-like world crawled to his mind.

"Yeah..." He faintly replied.

Raising his arm for his comrades yet before Julien could call for the elites, an unsure grasp kept the limb to rest.

"What is it?" Julien asked, willing to hear whatever Arminius had to say.

"It'll take more lives than we can count..." The latter began.

"But it's the only idea we can rely on."

As the younger lieutenants worked for the plan with Arber who retreated to the call of his name, unknown to the veterans of war. Adam, Ascot and Wojsław, stranded from the core of their headquarters in a brutal clash against Vasilevsky whose forces flushed from the treeline, stared at the intruding front.

"Vanguard!" Ascot commandeered the frontline with his still hand, hiding the trembling other.

"Amass a retreat across the bridge and rally with Reichner's cohort!"

His men followed Ascot's order, withdrawing without doubt; fleeing whenever they had found the hatches of escape in the human wave that rushed along the bridge towards the elites. Exposed to the flesh-eating elements, the officers were forgotten by their own in the senseless race to heaven.

"I may know defeat well, as if it were a close family." The major spoke to himself.

"However!" He erupted, thickening his veins.

"I am a soldier, no less so than a ship is a vessel." A composure seeped into the cracks in his skin.

Clearing his throat, Ascot clenched the shaft of his hammer with his shaking hand, rattling the polearm in its slumber.

"Wojsław. *Adam!*" He sharply boomed on the lieutenant's name.

The oncoming Confederates funneled into the narrow bridge, like oil, were clogged and slowed by the frontal stampede, biding time for Ascot to act as his hunches told him.

"Go, the both of you."

"Whilst I defend this bridge with my life." Calming once more, the major offered the passage.

Faking an assuring grin acted with a forced tone, Adam sniggered in denial of Ascot's resolution,

"Heh, hey now, don't be gettin' cynical on us, major."

"To give you the means to flee!" Ascot yelled, punching his

chest to stop his irritating spikes of frustration.

"That is my will." The man sharply exhaled.

Tossing away the beret over the low walls onto the rapids below, Ascot released a bitter sigh, as it was taken away, like a swift obscured pass into the next life. Shadowed by shades of swords and soldiers, the Confederacy pushed into the presence of the dismounting officer.

"At the very least, allow me to do something worthwhile," Ascot whispered.

"Major, I haven't accepted anythin' y'know!" Adam interrupted, flinging his arms about like Gin in the fever of winter.

"Just so ya do know, I'm not plannin' ta let ya fight alone—"

Wojsław chopped a hand into Adam's neck and put him to sleep with the one strike on the common weakness, catching him as he fell. Like a paralyzed man, the lieutenant held onto his weapons unletting for the blades to loosen from his grip.

"Wojsław." Ascot unemotionally addressed, bringing onwards his hammer that was charged with his eifer.

"No matter what, obey Arminius Reichner to your death."

"It *is* the general's desire." He firmly added to concrete the words that were to be stamped into Wojsław's head.

The protector nodded and pulled Adam on board, leaving no trace of remorse. Patting the stone bear, growling and shuddering from the fate he sensed from Ascot's olden aura, the beast took to the dash carrying the two soldiers, hurriedly down the bridge.

"We may be their guardians now..."

"But whoever saves you from defeat in the future..." Ascot remnicized the near past that had rushed.

"To hell with this!" The major let off one last uncontrolled shout from the bottom of his lungs.

Holding the grand hammer, gone alight with a cold, cruel blue, the single-manned defense held strong against the straining air of the Confederacy, nearing the edge of the curve on the bridge. As the first ranks arrived, their swords sprouted over the sea of heads, glistening under the revealing sun that showcased its lightening heart. It poured a jubilant ray onto the sprinting columns, leaving Ascot in the bleak colorless panel of a segregated painting.

The major dug deeper into his stance, sighing relievedly at the sight of his eifer that he prayed to appear. He smiled, for the second time in his pathetic life, and dashed down the declining straight with an airy launch. Slowed by his years of inactivity, the winds that passed him were weak and sometimes static. But Ascot charged from one leap to the next until reaching the line who exchanged positions with spearmen and bayonet-fitted rifles, unfrightened by the feeble soldier sprinting towards.

"Hold firm!" The frontal sergeant barked.

"This fat arse won't get far!"

At a sacrificial halt before meeting the blades, the major leaned away as he slid along the thin snow cover. Charging his aqua eifer, Ascot swung across with a heavy bash and the weight of his forward body. Blood gushed out of the fearless soldiers whose weapons were splintered, throwing wooden shrapnel into close by eyes, as their wounds ripped open before collapsing onto the ground.

"Tsk." Ascot sneered at his foes who flawlessly recovered the replacement of a young rank of soldiers.

A leaning tower of spikes from sharpened iron in a phalanx thrusted at the rusty major like a hidden trap that exposed itself to protect their comrades. In overwhelming waves, they rode on the attack, stealing Ascot's pedestal in a favorable, suicidal assault. Cut with shallow jabs that somehow eased his shaking hand, knotted with his own blood, Ascot leapt some paces back that gave his enemies the stagnant time to regroup before he decided his next dance.

Drawing his weapon to the side, parallel with the polluted ground, smeared in wine red, the major wearily panted. He placed both eased hands on his hammer and had the blunted but malicious edge pointed at the ranks, marching towards him en masse. Ascot forced a breath of burdened thoughts onto a train of steam and huffed twice when his eifer returned. Flowing eternally in his hammer, a razor coat of air and water extended across the polearm. The thin lining displayed an innocent face no eifer the soldiers had seen before. And though they knew the mirage had fooled their eyes, the mask unfolded into a sharp whistle of heroism.

"A meander in the cold stream falling from the highlands." His eardrums burst when he took to the sprint.

Skimming along the surface, a water droplet from the tip of the major's hammer formed a tapering tail, spinning as the body spun. With a dance-like motion, Ascot glided along the cobbled floor, and struck the frontline soldier, devastating the shoulder before moving to the following victim in fluidity. The major swiped up and split a face whose screams silenced before his voice could be ejected. Right and left, and in vertical arcs that left traces condensed into afterimages of clobbers. He sharply moved from person to person, jumping ranks into the valley his hammer had carved out yet was not bloodied by Ascot's swiftness, like nothing had ever touched the troops. Those smashed by the streamline paused, unknown about the ticklish feeling they felt until the many looked down, frozen numb by the ushering of collapsed stomachs. However his terror ran dry in the last he bisected. The final kei dissipated and Ascot was halted in his tracks on the forty-ninth victim.

Two dozen spears and swords threw themselves into the major's flesh, penetrating everything beneath the ailing skin from flesh to bone. Blood oozed from his wounds and once the executing severing slash across his spine ended all was dealt, Thomas Ascot fell to his fragile knees and came to a realization that he was to travel down the rails to the next station in isolation.

Bulked striding from the distance like an enormous steam train shaking the bridge with its heavy body, a brown bear, showing tissue white patches of fur, sprinted at the elite squad with Wojsław and Adam on its back. The warrior showed its axe, raised high up into the sky, and began waving it in circles for Arminius to see.

"Where's the major?" They all asked, squinting to spot whether there was another following from behind.

"Ain't that geezer with you?!" Drawing his sword, Gin stamped forward in a thin coating of blood, clotted by his exhaustion.

"Not now, Gin—" Arber raised his half spear against him, who looked down with a mild demeanor.

The warrior rushed nearer, crossing the half point mark when a storm of enemy troops appeared as mere shadows in the shroud of snowy powder kicked up from the stone bear's tracks. Punching his armored chest, Wojsław puffed his lungs, inhaling streams of air as if he was a turbine.

"Retreat!" Wojsław roared with his voice magnified ten times over, sounding like he had screamed it into their ears.

Echoing across the forest behind, the birds nested quietly in their straw and leaved homes flapped away in flocks overhead.

Of all times?! The squad stared at the crossing.

Soldiers posted on the safe bank nudged each other out of formation, whose mumbles stemmed into skeptical grumbles.

"I thought we had the general's support." A soldier complained.

Siegfried eavesdropped on his comrades who could not stop their discontented protesting.

"Don't they have the upperhand in the ambush?" Another unknowingly asked that stimulated even more unease.

The century of mouths babbled, stirring irritation among the ranks grown into restlessness at the sight of the approaching force that had already overrun Ascot's last stand. They peered down the narrow straight of the advance, screaming battle cries and playing a patriotic tune of hailing the empire. Unsure of the ensuing chaos, breaking apart the once too many broken morale of common soldiers alike, Siegfried turned to Arnau, hopelessly, with his terrified face of a child.

"What now?" Juggling his swords, Arnau asked himself, rotating to his side to see the three pondering over something.

Arminius glumly glanced down at his feet and those who had remained beside him. Layered with cuts to his arm that fought the most, Károly patted him, reminding Arminius of his following duty that preceded the wrath he feared would engulf his soul.

As Wojsław dashed down the bridge, his aiming eyes did not take a single look at Arminius and instead passed by at hastiness where the wind abruptly changed that blew against the lieutenant's back. His jacket fluttered. The unfolded hood gently brushed against his hair. The chipped sword he wielded was loosened from his hand that nearly scraped the hard stone bricks cracking from the overloading clash. Though the warrior did not speak with words, the foretelling of what the demon wanted to say pierced his mind,

Do whatever you want, child.

Releasing a dismal sigh, Arminius inspired himself with a cheer of his name, hallucinating a crowd that cried for him like a great general.

Well...I won't say no... He thought with his returning resolve steeled on the pivot around the footprints left in the snow.

"Julien," said Arminius, sharply.

"Yes?" Shocked by the familiar voice enlightening his considerate being, Julien flinched and froze.

"Evacuate the bridge and retreat north." His comrade offered the path to be gone.

The lieutenant directed all eyes towards the imposing forest that waved like a good protector as his friendly gesture dampened the clamoring,

"I'll join you once we're done here."

Despite the fears that surrounded Julien, worrying him about the blunders that he could make over small inaccuracies in his predictions and strategies if he ever led, the bestowed place yet again as a temporary commander burdened him with a role he had never wanted to attain from the onset of war.

"Alright..." Julien smiled at his counterpart and lightly pressed his fist against Arminius' chest.

"Arminius." Arber reminded him, pointing at the nearing blizzard of the Confederacy who had yet to slow.

The perfect opportunity presented itself before their very eyes as Arminius sent Julien on his duties whilst the lieutenants followed not knowing what they would live to witness that changing day. Hidden beneath the two menaces, their comrades, Julien pushed the cohort off the bridge and escaped the field of the stone structure that began to crumble. Pebbles disintegrated, dropping dust and icicles into the river below that splashed. The century halted in the next forest, able to witness the forming madness that was to follow on the rumbling crossing.

Being the final strength able to fight with his eifer, particles formed around Arber, holed at the tip of his glowing halved spear as long as a sporting javelin. Swapping from grip to grip, he readied a borrowed technique that Arminius recognized. Arber held his spear with a unique backhand-grip, between two fingers, that had a striking resemblance to Arminius' javelin hand.

"Sorry..." Arminius set aside to apologize.

Thinking it was for both times he had spilled his anger over himself, Arber was ready to blankly refuse for the greater good if not for otherwise,

"All of their deaths might defile you and stain your hands,

Arber."

Before the reserved soldier had a chance to open his mouth, Arminius continued as he allowed the Confederates to close the gap ahead.

"Remember when our teams competed in the finals?" He asked.

"Two birds and one stone." Arber directly replied with the only combination in mind that Arminius had performed in his childhood.

The devoted look in his eyes told Arber. That his courage to break free of his devout beliefs in saving even the worst of his enemies had arisen.

"If you can't hold all their blood in your two hands," said Arminius, trailing in counted steps along Arber's runway for he stopped at a sport court's distance with his sword laid like a stepping booster to fly higher than it was humanly possible.

"I have an extra pair to hold the sacrifices for this war."

Arber nodded, which sank the doubts in Arminius' heart. But for the time they had spent recalling the past, the Confederates had flooded into the last quarter. Though the lieutenants were equally aware that their limits should be pulled farther.

"Wait..." Arminius mumbled.

The tramping wait built as their vanguard declined the sloped bridge.

"Hold..." He whispered.

A lightning strike cackled in the distance, throwing volleys of booming claps that with it signaled the two youngsters.

"Now!" Arminius yelled down the pathway ushering an illustrious sign of a midnight blue eifer.

Dashing across the short length with a shockwave taken away by the wind, Arber rushed across the many tiles that broke beneath his slashing pulse like a jet skimming along the linear road. The stones cracked at the dashing pace he traveled with, maintaining a pure form of an offensive. The cold lieutenant's arms were flung back, like an eagle ready to lift itself from a nest. His eifer charged, finally taking to the space above his spearhead, being grinded into the dust from the immense heat it carried. Within half a second, his foot landed flawlessly on Arminius' sword and with a push backed by a scream,

"For victory, Arber!"

A second pulse circled the impact and who was propelled into the air with an explosive push from both his arms and the sword that already seemed distant as he soared above the Confederates' heads. All turned up at the shining sun, barely dimmed by the high-reaching soldier casting one shade that served as the target he aimed for. Arminius gave chase from below, leaping but without a distinct push, to a height beneath the extensive space between him and the other. Like a javelin player, Arber leaned back mid-air, impeccably balancing against the overriding gravity that began to pull him down. He held in a breath that saw no end. Exposing the vibrant honest blade radiating a storm around its tip that served as an eye, Arber ruthlessly launched it in a near vertical. It shot through the known sound walls, bursting into rings of clouds that formed its own natural circles. Though it was no Letalis, the severe gusts spun into a drill, burning the splinters that stabbed Arber's hands by a whirlpool exceeding the human range. Arminius grasped his sword tighter, locking his sights on the looming spear turned javelin. He spun the blade flat and jolted forward with two full spins, and at the point of perfection, struck the falling missile on the shaft's end. The contact blasted, accelerating the spear even quicker as those tragic soldiers below saw the final light for the spear touched the bridge.

It flew through the cobblestone, and the pillars that held the structure. And as the Confederates' faces finally showed reaction, the spear smashed into the ravaging river. Exploding into a flowerbed of rubble, the transient condensation cloud detonated the bridge like glass shattering with a fierceful punch upwards. Throwing Arminius and Arber out of their floating hold, bodies and boulders erupted volcanically into the sky before the litters of the dead dived down like a burned out asteroid. Mutilating the Confederacy's fictional victory, blood showers rained onto Regulus and Aurel's unshielded faces. None were distraught at the sight of what they both could have predicted but did not prevent from the wrathful happening that granted the Arminius they knew a new name.

Like a heroic epic poem from ancient Hëllat, Warneńczyk deflected the blows of the Summer Lion's sword, crashing into the old man restlessly when he noticed the condensed cloud blocking the sunlight shining into the forest where only he remained to duel the vice general. Slyly offering a slash that threw his enemy on guard, deforesting the lands around him, with his rear facing a small ridge, he stepped away.

"I promise I'll save you, Károly..." Sweat ran along his wrinkles, lined with swelling veins.

"Your mother won't forgive me if she sees you again in the next world..."

"Remember? Audrey too..." The general's bones started to ache as he panted even more, drying his throat.

The titanic scythe he defensively held proved to be the greatest shield and sword the general could wield. In the hour spent that tolled his aging body, not once was he cut, nor came close to death under Vasilevsky's enraged pace, quickening, for much he missed. Until he gave up near a falling tree, crashing into the snow that clouded Warneńczyk's vision.

"Old man." Vasilevsky growled before the foe's reach.

Lifting his heavy blade stuck in the mud, the vice general ordered his men to surround the general with rifles aimed and the iron of the sights bearing on his head.

"Don't you think it's about time to crawl into a coffin?"

Once the chalky smoke cleared, at least an entire century was unveiled, having Warneńczyk encircled who inched closer to the ridge, nearing the edge that broke away at each step.

"So were you the devil who aimed for my head at Sorrmul?" asked Vasilevsky, easing his stance as the Lekann general refitted his grip.

"Or was it simply by your elite squad's accord?"

Turning in his wrists, Warneńczyk held the war scythe near his face, ignoring the minor soldiers, holding their fingers on the trigger guards and the edge.

"I was bored by your inactivity." The general spoke.

"What did you say?" Vasilevsky's face reddened and his sword and shield steamed.

"Could an elder like myself really fight back?" Warneńczyk asked rhetorically, though his enemy answered nonetheless.

"You're digging your grave—" The Confederate threatened as his flames were presented on his shoulder, igniting the tree the man stomped into cinders.

"Then as a gravedigger, why have I deterred you for an hour?" Warneńczyk ridiculed him to no return.

Vasilevsky's eifer vented by his outraged self erupted, where his mind had told itself never to release its anger. It was exactly what his teacher said that he did not heed.

"You imbecile!" He roared, fanning his flames with a near strike.

Warneńczyk scouted the corner of his eyes that produced a sound of galloping hooves with a Lekann officer aiming his pistol at the Summer Lion. The distant soldier cocked the gun and fired twelve rounds into the crowd with each bullet striking its target that brought the distracted soldiers away from the general for a thin time that had him unattended. But soon realizing their error, the troops tried scurrying back into formation but were too late to settle.

As Vasilevsky froze from a battlefield paranoia, Warneńczyk swung his scythe into the ground and threw a thick dust cloud at the soldiers, impairing their vision over the cornered prey. Then grabbing hold onto the saddle that galloped by, the general was taken away, leaving two trails of snow clouds that opened Vasilevsky's eyes to another irritative loss.

"Are you hurt anywhere?" Florek attended to his commander, vigilantly keeping an eye on Vasilevsky who had not pursued.

"Not yet." Warneńczyk bluntly returned.

"As long as we have you, general," The colonel aide commended.

"Then the war is yet to be lost—"

"No..." said Warneńczyk who looked onwards, at the river path linked to the canal fortress of Tschrewen.

Issuing a long pause beneath the alternating shadows from the stripped branches dissecting the path of light, Florek questioned,

"How so?"

The general pondered, in the depths of thoughts about his grandson that he was so close to, who had then been stolen away from the committed fluke by his enemies. But truly, the entirety of the servants of an Aelon paradise troubled him most.

"Across the bridge..." Warneńczyk groaned.

"We had lost our greatest asset in this war."

XXV

10 APELYOTES 491

10.11.12017

Julien Carlstadt

The sea's close. I can feel the familiar salt in the breeze that flows into this room, over the empty road in the field of unyielded harvests. We had taken shelter in an old farmhouse whose kind owner allowed us to stay. But it was only because I could speak our language. The good farmer told us that it was another two hours' march to Medwen. A fort that sits protecting a strait to the three main islands of my home.

I'd never felt so excited yet anxious stepping onto native soil with the Confederates biting at our heels. The bridge we'd destroyed south of Lubek may have delayed the three great commanders pursuing us. Yet, it did little to stop them. Nor did the river through Kilunn do anything to slow their invasion. Colonel Eos, Third General Radilov, and General Vasilevsky. They made me wonder, at times. Why didn't I bother finding my grandfather or even smuggle myself across the sea on that day? Would it have been easier had I stayed home?

I guess...it never occurred to me that these options were there. Afterall...how Arminius felt...that was the same as my choice to stay with him on this tour.

The more I think about our journey, why we called this hell, the image before me clears. How the general was so protective of us crossing that bridge. Now, to our south was Vasilevsky's army group marching with six hundred thousand. The northern landing of one hundred and fifty thousand from the Confederate protectorate of Nurtözh. And to our west is occupied Sueken, under Kolchakov, mobilizing a few leagues from the capital. Once the chart had been laid in my mind, my understanding opened in despair, with no luck this time...

We had been encircled...

CHAPTER

26   PARANOIA

In the rocking wooden wagon, bumping along the unkept road, dragged by an old war horse, Julien and Károly sat on its benches. They looked outward into the empty channel feeding tranquility to their men. Hardly fifty-two. Fatigued and wounded. At a crawling pace behind the march, Wojsław and Adam guarded the rear, whilst the lieutenants gathered near the core, watching each other's backs. The rare sighting of the sun on the dreary kingdom colored the mood and the world around them was repainted with the contrasting seas of trees and the icy plains of white and blue.

As the files turned around the corner of a hedge-lined road, the rising morning sun struck Arminius' face like a motherly hand that slowly woke him as if it was another school day. He felt a shadow, gently loom over him, covering the sunlight that provided warmth besides from the blanket. The boy did not react. One side was warmer, under his fooled sense believing it was a fireplace. Yet his left, covered by a shade that was cold like hail, though was not unbearably so.

"Ngh…" Arminius moaned, stretching his arms that knocked against the edge of the wagon.

The fifty-two manned century ascended a bridge that was one full league, suspended over water, designed like a rib cage. It climbed until the steepness ended at the center where the road began to drop at a calm incline.

"Arminius…" Julien shook him awake.

The squad captain's sleepy eyes opened to an unbelievably freeing sky. Cloudless and coated with a new baby blue ceiling. Arminius realized that his comrade's wintry hands were laying on his shoulders as Károly heated the climate that burned his eifer orderly. The two looked over him and smiled with joyous intentions.

"Happy fourteenth birthday!" exclaimed Károly who retracted his eifer.

"Happy birthday." Julien congratulated.

For even Arminius had forgotten as his face was shocked into blushing cheeks, he stammered as his lips tried to seal itself,

"A-Ah...t-thanks."

"You wouldn't wake up no matter how we tried." recounted Julien, awkwardly grinning at the thought of carrying Arminius down the flight of stairs that he nearly stumbled on.

"So we borrowed this wagon from the old farmer."

"Was that necessary?" Arminius rubbed his sore neck and asked.

"We could always pay him back once we've earnt enough." Julien shook his head and leaned over his comrade's face, embarrassingly close.

As his friend gave way, Arminius sat up with his blanket rolled to one side. Noticing the sea of harsh currents flowing beneath the dangling bridge, his mind was in complete blur.

"Where are we?" Arminius wondered with he had not fully woken.

Julien gazed upon the famed late renaissance walls of Medwen, slowly revealing itself before their very eyes.

"The bridge to our allies," He answered, pointing at the reveling fort.

"Danen."

A bewildering first glance shone among the tired hunters, at last, who could see a sane part of civilization. The elites' jaws dropped as the officers gathered a breath to what their eyes held. Danen was more than a new world of Yurupe, heralding its gleaming chalk white coastal walls, manned with antique bronze cannons for every one hundred paces along the battlements. Towering over homes and camps settled behind, the walls were at least fifteen meters tall. Protecting its home, where they had found the material to erect such a magnificent structure, able to circle around the island, which at times was eighty leagues wide, remained a challenging feat, mysterious to the squad. On the short approach down the bridge towards the studded gate where the only keeper of the western battlements stood, the convoy slowed before the sheltering shades emerged where no light could reach further beyond. The shadow darkened their hair as they

neared the three grandiose flags, bearing the banners of the blank
cross over a red field, taller than the ducal and the barony's flag,
flapping like sails in the average wind.

The guards, in the light brownish tower, as if the timber had
been newly cut, trailed in cycles, rotating around their daily shifts
in dull manners. They were dressed in pantone red uniforms of
the kingdom. But despite the bright colors, everyone seemed
demoralized, and displeased, emphasized by their weak shuffled
and delayed changing of arms. Not one stood out among the
many who waited nervously for new orders from the capital. That
was either to retreat or to simply return home. And not even one,
looked like they had seen battle for the course of the war. Scared
and intimidated by the growing presence of the Confederate
fleets eyeing their island, they were far too few in numbers, like a
droplet of water in a sea of magma.

The atmosphere's dampened... Julien scouted the walls,
corrupt with dispiriting groans and yawns.

A lonely sergeant, in his late twenties, who looked to be
of the highest rank the squad had spotted, strolled along the
narrow corridor above the gate and halted before a recruit. He
jumped from the sergeant's appearance and wrongly saluted with
the opposite arm, held at a dipped angle. Biting his thumb, the
sergeant sighed, and corrected the conscript's awful attempt. As
even his uniform was dressed like poverty, his commander knelt
to tie his boots when the recruit spotted the approaching forces,
nearing them at an inoffensive march. Unknown to his allies'
colors that was unrecognized in whatever ill mind he possessed,
the youngster shouted in his native tongue,

"M-Mjen feletchvepele! (Sergeant!)"

"T-Tje fjente øs tëa Koenfeatëatchjoen (The enemies of the
Confederacy!)" He cried.

The commander sprung up and pressed against the low wall,
watching the traumatized unit with a dangerous glare. He could
not quite make out the blurred flags sewn into the officers' patches
and so assumed their allegiances too from the redness of the
banner.

"Uenmmeaclejk (Impossible!)" His thoughts blasted aloud.

"Øfkleåeauencstcheaupp?! Skoen ta?! (Scouts here?!)"

"What?! Why are they mobilizing—?!" Lev yelled over the
stomping footsteps, sprinting about the floors that he could not

count before his eyes.

Its section was chaos. Incapable of pulling a defense with the outdated rifles and chipped bows in the arsenal. Shaking and loading their rifles that the troops had forgotten to standby, shells and arrows fell everywhere. They tripped over their self-induced paranoia and fear, who acted no more than the children they were. Before the Blitshünntorkoeurt had the chance to explain, the building storm within the guards of the western gate had once collapsed on itself, rendering the tower useless if ever the Confederates truly were to show themselves.

The stamp on his landing drew all the Dannes' attention to him, having their trembling sights at the lieutenant. Seeing his shuddering, off-beating breath, Julien and Károly inched closer to the edge to the sound of blades being unsheathed. Raising his fist in the air that halted Gin who had his burning palms on the hilt, ready to draw first blood, Arminius tread. And as comrades, the squad followed the trio, in any case whatever the reckless did turned unfavorable. But carefully, entering a change in the tarmac road of a weathered shade until deciding it was far enough, he knew when not to provoke on the wrong side of the barrel. As Arminius gazed upwards at the impressive border that the kingdom held, without the sun in his eyes, it was clear why no one had ever dared invade the archipelago.

"What was it again…?" The lieutenant said softly.

Taking a deep breath that freed his mind, Arminius prepared himself to converse, and searched even higher for the sergeant who peeked out of the battlements, fidgeting the pommel of his sword. He gulped and took another gasp.

"Jkyen…kjen…(I'm…not an…)" Arminius cautiously began in a distinct foreigner's accent but had run aground after his second word before the flustered was eased of humiliation by a hand on his shoulder.

"Vjeayt pj tëa alljaens! (We're with the alliance!)" Julien brought himself, pressing his hand, flat along his left arm.

To that gesture of a country's faith, observed by all of the tower who rested their fingers on the triggers, they froze. Lowering their weapons, the soldiers looked at their comrades, unsure of what they should do. As if Julien's ties had saved his unit, both sides sighed to comfort the heavens.

"Keannën vjea enjktch jen tëa uenjfëasellën speåke speaekën? (May we speak in the universal tongue?)" The ally Danne requested as Arminius headed once more.

The sergeant disappeared behind the wall and consulted his petty soldiers, shrugging and shaking their heads for either they understood little or nothing at all. Appearing more over the parapet, the commander of the gatekeepers peered below.

"State…your allegiance!" He unsurely yelled.

"We're of the Winged Lance Army!" Arminius proudly told him as the sun revolved over the walls.

It climbed higher than anything and shortened the shadows that drew over the brightened squad, melting the crunching snow beneath their feet.

"Your commander?!" The sergeant asked in addition.

"Warneńczyk!" replied the lieutenant without hesitation.

The Danne commander frowned at his answer with an acceptable suspicion. Turning to his close advisors, he distanced himself from the elites ears and leaned back to confirm,

"Tje Cefleüceletchën Leaensën? (The Winged Lance Army?)"

"Jk taktche sje alle stchaeapën jen Stchettjen. (I thought they had been wiped out in Sedinn.)" One corporal brought, holding his chin.

There it seemed the news of the downfall knew no limits as within a matter of days, had already reached the eyes and ears of the troops across the sea. What forbade them to trust was only so natural.

"Ja, mjene cetaenkën sjent tje clejkën… (Yes, that was my first thought…)" Their commander agreed, returning to the force of no more than the injured.

He held the exhaustion of the Aelon in his eyes that never lied. The wounds the fifty-two had marched and sustained. Though for the possibilities that they were not to worry over the impossible threat, came a fresh stack of doubts, rewritten in his mind.

"Enuea tje ceattëa vjssën es? Sje keanntchën jene falle stchellën… (Who knows? They could spring a trap…)" Another added with a preying stare at the waiting.

"Tann, vjea solltchën øfpassën vas vjea sacën, mjen füeaëa.

(In any case, be careful what we say, sir.)" The corporal suggested.

Nodding to his comrades on guard, the sergeant returned to Arminius, restlessly glancing over his shoulders to make doubly sure that his men were with them.

"What is your name, good soldier of the Winged Lances?!" He confidently shouted in high hopes of revealing their believed intentions.

Arminius felt a tug on his jacket and paced back into the squad's center, surrounded by a counsel of opinions oceans divided.

"We don't have de time to be sittin' 'round answerin' 'eir questions." Gin whined, gifting the sergeant a frightful shock with his harming glare.

"Let's leave them be." Colt suggested.

"Look, we could just run 'way an' become mercenaries or somethin'." The brute added an odd recommendation.

"Den we won't have to be chased halfway 'round de continent."

The lieutenant felt a piercing poke against his back and as he turned around, Alexandria's menacing stare choked his soul.

"It may work for idiots like you in the short run."

"But what do you think will happen once this war's over?" She helped their minds ponder as the shaft was driven deeper against Gin's bones.

"Tsk." The latter slapped her blade away and walked for the wagon, steaming from his fear and annoyance of her provocation.

Between a similar strait of paranoia, splitting two lands wanting to unmask the truth behind the other, both fronts impatiently rejected either's questions or demands, and yet, even with a blockade, a few wanted to sail along the same path.

"We don't have a choice." Arminius briefly looked at Julien and returned to the sergeant.

They watched as he singled himself out of the crowd, before the soldiers wheezing and gasping in pain. Illustriously, he stood before the giant gates, as if used to transfer mechanized weapons, and shouted his rank and title,

"I'm Lieutenant Arminius Reichner!"

The walls went silent. As the factions wondered what he had said wrong when the lieutenant felt a small rock, no larger than half a finger, strike his head that knocked him towards his squad. Blood dripped in a stream down his face as Julien slid across the ice to him, stunned and stumbling.

"Arminius!" Julien ushered an aching cry.

Holding his cut above the right eye, the Danne withdrew Arminius into the protection of his comrades as the pointed weapons of the battlements and ground spun to be faced in a standoff on the checkpoint. The sergeant's subordinates hollered and read calls to the panicking soldiers whilst Colt yelled for the baking hearts of their supposed allies,

"Da hell?!"

"Don't fuck around!" A corporal on the walls threw his arms in the air and trailed back and forth, rubbing his head with a cigarette at hand.

"Jen leøtchenaentch?! (A lieutenant?!)" He glanced at his commander whose face was in fright from the outburst.

"At that age?!" The enraged soldier stamped into the cover of the officer's quarters.

The room's portable heater flushed warm air against the cold wind that shook the sergeant watching the squad tend to Arminius. Hearing the bickering between the two rival forces, Adam rode towards the core where the lieutenants crowded around Arminius, laid in the wagon to be treated.

"Koeapoeåle! (Corporal!)" The Danne sergeant commanded out of the blue.

"Jk vëate tjeses peaoplëmm jen jeae håente lëcën. (I leave this matter in your hands.)" told he.

His junior lazily slipped onto a chair and exaggeratedly sipped on a hot cup of tea as an ask clouded the air,

"Vojen cestch tu? (Where are you off to?)"

"Umm temm lëcatchën jenën pesuk apsustchattën. (To see the legate.)" The keeper of the gate answered boldly and bleakly.

In a compact room of a cramped two-storied house, beneath the tower, with its thatch blinds lowered that concealed the plain medieval colors layered below the smoky air, sat a hard-working

man, scribbling in the piles of documents that had been stacked on the side of his humble desk. His office was no simpler than a poor man's home and had little things that caught anyone's eye. As he flipped the pages of the logistics to a census under the province's name, *Sëleaent*, the door flashed open, releasing a brisk gust of wind over the sergeant's shoulder. The man stopped his writing hand as if he had been waiting.

"Yes?" He asked in the Nyozhormannik tongue, standing from the creaking chair.

The soldier need not salute and informed him without a proper address,

"An *allied* unit has shown itself outside the walls,"

"Numbering in the fifties." He told him with his hand holding the door.

Facing his aide, the legate clicked the pen and quietly clipped it onto a sheet of importance.

"My, my, that's a small number to have caused that large a ruckus." The commander commented in the fashion of a noble.

"I have indeed predicted our impenetrable walls to be thrown into disorder,"

"But not at such a scale." He fixed his plain silver armlet that had fallen to his wrist and adjusted it until the ring remained tightly wrapped around the forearm.

"Did they give you a name?" The man anxiously asked.

"Yes." His soldier covered his mouth and cleared his throat.

"Arminius Reichner."

"Arminius Reichner?!" The legate stormed around the desk and confronted him as he spun around the corner into the corridor.

"Prepare all legions for departure!"

His excited footsteps on the hollow floor echoed beneath, and scurried away at a quickening pace.

"Oh! And open the gates!" He ordered the puzzled sergeant and leapt down the stairs with his guards hurrying behind.

The tyrannical corporal argued with his theories beyond relief. Until another demand from his abuse was dejected again, he madly raised his sword. Its polished blade shined, reflecting those of the young terrified recruits trembling on standby.

"Any fool knows the Winged Lance Army's been devastated!"

The corporal's fascist voice could not be saved.

"Reveal your intentions, *Confederate* hounds!"

Waving his command in the air, the fortress locked their sights unto the elite squad who slowly inched back. With each layer of the wall and tower drawing their rifles and bows, knowing there was a fellow Danne at risk, the soldiers mumbled across the ranks that found displeasure among their common hearts.

"Pjst tu tjea sjkëa? (Are you sure?)" Some soldiers murmured below and above the corporal who flinched for each he heard some unrest.

"Sje hapën jenën laentsmmann. (They have a Danne on their side.)" Another said too loudly.

"Ëa hatch enjktch ueneaektch, (He's right you know,)" One backed as he held down the barrels in the range of his arms.

"Vueateuensytch pjcepeåktch uensëae jcënën su skütchsën? (Weren't we taught to protect our people?)"

Poking his head outside the battlements, he bravely watched the discord around them when the corporal's ears perked and furiously yelled at his oppressed men,

"Eaujc sjen, kaenoenënfuttëa! (Silence, conscripts!)"

"Heaeae enjktch øf tje tchøfele! (Do not listen to that fiend's lies!)" He spoke with his self-perception of the falsehood before.

"Tëa juence jstch jen ferråtchëa tes keaenjcs uent tëa enatchjoen! (He is a clear traitor to our state and king!)"

Lacking explanation, his speech was underwhelming under the squabbles, overpowering him. He felt a nerve to split and a vein to burst. The insane raged towards the nearest soldier of a small stature and an immature age, expanding a shadow over him.

"K-Koeapoeåle? (C-Corporal?)" The gendarme turned to a hand who grabbed him by the collar.

Dragging him to the edge of the wall, the corporal shoved the soldier against the parapet that cracked a rib and forced a cough from the young conscript.

"Ack!" With gasps that blued his face, he fought the officer's strangling grip.

The elites spotted him whose body was held away from ground. Unable to find his footing, he slipped and dropped further until his jacket started to tear from the corporal's unethical terror.

"He's lost it!" Gin swung off the wagon and rocked it gently that had Arminius to weakly rise around the fuss.

His searing headache fazed the foreground of his sights, as the bandage applied to him started to redden even more as Arminius thought about the blurred figure dangling from the walls. It started to clear when Julien scrambled towards him with a cloth bag filled with snow.

"You shouldn't be up," He kindly told him, applying the melting ice on Arminius' head.

"W-What's happening—?" Arminius asked when his memories shortly returned.

Whose eyes widened at the spotting of the soldier, endangered by the long fall under, the lieutenant's pupils quivered in disbelief, and sprung onto his feet, with watchfulness. Beside the wagon, Colt crossed his arms around the spear and disappointedly shook his head with a miserable joke.

"Look at what you'd call disposable." He said as the soldier was brought further into the wild air.

The corporal's devilish rant sustained its insanity that brought all eyes on him, with a fear condensing.

"It is by law to execute anyone who has trespassed our sanctity!"

"Even those who were once allies whom do not follow our superiors!" The cultist of the kingdom memorized a passage from the book of order that had rather confirmed his lunacy.

Swinging his sword beside the soldier's ribcage, the madman brought the blade closer against the jacket until his strained clothing tore more. Despite the kicking and vainly cries for help, his commander forced the steel onto the flesh whilst the poor soldier's comrades strayed from the madman. As the wound oozed, the youngster fell unconscious of pain and his battle ended.

"Venn tu enjktch fallën vjllstch, (If you don't want to be thrown off the wall,)"

"Sjelëen sje jeae fëatammtchën vaffën! (Aim your damned weapons at the enemy!)" The corporal threatened as the blood of his veins surged across the whites of his eyes.

Unable to withstand the torment of their leader, the soldiers gritted their teeth and fastened their barrels and arrows along the battlements. And in the second hold of doubt, it caught the unit, alarmed, with its innocent claws.

Wondering how it had come to be their supposed inviting welcome had turned so sour to swallow, the forgotten hospitality humiliated Julien's identity. He saw his squad start to scatter into a formation, and beside him, Károly inconspicuously had readied his three arrows, hidden from sight.

"I…uh…might need your plot armor if you don't mind." Colt laughed in the darkest minute.

Julien searched for his comrades, protecting him on the flanks. Whilst to his surprise, Arminius had already pulled Adam and Wojsław away from the growling stomach of the battlefield, who took those inept for battle and discreetly retreated towards the bridge.

This can only get worse… He watched the unwavering defenders mumble prayers in hopes for the gods to forgive them before an expected massacre.

We shouldn't be fighting at a time like this… The Danne lieutenant thought, clutching his jacket which wrinkled from his wringing grip.

Especially when the Confederates can show up behind our backs, we'd still be clueless in our deaths.

Moving his hand up to the collar and unbuttoning the top link, he exposed the noble tie that he had never taken off, waving as the winter winds surfed along the sea.

I didn't want to do this…

But we're at a dead end… Julien's resolve strengthened as he took hold of the glacial blue jewel he wore.

The Danne readied to reveal it as the gale sped, throwing branches and junk across the path that splitted the wall and squad.

"Heaeatch mjk, ëaënvëatche keajecëa, tëa stcholes uensëaes eajkes! (Hear, honorable warriors, pride of our kingdom!)" Single handedly, Julien grasped the ears of his countrymen with one swooping phrase that paused even the corporal.

"Keannën vjea enjktch ales fëapüentetche kåmmpfën?! (Can't we fight together?!)"

"Füea tën keaenjc?! (For the same king?!)" He offered the declaration of allegiance that began to stain the walls with ever greater questions.

Although he had been blessed with a cooperative silence for the meantime, the corporal could not rid the grudge with Julien. And in spite of the child of Danen speaking in their native tongue, the man was stubborn enough not to witness the defeat of his honor.

"Tu musst stchëapën vollën sjtch tu foen sjenemm enammën speajkstch! (You must wish for death to speak of our king!)" The dramatically sensitive corporal roared.

Julien quietened as he brought his hand to show, still tightly clenched with his penchant buried within.

"Jk pjen— (I am—)" The revealing answer of the continuing squabble halted when a shout from the wall's interior propelled a message at the tower.

"Enakcepën! (Open the gates!)" It commanded once.

"Skenellëa! Tën kaenale eaffenën! (Quick! Raise them!)" Another of a different tone followed second.

The ancient cogs and chains, rusted from the centuries of the elements creaked and clanked. Its levers that held it shut were carefully pulled by the fort's militia holed up within the gate tower. Looking desperately for answers, the corporal scouted the easing walls, and found a messenger sprinting his way. Knelt down beyond reach from his commander, the soldier delivered an order,

"Enakeajktch fomm lëcatchën, Leoeat Paulus Rantzau. (From the legate, Lord Paulus Rantzau)."

"Tsk." The corporal bit his thumb and flicked it at the young soldier.

Loosening his grip, he allowed the jacket to slip from his fingers, and the gendarme unknowingly plummeted towards his death. Falling from the height of the walls, the recruits on guard rushed to the side to see his declining body, endlessly dropping farther towards the earth. A reflexive lightning snap across the snow thrusted an enormous wave of purplish coils into the air and landed before the gate that left a narrow trail of sparks. Before the child reached the ground, a pair of arms, held under, rushed to his fall, latching onto his body as Arminius crashed into the gate that was an excruciating impact against the metal studs. Waking from mere seconds of blankness, he watched him, asleep, not wanting to look away from his steady breathing. Arminius released a comforting sigh when the titanic gates quaked behind him.

It dragged along the frozen mud by the levers which clicked, releasing a resounding boom as the wooden gates fiercely rubbed against the stone and soil. A cloud followed the path in the air, sucked into the encampment through the widening gap until the two doors were fully pushed away which revealed a welcoming party waiting beyond the shadows that shielded Arminius. With gratitude and relief, the lieutenant stayed knelt ahead of the man who smilingly stood, heading the few royal guards.

In his early thirties, Paulus Rantzau was a clean-shaven man. Yet with messy chestnut brown hair, he was proper, in which as if his legs were glued together as he bowed with one arm flat against his stomach. Though no one could ever tell where he was looking from his narrow eyes, like slits, however, never gave the impression of a sly gentleman. The legate was dressed as he acted, in humble aristocratic clothing. With a copper brown jewel on his bolo tie, he was a meager lord. Nothing was too out of the ordinary. Although addressed as a commander of his legion, Rantzau did not appear to be of the warrior sort. What gave away his ideals as an intellectual working man was that even in the sludge of mud and snow, he was not willing to change away.

The elite squad raced to Arminius' wings and kept in alerted stances, with their blades turned towards the legate who straightened his posture. Reaching out his hand into the shadow that separated the two parties, Rantzau apologized in a pleasing tone,

"Great warriors, I apologize if our soldiers have caused the slightest inconvenience."

Slightest? Gin frowned and glared, beast-like, at the noble party.

As if he growled, the lieutenant marched onwards, nearing the gate with what little patience he had and bouncing the sword on his slackened grip.

"Ya backtrackin' slant-eyed fuck…ya're de one in charge 'ere…" He mumbled before reaching the underside of the restless gatehouse, on edge, as its soldiers peered beneath them, at the wildling.

"Gin!" Arminius called for his comrade froze half a pace through the gate and looked over his shoulder.

"Eh?" He grunted at his leader.

Arminius stood upright on his drained, and numbed legs, bringing the conscript, clutched in his arms, to rise with him as he allowed the legate to speak.

"But nonetheless…" said Rantzau, meaning no trouble having his hand held against his chest.

"Welcome to the Three Kingdoms of Danen."

The path into Medwen opened, for the tried unit in the test of endurance. And although Adam and Wojsław were yet to trust the Dannes, they urged for their wounded's treatment. Flowing into the allied fort, symmetrical on all of its four sides, their wagons were prioritized for Arminius' force who were introduced to the warming hospitality that the squad had desired.

Upon entry through the closing gates, Arminius was faced with a settlement of both civil and military life, harmoniously living through industry and training. Its white stones and timber skeletons, roofed with multiple shades of brownish red tiles, were packed within the thick walls. Divided into four quarters, all houses or unique smiths and its two town roads led to one destination in the center that Rantzau aimed for. A sublime well, was where all paths converged into a paved roundabout that could date back to when the first bricks were laid as foundations to that grandiose fort. Albeit not in use, it was the single great beacon that any group could flock to whenever their callings required them to be.

As Arminius, who still had not removed the soldier from his care, basked in the city's lights of both modern street and traditional lamps that never turned off, Rantzau snapped his fingers and a pair of royal guards were summoned before the lieutenant. Both towered over Arminius as a guard reached his hands out.

"We'll take him, sir." One politely spoke for the other.

They looked down with their pickelhauben shielding their eyes, but for their professionalism, he could trust.

"Please take care of him…" Arminius seemed hesitant.

The guard took hold of the soldier from the lieutenant's hands and carried him away to the quarters of idle medics, with his comrade behind.

"We will do our best." He saluted before shortly marching away to join his fellow guardsman to a sigh of relief.

The open-topped trucks, coughing polluting smoke from its wheezing engines, that carried boundless waves of troops across the streets were watched by the evacuating populace. Whatever they could hold by hand such as the likes of baggages and dolls began the long march following the east-flowing winds. It was as if their arrival had signaled the mass retreat Arminius was witnessing who could not remove the burden of thoughts that it was plausible, in many forms that it laid with the unit's fault. In his eyes that reflected the last useless documents burning in tragic bonfires of rotting bandages, there was a gain in sickened false hope.

"Dey can't stop starin'." Gin clicked his tongue, and growled at the crowds who had their eyes fixed elsewhere over him.

"It's Lev and Miklós." said Arber, eyeing the two walking skyscrapers behind him.

"Who the hell would want to look at someone as stupid as y—?" Colt smirked when two demonic fists crashed into both their heads.

As Miklós dragged Gin away and Alexandria tugged the other by the ear, their black-haired comrade distracted himself with the restaurants that starved his mind. And of course the glimpses he caught of girls gazing at him.

Marching ever closer to the town's central monument, Arminius stuck his hands in his pockets and scavenged for cigarettes. Eventually finding one last eifer stick hidden beneath the packet, the lieutenant ignited it and puffed a heavy blanket of smoke into the bluish gray sky, darkened by the rising flames from the pits of hells, dotted around the town.

"Where's Károly?" Arminius remembered and turned to Julien.

A head rammed itself against Arminius' shoulders to his surprise that made him give the slightest cry.

"Ah! Who is it?" He looked back as a face sprouted into view.

"Look, look!" Siegfried was riding on Károly again, though

they had gone farther on an adventure that time.

"I found you a present!" The messenger exclaimed as he lifted a gun against the lieutenant's face.

"You're joking…" chuckled Arminius as he admired the weapon of the century-old legends.

It had an elegant carbon black body accompanying the slim barrel, and the slanted grip made of ebony wood that held perfectly in his hands. With no scratches or dents as far as he could see, it only meant that the Löbenitz pistol was newly manufactured.

"How mu—" He slowed down and felt another item fall onto his shoulder.

An attachable belt holster dropped into his other hand and with either full, Arminius spun around in glee and mumbled,

"You two…"

"No, no…" Károly dismissed his thanks with an awkward wave.

"Arnau suggested it as well!" Siegfried pointed towards the hiding lancer, whistling behind Lev's back.

Strapping the holster onto his belt, Arminius drove the pistol into its fitting home. And with the grip buckled in place, he could not hold his smile and pivoted ahead to keep his cheerfulness from sight.

"Thanks, all of you…" Embarrassedly, he uttered in clear words.

Both Károly and Siegfried faced each other, grinning, when they bursted into laughter that Julien joined. The unit commander's face reddened for he had received the first gift in his life.

Not distant from the center where the well had finally shown, the vanguard quieted and were divided once more. As Károly sprinted across the street with Siegfried, giggling and enjoying the blasts of breezes, Arminius and Julien could not take their eyes off the cityscape that to modern city-dwellers, such as them, the idealized world that the Dannes docked in was no more than a fantasy seen in novel epics. Even to the latter, he had never been exposed to that imaginative side of his home.

"I see that you are quite taken by the sights of Medwen." Rantzau interrupted their merry tour.

"Yes, sir." replied Arminius, in formality.

Reducing his pace to the both's enjoyed stroll, the legate cleared his throat.

"No need for such formalities. Speak freely however you wish." The humble man informed them.

At the town's core, Rantzau halted at the magnificent but breaking well where cracks in the stone were beyond repair though kept its pronounced beauty circled and tied into knots by vines of azure blue roses. The elite squad slowed and came to a stop before the legate, humming a country melody that was played in the back of his mind. Then exhaling a series of troubled thoughts, Rantzau remembered something of greater importance. He spun around, at his own leisure and firstly apologized sincerely,

"I must have forgotten!"

"Please excuse my rudeness, I have yet to introduce myself." Scraping one leg back, the legate placed a hand on his heart and bowed before the squad.

"I am the Mayor of Haven," He told.

"Lord Paulus Rantzau."

Astonished, it was not the fact that a noble had appeared before them because in truth any one would have knowingly seen one in their lifetime, but that his appearance in simple behaviors and an affectionate voice was not the typical tyrant that they had expected.

"A lord?" Scratching his face, Lev repeated.

"You sure don't act like one—"

Arber smashed his leg into Lev's knee within a flash and grabbed the latter's head to bow, conciliatorily.

"Forgive his insolence." pleaded the lieutenant.

"No, no, you can release your friend." laughed Rantzau, as he lifted his head to answer.

"I get that most times."

Lev slapped Arber's hand from him and shuffled closer to Miklós' sanctuary.

"But yes," The legate said as he rested his hands behind his back.

"I am the third son of the late Count of Utann, hence my title at birth."

Vehicles of utilities flowed across the waterlogged roundabout from melted snow that Siegfried was lowered to. Bringing the common elders and younger folk for the gate, the churning convoys chuckled their motors in endless cycles as the citizens bunched into lines ahead of the foreground the squad and Rantzau covered behind turning tracks.

"Speaking of introductions," Rantzau smiled at Arminius, exhaling warm smoke when he realized that a pair of eyes were upon him.

"I presume you are *Lieutenant* Arminius Reichner." The legate thought.

"Yeah..." Lowering his cigarette as the wind changed its course, Arminius faintly replied.

It brought a scent of herbs and coffee, intertwined into one that tickled Julien's nose into a small courtly sneeze.

"We had hoped what General Warneńczyk told us was the truth." Rantzau clenched his hands beside.

"The Battle of the Thousand." The legate recalled but to the squad, such a name for the last stand was an exaggeration of the glory earned in trade of death.

"Heh..." Gin had a stupid smirk, proudly thumping his fists together.

"Ya bet yer ass dat's the truth."

With another sneeze of Julien from the smoke, sniffling, his comrade tossed the burned stick onto the snow, crunched into ash by the wary chained wheels, skidding along the road.

"Then I suffer no more worries." Rantzau consoled himself, yet by pinching his tie, the legate still seemed as equally troubled.

"By the way..." He spoke.

Glancing at Julien who received a white and red handkerchief from Károly, Rantzau fidgeted his collar and the ties of his vambraces, then proceeded to ask,

"I heard from a sergeant there was a Danne within your party."

Almost as gentle as a dab, Julien wiped his nose and was held to straighten to answer in an energetic tone,

"Yes?"

Rantzau scoured Julien's rumpled uniform and the ruined Alba emblem, five-parts burned and five-parts stained by maroon patches of dried blood on his sleeve. What he dressed in was no different than that of his comrades yet the legate found him to be his stressed focus.

Could it be...? He thought, drawing a short breath to reset his fogged mind.

Bringing his hands forward though refrained from pointing, Rantzau questioned,

"May I ask..."

"What is it that you're wearing around your collar?" The gentleman pointed at the young Danne's chest.

An expression of the interrogated took a drastic turn into dismay as Arminius and Károly lunged forward. They stared at Julien's troubled face who kept his hands pinned by his side until there was silence among the elites. And for only then did he twitch that brought him for his bolo tie, grabbing firmly at its strings, though the lieutenant feared and confirmed,

"This?"

Never answering, Rantzau had still forced the lieutenant's hand. Clenched onto the hidden jewel, Julien slid away his thumb and uncovered its crystal blue shine. As the sun met the precious gem that shot a ray of glimmering light into the legate's reflective eyes, that he opened them as wide as he could, the man shuddered and flinched to the shocking revelation. The truth bore. Cold sweat ran down his cheeks and he pulled away until the wall met his coat.

Impossible... The corner of his eyes trembled who could not believe his thoughts nor reality.

Why...of all kingdoms...?

The cooling aura of Julien's lessened when he hid his tie, and whilst his comrades found the legate's mumbling mouth uncanny, the lieutenant could not. Pretending to clear his throat, Rantzau coughed in an intuitive pattern that calmed himself.

No matter for now, I must play the part...

"I-I see..." He adjusted to a forced smile that anyone found transparent.

"Well..."

Clearing a path before the well, Rantzau left a rooted footprint where he once stood and took to the pavement in the direction towards the eastern gate. In a pretensed calmness, the legate gestured for the squad to trail along.

"O-Our evacuation was an order by the Whirlwind..." Rantzau stammered.

"So I'm afraid we can't wait for the next carriage."

His sharp cuts in his usually silent walk shifted Arminius' curiosity, following Julien from the rear. He watched Károly jump into conversation, unhinging Julien's rigidity who seemed awfully paranoid about the tie he wore as everytime he tripped or stumbled into a dip in the road, there would be a search for the keepsake.

XXVI

13 APELYOTES 491
13.11.12017

Paulus Rantzau

My first impressions of Arminius the Lesser but, a great, is no more than an unmoving and lifeless painting. I sit here, beside my fire, alone, on the last beam of our march east whilst they bring me joy, seeing their human childhood that we nobles never live through. Oftentimes, the same defined ideas, like a lucid dream, come to challenge my mind that this lieutenant couldn't have been the one the general spoke of. He is so unknown, perhaps so endangered by the lower ranks in the hierarchy that his voice does not travel afar with a withstanding wall echoing nothing.

They are no more than local tales. Arminius' reckless deeds in Akülunnarchs remain a blank chapter. Sorrmul and the fatality by the royal blade driven into an exemplary third general is nothing but washed clean by a flash flood of exceeding events. And his latest debut that he strategized. The Battle of the Thousand. Every odds that the gods had gambled against him were flushed into the hells. Yes, he lost that dismal battle called a massacre, even with Warneńczyk's...ambushed...ambush. But Arminius Reichner was the massacrist that could only explain the lives lost then. The gross burden, that he personally sent nine hundred to their unplanned deaths, waiting for hours to be admitted into their following rebirths. If I was perverted towards pleasing deaths, then that number would be laughable. The Confederates' wait into the aftersea's crossing will number decades to complete. Thirty thousand. Of fifty thousand the deed was dealt.

In my ability, I would give everything to propagandize the truth to the world. Not just him. But of the squad and their warriors who have lived enough to become legends of a national epic. They lack a catalyst to amplify their glassy interrupted voices. I could...I will become that speaker in between ears and tongues.

How so do you think, my king? Could they?

CHAPTER

27   A DISTANT CHIME

The hanging lamp had not been extinguished. Captured in
place. Unmoving. On the slim channel of a wall between the
still windows, opposing the winter calmly settling into the razed
metropolitan under the monstrous barrages of across the narrow
strait where the cloud barrier had extended to the far reaches. As
if a circle of hell had ascended the capital. Within the tranquil
room, simple and half-alive, was a somewhat colorful interior
decorated by glazed walnut brown furniture. A smooth incense
burned, hugging the wardrobe standing against the wall that had
a single daisy flower pot overseeing the three entrenched in their
dreams.

One beside the other in a row along the raised step of the
room. With little choice, they rested on a thin mattress whilst
the stolen beds were melted into blades and bullets. Struggling
to move, Julien was clenched between Arminius and Károly as
the both evilly pulled their blankets away then spun about onto
his face. Flinging his arms to turn with him, another found itself
atop Julien's neck, as if to strangle the poor lieutenant who did not
wake.

The ruffling and fighting did not disturb Arminius. Yet much
like lately, was first to rise to a hint of grayness bursting through
the curtains. He launched up, with messy morning hair and a
drowsy expression to a depressed memory of the last dream. The
lieutenant had not bothered changing out of uniform, only that
his jacket was unbuttoned and nothing else. As he rubbed his
eyes, Arminius gave a short glance at the calendar resting beside
the steel plates on his hand.

14 Apelyotes. It read on the Zhormannik counter.

Yawning, a tear swept down his face as he slipped off the
platform into his pair of boots whose soles had been grinded
into a gripless base. His small knots were tied below his knees,

as the uniform fastened with the last button secured, and whilst
brushing the dust that had collected along the sleeves, he quietly
trailed towards the squarish table, set in the center of three chairs.
Snatching one of the two swords guarding a feather-wing-like
bow, Arminius also grabbed the greased pistol, holstered onto
his belt and took care not to make a noise when traversing the
creaking floorboards. Never looking back, he turned the door
knob slightly and unclicked the lock, revealing a way into the
corridor leading beyond the enclosed world.

In the open plains, there was not one blade of grass that stuck
out of the veil shielding the green, turned a white meadow. The
serenity was blank and pristine. Trees and bushes were brushed
onto the sketch as were some creatures lurking in the hollow
craters dotted around some ruins. Such scraps never belonged
there, but were litter flung from the Confederate's bombings.
Somehow, it was a grand addition to the calmness in the air
despite the storm blowing against Arminius' back pushing him
ever onwards.

Alone, on the smoke gray gravel path, the lieutenant strolled
straight for the exalted walls of a sinister shade. Perhaps from
the foreboding sky yet maybe was simply its concrete body. Far
below his tolerant cold, he heavily breathed, to relight a cigarette
he, himself had redesigned. And at times such as that wintry
morning, Arminius wished that his comrade were beside.

Julien, I should've asked for a bottle of tea... The lieutenant
shivered at the thought of the pleasant warmth of ginger.

Or your flames, Károly...

Skipping over a dent in the road, Arminius' burst in kei that
tingled the feeling of a growing eifer stayed dormant.

Eventually, such as that of every short journey, near the end
in sight, the walls were finally in his reach. Huffing warm air into
his hands, Arminius gazed, at its dominating presence that was
not to be challenged. As the one presented at Medwen was scaled
to a mere chapel, the wondrous construct of royal Haven, the

capital of the Kingdom of Danen, was nothing short of a dream-like cathedral.

Its design was irregular as it was built in layers of steps rather than a flat fat block of stone that gradually led to the battlements itself. There were no towers. And the guard posts were barren except that at calculated distances, there were signal posts manned by squads of ten who acted as redoubts to claw away any attackers. Even if any were to successfully dare cross the enchanting moat for suicidal victims, too wide even for a jet, the mix of smooth stones which made up the twenty-meter-high wall prevented any from scaling it with grapples. In other words, a colossal engineering flex on the capabilities of the great power.

Ascending the ninety-nine steps, Arminius took good care at each rise not to lean backwards into the vertigo. Such as with nothing reeling his body from a possible flaw in his advance, by the point he had reached the summit, his heart beated like a racing war drum strapped onto a competing dragon boat. Despite his unnecessary fears as a steel-willed soldier, Arminius turned around on the last step to a rewarding intake of a hellish place on earth.

Smoke and fires rose like sunrise on heaven from the eastern sector, reduced to crumbling houses and landing shockwaves that exploded shrapnels into the rubble. The only airport that had not fallen into Confederate hands was scarred into a grazing flatland for flesh eating insects, gnawing the charred bones of the burials. Transformed into a mass cemetery, it was a salient for death's hell creeping above the soil.

"Lieutenant." A man called him with his kind voice and an appearing smile.

"Lord Rantzau!" Arminius scrambled onto the heights and bowed as he was taught by Julien.

"Don't worry about your courteousness," The legate laughed, asking to awkwardly straighten his posture.

"Less so about the proper address."

The younger officer slowly approached the walls, minding every footing pressured beneath every doubt until his hands met the aligned parapet where each gap had been sealed by wooden barricades. He viewed the open terrain. Nearly emptied of anything had there not been the lone wrecked church that stood out before the vast deforested trek.

"Tell me, do you despise this kingdom yet?" asked Rantzau, in the same positivity.

"Wha—?" Arminius voiced as the former interrupted,

"Excuse my irrelevance,"

"That was an odd question." The legate apologized, sighing from his displeasement and held onto the wall with his gentle grip.

"How well did you find the hospitality of our capital?" He questioned, searching hopefully for his answer.

Arminius gazed at the clouds, skimming across the sky as if they were dragged by a chariot along the turbulent waves.

"I didn't expect too much…" Brightened, the lieutenant murmured.

"But it has its own comfort."

"Huh. I'm glad." Rantzau chuckled with the truest voice.

"Though I wouldn't deny I had hoped that your headquarters should be something more extravagant."

"Like a villa?" joked Arminius who soon relaxed his stiffened joints.

"Yes…something of the sort." The legate shared the good exchange.

Winter gulls who flew from not too far, pure white with some bands of dark taupe brown, glided overhead. Imitating a bomber formation, their terrifyingly accurate shadows attacked the lieutenant's unaware consciousness.

"Reichner." Rantzau soothingly began, tearing Arminius out of the trauma.

"Enlighten me, from one who has suffered such unprecedented commands," Taking no notice of the afraid expression peering up to him, he held.

With a switch into genuine seriousness, his voice was dampened in a flurry of snow, agitated by irregular gusts.

"Do you fear failure?" The legate questioned.

Trembling as a phantom eye, drooping viscous black liquid, glared at Arminius. He shoved his hands into his jacket's pockets and unsurely answered,

"Of course…"

"Every day…going into battle…" told Arminius as Rantzau listened respectfully, blurting no words as the younger spoke,

"Or not knowing when…where…how you are to be defeated."

"I can't imagine anyone with enough willpower not to..." Arminius clutched the insides of the pockets, scraping the armor over his fingers.

"Afterall...I was raised to fear failure."

A somber mood touched the officers' voices who could not escape their hesitant mouths. Rantzau's words became stuck, crushed behind his tongue which could not release anything more than drawn out breaths of dense mist. He gulped, to free a highway of cold blasts into his lungs, gazing across the ice moat and watched the spray of snow dwindle to a few fluttering flakes.

"I shouldn't have asked." The legate answered the lieutenant with remorse.

"No," replied Arminius again.

"It's the first time I've talked about my childhood."

"Though I thought it would be relieving." He added.

The vision of the thin-eyed man returned to his content face whose accepting light smile was like a beacon, hidden behind a waving shroud of hair to shield the pair of harmed and despaired eyes, sighting the desolate field.

"What about you, Lord Rantzau?" The lieutenant asked in return, netting Rantzau whose gesture seemed surprised by the will to converse the fears of the human soul.

"Do you fear failure?" Arminius repeated for the same.

To their backs, that the commander spun towards, the city of Haven was presented, corrupted beneath the streamline trails of artillery shells providing a heart-wrenching fireworks display of spirits withered by the blight.

"Often, if not always." An open confession sounded of the truth.

"Even now, I watch..."

"Unable to act." told the legate.

Arminius distanced himself from the walls, pacing every inch as he faced the burning capital too.

"As a noble...no...a commander even," said Rantzau, stumbling over words.

"There is only the failure to protect these loving people that frightens more than the pious."

Paused, to let a barrage speak. Its practice of massacre on the red brick tiles below near the rampant seas corroded the coastal walls, decaying into the waves washing mutilated bodies into the fast flowing currents.

"It is how you are to him, is it not?" Rantzau compared, grinning towards the flustered.

"J-Julien?" Arminius blushed, near to tripping over his one step back.

"Yes..." The legate seemed to forbid himself from ever mentioning the comrade's name.

Drawing a hefty breath, Rantzau glanced at Arminius by the corner of his quick eye, and confirmed with unusual modesty.

"The...no...Lieutenant Julien Carlstadt." Stammering, he furthered.

"You seem that way at the very least."

"I..." Arminius' voice began with confidence.

Then it quieted into near silence.

"That was only because..." And with uncertainty, his justification tried to exit in words.

Staring into the derelict void of fog, like a leviathan levitating over the Rus bluish gray waters, the legate shuffled away from the steps and released a soft chuckle, breaking the lieutenant's embarrassment.

"Nevertheless you have a heart of the iron cross." Rantzau complimented whom he faced.

"Such that I could also assume you know who he is."

Arminius' comforted eyes tensed at a split, feeling a shock surge outwards. Yet, managed to brighten his face when he answered the commander with a gated pledge,

"I can guess, but I won't ever say."

"I'm sure he has his reasons..." He pivoted on the crunching snow, and looked into Rantzau's narrow eyes.

"So I thought...that was..." Arminius bore a gentle shake of his head.

Holding his chin, Rantzau dipped his nose as their feet carried themselves towards the parapet once more. There was calmness among the two, who beamed at the clearing. The soaked ground reduced the clouds beneath the pillow of snow that had set after the short storm served its term, at least, the white carpet, over trees of ice and the rarest phenomenal happenings of snow rollers, doubled. Before them, and the walls were no longer flatlands of simplistic details but that of the darkest depthful lake submerging the tallest bushes. They stood, unwavering despite the harsh stinging cold, for the longest and serene minute of their lives.

"It may be rude to ask…" Arminius broke the mutual vow of silence.

"But why have you called me, Lord Rantzau?"

The legate freed a troubled sigh, as if it was the first time the man had been concerned with matters behind him, unable to be reached by his arms held out.

"It is not in my daily suit to wage war, you should know." He told, pointing onwards at the church stationed near the foot of the plateau.

"But to live and be nearer my people."

Rantzau lowered his arm as Arminius leaned ahead to ask,

"Then…how did you become the commander-in-chief?"

"That is only a temporary position." Wagging his finger, Rantzau rejected.

"However, even as *that*…" He gazed at the sky, into the innards of the heavens watching his head.

"I cannot save everyone trapped within this last defense."

The lieutenant rested his notoriously shattered hand on the wall, whose dusty armor provided a blurred reflection of a dejected face. Then, a bulb of kei sprouted from his intuition into a grand plan.

"You have an army of thirty thousand and another three million civilians." noted Arminius, convinced that the strategy would be the breakthrough against the marching bands of the Confederacy.

Before the legate could speak to contradict, he ranted,

"Why not march them to Tschrewen?"

"Avoiding Vasilevsky, it would only take eight days even if we marched slowly…" On the suggestion, he left a pause for Rantzau.

"That would work…" The legate agreed without the whole hive of his thoughts in acceptance.

"If only we had an *army* of thirty thousand." Rantzau emphasized with a firm glare at the ally.

Flinching no less from what he heard correctly, the displeasing words which were uttered, Arminius turned to the Danne man and mumbled,

"What do you mean…?"

"No more than conscripts," His commander informed.

"Are those you see guarding this eternal fortress."

As the light descended from the clouds if the omen meant wellness that made his hands quiver, Rantzau tightened his tie, though shakingly.

"Who may be older or younger than you."

"Recruited in the last second that leaves them untrained," He harshly spoke of the failings of the kingdom headed.

"They can't fight." It was disclosed in the disunity of beliefs.

Until the legate found the need to whisper, Rantzau carefully led away from the closeby bulge who now Arminius only discovered to be as the commander said. No more than forcibly recruited comrades his age, although joking and laughing, could have seen more than the lieutenant had in what tragic life they were born to.

"Whilst most may be war orphans," Rantzau briefly looked at Arminius whose eyes, doused by the sight of early blood, were the same as those cheerfully posted on the frontal walls.

"For all had lost family or their closest persons," The former told, lowering his voice further.

"They don't know anything outside of these walls."

Like stone cages that had trapped the Dannes from the cavity of truth however benevolently safe-keeping, the reality was said,

"Even without knowing that one fifth of our kingdom perished overnight."

The lieutenant's lips sealed and his sullen eyes shuddered which did not tell lies of what he pondered.

"They were encircled only a few days ago." Rantzau retold, keeping his hands locked together to stop the trembling befitting of the cowardly act he was not.

"A firestorm swallowed their burns in the burial of the living."

Only one marshal filled the category of the ideals who could so easily massacre over a million in one night. Gulped, as he knew, exactly, the name and title that fearless commander possessed, Arminius carried the thought,

Kolchakov?

He gritted his teeth in agony as the ghastly voices howled like ghouls within him, provoking the little devil's heart with panels he could somehow make out in the shadow of the darkest thoughts.

"I won't question you, but…" promised Rantzau, pacifying

the dread.

"To know that yesterday, the recruits were easy schoolchildren, scribbling with lead and ink."

"And have been given iron and steel to paint their hands red today."

Rantzau patted Arminius' shoulders and heaved an acknowledging sigh with the humble steam,

"It only reminds me of my unfitting role."

In the bitter attitude worsened by the dry wind, Arminius stared at the foundations holding him up high. Rantzau loosened his gaze and returned his hands behind his back.

"Is this the reason we couldn't have this meeting at the headquarters?" The lieutenant asked.

"So that no one knows the truth?"

The legate's smile lessened when he took half a step from the captain of the fifties.

"Let me be blunt, Lieutenant Reichner." With ironclad conviction, Rantzau pleaded relatively normal for the diligent man.

"My desire is for you to become commander."

Last singing hymns, the voices of the sea who chanted salt-filled air which brushed their hair silenced for the startling whirl of events unfolding before Arminius.

"Commander of what...?" He questioned though knowing the next answer.

"Commander-in-chief." said the resolute legate and there his voice was followed by a second common pause.

"W-Wait...wait a minute!" Arminius cried with his arms held out waving for Rantzau to halt.

"I know what you are thinking." The commander ignored his meanings and envisioned exactly as Arminius contemplated.

"A lieutenant and a legate."

The speeding heart came to a stop for Arminius gathered the stage of a stunned soul.

"That may be true if the conventions existed here." Graciously saluting, Rantzau proposed.

"But compared to you, I am merely a newborn in the arts of war."

"Wait...wait..." Arminius tried to slow him.

But upon shedding his skin of politeness, the lord babbled

without consideration for the counterpart, as required of the latter's traits was confounded by the steep escalation like a lift, could only aim for one way up or down.

"There will be a transition I had fashioned." Rantzau informed him, or rather, his voice often looked to stop, but was compelled to outspeak the lieutenant in denial.

"On the morrow, the whole kingdom's heart will know of you and your victories, never defeats."

"And that I hope would win the people's approval." For the arrangement had gathered to the displeased ears, the legate took a break for air.

"Stop…" Arminius murmured as he attempted to endure the lord's one-sided speech.

"I'd even written a four-paged thesis adopting you as a Danne citizen." Rantzau revealed more in an increasing ramble.

"Perhaps raise you to peerage so as to promote your legitimacy." He chuckled so breezily.

"But alas that recommendation could only be made by the Whirlwind, our king—"

"Legate!" The lieutenant yelled aloud which thundered across the battlements in the shocking halt that stayed the man's voice.

The recruits of the walls in range halted their chatter and peeked at the officers past their allies' shoulders and arms.

"You can't declare me as commander!" Arminius lunged at Rantzau that forced him one pace back.

"They'll never accept me!" He explained with unchallenged certainty.

"I've murdered too many thousands…"

"Aren't there others you've considered?!" Restlessly fighting onwards in a path of a journey that hoped to search for another alternative, the lieutenant asked.

"Like Julien?!"

"He's the perfect defense! Isn't that what you want?" The soldier grasped his own jacket, scrunching it as he would his heart, and cried.

From the constant shouts that drained his kei, ushered in the form of steamed haze, Arminius wearily panted. Stressing his grip for Rantzau spotted, the legate calmed as a still lake setting after the passing torrent.

"I…" The legate began apologetically with a relieved sigh that seemed to hush Arminius.

"I'm truly sorry."

"That was unlike me." Truthfully, he mumbled.

The sword swayed, in its scabbard rustling against his clothes. Arminius gasped for a breath, tempering him.

"But you must understand this one thing." said Rantzau whilst the lieutenant willingly listened.

"Carlstadt, as I could concur, is the perfect defense if you could say so."

"However in this battle," He worried the lieutenant whose core, although preserved in the improving weather, lay dormant for a second eruption.

"I desire someone who has the imperfect defense."

Smiling again as it felt to have been an eternity since he had given the slightest grin, Rantzau held his desire high with an upsurging pause,

"In other words,"

"The perfect offense." The legate judged.

His trapped voice loosened, although stammering, Arminius expressed,

"W-Why...?"

"To gain leverage." Rantzau answered.

"I..." His sights were set upon the short ridge running along the horizon whose abysmal beyond was unseen.

"We desire one who'd undoubtedly turn into a kraken in the shell of defense."

"Look at it this way, lieutenant." The legate reinforced his gaze at Arminius.

Taking hold of the lone circlet in the clouds, bursting a ray of sunlight into the gloomy orphanage's slums erected beside the liveliest street of all Danen, he mentioned,

"These people rest assured when the Confederates are beatable."

"And your victories, hence will reel the world within the baited words of propagandized truth." Rantzau tightened the knots on his vambraces and turned to Arminius with a fatherly expression, in the mantle as the protector of his people.

"If we are able to deal a serious blow,"

"Then it is by fate a peace treaty could be signed." He declared his intentions.

As afterall, there was no feasible way for such a humble man to accept subjugation in a reign of terror that Arminius knew well enough. The lieutenant steadied his breath who realized his wrong doings and repeated, in composed manner,

"A peace deal?"

Sharply exhaled, Rantzau took a sealed piece of cream white paper from his coat, with quick scribbles copied onto the envelope.

"Once we gain the *leverage* it needs, not divulging too far into the sadist spiral," The Danne explained.

"We will sign a truce."

"For how long?" asked Arminius, sounding too skeptical that such ambition would hold against the scheming dogs of the continents.

"Long-lasting enough for our allies to fight back." Rantzau assured with the hint of a smile before forcing the handwritten draft against Arminius' chest and offered,

"Take it."

Who dubiously received the sealed letter with both his hands, Arminius stared at it in predicament, held close and with a feeling of a swell in predictions. Some told a life of a fantasy in serenity whilst others pillaged through his mind that ousted any reassurances.

"It may last for years but it is to preserve our freedom." The legate reminded him with a looming burden cast onto his shoulders.

"When victory rings her bells, then we will launch a revolution."

Carefully, Arminius folded the treaty into his inner pocket and appreciatively heard he who added,

"I did notice...it was out of my person to have chosen this journey."

"But when three million lives are stranded within a ring of fire, we must dig a moat around us to quell its unforgiving spread." Rantzau watched the waves take off, when crashing against the promenade of corpses, sweeping clean the tainted rocks with overpowering swipes by their watery bodies plunging into the thawing cracks.

"Then do you understand why I cannot fulfill my duties?" returned Rantzau, to Arminius who replied,

"To preserve everything...?"

"Of course, I won't simply leave this command..." Rantzau allowed a brief chuckle, enlivening the damp atmosphere.

"A thousand-ton jewel to your crushing demise." He assured, holding out his hands.

Opening his fists that unveiled scarred palms, as it had been cut so deeply old fated lines had been severed, the legate concluded his purpose in life,

"I may reside behind this stage but its internal affairs will remain with me."

Behind his closed lips, Arminius' gritting teeth weakened and started to tremble as the touches of the breeze and the smooth streams of snow were revived.

"How am I supposed to command thirty thousand troops...?" But he allowed his lungs to gush the last opposition.

"Hah." Rantzau laughed again and tipped,

"I never asked you to command alone."

Arminius gazed into the lord's honest eyes, as if they were smiling with the beaming face, never judging the lieutenant. And when he had found the time to steady, intaking a deep breath that chilled his lungs, he said with a calming tone, revitalized into his old self,

"Thank y—"

"It's too early for that." Rantzau interrupted.

"Tell that to everyone who has fought with you when this war is over." The lord advised for the future.

Aiming for the grand fleet eyeing the city with their devilish guns who then laid under the catastrophic barrages propelled from across the straight, Rantzau continued,

"And remind yourself for every moment you are alive in this world,"

Arminius flinched from a scare as the legate's hand landed atop his head as if he was a frail son needed to be guarded beneath the warm palm of a father. Afterall, he was still a child.

"We mustn't forget that they are still human." The man reminded very lastly.

"In any case you do, then the path of a fiend might follo—"

The burst of a bullet shot through Rantzau's skull that pierced through the head, exploding a gusher of hot boiling blood from the impact. As the legate's eyes flickered into darkness behind the whites drowned in a sea of erupting veins, he fell, leaning towards the stairs until his body was tossed beyond Arminius, dismayed. When the humble hand lost its energy that tried to hold onto the lieutenant's soft hair, a geyser of blood ushered from the wound and painted the virgin face with a dash of scarlet liquid that was thick. Then, plummeting onto the hard iced battlements, the lifeless head was bashed against the edge of the stairs until his cold fall diminished.

The body did not twitch as it was so rapid. His final words were forgotten by one he had directed the plea to. Arminius' eyes shuddered with his stained, quivering hands. Distraught and staring roused by the waterfall sprinting down the painted stairs. His saintly sanity held no more humanity.

XXVII

1 JULYUS 471
01.07.11997

Paulus Rantzau

Well! Who would've thought? I was expelled today from the academy. Sorry. But I won't kill for the sake of my duty. For the sake of becoming a brainless soldier. Even when our ancestors roamed the lands in the name of King Sejr, they abided by the laws of humanity. It's only common sense to treat others like our beloved. Or else, we'd be no better than animals. Caring so much for blood and war.

But I've made a bet with the commandant! If I can't ever become the highest official in ten years time, then he can accuse me of treason. Then I can think of a way to escape him and this place.

In the meanwhile, won't you be proud of what I've achieved so far?

I understand my duties as the son of a count. I understand everything everyone has taught me to know. Even then, don't you think this kingdom deserves more than honor, glory, and the superior rights of the Dannes? Something to preserve our people. To keep us from dying...

Such as freedom...?

I pray everyday that your heart recovers until you can healthily travel to the capital for my birthday.

Get well, father...

CHAPTER

28   WRATH

The draw of a lever bolt snapped like the toll of a bell as the shell which held the assassin's bullet was tossed out of its searing chamber. Still in flames, the metal casing's bright orange heat was put out by the snow, too vast for all to be melted away within the shuddering church tower whose body swayed from the worsening wind.

"One..." The girl counted as she kept her scope steady near her sharpshooter's eye, whose unique tropical green pupil was a cross.

Prone on the half-burnt flooring laid the unusual sniper. That although aged, barely eligible for recruitment, younger than Arminius, did not falter when the giant bronze bell's rope snapped, tearing open a hatch into the sky from where the spire once stood. It came crashing into the earth that rocked the building from its legs to the core. But the assassin did not flinch. Her determined eyes, yet not cold-blooded, were peeled onto the one who was left in her scope.

Under a simplistic fur cap, her royal golden hair was tied into one lengthy braid. Whose graceful face of no scars hid the killer's expression demonstrated on the battlefield that did not waver nor portrayed the slightest concern for the cold. The wear was half-contrasting, that did not blend with the baking environment of charcoal and embers. For that she was certain of victory and that enemies would not find her lying in wait.

The assassin's gloved grip was steady, near the trigger when she reached for a box of ammunition, placed beside the rifle that was as long as the sniper was tall. And without moving the gun, she picked up a bullet charged with an eifer. Taking a glance at the shine, she swiftly locked the cold brass shot into the chamber and pushed the lever downwards to seal the bullet in place. Steadily exhaling, did she hold half a breath in her lungs as her victim remained clueless.

Staring at the lifeless body, laying with decaying warmth, slumped over the first step in decline to the ground, Arminius' hands did not shake. He stilled at every step back, petrified by the drained head shrinking as blood endlessly flowered like petals landing after spring.

"Y-You have...to be...no...w-what..." He stammered, leaving bloodied footprints in the snow as a demonic trail formed.

Splinters of bone and the sticking organ layered his face who looked unable to act. With a certain slime dripping down his cheeks, Arminius had paled. A stabbing echo drummed within his head which thumped the mind into an aching pain, loudly battling against the foreign shadows invading his remaining sanctity of the soul.

"N-Not...again..." In agony, the lieutenant held his head, tensely squeezing the corruption circulating him when the foul mouth of the heartless tree whispered into his blood,

Are you unknown to death or bound to it...?

The soulless being you will possess... It tortured.

Then, he felt a break in the air. As if someone tapped him on his shoulder, Arminius spun towards the church tower and in time to spot a glistening shine that he could not wrong.

To the hells with—! His mind shouted, readying both hands on the hilt and scabbard.

Constructing the swallowed air, sucked into the barrel until fog arose beneath the sniper's trigger, a waterspout erupted with the round which was fired. Issuing a flash of chained sparks and a wildfire-like whirlpool from the unmistakable barrel, the bullet's piercing tip exploded into a whistling arrow. Screened beneath the hefty mist, it pelted at Arminius with great ferocity that before the eye could see, the lieutenant aimed the pommel of his sword into the unknown.

When his eyes sharpened at the rush, the soldier stomped at the final stretch that the bullet charged into. As if the sniper released a sigh for too early a celebration, she became unaware of her victim's purest strength. Waiting until the murderous mist passed over the walls, Arminius' grip bursted before time could react and a storming slash cut upwards bisected the impossible shot with one swift divide through the perfect center. A first gale gently brushed away the snow beneath his sword then as the hellish landscape broke free, the second tidal wave of enraged blasts detonated, cracking the wall before the two parts of brass skimmed through the air past the soldier's face. Swirling into the city behind, the deceased bullets exploded on their impact, tossing flashfires that dissipated.

Where the scope only had the lieutenant's figure, whose shadow was obscured and his outlines unrecognizable behind the thick blanket of smoke rising from a blade, the sniper could not make out whether her unparalleled shot had struck the target.

"Did I get him?" She kept her hawk's eye at the ready.

Never blinking, the girl waited with her heart rapidly beating for a blade to appear beyond the cloud. Then an insignificant breeze exposed the cracks of the wall whilst the sniper gulped, patiently watching when a spot of a bloodied uniform caught her eye.

The assassin sighed, lifting her head from the scope with a self-proclaimed sense of victory,

"I should head back now—"

She began shifting out of position when the concealing fog was torn open by a rift of bladed winds, ripping the thin cloth of mist into narrow shreds which unveiled a well and alive lieutenant.

"What?!" The girl's eyes expanded in disbelief.

"I missed…?"

Hopping onto her feet, the soldier swung the slinged rifle around and pressed her hands against a buttoned holster, bringing a loaded flare gun.

"No," She shook the anger out of her head.

"That must be Arminius Reichner."

Raising her barrel into the air, with its shell aimed through the collapsing roof, the assassin could not remove her eyes from Arminius, who was stilled with his sword held static.

"I've failed…" The soldier annoyedly clicked her tongue.

"Aurel."

A bleached red flare lifted into the air. With a trail tailed from its behind that linked the church and sky, the war chant of the Confederacy ruptured into sights. Appearing over the ridge of many glamorous banners carried by the first columns showing their heads above the weak curvature, Arminius gazed unto the lines of infantry dragging howitzers and machines. Marching over the bushes, and trampling the forgotten place, they showed no care. However the alliance had learned their invaluable lesson never to introduce mechanized armor after Sorrmul. The force that summited the hill carried a legion of heavy shieldbearers protecting the frontlines and headquarters. But no matter how time tolled, or how quick the second hand ticked, the endless waves of troops would plummet into the bowl-like basin.

"T-They're here already...?" Arminius stuttered when his spirit shrunk into insignificance.

Unforgivable...it's unforgivable... The hateful voice rumbled.

Bathe with them...they in torment... His ghouls living in the underworld wheezed.

"Ach...!" Arminius yelled as he felt a bite in his human consciousness.

Shakingly, the lieutenant drove the sword into the wall to hold his enslaved body, pressed into his tested sanity more than the last throbbing injection that punctured his mind. The perception of guilt and anguish armored his soul with torturous pins dug into the spiritual body and as the pursuing sickness grew into a burning headache, Arminius placed one empty hand over his face, tightly clutching it until the hidden eifer thundered.

Have I never told of your bind to death...? asked a close death's aide.

They brought you into this world...

How could you be so still...? The master of all life rambled.

"Shut...up..." The lieutenant cried, grinding his teeth till blood spilled.

Devour the spirits under who have dragged your body through this hell... That fiendish whisper groaned, driving his freakish nails into Arminius' ribs as his world dived into a schism between paradise and a hell.

Let them suffer with gaping wounds...

The saddened construct flickered like the slum's street lights. From one world to the next, pulled apart by the gap he soon fell into and heard,

Has his death granted never enough…?

His eyes were removed of light as tears flowed like streams of spring. The eifer rampaging within had a sadistic scent that smelled too foreign to like.

"Stop…stop…" Arminius pleaded, whose hands drew his blade into a conflicted stance.

The more that the vast split between two minds diverged, the lieutenant stumbled closer to the parapet, dreading over the unrestrained lust for death.

Go wrestle for your place in our heaven and eclipse the lesser entities… To the soldier whose mind finally shattered, a scream tore the fiend from its shade,

"Q-Quiet…*Letum!*"

Arminius flicked his cold steel's blade before the city, as if to protect with its spine aimed at the Confederates. And with no run, the lieutenant leapt over the barricades with the particular goal ahead, he knew there was no return from the freeing fall. His Danne comrades leaned over one another, staring at the tears and blood lifted against the descent. A bloom of snow exploded like a thunderclap from the impactful landing as it sent a booming shockwave that fractured the ice on the moat. Quivered as the snow storm cleared, whilst his monstrous and sorrowful sights were laid on one direct path, Arminius rose.

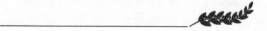

In the vast plain that all sides looked the same, his breath steamed between his teeth. And though the dreadful voices which hammered him into the cracks of inner earth with screeches, he restlessly sprinted into the terrible fire. Where the troops formed into a defensive crescent and halted with the headquarter's flag waving high on the ridge, they saw the lone warrior charging towards them with nothing but one standard sword, whose blade was dented and chipped like that of a pathetic bandit's. Their vanguard commander simply raised his arm, not needing to send a flare into the air, and directed every rank into packed rows, countless and wider than the walls itself. But no matter how many times Arminius' desire told never to attack, the lieutenant could not stop and had appeared over a slight rift in the terrain, sacrificing cover to a volley of lead and arrowheads.

Is this sacrifice enough to be branded a gateway...? The howls of the ghouls rung.

"Aarh...!" For the weakening of his knees, he cried with quick-flowing tears, tumbling into the snow.

Will you be granted a heavenly kingdom...? The devils asked.

Animalistic and sinister thoughts flooded the head that pushed him onwards in the dash and a torrid pain pounded his aching soul that only submerged him ahead of the phantom barrages. However many bullets and arrows were fired, Arminius only saw the murderous air ahead, shedding little care for the tips which missed. He launched a vertical strike, exempt of seeing, knocking a mysterious arrow out of its path and with a drugged and crying realization that the Confederates were only creatures deserving death by his blade, he casted a bolt of resentment, freezing the frontline in terror such as that of Medusa's glare, by the horrid, preying eyes. Sending a vortex of lightning in slashing crosses as he ran, the soldier deflected the killers' arrows and bullets, tirelessly.

Yet, allow that you were my child, I could toss yourself to the edges of our boundary... Wishful death spoke to him.

His blurred voice penetrated Arminius, throwing the poor boy into another endless pit of agony, rotating the fear and distraught that made him notice humanity. But the devils only found it amusing to see the dance of the smileless.

Let you alone to a bloodied feast, eternally dying... whispered the oracle of the other world.

"I told...you...to shut...it..." He lacked the strength even to speak, still was not reflected in his resolve to advance, driving arrows away.

The human wall tightened and locked itself into a hardy line, thumping plates of red steel that soundly held against the lieutenant approaching with agility. Volleys of hell shot after the other, leaving brief ravines of space for breath between each tide that devoured. And whilst none met Arminius' flesh, death degraded his innards until their black liquids, meant to be blood, oozed from a corner of his mouth.

Afterall...how could I be so bold to leave a protector... mumbled the lifeless tree.

Once the tenth chime of the rifles' clicks passed, and the

thunk of the bowstrings' vibrations silenced, spearmen slipped their blades through the cracks between shields in the mammoth wall and braced beside their comrades' shoulders. Presenting a colossal towering force shadowing over Arminius' speck of shade, he pushed his braking leg into the snow that flung a wall of white powder into the air. From where he slid, to where he halted, skinless arms of his victims crawled through the doomful earth and latched their fingers deep in Arminius' legs.

Kill...they who offered...to our lord... They provoked, mourning the fated welcoming as the branches of hands from the devils' tree spun and cracked their bones.

Whose lightning field sparked, Arminius remorsefully fused his kei into the sword that glowed. An electric bolt darted between the hilt and tip, until within itself, birthed thousands of coils that spanned the length of the blade. The lieutenant's colorless eyes were repainted into the shades which matched his eifer, but those were filled with sorry tears that converged with the blood dripping from his face.

"Forgive...me..." He apologized as the thunder erupted into a chaotic burst of charming lights, wrapped around by the loathsome hands.

I would not lend my eifer... It echoed into the weeping child.

If only you were human... The tree pressed on.

A highway of lightning vented from the snap up the hill. With the power of a whistling arrow of an ancient legend, fires and sparks exploded as the chain of bloodied streaks of strikes bisected the army. Both the godly and human eifers roared together as the massacre was proclaimed, thundering upon the headquarters who looked dismayed. The soldier's shockwave was still expanding from where the foot launched, and in the blink, the blade stayed pinned against the commander's neck. The vanguard officer peered at his inevitable death as the sword ran across the horizon. It divided the head from the body, severing the spine and hence it was blunted, ending the feeble life with a disastifying and brutal slash, like a bludgeoning, impaled the virtues of honoring the wishes of none suffering as the head was torn. And on the meeting of the otherside, a flash of blood fountains, of his victims driven a full distance into the formation, rocketed into the gray air with overwhelming cruelty that had carved faces, burning flesh and bone in the berserked rampage and bodies half-ripped apart, exposing their spillage of guts.

The hot ginger tea's aroma touched his nose with the rising steam. Sat beside the curtains, drawn before the window, Julien glanced at Károly, only with the protective look in his eyes as he sipped the warming drink. He rested his hand over an ornamented knife, that was nicely, not overly, decorated with a single sapphire in its royal white grip whilst its pure blade remained unseen, sheathed within a jet black scabbard that had one noble coat of arms planted upon. Sighing, Julien stared across the room. Daydreaming and longing for Arminius' return. However, he could not distract himself from hearing the rumblings of the cries of afar.

"That noise…" Julien grabbed the curtains, ready to reveal.

Though after a hesitant wait and a glance at Károly, shifting in his noiseless sleep, the lieutenant lowered his hand and decided not to wake him. Nearly falling asleep, Julien circled his hands around the metal mug to keep himself awake through its untouchable heat that he could not feel otherwise.

Although the lieutenant sat there, unmoving, leisurely enjoying the tranquility, the doors on the floor beneath slammed so powerfully that Julien's legs shook with the table and chairs. Bulks of footsteps stormed about the house then ended at the edge of the corridor. Then came a booming voice of Gin's waking everyone in the rooms next to his quarters.

"Y'all wake up!" Julien could hear the rampant soldier's muffled shout from above and eavesdropped on his comrades bouncing awake.

Blankets flapped, and he heard the quick stomps of boots, in the while, there was one who bashed their head on the doorway as they marched out.

"Ack! That hurt…" Being pushed out of the room, Lev complained.

"Why are Yurupe doorways so low?"

Stumbling in a hurry towards the stairs, Gin led on and rushed past the ground floor rooms like a hot-headed bull. He stamped furiously, almost ominously, onto the ascent into the second floor where Julien and Károly were.

"What is it n—?" asked Julien.

The door slowly unlocked, then slammed open vigorously to an uninvited soldier that Károly sprung up from the nightmarish awakening. Though realizing he was never under attack by a spray of shields bashing against his bones, the frightened sniffled and pointed his face in his blankets clenched ever tighter.

"W-What was that for…?!" Károly stuttered as he scolded, sounding to be in tears.

Hearing Siegfried chasing Arnau along the stairs, the archer dried his eyes to place ahead a cheery face for his cherished comrade who leapt through the doorway and excitedly greeted the lieutenant captain.

"No time to be moanin'." Gin ignored him and raced towards Julien as the squad caught him the disturbance in the commander's room.

All were unaware of the brute's strange behavior as their eyes told so. Yawning and half-awake, the squad followed his stream of golden kei into Julien's room as everything that the warrior seemed to know remained behind his closed doors, whose eyes were affixed on the curtains which were undrawn.

"What's wrong…?" asked Julien, leaning away on the chair from Gin's boiling path.

He kept the knife settled on the table and gave way when the fiery soldier swung open the curtains.

Light of the sun emanated into the intimate room, raided by both nature and torches with dying lamps. Julien slid further from the enchanting view and looked away for his eyes to adjust, covering one side with his hand. But as he gradually returned, he noticed the squad's stilled bodies, staring mindlessly, bewildered, past the window that reflected blots of fire along the concrete wall. Carefully withdrawing his fixed gaze on the interior, Julien turned outwards at the reveal of a haunting hold. His body numbed in fear, as the winter chills creeped through the glass, with unbelieving eyes shuddering at the picturesque horizon.

"I-Is that…?" Julien stammered.

The wall's braziers wildly burned, fueled under the slow whispering wind, and alight for all across the city to see whose bells chimed that threw the populace into mobilization. And whilst the craters laid submerged under the dense tarp of snow, the deathly cries and moans of devils and ghouls filled their ears. The rumblings that Julien heard growled louder until it became one with the choirs of screams. Though most fascinatingly, was the cloud that was borne beyond the wall.

Thunder clapping and lightning bolts terrorized the distant view that deepened in color from an ash gray day into a crimson night, covering the field of gore with splashes of blood that were ejected into the sky from an assault less and less humane.

"Explain what de fuck dat thin' is!" Unable to fathom the dreamlike world, Gin demanded with ever higher distress.

"An enemy attack?" Colt thought, moving closer to the sight.

"That's someone's eifer..." Arnau added, rubbing his head.

Waves of lightning flashed onto the earth that each was followed by a deafening cry for mercy as the massacre filled the clouds.

"Should we call for Adam and Wojsław?" voiced Lev, turning to Miklós who was ready to depart if in need of hurry.

"Wait." Arber butted in, holding still the squad as he took to the foreground.

"That would waste more time—"

"But we can't act alone even with the general's decree, right?" argued Lev, backed by the nods of Alexandria and the giant.

"Our autonomy disappeared with the Winged Lance—" Alexandria realized the pinch of the crisis.

"It doesn't mean we getta sit 'ere doin' nothin'!" Stomping towards his inexpressibly cold-faced comrade, Gin's yell blasted in the inner walls.

"Gah!" The lieutenant cried, heatedly flinging his arms about.

"Where's Arminius when we need him...?"

Their voices drowned under Julien's head, muting the squad's unstoppable bickering between every individual faction with one demanding defensive maneuvers as another fought with the implication to punch. Unable to bear either side, Károly slipped out of bed and skipped across the dusty floor to where his loyal friend was standing. Silently keeping his thoughts to himself when Károly leaned ahead for the unholy view, Julien's breathing ceased upon recognizing the descending fog of sparks.

"Don't tell me..." The Danne mumbled.

His comrades halted their infighting and weighed their eyes on Julien. Veins of lightning in the wreckage struck the many, tossing minced bodies, like the manifestation of a violent volcanic eruption, sporadically, across the charted skies as he heard, a distinct anguished cry.

"Arminius…!" Pained by his vision, Julien fled from the window.

He snatched the silver bow and sword, resting beside a chair and handed the former weapon to its master out of the blue.

"But it can't be…!" Károly received it under the blazing glow from the braziers outside without an answer.

As Julien squeezed past Gin and Arber, the archer called for his friend,

"Wait up, Julien!"

And too, rushed out of the room within a short notice that the squad found odd, Károly chased Julien down the flight of stairs that left the quieted squad mystified.

"What are they up to now?" Gin grunted near Lev's ear.

Thinking to make another joke, the Rus opened his mouth to blurt out another fleet of randomness when his maturity struck and reminded the lieutenant it was not the best of times.

"Anyways…" Lev spotted Arber's glare strengthening.

"We should follow them." He rolled his eyes and hastened through the doorway.

"They might end up in the red light di—"

A typhoon kick of behind funneled the Rus across the corridor that smashed him against the railings as his tall physique lost balance, Lev was close to performing a spin into the hardwood stairs.

"Ya lancers comin'?!" Gin asked for Arnau and Siegfried who watched Lev being dragged away by the ear.

With determination as their eyes were so, they surely tagged behind the elites to the marshlands of revelation in the unknown.

Winter flowers, and of snow petals, brushed along the highway air against their faces where they rode at a full gallop along the path that Arminius took towards the wall. The braziers grew, seeable past the short spruce trees, and standing astonished beneath the growling cloud were recruits who kept still enough to be statues. Settling on Julien's hands, latched tightly onto the reins, the white breeze worsened into compacted smoke, awkward to breath in as he felt it strangling his lungs. And though the wall was there to keep foreign entities at bay, it could not hold back the invasion of metallic scents, like that of an ocean's basket of blood.

Arminius...that's your eifer...right? Julien prayed, unable to soothe his shaking.

Ngh... He cleared his head and held,

I won't believe anything until I've seen it...

Nearing the foot of the stairs, the very same thoughts of the romantic portrait placed there distracted the squad from the violence in a snap, before returning to the truths which detailed the foul nature. The cries and clashing steel shrieked, not long since arriving, which noticeably attacked Julien's hope. Dragging himself off the saddle, the lieutenant rushed up the ninety-nine steps where his vision tunneled.

"Julien! Slow down!" Károly tried his best to match Julien's extraordinary pace though his comrade would not let.

Up the stairs, to a midway mark, they laboriously panted, but had not stopped for rest. Continuing his sprint into the skies despite losing his comrades to morning fatigue, Julien mumbled to himself repetitively,

"Almost there...almost there..."

"Slow down...Julien..." Károly repeated again, yet to no avail did the lieutenant slow.

"I need...to see...what this...is..." said Julien, close to the top when his ears detected vile squelches beneath him.

Before his kei was entirely diminished, the lieutenant bent over on the last dozen slabs, and gasped for breaths of desired air. With his eyes closed, he was defended from the sight of a hardened clump that his boot sunk into as the squad's footsteps dragged closer. Then at the feeling of a ripple drawing his breathing and heartbeats together, Julien relieved the weight on his head with quiet words of encouragement,

"Calm down...it's only a few steps more...until—"

His eyes gradually opened, when the lieutenant held a tensed pause. Squinting to behold a fazed rose red puddle. The blur cleared and showed a resolute smudge which soiled his purest mind.

"Aah!" Julien cried under a faint spell of shock.

He escaped his touch from the grossed frozen lump of colorless life with parts of shriveled brains and was almost to tumble had Károly not been there to catch him.

"You okay?" Károly sured him, holding his hands against Julien's back who he felt quivering.

Scouring from the puddle to the waterfall that had stained the stairs, the Danne responded with a breaking voice,

"Y-Yeah…"

Gathering their strength, the duo ascended, at a steady pace for the squad to finally catch. Along the blood creek, Julien painted gluey footprints that stuck to the snow, watching the stream widen the further they climbed. Until at the zenith, laid the deceased noble, whose face had been preserved under ice and snow. And although the body had been cold for an approximate eternity, the remaining drops of blood managed to seep through the smashed skull.

"Lord…Rantzau…?" Julien called, tugging Károly away from the mangled corpse.

A giant approached and knelt beside the head, and held a hand, like a plate, underneath the freezing wound.

"Eek! What's wrong with you, Miklós?!" Lev screeched as the tap filled Miklós' hand with viscid dark liquid that had the devils' stench puffed unto.

Yet, the demon warrior did not seem bothered at the least when he held the blood near his nose. Freakishly sniffing the pool, Miklós grunted once his scents processed. On the stainless settled snow, the soldier wiped his hands along the natural towel and stood to tell his comrades,

"Two hours…"

Gin pushed past the crowd surrounding the body and stomped on the battlements with fury.

"Are ya sure—?!" He asked.

"You all…" Arnau collected everyone's unwavering attention and strolled towards the parapet, where Julien had his gaze fixed on the horrendously painted ridge.

"Is this what you were searching for?" The lancer pointed ahead.

All the while, the elites ended their squabble and scrambled to the edge, looking over each other's shoulders and the barricades which shielded them from the shining blasts of lightning which only then, were their minds mesmerized and awed.

The transparent view, petrifyingly bitter in the taste of death and that of a brilliant massacre was blanketed on the hill. Whilst the strikes into the core of the Confederate army was unforgiving, there was a certain pain which followed behind the screams and murder vulgar. Seeming too apart from the ways that the berserker, in the center, whose values he followed to the book were found to be otherwise.

There's no way...that's impossible... Julien's singlemost discomforting thoughts filled himself.

Why...? He could feel the same tears that gushed out of Arminius.

Then, the wall jolted as the earth did too, throwing the squad onto the ground. When they stumbled, saw a beam shoot up that had an ally's colors radiating angelic lightning yet, not all were his own eifer. Raining into the army below, as if a meteor had struck its surface, an electric surfing wave pulsed across the basin, turbulently sweeping another great pile of bodies along the disheartened face of the battlefield. Hunks of new flesh splattered on the length of the wall in what could be described as death's valley. For even then, once the storm had settled, the survivors could not recover quick enough for the foreshadowing grim reaper shade had expanded along the dried grass, before hidden beneath the late snow. Its spiked screened edges detonated and sent the phantom of the skinless tree bellowing into a majestic body as the recollection of Arminius' eifer commenced into alternating flashes. Flickering left and right, his afterimages were too rapid to be caught, as he leapt between point and point, shockwaves boomed at each slash when the currents ripped grass and trees of their roots but not even the God of War's agility could compare to the lieutenant's barbaric assault.

"Was he hiding this strength all along?" Colt questioned, digging his nails into his flesh from a stink of envy.

"Arminius played us afterall." Gin singled himself with a proud chuckle, irritating the rival with the uncovering limits that their captain sprayed.

"Hah! With dat eifer, da Confederacy will find itself buried by the next winter!" Throwing his arm outward, he pointed at the gruesome figure with dangerous confidence and yelled.

"It could even challenge the Whirlwind..." Siegfried added, whose eyes reflected the unbeaten luminous rage, then looked at Károly who remained unnaturally silent.

Clenching his fists, spun aghast by the dashes of

bombardments, Julien despaired despite the words of praise,

"He'll…lose himself…"

Arber held his shoulder, hoping that it would ease him by words of a rare heart,

"But for our armies—"

"Arber!" Julien brought forth an outburst, taking the hand away, as he retreated from the edge.

"Not everyone needs to be a machine!"

Stubbornly sprinting for the northern signals where the cannons had been manned, traumatized by the presented bloodbath, the lieutenant gave a scowl to Károly, yet troubled and divided in his mind. But the decision to enter the plainest instinct chased his comrade who waved at the recruits gathered and guarding the gate's lever.

"Eaffene tas tchoea! (Open the gate!)" He shouted.

The soldiers hurriedly flocked to the lever, and had it not been for its rigidness, the device would have fallen from their wildly push on the lock.

"What're they doing now—?" asked Gin as Julien and Károly sprinted over the growling wall that began to shake.

"Look!" Arnau pointed at the stairs which shifted.

Unclogging the locked mechanism, the chains and pistons banged and clapped, drawing half the stairs beneath them towards the ground, and in the act of a snowstorm cloud that was pushed upwards like a steam vent, the stairs were swallowed into the contraption. However the further it sank was not all there was as the next cracks and booms ensued which rotated the block of dense concrete and stone onto its underbelly, opening the hidden gateway to be seen. And along, since its design was to be, the blockage, in the path before the bridge, had sunken.

"Károly!" Once the last thumps of the reaction ended, there was a shout beyond the dust clouds.

"Yeah, yeah!" The lieutenant captain answered as it was tailed by a bright whistle.

A sharp cutting wind of Arber's lagoon blue eifer blew the clouds from cover and cleared a way for the sounds of galloping horses racing past the new found gate. Realizing what the pair were to do, the squad inched ever so slightly ahead in disbelief and could barely watch as Károly raised a countdown,

"One, two, jump!"

They sprung onto the parapet and together, vaulted from the wall like two crows taking flight. Then as swift as they ran, Julien and Károly fell, in line, with their hopes solely resting on the appearing shadows. Holding their breath, the two thudded on the saddles, wrapping their hands around the reins, and rode across the bridge.

"Oh, no, no, no! I ain't doin' dat!" Gin watched his comrades' outlines shrink, farther away.

"They're at it again!" Colt slammed his hands onto the wall.

"Should we follow them?" asked Lev, unreasonably, drawing his spear.

"Whaddya mean?!" Gin yelled, skipping in flight down the stairs who abandoned the squad to their own.

"Of course we are!"

Shrugging, they let off a chastising sigh and hesitantly wandered to the first step when the bravest whisked across the ice with the avalanche-like chase.

At the foot of the abominable hill, the sea of corpses was loose but it could hold no more as the soil muddied and sank like quicksand from the terrorizing air it tried to withstand. The officers were reduced to a standstill and decided for the best to leave their ride hitched under a sheltering tree. Removing their feet from the rusting stirrups, they carefully settled themselves on the bed of bodies with a gut-wrenching sorrow worsening the sounds of the deep cracks and squashes of fragile bones and rotting organs. Julien scouted around his feet, were the chilling eyes, rolling about the obstacle course of torn rib cages and the sludges of bodily parts. Shriveled decapitated heads dried until their skin peeled under the soft wind. Dismembered limbs bursted pockets of blood onto his hands. Where some dead or perhaps alive but buried fingers, reached out of the pot of the horrific stew, twitched, Julien's voices led him to believe that there were fiends dragging him into the never idle pile of flesh. The sacred, though scared, started to asphyxiate as the drowned souls cried for sanctuary,

Help...save me...

Flee...flee...flee... The ghoulish spirits groaned.

"Aah…" Julien was near the height of breakdown when Károly reassured him with a tug on the sleeve.

"Julien." He called.

Shaking his head to be sure that the voices were only of his imagination, Julien unsurely answered,

"S-Sure…"

Károly led him from the cover of the spying tree whom they felt to have eyed them upon landfall, and nervously threaded through densest bulks of crisp skin and flesh. Over the crests and into pits, the journey through the pillaged hell furthered like a pebble beach until Julien stumbled into a hole. Nauseatingly, the paling boy slowly peered down at his leg which was stuck, at least knee-deep, within a batch of trampled entrails. Blood poured through the gaps into his boot within where there was a well of liquid that he was not so keen to discover.

"Kah!" The Danne cried as he pulled his trembling leg out of the pit.

Releasing a geyser of innards into the air, Julien wobbled his foot to rid of hanging guts whilst the other hiked up a kingly hill of the dead. From the eerie viewpoint, he could spot the lasting ridge of beings compressed into a grandiose cliff like lycoris.

"We're almost there." Károly lended a hand that Julien grabbed onto and pulled him onto the small sturdy dune of corpses.

"Thanks—" said Julien, stepping onto an unknown's chest when he felt something, that of a droplet, fall onto his face.

The lieutenant stopped in the bowels of the murdered and looked up to where a second drop fell. Refreshing rain, with the metallic texture of scarlet beads stormed in its return onto earth.

However disturbingly the field they had to wade through, both still climbed. With Károly pulling Julien along the entire way of the flooded hill, which for the mistakes in footing the latter made, a landslide of crimson remains cascaded into the slaughter basin. Latching onto a dangling arm close to the summit, Károly saw the squad entering the plains and so with the other hand, reached out for a distant body. Sticking his tongue out as he stretched outwards to the limit, the archer snapped his fingers, and like a lighter, sent a spark across that frenziedly ignited into a line of flames. The squad caught wind of the fluttering flared signal, and waved back, holding the duo to hasten their hike.

Along the death's ridge, the cliff steeped until it truly was a magnificent wonder to behold, grandly unfolding for the two scaling its heights. Upon meeting the overhang, Károly drove his arm into the stiffened carcasses, as a hook to latch onto, whose blood were still lukewarm. Then, pulling himself up, depleting his last breath, the lieutenant captain hopped onto ground where no more were as if the flooring rocked like a village fishing boat. Scouting the empty hill, where the last flag, not mutilated, flew, he knelt down over a bashed face and pulled his struggling comrade on board the saturated soil, which had materialized into a marsh.

The boys panted, seeing that the hill they had climbed inclined gradually from the rear, and slumped over on their knees. Not too far west where snow and grass resided, with the city to the east, from the old site where the vanguard's command was buried were a tiny contingent that could not be called an army.

In a rare instance, stragglers, rushed downhill, towards their forces with backs turned and screaming,

"He's a fiend!"

"The God of Death!" Another cried.

Witnessed by Julien and Károly, the few voices muted, and fleeing the carnage that backed them, some tripped from their numbed senses and were left to be murdered. Though eventually, they luckily gathered their breaths and escaped for their lives.

Tracing the path of crawling souls, longing to live on, to its origin, there was a single soldier, weeping aloud that Julien worriedly heard. It never sounded nor had it ever been in his memory that the voice was so in distress that drew him and Károly closer.

The smudges of grit and dirt which could not be evaporated, like the swathes of blood marks, tainted his shuddering body. His quivering hand, held onto a snapped sword that had a jagged blade, was bloodied by his nails' doing, deeply dug into and however otherwise, there was not one scar he suffered from the massacre.

"Arminius...?" Julien recognized him but was answered by an unfamiliar face.

The killer pivoted on the spot, with a possessed set of eyes crying streams of blood whose disastrous being frightened his supposed friends. Yet surrounded by his genocide, the expression cast upon the mournful face was like that of a victim's. Sluggishly shuffling closer to Julien under the heavy burden he bore, the maniac uttered,

"Another...human...?"

Arminius was blinded by a paint blanket over his sight that within, two others stood. He saw but could not differentiate from enemy and ally as the dwelling desire, to torment them, pumped. Another river of blackened blood spewed from his mouth and with a destroyed blade, sought to attack. Inching nearer, the unseen in Arminius' focus stayed remarkably still, when Károly nocked an arrow onto his swift bow.

Raising his sword, none spoke as Arminius' grip steadied, implying a sudden dash. Though before the lieutenant could swing his blade, a heaven-piercing arrow skimmed through the air and struck the hilt of the sword, disarming the provoked creature.

Stunned by fate, his sword had been thrown into the sky that plummeted, upright, into the mud behind. His selfhood swarmed death's wishes and emptied his mind of the devils' whispers. Sobbing, there was an occurrence that drained. The features which denoted his humanity, of the soreness and strain on his legs battling the broken conscience amassed inside. He dropped to his knees and was caught by Julien's loving embrace.

"Ju...lien..." Arminius whimpered under the returning light of victimized eyes.

Lifted off the cursed tree who released their grasp on the protector, he was tightly held in his good comrade's tender arms, pressing Arminius against his chest. Julien rested his head on the softened hair as the blood on his cheeks was washed out by a renewed river, running from his eyes. With humane and understanding tears, for what he had done, Arminius' voice cracked like a glass heart, into a regretful wail onto Julien, he hoped the ill-fated souls could hear.

XXVIII
15 APELYOTES 491
15.11.12017

Julien Carlstadt

The steam. The ripples. The warmth. It pained me…

The dead must feel the same…asleep…ablaze…

No matter how long it took for him to be rested underground, I watched. The legate, I wonder. Could he have saved him?

I never understood the scent that lingered on Arminius until this morning when I saw something greater than a curse. It did not seem human. Someone…somehow forced his hands. Was it the blood? Will Károly have to endure it too?

Only I have too many questions…

Rumors and the truth spread quickly in this city. The death was made known by noon and journalists were already writing about the victory after. They did not believe it knowing so much about the aftermath. And I was surprised at first. Before realizing this must have been Rantzau's will…

But if we're not careful, there would be a revolt from the Dannes. Divide and conquer. We wouldn't stand a chance against the Confederates like this. Without a commander-in-chief.

Should we simply disobey the mayor's wishes? An aide of his'? Adam could take up office. He's the highest ranking officer…that's impossible…he's not Warneńczyk…

What? Should I…? To betray Arminius…?

He's always been by those closest…

CHAPTER

29   KINGDOM

One iron gate, nailed into the hellscape, served as the beam that divided the finite space of the cavern reaching no ends. Studded with eyes which were shorn from their bodies, they gawked at the intruder, alone and laying. The leaking ceiling of branching arms swayed like leaves as blood ran down their exposed flesh, dripping beads of their juices into the shallow sea below, with their impacts as resounding as rain.

His hair was soaked and dyed red. Blood rained into the great polluted lake of gore that submerged his skin to where the poisonous unease rudely woke him ever so slowly with droplets splattering onto his cheeks. Arminius' eyes twitched. His pulsating heartbeat sent ripples in an arc over the surface as flooded lungs wheezed.

O' protector of all life... Death's figure shaped into the form of the disfigured tree, disgustingly growing another hundred eyes.

It eclipsed the shine of glazed and decapitated heads that made up the devils' world's shaded sun, sucking the kei of the dead into its lifeline by its roots made of curling spines.

Coughing blackened blood until his own waterfalled too, a punishing pain surged through his revival, forcing the lieutenant into the presence of the creature he despised whilst he recovered little.

Such lacking bloodshed could earn your gate... It said as Arminius staggered before he could stand without fail.

If you broke not so soon...

The blood levels heightened when the gates started to rumble, steadily pulling the fiend into the deepening sea. Before the horrible flood, the doorway that held back the tides bursted that flushed a tsunami of his victims into the judging calm. Completely drowning the tree with its bones and other bodily materials, the surge onwards halted by Arminius' face, terror-stricken.

A ghastly hand reached out of the abyss and grabbed his leg by the ankle. Where he could not escape, the lieutenant peered down to the anguished face, whose soul wept streams of blood.

"W-Wait…!" Arminius cried but none of his words reached the ghouls who sang a choir of their own mourning.

Help…us… His enemies hurtingly groaned as many more were forced into the realm.

Unfortunate souls latched onto Arminius who felt a shocking pain gnaw his legs. Then the first who caught him in its grip firmly squeezed until there was a bursting snap.

"Aaah!" The lieutenant released a distressing cry he knew could never equate to those of his victims.

It's cold…down here… They tortured him, climbing with accursed nails, and devils' claws, they pierced his skin as they dragged the shuddering body.

"N-No…stop…" Arminius broke into tears but however guilty his pleas were, the rotting sea only strengthened its hold.

Bones twisted in violence anyone could only have nightmares of. Fracturing and cracking wretchedly under each stale gasp of air which ended with a disturbing scream only he could hear. His flesh bruised and tore. Senses burned until the cruel pain was no more.

Why…? The victims asked, suffocating Arminius behind a mountain of hands piled atop his mouth and nose.

Have we ever…harmed you…?

He deteriorated into a watery burial, in a foreign world emptied into the paradise waiting below.

"Sorry…"

"Forgive…me…" said Arminius, remorsefully.

The blackness brightened and with a pained jolt to the head, he sprung awake, panting, to a home-like warmth. Its fiery lights of silent candles and lamps replaced the heated cavern, filling the room under a shroud of intimate steam from the neighboring bathroom underneath. A single tear ran down his face as the boy clenched the crumpled blankets, soundless. The headache was gone and he felt no more grief, strangely enough that little memories of anything in the nearest past had blanked alongside the pain.

Arminius' head was wrapped in a comfortable circlet of bandaged ice, whilst a thin layer of cloth, changed thrice over, was tied to his hands which had short stains of dried blood on the palms, though his wounds were nothing severe. In a casual red jacket and a white shirt that was not his belonging, he wondered, with his hurried heartbeat, why it was that his dream was so agonizing. Alas could not make of the world that had been purged.

What...was it...again? Arminius alone, wiping his tears before anyone could see.

"Armin!" A spirited voice called for him.

Looking up from his hands, the lieutenant spotted Károly, whom he had not noticed since awakening. Curled up on the corner of the mattress behaving in an unusual way that kept the active soldier still. When that archer shuffled closer to Arminius until they were only a fist's apart, the expression of his beaming face widened when the awoken one came to his senses.

"You okay?" asked Károly, swinging the two tails of his knitted cap.

They paused and after an awkward delay, Arminius responded,

"Hm?"

"Huh?!" cried Károly, worriedly.

Crawling about, he slipped his hands into the lieutenant's hair, without warning, and carefully committed his senses into feeling for missed wounds.

"W-What are you doing?!" Arminius stammered as he felt a chill down his spine.

"You shouldn't be up if you still feel light." Károly released his comrade from the nuisance inspection.

A slight snigger had come from another soldier leaning against the wall beneath a lamp and as the two turned towards the shadow, the light showed his grin.

"He might've hit his head too hard." The lieutenant chuckled with his arms crossed.

"Gin?" called Arminius.

But to his shock, he was not the single comrade in the room. The elites, in its entirety including the two lancers appeared in his once blurred sights who kept to themselves in their individual spaces dotted around the quarters. Some had already changed for the night in bland or washed-out colors yet others were in uniforms. However, so were the boring shades, the room was no matter illuminated by each plainly forced smile.

"Almost everyone's here..." Arminius mumbled when two officers revealed themselves out of the youthful backdrop.

"Adam and Wojsław too?" He took a guess as the uncommonly shaped shadow of the warrior gave away.

"Yer up runnin' quick ain't cha?" Adam greeted in the background, with a roll of newspaper clipped onto his belt.

He was juggling tape measures, though upon losing control, both were launched onto Gin's hardened head. A brutal feud like an underground brawl exploded between student and teacher, kicking and shouting at each other with their idiotic bickering. Comrades alike tried holding them back as the struggle swelled.

Though he could not laugh, the pumping heart of Arminius relaxed until the beats matched the average rest's. Bringing his legs out of bed and stretching them, as far as he could for his muscles to loosen as the calmness of the darkness encased the squad within somewhere like home he had only realized. Turned to the curtains, the lieutenant reached, ready to draw open the view behind the rattling window at his fingertips.

"It's night already?" He asked with a curious demeanor.

"Yeah.." Another boy stepped to block his wanted path.

Arminius gazed up to the lancer from his boots to the sword, kept buckled onto the rope tied around a fern green shirt.

"You've been asleep for a while, y'know." said Arnau, leaning against the wall that stayed the captain's hands.

Retreating to himself and from the sight of the outside world, Arminius returned onto the step and shyly sat upright.

"Right..." The lieutenant mumbled.

The timid knocking steps on the aging floor outside, although close, did not grow any louder than the distant marching. Gradually and through the gust of freezing breezes, the door before his eyes opened and stepped in the last member to show.

"Julien..." Arminius recognized him.

Even after a hot bath, his skin was only slightly red, whilst the neutral blue woolen sweater should have warmed him yet after such a brief time, the Danne was cooled. With the childhood penchant that had never left his neck swinging, Julien scrubbed his part-dried hair, under a white towel, in a bout.

"Evening, Arminius." His face pleasingly lit up with a sweet smile.

Nearing the bed, Julien tossed the towel onto a chair beside Arnau and slumped onto the step next to Arminius. He reached over his black shorts and stretched his arms to the buckles of his boots, yawning as the Danne watched Adam close the door, insulating whatever words they uttered to be guarded within.

All sat eerily silent, as if they waited for something to happen or perhaps it was the awkward atmosphere that kept their typically frequent mouths from opening, lest to say anything wrong or unwanted. He was not one to speak in the midst of serenity, however, Arminius held back no longer.

"What are all of you doing here?" The commander began in a reserved tone which dragged the squad's eyes onto him.

A similar silence filled the air as the few fidgeted their hands, awaiting someone to answer. Though no one seemed courageous enough to speak, leaving the fair room for another minute of quietness before a comrade moved.

"Hm...how should I put it...?" Gin grunted, removing himself from the light of the lamp, and thoughtfully trailed to the center of the room.

Gesturing for Adam's aid, his teacher's twisted aura menacingly forced him away with a demanding stare for the telling of the truth to be told by a friend.

"Listen...uh..." voiced Gin as he paced about.

The elites held their breaths, hoping that what the moron would say was not too revealing.

"That noble,"

"Rantzau...uh...he's dead." The lieutenant sped through his words which caught the room unguarded for the happening.

"Gin!" His squad harmoniously shouted, storming to their brash comrade who was backed against the wall.

Two fingers from the side pinched his ears and dragged him to a chair to be surrounded by looks of awe. Like an interrogation, Arber roughly grabbed Gin by the collar and lifted him for the squad to brazenly scold with tensing stares.

"Have you forgotten what we agreed on?" Arber hissed like no other.

"C'mon, what else was I supposed to tell 'im?!" Gin argued.

Though beyond Lev's shoulders, at the edges of his eye, he saw that Arminius was accepting the news peculiarly well, unexpectedly composed unlike the childish craze they had expected.

"I know..." Arminius interrupted, with his head lowered.

Beneath the clearing steam dissipating into the cracks of the house, the party stood bewildered, looking on at the comrade scrunching the blankets in slight distress. Yet, he was not to the point of a crazed outburst, nor was he ready to reject the fact. As if his entirety of the mind had been reversed, Arminius was accepting of the old commander's fate.

"How much...do you remember...?" Julien concernedly asked.

Gin shoved Arber away and the squad dispersed into their spaces nearer their leader. The room found itself to be more compact than it was. When Arminius held his head to recall, they stilled, but even then, he could not see past the fazed memories of the gunshot that blasted a coat of blood onto him which he envisioned, painted over his face.

Releasing a disappointed sigh, the lieutenant's head shook and told all listening with a hand cast over the washed stains of guilt,

"Not much past that..."

Adam lifted off the wall and strolled towards the group, though not too close, and unsheathed the roll of the national papers which he patted on his hands.

"Well, in dat case." He mumbled, tossing the newspaper overhead that spun onto Arminius' lap.

"Take yer eye on dis."

Need not glance to guess what the stored contents detailed, afterall, Arminius had remembered that Rantzau had informed him. But curiosity flipped the page onto its front anyways, and in revelling bold letters, his and the legate's name was printed across the paper accompanied with a question horde and glorified sketches of the mayor.

"Willin' ta become commander?" Adam joked, unbeknownst

of the actuality.

He retreated into the shadows with a smirk, shrugging, and shaking his head when the smile depressed into a click of the tongue.

What have ya done? Leaning against the same wall, the officer turned to the meditating warrior, sleeping feather-like lightly.

Ya've gone an' kicked da bucket. Now da army'll fall apart. Adam tapped his fingers stuck within his pockets.

Gazing at the rambling squad who spoke of many other alternatives or candidates, he let off a discreet smile, confidently showing.

"We all knew a succession was going to happen." Modestly suggesting, the single Danne pledged his heart under the words he told to the very few opposed to the selection although he who was in discussion was not given the brightest of rooms to speak within.

"Shouldn't we leave it to an election?" suggested Colt.

Slapped in the head, he fell onto the ground as Alexandria dragged him to stand.

"And what if it's an even match?" She implied the crisis to follow.

Before Arminius could breath, Gin tossed himself into the brawl among words that hardly suited him.

"The Dannes sure aren't gonna like it." He argued with an indifferent tone but upon seeing that Colt and others disapproved, soon grew wary of the candidates who were listed by the city's journalists.

"But look at it this way..." Gin raised his voice, taking a glimpse at Arminius who had simply swerved from the battle.

"If he ain't gonna do it, then who is?"

Pointing at one Lev had eyed and held a laughter for longer than he spoke, Gin bitterly made fun of the candidate,

"This bold butcher?"

As they took their patient turns reviewing the papers, and how it aged with new wrinkles, the squad strayed from the contained settlement, furthering the cause they fought for which were flattened by the march of their unstoppable voices. Like a merge of unsavory music, their arguments reached nowhere when Arminius stood.

Paused, the squad ceased the aimless mass debate in a stretch of mute awkwardness. He watched him tread, bare-footed across the floor to the closet. Opening its doors, the captain of the party removed a cigarette resting on the highest shelf and copying Károly's snap, ignited the stick balanced in his lips.

"That's my move!" Károly cried.

"I'm just *borrowing* it." Arminius, with the grayed expression, puffed pale mist that filled the room with an ambient climate.

"Seeing that this is getting nowhere,"

"I should tell you that it was Rantzau who asked whether I could replace him as commander-in-chief—" He recalled.

"He asked you?" Arnau confirmed as he crossed his arms.

"So it wasn't supposed to be questioned after all." Siegfried added.

Dragging his body across the smooth floor and who wandered towards the table, Arminius latched his hand onto a chair and swung the seat to face the squad.

"Then whaddya say?! Did ya accept it?!" Gin excitedly asked, leaning ever closer to the captain who sat under the coat of smoke.

"Eventually," said the latter.

"Haah!" Gin joyfully blasted whose voice journeyed into the fields where patrols could have heard him boom.

"I'd be lying if I weren't jealous, right, Arber?!" He wrapped his arms around his close comrade, unknowingly for a death's wish.

Who pushed Gin's jaw upwards that stunned him, Arber's whipped strike around his locked hands tossed the brute onto the quaking floor, thumping the dense body that threw a cape of dust into the air.

From the sprinkled murky powder, Julien courteously sneezed and covered his reddening nose as Lev appeared over Gin, casting a long shadow over the lieutenant with his arms and legs spread out.

"But no matter who does it," The Rus told.

"It'll make for a massac—"

Hesitating, Lev blinked hardly and waved his hand before lending help for deciding not to speak an ill word,

"Nevermind, nevermind."

"We're all gonna die here anyways," said Colt to the hopeless thinking but he found the storm humorous.

"I didn't think anyone had plot armor left."

The lieutenant was alone, given the flick of their shoulders, he awkwardly chuckled away to his poor joke.

Rising to the ceiling, and seeping through the window's gaps, the stagnant smoke inched into the wilderness, particle by particle. Clumped together as if were a gray steppe horde, it charged out of the room as Arminius huffed for the last. He crushed the cigarette into a little more than atoms and as he opened his fingers, emptiness revealed itself.

"Not necessarily." Arminius mentioned, holding out his spotless hand and challenged fate,

"But we won't die here."

His eyes were fueled with a passionate fire of ambition. But there was a fine rift between that and how it was three years ago. Such as that he had a somewhat visionary aim before remembering something of greater importance.

"I...!" Arminius straightened his posture and began searching his pockets for the valued item.

He heartened the squad, once glum and disunited, like a punch to the chest that enlivened the somberness.

"I had an envelope on me..." The lieutenant searched everywhere but the letter had disappeared.

Springing up, realizing what his comrade was searching for, Károly desperately tugged on his hooded sweatshirt and pulled a preserved letter from his warmth.

"You mean this?" The lieutenant captain held it up high in the light and saw an inked name spelt along the underside.

"Herr...foen...Kopën...åcën..." For it was Danne, he read aloud, flicking a knife beneath the seal.

"Don't open it!" Arminius panicked as the tip met the paper's edge.

The knife halted at the meeting, before the blade dug into the draft, and without question, Károly sheathed the weapon with a theatrical spin between his fingers and naively asked,

"What's so unique about this letter?"

Upon finding the eased heart to rest, Arminius sharply puffed, peacefully tapping his feet until the rattling of windows stopped. He, too, quieted. Swinging his legs back, the lieutenant clenched his fists and turned to the bare floor.

"It's the only draft we have..."

"Of Rantzau's peace treaty—" said he, bracing for a backlash.

Gin slammed his hand on the wall and yelled before thinking,

"Ya gotta be fuckin' 'round!"

"Don't tell me we're gonna sit by whilst everyone else are fightin' a war!" The enraged soldier spurted.

With a frightening kei, a hand grabbed his shoulder, whose pupils shrunk as the terror-ridden blood in him froze.

"Let him finish." Arber's voice did not sound as a question would do, but an oppressive demand.

"Whatever suits you…!" Gin hastedly calmed his mind.

And cared for when he spun away, not to bump into the inhumanly cold lieutenant, the dying storm in a pacific higher command allowed for Arminius' story.

"I don't intend to sign a treaty to distance myself from war." Their leader revealed.

"During that time of peace, we'll devote ourselves into an exodus."

An ambivalent, frightful that he would say anything wrong, lifted off the step to oppose, but not lacking good reason to do so. And with a judging gesture of his body advanced onward, Julien asked, keeping to his timidity,

"Do you mean to…call in our fleets…?"

Arminius shut his eyes, obscuring the world and merely heard Julien's voice in the dark.

"But, even if we did, they're all the way in the Tastschr Strait." The Danne reasoned.

"I'll force them through the Confederates no matter what it takes." Arminius surely replied.

"With the *leverage* we'll have." He tightened his fist, resting on his lap, until the armor felt near to burst.

Reaching out, the lieutenant held the squad, in a wholly confused stupor, within the palms of his hand. Though from his sights, Arminius had thought his comrades knew what his mind spoke of, but in the demoralizing reality, they looked to have shrugged and scratched their heads, evident of unknowing.

"Leverage?" asked the squad, which resonated in the walls, where the whispering echoes flooded into the lower floor.

"If we can damage the Confederacy enough," Arminius explained, raising the treaty between his eyes.

"Then they'd have no choice but to sue for peace."

The embers of the light fanned into ardent flames, by the whistle of the coming death, the house sat tranquil. Suddenly a punch of a hand crashed and the squad turned to the unexpected.

"I see!" Gin's mind shined as a bulb would do, believing with his own thoughts he had grasped the plan that perhaps even Colt found most strange.

"Den," The overjoyed lieutenant leapt into the center with his arms wide out like a television presenter and questioned,

"How are we gonna damage 'em?!"

Comrades released snickers and laughs for the stressed lungs to finally gasp, as it must have been unthinkable for anyone such as Gin to have understood.

"What?" Gin agitatedly spun around where Arber shed the first grin he could not hold back.

"What I've been saying about you all these years is right." Colt recounted in an antagonizing tone and a damning smirk.

"A fool can never change."

"You're one to talk." snarled Gin, holding a right hook as his insulting counterpart drew a left fist.

A colossal titan appeared from thin air and collapsed his shadow onto what he saw were shrimps. Bellowing as he grabbed their faces with his oversized hands, the giant ushered hot steam stored beneath his skin and butted Gin and Colt's heads where they dropped cold to the planks.

Flinching from the thump, Lev fled to the side and stayed afar, behind Julien, considerately glancing to make sure whether they were not lifeless shells.

"Deception." Julien told by the rules of nature.

"In other words…" said Arnau, balancing a knife on his fingertip whilst his eyes were closed.

"We'll be the ones to go on the offensive!" Károly and Siegfried shouted together, knowing this time was the truth.

Held a strong-willed salute, like a slash across the heart that would fill the buckets of war spoils, Arminius declared,

"Whilst we may appear unable, it's then when we'll strike."

Steadfast in his intentions, as the gale was blowing west, it vented crisp air into the tepid spring of the good hope. Smiled upon by the many allies he could call comrades, basking in the imagined glory they would receive as he detailed the plan.

"In simple terms, our forces will be divided into two sectors." He informed, lifting two fingers in the air.

"The assault from the west,"

"And the defense of the east." Withdrawing either, the commander leaned into the chair, rocking backwards until its spine met the table.

Gazing into the internal night sky, brightly contrasting the external world, Arminius exhaled as his mind engaged in the sport of strategy.

"I'll lead the western sector." The lieutenant informed the squad who naturally agreed.

Afterall, I can't stand being on the defense.

But the smile fainted when he mentioned the equal of the second front,

"As for the east…"

His chair plunged on its four stable legs, gently steadying. Though there his dimmed eyes, looking away, told true that he indeed held one name for the post yet was not willing to reveal it. The party felt so as the lieutenant in thought was centered as the elites pushed him forward.

It's only natural that he would take the west…

Then… Julien knew too then he swore with a hand on his chest,

"I'll command the east."

Held elsewhere, Arminius' eyes were not able to see the same glimmer the other had. The same ambition and desire to save the kingdom. Gritting his teeth, the leading lieutenant flicked his head away, and stingingly told his friend,

"Someone else should take it."

"How?!" The squad gave a cry of strain.

"Why not? The Confederates can't compare." First to voice, Károly wrapped his arms on Julien's shoulders and spoke, pointing to his face.

"You said so yourself."

"It's not that…" Arminius murmured though in the boiling temper, no one heard him.

"Don't you think that's unreasonable—?" Lev gently backed.

Through the gaps between his comrades, Arber weaved into the frame, shaded by a despising expression which advanced unto its attack.

"I thought you were over that tantrum." He openly confronted him.

Holding the silver plates lined along his fingers, the falling sweat ran down his neck as he gulped.

"That's not..." mumbled Arminius, whose words still remained unheard.

"Who else can if it ain't gonna be him, huh?" Gin hotly fussed when a hand crossed over, breaking the flaring outburst.

They searched, from his fingertips to the mindful self, and found the one in question lowering his arm. Slowly, not intimidating, Julien's footsteps were silent. Watchful over the shunned eyes which did not bother to face him, the consoling aura cooled the stifling atmosphere.

"After four years of wanting to..." The comrade recollected.

A wondrous short breath reminded Arminius under the shielding figure, blockading the light in producing his own.

"Are you going to deny my ambition in ending this war as well?" Julien soothingly asked.

"Do you still not..."

Whose memory started to flow, upon the demolition of a dam, Arminius' awareness of the devoted came to be in a cluster of previous pleas. For his humiliating rejection, the lieutenant removed himself from the frustrating sights.

What am I doing...? He calmly rose, knocking his ankle against the chair's leg as the squad made way.

Despite their hearts having built a fiery pillar waiting to be burned to ashes, they were not willing to, and simply let him be.

Under the realization time was needed to level his head, Arminius shuffled, in a curved trajectory, towards the door and placed his hand on the handle whilst the two officers resting against the wall were not looking. Swinging it open, the lieutenant prepared to depart when he thought it might have been rude had he not said anything. And so to his fellow soldiers, he announced with lessened passion and deserted pride,

"I..."

A suspended word to be said was not, but reflectingly changed his mind.

"Sorry..." Arminius apologized in a straight sincerity.

"Just decide by tomorrow which front you're going to fight for."

With a glimpse over the lamps who could barely see him, standing beyond the pale of flickering shadows, Arminius lowered his eyelids.

"And Julien…"

"Give me an hour…" The friend requested with uncertainty, nervously exiting the room and the shutting door was heard.

The coldest early morning, chirping for the rising sun concealed by the thick jacket of a dark expanse of smoke, and the house appearing taller than the distant walls stood. Brittle leaves, on the ride of a journey across the road of fallen ash and snow, melting as one into the earth who took its remains, like a mother holding her lifeless child. It bitterly blew on a cheerful face, staring into the solemn gray sky. His hair fluttered, and its individual strands softened to freely bask in the enjoyment of sea breezes no more like home. Hiking over the high coastal walls, the scent of wasting corpses, dumped into the sea, were salted by the waves playing an overture with the fleeting gusts. Cries of the common blood; joyous chants of war songs in a march in the disciplined streets, empty of rubbish but freckled with flesh and rubble. All seeped into his ears, although they were ignored. Knowing that the day would come for the liberal fight, the lives he sought to reward with the deaths prepared in the several thousands were longed for.

The smoke beyond the wall… He saw.

Peeling his focus off the fast-tracking clouds, Arminius had the elites before and beside him rested in uniform. Close to a supply wagon hardly filled, there were two lines of both the eastern and western sectors.

"Julien. Alexandria. Miklós. Lev…"

"And Colt?" Arminius listed the easterners.

Smirking, Colt cycled his spear in a spin overhead and landed the weapon on the concealed road.

"Heh, I heard there was only one bridge connecting Sueken and Danen." He eagerly answered.

"I'll have my fun there given the chance to be outside of your umbrella."

The appointed commander dipped his head and showed a

relieved smile,

"Then that leaves us with…"

Arminius peered down his avenue of lefts and rights, who formed a lengthier line, yet by their own rights, were only as powerful forces in the conducts of battles, and called for,

"Wojsław and Wojtek. Gin. Arber. Arnau. Siegfried. Károly—"

"Argh! Let's drink from their skulls!" Gin banged his fists and yelled too early in the day however, that fatigue and sickened smell of the graveyard air only filled the mad warrior with perhaps more kei.

Setting off towards the wall, Gin caught the elites off guard in his sprint and tore their attention one by one.

"Gin, hold on!" Siegfried and most chased after the foolish soldier with Wojsław who strolled down the path with a growling stone bear.

Károly raised an arm, nearly launching himself into the fray when Arminius held the elated archer by the collar until his fight weakened for Arnau to consider giving pursuit.

"Then! I'll see you after you've sorted the capital out!" The last lancer winked and sent his goodbyes with the flick of a hand, though he must have meant to conceal the massacre.

The figures in view shortly shrunk, and their voices were drowned by the furthering distance. Sighing, Arminius released Károly from his grip and kept him close as the eastern sector casually boarded the wagon, waving farewell to the opposite flank. But Julien had not.

Who was still, the Danne looked awkward.

"What's wrong?" asked Arminius, staring at his comrade's face.

"Can't leave us?" Károly popped out of cover and teased the blushing lieutenant.

"N-No, of course not…well…yes! But no!" Julien flustered when the one thing he had remembered came to mind.

Once the blush had gone with a few slaps to the face, he gave time to a sizable breath and gathered such courage to rummage for something hidden in his jacket. His hand halted, and brought out, only for the three to see, a mystical object unraveling into a gleaming work of art, decorated in extravagance. To the excessive shine even beneath the frosted heavens, Arminius and Károly's jaws dropped.

A knife, spectacularly designed, were its intricacies far more satisfying to gaze at. The sheath, fixed underneath the banner of a Leo with imperial red claws and a crown on one side. Whilst its pommel was golden, it was fitted with a single sapphire jewel carved into the shape of a Bawarann blue diamond as it was painted on a flag. The agarwood hilt ended at the start of the blade that was sharply revealed.

"It's made of a stone native to the Alpinnes." Julien described the glare of the cerulean metal.

"The same used for Napoleon's Eight Bladed Wheel."

"Here!" Pledging the knife to Arminius, stunned, he smiled tenderly,

"I think it belongs with you."

Arminius peered down, unbelieving that the magnificence was laying in his hands.

"Where did you...?" The commander asked, then abruptly turned to Károly, realizing that the poor lieutenant captain had not been gifted anything.

"What about Károly?"

Covering a hand over Arminius' mouth to stop his babbling or else he would not have otherwise, Julien replied with a slight giggle, returning his palm to himself,

"Don't worry about any of that."

"I hatched something with the royal blacksmith of this city." The Danne rested.

Shutting his eyes for the universal prayer, with one thumb slashing across from shoulder to shoulder; a drawing line from head to the stomach; and the third stroke along the ribs, Julien kissed the joint of his thumb and punched ahead.

"We should get going now." said he, jubilant of the turning day.

Looking at the hand cladding future triumphs, Arminius and Károly bumped their fists forming the trinity of their heavens.

"Lest we forget." They promised on the day for the memories when they age, where the morning moon would beam highest in the last halo before the shroud of raining ash.

XXIX

16 APELYOTES 491

16.11.12017

Julien Carlstadt

We had forgotten our ambitions in the smog of battles where what's occurring before our eyes deserved more. After four months of not remembering that dream, what is it that we had become? Shells in the drought on sand. I'm glad for Arminius that he has returned to his old self. For Károly to redress our wrongs.

Whilst we are no geniuses of war like Alexei von Roman or Regulus von Eos, the purposes which we fulfill as the offense and defense will satisfy the missing halves Arminius and I lack. With Károly smoothing our roughness and places we cannot reach alone. And as three, forms the mind of one sole genius needed to become worthy. This kingdom, this city, will not fall. I and the elites on the east, here, are stakes behind Arminius' back, to prevent a wrath of the Confederate cavalry. He, Károly and the elites on the west, there, are squadrons ready to take to the skies. So we must do the duty to protect them before ascending.

If we three were a bow, I would be its limbs; Arminius the bowstring; Károly the arrow. Without a part, we are nothing but junk.

CHAPTER

30   TIMED PEACE

Dual chariots of solar blazes beamed, dragged along the old forsaken road of bones, a highway along the washing tides. Its fires melted the withering bodies, unattended to, floating in the shallow emerald waters. Bloated after days the dead laid waiting, for a new frightful hunk piled atop. Suffocating its life which once lived in the sand, the coast had become desolate, near a town of massacre, burning and screaming that blighted the afternoon sky. The blood overflowed its streets and village houses, pouring like whitewater into the fjord. In several straits of streams, damning poison flowed, yet no one cared less when the victors, a small century, were its executors.

Galloping from the southern headland to the north, the entente lunged across the Confederate lines, shattered and routing before the furious chase that the Apollo's son gave. His eifer ripped through the very core, iron and steel, and engraved his burnt brand into the vanquished mind as the last present ahead of the drawing battle.

"Let's give 'em a show of de century!" yelled Gin, who had wrapped his jacket around the waist which exposed his able build.

Wielding two blades, one blunted and another sharpened, the warm steel, aglow, ignited into a vortex of rolling flames. Its waves twisted the air, emitting flickers of sparks where a golden hue of his ability flashed. Wildfires in line followed the tips of the swords, pulling his troops away to make grounds for the calamity. As the lieutenant's sweating grips slipped, fueling the fire with the dumbfounding heat, he tugged on the hilt.

An inviting death's smirk, godly but terrifyingly leered into the grail waiting to be gutted. The Confederates held their last prayers and dropped their weapons and, agreeing to fate, they watched Gin's hands rise. He swung up, against the resistant sand, and flicked a second of waves crashing into the skies as that water steamed and formed a cast of fires, in the creation of a striking image of his teacher's Sol. Two chariots stormed like trains into the destined ranks to be blasted, a fireball of the new seven rays, chained together, crashed and pillaged. Scorching the earth that drained its carved path of purged water, blood vaporized on the touch of the chariot. And who unlucky souls were there standing in the midst of the path or on its borders, unable to escape, were swallowed whole or only partly. Till the fire had been watered by the encroaching waves, the soldiers collapsed onto their spilling remains, splattering onto the sand that were washed into the sea.

Gin, in the embers of his dominant sea where he was king, a god to be revered by the howling winds, pulled on the reins and halted his wood brown horse, whose ears had been charred black. And looked out into the vast fjord covering the branching arms rushing into the open waters, his face was different. He was considerate. Not bathing in the dreading death under him, the lieutenant's hanging wave-like hair flapped as the breeze surfed.

A shine slapped his face which glimmered from the sweat. In the east it came and fell. What was white, but tinted a slight yellow. He watched for the smoke to dispel until making his move.

"Arber's done with 'is side too..." Gin murmured then faced his century, poking at the drifting stacks of corpses in a search for survivors.

"You've fought well today like any other!" The warrior shouted.

Clanking his blades for his soldiers' attention, he raised the sharper sword into the air and celebrated.

"With dis we're one step closer to paradise!"

His men stamped their spears and rifles in the tainted beach where the fast crawling tides closed. Their cheers were like the ripples in the water which were sent towards the strait.

"Den!" cried Gin with his voice sounding spirited.

"Remember to brag 'bout 'is in 'eir ears!"

The century managed an extra cheer, taking the spoils from looted bodies, the scattered soldiers hiked over the endless dunes. Carrying the exhausted groans and grins of glee among the oppressed whom their boots trampled, like crumbling carpets, without care.

Held onto the headphones which played symphonies of static in the room where no light exited or entered, the commander's face was determined to hear the breaks which sometimes sounded and ceased with a heavily accented voice. An ashtray, of a dozen cigarettes and a recent smoke pushed into the dust heap, rested on the map, rife with arrows and deceased plans, paled lines or words of many moons ago.

"Passed...blockade..." The static only worsened.

Arminius carefully adjusted the knob clockwise and once the frequency seemed to better, he listened closely with his aides looking on, anxiously.

"I...repeat, the Jarlsberg fleet has passed the third blockade."

"Gods we hope...will guide us true...." The man on the unclear microphone prayed.

"Five...hours...to..."

Then the radio terminated.

Throwing the headphones onto the desk, Arminius leaned back against his chair to release a clearing sigh. He spun a pen in a bout on his thumb for ten cycles that no one else could practice, and told the eager sergeants and corporals, standing at guard in the western headquarters, of the favorable news,

"That was the worst part down..."

Arminius tightened his top collar to fidget his trembling hands that the awaiting were clear to see. They gulped, bracing for the worst as their commander reassured,

"Jarlsberg will arrive tonight."

In a way of their own with grunts and shy nods, the leading officers sounded relieved, where the chatter amongst them ensured the release of tensed air in the stiff room. The curtains were finally drawn by one of the many and the sudden burst of the light decorated the space in the emancipation of dullness.

"The fleet only needs to make it past the fourth checkpoint now,"

"It won't be long..." An aide mentioned to his comrades where the binded atmosphere untangled farther.

The pen was settled on the files of papers to be filled, whilst it towered over the radio, intimidatingly staring at the lieutenant to provoke, he breezily ignored the stacks upon stacks and stood, pushing his chair back.

"Contact the eastern sector," Arminius ordered, resting his hands on the table.

"And make sure the port is clear for docking."

"Understood!" A corporal shouted and took hold of the radio's controls, prepared to signal the opposite front.

"Bruun. Proceed with *stage one* evacuation." The commander directed that brought another sergeant to salute.

Dashing up the stairs, the pair of hastening footsteps pulled the lieutenant from his much needed work, but upon the showing of the exotically colored hair, he knew who that was.

"Arminius!" The archer charged into the forefront alongside the rushing sergeant, and drifted along the floorboard to a halt, almost throwing himself across the corridor had he not caught the door frame.

"Károly?" Arminius expressed with great joy.

"You're early."

Braziers remained alight regardless of the settling enemy attacks. However any old fool could tell, the sun setting over the wall for another closing day, that it was anything but early. And in the event he had once more forgotten the concept of time, Arminius realized how much he had been engrossed into the late Rantzau's work.

I guess I could use a break... The lieutenant yawned, dragging his dagger along the table.

His comrade, the archer, was smudged in dirt and dried stains of enemy blood. panting energetically although his breath had yet to return, Károly smiled, widely.

The portal into the outer world, a panel door opened, guiding the last heated breezes through the widening gap and blew. A bustling encampment of bell tents, bland but colored, overwatched the lone headquarter's house on a meadow of sprouting spring flowers dressed like human faces. Lacking any motors, most carried goods and supplies in horse-drawn wagons which followed the three direct paths to the north, east and west. It was the least industrial, had there not been rifles to be held on marches and patrols across the jammed roads, then there was no telling apart from the ages gone and modernity. Except periodically, the height of gunmetal gray smoke rose above the factories' chimneys and blacksmiths' furnaces, arsenals and armories in the afar town center. It had grown ever so much in the past months that Haven had been reborn as a living fortress.

Along the widened avenue, paved with stones and gravel, that was seen to transport bountiful goods, Arminius and Károly strolled, individually taking in the ambient sights and noises of bolts being polished; sharpening swords; and the flickering braziers settled on the hacked tree stumps which used to line the path. It had gone to serve the pillars that erected the goliath lift built into the wall and could be seen, many leagues in any course.

"Have the others returned?" asked Arminius, stretching to make use of the halcyon breezes.

Vibrantly jogging, a squad from the opposite appeared out of the crowds, whose collars had iron cross pins denoting the one branch that was the heart of the Danne army.

The frontline? The two spotted and made way for the passing by.

"Afternoon, Lieutenant Reichner!" They blithely greeted, with the local salutes.

Though the lieutenant could not return the respected gestures for the squad had already run off, he smiled knowing that the people they protected unveiled acceptance.

"Nevermind." Arminius shook his head upon noticing the growing legions flocking to the lodgings, tired in the countering flow against the commander's path.

Conscripts and militiamen who were unfamiliar to the theory of discipline, roused the temporary garrison, creating ruckuses wherever the youngsters went, but most had almost immediately departed for the market avenue down the road. Yet it was precisely the obscure structure that the defense harbored which strengthened the hundreds of thousands fighting under a united front.

"I couldn't have imagined it turned out this way." Károly blissfully recalled, skipping to the shops not too far.

"Yeah…" Arminius gazed at the budding stars to the extent of the closing daylight hour.

"It sorta feels like a fantasy at times."

The commander held onto the silver pommel of a gilded sword whose hilt was wrapped in a thin layer of bandage cloth. It was branded by the coat of arms of the mayor's lordship.

"This would have been a different story had the Confederates rejected our conference." He told him, peering at the cracks and holes in the road.

"But it had cost us our luck and fortune."

"It'll be worth it!" Károly poked his comrade's back with the encouraging glimmer of his bow and sprinted ahead.

A stray cat, black and white, sat on the corner of a clinic's tent and purred for the boys to come. It was well-fed and inattentive to everyone else except for the archer who approached it at a slowing slide along the gravel ground. Károly stopped before and carefully knelt down for the roaming feline flipped and invited him to rub its furred chest.

"If we didn't sacrifice something," The lieutenant captain said to Arminius, who crouched to scratch the cat's chin.

"Who knows whether we could've stayed alive for this long."

From the tiring position, Arminius stood and tapped Károly on the shoulder.

"I guess you're right." The commander blankly muttered, pushing the archer onwards to the grand wall, looking back and forth, never wanting to leave the abandoned creature soon meowing wistfully.

It yearned for Károly's unforgettable warmth.

The summit of the hill ended at a plateau where the craters were abundant, used as training grounds. Towards the welcoming scent of the evening market stalls, below a new night, whiffed across the prosperous settlement. Petals and flowers hovered over the piping stoves and jugs, hence the subtle air allowed the forming of a florid ceiling that the hanging gardens of lamps could not match. The masses escaped the wonders of conflict and merged their bodies into the seas of cheers where the leg of the road was not so simply bunched by military personnel but their families and loved ones too. As gleaming life surged on the gravel that roared with laughter, knowing very well it was the day where the truce would be signed as jotted by the weekly papers, merchants and farmers pledged their life's work selling their plentiful harvests and produce.

Watching whilst walking oftenly catching both pairs of eyes, knowing there was something to fulfill, the duo's craving minds grumbled for a treat and distracted themselves under the mounted torches into the search for something to be had.

"Look at this!" Károly's overactive self bounced about the numerous shops.

Parlors of a variety of colorful street foods and drinks from rarely seen meat to baskets of candies and bread or hot fruitful drinks to warm the freezing nights, created a scenery all too confusing for the archer to withstand, attempting to hold in his desires knowing his friend was likely bankrupt.

But Károly's pleading eyes watered despite this, so did the drool leaving his mouth as one bar, whose queue interestingly snaked, found its way to attract the childish with its unique fragrance, steaming from its countless pots and fruit juice barrels.

"Arminius, what about it?!" The small youngster excitedly tugged Arminius' jacket and on the quick approach, found themselves at the drink's stall which served only one strange northern brew.

The pungent smell, pleasing, both alcoholic and of refreshing berries, flourished in the making of where the tables had been eroded by the shifting and outpours of boiling mixtures. Its mist had the feeling that it was unlucky Sedinn all again.

"Vjllkommën! (Welcome!)" Its keeper greeted them.

Noticing the commander scouring the simmering juices, the bartender called in a keen tone,

"Oh? If it isn't Arminius."

Does he know him? Károly tiptoed to see past the lieutenant who had entirely immersed himself in the easygoing atmosphere.

"Business is doing well as usual, Jonathan." said Arminius, casually leaning onto the counter.

The patriot, who wore a cook's bandana with a Danne flag, was an inch taller than he was, though only three years older. His hands had seen numerous boils but he did not swerve from the passionate work, and despite needing to spend eight hours a day standing for his old man's work, Jonathan's proof of verancy were the profane battle scars that defiled him.

"Of course!" Jonathan explosively shouted, shocking even Károly.

"Looking for some hot cleüvjen?" In suddenness, he calmed.

"Two cups." Arminius requested.

The bartender flamboyantly spun his hands around the bottomless wooden spoon and flipped it into the air, as a painter would to a brush, he flicked the hot drink into a figure of eight.

Károly's eyes could barely keep on its trail. Throwing mints and lemon peels into the balancing cups as the juice stayed floating, Jonathan launched the spoon across the sketched pattern and poured the steaming wine.

"Two bronzes, please!" He pushed the regular-sized cups ahead and pointed his finger like a gun after the artist's performance.

"Here." Arminius flipped two coins into the high air, clinking as it fluttered like its minted eagles' flight.

In the bleak darkness between the rows of egoistic mounted torches that hardly gave light, the pair wandered on the trail from the pit of civilization into the barren lands not too far. If the world was silent and if the war had never happened, then the fields would make for a stargazing plain, guiding them west of Polaris. Károly hummed a folk song tune, hidden from the world to hear the whispers of his home, the Mazhiar lands. Marching in time with each major beat, he kicked the pebbles on the broken path until the twenty-minute boredom caught his hand.

"You've never told me." The archer started a conversation.

"What was your home like?" He asked, slowing the lieutenant's hurried feet.

Holding onto his warming drink with both hands, Arminius sipped, as he admired the shining suns observing the mere beings crawling around the earth.

"Which one?" The commander countered, sighing heavily into the echoing cup.

Károly slid along the gravel and nudged the former in the ribs, intrigued by his inattentive expression, he curiously smiled at him,

"Hey, hey, how many homes do you have?"

"Don't get the wrong idea." Arminius looked away with a quick reply.

Covering his lips with the edges of the cup, the lieutenant bit onto the paper and mumbled to himself,

"We moved a lot when I was younger."

"Turunnt...Joku-dō...Rezhinn...Bristel..." But as he retained the places distant in the shelves of memories, his teeth mutilated the paper until it could bear no more and ripped, releasing an eifer-like cast pressing against him.

"Huh?" Károly peeped, to the dismayed comrade who could not stop shaking.

Where a calming draft latched onto him, Arminius steadied the pacing heart and punished himself with a bright slap to his face, knocking the needless thoughts piled above. In the everlasting cold, where spring felt closer to winter, Károly's awkward nature, afraid to pull the sensitive trigger, held his silence whilst how uncomfortable it was to do so was in his squirming and half-opened mouth. Then an unexpected hand, apparent that the only one who could be within reach, gently patted his head.

"Anyways..." Arminius changed his tone.

"Was it too hard getting the Confederates to comply?" The commander asked.

Károly aimed his eyes down the path, but never up nor down, whose gaze was like a straight arrow, rested his nose on the steam.

"Of course not!" He spoke into the drink and carefully savored the liquor.

"That was my fifty-sixth mission." The archer recalled and boasted, certain that he had done so rightly,

"There's no way it was!"

The path soon lost its paved tracks and they found themselves walking so slowly in the exchange over a border of gravel to dirt where near the opening of the avenue into a parading square, torches were replaced by bonfires that coughed storms of smoke wherever the wind fanned. The fumes were, however, annoyingly heavy that seemed to force anyone from.

"How many did you..." The gusts drowned Arminius' voice.

"My legion?" Károly leapt out of the endangering cloak and waited for his comrade to quietly appear.

"Yeah." The commander answered once the gale perished against the breezes from the sea.

Continuing on the path to the nearing wall whose blank outline was exhibited, Károly counted in his head for the indecisiveness as the number gradually came,

"Sixty..."

It was on the edge of his tongue when Arminius halted at the base of the titan tower.

"Sixty-two thousand!" Károly remembered, rubbing his head in embarrassment of ever forgetting his foes.

Of the two million... Arminius crushed the empty cup and tossed it onto the soil suffering a drought.

"I know, it isn't as impressive as Wojsław or Gin." The archer awkwardly chuckled who had not seen the lieutenant's frigid distress.

But for their families... Arminius leveled his head and spoke to himself in an alleviated manner, modestly tracking his thoughts visualized under every step.

The commander clenched his hands on the lever, and pulled with his entire body until the cogs choked and unlocked its gears where its chains brought down a platform that could hold half a battery of field guns.

There was tragedy... The devils spoke for him.

Its great tower it descended through was the ingenious structure, perhaps the grandest feat a city under siege could have masterminded. Taller than the twenty-meter-wall itself, the lift was a skeleton housing the single platform for the drive of the wall cannons onto the battlements. Whilst its chain of contraptions made the four parts of the system exist in reality, the design was hard to comprehend for a place which was so lacking. And how it stood and stayed upright remained another figure succeeding humanity.

"Arminius! Károly!" A dear lancer, waving and laughing in the joyous sight, cried ahead of his comrade, trying to keep to pace.

"Slow down...Sieg..." Arnau called for Siegfried, stumbling behind from the armory he dragged along.

"Sieg?! What are you doing here?" Károly asked as the youngest soldier leapt at him with a childish gladness, not answering the former.

The platform thumped and rocked the earth from its mammoth weight and once the mechanism slacked for the crew to enter, Arminius opened its gates for Károly and Siegfried, first to hop in as Arnau stalled at the foot of the tower, under the lights that shone on his fair face glistening from the dripping sweat.

"You forgot...your treaty..." The lancer held up the envelope, bent over, panting for his trickling stamina that widened his commander's eyes.

"So it was! I knew I had forgotten something before we left."
Arminius slapped his own head in disgrace and mumbled.

"Thanks, Arnau." He patted the messenger's back and lent
a shoulder to board the express which conveniently skipped the
stairs.

At the soaring heights where the lift rumbled, slowly
ascending the daring frame, wobbling at each quarter in where
the platform traded chains, the exalted lights of the urban sprawl
were presented a contrasting skyline where for the only night,
the eastern sector was not battered into an extermination ditch.
The skies were clear of the barrages and the heavens opened up
to where the moon ruled all that day in the cloudless populated
ocean of stars. Braziers were scattered for the anti-air defense
corps to maintain hold over the air whilst the coastal walls had
yet to see a breach. And when houses and streets were devoid of
electricity, people found themselves to other means of light and
invited the amber flow of homely lamps and carriages between
the renaissance roofs.

The two, Károly and Siegfried peered beyond the supporting
beams and watched the scene flicker like a recording tape, of the
serene artwork of a silent night whilst Arnau leaned onto the
short barrier that kept him from falling, beside Arminius who
gazed outwards too.

"I still can't get over a stupid hunch." Arminius broke the
sparse silence, resting his arms on the thin smooth rim.

"What is it?" Arnau concerned himself, hearing in his own
way with eyes shut.

To the lieutenant's conflicted speaking mind, the lancer
longed for an answer that became a question,

"What if the Confederates have been fooling us all along?"

"Eos and Radilov." The commander held their names in each
hand whom Arnau could recall.

A shot of stillness swam onto the platform and in the tame
swaying of the tower, frightened himself with goosebumps.
Arminius weakened his grip on the barricade whilst the lift
started to slow and thought,

"It shouldn't have been possible that they allowed us to *gain* so much."

On entering the final stage of the shift into a complete stop, the tower mildly rocked at its arrival, parallel to the battlements itself. When the gates were swung away by Arnau's quick hands, Siegfried was first to bring himself onto the single arched suspension bridge which laid unprotected on either side by a heart-aching plummet to the stairs below. Exhaling his questionably miserable luck, the lieutenant led on and brought the party to the advance upon the destination.

In the cosmic line of mounted defenses, of cannons and riflemen locked onto the lights that shone from the outside world, were an august column reaching no ends. It was to the extent of Arminius' plan that this grandiose sight was achieved and the braziers that targeted the wall every one hundred paces exaggerated the colossus bestowed to appear. Impeccable as it was, the conscripts and recruits were no more, refined into veteran defenders by Adam's instruction, they held true to the lines commandeering the battle front.

"You're thinking too much about it." Arnau rested him, with his vibrating paces taking to the battlements where the party was saluted on their forthcoming.

"They allowed the fleet past their blockades."

"And the attack on the east had stopped since yesterday." He noted, peeking past the parapets that provided the only setting that Arminius only needed to be assured with.

Rising winds climbed until a short exhilarating burst heaved like war drums when the commander's inspired face was exposed to a demon.

"If our victories were false, and knowing that we would win a defense any day,"

"Why would they appear in this form?" He showed the commander the true essence of raised hope.

A canopy of shining helmets on heads, swathed the graveyard basin, unknown to them that it was there where the massacre was executed. Half a million men piled into rows formed the carpet over the mud that must have stretched over and beyond the ridge with the lone tree. The luxurious army. Their armor sparkling from the torches, given spectacularly to showcase their prowess. They chanted and drove their spears into the old earth which enhanced the sights tenfold.

XXX

9 APRUDITE 492
09.04.12018

Arminius Reichner

Everything that was metal were melted for ammunition, blades and bolts. Trees were torn from their roots to make for our loss. Lakes shrunk to house new farms whilst our interior remains rich. In a way, this was the autarky so many states had wanted but failed to attain because of that lack of drive. This is our drive. For all three million to survive and see freedom at the end of an endless underwater tunnel.

Thirty thousand to three hundred thousand men. In the space of five months day by day they were trained by Adam. To the west, the Confederates were trapped under a sawfish's head. Károly's vanguard secured the bridge and encircled over two million for the rear guards of Gin and Wojsław to wipe out. Before Vasilevsky, Kolchakov, Eos or Radilov could show themselves, the lightning had ended. It was only then did the Confederates agree to sue for peace.

But...what if they were only toying with me? To never show and have me lower my guard...

I can't sleep. Not for the past week of being constantly reminded of the burden. Is this what it feels like to lead? To feel death for every soldier in every battle. Or is it the enjoyment of praise that I get out of victories?

Tomorrow, it will end. It'll be the day where the truce is signed. After fighting for nearly half a year for a country which was once foreign to me, this place has become another home.

Why is it that I still worry over the tiniest thing called luck?

Wherever I go, disaster follows. They might as well call me the god of calamity and death.

CHAPTER

31   AGONY

Rod's scepters, adorned with the gold of the rested sun were borne by the color bearers holding still before its fifty legions, summoned to the grand army presented beyond the wall. His brother, Dievas' reddish banners swayed in the stretch of a palatial panel thousands of paces along the ridge which shielded more heads than there were blades of grass. In the rear, settled on the hill were a crowded line of archers whose quivers outnumbered the defender's by twice. And more impressively, were that of all five hundred thousand soldiers uniform. The glimmer of metals and gold, like a Tsar's imperial army, under the moonlight sent a freezing shock heading along the wall that broke into Arminius' fear, feeling a piercing chest pain snap beneath his ribs.

How did they... The commander's cold sweat wept.

That reason, for which he thought, how and why petty militiamen could sweep a vanguard of two million was for that disclosure.

They had spent all this time mustering the elite guard...

"To break our spirits..." He said aloud.

The fanciful columns. The veterans' murderous aura arose into a black storm blanched the four faces. Not there for a peace treaty it seemed to them, but to snatch the city whilst the defender's guards were diminished by trickery. To the wise, the army was the red terror. To the foolish, it appeared weak. Either vision, the physique whom they saw did not lie.

"We should be careful." suggested Arnau, eyeing the distant eastern sector.

"This is their detachment."

Arminius held his breath as the tower shields behind the only crossing swung open, clamping into the saturated ground that created an only corridor of lucent battery torches no one had touched for years.

"By how much?" The lieutenant asked, tensing his clutch on the pommel.

A lean young man, casually dressed, was with a polearm as he escaped the daunting shadows who showed himself, but not his face, onto the fixed, and somewhat arched bridge.

"Four million less." Arnau informed when the one, so daringly faced the wall over eleven times his height, halted at the center.

Near the two pillars that held the minor crest above the slight waves on the moat, the three-pointed spear, and his devilish smile revealed themselves into the purest waning crescent moon's shine that reflected from the clear water surface. At his showing, Arminius' anguish waded into a full blast.

"W-Why...why is he here?" He retreated from the edge and cowered after a decline into a guilt-full shock.

"Arminius..." Aurel Radilov addressed.

The third general rested his spear, which in the dark appeared lapis blue, and he soothedly asked, without need to shout,

"Are you going to let me in?"

The decaying memories which had distanced from the present spurted and ruptured the gates encrypting the forbidden libraries where in the lieutenant's eyes, could see merely a hated enemy.

"Come..." Aurel moaned, lending an innocent hand pointed at Arminius.

"Can't we have tea over our talks?"

Dismayed by the uninvited presence of the cruel, the commander panted, under a feeling that his lungs were being smothered. The profound air that had him aghast clawed into his soul and struck the weakened heart. However in the company of comrades who could see why the lieutenant was unmoving, Arminius spoke in his usual tone,

"Arnau,"

"The pact." The commander requested, holding a hand out, across Károly and Siegfried's eyes.

They stared at the lancer, whose gaze had been set upon the third general for long, thinking in his dreamlike chasm, deprived of any freshening air.

"Arnau." Arminius repeated.

"O-Oh, sure..." His messenger returned and drove his hand

into his jacket and rummaged about.

The four watched as the letter was drawn, dusty and with a hint of beige. It neared the lieutenant's hand who had a clear intention of dealing the cards alone yet another keen messenger thought otherwise.

"Wait up!" Siegfried lunged forward, falling into Arnau's hand that caught his fall.

As the lancer found his footing off the barricades that saved him, Arnau lifted the letter away and handed the draft over Siegfried's head who bore his sights into the commander's, spirited to ask of him.

"Let me deliver it." The younger messenger urged, pleading with his bright eyes.

"You're kidding," Arminius subtly chuckled, leaning more so backwards as Siegfried pushed him to the brink in gifting him the duty of delivering the treaty.

"There's no way I'm letting you."

The lancer halted and spun to his good comrade, the archer, and appealed to him for aid with a shockingly feeble gaze. Siegfried, so heavily fixated on the letter, forgot his dream within the juvenile troubles, or was what they had thought.

"If I can deliver this message," Pointing at himself, he argued.

"Then you can trust me with anything in the future."

"We already do..." Károly stammered but it was taken as an agreement, for Siegfried drew closer and had his face uncomfortably nearer than needed.

"The König will know of me if I keep this up!" The latter excited himself that even the lieutenant captain could not keep up who was so eventually inclined to drive his support to the eager lancer, the remainder quieted.

"No," Arminius declined once more in his tunneled vision that disregarded the Confederates' standing, bored by the empty silence only they could sense.

"I don't want to command you everytime, but..." The lieutenant emphasized.

Yet the stubborn messenger did not give up, however high the winds were which battered his face, he found a way to quell it. Standing, in such a competitive form which reminded Arminius of Julien whenever they fought, Siegfried punched his own heart and offered again,

"Then let me do it."

"If he was Regulus von Eos, then I might've sent you." As he had done for numberless days, Arminius fought.

The commander pointed at the general, who polished his soles on the rocking bridge from the invasive waves, crashing into the wooden beams that retained its stand. From his eifer, locked into him, the impressive tides swashed against the foundations and threw an artistic rush of water high beyond his height. But it did not touch him.

"That's Aurel Radilov," Arminius relaxed his arm and looked into Aurel's cursed eyes, kindly admiring in return.

"Who knows what he might do."

Then feeling a tug on the letter, the commander peered down at a hand desperately holding on, to the soft paper's edge.

"Arminius, still..." Siegfried tried a last plea.

"What good is a messenger if he can't deliver a piece of paper?"

The atlas of Arminius' eyes widened to understand no boundaries, in the image that the divine wind gave. Delicately blowing from the east, the sea's whispers flicked his hair west as the treaty flapped in both their hands.

"Sieg..." Arminius called him by his shortened name, timidly.

And knowing he was left with little choice, the lieutenant sighed, divided among the gut feeling that told him otherwise, any preferable option but to accept the offer.

"I won't ever win an argument will I?" A chuckle matched his disbelieving expression.

Pressing the treaty against Siegfried's chest and before the latter was allowed to be away to consult the fiendish Radilov, the commander noted one last thing,

"If I withdraw you,"

"Don't hesitate." He said.

Siegfried's face lit cheerfully, and needless to show any fault, he determinedly snatched the draft from Arminius' hand and appeared to ready a leap. Feeling a gust press onto his back, the lancer held the letter closeby. As he hopped onto the parapet before anyone could notice, the energized boy scouted the battle lines, who undoubtedly had not seen anything of the likely view, and with a large, honest smile, took one step into the air and fell by his own grant.

"S-Siegfried!" The lieutenant and Arnau reached out, running to his aid but they were too late.

Leaning over the wall, they saw him, having plummeted a great way from safety, Siegfried braced for impact which he believed would have strained more than the shallow landfall which did not harm. A thin layer of dust crowded him, and upon seeing the sound lancer rise to brush his clothes, the two sighed, relievedly.

"Who taught him that?" Arminius glared over his shoulder to where Károly froze.

He pulled a wider smile and winked at Arnau from below and although catching a glimpse of the great Aurel on the same grounds where he stood, Siegfried inhaled a decent gasp of the constraining air, cooling his lungs and pumping blood.

So this is what everyone else has been fighting against... The lancer clenched his fists and in the narrow scale of time, he felt his heartbeat storm.

Like white pearls, eyes gawked from the shadows into the moonlight as the loyal messenger traversed onto the bridge, over the hushed moat where his comrades could see. The breeze lowered, to sweep by his feet, where the sheer crushing air sunk onto him as a battlefield would do. Clinging onto the treaty, Siegfried's arms started to tremble on the nearing over the slight hill where the bridge was highest and as the approach unclothed behind the lifeless wood, he finally saw the general. Who had tremendous aura, nothing that could be compared to what Arminius held, Aurel's sinister language, emitting from his soul, was frightening. That was both guiltless and sinful. Perhaps it was the harmless smile or the celestial spear he carried, everything about the warrior which was told afar ended at the shroud that shielded the truth.

"Oh...?" Aurel chuckled.

"Was Arminius too afraid to face me...?" Easing his grip on the spear, he dragged the polearm to hang beside him.

"So he sent a child in his stead."

With vigilance, the lancer closed the gap, until they met face to face. No words were exchanged between the two in the timeless muteness as created by the halted army. And despite Siegfried's mind in a cycle of reminders to calm, the messenger's heart spurred into serious thumps, stealing the lancer into unpreparedness for the iron fist that stamped into the encounter. It was Aurel who ruled over that bridge.

Gulping, showing a leer of a thousand eyes, that replied to the general, missing weakness, and grasping the lungs of himself, whose aura was borrowed from Arminius' enlarged breath, Siegfried inched a foot onward and sent an acute stare into Aurel's nerves.

"I'm not a kid, y'know." The lancer returned a ferocious response.

Aurel caught the startling reply with an appreciative grin and as he staggered, dipping his spear where the blade met the bridge, the general snickered.

"And, Arminius didn't send me because he's afraid or anything." Siegfried endlessly defended.

"That's only because I'm his runner."

Both voices appeared to have ceased, either amazed by the other or himself. Aurel shed no disregard for the sure messenger who had stolen his eyes' spotlight, shining of the youngster reflecting off his sparkling pupils.

"Kekekeh..." Aurel laughed, although bringing his spear upon his shoulder, he produced no killer's intent.

Instead, a set of particularly sharp canine teeth revealed one's self as the third general opened his mouth.

"Ah...I like you already..." said he in a youthful tone that Siegfried irresistibly blushed to.

Withdrawing his toughened stance, the lancer stepped back and gradually grew another pace of distance between him and the general, releasing his shaking grip on the paper, he rested easy within the influencing bubble Aurel had created. The heap of the trembling atmosphere had all but gone and the moat flowed as normal towards the north.

"Your name?" Aurel asked for.

The messenger hesitated, considering his purpose for he answered proudly,

"Siegfried."

"About that, Sieg..." Aurel shrugged, and requested beneath the clouded heavens that rushed across the night to shelter the moon,

"May I see the treaty?"

Holding out a pure empty hand for the letter, he charmingly smiled, that none could detest and in the shadows, the general in the limelight was the bulwark of a burning warmth that easily deceived Siegfried's apologetic eyes, for thinking him immoral. The lancer peered down at the treaty and as he was pledged to do, handed the envelope onto Aurel's hand who took it, absent of force.

Hence, the lancer's promise succeeded, for Arminius found his breath, and declined his reddened grip on the parapet. Turning to his comrades, they knew the encounter was far from gone, and administered for the Confederate's pending reply, overseeing the encounter for longer.

Aurel railed towards his forces, anxiously abiding with the slow-moving clock, whose shields had been brought to blockade the bridgehead but their spears were passively raised. Away from Siegfried who waited unmoving, the general slipped his thumb over the wax seal and with sufficient pull, drove the lock to snap open. However, he had already suspected the falsehood.

The document slid out of its hermit-like cave and landed in Aurel's hand, though it had an unusually sharp edge that gave the general a slight cut.

A copy...? He noticed, and on the turning of the thin page, his thoughts were confirmed.

Or a forgery...?

Its writing in a dense black ink, that Aurel nee nott hold up to the light and could tell, by that the words had not yet seeped through the page only drove him to be inclined towards his instinct. Nonetheless, he read through the contents, quietly enjoying the serenity that the defenders had provided him enough, and restored the page behind the seal.

You're being awfully discreet... Aurel mumbled, pointing the corners of his eyes at the lieutenant watching from the wall.

Arminius...

Retracing his steps to Siegfried, the third general paused at an arm's distance and looked him in his patient eyes. Aurel grinned, and leaked a restrained laugh, terrifyingly ringing and gently pushed the treaty onto the messenger's chest who caught it from gliding into faraway lands.

"Tell Arminius this..." told Aurel, raising three fingers into the cutting wind.

"We have three options."

The general stuck his hand into a pocket and relaxed his weight onto one foot.

"We could wait for the old dog, Kozlov, to sign the truce..." He suggested while the tone had changed into a chirp of a developing blight that refreshed Siegfried's conscience of the man ever being a yielding enemy.

"But..." Aurel shrugged once more.

"I'm not too keen on waiting..."

Siegfried's senses boiled in the flash of bloodlust that pained and bewildered him from the general who detailed the two remaining options,

"Surrender the city or..."

"We could scale the walls..."

"Then!" Aurel broke the placid waters with the first shout he had ever unleashed in an ending moan.

"Which one will it be, Arminius?" He questioned.

A burden crashed onto Siegfried's body, as if he was strung by burning ropes wrapped around the stones of a failing cliff. From the heartless glare, the lancer could not shift further away and had realized so as his trembling legs were glued to the bridge.

"I-I thought..." The messenger of Aelon stammered.

"Kakakah..." Aurel's chuckle loomed, placing one hand over half his face, he gawked at the lieutenant with an aching smile.

"Do I need to aid you, again...?"

Turning his wrists into the grip on the shaft, the young soulless warrior demonstrated in the audience of Arminius who slowly noticed until as memory served. The form. The stance. Aurel's intelligent grasp of the flow reminded of what the turbulent nature represented.

"Siegfried—!" Arminius and Károly yelled into the tranquility and however quick sound traveled in the early night, nearly reached the lancer who unfroze to witness the happening.

The curve of the bladed swing, carrying dimensions of the present world, rolled, thundering on the level with the arched bridge's apex where the spear's strong spine bent along the rapids that formed into sea waves crashing against the wooden planks. Swooping under the innocent's legs with its blunted edge which shattered his bones, it took Siegfried towards a deathly tumble onto the floor as the spear was held high in the darkening evening. Shining in the mirroring water, monstrously standing above the actual sea, the blade reflected a shattered boy who gasped for help but in the sphere of the ruthless fountain that the general's eifer was named, his crying voice emptied into null. In a swift and fluid pierce, Aurel thrusted the spear into Siegfried's chest, digging past the armor, the blade met flesh and ushered a veil of blood from his collapsing lung.

Lifting his spear from the bursted wound, spilling a fatal volume of the lancer's life which soaked through the bridge and dribbled into the moat below. For his lust had been fulfilled, Aurel giggled at the daunted militia, who could not find themselves to bring their weapons against the fiend where the blood of the choking boy streamed onto his hands whose grip widened. When a shadowed figure leapt to the above and eclipsed the smiling moon, he cried distressingly.

"Sieg!" Arnau's tears merged into tails that flew where the wind took it, above the gagging Siegfried clenching onto his chest.

Unsheathing two great longswords, driving the stinging metals from its scabbards like a braking train on a sparking railroad, the allied lancer held the blades above his head, bracing for a dual impact.

Like artillery fire, and the deafening screeches of a napalm strike, Arnau crashed his blades against Aurel's shaft and launched a shock across the rattled bridge as the embers of the rubbing steel exploded into a fury of booming slashes downward. Like blades of cutting grass, the swift whips mid-air began to slow from the flaming gusts that started to toll the bells of Arnau's limits.

Not yet... He endured until Aurel found a break in his attack.

The precise aim of where he needed to strike widened for the picking and had his eyes taunt Arnau into a vital stop and for a half a second, it had murdered the lancer's momentum. As the final slash came upon Aurel, the general deflected the blade into the open and flipped the spear onto its underside, thrusting the shaft into the lancer's stomach.

"Ack!" Arnau coughed as he was knocked senseless, into the air, but with his vision, the soldier quickly recovered.

Sliding his soles on the bridge, Arnau had his landing swift in a low twist of his toes, empowered by the collecting kei dormant within. And as his eyes sharpened by the stream of blood running from his mouth, he was awakened. Dashing like a winged lance of the past Kaiser's knights where the blast shone clearly unto the rumbling water, his blades were beneath Aurel's instinctive smile.

Whose spear recoiled from its jump on the wood, Aurel stretched his footing until their fighting legs locked and accelerated. The shaft's shoe rebounded into the air before the swords could meet any skin, and smashed its silver into his foe's ribs.

"Ngh..." Arnau gritted his teeth to withstand the pain leaking from his mouth and collected his swords into a cross.

In solidarity, the blades fell into the spear and divided the air between, forcing Aurel to leap back but yet, Arnau did not let up the battle of lightning. Diving each mountainous strike into the Confederate, each was weakened from the last as the tendency and patterns of the lancer started to unmask itself.

Ah...? Aurel casually blocked the predictable cuts and pierces who had begun to gain distance from his spear's arising blades.

Is this it...?

The single strike the general had awaited for, missed, and Arnau overextended his cut too far from the mark he always aimed for.

Damn! He yelled to himself that halted his advance and on the touch down, Aurel summoned a whistling slash that drove the lancer to a backward leap into the sky.

But behind his meander into a settlement like a floating fortress that Aurel gazed up towards, Arnau had returned his swords. And pressed between his fingers were half a dozen short trickster's knives. In an eruptive launch that fired a shockwave, breaking the covering clouds, the barrage of blades flung at Aurel. Who, in an ordinary human's eyes, watched, grinning at the angered downpour. However the steel coat snapped and left to fall were splinters that did no harm to the bridge it plunged onto.

When did he...? Arnau flustered as the glide took him to land on the wobbling bridge.

The lancer knelt on the discording planks before his comrade's cold shaking body. His arms felt heavy that could not draw his longswords and with eyes that shivered from the pain.

No matter...what I try... Spitting blood, tarnishing the wood, he realized, through the schisms, that his limit was nigh.

It feels like...I'm fighting my own shade...

"Out of breath already...?" Aurel mocked the exhausted enemy, flicking Siegfried's old blood from the edges of his blade.

Stains imprinted onto the spear stayed sharp as he stopped where the graves of the knives were. His laugh grew maniacally, holding his stomach, he leaned over the defiled bridge once the swift load of blood took him to the circles of the devils' hell,

"Kakakah..."

With the satisfaction of besmirching his face with a line of blood, Aurel's excitement composed. He trailed his red dyed finger into his mouth and smiled as he licked the sweetness of the juices of the eternally damned.

"You battle with agility..." The general had analyzed, pressing the shaft onto his back.

"But it's difficult, isn't it?"

"Not having an eifer..." He derided.

Sweat poured from Arnau's quivering hands which could not find their grip on the hilts. The thought he was subjected to before an executioner's face, delighted by his suffering, was to catch a breath that took a detour over the decaying space above the mortal aura. Aurel rotated his spear, with a simple flick, onto its blunted end, where the blade faced its back from battle and though the warrior kept a welcoming stance, he was as if to toy.

"What...are you doing...?" Arnau willed to wield a pair of lighter shortswords and eventually found the ground to stand.

"Kekekeh..." Aurel joyously giggled in secrecy and thrust the spear for the lancer's throat.

"There's no point in using a blade when your prey lacks a beating heart..."

The wandering disillusionment of the lieutenant's eyes told of sorrow. Reflecting the dubious stare that Károly gave to the view of Siegfried's twitching hands, they watched from above, within the safety on the walls, wondering why it was they could not act whilst Arnau had run to save his dying comrade.

Why didn't I say so sooner...? Arminius battered himself as his aching head started to throb damningly until a piercing cry of Siegfried's phantom-like voice was nailed into his ear from the ghostly smog.

"Aagh..." He cried, tugging on his own hair in a feeble attempt to neutralize the discomfort, crumbling to the befallen anguish.

"Armin!" Károly called, whose voice was on the softened verges of breaking, catching the commander's arm.

"Sir!" A sergeant shouted across the grand batteries, waving his flare into the air that with one eye, Arminius could spot.

The flare that would determine the battle which the riled officer of the guns held tightly on the trigger, unforgiving to the Confederates as it seemed from his clattering jaw.

Pulling Arminius to rise who clutched one hand over an eye yielding a masked droplet of blood, Károly stumbled.

"Your authorization...for the honor of our own!" The gunman stretched for the heavens and yelled.

"The shameless Confederates promised not to take another life and they do so now?!" Another sergeant hollered over the left to the dejected lieutenant climbing onto the parapet to witness the ensuing battle of the lancer.

Blades clashed and clanked, but every encounter ended with a snap or crack from the thumps of a blunted weapon. Yet without order, the militia could not stay their hands any longer by the honorable command of the individuals' selves. They raised the barrels and steel onwards, aimed at the Confederate rows in a menacing rank of towering shimmering metals. Reconsidering their superiors' orders, the foreign invaders contemplated and inched away from the moat that looked only to be a slump into a mudpit of gore.

Think! The Confederates haven't moved yet! Arminius firmly shut his eyes and punched the barricades with all his force, hoping to drive away the brewing storm.

It was Radilov! Just one person out of the five hundred thousand!

I can't kill them all... The commander argued with himself that endlessly spiraled into his downfall.

Of all the times! He frowned, on opening his eyes to a breeze passing under Károly's arm which tried to wrap itself around his comrade.

I thought I was over this...

"Hold your fire!" Arminius decided with an unsure

exclamation as his racing heart drummed.

To his men must have thought him mad, staring upon him with uncertainty, the commander explained,

"There's still a way to bring things back—!"

"Armin!" Károly shook the lieutenant to wake from the idealized dream and snapped his concious to look the archer in his tearing eyes.

"If we don't do anything now..." He slumped onto his knees, wringing Arminius' hands, the warrior wept over the commander's legs.

"He won't last..."

"At least, let us bring Sieg...and Arnau back..." The archer sobbed louder till the humming sky was stuffed with his gasping bawl.

Tears swept like flash floods from the torrential tropics which plagued Arminius to let off a shy droplet who doubled his grip on both Károly's head and the gilded sword.

Parrying the successive hits of Arnau's separating combinations of jabs and slashes, nothing seemed to pierce through the defense of Aurel's shield of the merciless spear where for every wrong, was corrected by a cruel bashing. The messenger coughed at a fracture of a bottom rib but pressed, with perhaps more vigor into the spear which repelled breezily. Arnau's footsteps tapped from the center, and leapt to the flanks, crashing into the railings upon discovering his loss in perception.

"Entertain me more..." Aurel moaned, holding his reversed spear.

Sieg... The lancer apologized, ahead of his sights splitting into unclear smudges as he stumbled.

I can't hold much longer...

Grasping the aiding beams, he wiped a blot of blood, smeared beneath his lips and disappeared from the naked eye in a sprint across the crossing. And at a sound-breaking jump that rocked the bridge, Arnau rocketed into a crescent hop into the form of a mechanized drill and dived towards his foe. Crossed slashing, however rapid, the cuts were all too shallow, easy to dodge and fend.

"Are you close to falling...?" Aurel taunted in the shower of sparks, pleasurably beaming.

The general toughened his grip, stirring Arnau to approach closer when once more, the latter's cut fell into his trap and plummeted towards the great whirling spear that brushed up gently. A burst of an eifer exploded from the ground and shot itself in an uppercut, charging as a battering ram would do, and crashed the spear's shoe into Arnau's face, sending a rash jolt to the head. His nerves fell half asleep. The shockwave blasted from the impact and dispersed a hefty layer of sweat where the lancer's hair sprung upwards and inept to cover his chest, Arnau was stricken by a second punch for the heart jumped, afflicting a leading suffering incomparable to anything else. He was tossed across the planks in a brutal roll, like a skipping rock, his body was hurled aloft at the breaks and dents of the bridge and eventually came to a halt as the messenger's face was bruised and cut by the splinters he took apart.

The dust cloud shrouded poor Arnau's rest, with his blades flung to the far reaches, he was entirely disarmed.

"Kakakah..." Aurel released a brief sadistic snigger, strolling nearer to the lancer.

"Can I torture you in peace now—?"

Arnau clenched his fists and forced his broken body to rise onto all four limbs. Shakingly, he coughed unstoppably, as rounds of viscous saliva, scarlet by the staining of his blood, shot.

"Oh...?" Aurel voiced.

"You can still fight?"

Lunging a leg ahead, and with his sapped strength, Arnau brought himself to stand with a coarse cry,

"Haargh...!"

The lancer lifted his head and bathed himself in the unclean air, providing a coaxing warmth to peace by the wishes of the moonlight holding his head.

It's no use... He gave his life to fate in his trembling arms and legs who could not run and could not fight.

"Arnau!" A voice yelled from the embankment, too far, it appeared, to save his comrade who looked back and found an imperial bolt, rumbling around a ring of soil lifted under the brimming eifer.

With the least hesitation, and a dumbfounded yet relieved

expression, Arnau leapt from the path that faced Aurel to his elation.

"Come..." The latter invited, reviving his spear into its bladed tip.

A spawn of a thundering creation discharged a voltage of a kingdom's supply, whilst the earth around cracked and levitated into a universal circle around the shocks. The seas of a snapping wave sailed into Arminius' veins, amplified by Zeus' wrath and at the crown of his oblivious boundary. His eifer of the lightning field tore the ripples of his shockwave into threads on the meteoric lift across the apparently impossible space. On the step into the leap, the water broke beneath the embankment. The flash, if it could be described in that manner, beyond light, acted like the stroke of a brush from the instability. There was no direct course, before the searing blade slashed into Aurel's unbreakable spear. A burst of the gale from the first impact impeded the course of the wild winds as it exploded into branches of ivory arcs which cut into the general's flesh, tearing a fresh canal of blood along the swift sword. Sliding into the utmost length that he could fly, Arminius turned his feet to grip the smoothened wood and burned his rubber soles with a screeching halt as the climax of time was reached. The waves of the displaced seas finally crashed against the opposite bank and like a chain, parts of the bridge smashed into chunks and committed to its descent into the slowing clamor of lightning in water.

The lieutenant guided his blade to the defense and turned the sword into his hands to keep a steady breath as the spray of the dirtied sea rained onto his face.

Ah...I've used too much... Arminius panted, whose arising heat took shape in the form of a stunning storm, making light of the numbness of his fingers.

I haven't fought in months...my body's forgotten how to move...

Aurel's wound cascaded as the beads dripped from his sweatshirt where one could wring it but it would not dry. Yet, the warrior did not stagger, over his blood pool of late. He pivoted on one foot and with deathly divine stare, he gazed into Arminius' torrid eyes.

The Confederates began to shuffle, ever closer towards the lieutenant's back, whom he found himself surrounded by enemies on all fronts with little space to escape.

"Now…" Aurel raised an arm and halted his army, who were riled by the sight of allied blood.

"Arnau." said Arminius, swinging his eyes between the ally and foe.

"Get Sieg out of here." He told, steeling the influx of his eifer.

Arnau climbed onto his feet by the aid of the shattered railings and coughed from the bothering affliction thudding on his chest.

"But…" The lancer tried but saw the predatory sharpness of his commander's pupils.

"Now!" Arminius commanded with his roaring voice tingling in Siegfried's head.

Despite his deepest willingness and desire to fight for his spirit still burned, Arnau turned away, limping over the wooden arch in pain, and mumbled behind Aurel's disheartening shadow,

"Understood, lieutenant…"

His departure, never desperate, marked a change in the storm, who the Radilov broke into a smile towards.

"Kekekeh…" The general warmed up with two bitter slashes to his flanks.

With the fierce waves bursting through the trails of fences that ripped the beams from its loosened nails, the attack threw the barricades into the turbulence that clawed the splinters to become one amidst the rapids were so stinging.

"Well…" Aurel blockaded the path to home which the lieutenant needed to pass, through Confederate blood or his own drowning.

"You're *my* toy anyways…" He pointed.

A detonative blast of the agile zip snapped into the air with an electric blade charged for a twister that found its prey. Arminius swooped, shallow as if a decoy, though the impact sparked, and made his fall, autumn-like. Reversing his grip that seemed to break the circuit of lightning, he sent a bolt past Aurel's spear and in an eight pointed star dashed in bursts of matchless energy. By the ascent he gradually climbed the stairs, awing both enemies and allies alike, of critical strikes and shot, after a shockwave busted a crumbling plank, into the high heavens that superseded the walls. At his grandest heights he witnessed slowly, that no matter how much he had fought, the Confederates had not moved, and so gave his thanks to the God of War who smiled with a sprint of thunder crashing through the clouds.

"Don't you find this pleasurable…?

"Arminius?" Aurel asked, peering up at the hastening firebolt.

He engaged his stance widely and twirled the spear into a sapphire plate that shielded the skies. With the whirlwind, waves conflicted at arches and interlocked at the point of the cursed blade to Arminius' drive towards the earth. The lightning snapped at the head of the advance, and unthinkably routed into a softened breeze.

What—! The commander had realized beyond return where his sword was weaved into the snare of Aurel's collected spear and with a good reminder the two were incomparable, the third general incited a splitting drive of eifer in Arminius' second of blunder.

Plunging the lieutenant, attached to the spear, with a ferocious blow into the fracturing bridge, the gusts of a scathing ring whisked around the tormented soul under the fiend's grasp.

Tributaries of blood flowed from his mouth. Young Siegfried, whose hands were gently held onto Arnau's, shaking beneath a blanket of the wintry cold that their warmth could not break through. Slumped against the wall, his legs were shattered, although unseen, were bruised into an ugly construct as if no bones remained. The gaping wound in the left chest, with each breath widening it, stained the stone with the painting of a comet's tail. To his best, was not enough, Károly's cloth did not stop the fountain-like spillage by the wrath of a crippled lung which was not to recover despite his comrades' great worthy cries.

"A-Arn…" Siegfried wheezed, crying from unaccepting death, whilst the blood choked him, he held his dear friend with many dreams to be had.

Shuddering in a red bath, the lancer clutched his collar, releasing wrestled gasps, trying to kick the pain but his legs would not move. When an opening showed itself with a torturous cough, an aqueous crimson waterfall spewed and painted a rose petal on Arnau's face. Siegfried's eyes, half-opened, lost its color and fell, swarmed with tears unto a stone deathbed, his head fell onto

Arnau's chest.

"S-Sieg…" The last lancer gripped strongly onto Siegfried's scent and pushed his head against himself with streaming tears,

"Sieg!" Károly could hear a muffled outburst, bringing his coat over his nose, he sobbed without noise.

Why…is it…like this…? The archer asked of the heavens watching upon them and cursed,

"This world…"

Arminius dragged his body to stand, where his shallowest cuts dribbled into the river over the edge. Like Arnau before him, he stumbled, yet whilst Aurel was in the clear for victory, the general did not seem much like so. Instead, the predator toyed with his rival.

Letting a deafening war cry, the lieutenant tightened his blood-soaked palm on the defiled sword and spun into a vertical blade. Leaping over Aurel's height, the Confederate grinned as the blades clashed, for the younger to inch ever closer until he tossed him away. Arminius wearily landed, pressing his hands against the bridge to break his fall. His eifer wildly charged and exploded into an illuminating burst of light where he took to a dash across the shaking floor. Three shocks busted the air into condensed clouds and at the slightest gap, he unholstered the gifted pistol, pulling the trigger before the aim had settled, firing eight shots through Aurel's hair. The bullets had missed.

"Kekekeh…" The general taunted, thrusting his spear through Arminius' hair that had skimmed his face.

The rampage was undying but Arminius' numbed slashes grew sluggish and powerless to turn the tides.

"This doesn't feel right…" Aurel flicked his spear down and caught Arminius' freed guard.

Punching upwards, the polearm rammed its bloodied shoe into the lieutenant's head and stunned him by the peak of the jaw, throwing Arminius into the sky who revived his broken mind and glared at his target. He clasped his teeth and with a hellish thunder that cladded the burning blade, the soldier of Aelon blitzed through the air and bombarded Aurel with a vivid fury that he felt sink into his bones. By the ignition of the thunderous field of crisp lightning, the wind splashed against the breaking bridge as cracks gave way.

"Don't you want to kill me, *Armin*?" Aurel provoked again who felt a sharp thrust in the denseness of Arminius' strikes.

However, which slowed, and unable to adjust his slipping grip, Arminius packed his last breath into the final act when the general calmly swooped a current of bladed waves where one made a swift mark at the commander's flesh.

"Ach..." His eyes quivered as he felt the steel hack through his torso.

Arminius could detail the very vicious twist that pushed him to the depths of agony until he was cast onto the bridge.

The sword dug into the wood to lighten the plummet, barely on both legs, and skidded many paces from his foe as he made for futile pauses to catch his breath when the same daubed blade broke the moon's glorious panel and struck with sparks, onto Arminius' nimble steel.

"Ngh..." He huffed, with his own sword burrowing into a shoulder.

His expression was both pained and deaf to defeat when stubbornness would cost him his life if he chained himself to the defensive.

"That's a cute face you're making..." told Aurel as the cut oozed further.

An inflamed arrow, stealing the night of its darkness, whistled towards the bridge as its course was set in stone. The general had nowhere to flee unless it meant breaking his strangling hold on Arminius' life. Aurel twirled his spear from battle and deflected the quick arrow, then almost as planned, his spear rounded about and knocked Arminius onto the Confederates' embankment with his swift turn. The Aelon commander thudded, face first on the ground and like a latch, the mud weighed him to fall.

Cannon fire of ancient black gunpowder; the draw of rifle bolts of the modern battlefield; and thunking bowstrings from the old lifted volleys and a barrage of piercing metals hurling towards the trapped enemies who could neither step back into their own comrades, nor forward into the burial-like moat. Their bodies were torn and limbs shredded; heads flung and organs gunned into the cardinal red sky, as holy as any night could be. The valley of a necropolis showed itself once more to let the blood seep into its muddied ground for the long dead grass to remember the preceding massacre. Screams cried and for once in Arminius' ears, their sounds were only human.

Whenever you may kill, Sekiya... A distant but hated voice of his injured childhood within the harbor of his sleep called out to him.

On any battlefield...

Remember to slay that is without suffering... The man said, shaded beneath the pink flowers of spring.

Is that why I had to...? Arminius' younger conscious asked whose lightness in his voice was innocent and foreign.

To suffer...? His older self told.

He woke to the sight of his hand that was clenched onto the sword, dimmed by Aurel standing before him, but his spear was not in a posture searching to end a life.

"It's beautiful..." Aurel bathed in the immaculate display of thousands of fireworks and splatter of bones and blood, warmed by the shells and their bodily heats.

Shooting from the alight wall that Arminius had armed to his own will, were the shrouds that protected him from the invaders who started to make their advance. They waded through the moat, and tried to crawl past the bridge but the gunfire was such too relentless that bodies dumped themselves into a blood wall of their own.

Arminius rose to his knees, simply to see the annihilation of human life who were never Confederates in his eyes. But the people who found a path to taste freedom from the raining bullets and cannon grape rounds.

"Too bad..." Aurel knelt to the lieutenant's eyes and gladly spoke.

"I wish I had taken something from you, before..."

"This..." He looked overhead to the picturesque purge and returned to his foe's eyes.

Touching Arminius' face, his hand printed an obvious color, which, with a surge of all circles of pains screeched yet the lieutenant was left perplexed, instead, undisturbed by the anguish. Who paid no will to the happenings around him, Arminius wondered why it was that a sadistic but warm hand felt like pins stabbing into his mind, and though it was soiled by blood, he discovered it to be understanding. Similar to a past he must have thought. But when he peered back, the young general had gone.

Kneeling helplessly beside a mountain of corpses, the

commander's heart collapsed. Gagging and choking, a forceful cough splatter a severe pond of blackened blood that shunned the small streams that once flowed.

"Aagh..." Arminius clutched his jacket over his heart and squeezed but the overflow worsened until his whole mouth ran with a deluge, spewing a dramatic downpour onto the earth.

The voices of the devils started to scream and the ghouls silenced the world for he was under a coat of allied shells, striking the Confederates who neared him.

"Armin!" Károly's tears remained for Siegfried and his hands rapidly released quivers' worth of arrows.

"Do not yield!" The keen sergeant commanded as too was aided by his own men.

"Protect the commander!" He yelled to the militiamen, desperately in the fire, being unable to bear the guilt if the cherished governor of their lives perished.

The renewed sparks flourished and covered the ceiling with fresh paint splattered onto the canvas. A human wave, steadfast with their chain rushed across the moat but there, they cowered, unable to do anything but to wait for artillery that had not appeared in the time of so many taken to the next life. To his greater dismay, a body thumped, ahead. Whose eyes paled and the soldier's jaw smashed to shards by an unfortunate dozen pellets into his mouth that hung open for the tongue to dangle in the free.

"S-Stop..." Arminius beseeched with his voice stuttering and eyes shuddering for he started to whimper, vomiting creeks of blood.

"I-I can't..." He stammered with his eyes closed, hearing bullets whizzing overhead.

The sound of death muted anymore cries, suffocating him with another disgorge, hurtling a flood when there was an expected silence.

Thus, the paradise of the reapers of a burgundy red hue, under the eternal shadow of the eclipsed sun held the floating island which was chained to the abyss of hell. A lone tree grew, ushering a river of old flesh, and regrew its bark and leaves with recent hands and skin. Nevertheless, its sap leaked. Knowing the place well, Arminius hugged himself in the chilling winds, breezing along his nakedness within the half-conscious world who was soaked by kneeling in the cascading lake.

"I-I don't need your paradise!" Arminius cried towards the judging eyes who gawked.

"Just...someone..." The boy whimpered, equating a thousand soft echoes that reverberated in the roots of the God of Death.

You're willing to use your tongue... The tree groaned, surprised in its monotone.

But alas...you are broken...

Its hands extended outward and reached for Arminius' shoulders who approached a calm in the ripples that he shuddered in, shyly weeping in the corner of his own.

Have I not told of your shattering mind? Death asked, dauntingly.

That may summon a hell.

Arminius sniveled, holding onto his body with a grip that slipped from his skin as the ghoulish hands approached his ears, mumbling from its mouths which lifted through the ruptures in the rotting flesh.

By your hand, a heavenly world shall be carved...

For you will become its god... It crept.

"Please..." Arminius wailed into the river where it was a stained mirror for him to look into.

Upon the high skies the clouded judgement will rest, They chanted at the roundtable hold of the gods.

And at the schism of your soul, the blood moon hears...

The Crimson God. The bellowing tree's words dampened and its figure dissipated upon the world falling on his revival into humanity.

Blood and embers of the massacre drenched Arminius' hair that became the color of the earth and sky that night. Which the real sound rain cleared at the landfall of a storm, he knelt, surrounded by corpses or dying souls. Confederate fighters flew daringly into the storm over the capital, and battled the guns against the aerial. A bombing run blasted the city and the fires raged. Mothers screamed and orphans bawled in the cleaved alleyways which were fueled by Arminius' softening cry.

"Károly…" Arminius felt a familiar presence approaching him, so he wept his name.

"Why…why did you…?"

The comrade, unknown to the limits of sorrow, lifted his head for the archer to see, who faltered on a step, having been frightened by Arminius' devilish tears of blood that peacefully flowed to his chin as the streams dripped.

"Armin…" Károly called for, reinforced by a squad of sharpshooters collapsing the lives around.

Then an echo of a boom breached the air, rinsing the sky of all screams. They peered north, at an explosion blasting a dune of winds from not too far. The cloud soared for all deities to see and the fire within burned into a demon that there only one's scent could have been.

Eos…

XXXI

10 APRUDITE 492
10.04.12018

Arnau Rieding

I was surprised to have found out that you only lived across the border, in the valleys that I pass weekly to serve my local lord. When we were in training, you spoke like you came from a fantasy that I could've only imagined to have been entirely different from mine. Though one thing I never understood was why you revered the König so much, all for wanting your family to be recognized and given a dynastic name.

Sieg was the fourteenth child of his family. His older siblings he had never met were killed in wars against Vrannken, Leken, Danen and more, spanning across a decade. Battling was a tradition or something along those lines. He was expected to follow the same path and his parents thought the unlucky number thirteen had gone, and that he would be the one to break the cycle. He knew his family had poured everything for his safety when he departed. Even the two gold pieces were the last coins of their home. If he told me earlier...then...

Remember...remember the face you made when you first saw the capital? I was hoping that you could make the same smile when...

What am I supposed to tell them...?

CHAPTER

32

SCOURGE OF THE HANNSEN

The shade of the cream yellow paper darkened and brightened in the ripples of the wind brushing along its words which were lightened by the distant lights of fire and beams. With the salt in the air of the changeable sea, he felt his hand tighten on the turn of a page. But he paid no care for that Julien was so engrossed that the rumbles of the distant fleets, and the mechas on the island fortress disturbed him not. The night was calm and the embers flickered. Alone in the sector that had seen a hurricane blow. And whilst the clouds rushed overhead, tugged by the hands of the unknown gods, his mind was clear as a cleaned lake was so.

"The Eastern Expedition…" Julien read from a box of its own, leaning against the chalk white parapet where the breezes fanned against his back.

"In five days time, the grand western fleet will embark on a voyage to relieve our forces in Jōngoku."

"Four hundred thousand have been recruited so far…" His eyes scrolled across its lines.

A crackle of thunder boomed across the city and the wind was suddenly sweeping, blowing the newspaper from his hands when he peered up and saw a row of sparks ignite the western wall.

"A-Artillery?" He frightened himself as the dozen who manned the battlements gazed across the roofs.

Then, to the cannon fire, where his eyes were set, the air converged into a dense fog and detonated into a swarm of fire forcing a black smoke cloud that pierced its head like a beacon to the stars. Debris shot across the city, with steaming trails landing boulders and sharpened pebbles on the unlucky folk. Who were crushed and smashed against the old town's paths, painting houses with a collage of flesh, a repulsive firestorm engulfed the beginning streets as from the cover entered the elitist cavalry. The scent their leader carried was familiar that Julien remembered. That was the taste of royal silver worth a thousand crowns, lingering within the flash of blood.

A squadron of jets colored on the tails and noses with bands of red and white, blasted their antique engines overhead and at a low passage, skimmed through the skies to burden the fleeing morale that the eastern sector maintained. As the hatches opened, batches of napalm bombs sprinted through a short freedom which were dumped at the people below, looking up, disoriented by the steel cloak binding their fates as the combustion charred the city. A gush of flames glowed in Julien's eyes where the infernal heat cried. Showers of coldness poured as rain unto the reflections at sea of the fiery barrages. Their attacks had restarted. The unpredicted storm washed the high waves against the breakwater stones, crashing old floating corpses back home.

Julien undid and pulled his cloak over his head, letting waterfalls take its course over the hang onto the emerging puddles beneath. The hollow mist, unseen on the battlements but had flooded into the streets, froze breaths other than the lieutenant's and in the far island of the middle fortress, the Confederates were found to be mobilizing.

"Did Arminius...fail...?" He thought, then turned to the outward sea.

"It can't be. Their attacks are too coordinated..."

The lieutenant pressed his body against the parapet and scouted the coastal bank. Although the spray was harsh, he could barely see the curve running around the city until two patrol boats showed, anchored at a small excluded pier. From his shallow pockets without much in store, Julien held a brass trench whistle and gasped to fill his lungs.

Where the mist was thickest, submerging the coast with murky shrouds laid atop in layers, was a pier, newly erected. The harshest waves, tattered by ripples of the brutish rain, rocked the wooden stilts that the platform was placed upon, and carried the ropes to strain on every wash away. Its docked vessels were neither large nor too frail for they sat upright from capsizing in the torrent. Gray, the boats blended with the fog where each mounted an aged machine gun on its bow with a little less than thirty rounds. Their ports and starboards were walled around the shielded helm whilst the sterns provided a narrow access to the cramped deck. But it was there, beneath the shadows of the night and wall, no one could see, that the four soldiers of distinct figures, were able to hide themselves from the light and hail of artillery.

The continual bridge shone with racks of electrical torches, marching towards the fortified island with stomps resounding into echoing streams of haze levitating above the pale waters. They stared at the fast mobilizing ranks, longing for the signal whilst cramped onto the confines of the howling pier.

"I didn't think the Confederates could last this long." Colt mocked who was the only to do.

A piercing whistle, high pitched and sharp through the lifeless rain, blew, tugging everyone's eyes to the commander's post. Awaiting the second to the chime, the small squad gulped when the one in thought huffed the next shrill shriek.

"That's the signal." As he opened the door to his boat, Colt pointed out with a quick glance.

"See! What did I tell you—?" said Lev, waving his spear about the rain drops.

"Get...on..." Miklós' giant's foot rammed Lev's back with the fury of a Spartan's kick, hurling him over the door onward where his face planted onto the deck as the titan leapt on board, gesturing for Alexandria and Colt to do so too.

Weighing their hands on the door handle to the pilot's helm, they entered through and were greeted by the intimate rooms. Surrounded with a ring of window panels, dated and rusting, the squad were not all too pleased to see the lack of seats, for that some legs were ready to collapse from waiting long. There was a rubber wheel, black, and was no wider than two usual hands which was settled beside a worn throttle in Colt's quarters, no different than Lev's in the bland, colorless interior. Their eyes complained at the sight of the dinginess.

"Gods, what were they thinking giving us this junk..." A master of whining, Colt, flicked the switches for lights, but the circuits hardly worked, whilst Lev's vessel shot a blinding beam into the dense sea.

"Alexandria, check the comms." The lieutenant signaled as he readied his hand on the engine switch.

His faithful comrade reached for the controls and analyzed every switch which was in Danne. And needed to memorize the colors and codes on the muddling panel instead, it was until she came across the one that seemed most likely. Alexandria turned the loosened dials before a wave of static flooded into their ears.

"Can you hear me?!" Lev blasted through the portable radio, with a deafening screech, and could hear his voice disorientingly replay past the raging rain and rattling windows.

A comedic silence held eerily sealed within the prison-like helmsman's booth when Colt clicked the transceiver.

"I can hear you! I can hear—" He blared before Alexandria rudely ceased the transmission with a click.

"Quiet." She demanded, leaning closer to prepare for a snatch as Colt flicked his hand from the girl's biting reach.

"Yes, mom…" The lieutenant teased.

Reaching down for Alexandria's hand, he put her aside and revived the links in the communications.

"Anyways, I have a question for all of you." The lieutenant stressed, switching the key left and right though the motor annoyingly stalled.

"About the plan." Doing away his soaked cape, he peered out at the shaded column of what appeared to be walls.

"Good that Julien posted us here, but…"

"How the hell are we supposed to fight off a fortress on our own?" asked Colt, pointing out the clearing fog by the gods' hands that wiped the mist from the revealing path.

The island of Salinn, a rocky behemoth that floated between the Suede port of Malmuzh and the Danne capital of Haven, was a star fort deserving the name as the maiden of the Hannsen. Its three hundred cannons could flay a fleet and wear its sailors as jewels in the five grand layers of the high castle, as the heights grew as the stone walls tightened. Whilst its sandstone barracks could provide home for a legion of ten thousand, the pillaged courts and ransacked palace of the summer retreat was shaped to prevent the bane of fires and deter shells from breaking into its complex of underground tunnels. No one who ever owned its control were to fall until the present, where unless modern navies allowed it to.

"Focus." Miklós spoke into the radio and steered Colt on

course.

"Just stick to the plan." Alexandria added.

Their engines finally gave its stubborn loyalty to the desperate flicks of the switch and rumbled, chucking suffocating smoke from its hard-working motor. Once the two pilots pushed the throttle to the half, the propeller spun, which started to drive the vessels onwards, leaving a trail of bubbling whitewater.

"The four of us?" Colt sniggered, sprinting the boat beside Lev's uneasy drive to the south.

"Might as well make this a suicidal mission." said he, pushing the throttle to its full to a diverging departure towards the east, skipping the hull over the roughened waves.

Over the humps of the prolonged prelude of the seas' orchestra howling at the battering of the fast sailing vessel, Colt held the wheel steady which shook and flinched for every lift over the crests into the air. Rocking his head back and forth from the hops which splashed a glaze onto the rattling windows, not caring less for it may pierce the boat, the lieutenant daringly latched onto the throttle, wanting to take flight.

Without the lights who tried its best to flicker, the Confederates never noticed the boat, even with the search from spotlights on the strait's colossal castle. The pair skimmed across the water like a harmless skipping pebble. But his playfulness would not allow to keep still and whilst Colt was at a steady pace, came on the approach of the westernmost bridge.

"Are you in position?" Lev shocked the two with his dark liveliness.

As Colt piloted the rudder to face the boding bridge, expressionlessly staring down upon him, he pulled the throttle towards himself and gently drifted to a halt. Letting Alexandria take her position near the machine gun's post, the lieutenant watched the girl closely as he picked up the radio.

"I'm sure I arrived earlier than you did." As lighthearted he could be, Colt joked before turning off the transmission, to gaze upwards at the drab structure.

The concrete pillars were many layers of heavens high, and at their feet, were towers of aged stone, covered by an algae coat that stretched to the boundless depths. Where the strait channeled through the gaps of the bridge, the foundations were tough, and the currents had to swerve around the manmade bulks of slabs in avoidance, for that the bridge stretched beyond the fog, it reminded him of an old home.

Knocking on the window, Colt gathered Alexandria and asked through the glass,

"You ready?"

Ignoring him, the girl turned her head towards the blank, soulless being whilst the columns of infantry and tanks endlessly rolled over the road with the intention of an invasion. Alexandria aimed her spear at the center of a stack of two pillars and weighed herself into a formidable stance.

"Just don't capsize the boat," Colt watched carefully.

"I'm not swimming back to shore."

Alexandria's hood fluttered from her head as the golden eifer of justice's kei sprung from the veins within, trailing through the wood of the shaft into the metal blade. Its zeal glowed. At the rumblings of the sea, her aura began to power and the charge weaved the future tales of carnage. Almost as if she was in prayer, the soldier closed her eyes.

Encouraging the most holy kei that Colt's sights were pinned upon, the sign of Libra of a balancing scale, burned into the air with all vigor. At the tip of the spear where the gold was brightest, the symbol calmly sunk into her mind having felt the recreation of the surrounding imagery, Alexandria's focus was ripe.

The capital eifer of a short glimmer corrupted the spear in a shaking spool of the hopeful gold discharging a ray, like lightning across the waves which made way for the shooting beam. The destructiveness of the shockwave blasted the sea into sound ripples, defeating the tides with their expulsion from the boat that was lunged backwards. Its thunderous echo traveled afar whilst a tunnel of water encased the hurtling streak. At its spearhead that drilled into the first then second pillars with ease, the cannon ripped a hole in its dazed body.

Its cracks widened and were on the collapse. The arches could hold no more until the pillars had snapped along the middle spines, and the concrete began to crumble and took the dwellers above in a ruthless surprise.

"Vasily..." A Confederate officer tapped his comrade's

shoulder, pausing him at the edge of the bridge.

"Can't you feel—?"

A calamitous explosion of a devil giant who gnawed at the furthest bridge engulfed the sky in an aurora of the Sorbe's hellfire, flowering through the clouds, the cover of fog, near the epicenter, surfed from the dread, taking the darkened helm of the fathomless jaw to swallow their entry into the capital unto the boiling pits of the demonic growl.

Then the cracks beneath them gave away and collapsed upon the seas with its rubble gushing a freakish crest. Colt pushed the throttle onwards and took to a sharp turn in the returning temper of the waves, shutting the door as Alexandria took her earned rest in the booth. They looked back, and saw the likes of falling scree. The chain of neverending bodies crashed onto the stones below, smashing their heads to burst open an array, rias of blood.

At the cover of a blind eye, a guard rotated his shift and turned his mark towards the worried barracks beholding the disasters to the east and west. Peeking from one flank to the other, to a ravine, bustling with fire of the leaking fuel the tanks had held, as the other had silenced. Their disbelief could not grasp the truth that was laid out as a dish on a table that the perpetrators' identities were so blatant. And whilst the command confused themselves amongst restless squabble, the food had cooled and they lost the tracks of whom those belligerents were and where they resided. The castle had noticed, all ten thousand, perfectly late, that the island was stranded unless the allied fleet were willing to aid. But their formation told the contrary.

Providing the opportunity for an access to the corners of the fortress where the shoreline wall was too high and too steep for any odd soldier to notice, Lev anxiously drove the patrol boat towards Colt's wave on the starboard of his vessel. And at the weary docking, Miklós flung the tangled rope across the gap and lassoed their boats together tightly until he was sure the vessels would not wander. The warrior knocked for Lev and stepped over the clashing bulwarks to a confrontation with a disgruntled lieutenant.

"Come on in to my home." Colt welcomed, leading the two

towards the helm's room that was too compact to fit more than four.

The hospitality was chilling.

"It sure is warm here." Lev played along, shuddering as the door was slammed to close.

"Lemme get straight to the point." said Colt with a shift that broke his worthless act.

Yet, he gave time for the squad to settle, leaning against the windows that sounded set to crack.

"We can't find the damned entrance." The lieutenant slammed a fist on the roof of the boat and scoured the seeping water soaking the bricks.

Pointing at the great wall that provided no pier nor a vent for them to infiltrate, they were simply faced under the shadow of a barren, straight cast that could not be scaled, painted onto the remaining lengths of the island's coastline that had nothing dissimilar.

"There's supposed to be a port here, isn't there?" Lev questioned, removing a neatly folded map from his luckily dry pockets.

Greedily, Colt snatched the paper off his comrade's hands and unfolded it for himself to see.

On the map detailing the island and the fort that was originally drawn by a steady hand, the borders were freshly printed whilst the copying machine had replicated its antique buff brown nature. But it was that which piqued Colt's interest. Why the map was fashioned so olden from the calligraphy to its traditional Zhormannik names.

Süd-Salzinsel...? The lieutenant thought.

"But this should be it..."

Then it all came to be as his eyes spotted a bland watermark signed along the corner.

"Lev!" Colt yelled, startling the black-haired boy.

The enraged lieutenant dragged Lev by the ear and pressed his face upon the map where the date was clear.

384. It was written.

Slapping the Rus' head with the roll of paper which was dropped onto Lev's hand, Colt eased his breath and looked outwards at the storm and wall who mocked him with the crash of thunder. The rain which struck the frontal windows fattened, dealing a bath which distorted the squad leader's troubled face behind the glass.

"It's probably been sealed off since then." He assumed when a gust stormed into the quarters.

"Move." Miklós shoved his comrades away and marched into the tears of the above.

"Miklós!" Lev called but the Sorbe was gone.

Trailing around the booth that sat the ones in the warming interior whose eyes followed Miklós to the bow, they scrambled to Colt's side and watched the giant's body pose himself before the wall. The warrior raised his spear at the horizontal and swayed back like a bat, pulling a leg to the rear until his foot bashed the booth with a shaking clank.

"Hey...Miklós...wai—" asked Lev, in an uptight pool of sweat.

His demon's eyes brightened and with a limitless gasp where the streams of air could be seen sucked through his teeth, the warrior stomped, jolting the boat. Pressing his grip into the splintering spear, he slashed the polearm in a furious arc which took a change in the wind, and crashed its blade against the wall. The booming shock, with the coincidental infuriated drum of thunder, bludgeoned the cold stone that carved open a crater. As Miklós' spear sharply snapped at the middle shaft, and was flung towards the spectral fog, the rocks and dust crumbled to clear unto the sea to unveil an expanding cave, where the gales of underground air blew slight rippling waves pulsating against the boats' hulls. Any could have heard the frightening crumble if not for the storm, as the way opened to unveil the harbor in the plan.

"Thanks...Miklós..." told Colt and Lev, bewildered.

The waters were a dump, stilled for a century, hence the reek and algae growing over the oil black surface. Stagnant and damp, that was the underground. Arched with well-preserved Rumann bricks layering the leaking ceiling, like an aqueduct, the port was flourishing of forsaken life that dripped from its pipes into the reeking waters. Whilst its buildings and piers had a hint of medieval constructs, the villas and the harbormaster's grand setting contrasted the drabness with the monotonal fire brick red tiles and limestone walls. Yet the further the squad traversed deeper into the cavern, the eras and ages started to show a landscape unlike another.

Stalactites were mounted from the ceiling, dribbling with the seeping rain onto the boats' drying decks. And however ancient these structures were, was renewed by the rust brown machines, like trees towering over the heritage site, that seemed foreign. It was nothing the Dannes had built for the definite distinctiveness in the smell of gas and metalworks. And at the slow admirable drift past a lost Zhormannik submarine, Lev spotted the iron eagle of the legendary king, Erwin.

"They haven't demolished the port..." Colt spoke over the radio that was badly echoed by the chortling motors and the churning waves as they entered the first pier's mouth, of the seven which were there.

On the reserved bringing of the boat near the port of half stone and half wood, Alexandria tossed a rope around a bronze green bollard and pulled the vessel to moore whilst the engine was flicked shut, awaiting the second pair, casually sailing.

"I guess it was never mentioned *how* it was sealed." Lev suggested, appreciating the sights when he spun to his comrade with his eyes off the helm.

"You were a step ahead of us, huh?" He acknowledged before scraping the unfortunate hull with a sour squeal.

"Hmph." The giant huffed, rocking the vessel on the approach to the dock.

The two boats were docked safely, and landfall was made. Onto the wetted ground that bred a terrible stench, Colt excitedly leapt off and found himself in the image that captured the renaissance mood, reimagining that decades and centuries ago there would be a population of lively folk settled on the port where it was no more. The torches were shunned from the dark where the last light would shine through the hole Miklós had made. Its chipped colors, which peeled like dead skin, irradiated off the reflections of the mud-filled water, displaying the bareness of sacked stores. Colt curiously trailed around the pier and discovered the wreckages of heretical stalls, gruesomely depicting the stains of slaves.

"This was a black market." The lieutenant presumed.

"Smells like it." Lev replied, hopping onto the pier with Miklós beside.

They prepared to depart when Alexandria called for the titan from the swinging deck,

"Dragosavac."

Halting on a step, Miklós turned back and caught an unbroken spear, thrown overboard that she left her hand vacant and wanting for the warrior's crippled spear.

"I'll keep watch." The girl declared with resolve, on the ask of her comrade's scrap.

"With what?" Colt loudly blared with a mocking chuckle that filled the den with his expansive voice.

"A stick?"

Snatching the splintered shaft tossed mid air by Miklós, Alexandria exempted her hearing of Colt and retreated herself into the booth alone.

"Suit yourself." Colt waved away Alexandria, who was meditating in the space of her own, and tapped his comrade's shoulders for the squad to follow on, leading them towards a perilous row of unsafe stairs.

Trekking the eroded path towards the tunnels' height, raised on a platform with two imperial podiums to the left and right, whose edges were blunted by the salt of the past high waves, Colt fearlessly jogged upwards until the summit was near. He stopped one step higher and cherished the time for witnessing the unreal cave before him, incomparably stunning and mystifying were the scalp of roofs, lining the narrow alleys he rested his eyes upon wondering what it would have been like to be born into that forgotten age.

"So now we just gotta find the arms depot." Colt mumbled to himself, skipping a block of steps with a powerful leap and delicately landed on the toppest slab, peering from one flank to the other, wasting longer for his misled stares.

"But...uh...which way is it?" He asked.

Lev and Miklós finally caught him, winded from what little action, to be confused themselves by the dual entrances to the underground system which blew unhelpful wind through its concrete tunnels with either sounding and smelling the same of nature's cruel odor.

"Heh." Lev wrapped his arm atop of Colt's shoulders and leaned his chin to be rested next to a displeased face.

"That's best left for this." The lieutenant figured.

Holding out a bronze coin before Colt's eyes, Lev inched the mark onto the edge of his thumb, readying for one purpose in mind.

"Let's say tails for left and heads for right." The Rus childishly recited as his playful eyes followed the flipping coin into the air.

On the twinkle of the reflective piece, returning to the ground at what sluggishness, the bronze clinked on Lev's flicker snatch who patted the change onto his other hand. Dramatically showing the rusting sparkle of the tiny coin, the Zhormannik eagle's wings revealed itself to be their promised fate.

"Alright!" Colt roared and pranced onwards to the entrance of a tunnel.

"Left it is!" He cried, pulling his comrades with a pointer to the brimming channel of ample white lights.

Nodding to the forward march, the operation proceeded, where the squad sprinted with their spears held aside, those three found themselves into the unending maze with a hostile bellow of destined winds.

Under the ceiling of trickling rain through the pipes of old, the squad of three sprinted down the iron panels which were drafted to layer the tunnels' base. Echoing and heavy were its sounds that made the atmosphere dire. On all sides were the walls of plates, with cables extending between the lamps, dangling on hooks and chains which swayed as they dashed in hurry. Their waves of winds flung through the system until the pathway sloped. The swamping stench had miraculously gone in the perpetual progression, in the one way towards the overground. Lev climbed first and Colt second, leaving the giant to cover their rears, but it was well, the fleeting run they made, that their paranoia became intuitive.

Halting at one corner, the vanguard stopped and held to show a muddied fist for his comrades to brake. Peeking around the dripping wall, where there were no shadows nor unfamiliar voices, he told his band,

"Clear."

And rotating his body, the lieutenant led onwards in a charge through the aisle on another approach, over the rivers and streams which splashed, that fed towards their departure, he paused at a dip in the mud and drove his back against the corner. Panting heavily, his breath was drained and dehydrated, losing little moisture and was locked at its capacity where Lev's sights started to blur. Yet, able to peer past the hidden corridor, the soldier checked the blind turn and did not spot a moving shade, thus prepared onwards.

"Clear—" He repeated, then feeling a sudden tug on the shoulder, a hand dragged him towards the cover of the walls.

"Clear your head." Colt slapped Lev's head and forced him to squat.

Collecting a handful of crisp cool water flowing from a puncture above, the lieutenant held the pool over Lev's head and doused him with the refreshing rain creeping through his fingers. The Rus shuddered and shook, flapping his hair to dry.

"Can't you hear their damn footsteps?" Colt steamed as the Confederates, no more than a squad of eight showed themselves around the distant pass.

"And music…?" The lieutenant turned towards.

In their drab uniforms, unbuttoned and delinquent-like, the soldiers were a lowly bunch of subterranean dwellers. They were oddly unprofessional, bumbling in their walk and playing at their loudest, a blast of pounding tunes.

Yurubeat! Colt's ears perked.

Noticing the commanding officer taking a brief and random turn, the lieutenant hid away and knelt, leaning into the dark as the blaring speakers and awful drunken singing boomed, flinging dust and dirt into the air from its heart-splitting bass.

"They're coming our way." He pushed his comrades farther.

"Crouch." told Colt, waiting for the Confederates to arrive, as he prayed that his enemies were too intoxicated to see anything but a smudge of darkness on the passing.

"Are you sure this will work—?" Lev muttered.

To a bold hand covering the Rus' mouth, Colt wagged his finger whilst his comrade had been silenced.

"Tsk tsk, it comes naturally from playing enough games." The lieutenant surely said, convincing himself with the foolish idea that the tactic would succeed.

"We'll never be spotted—"

A figure, the Confederate officer paced onwards from his

squad and at the beginning of an awkward shadow, he halted
and searched about the two alleys, not thinking much but for
his return to his quarters when he crossed the six gleaming eyes.
His breath stopped and stared down upon the squating trio,
ghoulishly blinking in the shade. The Confederate's pose told so
that he was clear to shout for help when Lev greeted in Rus with a
beam drawn across his face,

"Čaoy…(Hey…)"

A spear thrust through the Confederate's tongue and mouth,
bashing a few teeth along the ride to the edge of the skull, where
the blade which pierced swiftly so, displayed the mix of brain and
bones splattered onto the painted wall. His throat gurgled for a
tide of blood ran a marathon to the mud and loosened flooring
as the dead's comrades found themselves sober from the flashing
eifer around the corner.

"Haagh!" With the flesh skewer in his hands, Colt sprinted
out of his hiding.

Coloring the ceiling with his victim whose head was driven
and grinded along the cracking tunnel, the lieutenant's eifer
kindled a trail of emerald flash fire as his feet dashed where at the
burst of his eifer, the punctured skull began to disintegrate in the
heat that touched the Confederate squad into flames.

"You're not supposed to see me, fucking NPCs!" Colt raged,
as the streams near him started to clear and the sweat on his face
disappeared whilst the glowing blade exploded to become one as
a bluish drill, bulleting along the underground highway.

"Colt! This is supposed to be a covert op—!" Lev called for
as Colt's enlarged dragon was reborn into a flowering outbreak
through the earth towards the surface.

The soil quaked as the Confederates sought their stance,
unbeknownst to the final stops of the journeys' end at the eruption
of an azure spiral, rupturing the face of a jade green terra. Its blast
of a blazing dragon sprouted into a cone of extinction, fooling the
mere humans in its searing shadow that scorched half an island in
its detrimental wake.

From the screening fog, the discharged colors were shaded a
cerulean fire, with its cone extending to the cloud's soaring edges

that could not contain the igneous jewel. The skies were dispersed across the many directions on the spring of death. They watched, as enemies and comrades sympathized alike, on the illuminated platinum gray decks by the show of the night. All hands, the sailors and captains brought down their caps and gazed upon the devastating ruin performed.

At no further, were they, under the mist which cleared with a fierce expanding gust, the Confederate's gracious beauty and pride of the high seas, a kraken-like form of the grand fleet. Anchored near a headland's port, the Rus spared no spaciousness, and had filled the tub with a little more than fifty ships of destroyers and cruisers. But in the spearhead laid the battery of seven battleships, greater than any other machine of the known world. Though at the tip, fearless and cared not for the common rules of naval warring, was their daunting flagship.

The three hundred paces long and ninety thousand tonnes of the sheer behemoth, managed impossible buoyancy and an eerie stillness where the waves hardly moved it. And whilst her designer was mocked and ridiculed for proposing the mount of four triple barreled main guns, in the placement of cursing triangles, there it was, in reality and physical form that looked diabolical though perhaps one could think its firepower was merely an exaggeration. The rumors were not so true when beside the mountain-like control tower, were over two hundred cannons and anti-aircraft guns. With the crest of the Tsarevich's cross, made of gold but was a blackened silver, if she, Kalmar, the namesake of the exiled prince, was the goddess of the seas, then there would only be her as the one metallic deity.

Within the bridge of the steep and unnoticeably curved command tower, that was wrapped around by an exterior staircase, there was an elevator, facing the complex panels and controls of the officers' helm. And flanked on either side, were the highest ranking quarters for they seemed luxurious and guarded as a young ensign passed by. Into the main floorings of the headquarters, it was expansive and ornamented of decade-old equipment, on the panel which summoned all authority over the fleet it homed. Every moment he trailed the same path to deliver a word, the very few crew with one holding the wheel steady and another decrypting codes of the armies on land, would give him a quick glance before returning to their duties. It was certainly irregular, for the man on the humble throne, a worn chair, to have a scarce bridge that was so.

The admiral, lazing with his sights narrowed towards the island fort, held his hand around the third cup of coffee, piping with an Ätyope aroma arising, beside a traditional plate that served a few chocolate biscuits. Of the five, he picked one, and snapped the biscuit with his crunch as the ensign saluted and delivered,

"Sir! Report!"

"No need. I'm not blind." The admiral rudely returned with his mouth full.

Taking a sip of the warming drink, the one they named, the stout imperialist, and the Scourge of the Hannsen was Mikhail Radilov, rose from his seat. Aged forty-two years. Cleanly neat and formally proper. Yet having the demeanor of an egoist, the admiral was a tall figure, whose reserved hands were held behind. The marengo gray uniform he wore was less sophisticated and bore resemblance with enemies rather than allies. Not littered with decorations nor his rank and proudly so. The Radilov expected every being to know his name.

"I'd say I couldn't have predicted this maneuver." Radilov mentioned, turning to the ensign who calmly stayed his mouth.

"Especially at such rapidity."

The admiral lent an asking hand, overshadowing his close subordinate, and for he could not decline, unsurely passed the hastily scribbled, but unnecessarily detailed report. Skim reading through some pointless notes, Radilov found the number he desired to know and praised once more, the Aelon command,

"They must have quite the commander."

"Right, Tev?" He asked.

"Yes, sir." The second youngster replied, unconfidently, nervously holding the hilt of a gifted royal saber that was twice longer and wider than any standard backsword.

Stood to attention near the wall, the shy and lean fifteen-year-old of a stature like his brother's was enclosed and isolated to himself and his thoughts. Tiberis. Whose eyes' color were the same as the admiral's, a lush green, with the diluted brightness of the sights was where all that was said and written across his fair face doubted anything despite his being a captain. His short golden hair was messy, going no further than his ears which had regal earrings dangling a pair of malachite jewels, and had a distinct, olden scar which ran along the neck, within the shadow of his plated collar bearing the one aurelian star. Of the nobility, it was only by nature that he was in such striking black garb, with a cardinal ribbon around his waist. But uncaring of the fortune or if ever there were admirers flocking to his prettiness, the boy's spirit seemed fragmented. Neglected.

"In defense?" asked the ensign.

"Of course." Radilov answered surely.

"Look at its course."

He aimed towards the two fallen bridges and returned to his soldiers with a suggestion,

"They don't plan on retaking the island now, do they?"

Admiring the flush of lights displayed, the admiral's pupils shined from its glorious reflection and in the distant view, he looked towards, there was not a sign of support nor retaliation for the assault was so unforeseen, allies and enemies were equally caught out of the ring.

"The Danne fleet hasn't fired a single round," said Radilov.

"So, whoever that soldier is..." His words slowed in the upheaval of realization.

"Most definitely had the intention to eliminate our fortress, entirely."

Finishing the biscuit he held in his hand, Admiral Radilov cleared the crumbs from his fingertips and brushed the fine oils on his pants, with a gulp of coffee that helped swallow within the time he took to analyze the scenario.

"What say you, if we were to help them?" Radilov proudly blurted towards the captain.

"You don't mean to—" Tev interrupted, stepping out of the comforting shadow, and willed by his open hand.

"Don't bother yourself with your tutor's spew of shit." Radilov scolded over his shoulder who had not looked Tev in the eye, and that is for their lives, it had not happened once.

"You're a Radilov." The enraged man reminded his son.

"Your brother and sister know it well."

"And yet you're so snow-hearted." With scorn that reflected from the glass and metals of the helm, the admiral berated.

Tev stammered, though the words he wanted to say could not be flung out so easily in the presence of the commander.

Crestfallen and discouraged to argue any more, the captain retreated towards the frigid wall, cooled by the air conditioner exhaling onto his weakly fluttering hair.

"Do not believe in such things. Honor." The father harshly taught.

"It will dismember you and sink your body."

For his dejected look towards his feet, he replied timidly,

"Yes, father…"

Pondering whether he had done wrongly in his words, Radilov shook his head and watched, leaning onto the helm, the berthed fleet who withdrew their anchors in preparation for the scheme in design.

Joshua, do never dare berate me… The man remnicized a comrade lost.

He lifted his body from a calming rest and vigorously swung an arm along the horizon's axis until the island was marked, issuing the order,

"All hands on portside, ensign."

"And fire whatever you will, don't waste my shells." Radilov returned to be seated and waited for the command to pass.

The harmonious fleet blasted their engines and turned the rudders, settling them towards the starboard where the portside of guns were revealed. Their turrets and eyes revolved over the deck and at the lock in place, a grand battery was there, whose barrels extended beyond the reflections of the crescent moon. Shells and man, entered them, unto the duties which required a sacrifice of the same blood and people. Not knowing whom or what they were aiming for, only followed the barking officers and spun the wheels to drive the guns upwards.

With the muted pop of a flare by the ensign's following hand, the machines groaned and fired in chains of volley, undermining the waves of the sea that were broken into semi-orbs of shock. From the outburst on water to the skies overhead, a ceiling, the flight of the several hundreds added to the cover of dark and encased the local world with its fleet of a barrage, landing into the fortress that blasted awake into a combusting show at the hands of entertaining shells. Its percussion of colliding missiles into the fort sounded through the emptied air, engulfing the craters and buildings, flesh and mud into one loathing stream, battering in rows and where the depot, that the elites had aimed for, ignited with a dazzling flash, sent a gift to heaven of blood smoke, like plumes.

To the lieutenant in the maelstrom of a bonfire out at sea, on the battlements of the sheltering wall, Julien's eyes watered in disbelief, before his trembling body fell to a kneel. Sobbing in his sore pain, he clutched onto both the wall and his aching heart for the storm of souls emitted above the walled, incinerating grave.

XXXII

- - 508
- - 2034

Regulus von Eos

The House of Radilov was first documented in the year of three-twenty-one. But it was after, during the reign of young Alexei the Second that they rose to prominence. By serving in the Baltik with the Zhormanniks' Axis alliance, the Radilov's were loyal retainers to the Eos dynasty. We fought alongside each other for decades even after the Tsar's assassination and sought to protect the imperial family together.

However, upon the exile of the Romans, we merely became divided factions seeking for power within the new state and Confederacy. It had cost my family our legacy whilst the Radilovs became the Rus symbol of prowess and unity. Orthodoxy. Autocracy. Nationality. As I suspected, they were the new protectors of Rutenn.

During the days in my meetings with a pupil, Tiberis Radilov, I despised him through our indoctrination. It was natural to see the boy then throw a rampage with bloodshed. Yet he never fought back. In the while, his father, Mikhail Radilov, praised the toughening of his own son. Until his beloved sister, whom she was dear to everyone and protected by, called upon their eldest, Aurel, to strategize how to rid of I. I found the humiliation of being beaten senseless on occasional nights without consequences. And it would repeat before finding reason.

I never knew how it came to be, but there was a reversal.

The four members of this dynasty deserve thousand-paged stories each. Grandfather Mikhail. Uncle Aurel and Tev. Your mother, Athena. You might learn much from them, so do well remembering, Alexei...

CHAPTER

33   TORRENT

Drowning bodies, of living, and corpses, dragged beneath the crooked fire, thumped into the waves like falling meteors. They crashed through the waves and littered the waters with shrapnel and flesh. Skin, bleeding as the salt seeped into their wounds, where the sears forced their mouths wide, gurgling and drowning. For the fortuitous were the dead, who need not suffer in their sleep. It could not be said for another who found himself being pulled into the stillness awaiting judgement. His breaths bubbled, but his eyes were shut, finding the calmness beneath the rage to be something of a reminder. Where there was without marine life, forced away by an invasion of bloodied hunks, his mentor's senile voice spoke to him in a younger self,

Good child, how long will you be under this waterfall?

The scent of local herbs from a familiarity rested beneath his nose as he was discovered meditating beneath a holiest cascade.

As long as I can... A Colt, younger, replied with his eyes wholly covered by a drenched blue towel where the approaching footsteps injured him not, for the student's mind became engraved within the plunge pool.

Spirited...determined...patient... The teacher listed.

But you cannot simply master the Azure if you spend all day sitting here.

Came a slap of a cane that broke the valuable slumber, the old man waded through the waters, heard by the delicate emptiness of ripples, and pulled Colt by the ear, tugging the student who began their descent to the lower rocks as he mentioned for the ten thousandth time,

Nor merely being born into your prestigious family means that you might instantly become a genius.

Come along now, He said.

We might catch the ferry to the revolution.

Opening his eyes, slowly, in the descent to the unknown, a gush of the present sea flushed against his touch and sunk the spear further when Colt's grip could hold it no more. It disappeared, like a torpedo rushing towards the bottom, and he remained, eternally alone.

Where is this...? Colt questioned the gods of fate.

His flowing arms, and legs, were raised pointing upwards, waving for the flickering embers that neither had the tint of an azure cloud or any comrade's colors. It was the grave that absorbed the lieutenant's fixated eyes.

The water's emerald... He spotted, reaching outwards for a long, friendly arm who searched the abyss for a lost ally.

Like that place...it reeks of blood...

In the red current, his face followed the sinking of innocently torn and scraps of souls engaging themselves to the crimson dance which swirled and twirled about the sea. Limbs and eyes, ripped by a sprinkle of shrapnel, floated to rise, whose bisected torsos leaked a fortune of acids and intestines, to tie together the bundles of remains. Like the cosmos, as numerous as there were suns, carcasses declined around an aiding hand who latched onto Colt as he was brought to the above. A muffled shout called for his name when the surface became clearer,

"Colt...Colt!"

Soared above the burning waves, he was stinking of oil and flesh. Where the two pairs of hands grappled and pulled him to the hull, Colt lightly coughed and spat the salted taste of blood remnants stuck to the tongue before gasping for the stained air.

The chaos of kindled splinters and bodily parts enveloped everything his human eye could see, as far as the sights would allow. It loosened his proud expression on the seeing of the flooding fortress of chutes shooting to the smashing waves. The castle, although withstanding the judgement, was missing three-quarters from the series of Kalmar's shells. Indeed it was set alight to never last longer than a day, the behemoth will fall.

"C'mon...let's get you on board." Lev grunted as he and Miklós leaned against their supporting weights.

Hauling Colt over like a netted shark, the two counted for a final tug and yanked the squad leader onto deck, in a pool of a sorrowful mixture of blood and sweat. Lev leaned against the booth with Alexandria periodically peeking out to the one they had saved, who kneeled and bitterly shook his head, pouring a stream of water from each ringing ear.

"You're heavier...than I thought..." The Rus panted, as he slumped along the window.

"The Confederates have gone mad..." Colt told, punching the hull of the boat that sprung on the irritated waves.

"But..." The lieutenant lifted himself from the rocking floor and stumbled around until his shaking legs crippled, which took the soldier to tumble near the door.

Reaching high, stretching his body to latch a hand onto the handle, he entered himself to the compact quarters, at the least dried and warmer than the rain in the wilderness. Tailed by his comrades, Colt sat in a corner beside Alexandria as the door was shut.

"At least they did the job for us..." joked the lazing warrior, holding his stomach.

The squad were placed in an awkward absence of noise, between the usually rowdy duo. Who looked away from anyone, they clamored to their individual homes and waited for the flames to settle within the corners of their eyes.

"What now?" Lev faintly asked.

There was a brief peace till Colt snapped the still with a fake light-hearted chuckle. He glanced at Lev and returned his eyes upon the tarnished deck as an attempt to reconcile.

"We can't fight *both* the navy *and* army..." Colt admitted.

Then tapping Alexandria's heel which gathered her awareness, the soldier closed his eyes for a nap and decided off his accord,

"That leaves us with *that*."

The girl tightened her hands around the wheel and throttle, roughly pushing onwards the restart of the motor that hurled its choking smoke which smothered the skies. The propeller of the boat spun a narrow whirlpool near the bubbling waves and launched the vessel to its journey. Into the unusual change of steaming hail, the mist returned with an ever greater army of a surfing blood haze.

"Sorry..." Julien cried, whose hurt face was shielded by the flapping hood.

He sobbed over a puddle with a splashing reflection of his dripping tears and who clenched his fists on the battlement's coarse stone, the Danne lifted a quivering hand and clutched his thumping heart that was injured with a striking pierce he could not quite shun. In the sparse hail amidst the shower, his wail was light but never shallow.

"Forgive...me..." The lieutenant begged again, dipping his head lower until a few strands of hair were soaked in the pool.

The timidness of Julien's weeping swept across the empty wall, where his troops had gone to fight a closeby war. As he lamented, with a feeling of being deserted. Yet the more he mourned, his mind became near the fracture during the plague of battle, over the waves that drummed a death-like tune for it tolled like a graveyard's bell.

"I-I should've listened to Arminius..." He stammered and sniveled.

"I wasn't prepared..."

His tie, the aqua blue penchant, slipped and dangled to and fro, after the collar where his hand slowly moved until the necklace was within grasp. Shining onto the glass-like rain, the rays of the iced jewel flickered between the beating hail, hammering its surface before Julien intervened and covered the gemstone within his fist.

"Why are we fighting this war...?" asked the softening boy.

When the crackle of thunder struck the city from behind, Julien flinched, but did not see the lightning streak, in the seconds of existence, flash across the brick and tiled skyline, sparking an ignition of a burning voltage that tore across the narrow alleys, explosively clawing open a path for the shouts and cries of a distant voice to break onto the main street. As the cobblestones and paint of buildings were hurled into the air, bombarding the capital of inferno, Julien curled, pulling his tensing arms towards himself. The rumble of a sailing motor, gliding over the rampant sea suddenly came to be and halted its engine beneath the shadow of the wall where the boat was not too close to scrape its hull.

"Julien!" Someone finally called his name that the lieutenant had longed for.

Julien opened his eyes with a gasp, and released the strain strangling him by the chest.

"Are you up there?!" The soldier yelled again.

To that, with swelling hope, Julien crawled towards the edge and helped himself onto his feet before shyly peeking out to a thunderstorm. Blowing his cloak aside, the lieutenant grabbed on and lowered himself from the wind. At that height, he could see a strangely tall figure waving at him whose self was well-balanced on the rolling deck.

"Lev...?" Sniffling, he saw his face.

Wiping his tears away with a quick scrub from an arm, he leaned above the parapet and peered down at a comrade who was anxiously holding onto his head.

"Are you crying?!" Lev embarrassed the Danne.

"I'm going to tell Arminius when we see him!" He promised aloud.

The commander on the wall swiped his hand along his face and brushed the drops of tears into the storm, bearing a set of red marks beneath his eyes.

"That...Lev..." Holding a warming smile for himself to know or see, Julien murmured with the notes of his voice trapped on the tongue.

"He's seen me like this before..."

On the return to the spearman, he heard what the ally had to say,

"Anyways!"

"We should evacuate now!" Lev advised and glimpsed indoors where the resting giant had blocked the view of another.

"There's no way we'd be able to fight the sea, land and air!" He returned to tell Julien.

"I'm sure Arminius has the same idea!"

Gazing to his rear, the intruding Confederates were overwhelming the great defenses who had been broken on every lasting flank except for the direct west that remained stalwart in their stand. There at the viewpoint, Julien could pinpoint his very comrades and units which they led, where to the streets and roads the march went.

Arminius of the center guard, troubled by the aura of a hidden foe. They were to be outflanked if not for Károly's graceful vortex of arrows in a barrage of flames. Whilst Gin and Arber led with the axe heads of Wojsław and the stone bear, running a frenzy across the southern promenade and storming towards the western commander in the link of northern stars which the younger had forged. Of the crowded north, a human wave of cadets were driven south by Adam's command who lit the pathway under a golden heatwave of Sol's grand son, Apollo. All seemed to converge around the central command. To the true final bastion. A port, lest the Confederates were to hack open a gateway to the slaughterhouse.

"Julien!" Lev turned the lieutenant's hearing to him, excluding the terrible screams of the scorched homes.

"Let's meet up at the next pier!" The comrade suggested.

Julien returned to the downfall of Danen for a brief glance and resolutely nodded on his answer.

The two were reeled into the escape in their parallel ways, lunging themselves to perform a timed feat. Alexandria forced the throttle onwards and pushed the squad along the coast in the hopping boat across the sea of peril, thudding its shrieking propeller to the waves after a jump through the freeing air. As Julien took to his sprint, along the walled line and leapt at a block of stairs at the highest persistence that he thought to be the determining act if the Dannes and battle were to be saved. His eyes, whose redness was cleared in the cooling wind, were laid upon the grandeur of the evacuation fleet whose guns spun, fated to fire.

An ailing century of collapsing soldiers, into the cold of rubble and flow of streams, fled across streets but were trapped around every corner on the approach of Confederate columns nearing the thousands who marched between houses and stores. Their boots splashed about the muddied craters and uprooted bricks as buildings on either side collapsed upon some luckless heads, disintegrating to become less than clouds or ashes. The road, vast and direct, on two flanks lined with restaurants, was manned with the vulnerable fleeing who had been callously assaulted in waves of steel crashing against flesh and those who could bear no longer charged towards the barbarous fray.

In a zip, a thunderous bolt dashed. Exploding the automobiles and wagons with one shocking leap. Tearing the paint off the walls and rain to ripples, he brightened the avenue with the enchanting sparks. At near the burn of corpses laid beneath crushing rocks and trapping spite, the commander cleanly slashed awide a neck before the soldier could scream and felled another in a pierce between the eyes whose wounds hissed and gushed onto his hands as he brought upon a streamline dart, striking left and center like a sharp threading needle. Where at Arminius' lightning end, halted on the flick of the wetted blade. The cuts along the Confederates' vital lines flattened and rent for agony could not be felt in the fresh outpour. He took a chilling breath and peered down at his shivering hand holding onto a fatal ravine carved within him. That the blood had spilled for hours since Aurel's clash and yet he was to fall.

The innocents sat and watched, in the pool of families, maimed in the harshness, whose splintered bones showed beyond the skin, with skulls bashed until their brains leaked from noses. They crawled in the shadow of Arminius to plead for a savior's call when it was answered by the lieutenant himself,

"Everyone! Retreat to the port!"

"Get in whatever vessel you can find and sail for Jarlsberg's fleet!" He cried as the townsfolk began to stand and escaped the crumbling town.

"They can guarantee your safety out of Danen!"

An elder among the locals, who was holding the hand of a wailing child, brushed by a splatter of her parent's blood, approached the kind-hearted lieutenant with blessing and spoke to him in a frail tone,

"Thank you, good lord Reichner..."

Arminius dipped his head in appreciation and covered their departure towards the only alley that remained passable to the shoreline before letting his firm bluff to be away as the lieutenant's eyes withered in despair. The lancer from behind weaved past the soldiers of what remained to be the spirited in the diminishment and caught the commander staring ahead, towards the poor souls who knelt weeping amidst the stench of bodies.

"You're not looking too good yourself." Arnau glanced at the peaceful overflow of rain to wash the blood soaked ground.

With an ally he could not have abandoned, carried on his back asleep, the child's arms were wrapped around the lancer's shoulders.

"I-I can manage..." Arminius stammered when a despising cry from an alley revealed his shadow.

"Kirill! I'll send him to hell for you!" A Confederate youngster charged into the light with tears and a chipped short sword with the blade aimed for Arminius' life.

Then, a bursting beat of a bowstring thunked, and struck the soldier thrice. Arminius hurriedly sprinted to his aid and caught the failing boy in his arms when they both gasped from their pain. The soldier's eyes blanked and quivered as he reached for the lieutenant's face when the heartache took him from life. His sword clanked on the defeatist's drop and slumped his head onto Arminius. So for the blood of the two intertwined to leak for the earth upon resting the breathless onto the ground beside a row of comrades.

Arnau gazed up at the falling roof tiles and had Károly, panting with the silver bow at hand who peered along the street in search of the rush of footsteps that he had heard.

"They're here!" It cried.

That of Gin's wave around a corner, leading a sizable contingent beside Arber and Wojsław's flanks, whilst yet another officer heading a squad chased the ravine-like streets to the center force's position. Both sides yelled to burst their paces and gathered between the bloodstained boulders. The elites crowded beside Arminius who rose from the fallen and could only have listened.

"The last fort has fallen." Adam informed, sheathing his tapes as he reassured the commander,

"But I've sent everyone to the port."

"The south was overrun." Arber reservedly added.

"Fuckin' Confederates!" Gin cursed as he spotted the band of soldiers laying on the ground.

His foolish mind aimed towards the Confederate and made way for a kick.

"They dunno when ta—!"

The lieutenant's foot was halted by a furious stomp that nailed Gin in place who swore could have heard a crack of a bone when the stare of Arminius' mournful eyes froze his comrade's tension. Then releasing the latch onto Gin's rage, the commander looked away to ask,

"Has everyone crossed the river—?"

"Urgent report!" A desperate shout sprinted in the storm, whose hair and uniform were drenched.

He was of the few messengers who delivered himself across

the ponds and reeds of flesh chasing the wind towards Arminius and knelt at a distance to be heard.

"T-The Confederates have broken through the fallback line!" The messenger stuttered and lowered his head to the officers' displeasement.

"Already...?" Arminius faintly mumbled, unknown of what expression to portray, when his lips and face had paled.

From the roofs, touching the clouds, quite high, Károly leapt with the rain's current, and landed noiselessly that only sounded of a soft splash and hopped across the misted stones to his comrade's side as the weather chilled.

"How many broke through?" asked Arnau, who stepped in Arminius' wavering place.

"J-Just seventy!" The messenger replied as his voice deepened with fear to Arminius who saw his trembling breath weakening.

"And that number will only keep growing." said Arber.

In the brush of ghastly air, spotting the pungent scent of drowned flesh, Arminius nodded for the soldier's dismissal and sent him to be with the haven at port. Who rose and hopelessly saluted, the messenger took to a jog across the street and disappeared within the shading alley that would take him to his comrades and familiar faces.

"A-At this...rate..." Arminius slowly faded when he dropped onto his knees, chopping the blade of his sword into the loosened gaps of the pavement to hold himself.

"Reichner!" Gin shouted near his ear.

"Get a hold of ya self."

The lieutenant coughed and spewed blood that dribbled from his lips, recovering the sense of a stinging wound gnawing into his nerves. Arminius' sights started to wander and had divided whilst Károly flocked to help. The archer sheathed the winged bow and lifted Arminius to rise though to the commander, he thought it was not needed.

"I'm fine..." Arminius lied, pushing himself onwards even if the pain was damning sharp and changed the tone for it to not worry his comrades alike who watched on, unbelieving him.

"We...got to get to the port..." He grunted.

On that word, a roaring disturbance sounding of hooves echoed through the valleys of buildings unto the squad's ears and before they could speak or react, a silver horde of riders attached themselves to show around the corner and galloped like a fleet, rushing down the rivers of blood before the allied lines who watched in perplexity at their lances, strikingly tainted by patches of flesh, glued to the glimmering steel blades. The armor which layered every exposure of the cavalrymen's bodies proved a formidable sight of those pouring through the funnel in a wedge that seemed arranged to issue an assault to trample their foes.

But it was through the center, that the cavalry became divided and splitted into two forces flushing down the crossroads towards the lefts and rights that Arminius saw the exalted commander single one's self out of the pearl white ocean.

"Eos…" Arminius inaudibly muttered.

On his appearance in his dazzling armoring coat of Confederate scarlet red and silver, the extravagance of the colonel, Regulus von Eos, laid his eyes on Arminius, with the beaked helmet pointed at the rival in a stand-off.

"It is by fate that we would come to clash, soon in the future." Regulus reminded the lieutenant as his visor was raised, that his eyes were in view.

"And that future is the present."

He lifted himself from the war horse's worn royal saddle and removed his footing on the platinum stirrup, carefully drawing the glaive by the side to land. Unbuckling the helmet, carved to become that of a majestic falcon, Regulus rested the piece to hang beside his satchels, before a whistle sent the creature hurrying away. The air quieted, whilst the colonel trekked closer till he came to a halt and referred to Arminius once more as an odd and unheard name,

"Arminius von Regen."

"Are you to uphold your faith and duel me a sole?" He nobly pledged, crashing the shoe of the polearm towards the earth which cracked and rang on the impact.

Whilst Regulus was a patient warrior, so he waited for a desirable answer, the squad held their toes on edge as the brazen Gin advanced his step, ahead of Arminius and vulgarly clicked his tongue.

"This fucktard," Gin cursed, twirling his dual swords to forge a flaming wheel, until a stop, where one laid on his shoulder as the other pointed at Regulus.

"Did he think we weren't gonna intervene?!" The brute

boomed for the Confederate to know his presence.

"Gin…" Arminius held his comrade's shoulder who lowered the swords for himself to be revealed before Regulus to see.

"Ya don't plan…" Gin voiced his crude interruption.

"Head to the port…" Their allied commander tended closer to the frontlines where he halted at reason, within a heel-deep puddle.

"All of you." commanded Arminius.

A splash of water from the rear, with its droplets neatly falling, was followed by a tug on the arm to who Arminius looked back and found a hand clutching onto him tightly. With a blazing scent, the warmth was discovered nowhere else.

"You can't fight him…" Károly begged.

His tearing eyes were obscured by the fire-like hair that Arminius could tell from the archer's few sniffles. Each time fastening his grip on the commander's arm, as the streams ran down Károly's face and sprinkled on the stones below. But Arminius was not set on his beseeching friend. There was a predator ahead, in need of a purge.

"He's a reaper of war." Arber spoke against conflict, beyond his normality.

"There's no way in your crippled state—"

"What if I didn't hold back this time?" Arminius rejected and questioned Arber in a direct pursuit.

"Would it change the outcome?" He asked in succession.

The first dejected sigh from Arber exhaled, though hesitated in the schism, he gazed at Arminius' back for a final glance and had his mind and body eventually retreat from argument.

"Destroy this city if you have to." told Arber, who turned himself away and paced towards the exit's alleyway, that took the squad unable to comprehend his decision.

"But don't forget what you said."

The lieutenant sprinted into the dimmed path, leaving himself beyond battle and his comrades pinned between the moralities and honor that Gin wondered by his turns back and forth, disbelieving who Arber had abandoned.

"Arber?" Gin began to rile.

"We can't just—!"

The student felt a pair of fingers frighteningly hook itself on his collar and like a motherly cat, the teacher lifted Gin with little strength, minding that his junior weighed grossly.

"Are ya disobeyin' yer comman'r's orders?" Adam asked the doubtful century of troops on standby, reluctant to forget Arminius alone and carried Gin away to the one way road.

"He said he'll handle it, so he will."

Unwilling to evacuate as they looked around for their comrades. For those all wanting to stay and honorably battle to the death, they awkwardly peered down and made no contact besides themselves in the pools of reflections. Only when Arminius dipped his shadowed face, it pressed some to surrender and escape the closure as the century broke apart by the minute, along the lengthiest stretch of time. Whilst the rain unsteadily bellowed, the footsteps disappeared pace by pace, until Arnau, near last to depart, glanced at Arminius, and too found himself away. By the fifth, all who were there, was no more than one giant pair and another. Waiting.

"Why are you still here, Wojsław?" Arminius asked to a small growl of Wojtek.

"Warneńczyk's orders." The warrior bluntly replied who had lingered for long.

Károly sniveled, whose hand was still clinging onto Arminius as he wept without end, when the lieutenant spun to face him with no more than the same tear running down his eyes.

"Stop, Károly." said Arminius with a timid smile.

"Do you have so little faith in me thinking that I'll really die?"

"You...can't promise me that..." Károly wailed that loosened his speech that stuttered or shattered on every cry that cracked his voice.

For as a trembling Arminius saw in anguish, he brought the archer's head against his own chest, and rubbed his hair, doused, whilst the archer asked, sniffling onto the commander's coat,

"W-What about...the village...?"

"O-Or becoming...a general...?" The repeating voices of his own and new amidst Károly's were blurring the current of time.

"I'm only buying you a moment to evacuate..." told Arminius to assure the other stubbornness.

But with undeniably minimal intention to escape for himself, it was written across the words he crafted after all.

"Still..." Károly murmured.

"You won't leave will you...?" Arminius eventually stayed his hand and lifted a palm above the archer's back and warned when no answer arrived,

"Then..."

The lieutenant swung and smacked a cutting strike onto Károly's neck that merged a sodden slapping noise with the smacks of rain. His comrade cried as his eyes dulled and had fallen into sleep, to be caught by Arminius' arms. He saw, for the last time, with both eyes, how Károly could be still if in a slumber, and called upon Wojsław and the bear to carry the archer asleep. They lifted the lieutenant captain to be settled on the furred beast's back, and with a dip of Arminius' head, were directed away to the port in less than anything said.

Until the rivals came to be singled, like in a prose on battle, they stared along the straight street and kept each other within their sights. Whilst Regulus drew his stance, his enemy kept himself openly.

I...hardly have a drop of eifer left in me... Arminius thought alone.

"Károly...Julien..." The soldier called for them.

Gazing to the howling heavens, with a knowing tear, he spoke a few words which could not be heard, except for within Károly's distressed dreams who showed the streams flowing from his eyes and of Julien's illusional screech that reminded him aboard the fleeting vessel. Arminius turned the blade onwards to Regulus who accepted the challenge. The fated duel within the torrent tolled.

XXXIII

31 SEPIRUS 525
31.10.12051

Lycoris

Regulus von Eos. The genius. Who fought seventy-one battles before his fifteenth year. Half he masterminded. All he won. No record, or book in the present spoke ill of him. He could be defined as the reincarnation of the God of Honor. Everything Regulus had done seemed justified. It seemed that committing his actions to the Confederacy...was the only mistake...

Sometimes I wished, if it weren't for my studies, then my role would be as a warrior. Like him, battling in the snow beyond this palace, rather than cowering away in the warmth whilst those such as my father conquers this world. Compared to my ancestors, what have I done in these ten years of living? Nothing?

From the tales and rumors about the honesty he fought for or his reservedness when out of battle. Chamberlain Müller had even mentioned to me once that "Eos' calm demeanor was nothing like the creature he strived to be on a battlefield." Even when my father called him foolish, I could not believe so. He was someone I'd admire...to become stronger...at least...

But who knows the truth from fiction? I've never met him after all...

CHAPTER

34

DEATH AND DISHONOR

Chilled breaths sang clouds of ghost white steam into the spring of rain collapsing as if it were the sky that crushed the earth, like that of feathers from a felled freed dove whose wings were paralyzed by the fragrance of blood. They landed on the powers' wrists. Calmer, one and his loosened grip did not seem easy to duel by the lieutenant, found him worthy of a trap he could not overcome. No step back. As both waited amidst the mist and rippling puddles that took him and the unsteady heart to be strangled. Arminius' eyes being set upon the shrouded aura of the Confederate that released no instinct to kill befuddled him who could hardly keep his hands still. He trembled, and the sword rattled. The wound was not eased by the cracks and shattering of sliding roof tiles into the deceased piles.

He's not showing any openings... Arminius stayed his ground with something that told him to inch ever ahead.

Carelessly heaving, it was his weakened figure that seemed for he was unable to battle. But Regulus laid his sights solely on Arminius no matter how petite the threat looked to be. Concentrating a leer of the colonel when the genius found that the lieutenant had begun his advance, that on the draw of Arminius' blade to the left, the soldier had employed his uniquely silent however ominous kei into an executioner's bearing.

With one strike... He willed, peering down at the cut his hands had been led from.

The blood spilled endlessly.

My eifer's being depleted with each drop...

I need to make the first move... The lieutenant decided.

Arminius' eyes sharpened but there was a second of hesitation that revealed his ambition, with his slashed flesh tearing, over the exposed sparks of bleached purple lightning, the narrow field of battle became a playground of thunder. The stones lifted, in the whirlwind surrounding the cataclysmic store of eifer, bursted to the skies on the booming leap that snapped quicker as he skipped like a rapid on each landing boosting the dash onwards.

"Eos!" shouted Arminius, resolutely, progressing his sword that had the tail of a bolt chasing its tip.

For when the structures collapsed overhead like a curling wave that pulled all concrete and brick innards onto the street, the trail of gleaming embers ignited in the flash fire and sprouted above the rubble and hasting lightning through the shockwaves. Before the eifer could wholly collect, Arminius' mad sprint had arrived beside Regulus' head who maintained a composed face, shedding no unnecessary fear as the blade neared beneath his ribs. When the lieutenant thought to have the battle under his command, there sounded a disturbing clank.

"You gotta—!" Arminius knew the sound of doom, turning to the dread that arose to be true.

A spear was there, shielding the crash of the protected slash that produced petals of sparks, not blood. On the landing of his feet, slipping on the smoothened road, Arminius withdrew the discharge and spun the blade to the defensive. It was by surprise that caught him unwinded, a twister of a storming kick smashed itself upon the lieutenant, launching him paces in retreat as he skidded from balance.

"Ack..." Arminius coughed.

Lunging forward, he stumbled and gagged whilst he kept to the pain when a twirl of the glaive, howling more boldly than the rainstorm, swept from the ground at an incline to the air, taking with the shaft an arc of water that crushed the weapon into Arminius' stomach. The shoe hurled the Aelon upwards to a standstill. Before his rival could recover, yet Arminius did not seem like he could, Regulus glided along the puddles, splashing over a halt and batted the blunted edge of the glaive through the droplets, dividing the air with a swing faster than sound. The cloud rings exploded twice and drove its ringing steel onto the frail body whose injuries cracked.

Thrown, Arminius was propelled with a light spin onwards to the roofs and at the bounds of the street, and was blasted across the tiles in numberless rolls, tearing the burning buildings and skeletons of houses with him a dust cloud that marked the trail of ruin. Layering his skin with cuts, by the glass which shattered and disintegrating stones, he had finally barrelled to the end in reach and struck the dipped roof's overhang, launching him with great fury at a decline. Blasting into a nameless fountain that had dried once, still, it had been refilled by the torrent, Arminius was pressed to stop his flight. Saved before the statue when the warrior of Aelon was smacked against the creation that was hardly chipped. He slumped down, as a tide of blood poured from his mouth whilst the cuts blended. What truly was dire, the fading of life.

A fishing boat's motor churned heaps of dying exhausts into the black polluted air that formed a cloud of smog in its journey through the storm that bumped on the meeting of waves. Shaking the evacuation whose children screamed at the terror of swelling crests arising over the height of the single funnel.

The careful helmsman, Arnau Rieding, crossed his hands back and forth to manage the otherworldly controls of the shaking wheel and throttle whose nails were to fall apart. That no one helped him for. Its panels were ancient, had those been previously painted or marked with renewed letters, everything had been scraped away by the killing salt that weathered all. From the iron brown deck to the lanterns that often dimmed, the dreary quarters had nothing noteworthy. And though to command the largish vessel, for there to be a proper crew in that rusting junk was only natural. Arnau had been alone to fidget the hundreds of switches and that he did not know what changed, as his squad had selfishly retreated below the deck with Siegfried's silent body, through the hatch that housed a steep quivering stair. There was one who found himself useful on deck within the hurricane, and was oddly Gin, which Arnau had spotted, covering a distant light shining out of the accursed fog.

"Who is it now...?" The helmsman asked.

But as he squinted, its torches brightened. Past the gaps in the mist that blinked, whilst the lancer had yet to hear the motor or the thunking hull sailing at speed, he realized that they were a pace-long gap before collision, and tugged the throttle by his wits, pulling the boat to a stop.

Where the vessels glided alongside, with Gin leaning over

the deck to inspect who the supposed squad was, the other party seemed to do the same and declined their engine to a halt. Engaging the two boats until one was higher on the unpredictable and rough waves. Of curiosity, a soldier escaped the cramped quarters and doused himself in the fierce thunderstorm that was shielded by a bloating blanket of hail. At the reveal of his face when he peered upwards, holding tightly onto the fluttering hood, the brute looked down and yelled in amazement that they had survived the calamity,

"Julien?!"

"Gin?!" Julien replied with a brighter voice.

"Ya're headin' de wrong way!" told Gin, pointing at the vague shades of the naval machines that sat alert for the first arrivals.

"No, not yet," Julien shook his head.

"We're going to find the rest of the squad!"

The patrol boat rocked unevenly, as if it was attempting to throw the concerned lieutenant overboard, who swerved and stumbled about the deck until he found stable ground upon shuffling his legs to diverge not too far.

"By the way!" Julien gazed at the above again and shouted for the comrade.

Gin lunged further over the railings and heard over the batting wind.

"Is everyone there?!" asked the Danne, desperately.

The brute shuddered, who Julien's desire to concern himself piqued, and observed the quiet mist sat within Haven. Gin grunted for the untidy moments, slipping his hand into the hood to rub his itching head when he asked himself with vigorous scratches irritating him more than the sea ever did,

"Gah…how do I put this again?"

Returning to Julien, the lieutenant prepared himself for the brewing storm and revealed bluntly,

"Arminius' still fighting the horde of Confederates!"

That as anyone could have predicted, Julien's eyes shrunk on the hearing of Arminius' name, and reversed his course towards the helm steadfastly, from where his allies stared awaiting news, if not for he was stopped by Gin's call,

"Hey! Hold on will ya?!"

"Dat's not all!" The brute cried.

For it made Julien stay on the landing of a heel that knocked on the echoing hull with the thumps of raindrops which were nothing compared. And nervously, he waited for what his comrade was to inform him.

"He's dueling that white-haired noble, Eos!" Gin yelled.

A certain composure was nigh to break, as the speechless stare of the boyish face unbuckled into disillusioned fright. Julien had noticed. The screech of the distant omen was never false and that it rang, sounding of the reaper's bells.

Hidden behind the lowering haze, where the eroded fountain did not shake for long, the impact of a boy, whose body had slid half way into the murky water, dealt a crack in the marble sculpture. Rippling, as the debris and ash fell, a spray was delivered that sat a mystifying image of a twitching soul, bleeding ceaselessly for the cuts that had pierced through his shirt, ripped and leaked. His eyes were awake. But lifeless. That even the heavy rain could not wake him in the minute he laid there unmoving. Genuine were the sights which grieved upon failure, he modestly huffed.

Beyond the town of rubble, in flames and brimming massacre, was the modern promenade that shallow stairs led towards. Unlike the medieval eras of the historic capital, the coast was not filled with bricks and cobble, neither with chalk nor burning torches. Rather, the bland plains of the wasted port showed nothing of true value except for that the path provided the last arena with its glossy gray slabs along the hushed waterfront, beneath the extinguished lamps, where there was no end. A surge swept between the watchtowers that ended the wall's extent, which channeled into the cove-like harbor. The waves fervently crashed against the shores with a series of thunder and launched the devilish storm to the heights of the barred heavens. And whilst the street, being assaulted by the twists between hail and rain, had been emptied and abandoned. It provided for a commander, the ease in the air that whoever he had sent to depart, had evacuated.

"His strength..." He wheezed, punching his chest to dispel the pain.

How hard Arminius tried, a new wound would ache him in spite. Coughing and spewing, sprinkling blood onto the ledge that was flushed away by the tides. His hands gripped onto the sunken sword, underwater, that was bending within the wavering pool when he was woken by the unhuman aura which the scent was so acrid it smelled horrid and unlike an usual eifer.

"Is nothing like Aurel's..." Arminius squinted at the shadow on the roofs, above a structure that soon should collapse.

The intimidating but flattering silk white hair, seduced the night for the skies began to calm into little thicker than an early morning drizzle. Though it was only for him that the clouds silenced upon leaping from the tiles that started to crumple inwards. Regulus' drop slowed on the mediocre burst of a slash downwards, sending a cutting gale that cracked the stones for his landing to be elegantly placed. The storm restarted and gushed an awful downpour onto the rivals' heads.

As the colonel approached Arminius with unmatched ferocity carved into the shining glaive and his tenacious eyes, the lieutenant stomped to rise. Gaining a stronghold on his feet, he stood not wobbling with a choice to bring an offensive.

"Even...so..." said Arminius, rising onto the ledge of the fountain without showing his eifer.

Drawing the gilded sword that had not snapped under the sublime force, it was firmly held near his core, where the sharpest edge faced the Confederate's advance.

I still have a chance! Arminius declared, courageously.

At a stunning dash, the shocks in the raindrops fleeted as he recklessly thrusted. With the brushing wind, he landed beyond the polearm's reach and leapt, quaking the ground. A wave on the impact drove him through the storm and however did Regulus predicted, Arminius flicked aside and disappeared with the phantoms. Reappearing out of the flash, the lieutenant spun a high axe kick onto his stunned rival's glaive, and pushed his kei farther until he felt the tendons nearer to strain. Arminius contacted the ground and took flight again, lunging at the Confederate with the intentions of a fatal strike when an early defense made its first clash instead. Their eyes met before the grinding sparks. Where one who confidently emitted a rich stare of victory gradually gained his space by his push onwards, Regulus slipped a hand onto the shaft's shoe and catapulted Arminius towards the promenade. Bracing as he crashed past the fountain, bisecting the marble statue that had been bashed apart, with the quickening plummet over the stairs.

He rolled onto his feet with his soles scraping along the rugged stones and was close to a dive into the waves had his body not drawn forward to cease his slide. But when he had believed that the toss may have given him the second to recover, a shadow jumped over the crumbling fountain for the lieutenant sensed his heart stutter. Quickly, Arminius dashed from the fight yet the spurt of strength had cost him the rupturing wounds that diseased his flesh. His mind was jolted, but was contained with a bloodied hand resting on the deepest cut entrenching greater with each burdensome breath.

The Confederate touched from air to land, elegantly, and gazed down upon the stained path that Arminius took to be shaded by the coastal houses and decaying stalls, battered by the eastern winds. On the resonant steps that seemed immensely provocative, Arminius steadily trailed away to regain the paces for a defense. Although nevertheless knowing that wherever he fled, his rival would prevail in the chase.

"Prince of Regen," Regulus called the foe.

"You were never fit to battle."

Halted, ready to take another pace, he had chosen to keep afar. Spinning the thin glaive from flank to flank before the colonel opened his stance, the shaft pressed against his spine.

"Then why knowing that?" asked Regulus.

There was a crackle of the distant crashing thunder that would have struck some unknown tree of the vast northern forests. Though there was no lightning beside Arminius' hands for not even the remnants could show unless his heart forced the blitz out of slumber.

"You will be granted a brief sanctuary," Regulus reservedly suggested, motionless even when he spoke, and giving no gestures that did little to convince his rival.

"And we could duel another day."

Blood ran like a river of hell, from a source that had been smeared by a weak swipe of a hand, Arminius' body had been bruised but the captivating sparkles in his eyes were not to let down their master. The boy grinned whilst his crimson fluids flowed, and lifted his stubborn head to witness Regulus' collected face. Where the left was the lieutenant's faithful flank of warring everyday, Arminius peculiarly brought the blade to his right and engaged himself into relaxment. As if it was to taunt. Warring lightning coiled. The brushes of branching discharges flowered like the springing season they fought within, and withdrew the last drop of the warrior's kei to the vibrantly glowing steel and extremes of the feet. Whirling air formed a circle from the rumbling ground that shattered and lifted by blocks, surrounding the lieutenant on the promenade that had become his sacred field.

"Like hell...I'd run..." Arminius faintly uttered.

Upon a conflicted sigh, Regulus gently dipped his head and surely replied,

"If you desire it,"

"I will heed your wish." said he.

But before the colonel could return his vision unto the enemy, a thundering clap fired and rattled the distrubed air. Through the neutral mist was the bolt who fluctuated between a path to the next, dashing at a quickening rhythm. His blade was at its mark, and daringly slashed, though was disadvantaged, then came plummeting from a heavenly throw, a streak of lightning crashed towards the earth on the first impact. The pace of battle had been stolen. Arminius' brazen eifer rewinded and engulfed the clearing cloud with a second strike of lightning. Then as the lieutenant sped for six tremoring blows, unwinded, the angelic construct of his fortitude had been sketched into a painting of a romantic eight pointed star weaving its afterimages and lights through Regulus' stand like that of a pen's colored stroke. It was too shallow. Booms tore the stones. Ravaged. Where the remains had crumbled into dust from the roaring clashes of blades blowing clouds to be away. The clicks of thunder strengthened on the last godly strike and pounded at the final arrival of Arminius' landing which sent a gust with glints scattered across the storm.

"I-I...landed a strike..." Arminius stammered for his numbness settled upon him, seeing the blood on the shallow edge of his blade.

Belched rose fluids dyeing the streams beneath, he found his resolve to peer over his shoulder and saw Regulus, unnaturally calm. At the sight of his total defeat, the child of Aelon mumbled,

"But...that's not nearly enough..."

Regulus lightly touched the wound that had tainted his cheek and brought his right hand to show the smudge of blood which did not wash away. It was so little a scratch for him, he cared not the meager slash and muttered to himself,

"It's been five years..."

The blood beneath the opening bubbled, until the Confederate's flesh was diffusing red steam. His skin sizzled and miraculously began to seal, or was it to Arminius' fright, the curse, no one had ever wanted to compete, completed the healing as if nothing had passed. When the lieutenant saw the currents of blood rushing from the alleys and soaked streets of Haven towards Regulus' feet amassing such gore, Arminius began to pace back in utter awe. The colonel heeded the expression of the cowering enemy and chilled the poor boy's spine, freezing him on the step with the simple glare from the falcon's eyes. Whilst Regulus pulled on his glove, finger by finger, he removed the veil and revealed an absurd collection of scars. Of both new and old. Colorless or reddenned. The forever damned man, who seemed so humble, had been named the survivor of his eifer to have existed. Holding an exposed finger into his mouth that was clasped between his teeth, the dread emitted assaulted Arminius whose eyes appeared shaken.

"T-That's..." Arminius panted.

To the Diogenes' circle that flooded the street, the unbroken waves of blood seeped into the alchemist's incantations, printed against the ground which eventually glowed once the performance completed its journey. For the eldest of all eifers, the capital of human zeal.

"A...blood eifer...?" It was noticed.

As the liquids clotted, the circle sprouted upwards as crystals like ruby. There were imperfections amongst the mixtures that Arminius could not tear his eyes off the unreality, still for the eifer was not complete. For then when Regulus bit into his flesh that ruptured a schism to the bone, gushing a burst of his flesh and blood, that a pair of demonic wings flared into creation from his armored back. Arminius turned to the devil. With his mouth gaping. To the phantom that did not belong in the physical realm, dribbling its life from the edges of the yellowish bones which held together the thin scarlet skin tattered with pockets of holes. A ghastly scream deformed the skies and the explosion of blood was cast in a shifting mountain, at an arch through the ground and air. The torpedoes of crystals raced across the stretches of the depressed town and skimmed along the surface with no consideration when the Letalis had been unleashed.

"How—?" Arminius gasped upon casting a fury of firebolts and exhausted slashes at the impending waves which swept him.

Windows smashed and the bricks of houses dissolved. The standing walls were forced beneath the sheer shadowing colossus that swallowed its course, lifting floors and roofs to the storm above as a grant to the gods needing to witness what disaster. Engulfing even the streams of winds that could not compare, the force consumed the capital. Its city, that the decimating blood flooded below the rocks, was ripped from its very foundations. Perhaps it was luck for Arminius to have been plucked away earlier, than needing to be tormented by the dense burial later. But within his suffering shell where the eifer erupted, commited to a careless genocide, indiscriminating, Regulus' mind was split from the sole virtue of honor. Only that his elites of the cavalry could flee the sprinting carnage chasing the air wherever it seeped until from the high gliding scout planes, snapped thousands of photographs for the world to see. From the heavens there was a view. Laying was a foul crystal which had an old city encased within. But troubled, Regulus halted its advance.

Why did I have to push myself this far...?

What would they say...? The colonel questioned the will grasped in his hands.

The stained vapor rested and plunged the atmosphere to settle like mist, only a pace above ground whilst Regulus was drowned in regret. He finally chose a path to head and silenced the cries of his doomful eifer. The clots were purged and returned themselves into a sane deluge of liquid blood, raining upon an ancient haven.

Retching in bursts of foreigner blood, he knelt on the washing tides that flooded his boots where the kingdom was too near. If one was to ignore the wails of orphaned children or the tempest, the paradise of death would be first to remind Arminius who reeked of Regulus' abominable eifer. Shrouded within the red dust and rain which did not clear, the haunting aura kept his edges sharp as the lieutenant wiped his bruised face of the grainy blood.

Where...is he...? Arminius scouted the open crypt as he lifted himself to stand.

Feeling no pain from the fatal wound for his body was due a living graveyard of recent torture, Arminius gazed upwards, and found the exit beyond the foul-smelling cloud.

I...need...a better...view... The cold found its way into the soldier's lungs when he felt a brisk clean swoop of air strike his neck.

As he carefully poked his sights to where the wind had silenced, there, the silver glaive rested a finger away from his spine that hummed a hunter's tone. The battle calmed. Arminius was in defeat. But the ambition told not to stay his trembling hand.

"This battle was too one-sided to be deemed worthy..." told Regulus.

"I'm offering you safe passage so that we may—"

A set of gleaming eyes sharpened, and in the vortex of which the blood lingered, around the rivals, whirled towards the skies. The eifer exploded into charming sparks of the remaining lightning when Arminius glared at Regulus, whose soul was taken from the berserked stare that revealed the colonel's agitation as he withdrew his glaive. Sliding under the blade, the lieutenant swooped his legs along the waterlogged street and spun to meet his enemy above whose weapon was yet in hold.

"Hagh!" Arminius screamed, blasting his eifer for the final sprint.

The sword sailed over the surface of blood where the tip pulsated from the swiftness, and was rocketed upwards with death chiming. Regulus' mind snapped. On the verge of his downfall and the shackles that had been weighing him, for the past twenty years, broke free. The colonel bashed his shoulder against the lieutenant's chest and thrusted him away. Then with Arminius' momentum severed, Regulus tugged him with a monstrous pull. Jolting his shoulder out of its lock, they butted heads, as the glaive had spun a whirlpool. Without an alert, the shaft soared into a forearm and uprooted both bones which gruesomely pierced his elbow, splattering a short spring of blood whilst the youngster fell into a cold shock. Disarmed. The sword fell before Regulus dealt a mortal slash across the chest and ended the blade's journey opposite its departure.

As the colonel awakened from his frenzy, he noticed that

his glaive had been bathed by the life of the foe who stumbled farther with an unforgiving scowl. Held onto a shattered shoulder, he trailed to an unreachable range and halted where he thought Regulus could be hindered. Though twice it had been proven otherwise. He was no less, a genius, to vy for the title as the God of War.

"Regen." Regulus gritted his teeth who could not bear to look Arminius in the eye and presumed,

"We know it will never end."

Arminius discovered his will to glance at his gaping wound and sought more discomfort from the dangling limb that had been bruised and shattered many strikes over. Nothing could be felt on his right arm. There was no sense of the gusts. Nor the pellets of rain. The tendons had been cleaved and his revealing flesh drooled to the fingers he could neither move nor feel the creaking platings. When his touch had been diminished with death offering him to advance, the motor he had never heard skipped across the waterway and invaded the port with the blare of a horn.

"Arminius!" Julien cried behind Alexandria's mounted machine.

A rustic brass gun, with signs of carbon fillings, had its sights marked on Regulus' heart. The barrel began to steam as the gunner fortified her bastion with the trigger pulled to its closest, and at the rush over a wave, the rounds propelled. In repeating sparks, the bullets hurtled through the rain and like a spray, the missiles became a shroud for Arminius' escape. But it was so easily countered by a shielding whirlpool of Regulus' deflecting glaive that knocked the feeble embers from the air.

His...guard's down...! Arminius discovered an opening beneath the Confederate, and hastily steeled his unbroken hand on the hilt of the Bawarann knife.

Aimed, the shortened blade envisioned the arc towards Regulus. The blitz was smooth in the launch from its scabbard and even betted to strike when the colonel realized his ambition. Hence on the last bullet that had been stricken in half, he turned to face Arminius with the given acute glare that delayed the lieutenant again without a lesson learnt on hesitation. A silver blade rushed towards the skies and took a stream of blood along its tip.

All was sinisterly quiet. The boat swung around to welcome

its stern for Arminius to board. But he had been so silent that none knew what had happened. Then as he fell to his knees, Arminius sent a fierce cry of anguish that echoed across the city that had Julien shivering in tears when he found the friend laying his hand and knife over his bloodied face. A summer green eye squelched as it plunged to the ground. It was not cleanly gouged out of its cavern by that there was a distinct cut that severed the lens with a slight scent of steel pierced into the organ. The eyeball had been torn from Arminius. Whose right hollow crater repulsively leaked between his fingers.

With a lightened sigh, Regulus approached the lieutenant, swinging his glaive passively, turned from the crippled who had softened his cry. One half spilled tears. Another bled.

"Enough of this farce." The Confederate halted before the enemy.

"The loss of an eye." In the list of his doings, Regulus reminded him of the agony and sorrows.

Which drenched his knife and hand, the blood of Arminius dribbled from the emptied chamber.

"Any nerves of an arm." said the colonel, to the enemy's twitching limb.

When he finally surrendered to acceptance in victory, Regulus straightened his glaive to the heavens which thundered and burned for the standing warrior's announcement to the deities.

"There is a sole path to save your glory. Your reputation." He told the soldier of Aelon, tricked into the service for an alliance that was no less than a reich.

"Do not fret." Regulus pledged too.

"Regen and Shokuten will hear of your triumphs in this war."

Tightening his hands on the shaft, the strike was ready for the ritual as Arminius had performed for the honor of a general before.

"The God of Death grants you mercy in judgement—" The chant was hollow of expression that another filled.

The distress evolved into a fiendish chuckle. As his hand was drawn to reveal the haunting black hole, gaping amidst the rain, it gushed a blood waterfall. And though his strength was non-existent, the laugh was too haunting that kept Regulus' blade unwilling to cast the execution. It would be no mistake to assume he had been possessed. Arminius had never grinned with such sadism.

"Do you think...I'd give a shit..."

"After all of that...?" Arminius huffed, lifting his head to disturb Regulus with a deteriorating smile.

"Have you seen the God of Death?" With the resentful tremors of his voice, the fiend asked when the tone spun into a declaration,

"He's before you!"

A dagger, with a wave of rain and blood, was driven at the Confederate's face, who dodged aside before the blade met any flesh. But the spray had dazed him under a bitter blanket of vapor as a bolt was sent from scorching veins of Arminius' running blood to the cold steel. The sparks blasted a condensing cloud which obscured Regulus' sights in the while for the footsteps to carry the dying sound of Arminius' heavy gasps, wasting aura onwards to the awaiting vessel.

The bloodied colonel coughed, for the dust shortly settled. It eventually revealed the figure of his rival that had daringly leapt over the freakish waves which swept in curves. And that upon bounding himself for his comrades' grace, Arminius crashed, back first, through the shattered window to the startled booth.

"Arminius Reichner!" Regulus chased the sprinting boat where the elites tended to the collapsed soldier.

Yet the Confederate could not reach him. So he slowed to the eventuality of admitting failure in his grasp. When the vessel was beyond, far and shrinking, he halted on the very boundaries to the haven on the pier and looked outwards through the gates of the wall, to the darkening horizon eclipsed by the distant fleet.

"Death or dishonor?!" He yelled for Arminius' answer, but never knowing that the lieutenant could hear.

At the promenade's end, the shadow shrunk in the wintry color of his eye that faded alone. His skin was ghastly pale. The wounds were profound. But neglecting the slashed and bruised body of the own that burned with the heart, he weakly answered,

"Why not...both...?"

Laying on the bed of glass as the warring world had shaken him to wake, Arminius returned to a desolate slumber within the warmth of his blood.

Tis Hëllischucurlt bevurëtmj, Lycoris

YURUPE
KENNTOR

Jyar 488 wunn Zhormanniken
12014 Jyaren sinnke Hümannitjisbirtet

0   50   100   150   200   250   300

Distannke inn Lyazhuën

Thank you for reading!

I pray that you may find time for the coming second volume...